VALANCOURT CLASSICS

THE COMPLETE JUDITH LEE ADVENTURES

RICHARD MARSH was born Bernard Richard Heldmann in North London in 1857. He began his career publishing fiction for boys under his own name, but after a falling out with his editor, G.A. Henty, and a criminal conviction for fraud, he adopted the *nom de plume* of 'Richard Marsh', under which name he would go on to publish some eighty volumes of fiction and dozens of short stories beginning in 1888. Extraordinarily prolific, at the height of his output Marsh published as many as eight volumes in a single year: apparently his publishers could not keep up with the pace of his pen, since even after his death in 1915 further Marsh volumes continued to appear regularly through 1920. Though remembered primarily for the bestseller *The Beetle* (1897), a supernatural horror novel that initially outsold Bram Stoker's *Dracula* (1897), Marsh was active in many genres, publishing crime stories, romance novels, spy and adventure fiction, and humorous fiction. He was especially adept at the short story, particularly tales of the occult and supernatural, and was very popular in his time for his tales of the lip-reading detective Judith Lee and his stories featuring the clerk/war hero Sam Briggs. Marsh died of heart disease in 1915, perhaps brought on in part by overwork. Valancourt Books began publishing Marsh's fiction in 2007 and has so far issued thirteen volumes of his novels and stories.

MINNA VUOHELAINEN is Senior Lecturer in English Literature at Edge Hill University. She studied International History at the London School of Economics and English Literature at King's College London before completing a Ph.D. on "The Popular Fiction of Richard Marsh: Literary Production, Genre, Audience" at Birkbeck, University of London. Her current research focuses on fin-de-siècle print culture, literary representations of London, and the discursive overlap between gothic fiction and factual discourses at the fin de siècle. She is the author of a forthcoming monograph on Richard Marsh (University of Wales Press, 2015) and the editor of a number of Valancourt editions of Marsh's fiction, including *The Beetle: A Mystery* (2008), *The Goddess: A Demon* (2010), and *The Complete Adventures of Sam Briggs* (2013).

D1547192

RICHARD MARSH

THE COMPLETE JUDITH LEE ADVENTURES

Edited with an introduction and notes by
MINNA VUOHELAINEN

VALANCOURT BOOKS

The stories collected in this volume were originally published variously in *Strand Magazine* (1911-16) and in volume form as *Judith Lee: Some Pages from Her Life* (Methuen, 1912) and *The Adventures of Judith Lee* (Methuen, 1916)

First Valancourt Books edition 2016

Published by Valancourt Books, Richmond, Virginia
http://www.valancourtbooks.com

ISBN 978-1-943910-22-9 (trade paperback)

All Valancourt Books publications are printed on acid free paper that meets all ANSI standards for archival quality paper.

Set in Dante MT 11/13.2

CONTENTS

Introduction   vii

The Complete Judith Lee Adventures
    The Man Who Cut Off My Hair   1
    Eavesdropping at Interlaken   20
    Conscience   45
    Matched   68
    The Miracle   91
    "Auld Lang Syne"   118
    Isolda   139
    Was It By Chance Only?   164
    "Uncle Jack"   186
    The Restaurant Napolitain   210
    "8, Elm Grove—Back Entrance"   230
    Mandragora   250
    The Affair of the Montagu Diamonds   271
    My Partner for a Waltz   291
    Curare   319
    Lady Beatrice   344
    The Finchley Puzzle   368
    Two Words   393
    The Glass Panels   419
    On Two Trains   445
    The Clarke Case   476
    The Barnes Mystery   499

INTRODUCTION

Detective fever

In August 1911, the *Strand Magazine*, the most popular monthly fiction paper of the period, launched a new series of detective stories with the following editorial announcement:

> A new detective method is such a rare thing that it is with unusual pleasure we introduce our readers to Judith Lee, the fortunate possessor of a gift which gives her a place in detective fiction. Mr. Marsh's heroine is one whose fortunes, we predict with confidence, will be followed with the greatest interest from month to month.[1]

Judith Lee, the editor explained, "is a teacher of the deaf and dumb by the oral system, and therefore the fortunate possessor of the gift of reading words as they issue from people's lips, a gift which gives her a place apart in fiction."[2] Fourteen of Lee's adventures were initially published in the *Strand* between August 1911 and October 1916, illustrated by W.R.S. Stott (1878-1939) and J.R. Skelton (1865-1927). The first twelve of the *Strand* stories were in 1912 collected as *Judith Lee: Some Pages from Her Life* (Methuen), and another nine, including one of the remaining *Strand* stories, appeared in 1916 in *The Adventures of Judith Lee*, also published by Methuen. The final of the *Strand* stories, the posthumous "The Barnes Mystery," was never issued in volume form. Altogether, Lee's toll of adventures thus stands at twenty-two. Joseph Kestner rightly argues that "Lee is memorable because of her profession, her specific expertise at lip-reading, her adventurous travelling, her willingness to engage in physical self-defence, her quickness to perceive female criminality and her absolute independence."[3] In addition, Lee's frequent

---

[1] Richard Marsh, "The Man Who Cut Off My Hair," *Strand Magazine* 42 (August 1911), 215.
[2] Marsh, "Conscience," *Strand Magazine* 42 (October 1911), 449.
[3] Joseph A. Kestner, *Sherlock's Sisters: The British Female Detective, 1864-1913* (Aldershot: Ashgate, 2003), 212.

appearances in the *Strand*, a magazine closely associated with significant fictional detectives, particularly Sherlock Holmes, arguably also place her in a detective aristocracy.

The turn of the century was a time of great cultural and social change, which led to anxiety as well as excitement. The rise of detective fiction in this period is arguably closely related to the ways in which stories of crime addressed certain fin-de-siècle uncertainties, particularly the urban anxieties of an emerging lower-middle-class readership. The nineteenth century had witnessed rapid urbanization, in particular the expansion of London, but by the late century urban life was associated not only with wealth, consumerism, entertainment and trade but also with slums, disorder, crime, immigration and deviance. The Metropolitan Police's disastrous mishandling of the Bloody Sunday riots in 1887 and failure to solve the Jack the Ripper murders in 1888 had provoked widespread public distrust in official law enforcement, triggering the resignation of the Metropolitan Police Commissioner Sir Charles Warren in 1888.

These urban disturbances also coincided with Arthur Conan Doyle's creation of his famous consulting detective, Sherlock Holmes, in 1887, and it could be argued that the private detective, whether amateur or professional, emerged in this period as an imaginary rival to the official police force, exercising fictional crime control and providing readers with reassurance at a time when the police were increasingly perceived to be unable to control the urban chaos of London. Upwardly mobile lower-middle-class readers, protective of their material possessions and anxious about the social changes taking place around them, could find solace in stories which appeared to indicate that help, albeit of a fictional kind, was at hand. In creating the character of Sherlock Holmes, Doyle had hoped to reinvest the detective story with scientific vigor. Holmes was a rational hero for an age which witnessed the rise of the scientific profession, of statistics, of sociology, and of various branches of anthropology, including not only cultural and racial anthropology, which facilitated imperial administration, but also criminal anthropology, degeneration theory and sexology, which were deployed at home in an attempt to define the constitution of a desirable national stock through the classification of deviant physical and psychological features. Doyle's detective genius is, of course, well-known for his "deductive" skills: with the help of his panoptic gaze, Holmes sees the necessary clues and signs, makes connections, and provides a solution to the puzzle. With his omniscient knowledge of London, he is able to place the entire city under surveillance. Holmes uses logic, scientific rationalism and his knowledge of the city to establish codes and taxonomies, so that under the detective's gaze, the city and its criminal underworld can be analyzed and eventually contained.

Holmes's success is evident in the public hysteria surrounding Doyle's first two dozen stories, which appeared in the *Strand Magazine* in 1891-93. Initially designed as a short-story magazine "organically complete each month,"[1] *Strand* was instrumental in ushering in the golden age of the short story in Britain. Founded in January 1891 by George Newnes, possibly the most important enterprising publisher of the turn of the century, the *Strand* was supported by a powerful newspaper empire[2] and was commercially a resounding success.[3] Newnes, who famously claimed to be "the average man" and thus to know his literary needs,[4] had made his money out of *Tit-Bits*, a revolutionary penny weekly he had established in 1881 which dissected the world for its working- and lower-middle-class audience by digesting news into short snippets of information not too demanding for imperfectly educated readers. The *Strand* was a more challenging monthly venture, demanding greater levels of literacy from its readers but, at 6d., still offering excellent value for money. Apart from its plentiful illustration, the magazine was designed to sell by its lively contents, typically a mixture of short fiction, topical articles and celebrity interviews. Importantly, the *Strand* also offered contributors prompt editorial decisions and fair pay: Doyle, for example, had in 1891 earned a generous £4 per thousand words, or approximately £35 per story, from the *Strand*;[5]

---

[1] Reginald Pound, *The Strand Magazine, 1891-1950* (London: Heinemann, 1966), 30.

[2] On Newnes, see Ann Parry, "George Newnes Limited," in *British Literary Publishing Houses, 1881-1965: Dictionary of Literary Biography* 112, ed. Jonathan Rose and Patricia J. Anderson (London and Detroit: Gale Research, 1991), 226-32.

[3] Peter D. McDonald, *British Literary Culture and Publishing Practice, 1880-1914* (Cambridge: Cambridge University Press, 1997), 156.

[4] Pound, *Strand Magazine*, 25.

[5] McDonald, *British Literary Culture*, 140-42.

from the mid-1890s, he never received less than £100 per thousand words.[1] This was very good money indeed, and although Doyle's was an exceptional case, the *Strand* could afford to pay its favorite authors better rates than its rivals.

The *Strand* was from the first associated with detective fiction, most importantly Doyle's series of Sherlock Holmes stories, which ran in it from the summer of 1891. Doyle's detective duo Holmes and Watson had previously appeared in two moderately successful novellas, *A Study in Scarlet* (1887) and *The Sign of Four* (1890), but their adventures only became a phenomenon after Doyle's literary agent A.P. Watt sent six short stories featuring Holmes and Watson to the newly established *Strand* as a likely place of publication. Halfway between the serial *novel* and the *unconnected* short story, the serial short story simultaneously created continuity and produced a self-contained reading experience that could be completed in one sitting, even on public transport; it also made it possible for busy readers to miss an installment without losing the plot. As Doyle later explained,

> A number of monthly magazines were coming out at the time, notable among which was "The Strand," then as now under the editorship of Greenhough Smith. Considering these various journals with their disconnected stories it had struck me that a single character running though a series, if it only engaged the attention of the reader, would bind that reader to that particular magazine. On the other hand, it had long seemed to me that the ordinary serial might be an impediment rather than a help to a magazine, since, sooner or later, one missed one number and afterwards it had lost all interest. Clearly the ideal compromise was a character which carried through, and yet instalments which were each complete in themselves, so that the purchaser was always sure that he could relish the whole contents of the magazine. I believe that I was the first to realize this and "The Strand Magazine" the first to put it into practice.[2]

This format, pioneered by Doyle in the *Strand*, became a staple of the monthly magazine market at the turn of the century, and

---

[1] Pound, *Strand Magazine*, 74.
[2] Arthur Conan Doyle, *Memories and Adventures* (London: Hodder & Stoughton, 1924), 95-96.

Marsh, like many other popular authors such as Arthur Morrison, Guy Boothby and Grant Allen, exploited it fully in his series of stories featuring not only Judith Lee but also the lower-middle-class clerk Sam Briggs, whose adventures appeared in the *Strand* in 1904-15. The format offered these writers a readily accessible formula which proved particularly useful after Doyle, frustrated by constant requests for further Holmes stories, decided to kill off his detective genius at the Reichenbach Waterfalls in December 1893. Holmes would eventually return, but not until the 1901-02 *Strand* serial "The Hound of the Baskervilles"; in the hiatus left by his untimely demise, serial detective fiction provided commercial opportunities for a number of professional writers who attempted to create new detective figures to fill the gap left by Holmes. While retaining the successful plot formula of the stories, these fictional detectives also had to offer some novelty and innovation to distinguish them from Holmes and from one another. Thus, we encounter Arthur Morrison's trustworthy Martin Hewitt, William Hope Hodgson's ghost-buster Carnacki, Ernest Bramah's blind detective Max Carrados, Guy Boothby's double-dealing crook Klimo, and Baroness Orczy's grotesque Old Man in the Corner who solves crimes from his base in an ABC teashop—all different takes on the same commercially successful formula.

The female detective: a subversive figure

Another variation on the detective genre was the creation of the fictional female detective—an unusual and transgressive character because she is employed in a role traditionally considered unsuitable for a woman. The first female detectives had appeared as early as the 1860s, when the Sensation Novel was beginning to use investigator figures amongst its stock characters in uncovering the secrets lurking within respectable English homes.[1] Adrienne E. Gavin notes that the roots of these early female investigators go even further to the female heroines of eighteenth-century gothic novels, who often find themselves having to unravel mysteries.[2] The

---

[1] Carla T. Kungl, *Creating the Fictional Female Detective: The Sleuth Heroines of British Women Writers, 1890-1940* (Jefferson, N.C. and London: McFarland, 2006), 8.

[2] Adrienne E. Gavin, "Feminist Crime Fiction and Female Sleuths," in *A Compan-*

fin de siècle witnessed the appearance of a number of female investigators, including Catherine Louisa Pirkis's plain thirty-something
spinster Loveday Brooke, Baroness Orczy's Lady Molly of Scotland
Yard, Grant Allen's lively New Woman misfit Lois Cayley, Fergus
Hume's Hagar of the pawnshop, and Marsh's lip-reader Judith
Lee. The official female detectives and investigators of fin-de-siècle
fiction are figures of fantasy. Women did not work in detective roles
within the police force at the time, and there was never a female
detective, a Lady Molly, at Scotland Yard in this period.[1] Although
the Metropolitan Police had appointed two women in 1883 to
oversee female prisoners, women only gained full police status in
1918.[2] These real-life policewomen worked to ensure the protection
and custody of women and children and dealt with cases of wife-
beating and child prostitution; they did *not* solve jewel robberies,
murders, or spy cases.[3] Indeed, in the nineteenth century, middle-
class femininity was seen to be incompatible with the earning of
money in public-facing roles: for much of the century, the home
was the woman's sphere and women in public were seen as unwom-
anly and sexually suspect.[4] Middle-class women who were forced
to work for economic reasons, most often as governesses, were at
pains to emphasize that they were not interested in the salary and
were seeking the protection of the domestic sphere in exchange
for their employment: being paid for one's labor placed a middle-
class woman in a liminal social and sexual situation. Although the
fictional female detective is often led to detection by her wish to
help a man, she is, thus, a subversive figure: she works, often for
money, and, in order to solve crimes, she has to venture into the
public sphere.[5]

Carla T. Kungl correctly notes that critical readings of the female

ion to Crime Fiction, ed. Charles J. Rzepka and Lee Horsley (Chichester: Wiley-
Blackwell, 2010), 259

[1] Kungl, *Creating the Fictional Female Detective*, 25-27.

[2] Kestner, *Sherlock's Sisters*, 5.

[3] Michelle B. Slung, "Introduction," in *Crime on her Mind: Fifteen Stories of Female
Sleuths from the Victorian Era to the Forties*, ed. Michelle B. Slung (Harmondsworth:
Penguin, 1984), 16.

[4] Patricia Craig and Mary Cadogan, *The Lady Investigates: Women Detectives and
Spies in Fiction* (Oxford and New York: Oxford University Press, 1986), 21.

[5] Kungl, *Creating the Fictional Female Detective*, 56.

detective genre are often flawed by their Second-Wave Feminist bias and the assumption that the detectives are always either unattractive spinsters or end up married.[1] Such readings often ignore female detectives who fail to fit: Marsh's unconventional Judith Lee, for example, features in very few surveys of the female detective. Thus, for example, Kathleen Gregory Klein argues in her study of *The Woman Detective* that the female detective is undercut in one or both of her roles—that she is "either not a proper detective or not a proper woman" because she fails to conform to the patriarchal status quo.[2] Klein states that readers expect to see the female detective fail in her detective career because "[i]f she can be shown as an incompetent detective or an inadequate woman, readers' reactionary preferences are satisfied."[3] Klein's assumption appears to be that only conservative men read female detective stories. Patricia Craig and Mary Cadogan, somewhat similarly, argue that there were two types of female investigator in fin-de-siècle fiction: firstly, women who were able to solve crimes because of their specialized feminine knowledge and intuition; and secondly, women who were equal to male investigators but compromised their femininity in the process.[4] As they see it, neither type is quite "right" because one relies on that elusive feminine intuition and is thus derogatory of female ability, and the other appears to question the women's femininity. These critics also note that many female detectives end up married at the end of their respective story cycles, and that the relinquishment of their detective careers upon wedlock restores their femininity, which has become compromised by their public and economic status. Klein concludes that the stories thus also warn female readers not to challenge patriarchy by venturing into the public sphere.[5]

As Gavin notes, some female detectives "variously use knowledge and observation of domestic environments and human behaviour, female intuition, and their capacity for going unnoticed or

---

[1] Kungl, *Creating the Fictional Female Detective*, 5.
[2] Kathleen Gregory Klein, *The Woman Detective: Gender & Genre*. 2nd edn (Chicago: University of Illinois Press, 1995), 4.
[3] Klein, *Creating the Fictional Female Detective*, 5.
[4] Craig and Cadogan, *The Lady Investigates*, 12.
[5] Klein, *Creating the Fictional Female Detective*, 73.

being underestimated in solving crimes" to their advantage in their investigative careers.[1] Pirkis's ironically named Loveday Brooke, for example, is plain, aging and unattractive to men, and thus goes unnoticed both as a woman and as a detective. Her femininity and plainness make her invisible: whereas Sherlock Holmes is a master of disguise, Brooke is invisible to begin with. She also has an eye for detail, particularly for domestic detail, and this helps her solve cases of a domestic nature. However, there is, in reality, a good deal of variety within the fin-de-siècle female detective genre. The stories featuring female detectives deal with all manner of issues, including murder, theft, robbery and espionage. The detectives themselves are "independent, confident, clever women"[2] in a range of circumstances: single, married, or widowed; elderly spinsters or young and attractive; amateurs, adventurers, or professionals.[3] In particular before the First World War, they are young, single, middle-class and professional, whereas the Miss Marple type, the nosy elderly spinster amateur detective, emerges after the War.[4] Many of them *are* eccentric and sexually ambiguous, but eccentricity and enigma are common characteristics of all detectives: Holmes, for example, is an inherently problematic figure—a misogynistic, decadent drug user who somehow combines scientific knowledge with violin playing and boxing.

As noted above, the female detective emerges during the hiatus in the publication of Sherlock Holmes stories in the mid-1890s. She is, arguably, some fiction writers' attempt to create a fresh detective figure but also to make detective fiction attractive to female readers. However, the mid-1890s was not only a period during which Holmes was "dead" but also a period during which the New Woman, the independent young woman of the 1890s who demanded education, work and sexual equality, was very much alive. The fin de siècle was a time of intense debate over the rights of women and first-wave feminist agitation, and the female detective's public role and employment record point to notable links between

---

[1] Gavin, "Feminist Crime Fiction and Female Sleuths," 258.
[2] Gavin, "Feminist Crime Fiction and Female Sleuths," 258.
[3] Kungl, *Creating the Fictional Female Detective*, 3.
[4] Kungl, *Creating the Fictional Female Detective*, 12.

her and the controversial New Woman.[1] Like the New Woman, the female detective is typically educated, middle- or upper-class, and, besides her detective role, works in a professional, creative or white-collar employment; and, like the fictional New Woman, she has outspoken opinions on gender roles and appears to be sexually ambiguous. Furthermore, the female detective often fights for women's rights within the domestic sphere, a problematic space associated in the stories with violence and deception. Thus, Kestner rightly notes that female detectives "exercise surveillance over the culture, including its men, women, public institutions and private domestic spaces."[2] The narrative technique of the stories—usually either the detective's own voice or the voice of an admiring sidekick —creates an image of a woman as a protagonist with control over the storyline.[3] Thus, while some female detective stories certainly are conservative, others may be read as proto-feminist.

Richard Marsh and the magazine market

Although now best known as a writer of gothic novels, Richard Marsh (pseudonym of Richard Bernard Heldmann, 1857-1915) was in fact a prolific author of both short stories and of a wide range of genre fiction, including gothic, crime, adventure, spy, romance, juvenile and comic fiction. In an increasingly fragmented literary marketplace, it was imperative for writers to be able to target particular audiences with very different reading needs.[4] As Ian Small recognizes,

> [C]ommercial success depended not upon the understanding of
> the *individual* consumer and the insatiability of his or her wants,
> but rather upon identifying a *community* of taste. And, importantly,
> a community of taste presupposes certain *social relations* which

[1] Kestner, *Sherlock's Sisters*, 30.
[2] Kestner, *Sherlock's Sisters*, 226.
[3] Kestner, *Sherlock's Sisters*, 95.
[4] Patrick Brantlinger, *The Reading Lesson: The Threat of Mass Literacy in Nineteenth-Century British Fiction* (Bloomington & Indianapolis: Indiana University Press, 1998), 187; Peter Keating, *The Haunted Study: A Social History of the English Novel, 1875-1914* (London: Fontana, 1991), 340; Joseph McAleer, *Popular Reading and Publishing in Britain, 1914-1950* (Oxford: Clarendon Press, 1992), 24.

underlie and define it—a class or gender identity, for example.[1]

Marsh targeted a number of such communities through short genre fiction, never relying solely on the support of a solitary, potentially fickle, niche audience. In a career which lasted from 1880 to 1915, he published, under two names and also anonymously, 83 volumes of fiction and some 300 short stories. Much of this work was initially published in magazines, either in short or serial formats, and only subsequently issued in volume form as novels or short-story collections. Marsh's success as a professional writer was, thus, intimately connected to fundamental changes in the consumption of print at the fin de siècle, a transitional period in the print industry following the coming of universal literacy and the introduction of affordable 6s. first editions and of magazines specializing in fiction.[2] Writing in 1899, Walter Besant noted that

> There are at this moment in the country hundreds of papers and journals and magazines, weekly and monthly […]. The circulation of some is enormous, far beyond the wildest dreams of twenty years ago: they are the favourite reading of millions who until the last few years never read anything: they are the outcome of the School Board, which pours out every year by thousands, by the hundred thousand, boys and girls into whom they have instilled […] a love of reading.[3]

Marsh's career coincided with this proliferation of popular fiction magazines providing the public with inexpensive reading matter. Between 1888 and 1897 he published, sometimes anonymously, in a number of fiction papers, including at least *Belgravia*, *Household Words*, the *Cornhill*, *Gentleman's*, *Blackwood's*, *Longman's*, *Home Chimes*, *All the Year Round*, the *Strand*, the *Idler* and *Answers*. These early contributions were almost exclusively in the short-story format and thus exploited the enormous demand for short fiction

---

[1] Ian Small, "The Economies of Taste: Literary Markets and Literary Value in the Late Nineteenth Century," *English Literature in Transition, 1880-1920* 39.1 (1996), 14.

[2] Richard D. Altick, *The English Common Reader: A Social History of the Mass Reading Public, 1800-1900*. 2nd edn (Columbus: Ohio State University Press, 1998), 306-07; McAleer, *Popular Reading and Publishing*, 14, 27; Brantlinger, *The Reading Lesson*, 184.

[3] Walter Besant, *The Pen and the Book* (London: Thomas Burleigh, 1899), 54-55.

that characterized the publishing industry, particularly the magazine market, towards the end of the nineteenth century,[1] when the papers "call[ed] aloud continually for stories—stories—stories."[2] This early experience of writing short fiction allowed Marsh to develop into one of the leading producers of popular short stories of his day. He acknowledged the importance of such training in an 1891 article on the short story, in which he argued that

> The short story is the product of to-day. This is the age of condensation. You condense an ox into a spoonful of essence. You condense a three-volume novel into eighteen pages. In other words, you boil it down. People say that writers of short stories are born, not made. It is a mistake. They are made.[3]

In Marsh's case, it was the success of *The Beetle* that "made" him as a popular author, but from 1897 his efforts as short-story writer also began to pay off and he began to navigate towards the illustrated 6*d*. monthlies which flourished in turn-of-the-century Britain. These included the *Harmsworth Magazine*, the heavily illustrated *Pearson's Magazine*, the *Windsor Magazine*, and *Cassell's Magazine*, all powerful commercial enterprises with print runs of from 100,000 to a million monthly copies, each catering for a slightly different target audience. Of greater importance to Marsh than any of these, however, was the *Strand Magazine*,[4] where Marsh's first contribution appeared in December 1892 and where the Judith Lee stories would be published in 1911-16. From 1900, the *Strand* emerged clearly as Marsh's primary and, after 1910, sole, magazine contact, issuing sixty items by him between 1892 and 1916.

The short story was an extremely effective literary vehicle for the popular author at the fin de siècle, when a number of critics attempted to define it as "a definite species, having possibilities of its own and also rigorous limitations."[5] The short story theorists

[1] Nigel Cross, *The Common Writer: Life in Nineteenth-Century Grub Street* (Cambridge: Cambridge University Press, 1985), 208.
[2] Besant, *The Pen and the Book*, 136.
[3] Richard Marsh, "The Short Story," *Home Chimes* 12.67 (August 1891), 23.
[4] Pound, *The Strand Magazine*, 53.
[5] Brander Matthews, ed., *The Short-Story: Specimens Illustrating Its Development* (London: Sidney Appleton; New York: American Book Company, 1907), 3.

were led by the American Brander Matthews, who described the "essential unity of impression" of the "Short-story" which "deals with a single event, a single emotion, or the series of emotions called forth by a single situation."[1] The short story, Matthews maintained, "must do one thing only, and it must do this completely and perfectly; it must not loiter or digress; it must have unity of action, unity of temper, unity of tone, unity of color, unity of effect; and it must vigilantly exclude everything that might interfere with its singleness of intention."[2] Another critic, T. Sharper Knowlson, agreed that a "short story is a narrative in miniature, exhibiting the working and climax of a deep emotion, considered subjectively, and therefore giving a pre-eminent interest to one particular person."[3] While these literary critics attempted to define the short story as an elite form and thus to invest it with cultural capital, it was also a convenient commercial vehicle for popular authors—as Knowlson tacitly acknowledged in the title of his 1904 book, *Money-Making by Short-Story Writing*. Short fiction could be produced relatively quickly to ease financial pressure, and the magazine market was a means for an author to make himself known to different audiences. Short magazine fiction could also be used to experiment with new genres and audiences.

Marsh exploited the flexibility of the magazine market by using a broader generic range in his short fiction than in his novels. A topical interest in crime and criminality is evident throughout his career, from stories of degeneration in the 1890s to spy fiction during the First World War and, in one form or another, crime is a key element in most of his novels, whether primarily belonging in the gothic, sensation or thriller genres. Detection, while often a minor element in his novels, plays a major role in his short fiction. His first serial detective figure was the aristocratic Augustus Champnell, who featured in a number of stories and novels in the 1890s, including the novels *The Beetle* and *The House of Mystery* and the short story collection *The Aristocratic Detective*. However, the

[1] Brander Matthews, *The Philosophy of the Short-Story* (New York: Longmans, Green, 1901), 15-16.

[2] Matthews, ed., *The Short-Story*, 26-27.

[3] T. Sharper Knowlson, *Money-Making by Short-Story Writing* (London: Neuman and Castarede, [1904]), 19.

lip-reading female detective Judith Lee was a much more successful and innovative addition to Marsh's portfolio.

"The Adventures of Judith Lee"

With the exception of two stories, placed at the end of this collection, Judith Lee is a first-person narrator. This gives her agency but also leads the reader to accept her choices and interpretations without question. Lee's voice is remarkably direct. The first story begins thus:

> My name is Judith Lee. I am a teacher of the deaf and dumb. I teach them by what is called the oral system—that is, the lip-reading system. When people pronounce a word correctly they all make exactly the same movements with their lips, so that, without hearing a sound, you only have to watch them very closely to know what they are saying. Of course, this needs practice, and some people do it better and quicker than others. I suppose I must have a special knack in that direction.[1]

Lee's narrative moves chronologically, both within each individual story and within the series. In the first story, we meet her as a prepubescent girl, when she walks in on two burglars who tie her to a chair and cut off her hair; she speaks of her "rage" and "fury" at the "outrage" to which she is subjected,[2] and this "symbolic rape" acts as a motivation for her subsequent career in detection.[3] Kestner rightly notes its similarity to the fate suffered by Marjorie Lindon in *The Beetle* but also discusses Lee's swift recovery from her ordeal and her remarkable stamina in tracking down her attackers,[4] which point to a greater acceptance of female independence in an increasingly inclusive society. In the second story, Lee is a young woman of 17, and by the third story she is an independent, professional woman.

Lee is portrayed in the stories as an independent young professional. Her primary activity is as a teacher of the deaf and dumb,

[1] Marsh, "The Man Who Cut Off My Hair," 215.
[2] Marsh, "The Man Who Cut Off My Hair," 218, 220.
[3] Kestner, *Sherlock's Sisters*, 199.
[4] Kestner, *Sherlock's Sisters*, 210-11.

and in this capacity she travels widely with her pupils, attends conferences, and generally advises on the training of the deaf and dumb. She frequently reminds the reader that she is not a professional detective: "I have seldom set out," she tells us, "from the very beginning, with the deliberate intention of conducting an investigation."[1] Nonetheless, Lee's high-status career directly leads to her detective work as it is due to her professional training that she possesses the skills that allow her to solve crimes. Indeed, we could see Lee as a new type of scientific detective: it is her great skill at lip-reading, acquired through hard work and years of study as much as natural ability, that allows her to solve crimes. While her adventures come about by chance and she often acts on impulse, she does not primarily conduct her investigations through feminine intuition or knowledge of the domestic sphere but through her professional ability in lip-reading, a developing field bringing together pedagogy, medicine, and linguistic ability.

As was the case with the Holmes stories, the Lee stories follow a formula: the detective begins by reminding the reader of her lip-reading skills, then witnesses an exchange in a public place, uses the knowledge thus acquired to thwart a crime or a plot, usually on her own but occasionally with the help of the police, and then returns to her life as a teacher of the deaf and dumb. Lee essentially belongs in the public sphere, which does not intimidate her. We see her traveling independently, both in the UK and abroad, hear of her language skills in German and Italian, and witness her frequent outings to restaurants, shops, balls and entertainments of various kinds in London. Her characteristically direct voice takes these privileges for granted, assumes that she has a right to a place within the public sphere and to the material rewards resulting from her professional success. As she puts it herself, she is "seldom afraid of anything—I suppose it is a matter of temperament."[2] It is in the public spaces frequented by Lee—the street, the railway station, a hotel, a pier, a ball, the opera, a restaurant—that she witnesses private exchanges that were not intended for anyone else's ears. She, however, literally *sees* rather than hears the words exchanged: she is "constantly

[1] Marsh, "Lady Beatrice," in *The Adventures of Judith Lee* (London: Methuen, 1916), 77.

[2] Marsh, "The Man Who Cut Off My Hair," 218.

being made an unintentional confidante of what were meant to be secrets."[1] Marsh updates the classic detective story in which the detective's panoptic gaze spots clues or signs which lead him (or her) to solve the case: instead of snooping around with a magnifying glass, Lee watches the suspect's lips as a more direct source of information. The private and the public are blurred further when Lee communicates what she sees to the reader in her narrative. She tells us:

> To find out what people are saying to each other in confidence, when they suppose themselves to be out of reach of curious ears, may be very like eavesdropping. If it is, I am very glad that, on various occasions in my life, I have been enabled to be an eavesdropper in that sense.[2]

Many of Lee's acquaintances and adversaries see her lip-reading skill as bordering on the supernatural. It does not, of course: the success of Lee's investigations depends entirely on her ability to see clearly. However, Lee is in many ways an intriguing and liminal figure who seemingly fails to conform to early-twentieth-century expectations of acceptable feminine behavior. Her supposedly semi-supernatural professional success is just one facet of her unconventional personality and lifestyle. Her ethnicity, for example, is ambiguous: she seems equally at home in different corners of the world, easily masters any language that comes her way, and is described as small, dark and gipsy-like—a "black-faced devil's spawn"[3] as one adversary puts it. While she dresses well and attends balls and parties, she also fails to conform to conventional gender roles. Thus, Lee frequently mentions her attraction to beautiful young women but we never hear of any viable male suitor in her life, and, in fact, she repeatedly implies that she is not terribly fond of men at all following the violations and betrayals of trust described in the first two stories. She avows "[n]ever, never, never" to marry,[4] and no marriage concludes her adventures. While now and again assisted and even saved by Inspector Ellis of Scotland

---

[1] Marsh, "Conscience," 449.

[2] Marsh, "Eavesdropping at Interlaken," *Strand Magazine* 42 (October 1911), 304.

[3] Marsh, "Restaurant Napolitain," *Strand Magazine* 42 (October 1911), 312.

[4] Marsh, "The Miracle," *Strand Magazine* 42 (December 1911), 748.

Yard, Lee remains a solitary figure till the end of her adventures in the *Strand*.

We could, perhaps, question whether Lee's avoidance of romance puts her femininity into question, and this is to an extent borne out by references to her unfeminine skills in martial arts. However, this interpretation is challenged by the illustrations which accompanied the stories in the *Strand*, which portray Lee as an attractive, petite woman who is well-dressed and appears comfortable in the public sphere. She takes her independence, frequent ventures into the public sphere, traveling and work for granted and, while willing to acknowledge her mistakes, is never portrayed as a figure of fun. Nor is her ability ever questioned, apart from her own admission that she sometimes needs to take a holiday to escape the pressure of work. The narrative pattern of unwitting lip-reading leading to an adventure and detective work requires Lee to operate within the public sphere, and her voice presents this in such a matter-of-fact way that the reader, too, never questions Lee's right to independence. Perhaps it is this self-assurance which leads her enemies to describe her as "the most dangerous thing in England."[1]

As noted above, feminist critics of the female detective genre often argue that female detectives operate solely within the domestic sphere, drawing upon their stock of "feminine intuition." Many of the crimes Lee solves involve women, and she often comes to the aid of women who are subjected to violence or intimidation by men. However, Lee is not solely a domestic detective. She deals with a wide range of crime and deception, including theft, swindling, blackmail, coining, murder, poisoning, hypnotism, anarchism, bomb plots, espionage and even the provision of corpses for dissection. The stories feature criminals and immoral characters of both sexes, including predatory women. One recurring plotline involving forged checks supplies us with an interesting link to Marsh the author. For example, "The Miracle," a story which comments on female depravity and commodification of men within a marriage market dependent on purchasing power, introduces us to the marital plans of the unattractive, elderly spinster Miss Drawbridge, commonly known as "Gertrude," who intends to make

---

[1] Marsh, "The Finchley Puzzle," in *The Adventures of Judith Lee*, 113.

the dashing young Cecil Armitage her husband. In a moment of desperation following careless living, the young man has forged an acceptance, placing him at the mercy of blackmailers and within a hair's-breadth of imprisonment. Marriage to the wealthy Gertrude is Armitage's only escape—but to achieve it, he has to give up his real love Margery. Judith Lee so manages that the miracle of the story's title is achieved and the young couple are given a fresh start in America. In "The Barnes Mystery," forged checks are presented on the account of Mrs. Netherby, who has mysteriously disappeared from her cottage. A disguised stranger makes a purchase in Mrs. Netherby's name, pays with a large check, pockets the change, and moves on until the victim's bank account has been cleared.

Towards the end of his life and career, Marsh appears with this recurring plot pattern to be returning to a youthful misdemeanor committed some thirty years before. Born Richard Bernard Heldmann in London on 12 October, 1857, Marsh was the first child of an English mother and a German-Jewish father who was in 1857 involved in large-scale bankruptcy proceedings against his in-laws and employers. Marsh had initially begun writing boys' fiction under his real name Bernard Heldmann in 1880, and was making a promising career for himself on the staff of G.A. Henty's boys' paper *Union Jack* when, in 1883, Henty abruptly brought his connection with the weekly to a close. In March 1883, Heldmann had opened an account at the Acton branch of the London and South Western Bank and had been given a check book with a hundred blank forms. By May, the bank had to contact Heldmann to call "his attention to the irregular way in which the account had been kept," and the account was closed.[1] Heldmann, however, continued to issue checks against the now defunct account and soon went on to live on his wits in France, the Channel Islands and different parts of Britain, where he would pay for his expenses with a substantial check, pocket the change, and move on before the fraud was discovered—exactly like the criminals in "The Barnes Mystery." Soon he was "wanted at various parts of the kingdom for various frauds" committed in the guise of "a well-to-do gentleman" sporting various aliases.[2] No Judith Lee came to his rescue: Heldmann

---

[1] "'Captain Roberts' Sent for Trial," *Kent and Sussex Courier*, 20 February 1884, 3.

[2] "Capture of a Forger at Tenby," *Western Mail*, 12 February 1884, 4.

was eventually captured at Tenby in South Wales in February 1884 and tried at the West Kent Quarter Sessions on 9 April, where he was sentenced to eighteen months' hard labor for obtaining money, board and lodgings by false pretenses.[1] He served his sentence in full at Maidstone Jail and was released on 8 October, 1885. The Maidstone Prison Nominal Roll tells us that he was considered well-educated, declared his occupation to be journalism, had brown hair, and was 5 foot 5 inches tall.[2] Soon after his release, he settled down with a woman named Ada Kate Abbey, started a family, and adopted the penname "Richard Marsh," a combination of his own first name and his mother's maiden name, as well as the name of his maternal grandfather and, incidentally, of the trainer of the Prince of Wales's racehorses. He would never speak of his real identity, first career and subsequent disgrace and, for such a popular writer, appeared very little in interviews and celebrity features.

Marsh's fiction articulates a fascination with criminality which is essentially ambivalent in its implied understanding of the difficult circumstances which may drive individuals to crime. While in the conservative backlash of the late 1890s such sympathies were difficult, even dangerous, to voice, by the early twentieth century Marsh was articulating them increasingly vocally in a number of texts. *The Surprising Husband* (1908) is an essentially ambivalent account of a mixed-race man condemned by society; *The Master of Deception* (1913) appears to side with its double-dealing, murderous but charming protagonist; *Justice—Suspended* (1913) refuses to pass judgment on Mr. Justice Arkwright with his criminal past and on the jailbird protagonist Charles Bryant, a wonderful husband and father; *His Love or His Life* (1915) tells the story of an essentially good man who yet has behind him a prison sentence. With their ambivalent protagonist and progressive take on criminality, the Judith Lee stories are yet another example of Marsh's ventures into liminality in the early twentieth century. Marsh had high commercial

---

[1] *West Kent Quarter Sessions*, Wednesday 9 April 1884, 72. See also *County of Kent: Criminal Register: England and Wales 1884*, 284: "Return of all persons Committed, or Bailed to appear for Trial, or Indicted at the General Quarter Sessions held at Maidstone on the ninth day of April 1884, showing the nature of their offences, and the result of the proceedings."

[2] *Maidstone Prison Nominal Roll*, November 1883-November 1884, no. 2100: "Hildmann, Bernard" (*sic*).

hopes for Lee,[1] and her frequent appearances in the *Strand* suggest that she was indeed popular with its readers. While Lee's daring adventures would have appealed to the *Strand's* male readers, she is also a detective with whom female readers could identify. Lee's professional life could be interpreted as her strength with female readers, who would see in her a potential role model. Her popularity, and the success of Marsh's other controversial characters from the period, suggests that the pre-war audience of popular fiction was possibly more understanding of misfits and more receptive to stories of unconventional characters than previously thought.

MINNA VUOHELAINEN

A note on the edition

This edition, which was completed with support from the British Academy, is based on the fourteen Judith Lee stories published in *Strand Magazine* between 1911 and 1916. The *Strand* stories are accompanied by the original illustrations by W.R.S. Stott and J.R. Skelton. Additionally, eight unillustrated stories are taken from the collection *The Adventures of Judith Lee* (London: Methuen, 1916). Obvious printing errors have been silently corrected. Lee's twenty first-person narratives have been arranged in the order in which they first appeared, while the two stories told in the third person are placed at the end of this collection.

The stories were originally published as follows:

"The Man Who Cut Off My Hair": First published as "Judith Lee: Pages from her Life: The Man Who Cut Off my Hair" in *Strand Magazine* 42 (August 1911), 215-24; illustrated by W.R.S. Stott. Reprinted in *Judith Lee: Some Pages from her Life* (London: Methuen, 1912), 1-19.

"Eavesdropping at Interlaken": First published as "Judith Lee: Pages from her Life: Eavesdropping at Interlaken" in *Strand Magazine* 42 (September 1911), 292-304; illustrated by J.R. Skelton. Reprinted in *Judith Lee: Some Pages from her Life* (London: Methuen, 1912), 20-46.

"Conscience": First published as "Judith Lee: Pages from her Life:

[1] Robert Aickman, *The Attempted Rescue* (London: Victor Gollancz, 1966), 12-13.

Conscience" in *Strand Magazine* 42 (October 1911), 449-60; illustrated by J.R. Skelton. Reprinted in *Judith Lee: Some Pages from her Life* (London: Methuen, 1912), 47-69.

"Matched": First published as "Judith Lee: Matched" in *Strand Magazine* 42 (November 1911), 482-94; illustrated by J.R. Skelton. Reprinted in *Judith Lee: Some Pages from her Life* (London: Methuen, 1912), 70-92.

"The Miracle": First published as "Judith Lee: The Miracle" in *Strand Magazine* 42 (December 1911), 735-48; illustrated by J.R. Skelton. Reprinted in *Judith Lee: Some Pages from her Life* (London: Methuen, 1912), 93-120.

"'Auld Lang Syne'": First published as "Judith Lee: 'Auld Lang Syne'" in *Strand Magazine* 43 (January 1912), 3-13; illustrated by J.R. Skelton. Reprinted in *Judith Lee: Some Pages from her Life* (London: Methuen, 1912), 121-42.

"Isolda": First published as "Judith Lee: The Experiences of a Lip-Reader: Isolda" in *Strand Magazine* 43 (March 1912), 242-54; illustrated by J.R. Skelton. Reprinted in *Judith Lee: Some Pages from her Life* (London: Methuen, 1912), 143-74.

"Was It By Chance Only?": First published as "Judith Lee: The Experiences of a Lip-Reader: Was It by Chance Only?" in *Strand Magazine* 43 (April 1912), 433-44; illustrated by J.R. Skelton. Reprinted in *Judith Lee: Some Pages from her Life* (London: Methuen, 1912), 175-204.

"'Uncle Jack'": First published as "Judith Lee: The Experiences of a Lip-Reader: 'Uncle Jack'" in *Strand Magazine* 43 (May 1912), 554-66; illustrated by J.R. Skelton. Reprinted in *Judith Lee: Some Pages from her Life* (London: Methuen, 1912), 205-37.

"The Restaurant Napolitain": First published as "Judith Lee: The Experiences of a Lip-Reader: The Restaurant Napolitain" in *Strand Magazine* 43 (June 1912), 680-90; illustrated by J.R. Skelton. Reprinted in *Judith Lee: Some Pages from her Life* (London: Methuen, 1912), 291-317.

"'8, Elm Grove—Back Entrance'": First published as "Judith Lee: The Experiences of a Lip-Reader: '8, Elm Grove—Back Entrance'" in *Strand Magazine* 44 (July 1912), 54-64; illustrated by J.R. Skelton. Reprinted in *Judith Lee: Some Pages from her Life* (London: Methuen, 1912), 268-90.

"Mandragora": First published as "Judith Lee: The Experiences of a Lip-Reader: Mandragora" in *Strand Magazine* 44 (August 1912), 176-86; illustrated by J.R. Skelton. Reprinted in *Judith Lee: Some Pages from her Life* (London: Methuen, 1912), 238-67.

"The Affair of the Montagu Diamonds": First published as "The Affair of the Montagu Diamonds" in *Strand Magazine* 45 (February 1913), 190-

99; illustrated by J.R. Skelton. Reprinted in *The Adventures of Judith Lee* (London: Methuen, 1916), 248-70.

"My Partner for a Waltz": Published in *The Adventures of Judith Lee* (London: Methuen, 1916), 1-38.

"Curare": Published in *The Adventures of Judith Lee* (London: Methuen, 1916), 39-73.

"Lady Beatrice": Published in *The Adventures of Judith Lee* (London: Methuen, 1916), 74-107.

"The Finchley Puzzle": Published in *The Adventures of Judith Lee* (London: Methuen, 1916), 108-43.

"Two Words": Published in *The Adventures of Judith Lee* (London: Methuen, 1916), 144-79.

"The Glass Panels": Published in *The Adventures of Judith Lee* (London: Methuen, 1916), 180-215.

"On Two Trains": Published in *The Adventures of Judith Lee* (London: Methuen, 1916), 271-314.

"The Clarke Case": Published in *The Adventures of Judith Lee* (London: Methuen, 1916), 216-47.

"The Barnes Mystery": Published as "The Barnes Mystery: An Adventure of Judith Lee" in *Strand Magazine* 52 (October 1916), 407-17; illustrated by W.R.S. Stott.

A chronology of Richard Marsh

1854: Joseph Heldmann arrives in London from Bavaria via Paris, and sets up as a lace merchant.

1856: Marriage of Joseph Heldmann and Emma Marsh, daughter of lace manufacturer Richard Marsh, of Mansfield, Nottinghamshire, according to the rites and ceremonies of the Church of England (30 December).

1857: Joseph Heldmann becomes a naturalized British citizen. Birth of Richard Bernard Heldmann at 23, Adelaide Road, St. John's Wood, London (12 October). Joseph Heldmann becomes involved in bankruptcy proceedings following reckless trading (December).

1858: Joseph Heldmann is branded a "German adventurer" and refused a bankruptcy certificate. Birth of Henry ("Harry") Heldmann at Railway Terrace, Mansfield, Nottinghamshire (28 October).

1860: Birth of Sophia Alice ("Alice") Heldmann at 19 Scarsdale Terrace, Kensington, London (21 October).

1861: Joseph Heldmann is working as classical and language tutor in London.

1867: Birth of Ada Kate Abbey, daughter of journeyman stone carver Charles Abbey and his wife Hannah, in Walworth, Surrey (2 April).

1870: Joseph Heldmann is in charge of Brunswick House School at 19 Mayland Road, Hammersmith, London. Birth of John Whitworth Heldmann (20 October).

1871: Death of John Whitworth Heldmann (13 August). Edith Nesbit attends Brunswick House School together with her brother Alfred.

1880: Bernard Heldmann publishes his first signed fiction in the devotional periodical *Quiver*, in the religious juvenile paper *Young England*, and in the secular boys' paper *Union Jack*.

1881: Bernard Heldmann begins to publish serial school and adventure stories exclusively in G.A. Henty's *Union Jack*. His first volume-form novels, *Boxall School* and *Dorrincourt*, are issued by the religious publisher Nisbet.

1882: Heldmann continues to work for *Union Jack* and becomes co-editor with Henty (October). Publication of *The Mutiny on Board the Ship "Leander"* (Sampson Low); *The Belton Scholarship* (Griffith & Farran); *Expelled* (Nisbet).

1883: Heldmann is living at Seaton House, The Vale, Acton, West London. Heldmann's serial "A Couple of Scamps" is dropped by *Union Jack* in April and only concluded in July. The co-editorship is abruptly and publicly terminated (5 June). Heldmann begins to live a fraudulent life, presenting checks on an account that has been closed. Publication of *Daintree* (Nisbet).

1884: Heldmann continues to live on his wits until he is arrested at Tenby in South Wales on 12 February. He is tried at Maidstone, Kent on 9 April and sentenced to eighteen months' hard labor at Maidstone Jail for obtaining money, food and lodgings by false pretences.

1885: Heldmann is released from prison (8 October).

1887: Birth of Alice Kate Heldmann, first child of Bernard Heldmann and Ada Kate Heldmann, née Abbey (14 July). No marriage certificate has been found for the Heldmanns, who are living at 21, Shaftesbury Road, Richmond, Surrey. Bernard Heldmann is working as a journalist.

1888: "Richard Marsh" publishes his first signed short story, "Payment for a Life," in *Belgravia* (summer). Signed and unsigned stories follow in a number of weekly and monthly fiction papers. Death of Alice Kate Heldmann (24 March). Emma Heldmann disinherits Richard Bernard Heldmann in her will (15 June). Birth of Harry Randolph Heldmann (7 July).

1890: Birth of Mabel Violet Heldmann (24 May). The Heldmanns are living at 4, Kempson Road, Fulham, London.

1891: Birth of Madge Heldmann (5 August). The Heldmanns move from 2 Bedford Row, Worthing, West Sussex to New Street, Three Bridges, Sussex. Bernard Heldmann describes himself as "a professional author." Emma and Joseph Heldmann have given up Brunswick House School and are living at Worton Court, Isleworth, Middlesex, with Alice and Harry, now a stockbroker.

1892: Birth of Conrad Heldmann (12 October). Publication of "A Vision of the Night," Marsh's first story in Strand Magazine (December).

1893: "Richard Marsh" publishes his first novels, The Devil's Diamond and The Mahatma's Pupil (Henry).

1895: Birth of Bertram Max Heldmann (9 January). Publication of Mrs. Musgrave – and her Husband (Heinemann) and The Strange Wooing of Mary Bowler (Pearson).

1896: Death of Joseph Heldmann (12 April).

1897: Publication of The Mystery of Philip Bennion's Death (Ward, Lock); The Duke and the Damsel (Pearson); The Crime and the Criminal (Ward, Lock); The Beetle: A Mystery (Skeffington). Four impressions of The Beetle appear between September and December. Marsh is now signing all his magazine work.

1898: Publication of Tom Ossington's Ghost (Bowden); The Datchet Diamonds (Ward, Lock); Curios (John Long); The House of Mystery (F.V. White); Under One Cover: Eleven Stories by S. Baring-Gould, Richard Marsh, Ernest G. Henham, Fergus Hume, Andrew Merry and A. St John Adcock (Skeffington).

1899: Publication of Frivolities: Especially Addressed to Those Who Are Tired of Being Serious (Bowden); In Full Cry (F.V. White); The Woman with One Hand and Mr. Ely's Engagement (Bowden).

1900: Marsh issues eight volumes in the busiest year of his career: Marvels and Mysteries (Methuen); A Second Coming (Grant Richards); Ada Vernham, Actress (John Long); The Goddess: A Demon (F.V. White); The Seen and the Unseen (Methuen); A Hero of Romance (Ward, Lock); An Aristocratic Detective (Digby, Long); The Chase of the Ruby (Skeffington). Marsh begins to contribute to Strand Magazine annually.

1901: Marsh's publication pattern settles to an average three volumes a year. Publication of Amusement Only (Hurst & Blackett); Both Sides of the Veil (Methuen); The Joss: A Reversion (F.V. White). The Heldmanns are still living in Three Bridges. Only the youngest child, Bertram Max, remains at home.

1902: Publication of *The Adventures of Augustus Short: Things Which I Have Done for Others and Wish I Hadn't* (Anthony Treherne); *Between the Dark and the Daylight* (Digby, Long); *The Twickenham Peerage* (Methuen).

1903: Publication of *The Magnetic Girl* (John Long); *The Death Whistle* (Anthony Treherne); *A Metamorphosis* (Methuen).

1904: Publication of *A Duel* (Methuen); *Garnered* (Methuen); *Miss Arnott's Marriage* (John Long). Publication of "The Girl on the Sands," Marsh's first story featuring the lower-middle-class clerk Sam Briggs, in *Strand* (October).

1905: Publication of *The Confessions of a Young Lady* (John Long); *The Marquis of Putney* (Methuen); *A Spoiler of Men* (Chatto & Windus).

1906: Publication of *The Garden of Mystery* (John Long); *In the Service of Love* (Methuen); *Under One Flag* (John Long).

1907: Publication of *The Girl and the Miracle* (Methuen); *The Romance of a Maid of Honour* (John Long); *A Woman Perfected* (John Long).

1908: Publication of a seemingly new Heldmann novel, *That Master of Ours* (Nisbet), "by the author of *Dorrincourt, Boxall School, Expelled*, etc." Marsh publishes *The Coward behind the Curtain* (Methuen) and *The Surprising Husband* (Methuen).

1909: Publication of *The Girl in the Blue Dress* (John Long); *The Interrupted Kiss* (Cassell); *A Royal Indiscretion* (Methuen).

1910: Publication of *Live Men's Shoes* (Methuen); *The Lovely Mrs. Blake* (Cassell).

1911: Publication of *A Drama of the Telephone* (Digby, Long); *The Twin Sisters* (Cassell). Death of Emma Heldmann (11 July). Publication of "The Man Who Cut Off My Hair," Marsh's first story featuring the female detective and lip-reader Judith Lee, in *Strand* (August).

1912: Publication of *Judith Lee: Some Pages from Her Life* (Methuen); *Sam Briggs: His Book* (John Long); *Violet Forster's Lover* (Cassell).

1913: Publication of *If It Please You* (Methuen); *Justice—Suspended* (Chatto & Windus); *The Master of Deception* (Cassell).

1914: Publication of *Margot and her Judges* (Chatto & Windus), *Molly's Husband* (Cassell); *The Woman in the Car* (T. Fisher Unwin).

1915: "Sam Briggs Becomes a Soldier" appears in *Strand* in monthly installments throughout the year. Death of Richard Bernard Heldmann of heart failure and heart disease at The Ridge, Lucastes Avenue, Haywards Heath, Sussex (9 August). Funeral of Bernard Heldmann, St. Wilfrid's Church, Haywards Heath (13 August). Heldmann's estate is valued at £453 14s. Death of Harry Heldmann in action (25 September). Publication of *The Flying Girl* (Ward, Lock); *His*

Love or his Life (Chatto & Windus); *Love in Fetters* (Cassell); *The Man with Nine Lives* (Ward, Lock); *Sam Briggs, V.C.* (T. Fisher Unwin).

1916: Publication of *The Great Temptation* (T. Fisher Unwin); *Coming of Age* (John Long) and *The Adventures of Judith Lee* (Methuen).

1917: Publication of *The Deacon's Daughter* (John Long).

1918: Publication of *Orders to Marry* (John Long) and *On the Jury* (Methuen).

1919: Publication of *Outwitted* (John Long).

1920: Publication of *Apron-Strings* (John Long).

Further reading

Bernard Heldmann and Richard Marsh (biography and bibliography)

Aickman, Robert. *The Attempted Rescue.* London: Victor Gollancz, 1966.

Baker, William. "Introduction." In Richard Marsh, *The Beetle.* Stroud: Alan Sutton Publishing in association with the University of Luton, 1994: vii-x.

Brèque, Jean-Daniel. "Introduction." In Richard Marsh, *The Complete Adventures of Judith Lee*, edited by Jean-Daniel Brèque. Encino, Calif.: Black Coat Press, 2012: 7-13.

Dalby, Richard. "Introduction." In Richard Marsh, *The Haunted Chair and Other Stories*, edited by Richard Dalby. Ashcroft, British Columbia: Ash-Tree, 1997: ix-xxi.

———. "Richard Marsh: Novelist Extraordinaire." *Book and Magazine Collector* 163 (October 1997): 76-89.

———. "Unappreciated Authors: Richard Marsh and *The Beetle.*" *Antiquarian Book Monthly Review* 144 (April 1986): 136-41.

Davies, David Stuart. "Introduction." In Richard Marsh, *The Beetle: A Mystery.* Ware: Wordsworth, 2007: vii-xii.

Greene, Hugh. "Introduction." In *(The Penguin Book of) Victorian Villainies*, edited by Hugh Greene and Graham Greene. London: Bloomsbury, 1991: 7-10.

Höglund, Johan. "Introduction." In Richard Marsh, *A Spoiler of Men*, edited by Johan Höglund. Kansas City: Valancourt, 2009: vi-xviii.

James, Callum. "Callum James's Literary Detective Agency, Case #1: Why Was Richard Marsh?" *Front Free Endpaper*, 30 November 2009. http://callumjames.blogspot.com/2009/11/callum-jamess-literary-detective-agency.html

Kirkpatrick, Robert. *The Three Lives of Bernard Heldmann.* London: Children's Books History Society, 2010.

Pittard, Christopher. "'The Unknown! with a Capital U!:' Richard Marsh and Victorian Popular Fiction." *Clues: A Journal of Detection* 27.1 (2008): 99-103

Taylor, Michael Rupert. "G. A. Henty, Richard Marsh and Bernard Heldmann." *Antiquarian Book Monthly Review* 277 (August/ September 1997): 10-15.

Vuohelainen, Minna. "From 'vulgar' and 'impossible' to 'pre-eminently readable': Richard Marsh's Critical Fortunes, 1893-1915." *English Studies* 95.3 (2014): 278-301.

——. "Bernard Heldmann and the *Union Jack*, 1880-83: The Making of a Professional Author." *Victorian Periodicals Review* 47.1 (2014): 105-42.

——. "'Contributing to Most Things': Richard Marsh, Literary Production and the Fin-de-Siècle Periodical Market." *Victorian Periodicals Review* 46.3 (2013): 401-22.

——. "Introduction." In Richard Marsh, *The Complete Adventures of Sam Briggs*, edited by Minna Vuohelainen. Kansas City: Valancourt, 2013: vii-xxxvii.

——. "Introduction." In Richard Marsh, *The Goddess: A Demon*, edited by Minna Vuohelainen. Kansas City: Valancourt, 2010: vii-xxxiv.

——. "Richard Marsh." Victorian Fiction Research Guide 35 (Canterbury: Canterbury Christchurch University, 2009). http://www. victoriansecrets.co.uk/victorian-fiction-research-guides/richard-marsh/.

——. "Introduction." In Richard Marsh, *The Beetle: A Mystery*, edited by Minna Vuohelainen. Kansas City: Valancourt, 2008: vii-xxx.

——. "The Popular Fiction of Richard Marsh: Literary Production, Genre, Audience." Ph.D. dissertation, University of London, 2007.

Wolfreys, Julian. "Introduction." In Richard Marsh, *The Beetle*, edited by Julian Wolfreys. Peterborough, Ontario: Broadview Press, 2004: 9-34.

The publishing industry at the fin de siècle

Altick, Richard D., *The English Common Reader: A Social History of the Mass Reading Public, 1800-1900*. With a foreword by Jonathan Rose. Second edition. Columbus: Ohio State University Press, 1998.

Brantlinger, Patrick. *The Reading Lesson: The Threat of Mass Literacy in Nineteenth-Century British Fiction*. Bloomington & Indianapolis: Indiana University Press, 1998.

Eliot, Simon. *Some Patterns and Trends in British Publishing, 1800-1919*. London: The Bibliographical Society, 1994.

McAleer, Joseph. *Popular Reading and Publishing in Britain, 1914-1950*. Oxford: Clarendon Press, 1992.

McDonald, Peter D. *British Literary Culture and Publishing Practice, 1880-1914*. Cambridge: Cambridge University Press, 1997.

Pound, Reginald. *The Strand Magazine, 1891-1950*. London: Heinemann, 1966.

Detective fiction

Belsey, C. *Critical Practice*. London: Methuen, 1980.

Chernaik, W., Swales, M. and Vilain, R. (eds.). *The Art of Detective Fiction*. Basingstoke: Macmillan in association with the Institute of English Studies, School of Advanced Study, University of London, 2000.

Jann, R. "Sherlock Holmes Codes the Social Body." *English Literary History* 57 (1990): 685-708.

Knight, S. *Form and Ideology in Crime Fiction*. London: Macmillan, 1980.

Priestman, M. *Crime Fiction from Poe to the Present*. Plymouth: Northcote House/British Council, 1998.

The female detective

Craig, Patricia, and Mary Cadogan. *The Lady Investigates: Women Detectives and Spies in Fiction*. Oxford and New York: Oxford University Press, 1986.

Gavin, Adrienne E. "Feminist Crime Fiction and Female Sleuths." In *A Companion to Crime Fiction*, edited by Charles J. Rzepka and Lee Horsley. Chichester: Wiley-Blackwell, 2010: 258-69.

Godfrey, Emelyne. *Femininity, Crime and Self-Defence in Victorian Literature and Society: From Dagger-Fans to Suffragettes*. Houndmills: Palgrave, 2012.

Kestner, Joseph A. *Sherlock's Sisters: The British Female Detective, 1864-1913*. Aldershot: Ashgate, 2003.

Klein, Kathleen Gregory. *The Woman Detective: Gender & Genre*. 2nd edn. Urbana & Chicago: University of Illinois Press, 1995.

Kungl, Carla T. *Creating the Fictional Female Detective: The Sleuth Heroines of British Women Writers, 1890-1940*. Jefferson, N.C. and London: McFarland, 2006.

The New Woman

Ardis, A. *New Women, New Novels: Feminism and Early Modernism*. Brunswick, N.J.: Rutgers University Press, 1990.

Heilmann, A. *New Woman Fiction: Women Writing First-Wave Feminism*. Basingstoke: Macmillan, 2000.

Ledger, Sally. *The New Woman, Fiction and Feminism at the Fin de Siècle*. Manchester: Manchester University Press, 1997.

Pykett, Lyn. *The Improper Feminine: The Women's Sensation Novel and the New Woman Writing*. London: Routledge, 1992.

Richardson, A. and Willis, C. (eds.). *The New Woman in Fiction and Fact: Fin-de-Siècle Feminisms*. Basingstoke: Palgrave, 2001.

Showalter, Elaine. *Sexual Anarchy: Gender and Culture at the Fin de Siècle*. London: Virago, 2001.

Fin-de-siècle London, degeneration and crime

Fishman, W.J. *East End 1888: A Year in a London Borough among the Labouring Poor*. London: Duckworth, 1988.

Greenslade, William. *Degeneration, Culture and the Novel, 1880-1940*. Cambridge: Cambridge University Press, 1994.

Jones, Gareth Stedman. *Outcast London: A Study in the Relationship between Classes in Victorian Society*. Oxford: Clarendon Press, 1971.

McLaughlin, Joseph. *Writing the Urban Jungle: Reading Empire in London from Doyle to Eliot*. Charlottesville and London: University Press of Virginia, 2000.

Pick, Daniel. *Faces of Degeneration: A European Disorder, c. 1848-1918*. Cambridge: Cambridge University Press, 1993.

Schneer, Jonathan. *London 1900: The Imperial Metropolis*. New Haven and London: Yale University Press, 2001.

Walkowitz, Judith R. *City of Dreadful Delight: Narratives of Sexual Danger in Late Victorian London*. London: Virago, 2000.

Wiener, Martin J. *Reconstructing the Criminal: Culture, Law, and Policy in England, 1830-1914*. Cambridge: Cambridge University Press, 1994.

THE COMPLETE JUDITH LEE
ADVENTURES

THE MAN WHO CUT OFF MY HAIR

My name is Judith Lee. I am a teacher of the deaf and dumb. I teach them by what is called the oral system—that is, the lip-reading system.[1] When people pronounce a word correctly they all make exactly the same movements with their lips, so that, without hearing a sound, you only have to watch them very closely to know what they are saying. Of course, this needs practice, and some people do it better and quicker than others. I suppose I must have a special sort of knack in that direction, because I do not remember a time when, by merely watching people speaking at a distance, no matter at what distance if I could see them clearly, I did not know what they were saying. In my case the gift, or knack, or whatever it is, is hereditary. My father was a teacher of the deaf and dumb—a very successful one. His father was, I believe, one of the originators of the oral system. My mother, when she was first married, had an impediment in her speech which practically made her dumb; though she was stone deaf, she became so expert at lip-reading that she could not only tell what others were saying, but she could speak herself—audibly, although she could not hear her own voice.

So, you see, I have lived in the atmosphere of lip-reading all my life. When people, as they often do, think my skill at it borders on the marvellous, I always explain to them that it is nothing of the kind, that mine is simply a case of "practice makes perfect." This knack of mine, in a way, is almost equivalent to another sense. It has led me into the most singular situations, and it has been the cause of many really extraordinary adventures. I will tell you of one which happened to me when I was quite a child, the details of which have never faded from my memory.

[1] This technique of understanding speech by watching the movement of the speaker's lips has a history dating back to the sixteenth century.

My father and mother were abroad, and I was staying, with some old and trusted servants, in a little cottage which we had in the country. I suppose I must have been between twelve and thirteen years of age. I was returning by train to the cottage from a short visit which I had been paying to some friends. In my compartment there were two persons besides myself—an elderly woman who sat in front of me, and a man who was at the other end of her seat. At a station not very far from my home the woman got out; a man got in and placed himself beside the one who was already there. I could see they were acquaintances—they began to talk to each other.

They had been talking together for some minutes in such low tones that you could not only not hear their words, you could scarcely tell that they were speaking. But that made no difference to me; though they spoke in the tiniest whisper I had only to look at their faces to know exactly what they were saying. As a matter of fact, happening to glance up from the magazine I was reading, I saw the man who had been there first say to the other something which gave me quite a start. What he said was this (I only saw the fag-end of the sentence):—

". . . Myrtle Cottage; it's got a great, old myrtle in the front garden."

The other man said something, but as his face was turned from me I could not see what; the tone in which he spoke was so subdued that hearing was out of the question. The first man replied (whose face was to me):—

"His name is Colegate. He's an old bachelor, who uses the place as a summer cottage. I know him well—all the dealers know him. He's got some of the finest old silver in England. There's a Charles II. salt-cellar[1] in the place which would fetch twenty pounds an ounce anywhere."

The other man sat up erect and shook his head, looking straight in front of him, so that I could see what he said, though he spoke only in a whisper.

"Old silver is no better than new; you can only melt it."

The other man seemed to grow quite warm.

"Only melt it! Don't be a fool; you don't know what you're

---

[1] A dish for holding table salt dating back to the reign of Charles II (1660-1685).

talking about. I can get rid of old silver at good prices to collectors all over the world; they don't ask too many questions when they think they're getting a bargain. That stuff at Myrtle Cottage is worth to us well over a thousand; I shall be surprised if I don't get more for it."

The other man must have glanced at me while I was watching his companion speak. He was a fair-haired man, with a pair of light-blue eyes, and quite a nice complexion. He whispered to his friend:—

"That infernal kid is watching us as if she were all eyes."

The other said: "Let her watch. Much good may it do her; she can't hear a word—goggle-eyed brat!"

What he meant by "goggle-eyed" I didn't know, and it was true that I could not hear; but, as it happened, it was not necessary that I should. I think the other must have been suspicious, because he replied, if possible in a smaller whisper than ever:—

"I should like to twist her skinny neck and throw her out on to the line."

He looked as if he could do it too; such an unpleasant look came into his eyes that it quite frightened me. After all, I was alone with them; I was quite small; it would have been perfectly easy for him to have done what he said he would like to. So I glanced back at my magazine, and left the rest of their conversation unwatched.

But I had heard, or rather seen, enough to set me thinking. I knew Myrtle Cottage quite well, and the big myrtle tree; it was not very far from our own cottage. And I knew Mr. Colegate and his collection of old silver—particularly that Charles II. salt-cellar of which he was so proud. What interest had it for these two men? Had Mr. Colegate come to the cottage? He was not there when I left. Or had Mr. and Mrs. Baines, who kept house for him—had they come? I was so young and so simple that it never occurred to me that there could be anything sinister about these two whispering gentlemen.

They both of them got out at the station before ours. Ours was a little village station, with a platform on only one side of the line; the one at which they got out served for quite an important place—our local market town. I thought no more about them, but I did think of Mr. Colegate and of Myrtle Cottage. Dickson, our housekeeper, said that she did not believe that anyone was at the cottage, but she owned that she was not sure. So after tea I went for a stroll, without saying a word to anyone—Dickson had such a troublesome habit of wanting to know exactly where you were going. My stroll took me to Myrtle Cottage.

It stood all by itself in a most secluded situation on the other side of Woodbarrow Common. You could scarcely see the house from the road—it was quite a little house. When I got into the garden and saw that the front-room window was open I jumped to the very natural conclusion that someone must be there. I went quickly to the window—I was on the most intimate terms with everyone about the place; I should never have dreamt of announcing my presence in any formal manner—and looked in. What I saw did surprise me.

In the room was the man of the train—the man who had been in my compartment first. He had what seemed to me to be Mr. Colegate's entire collection of old silver spread out on the table in front of him, and that very moment he was holding up that gem of the collection—the Charles II. salt-cellar. I had moved very quietly, meaning to take Mr. Colegate—if it was he—by surprise; but I doubt if I had made a noise that that man would have heard me, he was so wrapped up in that apple of Mr. Colegate's eye.

I did not know what to make of it at all. I did not know what to think. What was that man doing there? What was I to do? Should I speak to him? I was just trying to make up my mind when someone from behind lifted me right off my feet and, putting a hand to my throat, squeezed it so tightly that it hurt me.

"If you make a sound I'll choke the life right out of you. Don't you make any mistake about it—I will!"

He said that out loudly enough, though it was not so very loud either—he spoke so close to my ear. I could scarcely breathe, but I could still see, and I could see that the man who held me so horribly by the throat was the second man of the train. The recognition seemed to be mutual.

"If it isn't that infernal brat! She seemed to be all eyes in the railway carriage, and, my word, she seems to have been all ears too."

The first man had come to the window.

"What's up?" he asked. "Who's that kid you've got hold of there?"

My captor twisted my face round for the other to look at.

"Can't you see for yourself? I felt, somehow, that she was listening."

"She couldn't have heard, even if she was; no one could have heard what we were saying. Hand her in here." I was passed through the window to the other, who kept as tight a grip on my throat as his friend had done.

"Who are you?" he asked. "I'll give you a chance to answer, but if you try to scream I'll twist your head right off you."

He loosed his grip just enough to enable me to answer if I wished. But I did not wish. I kept perfectly still. His companion said:—

"What's the use of wasting time? Slit her throat and get done with it."

He took from the table a dreadful-looking knife, with a blade eighteen inches long, which I knew very well. Mr. Colegate had it in his collection because of its beautifully-chased, massive silver handle. It had belonged to one of the old Scottish chieftains; Mr. Colegate would sometimes make me go all over goose-flesh by telling me of some of the awful things for which, in the old, lawless, bloodthirsty days in Scotland, it was supposed to have been used. I knew that he kept it in beautiful condition, with the edge as sharp as a razor. So you can fancy what my feelings were when that man drew the blade across my throat, so close to the skin that it all but grazed me.

"Before you cut her throat," observed his companion, "we'll tie her up. We'll make short work of her. This bit of rope will about do the dodge."

He had what looked to me like a length of clothes-line in his hand. With it, between them, they tied me to a great oak chair, so tight that it seemed to cut right into me, and, lest I should scream with the pain, the man with the blue eyes tied something across my mouth in a way which made it impossible for me to utter a sound. Then he threatened me with that knife again, and just as I made sure he was going to cut my throat he caught hold of my hair, which, of course, was hanging down my back, and with that dreadful knife sawed the whole of it from my head.

"HE CAUGHT HOLD OF MY HAIR, AND WITH THAT DREADFUL KNIFE SAWED THE WHOLE
OF IT FROM MY HEAD."

If I could have got within reach of him at that moment I believe
that I should have stuck that knife into him. Rage made me half
beside myself. He had destroyed what was almost the dearest
thing in the world to me—not because of my own love of it, but
on account of my mother's. My mother had often quoted to me,
"The glory of a woman is her hair," and she would add that mine
was very beautiful. There certainly was a great deal of it. She was
so proud of my hair that she had made me proud of it too—for her
sake. And to think that this man could have robbed me of it in so
hideous a way! I do believe that at the moment I could have killed
him.

I suppose he saw the fury which possessed me, because he
laughed and struck me across the face with my own hair.

"I've half a mind to cram it down your throat," he said. "It didn't
take me long to cut it off, but I'll cut your throat even quicker—if
you so much as try to move, my little dear."

The other man said to him:—

"She can't move and she can't make a sound either. You leave her alone. Come over here and attend to business."

"I'll learn her," replied the other man, and he lifted my hair above my head and let it fall all over me.

They proceeded to wrap up each piece of Mr. Colegate's collection in tissue paper, and then to pack the whole into two queer-shaped bags—pretty heavy they must have been. It was only then that I realized what they were doing—they were stealing Mr. Colegate's collection; they were going to take it away. The fury which possessed me as I sat there, helpless, and watched them! The pain was bad enough, but my rage was worse. When the man who had cut off my hair moved to the window with one of the bags held in both his hands—it was as much as he could carry—he said to his companion with a glance towards me: "Hadn't I better cut her throat before I go?"

"You can come and do that presently," replied the other; "you'll find her waiting." Then he dropped his voice and I saw him say: "Now you quite understand?" The other nodded. "What is it?"

The face of the man who had cut my hair was turned towards me. He put his lips very close to the other, speaking in the tiniest whisper, which he never dreamed could reach my ears: "Cotterill, Cloak-room, Victoria Station, Brighton Railway."[1]

The other whispered, "That's right. You'd better make a note of it; we don't want any bungling."

"No fear, I'm not likely to forget." Then he repeated his previous words, "Cotterill, Cloak-room, Victoria Station, Brighton Railway."

He whispered this so very earnestly that I felt sure there was something about the words which was most important; by the time he had said them a second time they were printed on my brain quite as indelibly as they were on his. He got out of the window and his bag was passed to him; then he spoke a parting word to me.

"Sorry I can't take a lock of your hair with me; perhaps I'll come back for one presently."

Then he went. If he had known the passion which was blazing in my heart! That allusion to my desecrated locks only made it

[1] Victoria Station, a major railway terminus in Central London serving the South of England, including the fashionable seaside resort of Brighton.

burn still fiercer. His companion, left alone, paid no attention to me whatever. He continued to secure his bag, searched the room, as if for anything which might have been overlooked, then, bearing the bag with the other half of Mr. Colegate's collection with him, he went through the door, ignoring my presence as if I had never existed. What he did afterwards I cannot say; I saw no more of him; I was left alone—all through the night.

What a night it was. I was not afraid; I can honestly say that I have seldom been afraid of anything—I suppose it is a matter of temperament—but I was most uncomfortable, very unhappy, and each moment the pain caused me by my bonds seemed to be growing greater. I do believe that the one thing which enabled me to keep my senses all through the night was the constant repetition of those mystic words: Cotterill, Cloak-room, Victoria Station, Brighton Railway. In the midst of my trouble I was glad that what some people call my curious gift had enabled me to see what I was quite sure they had never meant should reach my understanding. What the words meant I had no notion; in themselves they seemed to be silly words. But that they had some hidden, weighty meaning I was so sure that I kept saying them over and over again lest they should slip through my memory.

I do not know if I ever closed my eyes; I certainly never slept. I saw the first gleams of light usher in the dawn of another morning, and I knew the sun had risen. I wondered what they were doing at home—between the repetitions of that cryptic phrase. Was Dickson looking for me? I rather wished I had let her know where I was going, then she might have had some idea of where to look. As it was she had none. I had some acquaintances three or four miles off, with whom I would sometimes go to tea and, without warning to anyone at home, stay the night. I am afraid that, even as a child, my habits were erratic. Dickson might think I was staying with them, and, if so, she would not even trouble to look for me. In that case I might have to stay where I was for days.

I do not know what time it was, but it seemed to me that it had been light for weeks, and that the day must be nearly gone, when I heard steps outside the open window. I was very nearly in a state of stupor, but I had still sense enough to wonder if it was that man who had cut my hair come back again to cut my throat. As I watched the open sash my heart began to beat more vigorously than it had for a very long time. What then was my relief when there presently appeared, on the other side of it, the face of Mr. Colegate, the owner of Myrtle Cottage. I tried to scream—with joy, but that cloth across my mouth prevented my uttering a sound.

I never shall forget the look which came on Mr. Colegate's face when he saw me. He rested his hands on the sill as if he wondered how the window came to be open, then when he looked in and saw me, what a jump he gave.

"Judith!" he exclaimed. "Judith Lee! Surely it is Judith Lee!"

He was a pretty old man, or he seemed so to me, but I doubt if a boy could have got through that window quicker than he did. He was by my side in less than no time; with a knife which he took from his pocket was severing my bonds. The agony which came over me as they were loosed! It was worse than anything which had gone before. The moment my mouth was free I exclaimed—even then I was struck by the funny, hoarse voice in which I seemed to be speaking:—

"Cotterill, Cloak-room, Victoria Station, Brighton Railway."

So soon as I had got those mysterious words out of my poor, parched throat I fainted; the agony I was suffering, the strain which I had gone through, proved too much for me. I knew dimly that I was tumbling into Mr. Colegate's arms, and then I knew no more.

When I came back to life I was in bed. Dickson was at my bedside, and Dr. Scott, and Mr. Colegate, and Pierce, the village policeman, and a man who I afterwards knew was a detective, who had been sent over post-haste from a neighbouring town. I wondered where I was, and then I saw I was in a room in Myrtle Cottage. I sat up in bed, put up my hands—then it all came back to me.

"He cut off my hair with MacGregor's knife!" MacGregor was the name of the Highland chieftain to whom, according to Mr. Colegate, that dreadful knife had belonged.

When it did all come back to me and I realized what had happened, and felt how strange my head seemed without its accustomed covering, nothing would satisfy me but that they should bring me a looking-glass. When I saw what I looked like the rage which had possessed me when the outrage first took place surged through me with greater force than ever. Before they could stop me, or even guess what I was going to do, I was out of bed and facing them. That cryptic utterance came back to me as if of its own initiative; it burst from my lips.

"Cotterill, Cloak-room, Victoria Station, Brighton Railway! Where are my clothes? That's where the man is who cut off my hair."

They stared at me. I believe that for a moment they thought that what I had endured had turned my brain, and that I was mad. But I soon made it perfectly clear that I was nothing of the kind. I told them my story as fast as I could speak; I fancy I brought it home to their understanding. Then I told them of the words which I had seen spoken in such a solemn whisper, and how sure I was that they were pregnant with weighty meaning.

"Cotterill, Cloak-room, Victoria Station, Brighton Railway —that's where the man is who cut my hair off—that's where I'm going to catch him."

The detective was pleased to admit that there might be something in my theory, and that it would be worth while to go up to Victoria Station to see what the words might mean. Nothing would satisfy me but that we should go at once. I was quite convinced that every moment was of importance, and that if we were not quick we should be too late. I won Mr. Colegate over—of course, he was almost as anxious to get his collection back as I was to be quits with the miscreant who had shorn me of my locks. So we went up to town by the first train we could catch—Mr. Colegate, the detective, and an excited and practically hairless child.

When we got to Victoria Station we marched straight up to the cloak-room, and the detective said to one of the persons on the other side of the counter:—

"Is there a parcel here for the name of Cotterill?"

The person to whom he had spoken did not reply, but another man who was standing by his side.

"Cotterill? A parcel for the name of Cotterill has just been taken out—a hand-bag, scarcely more than half a minute ago. You must have seen him walking off with it as you came up. He can hardly be out of sight now." Leaning over the counter, he looked along the platform. "There he is—someone is just going to speak to him."

I saw the person to whom he referred—a shortish man in a light grey suit, carrying a brown leather hand-bag. I also saw the person who was going to speak to him; and thereupon I ceased to have eyes for the man with the bag. I broke into exclamation.

"There's the man who cut my hair!" I cried. I went rushing along the platform as hard as I could go. Whether the man had heard me or not I cannot say; I dare say I had spoken loudly enough; but he gave one glance in my direction, and when he saw me I have no doubt that he remembered. He whispered to the man with the bag. I was near enough to see, though not to hear, what he said. In spite of the rapidity with which his lips were moving, I saw quite distinctly.

"Bantock, 13, Harwood Street, Oxford Street."[1] That was what he said, and no sooner had he said it than he turned and fled—from me; I knew he was flying from me, and it gave me huge satisfaction to know that the mere sight of me had made him run. I was conscious that Mr. Colegate and the detective were coming at a pretty smart pace behind me.

The man with the bag, seeing his companion dart off without the slightest warning, glanced round to see what had caused his hasty flight. I suppose he saw me and the detective and Mr. Colegate, and he drew his own conclusions. He dropped that hand-bag as if it had been red-hot, and off he ran. He ran to such purpose that we never caught him—neither him nor the man who had cut my hair. The station was full of people—a train had just come in. The crowd streaming out covered the platform with a swarm of moving figures. They acted as cover to those two eager gentlemen—they got clean off. But we got the bag; and, one of the station officials coming on the scene, we were shown to an apartment where, after explanations had been made, the bag and its contents were examined.

Of course, we had realized from the very first moment that Mr. Colegate's collection could not possibly be in that bag, because it was not nearly large enough. When it was seen what was in it, something like a sensation was created. It was crammed with small articles of feminine clothing. In nearly every garment jewels were wrapped, which fell out of them as they were withdrawn from the

[1] While Harwood Street appears to be imaginary, Oxford Street is a major West End thoroughfare and shopping district.

bag. Such jewels! You should have seen the display they made when they were spread out upon the leather-covered table—and our faces as we stared at them.

"This does not look like my collection of old silver," observed Mr. Colegate.

"IN NEARLY EVERY GARMENT JEWELS WERE WRAPPED, WHICH FELL OUT OF THEM AS THEY WERE WITHDRAWN FROM THE BAG."

"No," remarked a big, broad-shouldered man, who I afterwards learned was a well-known London detective, who had been induced by our detective to join our party, "This does not look like your collection of old silver, sir; it looks, if you'll excuse my saying so, like something very much more worth finding. Unless I am mistaken, these are the Duchess of Datchet's jewels, some of which she wore at the last Drawing Room,[1] and which were taken from her Grace's bedroom after her return. The police all over Europe have been looking for them for more than a month."

"That bag has been with us nearly a month. The party who took it out paid four-and-sixpence[2] for cloak-room charges—twopence a day for twenty-seven days."

The person from the cloak-room had come with us to that apartment; it was he who said this. The London detective replied:—

"Paid four-and-sixpence, did he? Well, it was worth it—to us. Now, if I could lay my hand on the party who put that bag in the cloak-room, I might have a word of a kind to say to him."

I had been staring, wide-eyed, as piece by piece the contents of the bag had been disclosed; I had been listening, open-eared, to what the detective said; when he made that remark about laying his hands on the party who had deposited that bag in the cloak-room, there came into my mind the words which I had seen the man who had cut my hair whisper as he fled to the man with the bag. The cryptic sentence which I had seen him whisper as I sat tied to the chair had indeed proved to be full of meaning; the words which, even in the moment of flight, he had felt bound to utter might be just as full. I ventured on an observation, the first which I had made, speaking with a good deal of diffidence.

"I think I know where he might be found—I am not sure, but I think."

All eyes were turned to me. The detective exclaimed:—

"You think you know? As we haven't got so far as thinking, if you were to tell us, little lady, what you think, it might be as well, mightn't it?"

I considered—I wanted to get the words exactly right.

"Suppose you were to try"—I paused so as to make quite sure—"Bantock, 13, Harwood Street, Oxford Street."

"And who is Bantock?" the detective asked. "And what do you know about him, anyhow?"

[1] A royal morning reception.
[2] Four shillings, six pence. Up to 1971, the British pound was made up of twenty shillings, each shilling = twelve pence, the pound thus consisting of 240 pence.

"I don't know anything at all about him, but I saw the man who cut my hair whisper to the other man just before he ran away, 'Bantock, 13, Harwood Street, Oxford Street'—I saw him quite distinctly."

"You saw him whisper? What does the girl mean by saying she saw him whisper? Why, young lady, you must have been quite fifty feet away. How, at that distance, and with all the noise of the traffic, could you hear a whisper?"

"I didn't say I heard him; I said I saw him. I don't need to hear to know what a person is saying. I just saw you whisper to the other man, 'The young lady seems to be by way of being a curiosity.'"

The London detective stared at our detective. He seemed to be bewildered.

"But I—I don't know how you heard that; I scarcely breathed the words."

Mr. Colegate explained. When they heard they all seemed to be bewildered, and they looked at me, as people do look at the present day, as if I were some strange and amazing thing. The London detective said:—

"I never heard the like to that. It seems to me very much like what old-fashioned people called 'black magic.'"

Although he was a detective, he could not have been a very intelligent person after all, or he would not have talked such nonsense. Then he added, with an accent on the "saw":—

"What was it you said you *saw* him whisper?"

I bargained before I told him.

"I will tell you if you let me come with you."

"Let you come with me?" He stared still more. "What does the girl mean?"

"Her presence," struck in Mr. Colegate, "may be useful for purposes of recognition. She won't be in the way; you can do no harm by letting her come."

"If you don't promise to let me come I sha'n't tell you."

The big man laughed. He seemed to find me amusing; I do not know why. If he had only understood my feeling on the subject of my hair, and how I yearned to be even with the man who had wrought me what seemed to me such an irreparable injury. I daresay it sounds as if I were very revengeful. I do not think it was a question of vengeance only; I wanted justice. The detective took out a fat note-book.

"Very well; it's a bargain. Tell me what you saw him whisper, and you shall come." So I told him again, and he wrote it down. "'Bantock, 13, Harwood Street, Oxford Street.' I know Harwood Street, though I don't know Mr. Bantock. But he seems to be residing at what is generally understood to be an unlucky number. Let me get a message through to the Yard[1]—we may want assistance. Then we'll pay a visit to Mr. Bantock—if there is such a person. It sounds like a very tall story to me."

I believe that even then he doubted if I had seen what I said I saw. When we did start I was feeling pretty nervous, because I realized that if we were going on a fool's errand, and there did turn out to be no Bantock, that London detective would doubt me more than ever. And, of course, I could not be sure that there was such a person, though it was some comfort to know that there was a Harwood Street. We went four in a cab[2]—the two detectives, Mr. Colegate and I. We had gone some distance before the cab stopped. The London detective said:—

"This is Harwood Street; I told the driver to stop at the corner— we will walk the rest of the way. A cab might arouse suspicion; you never know."

It was a street full of shops. No. 13 proved to be a sort of curiosity shop and jeweller's combined; quite a respectable-looking place, and sure enough over the top of the window was the name "Bantock."

"That looks as if, at any rate, there were a Bantock," the big man said; it was quite a weight off my own mind when I saw the name.

Just as we reached the shop a cab drew up and five men got out, whom the London detective seemed to recognize with mingled feelings.

"That's queered the show," he exclaimed. I did not know what he meant. "They rouse suspicion, if they do nothing else—so in we go."

---

[1] Scotland Yard, the headquarters of the Metropolitan Police and the detective force.
[2] The hansom cab, a fast public two-wheeled carriage, was designed to seat two people.

And in we went—the detective first, and I close on his heels. There were two young men standing close together behind the counter. The instant we appeared I saw one whisper to the other:—

"Give them the office—ring the alarm-bell—they're 'tecs!"

I did not quite know what he meant either, but I guessed enough to make me cry out:—

"Don't let him move—he's going to ring the alarm-bell and give them the office."

Those young men were so startled—they must have been quite sure that I could not have heard—that they both stood still and stared; before they had got over their surprise a detective—they were detectives who had come in the second cab—had each by the shoulder.

There was a door at the end of the shop which the London detective opened.

"There's a staircase here; we'd better go up and see who's above. You chaps keep yourselves handy, you may be wanted—when I call you come."

He mounted the stairs—as before, I was as close to him as I could very well get. On the top of the staircase was a landing, on to which two doors opened. We paused to listen; I could distinctly hear voices coming through one of them.

"I think this is ours," the London detective said.

He opened the one through which the voices were coming. He marched in—I was still as close to him as I could get. In it were several men, I did not know how many, and I did not care; I had eyes for only one. I walked right past the detective up to the table round which some of them were sitting, some standing, and stretching out an accusatory arm I pointed at one.

"That's the man who cut off my hair!"

It was, and well he knew it. His conscience must have smitten him; I should not have thought that a grown man could be so frightened at the sight of a child. He caught hold, with both hands, of the side of the table; he glared at me as if I were some dreadful apparition—and no doubt to him I was. It was only with an effort that he seemed able to use his voice.

"Good night!" he exclaimed, "it's that infernal kid!"

On the table, right in front of me, I saw something with which I

"THAT'S THE MAN WHO CUT OFF MY HAIR!"

was only too familiar. I snatched it up.

"And this is the knife," I cried, "with which he did it!"

It was; the historical blade, which had once belonged to the sanguinary and, I sincerely trust, more or less apocryphal MacGregor. I held it out towards the gaping man.

"You know that this is the knife with which you cut off my hair," I said. "You know it is."

I dare say I looked a nice young termagant[1] with my short hair, rage in my eyes, and that frightful weapon in my hand. Apparently I did not impress him quite as I had intended—at least, his demeanour did not suggest it.

[1] A virago; a violent, troublesome female.

"By the living Jingo!"[1] he shouted. "I wish I had cut her throat with it as well!"

It was fortunate for him that he did not. Probably, in the long run, he would have suffered for it more than he did—though he suffered pretty badly as it was. It was his cutting my hair that did it. Had he not done that I have little doubt that I should have been too conscious of the pains caused me by my bonds—the marks caused by the cord were on my skin for weeks after—to pay such close attention to their proceedings as I did under the spur of anger. Quite possibly that tell-tale whisper would have gone unnoticed. Absorbed by my own suffering, I should have paid very little heed to the cryptic sentence which really proved to be their undoing. It was the outrage to my locks which caused me to strain every faculty of observation I had. He had much better have left them alone.

That was the greatest capture the police had made for years. In one haul they captured practically every member of a gang of cosmopolitan thieves who were wanted by the police all over the world. The robbery of Mr. Colegate's collection of old silver shrank into insignificance before the rest of their misdeeds. And not only were the thieves taken themselves, but the proceeds of no end of robberies.

It seemed that they had met there for a sort of annual division of the common spoil. There was an immense quantity of valuable property before them on the table, and lots more about the house. Those jewels which were in the bag which had been deposited at the cloak-room at Victoria Station were to have been added to the common fund—to say nothing of Mr. Colegate's collection of old silver.

The man who called himself Bantock, and who owned the premises at 13, Harwood Street, proved to be a well-known dealer in precious stones and jewellery and *bric-a-brac* and all sorts of valuables. He was immensely rich; it was shown that a great deal of his money had been made by buying and selling valuable stolen property of every sort and kind. Before the police had done with him it was made abundantly clear that, under various *aliases*, in half the countries of the world, he had been a wholesale dealer in stolen goods.

[1] A mild oath.

He was sentenced to a long term of penal servitude. I am not quite sure, but I believe that he died in jail.

All the men who were in that room were sent to prison for different terms, including the man who cut my hair—to say nothing of his companion. So far as the proceedings at the court were concerned, I never appeared at all. Compared to some of the crimes of which they had been guilty, the robbery of Mr. Colegate's silver was held to be a mere nothing. They were not charged with it at all, so my evidence was not required. But every time I looked at my scanty locks, which took years to grow to anything like a decent length—they had reached to my knees, but they never did that again—each time I stood before a looking-glass and saw what a curious spectacle I presented with my closely-clipped poll, something of that old rage came back to me which had been during that first moment in my heart, and I felt—what I felt when I was tied to that chair in Myrtle Cottage. I endeavoured to console myself, in the spirit of the Old World rather than the New, that, owing to the gift which was mine, I had been able to cry something like quits with the man who, in a moment of mere wanton savagery, had deprived me of what ought to be the glory of a woman.

EAVESDROPPING AT INTERLAKEN

I have sometimes thought that this gift of mine for reading words as they issue from people's lips places me, with or without my will, in the position of the eavesdropper. There have been occasions on which, before I knew it, I have been made cognisant of conversations, of confidences, which were meant to be sacred; and, though such knowledge has been acquired through no fault of mine, I have felt ashamed, just as if I had been listening at a key-hole, and I have almost wished that the power which Nature gave me, and which years of practice have made perfect, was not mine at all. On the other hand, there have been times when I was very glad indeed that I was able to play the part of eavesdropper. As, to very strict purists, this may not sound a pleasant confession to make, I will give an instance of the kind of thing I mean.

I suppose I was about seventeen; I know I had just put my hair up, which had grown to something like a decent length since it had come in contact with the edge of that doughty Scottish chieftain's —MacGregor's—knife. My mother was not very well. My father was reluctant to leave her. It looked as if the summer holiday which had been promised me was in peril, when two acquaintances, Mr. and Mrs. Travers, rather than that I should lose it altogether, offered to take me under their wing. They were going for a little tour in Switzerland, proposing to spend most of their time at Interlaken,[1] and my parents, feeling that I should be perfectly safe with them, accepted their proffered chaperonage. Everything went well until we got to Interlaken. There they met some friends who were going on a climbing expedition, and, as Mr. and Mrs. Travers were both keen mountaineers, they were very eager to join them. I was the only difficulty in their way. They could not say exactly how long they would be absent, but probably a week; and what was to become of me in that great hotel there all alone? They protested that it would be quite impossible to leave me; they would have to

[1] A picturesque international holiday resort in Switzerland, situated between the two lakes of Thun and Brienz.

give up that climb; and I believe they would have done so if what seemed to be a solution of the difficulty had not turned up.

The people in the hotel were for the most part very sociable folk, as people in such places are apt to be. Among other persons whose acquaintance we had made was a middle-aged widow, a Mrs. Hawthorne. When she heard of what Mr. and Mrs. Travers wanted to do, and how they could not do it because of me, she volunteered, during their absence, to occupy their place as my chaperon, assuring them that every possible care should be taken of me.

In the hotel were stopping a brother and sister, a Mr. and Miss Sterndale. With them I had grown quite friendly. Mr. Sterndale I should have set down as twenty-five or twenty-six, and his sister as a year or two younger. From the day on which I had first seen them they had shown an inclination for my society; and, to speak quite frankly, on different occasions Mr. Sterndale had paid me what seemed to me to be delicate little attentions which were very dear to my maiden heart. I had some difficulty in inducing people to treat me as if I were grown up. After a few minutes' conversation even perfect strangers would ask me how old I was, and when I told them they were apt to assume an attitude towards me as if I were the merest child, of which I disapproved.

What attracted me to Mr. Sterndale was that, from the very first, he treated me with deference, as if I were at least as old as he was.

On the third day after Mr. and Mrs. Travers had left Mrs. Hawthorne came to me with a long face and a letter in her hand.

"My dear, I cannot tell you how annoyed I am, but I shall have to go to England at once—to-day. And whatever will become of you?"

It seemed that her only sister was dangerously ill, and that she was implored to go to her as soon as she could. Of course, she would have to go. I told her that it did not matter in the least about me; Mr. and Mrs. Travers would be back in a day or two, and now that I knew so many people in the hotel, who were all of them disposed to be friendly, I should be perfectly all right until they came. She must not allow any consideration for me to keep her for a moment from obeying her sister's call. She left for London that afternoon; but, so far from everything being perfectly all right with me after she had gone, the very next day my troubles began.

They began in the morning. I was sitting on the terrace with a book. Mr. Sterndale had been talking to me. Presently his sister came through an open French window from the lounge. Her brother went up to her; I sat still. She was at the other end of the terrace, and when she saw me she nodded and smiled. When her brother came up to her, he said something which, as his back was towards me, of course I did not catch; but her answer to him, which was very gently uttered, I saw quite distinctly; all the while she was speaking she was smiling at me.

"She has a red morocco[1] jewel-case sort of a thing on the corner of her mantel-shelf; I put it under the bottom tray. With the exception of that gold locket which she is always wearing it's the only decent thing in it; it's full of childish trumpery."

That was what Miss Sterndale said to her brother, and I saw her say it with rather curious feelings. What had he asked her? To what could she be referring? I had "a red morocco jewel-case sort of a thing," and it stood on a corner of my mantel-shelf. I also had a gold locket, which, if I was not, as she put it, always wearing, I did wear pretty often. Certainly it was the only article in my jewel-case which was worth very much; and with a horrid sort of qualm I owned to myself that the rest of the contents might come under the definition of "childish trumpery." She said she had put something under the bottom tray. What bottom tray? Whose bottom tray? There were trays in my jewel-case; she could not possibly have meant that she had put anything under one of them. The idea was too preposterous. And yet, if we had not been going to St. Beatenberg[2] I think I should have gone straight up to my bedroom to see. I do not know how it was; the moment before I had been perfectly happy; there was not a grain of suspicion in the air, nor in my mind; then all of a sudden I felt quite curious. Could there be two persons in the house possessed of "a red morocco jewel-case sort of a thing," which stood on a corner of the mantel-shelf, in which was a gold locket and a rather mixed collection of childish trumpery? I wondered.

The evening before we had arranged to make an excursion to St. Beatenberg on the Lake of Thun—five or six of us. I was dressed ready to start when Miss Sterndale came through that

[1] Fine soft leather made of goatskin.
[2] A village located above the picturesque Lake of Thun, offering panoramic views of the Alps; approximately six miles from Interlaken.

French window. She also was ready, and her brother. Presently the others appeared. I was feeling a little confused; I could not think of an excuse which would give me an opportunity of examining my jewel-case. Anyhow, I kept trying to tell myself it was absurd. I wished I could not see what people were saying merely by watching their lips.

My day at St. Beatenberg was spoilt, though I kept telling myself that it was all my own fault, and nobody else's. Everyone was gay, and full of fun and laughter—everyone but me. My mood was so obviously out of tune with theirs that they commented on it.

"What is the matter with you, Miss Lee?" asked Mrs. Dalton; "you look as if you were not enjoying yourself one little bit."

I did not like to say that I was not; as a matter of fact, when they rallied me I said that I was—but it was not true.

When I got back to the hotel and was in my bedroom, I went straight up to that "red morocco jewel-case sort of a thing" and looked at it. It was locked, just as I had left it. Clearly I had been worrying myself all day long about nothing at all. Still, I got my keys and opened it; there was nothing to show that the contents had been touched. I lifted the two trays—and I gasped. I do not know how else to describe it—something seemed all at once to be choking me, so that it was with an effort that I breathed. In the jewel-case, under the bottom tray, was a pendant—a beautiful circular diamond pendant, of the size, perhaps, of a five-shilling piece. It was not mine; I never had anything so beautiful in my life. Where did it come from? Could Miss Sterndale have put it there? Was that the meaning of her words?

I took the pendant out. It was a beauty; it could not be a present from the Sterndales, from either the sister or the brother. They must have known that I could not accept such a gift as that from strangers. And then, what a queer way of making a present—and such a present!

As I looked at it I began to have a very uncomfortable feeling that I had seen it before, or one very like it, on someone in the house. My head, or my brain, or something, seemed to be so muddled that at the moment I could not think who that someone was. I had washed and tidied myself before I decided that I would go down with the pendant in my hand and, at the risk of no matter what misunderstanding, ask Miss Sterndale what she meant by putting it there. So, when I had got my unruly hair into something like order, downstairs I went, and rushed into the lounge with so much impetuosity that I all but cannoned against Miss Goodridge, who was coming out.

"Good gracious, child!" she exclaimed. "Do look where you are going. You almost knocked me over."

The instant I saw her, and she said that, I remembered—I knew whom I had seen wearing that diamond pendant which I was holding tightly clasped in the palm of my hand. It was the person whom I had almost knocked over, Miss Goodridge herself—of course! One of the persons in the hotel whom, so far as I knew anything of them, I liked least. Miss Goodridge was a tall, angular person of perhaps quite thirty-five, who dressed and carried herself as if she were still a girl. She had been most unpleasant to me. I had no idea what I had done or said to cause her annoyance, but I had a feeling that she disliked me, and was at no pains to conceal the fact. The sight of her, and the thought that I had nearly knocked her over, quite drove the sense out of my head.

"Oh, Miss Goodridge!" I exclaimed, rather fatuously. "You look as if something had happened."

"Something has happened," she replied. "There's a thief in the house. I have been robbed. Someone has stolen my pendant—my diamond pendant."

Someone had stolen her diamond pendant! I do not know if the temperature changed all at once, but I do know that a chill went all over me. Was that the explanation? Could it possibly be—— I did not care to carry even my thought to a logical finish. I stood there as if I were moonstruck, with Miss Goodridge looking at me with angry eyes.

"What is the matter with the child?" she asked. "I did not know you dark-skinned girls could blush, but I declare you've gone as red as a lobster."

I do not know if she thought that lobsters were red before they were boiled. I tried to explain, to say what I wanted to say, but I appeared to be tongue-tied.

"Can't you speak?" she demanded. "Don't glare at me as if you'd committed a murder. Anyone would think that you had been

"GET OUT OF MY WAY! DON'T YOU EVER DARE TO SPEAK TO ME AGAIN."

robbed instead of me. I suppose you haven't stolen my pendant?"

She drew her bow at a venture, but her arrow hit the mark.

"Oh, Miss Goodridge!" I repeated. It seemed to be all I could say.

She put her hand upon my shoulder.

"What is the matter with the girl? You young wretch! Have you been playing tricks with that pendant of mine?"

"I—I found it," I stammered. I held out to her my open hand with the pendant on the palm.

"You—you found it? Found what?" She looked at me and then at my outstretched hand. "My pendant! She's got my pendant!" She snatched it from me. "You—you young—thief! And you have the insolence to pretend you found it!"

"I did find it—I found it in my bedroom."

"Did you really? Of all the assurance! I've always felt that you were the kind of creature with whom the less one had to do the better, but I never credited you with a taste for this sort of thing. Get out of way! Don't you ever dare to speak to me again."

She did not wait for me to get out of way; she gave me a violent push and rushed right past me. It was a polished floor; if I had not come in contact with a big armchair I should have tumbled on to it. My feelings when I was left alone in the lounge were not enviable. At seventeen, even if one thinks oneself grown up, one is still only a child, and I was a stranger in a strange land, without a friend in all that great hotel, without a soul to advise me. Still, as I knew that I was absolutely and entirely innocent, I did not intend to behave as if I were guilty. I went up to my room again and dressed for dinner. I told myself over and over again as I performed my simple toilette that I would make Miss Goodridge eat her words before she had done, though at that moment I had not the faintest notion how I was going to do it.

That was a horrid dinner—not from the culinary, but from my point of view. If the dinner was horrid, in the lounge afterwards it was worse. Miss Sterndale actually had the audacity to come up to me and pretend to play the part of sympathetic friend.

"You seem to be all alone," she began. I was all alone; I had never thought that anyone could feel so utterly alone as I did in that crowded lounge. "Miss Lee, why do you look at me like that?" I was looking at her as if I wished her to understand that I was looking into her very soul—if she had one. Her smiling serenity of countenance was incredible to me, knowing what I knew. "Have you had bad news from home, or from Mr. and Mrs. Travers, or are you unhappy because Mrs. Hawthorne has gone? You seem so different. What has been the matter with you the whole of to-day?"

I was on the point of giving an explanation which I think might have startled her when I happened to glance across the room. At a table near the open window, Mr. Sterndale was sitting with Miss Goodridge. They were having coffee. Although Miss Goodridge was sitting sideways, she continually turned her head to watch me. Mr. Sterndale was sitting directly facing me. He had a cigarette in one hand, and every now and then he sipped his coffee, but most of the time he talked. But, although I could not even hear the sound of his voice, I saw what he said as distinctly as if he had been shouting in my ear. It was the sentence he was uttering which caused me to defer the explanation which I had it in my mind to give to his sister.

"Of course, the girl's a thief—I'm afraid that goes without saying." It was that sentence which was issuing from his lips at the moment when I chanced to glance in his direction which caused the explanation I had been about to make to his sister to be deferred.

Miss Goodridge had her coffee-cup up to her mouth, so I could not see what she said; but if I had been put to it I might have made a very shrewd guess by the reply he made. He took his cigarette from his lips, blew out a thin column of smoke, leaned back in his chair—and all the time he was looking smilingly at me with what he meant me to think were the eyes of a friend.

"It's all very well for you to talk. I may have had my suspicions, but it is only within the last hour or two that they have been confirmed."

She said something which again I could not see; his reply suggested that she must have asked a question.

"I'll tell you what I mean by saying that my doubts have been confirmed. A man was passing through this afternoon with whom I have some acquaintance—the Rector of Leeds." I wonder he did not say the Bishop of London. "He saw—our friend——" He made a slight inclination of his head towards me. "At sight of her he exclaimed: 'Halloa, there's that Burnett girl!' For a parson he has rather a free and easy way of speaking; he's one of your modern kind." I believed him! "'Burnett girl?' I said. 'But her name's Lee —Judith Lee.' 'Oh, she calls herself Lee now, does she? That settles it.' 'Settles what?' I asked, because I saw that there was something in his tone. 'My dear Reggie,' he said (he always calls me Reggie; I've known him for years), 'at the beginning of the season that girl whom you call Judith Lee was at Pontresina,[1] staying in the same hotel as I was. She called herself Burnett then. Robberies were going on all the time, people were continually missing things. At last a Russian woman lost a valuable lot of jewellery. That settled it—Miss Burnett went.'"

Miss Goodridge turned so that her face was hidden; but, as before, his reply gave me a pretty good clue as to the question she had asked.

"Of course I mean it. Do you think I'd say a thing like that if I didn't mean it? I won't tell you all he said—it wouldn't be quite fair. But it came to this. He said that the young lady whom we have all thought so sweet and innocent——"

Miss Goodridge interposed with a remark which, in a guessing competition, I think I could have come pretty near to. He replied:—

"Well, I've sometimes felt that you were rather hard on her, that perhaps you were a trifle prejudiced."

Miss Goodridge turned her face towards me, and then I saw her words.

"I'm a better judge of feminine human nature than you suppose. The first moment I saw her I knew she was a young cat, though I admit I didn't take her to be as bad as she is. What did your clerical friend say of her, of the Miss Burnett whom we know now as Miss Lee?"

I did not wait to learn his answer—I had learnt enough. What his sister thought of my demeanour I did not care; I had been dimly conscious that she had been talking to me all the while, but what she was saying I do not know. My attention had been wholly taken up with what I did not hear. Before he began his reply to Miss Goodridge's genial inquiry I got up from my chair and marched out of the lounge, without saying a word to Miss Sterndale. When I had gone a little way I remembered that I had left my handkerchief—my best lace handkerchief—on the table by which I had been sitting, Even in the midst of my agitation I was conscious that I could not afford to lose it, so went back for it.

Miss Sterndale had joined her brother and Miss Goodridge. Two

---

[1] A Swiss resort in the Southern Alps.

or three other people were standing by them, evidently interested in what was being said. I found my handkerchief. As I was going off with it Miss Sterndale turned round in my direction, without, however, thinking it worth her while to break off the remark she was making, taking it for granted, of course, that it was inaudible to me. I came in, as it were, for the tail end of it.

"... I am so disappointed in her; I have tried to like her, and now I fear it is only too certain that she is one of those creatures of whom the less said the better."

That these words referred to me I had not the slightest doubt. Yet, while they were still on her lips, presuming on her conviction that they were hidden from me, she nodded and smiled as if she were wishing me a friendly good-night.

The treachery of it! Now that I am able to look back calmly, I think it was that which galled me most. Her brother, with his gratuitous, horrible lies, had actually been pretending to make love to me—I am sure that was what he wished me to think he was doing. What a fool he must have thought me!

That was a sleepless night. It was hours before I got between the sheets, and when I did it was not to slumber. The feeling that I was so entirely alone, and that there was not a soul within miles and miles to whom I could turn for help, coupled with the consciousness that I had scarcely enough money to pay the hotel bill, and, what was even worse, that Mr. and Mrs. Travers had gone off with the return-half of my ticket to London, so that I could not go back home however much I might want to—these things were hard enough to bear; but they seemed to be as nothing compared to that man and woman's treachery. What was their motive, what could have induced them, was beyond my comprehension. It was a problem which I strove all night to solve. But the solution came on the morrow.

I soon knew what had happened when I went downstairs. Miss Goodridge had told her story of the pendant, and Mr. Sterndale had circulated his lie about his clerical friend. Everybody shunned me. Some persons had the grace to pretend not to see me; others looked me full in the face and cut me dead. The only persons who were disposed to show any perception of my presence were the Sterndales. As, entering the breakfast-room, I passed their table, they both smiled and nodded, but I showed no consciousness of them. As I took a seat at my own table, I saw him say to his sister:—

"Our young friend seems to have got her back up—little idiot!"

Little idiot, was I? Only yesterday he had called me something else. The feeling that he was saying such things behind my back hurt me more than if he had shouted them to my face. I averted my gaze, keeping my eyes fixed on my plate. I would learn no more of what he said about me, or of what anyone said. I was conscious that life might become unendurable if I were made acquainted with the comments which people were making on me then. Yet, as I sat there with downcast face, might they not construe that as the bearing of a conscience-stricken and guilty wretch? I felt sure that that was what they were doing. But I could not help it; I would not see what they were saying.

Later in the morning matters turned out so that I did see, so that practically I had to see what the Sterndales said to each other. And perhaps, on the whole, it was fortunate for me that I did. I had spent the morning out of doors. On the terrace the Sterndales were standing close together, talking; so engrossed were they by what they were saying that they did not notice me; while, though I did not wish to look at them, something made me. That may seem to be an exaggeration. It is not—it is the truth. My wish was to have nothing more to do with them for ever and ever; but some instinct, which came I know not whence, made me turn my eyes in their direction and see what they were saying. And, as I have already said, it was well for me that I did.

They both seemed to be rather excited. He was speaking quickly and with emphasis.

"I tell you," he was saying, as I paused to watch, "we will do it to-day."

His sister said something which, as she was standing sideways, was lost to me. He replied:—

"The little idiot has cooked her own goose; there's no need for us to waste time in cooking it any more—she's done. I tell you we can strip the house of all it contains, and they'd lock her up for doing it."

Again his sister spoke; without, because of her position, giving herself away to me. He went on again:—

"There are only two things in the house worth having—I could give you a catalogue of what everyone has got. Mrs. Anstruther's diamonds—the necklace is first-rate, and the rest of them aren't bad; and that American woman's pearls. Those five ropes of pearls are worth—I hope they'll be worth a good deal to us. The rest of the things you may make a present of to our young friend. The odium will fall on her—you'll see. We shall be able to depart with the only things worth having, at our distinguished leisure, without a stain upon our characters."

He smiled—some people might have thought it a pleasant smile—to me it seemed a horrid one. That smile finished me—it reminded me of the traitor's kiss. I passed into the house still unnoticed, though I do not suppose that if I had been noticed it would have made any difference to them.

What he meant by what he had said I did not clearly understand. The only thing I quite realized was that he was still making sport of me. I also gathered that that was an amusement which he proposed to continue, though just how I did not see. Nor did I grasp the inner meaning of his allusion to Mrs. Anstruther's diamonds and Mrs. Newball's pearls—no doubt it was Mrs. Newball he meant when he spoke of the American woman. The fine jewels of those two ladies, which they aired at every opportunity, were, as I knew perfectly well, the talk of the whole hotel. Probably that was what they meant they should be. When Mrs. Anstruther had diamonds round her neck and on her bosom and in her ears and hair and round her wrists and on her fingers—I myself had seen her wear diamond rings on all the fingers of both hands and two diamond bracelets on each wrist—she was a sight to be remembered; while Mrs. Newball, with her five strings of splendid pearls, which she sometimes wore all together as a necklace and sometimes twisted as bracelets round her wrists, together with a heterogeneous collection of ornaments of all sorts and kinds, made a pretty good second.

Not a person spoke to me the whole of that day. Everyone avoided me in a most ostentatious manner; and everyone, or nearly everyone, had been so friendly. It was dreadful. If I had had enough money to pay the hotel bill, as well as the return-half of my ticket home, I believe I should have left Interlaken there and then. But the choice of whether I would go or stay, as it turned out, was not to be left to me.

Depressed, miserable, homesick, devoutly wishing that I had never left home, almost resolved that I would never leave it again, I was about to go up to my room to dress for what I very well knew would only be the ghastly farce of dinner, when, as I reached the lift, a waiter came up to me and said that the manager wished to see me in his office. I did not like the man's manner; it is quite easy for a Swiss waiter to be rude, and I was on the point of telling him that at the moment I was engaged and that the manager would have to wait, when something which I thought I saw in his eye caused me to change my mind, and, with an indefinable sense of discomfort, I allowed him to show me to the managerial sanctum. I never had liked the look of that manager; I liked it less than ever when I found myself alone in his room with him. He was a young-ish man, with a moustache, and hair parted mathematically in the centre. In general his bearing was too saccharine to he pleasant; he did not err in that respect just then—it was most offensive. He looked me up and down as if I were one of his employés who had done something wrong, and, without waiting for me to speak, he said:—

"You are Miss Judith Lee—or you pretend that is your name?"

He spoke English very well, as most of the Swiss one meets in hotels seem to do. Nothing could have been more impertinent than his tone, unless it was the look which accompanied it. I stared at him.

"I am Miss Lee. I do not pretend that is my name; it is."

"Very well—that is your affair, not mine. You will no longer be allowed to occupy a room in this hotel. You can go at once."

"What do you mean?" I asked. The man was incredible.

"You know very well what I mean. Don't you try that sort of thing with me. You have stolen an article of jewellery belonging to a guest in my hotel. She is a very kind-hearted lady, and she is not willing to hand you over to the police. You owe me some money; here's your bill. Are you going to pay it?"

He handed me a long strip of paper which was covered with figures. One glance at the total was enough to tell me that I had not enough money. Mrs. Travers was acting as my banker. She had left me with ample funds to serve as pocket-money till she returned, but with nothing like enough money to pay that bill.

"' MY DIAMONDS HAVE BEEN STOLEN !' SHE CRIED."

"Mrs. Travers will pay you when she comes back, either to-morrow or the day after."

"Will she?" The sneer with which he said it! "How am I to know that you're not at the same game together?"

"The same game! What do you mean? How dare you look at me like that, and talk to me as if I were one of your servants!"

"I'm not going to talk to you at all, my girl; I'm going to do. I'm not going to allow a person who robs my guests to remain in my house under any pretext whatever. Your luggage, such as it is, will remain here until my bill is paid." He rang a bell which was on the table by which he was standing. The waiter entered who had showed me there. He was a big man, with a square, dark face. "This young woman must go at once. If she won't leave of her own accord we must put her out, by the back door. Now, my girl—out you go!"

The waiter approached me. He spoke to me as he might have done to a dog.

"Now, then, come along."

He actually put his hand upon my shoulder. Another second, and I believe he would have swung me round and out of the room. But just as he touched me the door was opened and someone came rushing in—Mrs. Anstruther, in a state of the greatest excitement.

"My diamonds have been stolen!" she cried. "Someone has stolen my diamonds!"

"Your diamonds?" The manager looked at her and then at me. "I trust, madam, you are mistaken?"

"I'm not mistaken." She sank on to a chair. She was a big woman of about fifty, and, at the best of times, was scant of breath. Such was her agitation that just then she could scarcely breathe at all. "As if I could be mistaken about a thing like that! I went up to my bedroom—to dress for dinner—and I unlocked my trunk—I always keep it locked; I took out my jewel-case—and unlocked that—and my diamonds were gone. They've been stolen!—stolen!—stolen!"

She repeated the word "stolen" three times over, as if the heinousness of the fact required to be emphasized by repetition. The manager was evidently uneasy, which even I felt was not to be wondered at.

"This is a very serious matter, Mrs. Anstruther——"

She cut him short.

"Serious? Do you think I need you to tell me that it's serious? You don't know how serious. Those diamonds are worth thousands and thousands of pounds—more than the whole of your twopenny-halfpenny hotel—and they've been stolen. From my trunk, in my bedroom, in your hotel, they've been stolen!"

The way she hurled the words at him! He looked at me, and he asked:—

"What do you know about this?"

What did I know? In the midst of my confusion and distress I was asking myself what I did know. Before I could speak the door was opened again and Mrs. Newball came in. And not Mrs. Newball only, but six or seven other women, some of them accompanied by men—their husbands and their brothers. And they all told the same tale. Something had been stolen from each: from Mrs. Newball her five strings of pearls, from Mrs. This and Miss That the article of jewellery which was valued most. I am convinced that that manager, or his room, or probably his hotel, had never witnessed such a scene before. They were all as excited as could be, and they were all talking at once, and every second or two someone else kept coming in with some fresh tale of a dreadful loss. How that man kept his head at all was, and is, a mystery to me. At last he reduced them to something like silence, and in the presence of them all he said to me—pointing at me with his finger, as if I were a thing to be pointed at:—

"It is you who have done this! You!"

Someone exclaimed in the crowd: "I saw her coming out of Mrs. Anstruther's room."

The manager demanded: "Who spoke? Who was it said that?"

A slight, faded, fair-haired woman came out into the public gaze.

"I am Mrs. Anstruther's maid. I was going along to her room when I saw this young lady come out of the door. Whether she saw me or not I can't say; she might have done, because she ran off as fast as ever she could. I wondered what she was doing there, and when my mistress came I told her what I had seen, and that's what made her open her trunk."

"What Perkins says is quite true," corroborated Mrs. Anstruther. "She did tell me, and that made me uneasy; I had heard something about a diamond pendant having been stolen last night, so I opened my jewel-case, and my diamonds were gone."

"Mine was the diamond pendant which was stolen by this creature last night," interposed Miss Goodridge. "She came to my room and took it out of my trunk. Since she did that it seems not impossible that she has played the same trick on other people to-day. If she has, she must have had a pretty good haul, because I don't believe there is a person in the hotel who hasn't lost something."

The manager spoke to an under-strapper.

"Have this young woman's luggage searched at once, in the presence of witnesses, and let me know the result as soon as you possibly can."

As the under-strapper went out I noticed for the first time that Mr. Sterndale was present with the rest, and almost at the same instant his sister came in. She looked about her as if wondering what was the cause of all the fuss. Then she went up to her brother, and he whispered something to her, and she whispered something to him. Only three or four words in each case, but my heart gave a leap in my bosom—I mean that, really, because it did feel as if it actually had jumped—courage came into me, and strength, and something better than hope: certainty; because they had delivered themselves into my hands. I was never more thankful that I had the power of eavesdropping—you can call it eavesdropping, if you like!—than I was at that moment. Only a second before I had been fearing that I was in a tight place, from which there was no way out; which would mean something for me from which my very soul seemed to shrink. But God had given me a gift, a talent, which I had striven with all my might to improve ten, twenty fold, and that would deliver me from the wiles of those two people, even when hope of deliverance there seemed none. I feel confident that I held myself straighter, that trouble went from my face as it had done from my heart, and that, though each moment the case against me seemed to be growing blacker and blacker, I grew calmer and more self-possessed. I knew I had only to wait till the proper moment came, and the toils in which they thought they had caught me would prove to be mere nothings; they would be caught, and I should be free.

All the same, until that moment for which I was waiting came, it was not nice for me—standing there amidst all those excited people, between two porters, who kept close to either side of me, as if I were a prisoner and they had me in charge; though I dare say it was as well that they did keep as close to me as they did, because I fancy that some of the injured guests at that hotel would have liked to give me a practical demonstration of what their feelings towards me were.

That under-strapper came back in a surprisingly short space of time with a hand-bag—a brown bag, which I recognized to be my own.

The agitated guests crowded round him like a swarm of bees. He had difficulty in forcing his way through them. The manager did his best to keep them in something like order—first with a show of mildness.

"Ladies, gentlemen—gently, gently, if you please." Then, with sudden ferocity: "Stand back, there! If you will not stand back, if you will not make room, how can anything be done? Keep these people back!"

To whom this order was addressed was not quite clear. Thus admonished, the people kept themselves back—at least, sufficiently to enable that under-strapper to pass with my bag to the table. The manager said to him:—

"Go to the other side; what have you in that bag?" When, as he said this, his guests evinced an inclination to press forward, he threw out his arms on either side of him and positively shouted:—

"Will you not keep back? If you will keep back, everything shall be done in order before you all. I ask you only to be a little sensible. If there is so much confusion, we shall not know what we are doing. I beg of you that you will be calm."

If they were not precisely calm, the people did show some slight inclination to behave with an approach to common sense. They permitted the bag to be placed on the table, and the manager to open it, having first put some questions to the young man who brought it in.

"Where did you find this bag?"

"In her room." I was the "her," which he made clear by pointing his finger straight at me.

"Was anyone else present in the room at the time you found it? Did you find anything else?"

"There were three other persons present in the room. That bag was the first thing I touched. When I opened it and saw what was inside, I thought that, for the present, that would be enough. I think you also will be of my opinion when you see what it contains."

Then the manager opened the bag. He looked inside, then he turned it upside down and allowed the whole contents to fall out on to the table. Of all the extraordinary collections! I believe there were articles belonging to every person in the hotel. When you came to think of it, it was amazing how they had been gathered

together—in what could only have been a short space of time—
without the gatherer being detected. As for the behaviour of the
guests of the hotel, it was like Bedlam broken loose.[1] They pressed
forward all together, ejaculating, exclaiming, snatching at this and
that, as each saw some personal belonging.

" HE TURNED IT UPSIDE DOWN AND ALLOWED THE WHOLE CONTENTS TO FALL OUT ON TO
THE TABLE."

"Keep back! Keep back!" shouted the manager. "Will you not
keep back?" As he positively roared at them they did shrink back as
if a trifle startled. "If you will only have a little patience each lady
shall have what belongs to her—if it is here."

Mrs. Anstruther's voice was heard above the hubbub: "Are my
diamonds there?" Then Mrs. Newball's: "And my pearls?"

The under-strapper was examining the miscellaneous collection which my bag had contained with all those women breaking
into continual exclamations, watching him with hungry eyes. He
announced the result of his examination.

"No; Mrs. Anstruther's diamonds do not appear to be here, nor
Mrs. Newball's pearls; there is nothing here which at all resembles
them."

The manager held out towards me a minatory finger;[2] everyone

[1] It was complete chaos.
[2] Threatening, menacing.

seemed to have developed a sudden mania for pointing, particularly at me.

"You! Where have you put Mrs. Newball's pearls and Mrs. Anstruther's diamonds? Better make a clean breast of it, and no longer play the hypocrite. We will find them, if you do not tell us where they are, be sure of it. Now tell us at once."

How he thundered at me! It was most embarrassing, or it would have been if I had not been conscious that I held the key of the situation in my hand. As it was, I minded his thunder scarcely a little bit, though I always have hated being shouted at. I was very calm—certainly the calmest person there—which, of course, was not saying very much.

"I can tell you where they are, if that is what you mean."

"You know that is what I mean. Tell us at once! at once!"

He banged his fist upon the table so that that miscellaneous collection trembled. I did not tremble, though perhaps it was his intention that I should. I was growing calmer and calmer.

"In the first place, let me inform you that if you suppose I put those things in my bag—the bag is certainly mine—or had anything to do with their getting there, you are mistaken."

My words, and perhaps my manner, created a small diversion. "What impudence!" "What assurance!" "Did you ever see anything like it?" "So young and so brazen!" "The impudent baggage!" Those were some of the things which they said, which were very nice for me to have to listen to. But I was sure, from a glimpse I had caught of Mr. and Miss Sterndale, that they were not quite at their ease, and that was such a comfort.

"No lies!" thundered the manager, whose English became a little vulgar. "No foolery! No stuck-up rubbish! Tell us the truth—where are these ladies' jewels?"

"I propose to tell you the truth, if you will have a little patience." I returned him look for look; I was not the least afraid of him. "I am going to give you a little surprise." I was so conscious of that that I was beginning to feel almost amused. "I have a power of which I think none of you have any conception, especially two of you. I know what people are saying although I do not hear them; like the deaf and dumb, who know what a person is saying by merely watching his lips."

There were some very rude interruptions, to which I paid no notice whatever. An elderly man whom I had never seen before and who spoke with an air of authority, advised them to give me a hearing. They did let me go on.

I told them what I had seen Miss Sterndale say to her brother on the balcony the morning before. It was some satisfaction to see the startled look which came upon the faces of both the brother and the sister. They made some very noisy and uncivil comments, but, as I could see how uncomfortable they were feeling, I let them make them. I went on. I told how unhappy I had been all day, and how, when I returned, I found under the bottom tray of my jewel-case the diamond pendant. How, astounded, I went down to ask Miss Sterndale why she had put it there, and how, encountering Miss Goodridge bewailing her loss, utterly taken aback, I held out to her her pendant in a manner which, I admitted, might very easily have seemed suspicious.

By this time the manager's room was in a delightful state of din. Mr. and Miss Sterndale were both of them shouting together, declaring that it was shocking that such a creature as I was should be allowed to make such monstrous insinuations. I believe, if it had not been for that grey-haired man who had suddenly assumed a position of authority, that Miss Sterndale would have made a personal assault on me. She seemed half beside herself with rage— and, I was quite sure, with something else as well.

I continued—in spite of the Sterndales. I could see that I was creating a state of perplexity in the minds of my hearers which might very shortly induce them to take up an entirely different attitude towards me. I told of the brief dialogue which had taken place between the sister and brother that very morning. And then you should have seen how the Sterndales stormed and raged.

"It seems to me," observed the grey-haired man to Mr. Sterndale, "that you protest too much, sir. If this young lady is all the things you say she is, presently you will have every opportunity of proving it. Since she is one young girl among all us grown-ups, it is only right and decent that we should hear what she has to say for herself. We can condemn her afterwards—that part will be easy."

So I went on again. There was very little to add. They knew almost as much of the rest as I did. Someone had effected a wholesale clearance of pretty nearly every valuable which the house contained. I did not pretend to be certain, but I thought it extremely probable that it was Miss Sterndale who had done this, while her brother kept the owners occupied in other directions. At this point glances were exchanged. I afterwards learned that Mr. Sterndale had organized a party for an excursion on the Lake of Brienz, which had been joined by nearly everyone in the place with the exception of Miss Sterndale, who was supposed to have gone for a solitary expedition up the Schynige Platte.[1] When Miss Sterndale saw those glances, as I have no doubt she did, she commenced to storm and rage again, and continued to the end. I do not think, even then, she guessed what was coming; but she was already more uncomfortable than she had expected to be, and I could see that her brother felt the same. His face was white and set; he looked like a man who was trying to think of the best way in which to confront a desperate situation.

I went on to explain, quite calmly, that as, owing to the machinations of Mr. Sterndale and his sister, everyone in the house had come to look upon me as a thief, their evident intention was to allow suspicion to be centred on me, and that that was why they put those things in my bag.

"But what were they going to gain by that?" asked the grey-haired man, rather pertinently. His question was echoed in a chorus by the rest—particularly, I noticed, by the Sterndales, who laid emphasis on the transparent absurdity of what I was saying.

"If you will allow me to continue, I will soon make it perfectly clear to you what they were going to gain. If you remember, when Mr. Sterndale was talking to his sister on the balcony this morning, I saw him say to her that there were only two things in the house worth having——"

Here Mr. Sterndale burst into a very hurricane of adjectives. The grey-haired man addressed him with rather unlooked-for vigour.

"Silence, sir! Allow Miss Lee to continue."

Mr. Sterndale was silent. I fancy he was rather cowed by what he saw in the speaker's eyes. I did continue.

[1] Regular boat cruises had taken place on the dramatic Lake Brienz with its steep banks since the 1830s; the Schynige Platte is a mountain region offering good views of the Alps.

"The only two things which, according to Mr. Sterndale, were worth having were Mrs. Anstruther's diamonds and Mrs. Newball's pearls. If they put the whole of the rest of the stolen things into my bag it would be taken for granted that I was the thief, and they would be able to continue in unsuspected possession of the two things which were worth much more than all the rest put together."

The moment I stopped the clamour began again.

"And where do you suggest, young lady," asked the grey-haired man, "that those two articles are?"

"I will tell you." I looked at Miss Sterndale and then at her brother. I believe they would both have liked to have killed and eaten me. They can scarcely have been sure, even then, of what I was going to say, but I could see that they were devoured by anxiety and fear. "I have told you that I can see what people are saying by merely watching their lips. When Miss Sterndale came into the room she whispered something to her brother, in so faint a whisper that her words could have been scarcely audible even to themselves; but I saw their faces, and I knew what they had said as plainly as if they had shouted it. He told her that he had Mrs. Anstruther's diamonds in the pocket of the jacket he has on."

I paused. The first expression on Mr. Sterndale's face was one of blank astonishment. Then he broke into Billingsgate[1] abuse of me.

"You infernal liar! You two-faced cat! You dirty little witch! I'm not going to stay in this room to be insulted by a miserable creature——"

He made for the door. "Stop him!" I cried. As he reached the door it was thrown back, almost in his face, and who should come into the room but Mr. and Mrs. Travers. How glad I was to see them! "Stop him!" I cried to Mr. Travers. "Stop that man!" And Mr. Travers stopped him. "Put your hand into the pocket of his jacket and take out what he has there."

Mr. Travers, knowing nothing of what had been taking place, must have been rather at a loss as to what I might mean by such a request; but he did as I told him, all the same. Mr. Sterndale struggled; he did his best to protect himself and his pocket; but he was rather a small man, and Mr. Travers was a giant, both in stature and

---

[1] Vulgar, obscene, abusive, foul, after the East London fish market.

in strength. In a very few seconds he was staring at the contents of his hand.

"From the look of things, this gentleman's pocket seems to be stuffed with diamonds. Here's a diamond necklace."

" FROM THE LOOK OF THINGS, THIS
GENTLEMAN'S POCKET SEEMS TO BE STUFFED WITH DIAMONDS."

He held one up in the air. Heavy weight though she was, I believe that Mrs. Anstruther sprang several inches from the floor.

"It's my necklace!" she screamed.

"And where are my pearls?" demanded Mrs. Newball.

"Miss Sterndale whispered to her brother that your pearls were inside the bodice of her dress."

The words were scarcely out of my lips before Mrs. Newball sprang at Miss Sterndale, and there ensued a really painful scene. Had she not been restrained, I dare say she would have torn Miss Sterndale's clothes right off her. As it was, someone opened her bodice, and the pearls were produced.

The scene which followed was like pandemonium on a small scale. It seemed as if everyone had gone stark, staring mad. Guests, manager, and staff were all shouting together. I know that Mrs. Travers had her arm round me, and I was happier than—only a few minutes before—I thought that I should ever feel again.

We did not prosecute the Sterndales—which turned out not to be their name, and they were proved not to be sister and brother. Law in Switzerland does not move too quickly; the formalities to be observed are numerous. I did not very much want to have to remain in Switzerland for an indefinite period, at my own expense, to give evidence in a case in which I was not in the faintest degree interested. The others, the guests in the hotel, did not want to do that any more than I did. Their property was restored to them— that was what they wanted. They would have liked to punish the thieves, but not at the cost of so much inconvenience to themselves. So far as we were concerned, the criminals got off scot-free; but, none the less, they did not escape the vengeance of the law. That night they were arrested at Interlaken on another charge. It seemed that they were the perpetrators of that robbery in the hotel at Pontresina which, according to Mr. Sterndale, his apocryphal clerical friend had laid at my door. They had passed there as Mr. and Mrs. Burnett, and were found guilty and sentenced to a long term of imprisonment. I have not seen or heard anything of that pseudonymous brother and sister since. I hope I never shall.

To find out what people are saying to each other in confidence, when they suppose themselves to be out of the reach of curious ears, may be very like eavesdropping. If it is, I am very glad that, on various occasions in my life, I have been enabled to be an eavesdropper in that sense. Had I not, at Interlaken, had the power which made of me an eavesdropper, I might have been branded as a criminal, and my happiness, my whole life, have been destroyed for ever.

CONSCIENCE

I had been spending a few days at Brighton, and was sitting one morning on the balcony of the West Pier pavilion,[1] listening to the fine band of the Gordon Highlanders. The weather was beautiful—the kind one sometimes does get at Brighton—blue skies, a warm sun, and just that touch in the soft breeze which serves as a pick-me-up. There were crowds of people. I sat on one end of a bench. In a corner, within a few feet of me, a man was standing, leaning with his back against the railing—an odd-looking man, tall, slender, with

"PRESENTLY ANOTHER MAN CAME ALONG THE BALCONY AND PAUSED CLOSE TO HIM."

[1] Brighton, a major seaside resort on the South coast of England, approximately 50 miles south of London, had two piers in 1911: The West Pier, opened in 1866, and the Palace Pier, opened in 1899.

something almost Mongolian in his clean-shaven, round face. I had noticed him on that particular spot each time I had been on the pier. He was well tailored, and that morning, for the first time, he wore a flower in his buttonhole. As one sometimes does when one sees an unusual-looking stranger, I wondered hazily what kind of person he might be. I did not like the look of him.

Presently another man came along the balcony and paused close to him. They took no notice of each other; the new-comer looked attentively at the crowd promenading on the deck below, almost ostentatiously disregarding the other's neighbourhood. All the same, the man in the corner whispered something which probably reached his ears alone—and my perception—something which seemed to be a few disconnected words:—

"Mauve dress, big black velvet hat, ostrich plume; four-thirty train."

That was all he said. I do not suppose that anyone there, except the man who had paused and the lazy-looking girl whose eyes had chanced for a moment to wander towards his lips had any notion that he had spoken at all. The new-comer remained for a few moments idly watching the promenaders; then, turning, without vouchsafing the other the slightest sign of recognition, strolled carelessly on.

It struck me as rather an odd little scene. I was constantly being made an unintentional confidante of what were meant to be secrets; but about that brief sentence which the one had whispered to the other there was a piquant something which struck me as amusing—the more especially as I believed I had seen the lady to whom the words referred. As I came on the pier I had been struck by her gorgeous appearance, as being a person who probably had more money than taste.

Some minutes passed. The Mongolian-looking man remained perfectly quiescent in his corner. Then another man came strolling along—big and burly, in a reddish-brown suit, a green felt hat worn slightly on one side of his head. He paused on the same spot on which the first man had brought his stroll to a close, and he paid no attention to the gentleman in the corner, who looked right away from him, even while I could see his lips framing precisely the same sentence:—

"Mauve dress, big black velvet hat, ostrich plume; four-thirty train."

The big man showed by no sign that he had heard a sound. He continued to do as his predecessor had done—stared at the promenaders, then strolled carelessly on.

This second episode struck me as being rather odder than the first. Why were such commonplace words uttered in so mysterious a manner? Would a third man come along? I waited to see—and waited in vain. The band played "God Save the King," the people rose, but no third man had appeared. I left the Mongolian-looking gentleman still in his corner and went to the other side of the balcony to watch the people going down the pier. I saw the gorgeous lady in the mauve dress and big black picture hat[1] with a fine ostrich plume, and I wondered what interest she might have for the round-faced man in the corner, and what she had to do with the four-thirty train. She was with two or three equally gorgeous ladies and one or two wonderfully-attired men; they seemed to be quite a party.

The next day I left Brighton by an early train. In the compartment I was reading the *Sussex Daily News*, when a paragraph caught my eye. "Tragic Occurrence on the Brighton Line." Late the night before the body of a woman had been found lying on the ballast, as if she might have fallen out of a passing train. It described her costume—she was attired in a pale mauve dress and a big black picture hat in which was an ostrich-feather plume. There were other details—plenty of them—but that was enough for me.

When I read that and thought of the man leaning against the railing I rather caught my breath. Two young men who were facing each other at the other end of the compartment began to talk about the paragraph in tones which were audible to all.

"Do you see that about the lady in the mauve dress who was found on the line? Do you know, I shouldn't wonder a bit if it was Mrs. Farningham—that's her rig-out to a T. And I know she was going up to town yesterday afternoon."

"She did go," replied the other; "and I'm told that when she started she'd had about enough cold tea."

[1] A decorated, wide-brimmed hat.

The other grinned—a grin of comprehension.

"If that's so I shouldn't wonder if the poor dear opened the carriage door, thinking it was some other door, and stepped out on to the line. From all I hear, it seems that she was quite capable of doing that sort of thing when she was like that."

"Oh, quite; not a doubt of it. And she was capable of some pretty queer things when she wasn't like that."

I wondered; these young gentlemen might be right; still, the more I thought the more I wondered.

I was very much occupied just then. It was because I had nearly broken down in my work that I had gone for those few days to Brighton. I doubt if I even glanced at a newspaper for some considerable time after that. I cannot say that the episode wholly faded from my memory, but I never heard what was the sequel of the lady who was found on the line, or, indeed, anything more about her.

I accepted an engagement with a deaf and dumb girl who was about to travel with her parents on a long voyage, pretty nearly round the world. I was to meet them in Paris, and then go on with them to Marseilles, where the real journey commenced. The night before I started some friends gave me a sort of send-off dinner at the Embankment Hotel. We were about half-way through the meal when a man came in and sat by himself at a small round table, nearly facing me. I could not think where I had seen him before. I was puzzling my brain when a second man came across the room and strolled slowly by his table. He did not pause, nor did either allow a sign to escape him to show that they were acquaintances, yet I distinctly saw the lips of the man who was seated at the table frame about a dozen words:—

"White dress, star in her hair, pink roses over left breast. To-night."

The stroller went carelessly on, and for a moment my heart seemed to stand still. It all came back to me—the pier, the band of the Gordon Highlanders, the man with his back against the railings, the words whispered to the two men who had paused beside him. The diner in front of me was the Mongolian-looking man; I should have recognized him at once had not evening dress wrought such a change in him. That whispered sentence made assurance doubly sure. The party with whom I was dining had themselves been struck

"I COULD NOT THINK WHERE I HAD SEEN HIM BEFORE."

by the appearance of the lady in the white frock, with the diamond star in her hair and the pink roses arranged so daintily in the corsage of her dress. There had been a laughing discussion about who was the nicest-looking person in the room; more than one opinion had supported the claim of the lady with the diamond star.

In the middle of that dinner I found myself all at once in a quandary, owing to that very inconvenient gift of mine. I recalled the whisper about the lady in the mauve dress, and how the very next day the body of a lady so attired had been found on the Brighton line. Was the whispered allusion to the lady in the white dress to have a similar unpleasant sequel? If there was fear of anything of the kind, what was I to do?

My friends, noticing my abstraction, rallied me on my inattention.

"May I point out to you," observed my neighbour, "that the waiter is offering you asparagus, and has been doing so for about five minutes?"

Looking round, I found that the waiter was standing patiently at my side. I allowed him to help me. I was about to eat what he had given me when I saw someone advancing across the room whom I knew at once, in spite of the alteration which evening dress made in him—it was the big, burly man in the red-brown suit.

The comedy—if it were a comedy—was repeated. The big man, not, apparently, acknowledging the existence of the solitary diner, passed his table, seemingly by the merest chance, in the course of his passage towards another on the other side of the room. With a morsel of food on his fork poised midway between the plate and his mouth, the diner moved his lips to repeat his former words:—

"White dress, star in her hair, pink roses over left breast. To-night."

The big man had passed, the morsel of food had entered the diner's mouth; nothing seemed to have happened, yet I was on the point of springing to my feet and electrifying the gaily-dressed crowd by crying, "Murder!"

More than once afterwards I wished I had done so. I do not know what would have happened if I had; I have sometimes asked myself if I could say what would *not* have happened. As a matter of fact, I did nothing at all. I do not say it to excuse myself, nor to blame anyone, but it seemed to me, at the moment, that to do anything was impossible, because those with whom I was dining made it so. I was their guest; they took care to make me understand that I owed them something as my hosts. They were in the merriest mood themselves; they seemed to regard it as of the first importance that I should be merry too. To the best of my ability I was outwardly as gay as the rest of them. The lady in the white dress, with her party, left early. I should have liked to give her some hint, some warning—I did neither; I just let her go. As she went across the room one or two members of our party toasted her under their breath. The solitary diner took no heed of her whatever. I had been furtively watching him the whole time, and he never once glanced in her direction. So far as I saw, he was so absorbed in his meal that he scarcely raised his eyes from the table. I knew, unfortunately, that I could not have mistaken the words which I had seen his lips forming. I tried to comfort myself with the reflection that they could not have referred to the vision of feminine loveliness which had just passed from the room.

The following morning I travelled by the early boat-train to Dover.[1] When the train had left the station I looked at my *Telegraph*. I read a good deal of it; then, at the top of a column on one of the inside pages, I came upon a paragraph headed: "Mysterious Affair at the Embankment Hotel." Not very long after midnight—in time, it seemed, to reach the paper before it went to press—the body of a young woman had been found in the courtyard of the hotel. She was in her night attire. She was recognized as one of the guests who had been staying in the hotel; she had either fallen or been thrown out of her bedroom window.

Something happened to my brain so that I was unconscious of the train, in which I was a passenger, as it sped onwards.

What did that paragraph mean? Could the woman who had been found in her night attire in the courtyard of the Embankment Hotel be the woman who had worn the white dress and a diamond star in her pretty brown hair? There was nothing to show that she was. There was nothing to connect that lightly-clothed body with the whispered words of the solitary diner, with a touch of the Mongol in his face; yet I wondered if it were not my duty to return at once to London and tell my story. But, after all, it was such a silly story; it amounted to nothing; it proved nothing. Those people were waiting for me in Paris; I could not desert them at the last moment, with all our passages booked, for what might turn out to be something even more fantastic than a will-o'-the-wisp.

So I went on to Paris, and, with them, nearly round the world; and I can say, without exaggeration, that more than once that curious-looking gentleman's face seemed to have gone with me. Once, in an English paper which I picked up after we had landed at Hong-Kong, I read about the body of a woman which had been

[1] A train from London connecting with a ferry across the English Channel at Dover; a convenient way of reaching the Continent.

found on the Great Western Railway line near Exeter station—and I wondered. When I went out into the streets and saw on the faces of the people who thronged them something which recalled the solitary diner at the Embankment Hotel—I wondered still more.

More than two years elapsed. In the summer of the third I went to Buxton,[1] as I had gone to Brighton, for a rest. I was seated one morning in the public gardens, with my thoughts on the other side of the world—we had not long returned from the Sandwich Islands[2]—and I was comparing that land of perpetual summer with the crisp freshness of the Buxton air. With my thoughts still far away, my eyes passed idly from face to face of those around me, until presently I became aware that under the shade of a tree on my left a man was sitting alone. When I saw his face my thoughts came back with a rush; it was the man who had been on the pier at Brighton, and at the Embankment Hotel, and who had travelled with me round the world. The consciousness of his near neighbourhood gave me a nasty jar; as at the Embankment Hotel there was an impulsive moment when I felt like jumping on to my feet and denouncing him to the assembled crowd. He was dressed in a cool grey suit; as at Brighton, he had a flower in his buttonhole; he sat upright and impassive, glancing neither to the left nor right, as if nothing was of interest to him.

Then the familiar comedy, which I believe I had rehearsed in my dreams, began again. A man came down the path from behind me, passing before I had seen his face, and under the shady tree paused for an instant to light a cigarette, and I saw the lips of the man on the chair forming words:—

"Grey dress, lace scarf, Panama hat;[3] five-five train."

His lips framed those nine words only; then the man with the cigarette passed on, and I really do believe that my heart stood still. Comedy? I had an uncomfortable conviction that this was a tragedy which was being played—in the midst of that light-hearted crowd, in that pleasant garden, under those laughing skies. I waited for the action to continue—not very long. In the distance I saw a big, burly person threading his way among the people towards that

---

[1]   A Derbyshire spa town.
[2]   Hawaii.
[3]   A hat made of straw, intended for warm temperatures.

shady tree, and I knew what was coming. He did not pause even for a single instant, he just went slowly by, within a foot of the chair, and the thin lips shaped themselves into words:—

"Grey dress, lace scarf, Panama hat; five-five train."

The big man sauntered on, leaving me with the most uncomfortable feeling that I had seen sentence of death pronounced on an innocent, helpless fellow-creature. I did not propose to sit still this time and allow those three uncanny beings, undisturbed, to work their evil wills. As at the hotel, the question recurred to me—what was I to do? Was I to go up and denounce this creature to his face? Suppose he chose to regard me as some ill-conducted person, what evidence had I to adduce that any statements I might make were true? I decided, in the first place, to leave him severely alone; I had thought of another plan.

Getting up from my chair I began to walk about the gardens. As had not been the case on the two previous occasions, there was no person in sight who answered to the description—"Grey dress, lace scarf, Panama hat." I was just about to conclude that this time the victim was not in plain view, when I saw a Panama hat in the crowd on the other side of the band. I moved quickly forward; it was certainly on a woman's head. There was a lace scarf spread out upon her shoulders, a frock of a very light shade in grey. Was this the woman whose doom had been pronounced? I went more forward still, and, with an unpleasant sense of shock, recognized the wearer.

I was staying at the Empire Hotel. On the previous afternoon, at tea-time, the lounge had been very full. I saw a tall lady, who seemed to be alone, glancing about as if looking for an empty table. As she seemed to have some difficulty in finding one, and as I had a table all to myself, I suggested, as she came near, that she should have a seat at mine. The manner in which she received my suggestion took me aback. I suppose there are no ruder, more ill-bred creatures in the world than some English women. Whether she thought I wished to force my company upon her and somehow scrape an acquaintance I cannot say. She could not have treated my suggestion with more contemptuous scorn had I tried to pick her pocket. She just looked down at me, as if wondering what kind of person I could be that I had dared to speak to her at all, and then, without condescending to reply, went on. I almost felt as if she had given me a slap across my face.

After dinner I saw her again in the lounge. She wore some very fine jewellery—she was a very striking woman, beautifully gowned. A diamond brooch was pinned to her bodice. As she approached I saw it was unfastened; it fell within a foot of where I was sitting. I picked it up and offered it to her, with the usual formula.

"I think this is your brooch—you have just dropped it."

How do you think she thanked me? She hesitated a second to take the brooch, as if she thought I might be playing her some trick. Then, when she saw that it was hers, she took it and looked it carefully over—and what do you suppose she said?

"You are very insistent."

That was all, every word—in such ineffable tones! She was apparently under the impression that I had engineered the dropping of that diamond brooch as a further step in my nefarious scheme to force on her the dishonour of my acquaintance.

This was the lady who in the public gardens was wearing a light grey dress, a lace scarf, and a Panama hat. What would she say to me if I told her about the man under the shady tree and his two friends? Yet, if I did not tell her, should I not feel responsible for whatever might ensue? That she went in danger of her life I was as sure as that I was standing there. She might be a very unpleasant, a very foolish woman, yet I could not stand by and allow her quite possibly to be done to death, without at least warning her of the danger which she ran. The sooner the warning was given the better. As she turned into a side path I turned into another, meaning to meet her in the centre of hers and warn her there and then.

The meeting took place, and, as I had more than half expected, I entirely failed to do what I had intended. The glance she fixed on me when she saw me coming and recognized who I was conveyed sufficient information. It said, as plainly as if in so many words, that if I dared to insult her by attempting to address her it would be at my own proper peril. None the less, I did dare. I remembered the woman in the mauve dress, and the woman in the white, and the feeling I had had that by the utterance of a few words I might have saved their lives. I was going to do my best to save hers, even though she tried to freeze me while I was in the act of doing so.

We met. As if scenting my design, as we neared each other she quickened her pace to stride right past. But I was too quick for her; I barred the way. The expression with which, as she recognized my intention, she regarded me! But I was not to be frightened into dumbness.

"There is something I have to say to you which is important—of the very first importance—which it is essential that I should say and you should hear. I have not the least intention of forcing on you my acquaintance, but with your sanction——"

I got as far as that, but I got no farther. As I still continued to bar her path, she turned right round and marched in the other direction. I might have gone after her, I might have stopped her—I did move a step or two; but when I did she spoke to me over her shoulder as she was moving:—

"If you dare to speak to me again I shall claim the protection of the police, so be advised."

I was advised. Whether the woman suffered from some obscure form of mental disease or not I could not say; or with what majesty she supposed herself to be hedged around, which made it the height of presumption for a mere outsider to venture to address her —that also was a mystery to me. As I had no wish to have a scene in the public gardens, and as it appeared that there would be a scene if I did any more to try to help her, I let her go.

I saw her leave the gardens, and when I had seen that I strolled back. There, under the shady tree, still sat the man with the touch of the Mongol in his face.

After luncheon, which I took at the hotel, I had a surprise. There, in the hall, was my gentleman, going through the front door. I spoke to the hall porter.

"Is that gentleman staying in the house? The porter intimated that he was. "Can you tell me what his name is?" The porter answered promptly, perhaps because it was such an unusual name:—

"Mr. John Tung." Then he added, with a smile, "I used to be in the Navy. When we were on the China station I was always meeting people with names like that—this gentleman is the first I've met since."

An idea occurred to me. I felt responsible for that woman, in spite of her stupidity. If anything happened to her it would lie at my door. For my own sake I did not propose to run the risk. I went to the post-office and I sent a telegram to John Tung, Empire Hotel. The clerk on the other side of the counter seemed rather surprised as he read the words which I wished him to wire.

"I suppose this is all right?" he questioned, as if in doubt.

"Perfectly all right," I replied. "Please send that telegram at once."

I quitted the office, leaving that telegraph clerk scanning my message as if he were still in doubt if it was in order. In the course of the afternoon I had another idea. I wrote what follows on a sheet of paper.

"You threw the woman in the mauve dress on to the Brighton line; you were responsible for the death of the woman in the white dress at the Embankment Hotel; you killed the woman who was found on the Great Western line near Exeter station; but you are going to do no mischief to the woman in the grey dress and the lace scarf and the Panama hat, who is going up to town by the five-five.

"Be sure of that.

"Also you may be sure that the day of reckoning is at hand, when you and your two accomplices will be called to a strict account. In that hour you will be shown no more mercy than you have shown.

"That is as certain as that, at the present moment, you are still alive. But the messengers of justice are drawing near."

There was no beginning and no ending, no date, no address—I just wrote that and left it so. It was wild language, in which I took a good deal for granted that I had no right to take; and it savoured a good deal of melodrama and highfalutin. But then, my whole scheme was a wild-cat scheme; if it succeeded it would be because of that, as it were, very wild-cat property. I put my sheet of paper into an envelope, and I wrote outside it in very large, plain letters, "Mr. John Tung." Then I went into the lounge of the hotel for tea —and I waited.

And I kept on waiting for quite a considerable time. It was rather early for tea, but as time passed and people began to gather together, and there were still no signs of the persons whose presence I particularly desired, I began to fidget. If none of them appeared I should have to reconsider my plan of campaign. I was just on the point of concluding that the moment had come when I had better think of something else, when I saw Mr. John Tung standing in the doorway and with him his two acquaintances. This was better than I had expected. Their appearance together in the public room of the hotel suggested all sorts of possibilities to my mind.

I had that missive prepared. I waited until I had some notion of the quarter of the room in which they proposed to establish themselves, then I rose from my chair and, crossing to the other side of the lounge, left on a table close to that at which they were about to sit—I hoped unnoticed—the envelope on which "Mr. John Tung" was so plainly written. Then I watched for the march of events.

What I had hoped would occur did happen. A waiter, bustling towards the new-comers, saw the envelope lying on a vacant table, picked it up, perceived that it was addressed to Mr. John Tung, and bore it to that gentleman. I could not hear, but I saw what was said. The waiter began:—

"Is this your letter, sir?"

Mr. Tung glanced, as if surprised, at the envelope which the man was holding, then took it from between his fingers and stared at it hard.

"Where did you get this?" he asked.

"It was on that table, sir."

"What table?"

"The one over there, sir."

Mr. Tung looked in the direction in which the man was pointing, as if not quite certain what he meant.

"How came it to be there? Who put it there?"

"Can't say, sir. I saw an envelope lying on the table as I was coming to you, and when I saw your name on it I thought it might be yours. Tea, sir?"

"Tea for three, and bring some buttered toast."

The waiter went. Mr. Tung remained staring at the envelope as if there were something in its appearance which he found a little puzzling. One of his companions spoke to him; but as his back was towards me I could not see what he said—I could guess from the other's answer.

"Some rubbish; a circular, I suppose—the sort of thing one does get in hotels."

Then he opened the envelope, and—I had rather a funny feeling. I was perfectly conscious that from the point of view of a court of law I had not the slightest right to pen a single one of the words which were on the sheet of paper inside that envelope. For all I could prove, Mr. Tung and his friends might be the most innocent of men. I might find it pretty hard to prove that the Mongolian-looking gentleman had whispered either of the brief, jerky sentences which I had seen him whisper; and, even if I could get as far as that, there still remained the difficulty of showing that they bore anything like the construction which I had put upon them. If I had misjudged him, if my deductions had been wrong, then Mr. Tung, when he found what was in that envelope, would be more than justified in making a fine to-do. It was quite possible, since I could not have eyes at the back of my head, that someone had seen me leave that envelope on the table, in which case my authorship might be traced, and I should be in a pretty awkward situation. That woman in the grey dress would be shown to have had right on her side when she declined, with such a show of scorn, to allow me even to speak to her. So, while Mr. Tung was tearing open the envelope and taking out the sheet of paper, I had some distinctly uncomfortable moments. Suppose I had wronged him—what was I to do? Own up, make a clean breast of it—or run away?

I had not yet found an answer when I became perfectly certain that none was required. My chance shot had struck him like a bombshell; the change which took place in his countenance when he began to read what was written on that piece of paper was really curious. I should have said he had a visage over whose muscles he exercised great control—Mongols have as a rule. But those words of mine were so wholly unexpected that when he first saw them his expression was, on the instant, one of stunned amazement. He glanced at the opening words, then, dropping his hands to his sides, gazed round the room, as if he were wondering if there were anyone there who could have written them. Then he raised the sheet of paper again and read farther. And, as he read, his breath seemed to come quicker, his eyes dilated, the colour left his cheeks, his jaw dropped open. He presented a unique picture of the surprise which is born of terror.

His companions, looking at him, were affected as he was,

" HE PRESENTED A UNIQUE PICTURE OF THE SURPRISE WHICH IS BORN OF TERROR."

without knowing why. The big, burly man leaned towards him; I
saw him mutter:—

"You look as if you'd had a stroke. What's the matter? What's
that you've got there? Don't look like that. Everyone is staring at
you. What's up?"

Mr. Tung did not reply; he looked at the speaker, then at the sheet
of paper—that time I am sure he did not see what was on it. Then
he crumpled the sheet of paper up in his hand, and without a word
strode across the lounge into the hall beyond. His two companions
looked after him in bewildered amazement; then they went also,
not quite so fast as he had done, but fast enough. And all the people
in the lounge looked at each other. The manner of the exit of these
three gentlemen had created a small sensation.

My little experiment had succeeded altogether beyond my
anticipation. It was plain that I had not misjudged this gentleman. It
would be difficult to find a more striking illustration than that presented by Mr. John Tung of the awful accusing conscience which
strikes terror into a man's soul. I could not afford to let my acquaintance with these three interesting gentlemen cease at this moment;
the woman in the grey dress must still not be left to their tender
mercies.

After what seemed to me to be a sufficient interval, I left my tea and went after them into the hall. I was just in time. The three men were in the act of leaving the hotel. As they were moving towards the door a page came up, an official envelope in his hand.

"Mr. John Tung? A telegram for you, sir."

Mr. Tung took it as if it were some dangerous thing, hesitated, glanced at the men beside him, tore it open, read what was on the flimsy sheet of pink paper, and walked so quickly out of the building that his gait almost approached a run. His companions went after him as if they were giving chase. My wire had finished what those few plain words on the sheet of paper had begun.

I was lingering in the hall, rather at a loss as to what was the next step that I had better take, when the woman in the grey dress came out of the lift, which had just descended. A cab was at the door, on which was luggage. Although she must have seen me very clearly, she did not recognize my presence, but passed straight out to the cab. She was going up to London by the five-five train.

I no longer hesitated what to do. I, too, quitted the hotel and got into a cab. It still wanted ten minutes to five when I reached the station. The train was standing by the platform; the grey-frocked lady was superintending the labelling of her luggage—apparently she had no maid. She was escorted by a porter, who had her luggage in charge, to a first-class carriage. On the top of her luggage was the tell-tale thing which has probably done more harm than good—the dressing-bag which is so dear to the hearts of many women, which ostentatiously proclaims the fact that it contains their jewels, probably their money, all that they are travelling with which they value most. One has only to get hold of the average travelling woman's dressing-bag to become possessed of all that she has—from the practical thief's point of view—worth taking—all contained in one portable and convenient package.

At the open door of the compartment next to the one to which the porter ushered her, the big, burly man was standing—rather to my surprise. I thought I had startled him more than that. Presently who should come strolling up but his more slightly built acquaintance. Apparently he did not know him now; he passed into the compartment at whose door he was standing, without a nod or sign of greeting. My glance travelling down the platform, I saw that standing outside a compartment only a few doors off was Mr. John Tung.

This did not suit me at all. I did not propose that those three gentlemen should travel with the grey-frocked lady by the five-five train to town. Rather than that I would have called in the aid of the police, though it would have been a very queer tale that I should have had to tell them. Perhaps fortunately, I hit upon what the old-time cookery books used to call "another way." I had done so well with one unexpected message that I thought I would try another. There were ten minutes before the train started—still time.

I rushed to the ladies' waiting-room. I begged a sheet of paper and an envelope from the attendant in charge. It was a sheet of paper which she gave me—and on it I scribbled:—

"You are watched. Your intentions are known.

"The police are travelling by the five-five train to London in attendance on the lady in the grey dress. If they do not take you on the road they will arrest you when you reach town.

"Then heigh-ho for the gallows!"

I was in doubt whether or not to add that last line. I daresay if I had had a second or two to think I should not have added it; but I had not. I just scrawled it off as fast as I could, folded the sheet of paper, slipped it into the envelope, which I addressed in large, bold letters to Mr. John Tung. The attendant had a little girl with her, of, perhaps, twelve or thirteen years old, who was acting as her assistant. I took her to the waiting-room door, pointed out Mr. Tung, and told her that if she would slip that envelope into the gentleman's hand and come back to me without having told him where she got it from, I would give her a shilling.

Officials were examining tickets, doors were being closed, preparations were being made to start, when that long-legged young person ran off on her errand. She gave Mr. Tung the envelope as he was stepping into the carriage. He had not time even to realize that he had got it before she was off again. I saw him glance with a startled face at the envelope, open it, hurriedly scan what was within, then make a dart into the compartment by which he was standing, emerge with a bag in his hand, and hurry from the station. Conscience had been too much for him again. The big, burly man, seeing him going, went hurrying after him, as the train was in the

"I TOOK HER TO THE WAITING-ROOM DOOR AND POINTED OUT MR. TUNG."

very act of starting. As it moved along the platform the face of the
third man appeared at the window of his compartment, gazing in
apparent astonishment after the other two. He might go to London
by the five-five if he chose. I did not think it mattered if he went
alone. I scanned the newspapers very carefully the next day; as there
was no record of anything unusual having happened during the
journey or afterwards I concluded that my feeling that nothing was
to be feared from that solitary gentleman had been well founded,

and that the lady in the grey dress had reached her destination in comfort and safety.

What became of Mr. Tung when he left the station I do not know; I can only say that he did not return to the hotel. That Buxton episode was in August. About a month afterwards, towards the close of September, I was going north. I started from Euston station. I had secured my seat, and, as there were still several minutes before the train went off, I strolled up and down the platform. Outside the open door of one of the compartments, just as he had done at Buxton station, Mr. Tung was standing!

The sight of him inspired me with a feeling of actual rage. That such a dreadful creature as I was convinced he was should go through life like some beast of prey, seeking for helpless victims whom it would be safe to destroy—that he should be standing there, so well dressed, so well fed, so seemingly prosperous, with all the appearance about him of one with whom the world went very well—the sight of him made me positively furious. It might be impossible, for various reasons, to bring his crimes home to him, but I could still be a thorn in his side, and might punish him in a fashion of my own. I had been the occasion to him of one moment in which conscience had mastered him and terror held him by the throat. I might render him a similar service a second time.

I was seized with a sudden desire to give him a shock which would at least destroy his pleasure for the rest of that day. Recalling what I had done at Buxton, I went to the bookstall and purchased for the sum of one penny an envelope and a sheet of paper. I took these to the waiting-room, and on the sheet of paper I wrote three lines—without even a moment's consideration:—

"You are about to be arrested. Justice is going to be done.

"Your time has come.

"Prepare for the end."

I put the sheet of paper containing these words into the envelope, and, waylaying a small boy, who appeared to have been delivering a parcel to someone in the station, I instructed him to hand my gentleman the envelope and then make off. He did his part very well. Tung was standing sideways, looking down the platform, so that he did not see my messenger approaching from behind; the envelope was slipped into his hand almost before he knew it, and the boy was off. He found himself with an envelope in his hand without, I believe, clearly realizing whence it had come—my messenger was lost in the crowd before he had turned; it might have tumbled from the skies for all he could say with certainty.

For him the recurrence of the episode of the mysterious envelope was in itself a shock. I could see that from where I stood. He stared at it, as he had done before, as if it had been a bomb which at any moment might explode. When he saw his own name written on the face of the envelope, and the fashion of the writing, he looked frantically around, as if eagerly seeking for some explanation of this strange thing. I should say, for all his appearance of sleek prosperity, that his nerves were in a state of jumps. His lips twitched; he seemed to be shaking; he looked as if it would need very little to make him run. With fingers which I am sure were trembling he opened the envelope; he took out the sheet of paper—and he read.

When he had read he seemed to be striving to keep himself from playing the cur; he looked across the platform with such an expression on his face and in his eyes! A constable was advancing towards him, with another man by his side. The probability is that, scared half out of his senses, conscience having come into its own, he misinterpreted the intention of the advancing couple. Those three lines, warning him that he was about to be arrested, that his time had come, to prepare for the end, synchronized so perfectly with the appearance of the constable and his companion, who turned out to be a "plain clothes man" engaged in the company's business, that in his suddenly unnerved state he jumped to the conclusion that the warning and its fulfilment had come together—that those two officers of the law were coming to arrest him there and then.

Having arrived at that conclusion he seems to have passed quickly to another—that he would not be taken alive. He put his hand into his jacket pocket, took out a revolver, which had no doubt been kept there for quite another purpose, put the muzzle to his brow, and while the two men—thinking of him not at all—were still a few yards off, he blew his brains out. He was dead before they reached him—killed by conscience.

They found his luggage in the compartment in which he had been about to travel. The contents of his various belongings supplied sufficient explanation of his tragic end. He lived in a small flat

"HE WAS DEAD BEFORE THEY REACHED HIM—
KILLED BY CONSCIENCE."

off the Marylebone Road[1]—alone; the address was contained in his
bag. When the police went there they found a miscellaneous collection of articles which had certainly, in the original instance, never
belonged to him. There were feminine belongings of all sorts and
kinds. Some of them were traced to their former owners, and in
each case the owner was found to have died in circumstances which
had never been adequately explained. This man seemed to have
been carrying on for years, with perfect impunity, a hideous traffic

[1] A major thoroughfare in North-Central London.

in robbery and murder—and the victim was always a woman. His true name was never ascertained. It was clear, from certain papers which were found in his flat, that he had spent several years of his youth in the East. He seemed to have been a solitary creature —a savage beast alone in its lair. Nothing was found out about his parents or his friends; nor about two acquaintances of whom I might have supplied some particulars. Personally, I never saw nor heard anything of either of them again.

I went on from Euston station by that train to the north. Just as we were about to start, a girl came bundling into my compartment whom I knew very well.

"That was a close shave," she said, as she took her seat. "I thought I should have missed it; my taxi-cab burst a tyre. What's this I heard them saying about someone having committed suicide on the platform? Is it true?"

"I believe there was something of the kind; in fact, I know there was. It has quite upset me."

"Poor dear! You do look out of sorts. A thing like that would upset anyone." She glanced at me with sympathetic eyes. "I was talking about you only yesterday. I was saying that a person with your power of what practically amounts to reading people's thoughts ought to be able to do a great deal of good in the world. Do you think you ever do any good?"

The question was asked half laughingly. We were in a corridor carriage. Two women at the other end of it suddenly got up and went, apparently, in search of another. I had been in no state to notice anything when I had got in; now I realized that one of the women who had risen was the one who had worn the grey dress at Buxton. She had evidently recognized me on the instant. I saw her whisper to her companion in the corridor, before they moved off:—

"I couldn't possibly remain in the same compartment with that half-bred gipsy-looking creature. I've had experience of her before."

I was the half-bred gipsy-looking creature. The experience she had had of me was when I saved her life at Buxton. That I did save her life I am pretty sure. I said to my friend, when they had gone:—

"I hope that sometimes I do do a little good; but even when I do, for the most part it's done by stealth, and not known to fame; and sometimes, even, it's not recognized as good at all."

"Is that so?" replied my friend. "What a very curious world it is."

When I thought of what had happened on the platform which we were leaving so rapidly behind, I agreed with her with all my heart and soul.

MATCHED

This gift of mine of entering into people's confidence, even against their will, has occasionally placed me in the most uncomfortable situations. Take, for instance, what I will call the Affair of the Pleasure Cruise, or Matched.

The story began at Charing Cross Station.[1] I had just entered the station and was looking about for the platform from which my train was going to start, when I saw one man hurrying up to another. I do not know what it was which caused him to catch my eye, unless it was that he was in such desperate haste, and was so covered with freckles, and had such a very red moustache; but I distinctly saw him say to the other—what he meant I had not the dimmest notion; some of the language he used was strange:—

"She's done a bunk all right, and is away with the best of the swag. Here's her brief." He handed to the other man what looked to me like a Continental railway-ticket. "I don't fancy the bloke is going; you'll have to go on and get the lot out the other end. It's worth having, you know; we'll be able to plant it easily. You understand? Move yourself; the train's just starting."

The man addressed did move himself, tearing through a gate over which was a board inscribed "Folkestone Harbour and Continent." His doing so made me think of Mr. Brookes. I had been to his wedding that morning, and had, indeed, only just come away from the reception which followed. I had gathered that he and his bride were to travel by that boat-train.

Thinking thus about the bride and bridegroom, who, since the train had started, I took it for granted were already on their way, what was my surprise to see coming through the wicket on to the platform which the boat-train had just quitted—Mr. Everard Brookes! He had discarded the orthodox "frocker"[2] in which he had been married, and in which I had seen him last, for a grey tweed suit —but it was he. And he seemed to be in a state of great disturbance,

---

[1] A major railway station in Central London.
[2] A frock coat, a man's fitted, knee-length coat.

as if he were looking for someone he could not find. A railway official was on either side of him, each of whom seemed doing his best
to calm his obvious agitation. What struck me as the strangest part
of it was that he was alone. An idea occurred to me as I walked
towards him.

"Mr. Brookes," I asked, "have you missed your train? You haven't
let your wife go off alone?"

"I TELL YOU I SAW HER GO THROUGH THE GATE AS CLEARLY AS I SEE YOU NOW."

"She hasn't gone on alone," he rejoined. "She isn't in the train at
all."

"She might have been in the train, you know, sir," struck in one of the officials. "It's not easy to make out everyone who's travelling in a long train like that."

Mr. Brookes turned on him with a show of anger which I knew was quite foreign to his character.

"I tell you I saw her go through the gate as clearly as I see you now, but though I watched for her to come back she never returned, although I never once took my eyes off the gate; that I am prepared to swear."

He turned to me with an explanation of his discomposure which filled me with surprise.

"We were standing, my wife and I, outside the compartment in which I had reserved our seats, when, about ten minutes before the train was due to start, she said to me: 'Everard, I've forgotten something. I must go and see about it at once. I'll be back in a moment.' She got into the compartment, took her travelling-bag off the seat, and was about to hurry down the platform. I asked her what she had thought of so suddenly; if it was something she wanted I offered to go and get it for her. She laughed at me. 'You stay where you are and let no one get into our carriage. I'll be back in less than a minute.' She was off before I could stop her. I thought it rather odd that she had thought of something so very pressing at the last minute, and had actually taken her bag with her, which contained all her belongings. I saw her go down the platform and through the gate; then, when I had waited two minutes, I strolled down the platform to see if I could discover her. I could see nothing. I was afraid to go through the gate lest we should miss each other, so I stood close to the gate, and I'll swear that no one the least like her came through it."

Mr. Brookes took off his bowler hat and passed his handkerchief across his brow. I had never seen him so disturbed.

"It occurred to me, after I had been waiting some little time, and the train was due to start, that, at her suggestion, I had put the tickets in her bag and practically all my money. I did not know what to do. I had never been in such a position in my life; I had not dreamt that I could be in such a position. They were calling out, 'Take your seats,' and were shutting the doors. What had become of Clare? I could not imagine. I could not go without her. Our luggage was in the train, I could not ask the officials to delay the train on our account, and while I was in a state bordering on distraction the issue was taken out of my hands—the train started; and now," turning to one of the officials, "this man wants me to believe that she was in the train after all. I am perfectly certain that she was nothing of the kind. What has become of her I don't know, but I'll swear she wasn't in that train."

The amazing part of it was that he never did know what had become of her—the bride had left the bridegroom on the eve of their wedding journey and vanished into space. Unfortunately, there were one or two suspicious circumstances about that vanishing. She had taken her brand-new dressing-case with her, a present from him, which contained all their portable property which was worth having—besides two hundred pounds in English money which was to have been spent upon the honeymoon. Mr. Brookes never saw any of that again. The heavy luggage which had gone on by the train, was claimed at the Gare du Nord[1] by an individual who produced the checks for it, as well as the keys, which permitted of the Customs examination—and that vanished. The wedding reception had been held at a South Kensington[2] hotel, at which the presents had been exhibited. Before Mr. Brookes got back to it someone called for the presents, armed with a letter from Mrs. Brookes— it seemed that she had made arrangements with the hotel people before she left to hand over the presents to someone who was to call for them—and they were never seen again.

The thing was very well done; Mr. Brookes found that he had been robbed in almost every direction in which he could have been robbed. To an onlooker it had its comical side, but it was a tragedy to him. He told me afterwards that, in one way or another, he reckoned he had been done out of more than a thousand pounds—to say nothing of the wife.

He had gone on one of those cruises which are so in vogue nowadays, to the Norwegian fiords. On the boat was a most charming lady, a Miss Clare Percival. He was a well-to-do bachelor, about forty years of age—the lady struck him as being the wife he had been looking for for years. Affairs of that sort on yachts I believe grow rapidly. Ere long she owned that she liked him, when he asked

[1] A railway terminus in Paris, serving passengers from London.
[2] A wealthy residential district in West-Central London.

her; before they reached England—I think it was a twenty-eight-day cruise—the liking had turned to love, or so she said. Three weeks after they were back in London they were married—that episode at Charing Cross Station was the result. The whole affair was decidedly funny—except for the mourning bridegroom.

About eighteen months afterwards I went for a yachting cruise —mine was to the Morocco coast and all sorts of pleasant-sounding places. Our party—we were called a "party"—consisted of about fifty persons. We had not been two days at sea when I had become impressed by two facts. One was that we had on board the proprietor of "Ebenezer's Grey-Blue Pills" and samples of his large and ebullient family, and the other was that among the passengers was a lady whose appearance had the most singular effect on me. The moment I saw her I had a feeling that I had seen her somewhere before, but for the life of me I could not think where and when.

She was a delightful person; full of resource, skilled in all sorts of what are known as "parlour tricks"; she could sing and recite, tell funny tales, perform conjuring tricks, and play on the piano and the banjo and the fiddle and, what was then the latest craze in musical instruments, the balalaika. She was good at bridge—some of the people said she was the best lady-player they had seen, and her knowledge of the sort of games which are calculated to amuse a general company was simply abnormal. She seemed to have lots of money, and some pretty dresses and some nice jewels. Before we were out of the Bay of Biscay she was the most prominent and popular person on board. By that time she had given people to understand, in a casual kind of way, that she had been an actress, and that she had been a singer, and that she had been an entertainer, and that she had written things and painted things—but I was commencing to wonder if she had ever been Mrs. Everard Brookes.

I frankly admit that the idea first came into my head because of the similarity of the cases; Mrs. Brookes had once been a single lady on a yachting cruise, and here was Marianne Tracy—she took pains to explain exactly how "Marianne" ought to be spelt—occupying precisely the same position. Of course, that was merely a coincidence; lots of single ladies go on yachting cruises, and they are all of them charming and respectable; and beyond that coincidence there was nothing, absolutely nothing. She bore no physical resemblance, from what I remembered, to Mrs. Brookes. I had only seen that lady once, and that was at her wedding, and I had a more or less vague recollection that she had fair hair, which matched her complexion, and that she was tall and slender, and, to my mind, uncomfortably prim; just the colourless sort of person one would expect Mr. Brookes to marry. Miss Tracy was black as night—black hair, black eyes, black eyebrows, and even the faintest shadow of what might be a black moustache. She was no taller than I was, but she was much plumper, and she was full of vivacity and high spirits; and as for prim—I do not wish to do the lady an injustice, but even by abuse of language one could not call her prim. She was hail fellow with everyone on board—the officers, the passengers, the stewards, the crew, and, I dare say, the stokers down below; she had a knack of making friends with everyone with whom she came in contact. Seeing, as I do, a great deal more than many people suppose, I was not a little tickled by some of the conversations in which I saw her take a very active part. She was a flirt. Before we were out of the Bay I believe that most of the male creatures on board, of all sorts and kinds, were under the impression that she was in love with them.

It was that faculty which I possess of seeing so much more than many folks guess which caused my vague suspicion to take, by degrees, a very concrete form. It was the evening on which we were leaving Gibraltar, where we had spent the day. Most gorgeous weather—the sky was ablaze with stars. I was prowling about the ship when, in a corner on the lower deck, I came upon an individual the sight of whom gave me quite a start. He was in a steward's uniform, but I had certainly never seen him on board before. Whatever his duties might be, they had never brought him into the passengers' saloons; I should have recognized him on the instant if they had. His was a face which, once seen by an observant pair of eyes like mine, was not likely to be forgotten, even after a lapse of eighteen months—and that period of time had passed since I had seen him.

The last, and first, time I had beheld that gentleman was at Charing Cross Railway Station on the afternoon on which Mrs. Everard Brookes had disappointed her husband by vanishing on the eve of their honeymoon. He was the individual who had hurried up to a masculine acquaintance and told him, right in front of me, that someone feminine had "done a bunk all right," and was "away with the best of the swag"; and had handed him what he called "her brief," and which had seemed to me to be a Continental railway-ticket. There was no mistaking those freckles and that flaming moustache—or, indeed, the man as a whole.

My surprise at seeing him there was so great that for some seconds I did not realize whom he was talking to; then I saw that it was Miss Marianne Tracy; and, as I watched what they were saying, I began to understand. He said to her:—

"The best of the old girl's things he takes care of; those diamonds and pearls which we got the office about, which the old girl flashes around, are in a bag which he keeps in his locker. Some of the girls' things are in it too; I dropped into the cabin as if by accident the other morning, and I saw him put them into his bag."

The man winked at her when he said "by accident"; I have no doubt that Miss Tracy grasped his meaning. I had had no intention of playing the spy—I had made no attempt to conceal myself; so that when Miss Tracy looked round, as she did just at that moment, she saw me at once. With perfect presence of mind she came straight up to me.

"Taking a stroll about the ship, Miss Lee?"

I do not know what possessed me; I do sometimes yield to impulse, and I did then. This person did seem to me to be such an impudent piece of goods that, without counting the cost, I felt bound to have a shot at her—and I did then and there. I looked her very straight in the face, and with what I am sure was the most perfect civility I asked her a question.

"Aren't you Mrs. Everard Brookes?"

She did not change countenance—the baggage! She must have had a front of brass. She just looked at me inquiringly, and she smiled, and she said:—

"So! We have met before, Miss Lee!"

She put her lips together, and she gave a tiny little whistle; it was scarcely audible, but I fancy it was heard by someone, because, without a moment's warning, someone, stealing on me from behind, put something over my head which blocked out all the light and made it difficult for me to breathe, and I was dragged down backwards on to the deck. I would have screamed when I got there,

"SOMEONE, STEALING ON ME FROM BEHIND, PUT SOMETHING OVER MY HEAD WHICH BLOCKED OUT ALL THE LIGHT AND MADE IT DIFFICULT FOR ME TO BREATHE."

only a hand was pressed against my mouth, on the outside of the stuff which covered my face, and I could not utter a sound. The same hand held me down tight, another took me by the throat and almost choked me, while a second pair of hands took hold of my wrists and tied them together, and then did the same to my ankles. I could not struggle, because the pressure on my mouth and throat seemed to be driving the sense all out of me. Then two hands were slipped under the cloth, my jaw was forced open, something was thrust into it—and there was I as helpless as a trussed fowl, and incapable of uttering a sound.

I am free to admit that it was very well done, evidently by persons who had done that sort of thing before. I had not the use of my eyes, but, if I could trust my ears, not a word was spoken nor an instant wasted. Presently two pairs of hands lifted me by the head and heels; I was carried a few feet, and deposited under what I have no doubt was cover, and there I remained for I have not the faintest notion how long. And in the cabin, as I was perfectly aware, they were waiting for me to make a four at bridge. I could picture Miss Tracy explaining how I had been overcome by a sudden headache, and how I had asked her, with their permission, to take my place; and as I continued to lie in that ignominious position I have no doubt that the creature who had been chiefly instrumental in putting me there was playing my hands.

Time passed; the hours went by—they seemed to me years—and as I was wondering if I had become an old woman and my hair had turned grey, I was lifted again by two pairs of hands, though I had not heard a sound of anyone approaching. I was carried this time some distance; a rope was tied round my waist, and immediately afterwards I became pleasantly conscious that I was being lowered over the side of the ship. I took it for granted that my two friends, desirous of avoiding the noise of a splash, had adopted this method of dropping me into the sea. I feared my end had come, and was momentarily expecting to come in contact with the water, when I went plump against something solid instead, and on what I had bumped against I stayed. The tension of the rope ceased. I was being lowered no longer; apparently I was on, or in, something. I suppose I was there some minutes before I discovered that the ligature which bound my wrists together was not so taut as it had been, and it did not take me very long after the discovery was made to wriggle both my hands loose. Then I put them up and pulled that covering off my head and face. I found it was a canvas-bag which had contained something undesirable, because my eyes, and nostrils, and mouth were full of grits, and something gritty was worrying my hair and skin. I took the gag out of my mouth; they had actually used a piece of cotton waste. Then I sat up, and I learned that I was in a small boat, which was all alone on what—literally to me—was a trackless ocean. My sensations on making this discovery were of the most exhilarating kind. I would have cried if I had thought it would do any good. As a matter of fact, I was consumed with rage; my one craving was to get that freckled man and that false woman by their throats, one hand at the throat of each, and knock, knock, knock their heads together; there would not have been much left of them if I had had a chance of knocking them together then. I would have just smashed them up like egg-shells.

I nursed my pleasant dreams of being revenged on them for quite a while. Then I untied my ankles, got on the one seat in the boat, and looked around. There was nothing to see, except water; and there was too much of that. I must have been lying for hours with that disgusting bag over my head, because it was clear, from the appearance of the heavens, that the dawn was on the point of breaking. It did break; I floated on, and on, and on. All of a sudden I saw something straight in front of me which caused me to get on to my feet and stare with all my might.

It was land—I believed it was land; I was sure it was land. It was ever so far away; but if I only had—then I realized that there was a pair of oars on board that boat. Whether that pretty couple had put them there on purpose, with the intention of giving me a chance to save my life, I have never known—but there they were. Presently I put them in the rowlocks, and I was pulling for dear life. I can row, but never before or since have I rowed as I rowed then. I sincerely hope I shall never have such a long pull again. I reached land, or I should not be telling the story. When I did I just lay down and felt as if I were as good as dead. If there had been so much as a ripple on the sea, I doubt if I should ever have gained the shore at all—my strength was utterly spent; but not only was the sea as calm as a mill-pond, but I have been told since that there is a strong current in that part of the world which sets towards the land. No doubt that helped to carry me in as much as my straining at the oars.

I want to get over this part of the story as fast as possible. I don't like to think of it even now. After a while I became conscious that people were standing by and looking down at me. I never knew quite who they were, but I suppose they were Moors, because I had got ashore in Morocco. They could not speak English, and I could not speak what they spoke, so neither side understood a word of what the other side said; but I followed them, because a man took me by the wrist and made me go to a disreputable-looking sort of village, which I dare say an artist would have called picturesque; but I like my villages to be clean and wholesome, and that certainly was not. There I met an old man who had some English, of rather a

"NEITHER SIDE UNDERSTOOD A WORD OF WHAT THE OTHER SIDE SAID."

curious kind; he must have acquired it in some strange company, because every third or fourth word was an oath; still, it was better than nothing. I knew, of course, that the yacht was making for Tangier, and I asked him how far that was. As far as I could gather from what he said, it was about six months' journey; but I did not believe it was anything of the kind, because I knew that the yacht expected to get there early that day, and in that cockle-shell of a boat I could not possibly have gone very far out of its course.

As a matter of fact it was four days before I reached Tangier. The sight I must have presented when I got there! I walked nearly all the way. I had never had a wash, or been able to brush or comb my hair —considering when I was lowered into that small boat I was in full evening-dress. I had on a costume of sky-blue satin covered with chiffon, the corsage cut low, no sleeves, a pair of blue silk stockings to match, and the flimsiest of shoes. When you have got those details clearly in your mind, and remember that I had spent a night at sea, rowing in a small boat, and that afterwards I walked for four days on the roads of Morocco, without once coming within sight of soap or water, brush or comb, I don't think I need say any more of what I looked like when I reached Tangier.

I created a sensation when I did get there; for that matter, I created a sensation all along the road. I was the centre of a highly-amused mob of the inhabitants of the place, when, of all people in the world, who should I encounter but the proprietor of Ebenezer's Grey-Blue Pills, his wife, his son, his two daughters, together with other passengers from the yacht which I had so unintentionally quitted. And they fell on me all at once, not with sympathy, but with accusations of robbery and theft.

We all adjourned to the house of the British Consul, and half the population of the town seemed to be waiting in the street without. There I was informed that jewels, and other valuables, belonging to John T. Stebbings, had been taken out of his cabin on the night I had gone, and everyone took it for granted that they had gone with me. So there I was, charged with leaving that yacht of set purpose and intention, with no end of valuables belonging to other people.

Looking back, I find that I have omitted something; it comes back to my mind at this moment just as it did then. It is not very much—just a trifle; but one of those trifles which turn the scale.

As, on that eventful night, Miss Marianne Tracy looked round and beheld me, she was in the very act of saying something to her freckled friend. I only saw her lips form part of the sentence; how it began I do not know, and it never ended. The words I saw her lips form were only these:—

"... the Villa Hortense, in the Street of the Fountain——"

In the excitement of the thrilling moment which immediately ensued I think I scarcely realized that those words had reached my brain—anyhow, I should not have known to what they referred. But in that room in the Consul's house, confronted by my accusers, they came back to me. I even had some inkling of what they might mean.

I told my tale. They listened with an amazement which grew; then, when I had come nearly to an end, and I felt that I had made some sort of impression, I asked the Consul a question:—

"Is there in this town a Street of the Fountain?"

He said there was; he ventured on a statement, eyeing me sharply.

"You have been here before—this is not your first visit to Tangier?"

I told him not only that it was, but that I hoped it would be my last. I explained the circumstances in which I had seen the words uttered. How he stared, and how they all stared, as if I were some wonderful creature! It is a continual source of amusement to me how many people think I am doing something wonderful when I am merely putting into practice the principles by the teaching of which I make my living.

"I understand," I added, "that Miss Tracy left the yacht the night before last, to spend a day or two ashore. I think it possible that you will find she prefers to remain ashore when the yacht goes." I put another question to the Consul: "Do you happen to know, sir, if in the Street of the Fountain there is a house called the Villa Hortense?"

"By repute I know it very well. It is a house which, at various times, has had some curious occupants—persons of whom somewhat queer tales have been told. I believe that at the present moment it is without a tenant."

"I venture, in spite of your belief, sir, to express my belief that if Mr. John T. Stebbings would like to learn something about the jewels belonging to Mrs. Stebbings and the Misses Stebbings, he cannot do better than make inquiries at the Villa Hortense, in the Street of the Fountain."

"AS I MADE A DASH AT HER SHE
SHUT THE DOOR WITH A BANG."

They all trooped off to that poetically-named street; I tried to get it into their heads that that was not the most desirable way of making what ought to have been a discreet approach. Each was willing that someone else should stay behind, but was bent on going him or her self. So they all of them went together. Someone, I do not know who, had lent me an aboriginal sort of wrap which I believe was called a burnous;[1] that covered the worst of me, but there was still enough of me visible to make me one of the most striking figures in that singular procession.

The Street of the Fountain proved to be very narrow, so the procession had to tail off, whether it wished to or not. From the outside the Villa Hortense seemed to be quite a good-sized house. While people were wondering how we were going to get in I turned the handle and opened the door. The door led directly into a room. As I entered I saw a feminine figure passing through a door which was on the other side. Although she looked quite different, I knew that she was Miss Marianne Tracy. As I made a dash at her she shut the door with a bang, I heard a key turned in the lock, and bolts shot home. As the door was a solid construction, apparently six inches

[1] A hooded cloak used by Arabs.

thick, my desire to get through it had to be postponed. Others had come in after me, and they were eyeing with surprise the contents of the room—which certainly were rather amazing. There were articles of clothing which had undoubtedly belonged to Miss Tracy, and what is known as a "transformation,"[1] which had probably belonged to her too, to say nothing of some odds and ends of an extremely intimate kind. The great discovery was made by Mrs. Stebbings and her two daughters; they dashed forward with a chorused cry: "Father's bag!"

There, on a sort of stool, was the bag which Mr. Stebbings had kept in his locker, and which had contained the most valuable possessions of the feminine part of the family. There were some of them left still—what the family seemed to regard as unconsidered trifles; the articles really worth having were there no more. They had probably gone with the lady who had locked and bolted—on the other side—that extremely solid door. While we were assimilating this interesting fact a person garbed as a sailor appeared in the doorway and informed us, at the top of his voice, that if we wanted to continue our yachting cruise we had better get on board at once, as the boat was on the point of starting.

There was a nice to-do. Everyone seemed to be strongly of the opinion that the captain was an exceptionally unreasonable person; but, as no one wished to be left behind, a common inclination was shown to rush to the shore. As nobody was more eager to get on board than I was, for divers reasons, I kept well to the front. We reached the quay just as the ship's boat was about to put off, and I was the first one in. They all came tumbling after me. We discussed the captain's conduct on the way to the ship, and we kept on discussing it to the end of the voyage. He was tried by a sort of court-martial, no two members of which agreed.

Mr., Mrs., the Misses, and Master Stebbings were of opinion that the captain ought to have kept the ship at Tangier while search was made for that disreputable woman, and at least endeavoured to recover their valuable property. As the ship had stayed there already much longer than she ought to have done, the captain made it quite clear that his first duty was to the owners, and that if the Stebbings

[1] A wig.

family had wished to remain they might have done so and come on by another ship. But as their remaining property was on board and they had only a few pounds on their persons, it was not strange that they had not seen their way to act on the captain's suggestion. Mrs. Stebbings asked him pointedly if he thought she could live for a fortnight in the clothes she stood up in, and the young ladies hinted that he was not the kind of person they had taken him for. So the captain retired, and I should not be surprised if he bullied the crew. I believe efforts were made by wireless to ascertain the woman's whereabouts and to regain the Stebbingses' gems, and that directions were given to leave no stone unturned which should bring these things about. But, so far as I know, nothing ever came of what was done.

The yachting cruise went on, under a sort of blight. Everything seemed different without Miss Tracy and the Stebbingses' gems. The numerous inquisitions which were held on me, and the myriad questions which I had to answer, caused me seriously to consider whether it would not be desirable to remain at one of the ports at which we touched and continue my journey later. But the truth was that I had had enough of yachting, and the one thing for which I craved was to have done with that pleasure trip and get back home. I did get back home—we all got back home—and I think that most of us parted from each other in the hope that we might never meet again.

This story is episodical, with an interval between each episode. There was another interval of about eighteen months, during which I managed to keep myself alive, though, for the most part, I was badly overworked; and one afternoon I went to call upon a friend who was staying at the Hotel Metropole in town. I stayed in the lounge as she went to write some letters. Right on the other side was a party of Americans. They seemed to be so much amused by what they were talking about that I could not help watching them, and I saw one of them tell this story. He struck me as a man who had been in this world about sixty years, and who had lived them every one.

"Have I told you about Alexander King?"

He asked the question, and with one accord his listeners said that he had not; so he told them then.

"Last fall Alexander went on a pleasure cruise to the coast of Florida. On board there was a lady—I don't mean that there weren't other ladies on the ship, but she was the only one for Alexander. Alexander had had three wives already, and he told me himself that he thought enough was as good as a feast; but the sight of her made him think he'd try again. All the way there and back he made hay of that young female's heart to such an extent that, when he got back to New York, nothing would suit him but that he should rush off to the first handy place, and make her the fourth Mrs. King. But she was not taking any; she was a modest creature, and wanted time to prepare her mind. So he gave her time, as little as she would let him give her, and he spent most of it in buying such articles as New York had to sell; so that when they had the wedding he had quite a nice collection to pour into the lap of his bride. They were going to Tennessee for the honeymoon, and they went down to the depôt, and they boarded the train. And just before the train was going to start she remembered that she had forgotten something somewhere, and she caught up a bag which contained all he had worth having, as well as some trifles of her own, and she started off to get it. And she left Alexander alone in the train—and he's been alone ever since. Yes, boys, he has. That train started with Alexander alone in it, without even his bag. She had recommended him, like a good and thoughtful wife, careful of her husband's interests, to put all his cash into that bag, and everything he had worth taking; and he had acted on her advice, and now the bag was gone, and she with it. That's the last he's ever seen of either. Yes, boys, that's a fact. What honeymoon he had he spent all alone, which didn't amount to much; and, from what I have heard, it would seem that he has been spending most of the money he had left on telegraphing descriptions of the bag and the lady to every part of the world. He has met with no success so far, and I take it that his money will give out before he does. So he's a widower once more."

His hearers laughed, and I had to laugh—he had such a comical way of telling a story—but I laughed with rather a wry face. I had no doubt that Mrs. Everard Brookes, and Miss Marianne Tracy, and Mrs. Alexander King were one and the same person. The audacity of the creature was almost incredible! I believe I should have gone across to them and told them so, only just then my friend came up and insisted upon bearing me off without giving me a chance to explain.

A few days afterwards I was in Bond Street,[1] when a beautifully-attired lady came out of a shop, and stopped to stare at me. I could not believe my eyes—it was Marianne Tracy, though transformed into quite another being. Her coolness was almost supernatural.

"It is Miss Lee, isn't it? I thought it was. I'm so glad to have met you."

That was all she said, in the sweetest tone of voice. Then she got into a gorgeous motor-car, which I had been conscious had been standing at the kerb, and as she pulled the door to she leaned over and said:—

"BY THE WAY, HOW DID YOU ENJOY THAT LITTLE TRIP TO SEA?"

[1] A fashionable shopping street in Central London, just off Oxford Street.

"By the way, how did you enjoy that little trip to sea?"

Before I could answer the car was off. What was I to do? I could not run after it; it was lost in the traffic before I had got my wits about me. I could not give a description of the car—I had scarcely noticed it; I was not sure either of the shape or colour. That woman had slipped through my fingers, merely because her presence of mind was greater than mine. If I had only kept my head enough to take her by the throat in the middle of Bond Street!

A week afterwards I had a call from Mr. Everard Brookes. He began to talk about his wife—he still called her his wife. The man struck me as being more than half a lunatic. He told me that he had more than once thought of going into mourning. The very notion! I thought of what her feelings would have been if she had seen him in widower's weeds. He said that he felt that in the first flush of his agitation he had misjudged her; he was sure that she had cared for him; he had had proofs of it. I wonder what they were. He was nearly convinced that she had been the victim of one of those tragedies of which one reads in the newspapers; she might have been run over by a motor-bus; he had a morbid feeling that he himself would one day be run over by a vehicle of that description. Something had happened to her, he believed; one day it would be made known what it was.

I hoped that it never would, for his sake. He was one of those men who—because nothing ever has happened to them—like to think that something has happened to them at last—something wonderful, altogether out of the common way; that they have been the victim of some supreme tragedy. I doubt if he would have made much of a husband, anyhow. He was actually happy under the delusion that some strange, mysterious fate had in some altogether incomprehensible way robbed him of what might have been his life's bright star. His existence might have been so blissful had Destiny only stayed its hand. It is my belief that he endeavoured to make this clear to everybody he met after five minutes' acquaintance; so that, if he lost his wife before she was really his, at least he had an object in life.

The next morning I met William B. Stebbings, the son of Ebenezer's Grey-Blue Pills, and, as soon as he had made up his mind who I was, the very first words he said to me were:—

"I say, Miss Lee, I'm going to be married—yes, I am; and I hope to see you there; you must have a card. It's on Tuesday week." Then, though we were out in the open street, he closed his left eye and winked. "Have you ever heard anything of Miss Tracy? She was a dandy of a girl, she was; and, between ourselves, I believe that she didn't object to me. If it hadn't been for that little upset, matters between us might have gone farther than—— Well, strictly between ourselves, I don't mind telling you that she told me herself that she would like to be my wife; she meant it, too. She was fond of me, that girl was. Pity she made such a mistake."

I did not know to which mistake he alluded, and I did not ask him. I did not want to know. He was an extremely plain, clumsily-built, stupid young man; and I was half inclined to wish that she had married him. Where women are concerned, men are the most amazing things. What all those men, of different ages, different tastes, different altogether, saw in her was beyond my comprehension. The proof that she had a fatal fascination for the male animal came to me in still stranger shape only a few days later.

I was standing in one of the Tube stations,[1] when a decently-dressed young man came up to me and took his cap off.

"Excuse me, but aren't you Miss Lee? I don't suppose you know who I am, but I remember you because of Miss Balfour."

"Miss who?" I asked. I was quite certain I had never seen him before; he was almost a gentleman and quite nice-looking, about twenty-three or four.

"Miss Balfour spoke to you in Bond Street, now rather more than a fortnight since. You were passing when she came out of a shop and spoke to you, and then she got into the motor-car. I was the chauffeur. She told me afterwards who you were."

"So she calls herself Miss Balfour now, does she?" A light was beginning to dawn on me. "I shall be very much obliged if you can tell me where Miss Balfour is to be found at the present moment."

He pulled rather a long face.

"I wish I could; that is what I hoped you would be able to tell me."

"No one is less likely to be able to tell you about the movements

---

[1] London's deep-level underground network was constructed inside tube-like circular tunnels. The first of the deep underground lines had opened in 1890.

of the woman who, according to you, now calls herself Miss Balfour than I am. Are you no longer in her employ?"

He shifted his cap a little to one side and scratched his head. I thought what a rueful-looking object he was all at once.

"Well, it's rather a long story. It's like this." He paused, as if to try back to the beginning. "I wasn't exactly in her employ; the fact is, an uncle of mine left me a legacy, and I laid it out in buying a motor-car, meaning to hire it out to people who wanted one. It's a first-rate car, and I wanted to get at people of better class. Miss Balfour hired it—first by the day, then by the week, and then by the month. We used to go off together for tours in the country, and"— he began to look sheepish—"she made herself very pleasant to me. Of course, she paid my expenses, and nothing would suit her but that we should take our meals together—late dinner and all that; and—well"—he looked more sheepish—"she began to make out that she had taken a liking to me, and, of course, I liked her; so then I gave her the motor-car."

"You did what?" I almost shouted in that Tube station.

"You see, we were going to be married——"

"Oh, you were going to be married!"

"Of course; I knew she'd got lots of money, and that it would be a first-rate thing for me, and so I thought, there being only one thing I could give her worth having, that was the least I could give her, so I gave her the motor-car, thinking," he quickly added, "that, as what was hers would be mine, it would make no difference, and that it would be as much mine as ever; only the mischief was I gave it her before witnesses; and that very same night, if she didn't get up in the middle of the night, and go down to the garage, and take the car out, and drive off with it, and I've seen nothing of either of them since."

This was such an astounding story that if it had not been for the sincere air of depression which marked the man I should have thought that he was having a joke at my expense; but he was serious enough, as he had good reason to be.

"It was no use my going after her, even if I had known where she was, because, of course, she hadn't stolen the motor-car, seeing that I had given it to her in the presence of witnesses—and that's how it was."

"Do you mean to say you've lost your motor-car?"

"It looks as if I had. I did hear by a sort of side-wind that she's taken it to France, but, seeing that it's hers, I don't see what I can do to her if she has. She's had me fairly. It was one of the best motor-cars that money could buy; I didn't grudge anything in the way of fittings."

He sighed. My train came up, and I left the youth lamenting. He was only another example of what absolute idiots all sorts and conditions of men, old and young, can make themselves over a woman.

It was not very long afterwards that a letter reached me which bore the Paris post-mark. As a specimen of—I will call it courage—I give it verbatim. There was no date and there was no address.

"My dear Miss Lee—may I call you Judith?———"

It was at this point that I realized that the letter was from that woman. Might she call me Judith! I read on—with my teeth set pretty close together.

"When I saw you the other day in Regent Street[1]—I don't know if you saw me; I was in a motor-car and you were walking—quite a wave of emotion passed over me. It was so sweet to see again one of whom one has such sunny memories. And you were looking so well; a little older, perhaps, but a few years more or less would make no difference to your appearance. I should have liked to stop my motor-car and begged you to have a cup of tea. I cannot help sending you just a line to say so, if only to recall to your recollection one who I hope you look upon as an old friend.

"A great change is about to take place in my life. I am shortly to be married—to a Russian merchant of immense wealth. One has to be married some time. I wonder if you will ever be? There are men who will marry anything—who knows?

"I had no idea until the other day that you were the famous Judith Lee. It was a surprise. I had heard so much about you—about how wise and clever and wonderful you were. You are not in the least like what I expected. And yet how beautiful it must be to be able to read people's thoughts, even the secrets of their hearts, as I am told you can. Who would have thought it? I shall look forward to meeting you again some day, in order that you may teach me

[1] A fashionable shopping street connecting Piccadilly Circus and Oxford Street in Central London.

some of the strange magic—I am bound to call it magic—of which you are such a mistress. You will find me an apt pupil; don't you think you will?

"You must be able to do a great deal of good in the world with such a gift as yours. I love doing good—don't you? It must be so nice to detect an improper person directly you see one. Your friendship for me was almost a certificate of character. If only it had not been so brief—but the night was fine, and the boat was handy, and we did not tie you very tight.—Your affectionate friend, MARIANNE TRACY.

"Pray remember me to the gentleman whose name you once mentioned to me—Mr. Everard Brookes. Is he married?"

The audacity of the woman in writing to me at all! And such a letter, with such innuendoes! I could hardly contain myself till I got to the end. For quite two days after I had received that effusion I could hardly bring myself to speak civilly to a single person I came across. And even now sometimes I tingle all over when I think of it—and that was ages ago, and I have never heard of nor seen the woman since.

THE MIRACLE

People sometimes say that they envy me because, with my power of reading thoughts—that, they say, is what it comes to—I must have so many opportunities of doing people good. It must be so sweet, they add, with what I occasionally feel to be an irritating smirk, to be able, with very little trouble to oneself, to benefit one's fellow-creatures. That sort of remark is very easy to make, but it is not easy to benefit one's fellow-creatures. And as for doing people good, it is surprising how many people would rather not be done good to. Take that case of what happened at Dieppe.

I was spending my summer holidays at Dieppe. I had been there about a fortnight. One evening I was sitting, all alone by myself, on the terrace outside the Casino. I had been dancing; my partner had gone to fulfil another engagement, and, as I was not engaged for that dance, I had asked him to leave me where I was. I was taking my ease in a long chair close to the sea-wall. In front of me, in the glow of the electric light, people were seated at little tables having refreshments. At one of these was a gentleman whose name I knew, talking to one who was to me a complete stranger.

The first gentleman's name was Armitage—Cecil Armitage. He was an amazingly handsome young man, perhaps in the late twenties. He was staying in my hotel, and was the cause of no little amusement to some of the other visitors. He, a young man of seven or eight and twenty, evidently of birth and breeding, was paying the most marked attention to a woman who was one of the greatest jokes in Dieppe—Miss Drawbridge.

Miss Drawbridge, commonly known as "Gertrude" to people who had never spoken to her in their lives, was a sort of standing dish at Dieppe. She was supposed to have been there longer than the oldest inhabitant; she had certainly been a frequenter for quite a number of years. What I had seen of her I rather liked. She was staying at my hotel, and there was a time when she had asked me to share her table; and, although that time had passed and she never asked me to share it now, we were still on quite good terms. She was certainly a curious person—people who haunt the same foreign watering-place year after year generally are; and what an extremely presentable young man like Cecil Armitage could see in her was a mystery—unless it was her money.

Imagine the sensation which stirred the air when it became known that this perfect Adonis was engaged to "Gertrude." Had not Miss Drawbridge announced the fact herself, I fancy few people would have believed it. And the things which were said of Miss Drawbridge, especially by some of the women! The men just sneered.

There was I on the terrace, in my long chair (I could say things about men, but I think I had better get on with my story), and there was Mr. Armitage, drinking what looked to me very like absinthe[1] —fancy drinking absinthe at that time of night, or, so far as that goes, at any time!—and talking to a perfect stranger. Of course, the man was quite entitled to be a stranger; but I have seldom seen a man whose looks I liked less. The contrast between him and Mr. Armitage was amazing. He was a sallow, hatchet-faced man, with an upturned moustache—which I hate!—and something the matter with one of his eyes which made him seem to be looking in two directions at once. Nor did I like his manner towards Mr. Armitage; he seemed to me to be positively bullying him. That was one reason why I watched what they said, and some very surprising observations—I cannot say I heard—I saw. And, as always is the case on such occasions, I could not have gained a more intimate acquaintance with them had they bawled them in my ear.

The first thing I saw was the stranger's thin lips contorting themselves as, in what I imagined to be an angry undertone, they formed these words, which I have no doubt, judging from the expression of his face, he snapped out at Mr. Armitage as if he were an angry terrier:—

"Don't you make any mistake about it, my boy. I've not come over to Dieppe to be fooled with. I'm either going to have you or the money in four-and-twenty hours. If I have to have you, it will be penal servitude, and then the smile will come off that pretty face of yours."

[1] An anise-flavored green spirit, highly alcoholic and associated with addiction and decadence.

Mr. Armitage was not smiling at that particular moment, as anyone could see; on the contrary, he looked very much disturbed. The way in which he leaned across the table helped me to realize the earnestness which I felt sure was in his voice as he replied to the other's threat, in words which, as I saw each fresh one shaped on his lips, surprised me more and more.

"Don't be absurd, Clarke. I can't perform the impossible. I can't get it in four-and-twenty hours; but you shall have your money, with a thumping interest, if you will only give me reasonable time."

"And pray, what do you call reasonable time, my beautiful— forger?"

"It won't take very much to make me break this glass against your face, Clarke. You may have the whip-hand of me, but I'll break your neck before you get a chance of laying the lash across my back."

I held my breath, expecting every moment to see something dreadful happen. The way Mr. Clarke snarled back at him!

" YOU MAY HAVE THE WHIP-HAND OF ME, BUT I'LL BREAK YOUR NECK BEFORE YOU GET A
CHANCE OF LAYING THE LASH ACROSS MY BACK."

"That's the tone you take, is it? You talk to me like that again, and I'll have you jailed to-night. Do you think you can both rob and murder me? I say you're a forger—forger—forger! Now you touch me with a glass, or anything else, if you dare. This will be the last time you ever show yourself in a decent place if you do."

There was a pause. Mr. Armitage leaned so far forward that I quite expected that he would take the other by the throat and strike him with his glass. I was just on the point of jumping up and doing something which would divert his attention, when he seemed all at once to change his purpose, and, leaning right back, positively laughed.

"What nonsense it is, Clarke, our talking like this. You'll do no more good by calling me names than I should do by knocking you down. I tell you again, you shall have your money, with thumping interest, if you'll wait."

"I know a good deal about you, my lad—about all there is to learn—but I don't know where you're going to get anything like that amount of money from, unless you've found someone else to rob."

I thought Mr. Armitage would resent this remark as he had done the others, and I believe that for a moment it was his intention to do so, but again he changed his purpose, and I saw these remarkable words come from his lips instead:—

"I have—I've found a woman."

It was not strange that Mr. Clarke looked at him as if he wondered if he was in earnest; then he asked, with a smile which made him an even more unpleasant-looking person than before:—

"What woman have you found this time?

"If you are suggesting, as you appear to be, that I ever have robbed a woman up to now, I can only inform you, Clarke, with all possible courtesy, that you are a liar. I have not always treated women well—few men have; but no woman has ever suffered in pocket because of me up to the present time of speaking."

"That's between you and your conscience. Who is the woman you purpose, according to your own statement, to rob, at the eleventh hour?"

"It's the woman I intend to make my wife."

"Oh, so there is a woman you're going to make your wife—at

last. What about——" I do not know what he was going to say; Mr. Armitage stopped him so suddenly, and positively shook his fist in his face.

"Stop that, Clarke; don't you mention any names. You keep your tongue between your teeth. I'm going to marry the woman I'm going to marry because I'm a thief, and because I'm such a cur that I shrink from paying the penalty. She's a wretched old fool who comes all to pieces; Heaven knows what's left of her when the various aids to beauty are put away for the night; but she's got money, and she's willing to give me money, enough to be rid of you and save myself from the treadmill. That's why I'm going to enter the bonds of holy matrimony, and that's a perfectly frank confession; franker, I daresay, than most men make in similar circumstances."

"This sounds as if it were going to be a marriage of real affection; a genuine love-match." The sneer which was on Mr. Clarke's face as he said this; the indescribable look which was on Mr. Armitage's as he replied:—

"If you only knew how I hate the woman; how every pulse throbs with loathing when she comes near me." He gave what seemed to me to be a great sigh. "As I live, it's a comfort to say that to someone. It makes me ill to be in the same room with her—got to that stage already. Heaven knows how far it will go by the time we're married. I shouldn't wonder if I were to murder her on our wedding night."

"Is that so really? What a honeymoon you'll have if you do. Is the lady young?"

"Young! I shouldn't care to ask her age for fear of the depth of the lie she'd tell me; she's at least old enough to be my mother—my grandmother, for all the woman that's left in her."

"What a very charming couple you will make—full of vivacity! Has the lady physical charm?"

"She never had. I tell you she takes all to pieces nowadays. She is one of those women the ladies' papers always suggest to the masculine mind; she gets her hair from one of the persons advertised on the back pages; her complexion from some wretched harridan whose advertisement is to be found a page or two in front; her figure from a person the editor specially recommends—at so much a time; and her teeth from the Lord knows who. Oh, she's a regular specimen of love's young dream."

"Is she really? She must be a walking nightmare. What is the fortunate lady's name? I take it she has tons of money."

"Her name is Drawbridge, and she has, at any rate, enough money to pay you, Clarke."

"I hope there will be a little left for you when I am paid, I do really, my dear boy."

"Well, there may be or there mayn't; but I'm marrying her to get the money to pay you, and that's the whole, plain truth."

Mr. Armitage was about to rise from his chair when the other leaned right over the table and stopped him.

"One moment, Armitage, one moment. When are you going to touch that money, eh?"

"I can't tell you the exact day now, can I? I only proposed to her yesterday. It was your telegram that brought me to the sticking-point."

"I'm afraid I shall have to push you a little beyond the sticking-point. I'm in a hole myself. I'm pressed for money. I've got to find at least five hundred pounds in four-and-twenty hours."

"Is that true?"

"Perfectly true. I shall be in a very inconvenient position if I don't find it; and it's got to come from you. You'll be in a more inconvenient position than I shall if it doesn't; so that's plain. I've come all the way to Dieppe to make it clear to you that it is plain. Can you get five hundred pounds out of your fair lady between this and to-morrow night? If you can I'll wait a few days for the rest, but five hundred I've got to have before I go to bed to-morrow night; or —you know the alternative if I don't. That engagement will be off; I don't suppose even she will want to marry you after you've done a term of penal servitude. There's something else—I should like a hundred to-night."

"I haven't ten pounds left in the world. I'm practically broke; I've been losing steadily ever since I've been at this place."

"Then it looks as if you'll have to get a hundred for me and a bit over for yourself. I've got to have my hundred, and the other four to-morrow."

Mr. Armitage, looking steadily at the other, seemed to see something in his face which made it clear that he meant what he said. A grim look came on his own face as I saw him say: "I'll see what I can do."

"You'd better. Where is the lady?"

"Punting, in the club; playing baccarat."

"Then you'd better cut off to the club as fast as ever you can, and take her by the scruff of the neck and squeeze that hundred out of her while she's got it to squeeze. After you're married you're not going to let her play baccarat with your money, are you? She'll make a pauper of you if you don't take care."

"You mind your own business, and leave me to manage my matrimonial affairs after my own fashion." Mr. Armitage got up from his chair. "Where shall I find you, at the hotel or here?"

"You'll find me all over the place, my lad, don't you make any mistake. I'm not going to lose sight of you till I've got my money, or got you in jail. You can go, but just you understand I shall be close behind you—and I'm not the only one who'll be close behind you either. If you keep looking over your shoulder you'll see two or three—friends of mine."

Mr. Armitage took himself off, with an air of indifference which was very well done; he could not have had a very careless feeling in his heart. Almost immediately Mr. Clarke followed with the evident intention of dogging his steps. And I was left alone, nearly overcome by feelings which were altogether indescribable.

What on earth was I to do? It was no business of mine, this affair of the old maid and the young bachelor. She must have known what a risk she was running when she agreed to his preposterous proposal. If, by what I will call an accident, I had become acquainted with facts which made the gentleman's position in the matter abundantly clear—still it was no concern of mine.

But it was no use my talking to myself like that. I could not allow a person of my own sex to enter into what I knew would be such a hideous marriage without making some attempt to lay before her the facts upon which my knowledge was based. In other words, here was one of those opportunities for doing good of which people were so fond of talking; and, if the thing was in my power, good should be done.

I got up from my seat and went in search of Miss Drawbridge; finding her, as I had expected, in that part of the building which is found in every French casino, and which—I presume ironically—is called "Cercle privé," as if it ever is, in any sense of the word, a "club," or has anything "private" about it. She was seated at one of the baccarat tables, and I could see at a glance that she was winning; she had quite a quantity of bank-notes in front of her, and kept adding to the store. Presently the bank was closed and the players rose. Miss Drawbridge rose too, with her spoils in a white satin handbag. As she moved towards the door Mr. Armitage came into the room, with Mr. Clarke not very far behind him. When he accosted her, I thought, as I suppose everyone else did in the room, what an extraordinary couple they were—to think that they were ever going to be married. I saw him ask her, with an attempt at a smile:—

"Well, what luck? How many banks have you broken?"

Her back was towards me, so that I could not see her answer, but I guessed what it was from his rejoinder.

"That's great news." I fancy he hesitated. Would he have the assurance to ask for that hundred pounds for Mr. Clarke without a moment's warning? He approached the subject by what I suppose he meant to be a delicate way. "I'm awfully glad you've had a bit of luck, because the fact is it's all the other way with me; I can't do anything right, and, between ourselves——" I saw him hesitate again; I imagine that the decent man which was in him made it difficult for him to ask a woman for money when it came to the pinch.

What she said I could not see, but I conceive of her as saying, struck by his hesitation: "Well, and what is it between ourselves?"

He made a stumbling effort to explain what it was he wanted.

"You know, it's like this: I'm awfully pushed for coin. If you could manage to lend me, say, a hundred out of those winnings of yours——"

She cut him short. I could not tell with what words, but her hand dived into her white satin bag just as they passed through the swing-door out of sight.

Two or three minutes afterwards, when I returned to the Casino, I saw in the crowd round the "little horses" Mr. Clarke sidle up to Mr. Armitage. Both their faces were in plain sight. I could see Mr. Clarke ask:—

"Well, have you got it? Has the sweet young thing been kind?"

Mr. Armitage turned away, as if the other's gibe had roused him to sudden anger; but I saw him hand his companion something as he moved away, and I knew what it was. A few minutes later I saw Mr. Armitage again, going towards the club. He was addressed by a fat, florid-looking man, with an exaggerated moustache. A moustache sometimes screens a man's mouth almost completely; but his was so formed that, despite the absurd dimensions of that hirsute adornment, I could see his lips distinctly. He said to the man he had stopped, with what I fancied was an evil gleam in his bold, bloodshot eyes:—

"I'm sure Mr. Armitage has a five-pound note which he can spare for an old friend who's a little on his uppers."[1]

Mr. Armitage recognized him with what was evidently not a start of satisfaction.

"So it's you, Morgan, is it? What on earth are you doing here? I thought you were——"

Mr. Morgan raised his finger to his lips, to prevent the other bringing his sentence to a close.

"Quite so—we won't say where. How about a five-pound note, Mr. Armitage, for a very old friend?

Mr. Armitage looked at him angrily for a few seconds, then grabbed something out of the pocket of his dinner-jacket which might have been a hundred-franc note. He thrust it into the other's hand and, without waiting for a word of thanks, went quickly on. Mr. Morgan looked at what he had been given, then he looked after the donor—the expression on his face was not that of a grateful man.

I found Miss Drawbridge sitting at the very table on the terrace which had been lately occupied by Mr. Armitage and his friend. As I took the chair in front of her she said to me:—

"That's right, come and talk to me—and have something." She herself was having some curious concoction in a big glass; for me she ordered a lemon-squash. "I've had a good night, my dear. It seems as if I can't lose at baccarat lately—as if my luck had turned; I'm sure it's about time it should. You look a little moped. What's been troubling you?"

I considered for a second or so; then I decided, by degrees, to make the plunge. I approached the subject by what I meant to be a roundabout fashion of my own.

---

[1] Impecunious, badly off.

"I've just learnt something rather disagreeable."

"Have you? That's easy; the difficulty is to learn anything else. Is it private, or for publication?"

"I've just learnt that a man who I thought was rather a decent sort is a thief and a rogue, and two or three other things which are rather worse."

"When you've had my experience of life, my dear—which Heaven forbid you ever will—you'll know that that sort of thing is quite common with a man—you must take a man at his own valuation, my dear. We should never get one at all if we took them at ours."

"This man is not only going to marry a woman for her money, but because he doesn't know where he will get money from if he can't from her, and if he doesn't get her money at the earliest possible moment he'll be sent to jail. He's a thoroughly all-round bad lot, the man is, though he doesn't look it."

Miss Drawbridge had her fish-like eyes—they always looked as if they had been boiled—fixed on me with a watery stare.

"What's the gentleman's name?" I knew from her manner that, as the children have it in their game, she was "getting warm." "Does it begin with the first letter of the alphabet?"

"I'm afraid that it does."

"What have you found out about Mr. Armitage? Stay—before you speak I ought to tell you that what you say will in all probability be repeated to him; and while I'm about it I ought, perhaps, to tell you something else—and that is not a very easy something to say."

She sipped at her glass; then she took a cigarette out of a gold case and began to smoke. I thought what an extremely unprepossessing person she seemed. I wondered by what process of evolution a sweet, simple, fresh, clean young girl had become transformed into such a being. Rather to my surprise, and a good deal to my confusion, she showed an unexpected capacity to read my thoughts.

"You don't think I'm very much to look at, do you? I'm not; I never was. Time has not improved me, either outside or in. When I was young I was very poor. For seven years I was a governess at sometimes twenty, sometimes thirty pounds a year, and lived upon my earnings—if you know what that means. I couldn't expect to get married on that, could I? And no one wanted me anyhow, though I wanted to marry very badly. I never remember the time when the one thing of which I dreamed was not to become some decent man's wife. It sounds funny, doesn't it? Isn't it a shocking confession to make? I wonder how many women would make it if they told the truth?"

She flicked the ash from her cigarette. I was beginning to wish that I had left her alone, that I had not embraced an opportunity of doing her good.

" YOU DON'T THINK I'M VERY MUCH TO LOOK AT, DO YOU ?"

"When I was about thirty-eight I came into a lot of money from an uncle, whom I don't remember to have ever seen. It turned my head; I thought that money could do anything. I decided that now I would marry, and that I would marry just the sort of man I had always hoped I would do. You see, I had practically no knowledge of the world at all—how can a woman have who has lived a life like mine? It took seven or eight years to make it clear to me that, in thinking because I had got money I could marry the sort of man I wanted to, I was a fool."

She smiled, and the whole of her face seemed to be dislocated to enable her to do so, and she beckoned the waiter to fill her glass.

"Men wanted to marry me—oh, yes; but they were the kind of men whom I would not, as the saying is, have touched with the end of a barge-pole. I sent them about their business. Whenever I saw a masculine creature to whose appearance I particularly objected, I knew that, sooner or later, he would ask me to be his wife—which was nice. No one else ever did, so I made a fool of myself by way of seeking consolation. I know they call me 'Gertrude' here, and some equally silly name at other places which I favour regularly with my society. As a matter of fact, my name is Elizabeth. Since my mother died, when I was a girl, no one has ever called me by my Christian name—think of that!"

The waiter brought her a fresh edition of that curious concoction; she put the glass to her lips.

"Don't suppose that my desire to marry grew less as my years grew more; that's a silly notion which some young girls seem to have. If I have to advertise for a husband, I'm going to have one before I die; so you can imagine what it means to me that Cecil Armitage has asked me to be his wife. I don't know that I'm particularly fond of him; I'm quite aware that he isn't at all fond of me. But he's so young—you don't know what a young man means to a woman like me—and so handsome, so beautiful, so healthy, so strong, so well shaped! In my most sanguine moments I never dreamed that I should have such a perfect specimen of a man for my very own. Of course, I shall have to pay for him—you needn't tell me that; my experience is that one always has to pay for anything that's worth having—and generally through the nose. I expect to have to pay through the nose for him. I've got more money than some people think, or, I believe, even than he suspects. I believe he thinks that I've got two or three thousand a year; I'm a rich woman, my dear. My money has gone on increasing and increasing, and now I don't spend a tenth of my income. I don't mean to let him know how much money I really have; he'd want too much if I did. I don't suppose for a moment that he isn't what I've seen described as 'shop soiled'; he wouldn't want to get money out of me at the price of making me his wife if he wasn't in a nasty hole. And, bless you, I don't mind that; I've grown out of all my illusions. You can tell me all you know against him if you like, though I don't know how you found out; it will give me a pull over him when it comes to talking matters over a little later on. Nothing you can tell me to his discredit will surprise or hurt me in the least. I'm prepared to pay a good lump sum to get him clear of all his messes, then I'm going to have one of the finest weddings ever seen in town; I've had a special sum set apart for it for years. Won't he make a picture of a bridegroom? I never dreamed that I should marry a man like him."

Her cigarette being nearly consumed, she lit another, while I looked at her with, I have no doubt, amazement in my eyes and something like terror in my heart. I had never supposed that there were such women as she existing in the world, who looked at what, to me, were sacred things from such a point of view. It seemed to me that I was listening to someone in a nightmare when she went on.

"There will be crowds of people at my wedding; you can always get crowds of people if you don't care what it costs to get them. And the papers will be full of it; the ladies' papers send their own lady reporters to weddings, and give pages and pages, and lots of illustrations, if you make it worth their while. It's all a question of making it worth their while. I tell you that with such a bridegroom I'm going to have the wedding of the season; and I do believe you thought you were going to choke me off him by telling me that he is what you call a thief. You funny little thing! How many really honest men do you suppose there are, if the truth were known?"

I had nightmares because of Miss Drawbridge that night—real nightmares. I had a broken and disturbed night absolutely on her account, and I got out of bed with the feeling strong upon me that, if I could possibly help it, that, to my mind, impossible marriage should not take place—I would do that unfortunate woman good in spite of herself.

When I got down almost the first person I saw was Mr. Cecil Armitage, looking so glum, so unhappy, so desperate, and, I could not but think, so ashamed of himself, that my resolution was strengthened—particularly when, as I was having my coffee and roll, the man Morgan, with the huge moustache, came and planted himself at my table, and actually began to talk to me.

"I rather fancy, Miss Lee, that you are interested—shall I say?—in our mutual friend Armitage?"

He seemed to have got my name off pat, though where he had got it from I could not think; how he dared to address me I could not think either. I had never seen the man except the night before in the Casino for about thirty seconds—and then at a distance. I did not answer him, I just looked at him; he went on:—

"I may mention that I am Captain Morgan, of the Fusiliers." I think it was the Fusiliers, I know it was some regiment—as if I cared. "I'm an old friend of Mr. Armitage, and if you like I can place you in possession of certain facts concerning that gentleman——" I did not wait for him to finish. I got up and walked off, leaving my coffee and roll unfinished. I daresay if I had stopped to finish them he would have offered to sell me secrets about Mr. Armitage for five pounds apiece. I had an instinctive feeling that he was that kind of man.

It is quite the thing at Dieppe to go down to the quay to see the boat come in from Newhaven. After *déjeuner*,[1] as there was a pretty stormy sea, I thought I would go and see what the passengers looked like. As I was going I fell in with Mrs. Curtis, one of the dearest old ladies I have ever met. She was an American, and, so far as I could make out, had been doing Europe very much on her own, although she had a husband who everybody said was a millionaire. It seemed that he was coming to Dieppe by that very boat.

"I haven't seen him," she told me, "for more than six months. He's so occupied with business that he hasn't time to spare for such a trifle as a wife, except between whiles. I understand that he's been making another million dollars. I wish he wouldn't; every fresh million he makes only seems to fill him with the desire to make more; and as we've neither kith nor kin, and are just a lonely old couple, what we're going to do with all the money I can't think."

---

[1] Lunch (French).

It was a funny thing to say, but then people do say funny things, and there are such funny people, and so much of the world does seem queer. A few people have too much money and so many have nothing like enough—it's all a jumble.

When the boat drew up at the quay she began to wave her hand-kerchief with all her might to an elderly gentleman who stood on the deck, and he began to wave his to her; so I drew off in order that they might meet without being worried by a stranger. As I was strolling off the quay after most of the people had gone, a girl who had a small brown bag in her hand looked at me as if she wondered if I were very dreadful, and then, as if thinking that perhaps I was not, summoned up courage to speak to me.

"Can you tell me," she asked, "the name of a cheap and respect-able hotel where—where I can go alone?"

I told her of one which I thought answered that description—I offered to show her where it was. She was quite the prettiest girl I had seen for ages, with a face, I thought, which had character and strength, as well as being good to look at. I fell in love with her at sight. She did not accept my offer to show her to the hotel, but she thanked me for giving her the name; and then, after favouring me with a further inspection, she made a remark which took me aback.

"I believe that in these foreign places, if they have been there any time, English people begin to know each other by name as well as by sight. Will you pardon my asking how long you've been here?" I told her. Then came a staggering question: "Can you tell me if there is now staying in Dieppe a gentleman named Cecil Armitage?"

I informed her that to the best of my knowledge and belief there certainly was. I do not know what there was in my tone which she resented, but there seemed to be something; because, barely thank-ing me, she gave me a cold little nod and walked on.

That evening, after dinner, I was sitting in the Casino gardens, when I saw a fragment of conversation between Mrs. Curtis and her newly-returned husband which both amazed and tickled me. I may say at once that, unless I blindfold myself, whether I want to or not I cannot help seeing what people are saying whenever I look out of my eyes. I was rather in the shadow, and they were in the full glare of the electric light, so that I could not help seeing them. The old lady was speaking when I saw them first.

"So you've been making more money?" she said; and as she said it she looked at her husband rather severely.

"'SO YOU'VE BEEN MAKING MORE MONEY?' SHE SAID; AND AS SHE SAID IT SHE LOOKED AT HER
HUSBAND RATHER SEVERELY."

"I've been making a pile, Elinor; a regular pile. I wish money wasn't so easy to make, or that I hadn't the knack of making it."

As he said it, he looked to me as if he groaned. In spite of the severe expression on the old lady's face I daresay there was a twinkle in her eye.

"And what are you going to do with it now you've made it?"

"I'm hanged if I know—I'll be bothered if I do. It's of no use to me; and I suppose it's of no use to you, is it?"

"None whatever. I've all the money I'm ever likely to need and rather more; it's piling up at the bank as it is, so that I'm ashamed to look my bank-book in the face, there's such a lot of it. I wonder you can't find some better occupation for your time than making money when you've got more than you want already."

The old gentleman, bending towards her, took her hand in his.

I could see how his face softened as he touched her, and how hers softened too.

"I tell you what I should like to do with some of that last money I've been making—I'd like to do someone a good turn. Do you think it would be easy? I don't mean just give it away to the first Tom, Dick, or Harry who thinks he wants it—there are plenty of them. You don't happen to know of a man, woman, or child to whom a certain amount of money would mean the difference between heaven and hell? There must be such people in the world somewhere. Wouldn't you like to set some fellow, who wasn't quite a bad one, on his legs, or give some woman, who was very much in need of it, happiness—if money could do it?"

She did not answer, but I fancy she pressed the hand which was holding hers, and I stole off. I did not dare to stay longer for fear I really should be intruding.

I walked as far away from them as I could get, to the other end of the terrace, where I was a witness of quite a different scene. There was Mr. Armitage, standing close up against the sea-wall, looking out across the night-black sea; and somehow his attitude told me that it could not be blacker than his mood. I paused a little distance from him and sat on the wall itself. I wondered how long he would stay. I did not wish to intrude—I had nearly been intruding at the other end—but I did not wish to go; I had a right to be somewhere. After a while he turned, and I thought he was going; then out of the darkness there came—I knew no more than he did from where —the figure of a woman. When she saw him she stopped, and he stopped also. There was a lamp close to the sea-wall which let me see their faces, and how, at the sight of each other, they changed. Then I saw each pair of lips form at the same moment a Christian name—"Cecil!" "Margery!" and in an instant they were in each other's arms. I had to stop and look at them, because this was the girl I had met on the quay, to whom I had lost my heart. They were silent for quite a perceptible period, as if each was content to know that the other was there. Then, as he held her at arms' length, I saw him ask her:—

"Margery, how do you come to be here?"

And I saw her answer, with the light of love all over her:—

"I came for you."

"For me? Good God!" The hands which had held her fell to his sides; he seemed to stagger as if he had been dealt a blow. "Margery, you shouldn't have come."

"I had to come; I couldn't help coming; I couldn't stay away. I thought you might want me."

"Want you? As if there's ever likely to be a time when I don't want you! I was half beside myself for want of you then." She moved forward; he put up his hands as if to stop her. "You mustn't, you mustn't." He drew himself a little more erect. "Margery, I'm going to be married."

There was a look on her face as if she were bracing herself to bear.

"Is that true? Is it quite, quite certain that you're going to be married?"

"It's either that or jail."

"You are sure—perfectly sure?"

"Absolutely. Clarke is here; he wants his money; he'll take a warrant out if he doesn't get it soon. I can only get it from—her."

There was such an accent on the pronoun—I knew it from the look which was on his face. I could see she winced.

"I know; I've heard all about her. I don't know what to advise you to do. You know you will be committing a great sin—if you marry her." I noticed that both parties seemed to avoid mentioning her name. "I know you, Cecil, your weakness and your strength. I do not think you will ever cease to love me."

"I am as sure of that as that you and I are standing here; it's the only thing of which I am sure. You are part and parcel of my life, of my very being."

"That being so, do you think you ought to marry—her, even to save yourself?"

"It's not only to save myself—it's to save you. If I don't marry her I shall be sent to jail—there's no alternative. Then, when I come out, as likely as not I shall marry you."

"Well—what then?" The smile which lighted up her face was one which, my instinct told me, only comes to the woman who holds the world well lost for love. Her question made him flame into anger.

"What then? Everything then! Margery, you sha'n't marry a jailbird—you shall not. If I'm to be branded as a felon, I'll never carry on the brand to you, and to our children—never, never. As God is my witness, you shall not be a felon's wife. So the thing resolves itself into this: If I don't marry this woman I shall become a jail-bird—Clarke will make me one; then—you'll be such a temptation to me, Margery. I've been tempted once and I've fallen, but what was that temptation compared to you? I'll not dare to risk it. So it's good-bye, Margery. I've no right to kiss you; the mere thought of your lips against mine drives me mad. I'm going—I'm going to marry that woman—and I'm going to her now."

And apparently he went—he positively ran. And the girl never turned even to follow him with her eyes, but remained stock still where he had left her; then did as he had done—looked out across the night-black sea.

I sat still and watched her till I could bear it no longer; then I went to her and said:—

"Will you come with me, please, while I speak to some friends?" She glanced at me as she might have done at a ghost; I do not think she quite realized that I was a creature of flesh and blood. So I reached out and took her by the hand and said to her again: "I—I think I can help you if you'll come with me while I speak to some friends."

She did not utter a sound, or try to. I think her heart was broken. She just let me take her by the hand and lead her where I would; she moved as if she were a docile child. I saw, in the distance, that Mr. and Mrs. Curtis were still where I had left them; so I placed her on a chair within sight, and I said, as if I had been speaking to a child:—

"Sit there, please, and don't move; in a few minutes I hope I'll be able to come to you again with some good news."

She sat down with meek and heart-rending obedience—she was such a picture of misery I could have cried; but I bore up till I got to Mr. and Mrs. Curtis, even though I believe there was something moist in the corners of my eyes. I got to the heart of my subject without any sort of preamble.

"You know, Mrs. Curtis, I told you that I was a teacher of the deaf and dumb, and that I could tell what people are saying by watching their lips?"

"Of course you did, my dear. This is my husband, who has just come to me from New York City. Fred, this is Miss Judith Lee, of whom I was speaking to you. She's a very wonderful young woman, and I hope she's going to be my very dear friend."

I did not wait for Mr. Curtis to speak; I just went on. I could see he was beginning to look at me with a sort of wonder.

"I just saw you and Mr. Curtis talking, and I saw him say to you that with some of the money he had just been making he would like to set some fellow, who wasn't quite a bad one, on his legs, and give some woman, who was very much in need of it, happiness. Well, I know just such a pair, and if he meant it I can give him a chance of doing, right now, exactly what he said he wanted to do."

They looked at me, and they looked at each other, which I did not wonder at—I was so hot and eager, so very much in earnest. With that girl sitting there, right in my line of vision, I felt that I had got to take these people's hearts by storm; and I was not going to stick at a trifle in doing it. Mr. Curtis asked, with something in his voice which made me wonder if he was quizzing me, but I did not care if he was:—

"Who are your deserving couple, Miss Lee?"

Then I told them all about it, in just as few words as I could, and as close to the point as I could get them. It did me good to see how quick he was at getting at my meaning. I had heard a deal about American quickness; I saw an example of it then. I believe that before I had finished he understood it all—just got at what I wanted him to get. The quizzical note was still in his voice when he made what, from an Englishman, would have seemed a simply amazing speech, but which seemed to come quite naturally from him.

"If fifty thousand dollars—that is, ten thousand pounds sterling —would do for this lady and gentleman what you want to do, you can have the cash to-night, on one condition, Miss Lee—that you don't say from whom it comes. You're to regard that as your secret and mine."

In about three minutes I went tearing off after Mr. Armitage. I found him sitting at a table in a corner of the restaurant, a suspicious-looking glass in front of him and a most dismal expression on his face. Just as I reached him I saw Mr. Clarke coming in at the other end, but I paid no attention to him.

"AND I BORE THAT YOUNG MAN RIGHT PAST HIM."

"Mr. Armitage, I want you to come with me at once, on business which is to you almost a matter of life and death."

He looked at me as if amazed, which was not odd. I fancy I seemed pretty excited, and my acquaintance with him was of the slightest. But I gave him no chance to talk. Almost before he knew it, I was sailing down the room with him at my side. We encountered Mr. Clarke, who tried to stop us.

"Armitage, there's something which I've got to say to you."

I gave him no chance either.

"Then you'll have to have something. Mr. Armitage has business which won't permit of an instant's delay."

And I bore that young man right past him. I daresay they both of them thought I was mad. I was conscious that Mr. Clarke was looking after us as if he would like to bite me, but did not dare; he did not even dare to try to speak to Mr. Armitage again. I believe Mr. Armitage did ask some questions, but he got no answers; I took him at such a pace to my hotel that he had not time to ask many. I had arranged with Mrs. Curtis that she should carry off the girl to her private sitting-room. As I opened the door, with the young gentleman in tow, she came out, and she slipped into my hand what I knew to be a wad of notes. Then I showed Mr. Armitage into the room, and when he saw the girl and the girl saw him their faces were a study.

Off I went, without any preamble, as hard as I could to the point.

"I have no time to waste in explanations—at least, not now; I merely want you to understand that owing to circumstances over which I have practically no control I know all about you—and that's all. I believe, Mr. Armitage, that you have some regard for this young lady, whose name I don't happen to know, except that it's Margery. Is it correct that you have a regard for her?"

The bewildered look with which that young man regarded me, as if he wondered if something had happened to the foundations of the world!

"I have only the pleasure of knowing you very slightly, Miss Lee; I'm afraid I don't understand——"

I stopped the flow of his eloquence with a wave of my hand.

"We shall be able to talk about all that later. In the meanwhile, may I ask you to inform me if you have a regard for this young lady? You'll find it worth your while to say just 'Yes' or 'No.' I know you are supposed to be engaged to Miss Drawbridge, but that doesn't matter. Will you please answer my question?"

"I don't know what use you intend to make of the information, but I have no objection, since you appear to know already, to telling you that Miss Stainer is dearer to me than anything else in the world."

"I knew it, but I preferred to get the fact from you. Without thrusting myself too much upon your confidence, may I ask, Miss Stainer—I should prefer to call you Margery, but as it seems your name is Stainer——"

"Please call me Margery," she murmured—just murmured; I could see the words better than I could hear them.

"May I ask, Margery, if you have in the least degree any feeling of the same kind for Mr. Armitage?"

She did not answer—she looked at me. I don't know what she saw on my face, but she seemed to see something which induced her to draw close and take my right hand in both of hers, and—that was all; but I understood; as I immediately made clear.

"That being the case, it is evidently desirable that you should be married at the earliest possible moment"—you should have seen their faces—"and a friend has placed funds at my disposal which will enable you to do so. Please don't speak, not yet. Mr. Armitage, you've been doing something disgraceful; I'm ashamed of you. How much do you owe that man Clarke?"

That bewildered look on his face was increasing; he seemed all eyes.

"How do you know I owe him anything? Has he been telling you?"

"He has not; and I'm the only one who is to ask questions. You can ask all you like later on, but at present please content yourself with answering mine. How much money do you owe that objectionable Clarke person?"

"It was eight hundred, but now he makes it out to be a thousand."

I did not ask what hold the man had over him, not out loud; but I daresay the question was formulated in my brain. I cannot explain how it was, but I seemed to see the answer in his eyes, or somewhere: "He's got a forged acceptance."[1] And it gave me such cold shivers down my back that I went hurrying on.

"Mr. Clarke will be paid his thousand pounds; and you will sit down at that table and write on that sheet of paper a list of the moneys you owe; they will all be paid—out of the fund which I have at my disposal. Now, do not ask questions, but do as you're told.

[1] A forged cheque or bill, a legal document which transfers property without the said property leaving the seller.

Yes, it is a miracle if you like to think it so, it's the miracle which is going to be the making of you. Now, sit down and write."

He sat down and wrote; it took him some minutes. A young gentleman cannot be expected to set down all he owes in an instant; I daresay there were omissions in that list of his when it was finished, though it came to a nice little total as it was.

"That's a very great deal of money," I told him when I glanced at it. "Nearly three thousand pounds. It's dreadful that a young man who is practically penniless should owe all that. If, by a miraculous interposition, it is paid, is this sort of thing going to recur? Wait before you answer. You will leave Dieppe to-night, by the boat which starts at half-past one. Miss Stainer will leave also, in charge of a lady who is a very dear friend of mine. You will go to London, there you will obtain a marriage licence, and the day after to-morrow, which will be Thursday, you will be married."

"Oh!" Margery gasped; I had to put an arm round her waist to hold her steady.

"You will book two berths by the boat which starts for New York on Saturday. On your arrival there employment will be found for you, and you will be provided with funds which will enable you to live until your salary falls due. The future will be in your own hands. Live decently, keep out of debt, work like an honest man should do who has given hostages to fortune, and there's no reason I know of why you shouldn't be the happiest couple in the world—because you are starting with a very valuable capital, your love for each other. Now, Margery, you're not to do that."

The girl, having come close up to me, had laid her head against my breast and was crying. I had to comfort her.

"Now, my dear, you must keep your head; you mustn't give way; there are heaps of things you must do. To-morrow you must buy your trousseau, and all sorts of things you will have to have; and —now, Margery, if you will keep on crying you'll make me cry too, you will—and I won't."

And I did not cry; I never do. I look upon crying as an absurd feminine weakness; and if I did, it was nothing to speak of.

Everything happened as I intended. They left by the early morning boat—Mr. Armitage was so shame-faced. He was still bewildered; even as the boat was starting I believe he had a sort of feeling that his brains were addled. Mrs. Curtis shared a cabin with the girl. And Mr. Curtis stayed behind with me.

The next morning I interviewed Mr. Clarke. I sent for him to Mr. Curtis's sitting-room, and he came. Mr. Curtis was present to see that everything was fair. I began at the visitor before his nose was well inside the door—I did have such an objection to the man.

"Mr. Clarke, I presume you're aware that you have placed yourself in a very serious position?"

He glared at me as if he wondered who I was; then he looked at Mr. Curtis, and perhaps that kept him from saying some of the things he would have liked to say.

"You have in your pocket a forged bill of acceptance which you received, well knowing it to be forged, and which you have used for the purpose of extorting blackmail. I need not tell a person of your experience that by so doing you have placed yourself within the reach of the criminal law."

He began to bluster.

"WHO THE DEUCE ARE YOU, AND WHAT DO YOU MEAN BY TALKING TO ME LIKE THIS?"

"Who the deuce are you, and what do you mean by talking to me like this?"

"Mr. Armitage has instructed me to act on his behalf." I laid some notes on the table. "There is the money he owes you. You'll give me the bill you hold and a quittance in full of all the claims you have against him."

The man made quite a pretty little scene—or, rather, he tried to; because a few remarks from Mr. Curtis brought him to before he had really got under weigh. When he left that room he had got his money, and I had the bill and the quittance and everything I wanted. Then I interviewed Miss Drawbridge.

I found her in the courtyard of the hotel having what she called her aperitive. As always, I came to the point with her at once.

"Miss Drawbridge, Mr. Armitage wishes me to tell you that the engagement which he entered into with you is at an end. As you made it clear to me that there was no sentiment about the matter, I am sure you will excuse my treating it as a business proposition —which is off."

She did not seem to mind my talking to her like that in the very least. She was a most extraordinary woman. Instead of my taking her aback, she took me.

"That's all right. I've been turning matters over in my mind, and I think myself that it would be better to cut the loss. Between ourselves, I've almost decided to marry Captain Morgan. He's a gentleman I've known for some considerable period. Every time I meet him he asks me to marry him, and I think, on the whole, he will suit me better than Cecil Armitage; he's more my sort."

I believe my breath failed me. The rapidity with which she adjusted herself to fresh matrimonial prospects was a trifle startling. I saw that the person whom she called Captain Morgan was coming out of the hotel.

"You were so kind as to lend Mr. Armitage a hundred and fifty pounds, which he returns, and for which he thanks you. I think you'll find that correct."

I laid a hundred and fifty pounds in banknotes on the table and tore off. Captain Morgan was within a yard or two.

I left with Mr. Curtis by the afternoon boat for London. The next day that affectionate pair were married. Mr. Curtis gave the bride away, and I was her bridesmaid. Afterwards we had quite a festive time with Mr. and Mrs. Curtis. On the Saturday Cecil and Margery sailed. I doubt if they had realized the situation even then. I believe they still thought it was a miracle—and it was.

It was a miracle which materialized and, if I may mix my metaphors—and I shall if I choose—bore fruit and flourished. Mr. Curtis, that miracle-worker, gave Cecil a post in his own business—a small one at first, but which rapidly grew in importance. Cecil Armitage proved himself to be an excellent man of affairs; hard-headed, shrewd Mr. Curtis both trusts and likes him. Margery wrote to me only the other day that she and Cecil were the happiest pair in the United States of America. That seems a tall order; I hope there are lots of couples who are as happy as they are—but they are happy.

The same mail brought me a letter from Mrs. Curtis. She said she hoped to see me before very long with a husband of my own. She never, never will. Never, never, never!

"AULD LANG SYNE"

One of the few cases in which I had any association with the police was in connection with the affair of the shooting in Great Glenn Street.[1]

There was, about that time, an epidemic of shooting in that part of London in which the inhabitants, for the most part, are certainly not natives of the great city. The police had made a raid upon a club which they had reason to believe was in reality nothing but a gambling house. On their gaining entrance the lights had been extinguished and firearms had been used by persons who, in the darkness, had been invisible. Three of the constables had been shot —one of them had been killed on the spot, the two others seriously wounded. In the confusion the assassins had escaped. My connection with the matter began on a Tuesday morning, some three weeks after the tragedy had taken place. On the preceding afternoon an arrest had been made in a house in Park Street.[2] The man had made a desperate resistance; there had been shooting on both sides. He had actually killed two officers before he himself was rendered helpless. On the Tuesday morning of which I speak I had business in the City.[3] I learnt, casually, that Park Street was quite close to the spot to which my business took me. I thought I would go and see what sort of place it was; but only persons who could prove that they had business there were allowed to pass into it.

When I saw the crowds which thronged the approaches I wished to go no farther. I never saw such faces. Seldom has that gift of mine for reading what people are saying merely by watching their lips had on me a more curious effect.

On the fringe of the crowd on my right was a thin, undersized,

---

[1] Seemingly imaginary. However, the story references the Houndsditch murders of December 1910 and the subsequent Sidney Street siege in Stepney in January 1911. An armed battle took place in East London between the police and a gang of anarchists and burglars, who had shot dead two police officers following a bungled burglary.

[2] Possibly a street in Southwark, on the south of the River Thames.

[3] The financial district of London, situated across the river from Southwark.

yet intellectual-looking man, on whose sallow cheeks the blue beginnings of a beard lent him an appearance which was almost ghastly. There could be no doubt that he was a foreigner, and one who was ill at ease. He kept giving furtive glances round him, as if he feared that something unpleasant might come at any moment from either side. Presently something did come. A ginger-haired man,

"MOVING STEALTHILY TOWARDS THE MAN WITH THE SALLOW CHEEKS, HE GRIPPED HIM BY THE SHOULDER."

with a greasy cloth cap on the back of his head, came shambling past me. He paused as if to look about him. A more unpleasant-looking person one could hardly imagine. Suddenly he caught sight of the individual I had been observing. As he did so his whole being changed. It reminded me of what one reads of the wild beast which bristles and quivers at the sight of its prey. Moving stealthily towards the man with the sallow cheeks, he gripped him by the shoulder. The man, springing from the ground, leaped forward as if to tear himself free, but he of the ginger hair had him in too fast a hold. They eyed one another. Words came from the sallow man's lips, a torrent of them; I could see them, but what they meant I had no notion. They were in a language of which I had no knowledge.

One thing was evident from the words I saw him utter—he spoke with a strong accent. I had a vague general idea, but his exact words I could not have reproduced. The ginger-haired man turned round so that I could see the whole of his face. There was no mistaking what he said. The words he uttered were sufficiently startling:—

"I've only got to say a word to these blokes here, and they would tear you to pieces. You mind what you're saying."

Whatever the other might have been saying, the ginger-haired man's words affected him in a manner which it was not pleasant to see. There was an odd movement in his throat, as if there were something the matter with the muscles. Then he spoke again, just two or three words. That time I could see what he said.

"You go away—you let me go."

"If I let you go, where shall I see you tonight? Don't you make any mistake about it, I've got to see you."

The other replied:—

"Why have you got to see me? What for?"

"Someone will be on the road to the gallows by this time to-morrow if I don't see you to-night—and you know who." It was obvious from the sallow man's bearing that he did. I was conscious of an uncomfortable sensation as I realized the fact. The ginger-haired man went on: "That is, if they don't out him before the hangman does. I've only got to say half-a-dozen words and the hangman will never have his chance—these here coves would do him out of his job."

The look in the sallow man's eyes became accentuated, but for the moment the faculty of speech had gone. The ginger-haired man continued instead.

"All right, you needn't speak if it hurts you to try. I shall be at Sam's to-night at ten sharp. I sha'n't stop if I don't find you there; I shall go straight off and make a few remarks to some gentlemen who will pay me handsomely for every one of them—and don't you make any mistake about it."

The instant he disappeared the sallow-faced man slipped into a street which was in front on the right.

I also departed—in a singularly disturbed state of mind. In the first place, I wished that I had never come; and in the second, I had a most uncomfortable feeling that by my coming I had placed myself in possession of information for which, figuratively, all London was groping. This feeling of discomfort was strengthened by an incident which immediately followed.

A few paces ahead two men were strolling side by side. They were apparently foreigners of the decent mechanic class. At the end of the street they stopped. One of them turned towards the other. I saw him say:—

"Come into Sam's; I'll introduce you."

At the corner where they were standing was a shop-front which reminded me of a type of *café* one finds abroad. There was a good-sized window; the lower half was painted a deep chocolate colour; across the upper half a muslin curtain was drawn which badly needed washing. It was to the building to which this window belonged that the speaker had referred with a motion of his hand. Sam's? The ginger-haired man had advised the sallow-faced alien to meet him at Sam's at ten o'clock. Could this be the Sam's to which he had referred? The pair in front passed through a swing-door. I hesitated. There was nothing to show what the place might be —no name, no sign, no anything. I saw two constables advancing towards me. I addressed them.

"Can you tell me what that place is?"

I motioned towards the window at the corner of the street. They eyed me with what seemed inquiring glances.

"That's Sam's," said one; as he said it he smiled, as if something in my question had amused him.

"Are ladies admitted?"

"Ladies? Well, I don't know about ladies—it depends upon what you call ladies. Chaps take their wives and sweethearts, and plenty of women—respectable women—go in there by themselves; but as for ladies—well, begging your pardon, I don't suppose many of Sam's lady customers pay quite so much for their frocks as I dare say you do."

"Is the proprietor's name Sam?"

"I don't suppose he pays rates and taxes under that name, if that is what you mean. I fancy he is a Pole or a Russian, though he speaks English as well as you or I do; but everybody about here knows him as Sam."

That night I paid a visit to Sam's. I had to go, drawn there by a magnet which was stronger than I. The compelling cause was the little scene which I had witnessed between those two men. If they would be there I felt that I must be; that I had to be there, if only to see if they were. I could not make up my mind whether I should, or should not, communicate with the police. I had an intuition that if that meeting did take place, confidences might be exchanged which the police might consider it extremely desirable that they should share. And yet—I could not decide. Not improbably a telephone was available at Sam's; in a moment a message might be sent to the nearest station; I could give them notice, at the last minute, that assistance might be required, in time for it to reach me.

It was about twenty minutes to ten when I arrived at Sam's. I need hardly say that I was not wearing the frock to whose cost the policeman had rather pointedly alluded, for I had no wish to have the attention of Sam's customers attracted to the splendours of my costume. I passed the place four or five times before I actually entered.

When I was in I wondered why I had hesitated as to entering. It seemed quite respectable and fairly clean; and some of the customers, both male and female, were of a better class than I had expected from what the policeman said.

The apartment into which one came after passing the doors was a good large one. I dare say there were between twenty and thirty marble-topped tables, some of them quite large ones. At nearly all of them people were seated; trade was brisk, and there was a babel of voices. I took my seat at a table at which there were already a couple seated. In the hasty glance which I had given round the place I had been unable to discover either of the actors in the scene of the morning. Most of the people seemed to be drinking coffee. I ordered a cup. As it was being brought I looked carefully round; the whole place was visible from where I sat; it was certain that neither of the men was there. I glanced at the clock. It wanted four or five minutes to ten. I sipped my coffee when it came, and found it surprisingly good.

What the people around were talking about I had not a notion; watching their lips told me nothing. I had a feeling that more than one language was being spoken. If there were a dozen, they were all equally unknown to me.

The minutes passed. It was just on ten o'clock when the swing-door opened and the man with the ginger hair looked in. He was probably the only Englishman there. I thought of what I had heard of the unpleasant type of countenance found among low-class aliens. He was to my mind by far the most unpleasant-looking creature there. He glanced round. Not seeing the person he sought, he came farther in and searched more minutely. He glanced at the clock, hesitated, then took a seat at a table near the door. He ordered a cup of coffee from the waiter. When it came he began to swallow it in little gulps, glancing every moment at the clock. The minute-hand marked ten minutes past. He emptied his cup and rose to his feet, muttering something to himself. He might as well have shouted at the top of his voice; it could not have been more audible to me. His face seemed to be distorted by a sudden frenzy of rage.

"I'll pay him!" Those were the three words he muttered; they were followed by a string of oaths. Then he moved as if to go, and as he did so the sallow-faced man came in.

In the white glare of the electric light he seemed sallower than ever. He was a curious figure as he stood there with one hand still on the swing-door; so short, so slight, such a bundle of nerves; yet, as it were, all instinct with electricity. When he saw the ginger-haired man he held himself straighter, as if he had stiffened; as in the morning, a look came into his eyes which was half rage, half terror. No greetings were exchanged. The new-comer placed himself on a vacant chair. The ginger-haired man sat down on the opposite side of the table. From where I was I could see them perfectly. Then the ginger-haired man said:—

"Another half minute and you'd have been too late."

The sallow man, resting his arms on the table, seemed to consider the other's face. Then he spoke in what was no doubt a whisper, which only reached the ears of the man whom he addressed. His accent must have been less marked than it had been in the morning, because I saw so clearly what he said.

"What do you think to gain by going to the police?"

"They offer a reward, don't they?"

"I see—it is like that—it is the money you are after; so!"

"You take care what you're saying; you keep a gag on that tongue of yours, or you'll be sorry."

"You continually threaten. If it was me you threatened I would not mind—not that." He made a little movement with his hand. "But my friends—my brother—that is another thing." The speaker leaned farther forward; probably he dropped his voice still more. "You are a brave man to threaten, to my face, to sell my brother to the police for money."

The only effect which his words had on the ginger-haired man was to make him angry.

"Do you think I'm afraid of you, or of your friends either? I'll learn you, if you talk to me like that. I'll call Sam over here and tell him right out what will settle you and your brother too!"

"My brother did not mean to shoot them."

"What do I care? You tell that to the police; it don't interest me."

"He was a fool. He meant to frighten them; but he had the wrong pistol, and in the dark he did not know it. He thought the pistol was loaded with blank cartridge."

"I say again, you tell that to the police; it don't interest me. I don't care what he meant to do or what he did; that's his affair, not mine. It's business I'm after."

"What do you mean by 'it's business you're after'? What do you want from me?"

The ginger man had been sitting back in his chair. Now he also leaned over the table, so that their faces almost met. He uttered one word: "Money!"

"So! It is money you want from me? You know very well I have no money."

"I know that I want a hundred pounds from you—and I know I'm going to get it."

"You're a fool! I have no hundred pounds, nor have I the moon."

"You're going to pay me by instalments, so much a week, until the whole is paid. You're going to start by giving me this week five golden goblins."

"I tell you I have not the money; I do not know where to find it."

"How much have you got on you?"

"Three or four shillings—and that is all the money I possess."

"Hand it over."

The sallow-faced man stared as if he did not comprehend.

"But if I give you all that I have got I shall have nothing left. I do not know where the next money is to come from; I shall have none with which to buy food for to-morrow."

"You hand over what you've got, and you turn your pockets inside out to prove that it's all you've got."

"Do you think I am the sort that will let himself be robbed by such as you? And if I say 'No,' what then?"

"Your brother will be in quod to-night—that's what then. I'll begin by telling Sam and the blokes here that you're the brother of the chap that's wanted for the shooting in Great Glenn Street; they'll look after you. Then there'll be someone who'll get him—don't you make any mistake about it."

The sallow man's big eyes seemed to have grown on a sudden still larger, as if they had been distended by the stress of his emotion. His lips twitched.

"You don't know where he is!"

The ginger-haired man did not respond upon the instant. Possibly, realizing how the other hung upon his expected answer, he chose to play upon his feelings. When he did speak it was with that hideous grin which made his evil face seem positively diabolical.

"Oh, yes, I do know; I know as well as you do—perhaps better."

"Then where is he?"

"You precious brother is at No. 3, James Buildings, in the third-floor front—that's where he is. The room don't belong to him; it belongs to a lady, and the rent's a week behind. Perhaps that's news to you. The lady is trying to find the money to-night to pay the rent in the morning."

"How do you know?"

"That's tellings, how I know. I've a way of finding out things when I want to. Look here, I've had enough of talking. Are you going to hand over?"

"I will give you a shilling to-night, and I will see if I can find some more for you in the morning."

"A shilling! My crikey, there's generosity! A shilling for your brother's life! Chuck that! You'll not only hand over all the coin you've got, you'll give me your watch and chain and every blessed thing you've got about you. And if you can't find me some more by the morning, I'll have the clothes off your back. That's what you're going to give me as a start for your brother's life, my lad. Quick, too! Hand over, now, or I'll call Sam. Which is it to be?"

The ginger-haired man stretched out a huge, filthy hand, palm uppermost, across the table. The other met his eyes, saw what was in them, then proceeded to empty the contents of his pockets into the upturned palm—a pocket-knife, a wooden pencil, a packet of cigarettes, all sorts of oddments, even to his pocket-handkerchief. Still the ginger-haired man was not satisfied.

"Sure that's all? There's not much here, you know. You haven't got a revolver? It's not a nice thing to carry about with you if it's loaded."

"I have nothing of the kind, I swear to you. I never had such a thing; I am not that sort of man."

"I thought you might have your brother's. If you haven't, perhaps you'll be able to get it for me. I shall be at the corner of Market Street[1] at half-past eleven to-morrow morning. I am going to have five pounds out of you somehow this week, or—you know what. And don't you dare to be ten minutes late."

The ginger-haired man rose from his chair, thrusting the other's miserable belongings into the side-pocket of his jacket as he did so. Then, pushing the swing-door back, he passed into the night.

I was endeavouring to make up my mind what course I ought to pursue. As I watched the sallow man I kept repeating to myself,

[1] Possibly imaginary; there were Market Streets in Barking and Woolwich in East London.

"3, James Buildings." There could be no doubt who was the occupant of that third-floor front; or, at least, it seemed to be clearly my duty to give the police the earliest possible opportunity of resolving what little doubt there was. I asked the waiter, who was a dwarf-like person with scarcely a hair on his parchment-coloured scalp, if there was a telephone in the house. He informed me that there was not, but that there was a public telephone within a couple of minutes' walk. While I was speaking to the waiter the sallow man, getting quickly off his chair, went swiftly through the swing-doors. Following him in less than half a minute, I found him on the pavement without, talking to a young woman who had a check shawl drawn over her head. They were carrying on what seemed to be an animated conversation, in what was probably a foreign tongue. Cutting it suddenly short, he went hurrying down the street at what was very nearly a run. The girl stood looking after him. Then, I presume, hearing my footsteps, she glanced round towards me. She had quite a pleasant face; was scarcely more than a child—possibly seventeen or eighteen; but in her eyes was that uncomfortable look of something more than terror which had lent such grisly character to the face of the man I could still see hurrying through the street.

I left her there and went to seek the telephone. It was in a small tobacconist's shop. The people at the exchange put me on at once.

"Is that Scotland Yard?" I asked. "Who is that speaking? Put me on to Inspector Ellis. I am Judith Lee. I have an idea that I can put you on the track of the man you want for the shooting in Great Glenn Street."

There came along the wire a sound which was very like an ejaculation of surprise, even of incredulity.

"Are you serious, Miss Lee? Where are you speaking?"

"I want you to send half-a-dozen men in plain clothes, made up to look as little like policemen as they can manage, to the corner of Perrivale Street[1] as soon as possible. Let them go singly and appear not to know each other when they get there. I fancy it's a ticklish job they'll have to handle. The great thing is not to arouse suspicion till the thing is done. You had better come with them. How long will it be before you are there?"

---

[1] Apparently imaginary.

"I'll be there as soon as a taxicab can bring me."

"Will you be there, say, in fifteen minutes?"

"Before that—probably in less than ten."

When I came out of the telephone-box there were two women standing under a lamp-post on the edge of the pavement. I recognized one as the girl with a shawl over her head who had been outside Sam's talking to the sallow man. The other was bareheaded, so that I could see her scanty grey hair and how her face was seamed with wrinkles. They were so absorbed in what they were saying that they did not notice me standing at the door of the telephone-box. They seemed to be in a state of almost hysterical agitation; unless I erred, tears were in the voices as well as in the eyes of both. I looked at their lips, expecting to find that they were still speaking in that unknown tongue, and that, therefore, what they were saying was sealed from me. After watching them a moment, however, it struck me that, while they were not speaking in English, some of the words they uttered were not unfamiliar.

A few months before the occurrences of which I am writing I had received an invitation from certain persons who were starting an institution for the education of deaf-mutes in the town of Posen,[1] in the province of that name, in that part of Eastern Germany which is adjacent to Poland. I was invited for a month, but I stayed four. I had a fair knowledge of German before I went, but the variety of the language which was spoken in that part was new to me. Before, however, I came away it had become more familiar. I had only to watch the two women standing under the lamp-post closely for a few seconds to perceive that that was the tongue they were speaking.

At first I merely caught a word here and there. Only by degrees did I obtain anything like a clear insight into what they were saying. When I did understand I lost words here and there, so that I had to guess at them, but I learnt sufficient to render me thankful that I had been able to learn so much.

One of the first words I caught was "bomb"—which in German is "Bombe." My interest in their conversation grew when I realized that the word was being formed on the younger woman's lips again

[1] A town in the Prussian province of the same name, with a substantial Polish and Jewish population.

and again, and the sense in which it was being used. She repeated the same statement two or three times.

"I TELL YOU HE HAS GOT A BOMB ON A LITTLE TABLE BY HIS BED."

"I tell you he has got a bomb on a little table by his bed."
"But why a bomb?" the elder asked.
"Because he will not be taken. I have a particular way of enter-

ing the room; he would know in a second if it was anyone else who wished to enter. He says that if anyone tries to enter the room, someone who is not me, he will push the bomb over on to the floor —and that will be the end of everything."

"He must be mad to have a thing like that at his bedside. Suppose the table were to tumble over?"

"That would be the end! I tell you I am afraid to go near it, to look at it. I would not touch it for all the money in the world. It is made of some sort of glass; he says that if you hold it in your hand and squeeze, closing your fingers on it sharply, like that"—she demonstrated her meaning with her outstretched hand—"that would be enough. What I have suffered because of that thing!"

The girl covered her face with the edge of her shawl, as if to hide from herself the dreadful picture her imagination had conjured up. The tears were streaming down the old woman's wrinkled cheeks.

"He must be mad," she wailed, "to have a thing like that beside his bed."

"That is not the worst," continued the girl. "How can I tell you what I suffer when I return? When I am going up the stairs my knees tremble so that I can scarcely mount them; I tremble so that I can hardly think of the signal which tells him it is I. Consider what would happen if I made one little slip; he would not wait to give me a chance to put it right—he has sworn it. That same moment the bomb would fall."

The two women were reducing themselves almost to a state of nervous collapse by their own words. They both of them trembled and cried.

"What is the signal which you give?" asked the elder.

"It begins when I enter the house. I give one whistle—like that." She gave utterance to a clear, bird-like note. "As I ascend the stairs I sing, something different nearly every day. He is so afraid that someone will hear me and imitate that he makes me continually change. To-night it is to be a verse of an English song—like this."

As I stood on the step of the telephone-box she sang, just above her breath, so that the air reached me, the chorus of "Auld Lang Syne," with the strangest accent.

"It is an English song; I do not know what it means. He sang it to me—you know how well he sings."

"He can still sing?" There was an anxious note in the elder woman's voice.

"Yes, a little; enough to make me understand. I do not ask him to explain; I copy him as nearly as I can; for him that is sufficient. I sing this song as I am ascending, my knees shaking, my tongue dry in my mouth. When I reach the top, I pronounce what he calls the password loud enough for him to hear it on the other side; to-night it is 'Gruss.' Then I knock on the door, three times; first one tap, then two taps, then three taps; then I go in, and I sigh with thankfulness because I am still alive. Then I see the bomb upon the table, and I am worse than ever, because the sight of it terrifies me more than I can tell you."

"But there are other people in the house; they cannot go through all this performance each time they go in or out?"

"That is where you are wrong; there is no one else in the house; except that one, all the rooms are empty—that has been arranged. See, I have here the street-door key; with that I let myself in; and——"

The elder woman interrupted her, without glancing in my direction; so that if I had not been observing her lips I should not have guessed that it was to me she referred.

"Why does that woman stay so long upon the step? You see how she is watching us?"

The younger answered not a word. Without a look in my direction she glided away, up the street on my left; while, without so much—so far as I could perceive—as a peep towards me, the elder went trudging past me on the right.

Within a very few minutes I was at the corner of Perrivale Street. As I neared it a man came and accosted me.

"Miss Lee? I thought that you were not coming, that some hoax had been played. I am Mr. Ellis—you telephoned to me just now."

"Where are the men I asked you to send?"

"They are about the street, separately. They will gather at a word from me. They are in charge of Inspector Davis, who is standing in front of that shop-window smoking a pipe."

I noted the burly figure to which he referred. So far as I could judge, there was nothing to point to the presence of his six policemen. He went on:—

"Where is this man of whom you spoke? Are you sure that you are on his track, or is it merely surmise?"

"This is going to be a much more delicate business, Mr. Ellis, even than I supposed. The man who tries to arrest him will do so not only at the peril of his own life, but of the lives of others."

"Do you mean that there will be more shooting? We are prepared for that."

"I do not mean that there will be more shooting."

I told him of the conversation with which I had just been made acquainted. He heard me with growing amazement.

"Do you mean to say that the fellow has a bomb with him in his room, which he will explode if anyone tries to take him? He will do for himself if he does. Where's the gain?"

"That I cannot tell you. These people seem to have their own ideas. He will not only do for himself and his would-be captor, or captors, but he'll work wholesale havoc in the neighbourhood. That is a consummation not to be desired."

Mr. Ellis's manner suggested that he was excited.

"But, even if you are right, even if the fellow is such a hideous monster—because he is a hideous monster, is he to defy us, to escape us? Are we not to take him? What are we to do?"

"I'll tell you what we will do. I will take him."

"You! You will take him! What do you mean by you will take him? Do you imagine that we will allow you to do our work, to do what we dare not do, to run a risk which we should be afraid to take? You are dreaming."

"I am not dreaming. It is because I am very wide awake that I make the proposition. There will be not only risk in your case, there will be certainty. It would be absolutely certain that you would bring destruction upon innocent heads; while, in my case, there will be practically no risk at all. Let me explain."

He condescended to listen as I went scampering on.

"This girl, from whom I learnt about the bomb, is the only person who is allowed to approach his room. You must remember that the house is empty. She is the only person he permits to enter. I propose to pretend to be her."

"Do you mean that you're going to make up to imitate her? He would probably detect you in an instant."

"Not at all. I'm not going to try to imitate her in appearance. Haven't I been telling you about the elaborate series of signals by which she announces to him her coming, and how she described them in detail to the other woman? They're what I'm going to imitate. I know them off by heart. Before he's begun even to suspect that there's anything wrong I shall be in his room."

"There is, I am free to admit, a certain amount of sense in your suggestion. The idea of imitating the girl's signals is not bad; but if you try that we shall have to enter the house with you—some of us, at any rate; and, keeping close at your heels, go into the room with you, and trust to luck to down him before he's reached his bomb. There are women in the force. I'll get one here. You can tell her about the signals, she can work them instead of you. It's her business—as I said, each to his job."

"And don't you realize that by this time that girl has probably gone back to him, or may go back at any moment, and that then your chance is lost? If anything is to be done, it must be done at once—now, and I will do it."

"Where's the fellow to be found?"

"He's at 3, James Buildings, in a room on the third-floor front."

"That's just round the corner, less than a minute from here. If you and I go on in front, my men will follow."

He turned into a narrow side-street. There was not a soul in sight. A woman came out of a doorway on the left perhaps a dozen yards in front of us. I whispered to my companion:—

"That's the girl—the one I saw talking about the bomb. She is probably going to him now; if she gets to him first we are done."

Mr. Ellis made a curious sound—I think he did it with his tongue between his teeth. The girl hurrying along in front stopped and looked round, as if to see from whom it came. Two men, appearing from what I take it was an alley on the right, were on her before she could move. Each had her by an arm.

She never uttered a sound or attempted to struggle. When we got to her she seemed paralyzed with terror—trembling as if, without the support of her captors, she would have fallen.

Mr. Ellis spoke.

"You two had better look after her—take her to the station; detain her till I come." He addressed the girl. "Do you speak English?"

"I have no English." It was with difficulty that she spoke. Then she saw me. "You!" she exclaimed in German. "You were on the step."

" ' YOU !' SHE EXCLAIMED IN GERMAN. ' YOU WERE ON THE STEP.' "

I said to Mr. Ellis:—

"Can't I have her shawl? It might enable me to carry the deception a little farther if I have it. He'll spot the trick at once if I enter the room with a hat and jacket on. Apparently she wears neither."

They took her shawl. Removing my hat and jacket, entrusting them to the men who had her in charge, I donned the shawl in their place. A notion seemed to dawn on her of what the proceeding meant. She began all at once to struggle violently, breaking into voluble speech.

"Off with her," directed Mr. Ellis. "We don't want any fuss here."

I sped on in front. After a second or two he joined me.

"James Buildings is the next turning on the left," said Mr. Ellis. "You had better go on ahead. When you have got the door open we will follow—my men are all here. But for Heaven's sake run no more risk than you can help."

His words were sounding in my ears as I stole down the narrow street. All the windows seemed to be in darkness; there was not a creature to be seen. As I went a thought suddenly occurred to me —I had no key. The girl had spoken about gaining admission with a key. It seemed that the only thing to be done was to go back to her in search of it.

As I decided that the only thing to be done was to return and tell Mr. Ellis of my stupidity I drew the shawl closer around me and— something struck me quite a smart blow over the breast as I swung the corner over. There was something concealed in the shawl. I felt for it; something hard was tied in a knot in the corner. I unloosed it. It was a key—possibly the key I wanted.

I hurried on with the key in my band. Odd numbers were on one side of the street, even on the other. The door of No. 3 was in a shocking state. I could see how grimy the windows were, and how the blinds which veiled them were in keeping. There was not a glimmer at one of them. I was just about to insert the key into the lock when I thought of the whistle the girl had said she always gave before she did so. I am rather a good whistler; but it was odd how, on a sudden, I had become doubtful of my capacity. With difficulty I produced the note. I had not intended it to be a loud one, yet it seemed to me that it must have been audible streets away. Then I put the key into the lock and opened the door.

As I did so someone came up behind me. It was Mr. Ellis. I had seen him coming, but so noiselessly had he moved that I had heard nothing. Four other men came after him. We entered the hall—I first, Mr. Ellis and his four men after me. The moment my foot crossed the threshold I began to sing the chorus of "Auld Lang Syne." The girl's voice had been soprano; hers had struck me as being very soft and sweet; I felt that mine was shriller. I tried to pronounce the words as she had done, so that they seemed to an English ear to be so much gibberish. I do not know to what extent I succeeded in rendering it as she would have done; I do know that singing that immortal chorus under such conditions had on me the most singular effect. I wondered what effect the performance was producing upstairs.

One of the constables had a dark lantern, by whose light we ascended the uncarpeted, rickety staircase. Two men remained below to keep an eye on the street; Mr. Ellis and the two others went up with me. Not a word was spoken; my singing was the only sound there was. I was through the chorus before we were up the second flight of stairs, so, in order to cover a possible stumble on the part of the men behind me, I started it again.

We reached the third floor. There was a door immediately in front of us. As I paused my heart was beating so noisily that it seemed to me it must be audible to whoever might be within.

I gritted my teeth as I knocked at the door—one tap; then knocked again—two taps: another interval—three taps. Then I grasped the handle, turned it, opened the door, and went into the room, with my heart in my mouth.

The programme we had arranged was that I was to enter the room alone, divert the attention of the man within, then give a tiny whistle, and Mr. Ellis and his companions were to appear, and ensure his never reaching the bomb at all.

When I opened the door it was to find that there was darkness in the room. This was unlooked for. I had expected to find a light of some sort, if only a candle or a lamp. It was a strange sensation to enter a room of which I knew nothing and could see nothing, with the consciousness strong upon me that it was occupied by a desperate, blood-stained wretch, who had that hideous weapon of destruction within reach of his fingers. No words of mine could describe my feelings. I did not know whether to move or to speak, or what to do. Any instant, in the darkness, before we knew what he was about to do, the bomb might be thrown—death would be on us.

I longed for a light; yet how was I to get one, ignorant as I was of the geography of the room and of what it contained? I ventured to move, and struck against the back of a chair. He must have heard. I had a sudden feeling that the dreadful silence could not continue. I summoned up my knowledge of the sort of German the girl had spoken.

"Where are you? Why do you not speak to me? Why are you hiding? Why is it so dark?"

When I had put my four questions I had a fresh access of fright.

Now I felt the bomb must come, but it did not. The silence continued, and on the instant I became conscious of a quality in the silence which made me behave as if I had lost my head. I broke into reiterated exclamation, throwing open the door.

"Give me a light! Give me a light! Give me a light!"

The constable turned the shutter of his dark lantern, and allowed its light to travel round the room.

"What's that," he asked, "upon the bed?"

The light was resting on what seemed to be a truckle bed, on which something was lying. It was a man, huddled up anyhow, partially dressed, amid some filthy, scanty bed-clothes. I thought for the moment he was dead. But as we looked he turned slowly over on to his side, and stretched a lean, brown hand towards an old deal table within a foot of his bedside, on which was a quantity of the sort of wool which they use for stuffing chairs. Resting on this was what looked like one of the gleaming glass balls which serve as decorations for Christmas-trees.

It burst on me what it was. Ere his hand got there I snatched it up. As I did so he rolled off rather than rose from his bed, jerking towards me his claw-like fingers. I shrieked; I had to. Mr. Ellis and his men rushed forward. Someone caught the man by the shoulder. The instant he was touched he collapsed on the floor—dead. So near he had been to dying when we came in.

Later inspection by experts made it clear that the glass ball I had caught up was a bomb of a particularly diabolical sort. Had it been exploded in that small room the whole of James Buildings might have been destroyed with their inhabitants. Death, however, removed its owner before he had been able to put his benevolent design into execution.

The girl whose shawl I had annexed made a statement to the police, by which it appeared that the man's name was Stepan Grilovitch. His chiefly had been the hand which had dealt out death in Great Glenn Street. There the shooting had taken place in a darkened room. As, in the circumstances, was not surprising, a shot from one of his friends had struck him; he had been conveyed to that upper room, where he had been in charge of the girl ever since. The wound had gangrened. A doctor might have prevented it; on the other hand, a doctor would almost certainly have sent him to the gallows. He preferred to die in another way instead. What became of his brother I do not know; he has never crossed my orbit since. Nor, thank goodness, have I seen anything more of the man with the ginger hair.

I shall never forget mounting that rickety staircase, singing "Auld Lang Syne"; or those awful moments in the pitch-black room.

It was only afterwards I remembered that when I reached the top of the staircase, before tapping at the door, I had omitted to give what the girl said Stepan Grilovitch called the password: "Gruss!" What a shudder went all over me in the first shock of recollection! Sometimes that shudder comes over me still.

ISOLDA

Experience has taught me that people discuss the most confidential matters in public places; chiefly, probably, in establishments in which persons eat and drink together. I have often been disconcerted in a restaurant by the discovery of the amazingly intimate themes of the conversations which are being carried on around me. It is on such occasions that the gift I have of learning what people are saying by merely looking at their faces becomes a very questionable possession. I have had to keep my eyes fastened on my plate to avoid having observations forced upon me which were certainly intended for no one but the individual to whom they were addressed. Once when I was lunching with Mr. Carryer at the King's Restaurant, I actually saw a girl proposing to a man. She was quite a pretty girl, too; I had been admiring her hat. I saw her say to the man with whom she was sharing a table:—

"Arthur, won't you marry me? Say you will. I don't believe you have any idea how fond I am of you; I'd love to be your wife."

I did not see what his reply was; I looked away, feeling that this was certainly a case in which a third person was not company. I had scarcely got over the embarrassment which my unintentional eavesdropping had occasioned when Harry Carryer said:—

"You see that fellow over there? That's Isolda."

"And who may Isolda be?" I inquired, looking in the direction indicated.

"I thought everyone knew who Isolda was. He's the fortune-telling Johnny, chiromancer, palmist, or whatever he calls himself, whom everyone is rushing to consult. Women tell me that they think he is so beautiful, and are quite rude when I tell them that I don't think so."

Isolda was a tall, narrow-chested, thin-faced, large-lipped, big-eyed, long-haired, dandified individual, who, I felt sure, freely used perfume. Presently a man crossed the restaurant and took a seat at Isolda's table. In appearance he was a contrast to Isolda— short, thick-set, red-cheeked, blue-eyed; even at that distance I was convinced that he reeked of the country and the open air. Harry Carryer proceeded to regale me with a variety of anecdotes in which Isolda was the chief character; some of them were such odd ones that I glanced at him again. The red-faced man was speaking with such emphasis that I had to see what he was saying.

"You understand, I am going to post you up in everything about her, and you must let it off on her as if you had got it from the stars. You are to tell her that the consumption of which her sister Elsie died was brought on by a broken heart, because she was in love with a dark man with a slight cast in one eye—that's Tom Harvey. I know she was spoons on him; she couldn't marry him because he had got no money. Then you are to tell her that her fate is mixed up —well, describe a man like me. Lay it on thick. Tell her I have proposed to her five times, which I have; and that if she don't take me when I make it the sixth there'll be no end of a rumpus. And look here; this is what I particularly want you to tell her."

The speaker, leaning over the table, I have no doubt dropped his voice to a whisper; he had grace enough to do that.

"Tell her that she once cheated at baccarat, that the secret is known to one person, and that the only way she can save herself from a scandal is by marrying me. Tell her also that she owes money for bets—so she does, a good bit—and that exposure is bound to come unless she protects herself by becoming my wife. Make it as hot as you please; you can invent two or three things for yourself if you like. She's expecting such a lot from coming to see you that she'll swallow anything. My idea is that you'll give her a regular fit of the blues. If you manage things properly, when I propose to her again—to-night or to-morrow—she'll accept me right away and if she does accept me I'll give you fifty pounds."

Isolda made merely one remark.

"Fifty pounds is not a large sum—for a wife."

The red-cheeked person was staring at the palmist as if he would have liked to hit him.

"Fifty pounds isn't bad for a few minutes' talking. You will have to say something to her, anyhow. I'm giving you a distinct leg-up by dropping you a hint or two."

Isolda said nothing; he was apparently engrossed with the contents of his plate. The other plainly resented his silence.

"Well, aren't you going to tell her what I want you to? I would never have sent her to you at all if I'd thought you were going to turn up rusty. You've done this sort of thing for me before."

"At your request I told a friend of yours that a certain horse would win a race which you knew it would not win, and it didn't. It is possible that she lost a considerable sum of money by backing it."

The other smiled evilly.

"She did—a potful; she came a regular cropper. Served her right. I owed her one; that made us even. Are you going to do this for me now?"

"I tell you again that fifty pounds is not a large sum—for a wife."

"How much do you want?"

"At least a hundred."

"Very well, you shall have a hundred; only mind—I trust you."

The speaker produced a blank cheque and a fountain pen. As he was filling up the cheque the palmist asked:—

"What is the lady's name—this time?"

"The lady's name—this time—is Lucille Godwin. She is coming from Hyde Park Gate.[1] I impressed on her the necessity of being punctual; she will be with you at three-thirty sharp. I told her to wear a sprig of white heather. As I believe it's not your custom to ask your clients for their names—it impresses them so much more to find that you know them without asking—that sprig of white heather will tell you who she is."

"And if she doesn't wear the sprig of white heather?"

"She'll have cornflowers in her hat; cornflower-blue is her favourite colour; it does become her. She thinks cornflowers bring her luck; she's always got one stowed away somewhere about her."

"That's the most significant item of information you've given me yet; it's possible that I may be able to make more of that than of anything else. I wish you good morning."

As they left I glanced at the watch on my wrist. It was just after two. I wondered if I could communicate with Miss Lucille Godwin before she started for Isolda. I asked the waiter for the telephone call book. Harry surveyed me, as I searched its columns, with disapproving glances.

---

[1] A prestigious address just south of fashionable Hyde Park.

"I'm looking for a person named Godwin. Ah, here we are—Godwin. There seems to be lots of them, they are all over London. Hyde Park Gate—that looks like the one I'm after. If you don't mind, I rather want to send a telephone message."

I went out and sent it. This is the sort of dialogue which took place:—

"Yes? Who's there?"

"Is that Mrs. Godwin's? I want Miss Lucille Godwin."

"I'll go and fetch her. What name, please?"

"Ask her to be quick—I've something very important to say to her." I ignored the question; the person at the other end departed. Apparently I had hit upon the right Godwin the first time of asking. I waited for several seconds. Suddenly the sound of a girlish voice reached my ears.

"Yes? Who are you? What do you want? I'm in a hurry; I've got an appointment. I'm just rushing off to keep it."

"You are going to Isolda." There was a note of surprise in the clear young voice.

"How do you know that? Who are you?"

"You are wearing a sprig of white heather for luck."

"Who told you that? What do you mean? Whoever are you?"

"I want you to pay particular attention to what Isolda says to you. He has been told to tell you that your sister Elsie really died of a broken heart, because she was in love with a Mr. Harvey."

"Good gracious! Who told you that? Will you tell me who you are?"

"He has also been told to tell you that your fate is mixed up with a short, square man, with red cheeks and blue eyes, whom you will recognize from his description."

"Why, that's George Ratton. This is awful! Before you say another word will you please tell me who you are?"

"He's also been told to tell you that you once cheated at baccarat."

"Oh!" A shriek came over the wire. "Please—please tell me who you are."

"Also that you owe money for bets; that cornflowers are your favourite flowers, and that you carry a cornflower about with you for luck. Isolda has been told these things about you in order that he may convey to you the idea that he has occult powers which he doesn't possess. The blue-eyed person has proposed to you five times; he hopes, with Isolda's help, that you will accept him at the sixth time of asking. Be on your guard. Good-bye."

I hung up the receiver and walked away. Something had constrained me to give Miss Lucille Godwin a friendly warning; a man who could conspire with such a creature as Isolda against the girl he professed to love was the kind of person one ought to be warned against. Having conveyed that warning I felt that I had done all that was required of an utter stranger.

Some days afterwards I was glancing down the advertisement columns of a daily paper when these words caught my eye:—

"Will the stranger who sent the telephone message to L. G., about two-fifteen on Friday last, communicate at once with L. G. at her address, and so render a very great service?"

"L. G."? I considered a moment. Clearly those were the initials of Lucille Godwin. About two-fifteen on the previous Friday I had sent a telephone message to Lucille Godwin. Could the advertisement refer to me? I was reading the paper in my own sitting-room, after breakfast; there was a telephone at my elbow. I should not be likely to do much harm by ascertaining. I again looked up Miss Godwin's number, found it, and was presently informed that the connection was made. There came, unless I was mistaken, the same voice over the wire.

"Yes? Who are you?"

"Can I speak to Miss Lucille Godwin?"

"I don't know about Miss Lucille, but I dare say you can speak to Miss May. What name, please?"

"If Miss Lucille can't come, send Miss May." I wondered why Miss Lucille could not come. All at once there came a voice which was very like the one I had heard on Friday, but not quite the same.

"Yes? Who are you? I am May Godwin."

"Do you happen to know anything about an advertisement which appears in to-day's *Morning Post*?"

"Oh, dear; are you the person who telephoned on Friday? Please tell me who you are. Come and see me, or let me come and see you; I'm in such frightful trouble." Something in her voice suggested distress.

"Are you Miss Lucille Godwin's sister?"

"Of course I am; you know I am. Please tell me to whom I am speaking." Then, with a sudden burst which somehow made me wonder if it were a child who was speaking, "Oh, please, will you come and help me? Lucille told me all about what you said to her —it was she who put the advertisement in, and now she's disappeared."

"Disappeared? What do you mean by disappeared?"

"She went out two days ago, and nothing has been seen or heard of her since. Suspense is driving me half out of my mind."

The speaker's voice was broken by what sounded very like a sob.

"Have you no friends to whom you can apply? I am an utter stranger."

"That's one reason why I want you to come. If I go to any of our friends they're sure to give Lucille away, and then I don't know what will happen. I like the sound of your voice; I can hear that you're a woman, and I'm sure that you can help me. Oh, please—please do come!"

As the tearful, eager young voice kept flashing her entreaties along the wire I was turning things over in my mind. I had nothing very particular to do that morning; the speaker's anxiety and distress seemed genuine enough; after all, there was no real reason why I should not run round and see what all the pother was about; why and where Miss Lucille Godwin had disappeared, and what help this frantic young lady supposed I could render. I said:—

"I'll be with you in about twenty minutes; will that suit you?"

There came to me what almost amounted to a scream of joy.

"Oh, thank you! thank you! thank you! Please do come as fast as ever you can."

About twenty minutes afterwards I was knocking at the door of a big house at Hyde Park Gate. It was opened by a footman.

"Can I see Miss May Godwin?"

A slender figure came rushing across the hall; an eager face looked at me in the open doorway. "Are you——"

"I've just been talking to you over the telephone."

"Of course—yes—please come in."

She led me to a pretty sitting-room on the second floor, evidently the sanctum of something both feminine and young.

"Please will you sit down? May I ask for your name?"

The speaker assumed a dignity which became her rather well. The telephone had not misled me—she was extremely young. I set her down as just about seventeen; her skirts barely reached the ground. She was quite small—I dare say not much over five feet, very slight and dainty.

"My name is Judith Lee."

"I am May Godwin."

"So I imagined; I recognized your voice."

"Didn't you send a telephone message to Lucille last Friday?"

"I did."

"DIDN'T YOU SEND A TELEPHONE MESSAGE TO LUCILLE LAST FRIDAY?'

"Then you must know something about us, because you told her the most private things, some of them known only to herself, and some, at most, to two or three others."

"Before I answer your questions, will you tell me if I understood you rightly that your sister has disappeared?"

"She went out two days ago, and I've seen and heard nothing of her since."

"Is your sister older than you?"

"Of course she is; she is nearly four years older; she has just turned twenty-one."

"I don't wish to encroach upon your confidence. What I said to your sister over the telephone I learnt by the merest accident. Did she go to see Isolda?"

"Of course she did. He told her exactly what you said he would. He made her so wild that she told him that she knew he was going to say it, and there was quite a scene. She said that she felt that he would like to kill her."

"What has happened since? Understand, tell me nothing if you'd rather not."

She knit her brows in dire perplexity.

"I've simply got to tell someone. Things can't go on as they are; to tell any of our friends would be to give Lucille away." She eyed me very hard, as if she were trying to discover what kind of person I was. "Can I trust you?"

"You can."

"Then I will. I liked your voice, and now I like your looks, Miss Lee. I'll tell you everything."

Then she drew a long breath, as if she sighed with relief.

"George Ratton—you know George Ratton?"

"Short, square, red cheeks, blue eyes?"

"That's George. Then you do know him?"

"I saw him once."

"When Lucille came back from Isolda she wrote him such a letter! When he came over the next morning, she wouldn't see him. He wrote a note in the hall; when he sent it up by Tomkins she sent it back unopened. Then he sent her a telegram; she had to open that, because, of course, until she opened it she didn't know who it was from. Such a telegram! In that telegram there were over a hundred words—and there was a reply paid. She made me fill it up with just seven words: 'Wire received. Lucille has nothing to say.' Soon after there came another telegram. She made me open that, and when I told her who it was from she wouldn't let me read it. Then he called to see me, and she wouldn't let me see him."

"May I ask if you two girls are in the house alone?"

"The fact is, we've been a pair of perfect idiots. I may as well admit it, as that is where all the trouble began. Mother and father are abroad. We didn't want to go, so they put Mrs. Cotterill in charge. Of course, Mrs. Cotterill is quite nice, but we found her rather trying, so we got up a scheme to get rid of her, so that we might have a fortnight's perfect time before the mater and pater came home; but almost from the moment that Mrs. Cotterill left the house everything began to go wrong. Lucille quarrelled with Jack——"

I ventured to intrude a query. "May I ask who Jack is?"

"Jack? Oh, well, Jack's Jack; he's the one that Lucille is really in love with, and everyone approves of. They are engaged, and were to be married this year; but now, of course, it's impossible to say. Sometimes Lucille is rather trying; it can't be expected that Jack is to put up with everything. So when he told her, as far as I can make out, quite politely, that he really couldn't, Lucille declared that she would never speak to him again; and that's how the trouble began. She started encouraging George Ratton, who may be fond of her, but I'm nearly sure is fonder still of her money—she's got some now and will have a great deal more. Everybody says how frightfully hard-up George is; and, anyhow, he's not a very nice person, or he would not induce her to gamble and bet. She has always been mad to go to one of these palmist people, but both mamma and papa have forbidden her. Of course, everyone is full of Isolda; we know lots of people who have been to him, and George Ratton so cracked him up that nothing would satisfy her but that she should go. Just as she was starting there came your telephone message. How did you find out those things you told her?"

I explained. The excitable child broke into rhapsodies.

"Oh, how wonderful! Oh, how I should like to be you! How lovely it must be to be able to tell what people are saying!"

I cut her short. "There are one or two matters which require my attention. Would you mind telling me what has happened to Lucille?"

"I was getting to it. When she came back from Isolda she was as mad as a hatter. She can fire up when she likes, and there must have been quite a scene. This is Thursday. On Tuesday morning she had a wire from Jack Upcott telling her he had been frightfully unhappy, begging her to forgive him, entreating her to meet him—of all places in the world—in Richmond Park."[1]

"There may be a very simple explanation; she may be staying with Mr. Upcott's friends. There must be lots of persons who would be willing to have her as a guest."

"Of course there are; that's just what I thought she was doing, though I thought it jolly mean of her to leave me all alone in the house after the plans we had made. But last night there came a letter for her in Jack Upcott's handwriting, postmarked Nice. It seemed queer that he should be writing to her from Nice on the same day on which he had been telegraphing in town asking her to meet him in Richmond Park. I hesitated, and hesitated, and hesitated; then at last I opened the envelope. Then I saw at once that somewhere there must be something wrong. It was just a short note to say that, since she didn't want him in London, he thought he had better try Nice for a change, and that when she did want him she had only to send a wire, and he would return at once. I didn't sleep a wink all night, wondering where Lucille was. This morning, while I was having breakfast in bed, someone came with one of Lucille's visiting-cards, and said that she had sent him for the desk which stood on her writing-table, her jewel-case, and her dressing-bag. I said I would be down as soon as I could to see the messenger, but when I did get down he was gone. Tomkins says that he was quite a respectable-looking person, in a light overcoat and a grey felt hat; but evidently he had not courage enough to wait and see me. Here is the visiting-card he brought."

As I looked at the card she handed me I saw that there were three lines pencilled on the back in very minute writing. "Desk on writing-table. Jewel-case in drawer. Dressing-bag in wardrobe."

"Is this your sister's handwriting?"

"Not the least bit like it; she writes a great, big, sprawly hand. I've never seen that writing before; I'm sure I should remember if I had —it is so very tiny. Who can that man have been who brought the card? Where can he have got it? What did he want those things of hers for? Why didn't he wait for them?"

[1] A large park in Richmond, west of London, with views of the River Thames; a popular destination for day-tripping Londoners.

"I fancy that the answer to your last two questions is pretty obvious. But when do you say your parents are returning?"

"To-morrow. If Lucille isn't back before they arrive there will not only be a frightful rumpus, but they will probably find out all sorts of things that will put us into their black books for ages to come. I tell you we've behaved like a pair of perfect idiots."

That at least was clear enough; I only hoped that nothing worse would come of their folly than what she called a "frightful rumpus." I went up to a large photograph of a very pretty girl which stood on the mantelshelf.

"That's Lucille," the girl informed me. "How odd that you should know so much about her and yet have never seen her! She's tremendously pretty—very, very fair; her hair is almost white, and shines. When it's parted in the middle she looks a perfect saint, as if butter would never melt in her mouth—but it does. She says that she's as full of life as a kitten; and I tell her, and also of mischief—then she tries to scratch me. But, truly, she's a real good sort, and if you only stroke her the right way there's nothing she wouldn't do for anyone."

The girl was perhaps a trifle incoherent but she gave me a pretty clear idea of the person in the photograph.

"Obviously, the first thing we have to do is to find out where your sister is," I told her as I went. "I promise nothing, but I think it's possible that I may be able to do that before very long—in time to permit of her reappearance before Mr. and Mrs. Godwin return to-morrow."

After leaving the house I went to lunch at the King's Restaurant. I gathered, from certain trifles which I had noticed on the preceding Friday, that this was the place at which Mr. George Ratton, the short, square, red-cheeked, blue-eyed young man, made it his custom to lunch.

I had not been seated five minutes before he came in, going straight to a table which was evidently reserved for him, and which was not quite so well in my line of sight as I might have wished. Other tables were in the way, so that I could only see him clearly when he was in certain positions. It struck me that he looked worried, and that it was with an effort he smiled as he nodded to various acquaintances who were possibly, like himself, *habitués.*[1] Nothing happened, except that food and drink were brought to him, which he seemed to enjoy. As both his meal and my own drew towards a conclusion, a person, whom I had already noticed, moved towards the table at which he was seated.

This person looked as if he might be an actor—a comedian for choice. He was of barrel-like proportions; a small, almost bald head, shaped like a Gouda cheese, and nearly of the same colour, was set on a short, thick neck, as a climax to his enormous body. His attire was striking. The ends of a bright blue necktie, tied in one of those exaggerated bows which are dear to a certain type of French student, flowed loosely over an extensive shirt-front, which was of another shade of blue. He carried a wide-brimmed straw hat in his hand, and as he approached Mr. Ratton he waved it at him as a sort of salute. He stood where I could see him clearly—there was no mistaking what he said.

"Excuse me, Sir, but might I have a word with you? I believe you are Mr. Ratton—George Ratton."

There was something flamboyant in the words he chose, in the way he pronounced them; if he was not an actor, he ought to have been. Mr. Ratton seemed to eye him rather askance.

"My name is Ratton, sir—but I have not the pleasure, I think, of knowing you."

"I came here, Mr. Ratton," said the stranger, "in the express hope of seeing you; I have something to say to you which, I venture to assert, you will not only find interesting and important, but also to your advantage."

"What may that something be? May I ask your name?"

"My name does not matter, sir—no, it does not matter." The speaker made a movement with his hat as if to signify how little it did matter. "With your permission, Sir, I will take a seat."

When he did sit down, without, so far as I could judge, having permission accorded him, I had to move my seat in order to get anything like a satisfactory sight both of Mr. Ratton and of him. This took some seconds, and I had to pick up the conversation at a point which necessitated my guessing at what had been already said. The

[1] Regulars (French).

stranger was leaning right over the table, and Mr. Ratton was still very red, as if he resented his words and manner, and his appearance altogether. The barrel-like man was saying, in what, no doubt, were bland, unctuous, softened tones:—

"He was naturally hurt by the feeling that you had sold him."

I fancy Mr. Ratton's tones were considerably louder, and were certainly less bland.

"I told him, and I tell you, that I won't have it said that I sold him —I'll allow no one to say it."

"You tell him what to say to the young lady, then you tell the young lady what you said to him—what is the inference one draws? In consequence, he is placed in an extremely unprofessional position—by you."

Mr. Ratton seemed to be growing momentarily redder in the face.

"What he meant, and what you mean, by saying that I said a single word to the young lady is beyond me altogether. I told him it was a lie. I don't know who you are, but I tell you the same."

"DISAPPEARED? WHAT DO YOU MEAN BY TELLING ME THAT THE YOUNG LADY HAS DISAPPEARED?"

The stranger gave a little movement of his hand, as if deprecating the other's warmth; he seemed calm enough.

"However that may be, he was placed in an unprofessional position by someone—the fact remains. The young lady as good as told him he was a humbug. No man in his position cares to be spoken to like that, especially by a client on whom he had every reason to believe he was about to make a profound impression. No one, I am sure, can exaggerate the pain the whole affair has caused him—it touched him on his tenderest spot. He vowed he would be even with you both—for his reputation's sake. The consequence is that the young lady has disappeared."

"Disappeared? What do you mean by telling me that the young lady has disappeared?" said Ratton, hastily rising.

The big man, touching the tips of his fingers together, moved them softly to and fro.

"The young lady has disappeared. That, Mr. Ratton, is what I mean."

"If he has been playing any of his hanky-panky tricks with her I'll wring his long-drawn-out neck—that to begin with."

"Why should there be what you describe as 'hanky-panky tricks'? My dear sir, I come with an olive branch, not a sword. I believe that the dearest wish of your life is to marry this young lady. Very well; I'm as good as authorized to say that opportunity can be afforded you to marry her at once."

Mr. Ratton eyed the speaker in a very curious way, as if he heard what he said with emotions which were too strong for expression.

"I can't talk about that sort of thing in here. I don't know who you are; but, whoever you are, you will be so good as to come to my rooms and I'll talk to you there."

"Nothing could give me greater pleasure, Mr. Ratton, than to come to your rooms. There we shall be able to arrive at an understanding of the most cordial kind in a very brief space of time."

Mr. Ratton led the way across the restaurant, looking like a very excited country gentleman; the barrel-shaped man followed, apparently enjoying to the full a delicious piece of comedy. I watched them go in a rather uncertain frame of mind; their precipitance was unexpected. I hardly knew whether to remain where I was or to follow them. A moment's consideration—and I remained. Instead of hurrying away, I took my time over what remained of my luncheon. I was putting two and two together after a fashion of my own; the more I reflected, the less hazy the situation became. If my inferences were right, I ought to be able to treat these gentlemen to another act in the comedy which the barrel-shaped man seemed to be enjoying.

To begin with, I sent a telegram to Miss May Godwin, as follows:—

"I am coming to dine with your sister and you to-night. Trust that eight o'clock will be convenient.—Judith Lee." Then I summoned the head waiter.

"Do you know a palmist who calls himself Isolda?"

The man smiled benignantly; I fancy he thought he saw something in my words which was not there.

"Very well indeed, madam. He's one of our regular customers."

"Do you know where he lives? I thought you might be able to tell me."

"As to where he lives, that I do not know; but the address at which he receives clients, that I do know. I will write it down for madam."

He wrote it down. Isolda's studio, as he called it—there are studios of so many different kinds—was in Bond Street, that popular resort of curious characters. At a quarter to four I paid him a call. His "studio" was, it seemed, on the first floor. At the top of a rather steep flight of stairs was a door painted black; near the top, on the right-hand corner, in small red letters, was the word "Isolda." I knocked. The door was almost instantly opened by a youngish man. I entered without waiting for the invitation which something in his manner suggested that I might not have received. He eyed me askance.

"What is your business, madam?"

I did not answer; I was looking about me. I was in a sort of anteroom, apparently the young man's own quarters. On some pegs in a corner were a grey felt hat and a light-grey overcoat; their presence gave me the clue I wanted. He repeated his question, it struck me, rather surlily.

"I asked, madam, what your business was."

"I wish to see Mr. Isolda."

"Has madam an appointment?"

"I have not."

"Then it is impossible that madam can see him. Mr. Isolda only sees clients by appointment made several days ahead."

"Is that so? I rather fancy that he will make an exception in my case. I am going to see Mr. Isolda now."

The man seemed doubtful, as if he did not know what to make of me.

"I assure madam that it is impossible. Mr. Isolda only sees clients who have no appointment under very special circumstances for a very special fee."

"Mr. Isolda will see me without any fee at all."

The young man sought in another direction for an explanation for what clearly struck him as my peculiar manner.

"Perhaps madam is a friend of Mr. Isolda?"

"I am not—thank goodness! I am very much the other way. Young man!"

He started at the tone in which I said "Young man!" He was probably older than I was.

"Madam!" he exclaimed, as if about to remonstrate with my inclination towards over-familiarity. I allowed him to go no farther.

"This morning," I told him, "you called at a house in Hyde Park Gate, and you endeavoured to obtain, by false pretences, a writing-desk, a jewel-case, and a dressing-bag. Is there any reason why I should not at once give you into the custody of the police?"

The change which took place in that young man's manner! All at once he seemed to go at the knees, as if a couple of inches had gone from his stature.

"I—I—I think you are making a mistake," he stammered. Apparently he was under the impression that he had to say something, and, as he didn't know what to say, he said that.

"Oh, no, I'm not, as you're perfectly well aware. Let me give you a piece of information. It is not impossible that the police will be here in a few minutes, on business with which you are not immediately concerned. If you are on the premises when they arrive you will certainly be arrested with your principal, and unpleasantness will probably follow. If you prefer not to be found on the premises you can take yourself off. You are the best judge of which course you prefer."

He looked about him like a rat which seeks a way out of a trap; glanced towards the door at the other side of the room.

"No, you can't give Mr. Isolda warning. If you don't want to be

" 'I—I—I THINK YOU ARE MAKING
A MISTAKE,' HE STAMMERED."

found, you'll make yourself scarce inside of thirty seconds by my
watch."

When he saw how I regarded it, he went straight to those pegs,
took down the grey felt hat and the grey overcoat, put the hat on
his head, the coat over his arm, and, without even so much as a
word, went hurriedly out of the door through which he had admitted me—still another illustration of how conscience can make
a coward of a man. Within ten seconds of his going through one

door I crossed the room and passed through another. It opened into a sort of passage-way, on either side of which were what I can only describe as cubicles, screened by heavy curtains. I presume that in them expectant clients waited until it pleased the great man to admit them to his presence. At the farther end of this passage-way a corridor branched off to the right and left; there were doors in both directions. I stood still and listened; voices were coming from a door on the left. I walked up to it, turned the handle, and ushered myself in.

I found myself in what Isolda probably intended to be a really remarkable room; it struck me as rather worse than tawdry. What appeared to be black velvet screened both the walls and ceiling; a green carpet covered the floor; in the centre was a table covered with a scarlet tablecloth; on this table was what seemed to be a large, solid glass sphere. I believe that in Isolda's trade an article of that kind is known as a "crystal." There were odds and ends about the room which were perhaps meant to be awe-inspiring, but which were merely silly. There seemed to be no window to the room, which reeked of what, perhaps, was some variety of incense. Although it was broad day outside and the sun was shining, a single electric light flamed in the ceiling.

Three men were the occupants of what seemed to me to be this stuffy and extremely undesirable apartment—and as I stood there in the doorway facing them an exceedingly surprised three men they seemed to be. One was the great Isolda himself, another was Mr. George Ratton, and the third was the man with the barrel-body and the cheese-shaped head. They had, apparently, up to the moment of my entrance, been engaged in an animated discussion, which my unlooked-for appearance in the middle of it brought to a very awkward close. The great Isolda was the first to speak.

"Who are you, and what do you want in here?"

He struck a bell which was on the scarlet-covered table.

"It's no use your ringing that bell," I informed him. "The tool whom you sent to Hyde Park Gate this morning on a felonious errand has deemed it discreet to fly from the wrath which is coming."

My words seemed not only to add to their surprise, but to confuse them. The long man and the round man eyed each other as if in doubt what this thing might be. Mr. Ratton said:—

"BEFORE HE KNEW WHAT HAD STRUCK HIM HE WAS ON HIS BACK
ON THE FLOOR."

"Isolda, who is this young lady?"

I answered for the great Isolda.

"I, Mr. Ratton, am Nemesis.[1] Mr. Isolda, if I may add what seems to be an unaccustomed prefix, is a worker of wonders; I represent that power which brings those wonders to naught, proving them to be the poor antics of a clumsy charlatan."

[1] The Greek goddess of revenge or retribution.

Isolda cried, with what he probably meant to be crushing dignity:—

"Brayshaw, put this woman outside at once!"

The command seemed to be addressed to the barrel-shaped person. There was dignity neither in the manner of his approach nor in the words he used.

"Now, young woman, out you go! We've seen your sort before; we want none of your nonsense here. Not another word—outside! I don't want to touch you, but I sha'n't hesitate to do so if you make me."

I smiled at the barrel-shaped man. The idea of such a creature putting me out of the room really was too funny.

"I will recommend you, Mr. Brayshaw, not to touch me, unless you wish to discover what an extremely ugly customer a woman can be."

He tried to touch me, stretching out his hand with, I fancy, the intention of taking me by the shoulder. I am quite sure before he knew what had struck him he was on his back on the floor. The others stared as if they had witnessed some remarkable feat; as a matter of fact, the man was as incapable of offering resistance to a normally robust person who had had even a smattering of physical training as if he had been a barrel of lard.

"If you will be advised by me, you will allow me to make the remarks I intend to make without any interruption, because, in any case, I intend to make them."

Mr. Ratton made a movement as if to induce the great Isolda to act on my advice.

"Let her speak. The lady seems to be a bit of a character. Are any of those remarks of yours meant for me, or would you rather I went?"

"I would rather you stayed. You, Mr. George Ratton, have conspired with this—creature against a young girl, whose honour and happiness it should have been your first duty to guard at the risk of your own."

Mr. Ratton again went very red in the face—it was queer how red he did go. "What the dickens do you mean?" he muttered.

"Last Friday afternoon you bribed him to make certain statements to her, which you hoped would induce, and indeed, practically compel, her to become your wife. A monstrous marriage it would have been!"

I then told him what some of those statements were.

"How in thunder do you know that I said anything of the kind?" He turned to Isolda. "Did you tell her? Is that the secret of your pretending that I gave the show away? If you did——"

He clenched his fists—for the instant it looked as if matters might be breezy. I interposed.

"Mr. Ratton, God sometimes uses the foolish to confound the wise, and gives to the weak power to bring the strong to confusion. Your accomplice charges you with having, to use your own phrase, given the show away. You attribute to him the same offence; whereas it was I who gave you both away. I saw what you said; I warned your intended victim over the telephone. She came to this man armed with a knowledge which enabled her to convict him of imposture out of his own mouth. The shame of his detection and of her plain speaking rankled. He sent her a telegram signed by the name of the man whom she intends to marry, asking her to meet him in Richmond Park. In Richmond Park she was met by one of this man's emissaries, who drugged and kidnapped her. He holds her at present in confinement, and sent this man just now to the King's Restaurant with a proposal to hand her over to you for a consideration, so that you might practise such vile arts as you thought proper to force her to become your wife and use her money to pay your debts—which are, some of them, as you are aware, of a very peculiar kind—and give you something approaching a respectable position in society. How the law punishes such offences as yours you know; I would put it instantly into action were it not that I am reluctant to allow that ignorant, innocent, unsuspecting child—in everything that counts she is but a child—to run the risk of becoming the leading figure in a hideous public scandal. If she is back again in her own home, sound in mind and body, this evening by seven o'clock sharp, I may keep silent. If she is not, by a quarter past warrants shall be issued against all three of you."

On that I went, leaving them to make such comments on their visitor as they might think most appropriate. More than once during the intervening two or three hours I wondered if I had been wise; if, for the girl's sake, I ought not to have taken more active steps to bring them to a proper sense of what the situation required. It was with feelings which were distinctly mixed that I alighted from the taxi-cab which drew up at the door of the house in Hyde Park Gate a few minutes before eight. The moment, however, that the door was opened I knew that my knowledge of masculine human nature had not been at fault, and that my fears, at least in one direction, had been baseless. As I entered the hall I saw May's dainty face peeping over the staircase. When she saw who it was she came rushing down the stairs, two or three at a time, and tore towards me. When she was, to all intents and purposes, in my arms, she whispered:—

"Oh, Miss Lee! Miss Lee! Lucille has come home. Do come upstairs and see her."

I went upstairs, and on the threshold of the drawing-room there stood a tall, slim maiden, dressed in some wonderful concoction of cornflower-blue, with flaxen hair, in which there was a natural waving ripple, which was parted in the middle and brushed close to her well-shaped head. I thought of what her sister had told me. In a sense she certainly did look as if butter would not melt in her mouth; all the same, as May had admitted, I felt sure that it would. There was that light and laughter in her eyes which, when one is very young, goes hand in hand with mischief.

"I am Lucille Godwin; it was you who sent me that telephone message? I put an advertisement in the paper asking whoever it was to communicate with me. It is just as well you did, because I meant to put it in again and again until you answered."

"Have you anything to do," asked May, "with her being here now?"

"There have been certain incidents since I saw you this morning. I don't know if there will be time to speak of them before dinner is ready."

"Dinner won't be ready till at least half-past eight, so just you tell us everything. Please—please! I'm simply boiling over with wanting to know."

I told them what had happened since the morning. Their excitement was amusing. They interrupted me with interjections, ejaculations, exclamations of horror and surprise. When I had finished Lucille clasped her hands in front of her with what might almost have been the rapt enthusiasm of a mediæval saint; she looked the character, too.

"Oh, it's just simply wonderful. Listening to you sends little thrills all up and down my back. Do you know you're a miracle-worker, Miss Lee?"

"Should I be intruding myself upon your confidence if I ask where you have been since last Tuesday?" I replied.

"That's just it—I don't know. Isn't it awful? But I tell you what I do know. I took a cab up to Richmond Park gate. Instead of Jack, whom I was dying to see, a dapper little man, in a grey overcoat and a grey felt hat——"

"The same man," interposed May, "it must have been, who wanted her jewel-case and things."

"I saw that grey overcoat and grey felt hat this afternoon," I observed.

"He said that Jack was waiting with a motor down by the Penn Ponds.[1] Something had happened to the engine, and he was waiting to see it put right. Would I mind walking down to him? I thought it rather odd, but I didn't see what else I could do, so I walked down. As we went—I remember we were right off the road, close to a plantation—the man took a box out of his pocket, and said Mr. Upcott had told him to give it to me. When I opened it there were chocolates inside. Of course, Jack knows how fond I am of chocs, and I supposed he sent them to beguile the way. I put one in my mouth and I bit it in half. It seemed to be full of some queer-tasting liqueur, which I had swallowed before I knew it, and—that's all I remember."

"What do you mean by 'that's all I remember'?"

"I mean what I say. The next thing I do remember is that I had rather a headache and was feeling stupid, and couldn't make out where I was. Then all at once I realized that I was in a railway carriage which was standing at a platform, and that an official of some sort was at the open door of the compartment, looking at me as if he wondered what was wrong. 'Your ticket, please, miss. Isn't that it in your hand?' There was something in my hand; I held it out to him; he took it, and off he went, so I suppose it was my ticket; but how it

---

[1] Two large ponds in the middle of Richmond Park.

got there, or where it was from, I have not the vaguest notion. Presently the train stopped again. I asked a porter who came to the door what station it was. 'Waterloo,[1] miss. Any luggage?' I told him that I had no luggage, but I wanted him to get me a taxicab. He got me one; and here I am. That's every bit I know about it. Who's that at the front door? It can't be——"

Who it could not be she did not say. These were lively young ladies. May rushed to the door and listened. Footsteps were heard ascending the staircase. May threw the door wide open and a tall young man came in, his countenance wreathed in smiles.

"Oh, Jack!" cried Miss Lucille Godwin. "Oh, you darling, darling Jack!"

Almost before I knew it, and quite regardless of my presence, she was in the newcomer's arms. He seemed a hearty young man.

"You are a nice sort," he told her.

"Directly after I wrote you that note from Nice, I won a handful at the tables; with it I bought a necklace, which I felt bound to bring you straight away; so here I am, and here's the necklace."

He held out to her a string of gleaming stones which he had taken from a leather case.

"Oh, Jack, what a beautiful necklace! What a treasure you are! Please will you put it on?"

As we watched he fastened it round her lovely neck. For all they seemed to care, May and I might not have been present. The girl said to him, with a demure look:—

"Now, Jack, I forgive you. If you only knew what a wretch I've felt, and how I've wanted you!"

"Well you won't have to want any longer."

As the young man was saying this, in what I take was his heartiest manner, a footman appeared at the door to inform us that dinner was served. Jack took me down, the two girls following arm in arm behind. I have seldom spent a livelier evening.

The next morning, when I went to Bond Street, I found that Isolda was missing, as I had anticipated might be the case. It seems possible that he had kept that helpless girl unconscious for two whole days by means of repeated injections of one of the numer-

---

[1] A major railway station in Central London.

ous preparations of morphine, as doctors nowadays keep patients in the later stages of cancer oblivious of their sufferings sometimes for weeks; nor might it have been the first time he had tried the same villainous trick. He probably still practises on feminine credulity elsewhere; but, so far as I know, he has not reappeared in London. Nothing has been seen either of him or of his barrel-shaped friend.

Lucille Upcott—she has not long been back from her honeymoon —told me the other day, with that demure air which, where she is concerned, may mean anything, that she had recently heard that Mr. George Ratton had established himself on a ranch in Argentina. Whether Mr. Upcott had been made acquainted with the various passages which marked a certain week I cannot say—whenever I see him he seems to radiate happiness.

WAS IT BY CHANCE ONLY?

It is not easy to determine what part accident plays in the affairs of daily life. I have not been able to decide where, so far as I was concerned, it began, and where it ended, in what was known to the public as the Fulham Mystery.[1] Who can say, for instance, that it was not by design—the design of a force beyond our ken—that I entered that tea-shop in the Brompton Road?[2] Was it by chance that two persons were seated at the table next to mine? Anyhow, there they were—a dark-haired girl and a red-headed youth.

The girl was, after a fashion, good-looking. But her nose was too thin; her eyes, though undoubtedly fine ones, were to my mind too big—I have seldom seen larger ones. They were what I call roving eyes.

What first attracted my attention towards their table was not only the singularity of their appearance—and the fiery-headed youth, with his thin face, high cheek-bones, small eyes, deep set in a web of freckles, presented an even more remarkable appearance than the girl; what really, in the original instance, caught my eye was the pantomime the girl was going through. She had a handkerchief in her hand, with which she was going through some quite singular evolutions. Her lips, which were very red, were rather prominent; the sort of lips which, from my point of view, when she was speaking, were as easy to read as large print.

I saw her say to the red-headed youth, in a whisper which was so faint that I am sure it only just reached his ears:—

"There are all sorts of ways of signalling; you can signal with anything. Soldiers have found out that. You can signal with a blind. Almost any information can be conveyed to a passer-by by the way in which you draw it up. Now, take your case—it's impossible to meet you again. I'm only meeting you now by a tremendous risk."

The youth said something; he had his hand up to his face, so that

[1] A wealthy suburban residential district in West London.
[2] A thoroughfare connecting the Western suburbs and fashionable Knightsbridge via South Kensington.

I could not see what it was, but I guessed it was something tender. His whole attitude was that of an adoring lover. The girl went on:—

"Of course I care for you. You know I care for you. Should I ask you to do this for me if I didn't?"

The youth said something which I also lost—and again the girl went on:—

"My dear Dan, if you only knew how, when you talk like that, you make me quiver! But we mustn't speak of such things now—there really isn't time enough for me to try to make you understand —so pay particular attention. You want to know when the coast is clear, don't you?"

What he answered I could not say. She continued:—

"If you want to do this thing for me—and if you care for me as you say you do you must want to—it must be done at the first opportunity which offers. And as I may not be able to get at you in any other way——"

He took his hand away from his mouth, so that I could see what he said.

"Couldn't you write?" he asked.

"My dear Dan!" She looked shocked. "Think of the danger. Do you want me to place myself in your hands as I have done in his? Of course, I know I can trust you—you needn't fly out! But I shall never be easy in my mind again. No, no, no, writing is out of the question; we must try some other way, so pay attention to me. You know the window of my room?"

"I've looked at it often enough."

"Then look at it more carefully than ever each time you pass. If the blind is drawn right down or right up it will mean nothing; if it is half drawn, a little crooked, at an angle like this"—she demonstrated with her handkerchief—"it will mean, meet me here, at this tea-shop, this afternoon at four. If—now pay particular atten-tion—if it's drawn up more than half-way, and is crooked on the other side, like this—that will mean that the coast will be clear, and the angle at which the blind is set will tell you the day and the hour. Now, just you notice very carefully."

She was going to manipulate her handkerchief, and I was watch-ing with some curiosity to see how she was going to do it, when she changed the subject altogether, and said:—

"There's the girl at the table next to you staring at us in a way which I don't quite like. Of course she can't hear, but I think I'll just wait and see how long she's going to stay."

Clearly I had been staring at them more intently than I had supposed. So I called the waitress, paid for my tea, and went.

Two days afterwards I went to lunch with some friends near the Boltons.[1] When I left them I walked to the Fulham Road.[2] On my way I passed down a street of rather shabby-looking houses, in which there was only one other pedestrian. As he came nearer I recognized that it was the red-headed youth of the tea-shop in the Brompton Road. His glance was fixed on the houses on the other side of the way—there was something in his attitude and in the way he stared which suggested considerable agitation.

Immediately facing him was a house which was like its fellows, but rather less shabby, perhaps, as if it had been more recently painted. My eyes, passing over its front, rested on one of the windows of the upper floor, on the other side of which was a very crooked blind. That blind quite startled me. I thought of the girl with the handkerchief, and how she had explained how one could signal with a blind. Did she live in the house at which he was staring, or who did live there? Was someone signalling to him with that crooked blind?

He stood gazing, as if unwilling to credit his eyes. Then, as if conscious of my approach, he broke again into movement, and, quickening his pace, went past me at a speed which was very nearly a run.

The next day the papers were full of what came to be known as the Fulham Mystery.

George Ryder had been murdered in a house in Helena Grove, Fulham,[3] not very far from the road in which I had met that red-headed youth. George Ryder was a young man of thirty-seven. Not long before he had been knocked down, at night, presumably by some sort of motor vehicle. He was picked up near Barnes

---

[1] An oval-shaped street with a garden in the middle, located between Brompton Road and Fulham Road.

[2] A thoroughfare running parallel to but to the south of Brompton Road.

[3] Seemingly imaginary.

Common[1] insensible; he had concussion of the brain. When, several days afterwards, consciousness returned, he could only say that he had been crossing to the other side of the street at a point where four roads met, and that a car, coming round one of the corners, had knocked him down.

" HE WAS LYING ON THE FLOOR, DEAD."

He had nearly recovered from the effects of this accident when he was murdered—at five o'clock on an April afternoon. He was alone in the house—by what really seemed to be a most curious chance. It was the servant's afternoon out; the nurse who had charge of his case had gone out to take tea with a friend; his wife and four-year-old child were left at home. Just before five a telegram was brought to his wife, informing her that her mother, who

[1] A large green space in the Western suburb of Barnes, some two miles west of Fulham.

lived at Hampstead,[1] was dying; if she wished to see her alive she must go at once. Mrs. Ryder showed the telegram to her husband. Both the maid and the nurse were to be back at six. He declared that he wished to rest, that he would be all right till they returned, and that she was to go without delay to see her mother. She left the house between a quarter and twenty past five, taking her little girl with her. The nurse, whose name was Verrion, returned before her appointed time. She entered the house with a latch-key at about a quarter to six. She was going into her bedroom when, struck by the silence of the house, she opened the door of Mr. Ryder's room to see how her patient was. He was lying on the floor, dead; someone had struck him a heavy blow on the temple with an electro-plated[2] candlestick which lay beside him.

The whole tragedy had taken place inside twenty minutes—the twenty minutes which intervened between Mrs. Ryder's going out and Nurse Verrion's coming in. Nurse Verrion fetched in a doctor who lived on the other side of the street, who gave his opinion that Mr. Ryder had been dead about a quarter of an hour.

Just before seven a taxi-cab drew up in front of the house, and Mrs. Ryder came rushing out of it; that telegram which had reached her just before five had been a hoax. She had found her mother, if anything, in better health than usual. Wondering what the thing meant she had rushed back home—to find her husband dead.

This, succinctly, was the Fulham Mystery as it was presented to the public. Not a trace of the murderer was discovered. There were those who suspected both the wife and the nurse. It was, however, made perfectly clear that husband and wife were on excellent terms; there was, besides, the almost unconscious testimony of the intelligent four-year-old child, who told how her father had gone to the door to see them off, and kissed her before she started; so that he must have been alive when his wife went out. Nurse Verrion, on her part, established two facts—that she was accompanied by a friend to the house, who only left her as she opened the door, and that within three minutes she was at the doctor's on the other side of the way.

[1] A wealthy garden suburb in North London, seven miles from Fulham; thus, a considerable distance.
[2] Coated in a thin layer of a different metal.

For reasons which I can hardly define, I took more interest in the Fulham Mystery than I generally do in matters of the kind. Of course, it was the merest coincidence, but it did strike me as odd that I should have met the red-haired youth that same afternoon, and have been puzzled by the agitation he showed as he stared at the signalling blind. I suppose I met him, so far as I could judge, at about half-past three, some two hours before the murder took place within a quarter of a mile of where I saw him. I recalled what the girl had said at the tea-shop—that her object was to let him know, as I took it, by means of a signal conveyed by the blind in her room, when "the coast was clear." Two hours afterwards the coast had been cleared in Helena Grove in a truly singular manner.

Whether, again, the second chapter of this strange story owed its inception to mere chance, he would be a bold person who ventured positively to affirm. I was spending the week-end on the cliff at Boscombe.[1] George Ryder had been dead two years; the Fulham Mystery, still unsolved, had practically slipped from the public mind. I arrived on the Friday, and had to leave on the Monday afternoon. On Monday morning I enjoyed the open air in the pretty, sheltered public gardens. I occupied a chair under a tree. On the other side of the path a lady was the sole occupant of a seat. We were both of us reading. An exclamation caused me to glance up from the page of my book. A lady, holding a child by each hand, had come along the path; at sight of her the occupant of the seat had sprung up; the two women were staring at each other, as if each saw in the other a ghost.

The woman with the two children seemed to be the more amazed; it was she who had uttered the exclamation. I judged her to be perhaps thirty years of age, but she looked so worn and worried that she might have been younger than she seemed. Her clothing was old and shabby.

The person who had risen from the seat was the first to speak; though I could not hear her, I could see distinctly what she said. Her expression was one of sheer bewilderment, as if she were still in doubt of the other's identity.

"Annie! It is you! Have you tumbled from the sky? Where have

---

[1] A seaside resort near Bournemouth in Dorset.

you been hiding? What are you doing here? And who are these—these two young people? Where is your own small daughter? Surely this is not she?"

The woman addressed as Annie seemed to be so overcome by the other's unexpected appearance as to be almost incapable of speech. When she spoke, although I heard nothing, I could see from the twitching of her lips that her voice was tremulous.

"Laura, I—I never expected to see you. I—I can't stop now, but I—I want to speak to you very much. I've got to take these two children to a friend's, just—just over there; but I'll be back in—in ten minutes, if you'll wait for me—here. Laura, say you'll wait for me."

Her friend's bewilderment seemed to be growing. The expression in her eyes showed clearly that she could not make the speaker out.

"Stay for you?" She smiled, as if to reassure her. "Of course I'll stay for you—ten minutes, or as long as you like."

The woman, with her two charges, hurried off.

I imagine that it was nearer twenty than ten minutes before the other returned; when she came she was nearly running.

"They—they kept me longer—than I thought they would. I—I'm not my own mistress, and—and when people want me to stay—I have to."

"But, my dear Annie, what do you mean by you're not your own mistress?"

"I'm—I'm a nursery governess. Didn't you know I was a nursery governess?"

"A nursery governess?" The speaker's surprise was so marked that she gave a little bound on her seat. "You! Annie! A nursery governess! But I thought that George Ryder——"

The other put her hand upon her arm, glancing about her as if in sudden terror.

"Hush! I'm not Mrs. Ryder now—at least, I don't call myself that. I—I call myself Mrs. Brown."

"You call yourself Mrs. Brown? Annie—I understand you less and less. Are you ashamed of your husband's name?"

"Indeed no. But when I told people that I was Mrs. Ryder they began to ask me questions; and when they found out that I was Mrs.

George Ryder, and—and that it was my husband who was—murdered, they didn't want to have anything to do with me."

"But why ever not? It wasn't you who murdered him."

"Laura, I have to live. And when people found out who I was, they wouldn't give me a chance; so—I call myself Mrs. Brown."

"But what do you mean by you've got to live? Didn't your husband leave you plenty of money?"

"Not a penny—or, at least, only a few pounds. And shortly after my mother died, and she left nothing."

"But I thought that your husband not only had money of his own, but that he had excellent expectations?"

"He did; but nobody seems to have understood, and that has made it so much harder. His aunt, Mrs. Dawson, told him herself that she had left him all her money; and so she had, but her will was rather oddly worded. She left all her money to her nephew, George Ryder, but if he died before she did, then all her property was to go to her other nephew, Athelstan Ward. She was ill when George was—killed. Someone, stupidly enough, went blundering into her bedroom, crying out that George had been murdered. The shock had such an effect on her that it brought on a paralytic seizure, from which she never recovered. In less than a month afterwards she was dead. By her will, as I have explained, she left nothing to George, who was dead, and nothing to me, or to Daisy either. Everything went to Mr. Ward."

"What a very unfortunate state of affairs for you! Did Mr. Ward do nothing? He must have seen the iniquity of such an arrangement."

"Athelstan Ward had never expected to inherit anything. He and his aunt did not get on at all; he had offended her in all sorts of ways; at the last upset they had she had told him that she would leave him nothing. He knew that everything was left to George, who was her favourite nephew. When she died he was a clerk in the City, at a salary of something over a hundred a year. He told me to my face —gratuitously—that I would never get a farthing[1] out of him. He said that George would have stuck to the lot, and he meant to do the same."

---

[1] A quarter of a penny; thus, a very small amount of money.

"But what has become of the man? What a dreadful creature he must be!"

"He's married, that's all I know about him. He married Miss Lisle."

"What, Lily Lisle? The girl with the dreadful eyes, who acted as Mrs. Dawson's companion?"

"Mrs. Dawson liked her well enough, I believe; though in the end, in a sense, she was the actual cause of the old lady's death, because it was she who rushed into her bedroom screaming out that George Ryder was murdered. It turned out that she and Mr. Ward had been engaged, under the rose, for ages. After the will was read they were married—within a week or two. Everyone believed that the old lady was well off, but no one guessed how well off until things were gone into. I'm told that she left over two hundred thousand pounds. Think what even a little of it would have meant to Daisy and me. I'm getting twenty-five pounds a year, and out of that I have to clothe myself and keep my child."

"How long are you free now? I'm staying at the Burlington Hotel. Can't you come and lunch with me?"

"I'm free for this afternoon. If—if I'm not too shabby, I should like to come and lunch with you very much."

The two got up from their seat and walked away. I remained where I was, thinking. It did seem extraordinary that I should have been there when such things were being talked about—things which brought back such odd memories. The girl with the "dreadful eyes"—could she, by any chance, have had any connection with the young woman whose singular eyes had attracted my attention in the tea-shop in the Brompton Road? And Mr. Athelstan Ward—was he red-headed? I wondered.

Suppose that those two chance encounters, in the tea-shop, in the Boscombe public gardens, had put into my hands the key to the unsolved mystery—would that not be something very like a miracle? If I had had anything tangible to go upon, I would have spoken to those two women then and there. But I endeavoured to dismiss the whole subject from my mind, and went up to Waterloo by the afternoon train.

" I BOUGHT NEARLY ALL HER FLOWERS ; HER GRATITUDE WAS PITEOUS."

Nearly another two years elapsed, and I was at Eastbourne,[1] staying with some friends at a big hotel on the front. My friends had gone up to town for a day or two, and I was left in sole possession of their apartments. One morning, as I was walking rapidly along the Parade, I was accosted by a woman selling flowers. Something about her method of address and manner caused me to look at her. Where, I asked myself, had I seen her before? Her face seemed familiar. I had gone past her perhaps half-a-dozen steps when it

[1] A seaside resort on the south coast of England.

came back to me. The Boscombe public gardens; the two women on the seat—surely this was Mrs. George Ryder! And yet it seemed impossible.

I must have been mistaken; a chance resemblance had taken me in. I thought I would go back and, while buying some of her flowers, have a good look at her.

It was Mrs. Ryder—or the resemblance was supernatural. Of course, she had altered. She had grown so thin; her cheeks were hollow; her eyes cavernous, even hungry; her skin seemed to be all furrows; yet that she was the woman whom I had seen sitting on the seat, telling her friend the tragic story of the will which had passed her by, I was certain. What to say to her; what to do—these were points on which I could not make up my mind. I bought nearly all her flowers; her gratitude was piteous. Then I gave an order for more, and directed her to bring them to my hotel the next morning at a certain hour. I left her there, standing in the bitter east wind, which I hoped she did not feel to be quite so bitter as before, while I walked away, wondering by what possible means she could have reached so dreadful a position.

I kept thinking of her, even when I got back to the hotel; she was with me all that day; when I was dressing for dinner, as I was going down to the great meal of the day.

In the absence of my friends I was the solitary occupant of their table. I was down early, and watched the people coming in. I had just finished my fish course when four or five persons came down the room, at the sight of one of whom I almost jumped.

It was the girl of the tea-shop—she of the dreadful eyes. I was sure it was she, though she was altered out of all conscience. To begin with, she was beautifully dressed—rather too well dressed, in fact, for such a place. Her hair was done in a way which was really an exaggeration of the latest fashion; she held herself as if she were a person of importance—she had filled out, grown plumper; in many respects she had altered altogether. Yet it was she—surely no other woman in the world could have such eyes as she had. They seemed to have grown larger; they roved as much as ever.

I observed the other members of her party as they took their seats. One thing I saw at once—the red-headed youth was not there. There were three men and two other women. One of the men was her husband. I was sure of it from the obvious way in which he was acting as host.

The man who I was convinced was her husband was the antipodes of the red-headed youth. He was rather undersized; his scanty brown hair was parted in the centre and plastered down at the sides; he wore glasses; his clothes did not seem to fit, and his shirt-front bulged.

The head waiter was coming down the room; he and I were old acquaintances.

"Can you tell me who those people are who have just come in?" I asked.

His manner as he answered was most discreet.

"It's a dinner-party. The lady and gentleman who are giving it are Mr. and Mrs. Athelstan Ward; they arrived this morning; old customers; this is their fifth or sixth visit."

So, actually, this was Mr. and Mrs. Athelstan Ward, and my wild surmise had been right. The crooked blind in the top window of the house in the street leading off the Fulham Road—the girl whom I had seen demonstrating with her handkerchief how one may signal with a blind had done it; it had been crooked because she had carefully arranged it at the precise and proper angle. In that house Mrs. Dawson had lived, the aunt of the man who had been murdered two hours after I saw that crooked blind. At that time, if what Mrs. George Ryder had told her friend in the public gardens at Boscombe was true, this girl was engaged to the other nephew, who, in a certain eventuality, of which he seemed to have been ignorant, was to benefit by his aunt's will; that eventuality, by which the girl was to benefit as much as Mr. Ward, occurred within two hours of that crooked blind having been seen by that red-headed youth, with whom she had arranged that particular signal. For what purpose?

A cold something stole up my spine as I groped about for an answer. She knew the delicate state of Mrs. Dawson's health, she was her companion; the physicians had laid on her a special charge; yet the moment the news of the tragedy reached her, well knowing that she ought to do nothing of the kind, she rushed into the presence of the aged invalid and struck her down by yelling out the news at her.

Things began to look very ugly. Was it by accident, or design, that I was stumbling on these things? What I still had to understand was the relation between the red-headed youth and the girl. That, when I saw them together in the tea-shop, he was her lover, I was convinced. Could she have used him as a tool and then thrown him over? Unless I erred, she was that sort of girl. What had become of the red-headed youth? The widow of the murdered man was selling flowers in the gutter.

A page came down the room with a telegram on a waiter. He handed it to Mrs. Athelstan Ward. I do not think I ever saw such a change take place on a woman's face in public as took place on hers as she read that telegram. What was the dominant expression on her countenance I could not say; fear and rage were two. She seemed unconscious that the boy was waiting, that her guests were looking at her, until her husband's voice recalled her to herself. He was facing me; and I saw clearly what he said.

"My dear Lily, from whom is your telegram? It appears to be of absorbing interest. Permit me to see it."

He held out his hand across the table; then she came back to herself, after a fashion. She looked, or rather she glared, at him. When she saw his outstretched hand and caught his meaning, she crushed the telegram up into a ball, thrust it into the bosom of her dress, and turned to the page, who instantly departed. She was sitting sideways to me, so that it was not easy for me to read the reply which she made to her husband.

I resolved to keep my eye on Mrs. Athelstan Ward. By way of a beginning, I thought it might be just as well to see if she would recognize me. To reach the private sitting-room which my friends had at the other end of the building it was necessary for me to pass her table, which I presently did, with something like ostentation. As I approached she looked at me, and I at her. I could see that she recognized me, and was aware that I did the same to her. Her face changed again, and a look came into her eyes which haunted me long after I had quitted the room.

The next morning I got up early. My window looked out across the garden. As I peeped to see what sort of weather it was I saw Mrs. Athelstan Ward come through the great front-door of the hotel. She was dressed for walking. Crossing the garden to the street, turning to the right, she moved quickly in the direction of Beachy

Head.[1] I had one of those intuitions to which I am subject, and was out in the street in I am afraid to say how many minutes. Mrs. Ward was out of sight, but I knew the direction in which she was going, and off I tore.

Presently I saw her. She was nearly at the point where one begins to ascend the grassy slopes towards Beachy Head. That some special attraction was drawing her to Beachy Head at seven o'clock in the morning I felt convinced. The ascent at the part at which I took it was pretty steep. I was a little short of breath when I gained the ridge, and was sufficiently on the level to enable me to see what was ahead. There was Mrs. Ward some distance in front, striding rapidly along what I knew to be the better path. She was nearly out of sight when I gained the point from which one can see the top of the Head. A minute or two later someone came out of the little hotel which lies in the hollow on one side, and crossed to her. So this was it; she had an appointment with something masculine. It was a man who had joined her, on the top of Beachy Head, at an hour when they were likely to have it all to themselves.

I had with me a pair of those folding opera-glasses which lie down flat, so that they occupy scarcely any space at all. I focused them on to the pair in front. I was anxious to see who the man might be. Something within me gave quite a little jump as I recognized the red-headed youth of the tea-shop and the signalling blind. Their backs were towards me, so of course I could not see what they were saying; but one had only to observe the man's gestures to be able to form a very shrewd guess that the subject under discussion was of paramount interest to him. He was talking both with heat and volubility.

Presently they stopped on a little knoll which was just on the other side of the lighthouse. Down I dropped in a grassy dell which was just large enough to contain me as I lay full length, face downwards, and raised myself sufficiently on my elbows to permit me to have a view of the knoll in front.

I was particularly anxious that they should not see me. That the Fulham Mystery was going to be solved at last some instinct told me, and by that pair ahead. I did not intend to run any risk of losing

[1] A chalk headland, rising 530 ft above the sea, near Eastbourne; a notorious suicide spot.

what I had so long sought. With the aid of that pair of opera-glasses I watched their faces.

They were good glasses; the definition was excellent; the morning was clear. They were at a distance, as the crow flies, of perhaps under a hundred yards. When they turned my way I could see even the slightest movement of their lips as well as if they had been within a dozen feet.

It was some seconds, however, before they did turn my way. Then, suddenly the woman stood fronting the man and also me, and I saw her say, as distinctly as if she had been speaking within reach of my hand:—

"It's no use your ranting. What I've said I've said, and as I've no more to add, there's an end of it."

He was silent for an instant. Then he also turned slightly; occupying such a position that, while he faced across the sea, his mouth was as visible as if he had looked at me. I followed his answer through the glasses:—

"Lily, if ever there was a heartless devil in the shape of a woman, you are she."

She replied, with a little flick of the cane she was carrying:—

"You've told me so before. The remark is not in the least novel. Have you brought me here to make it again?"

"You have lied, and lied, and lied to me." His gesticulations recommenced. "You have fooled me practically my whole life long. I have stolen for you; you know how often you have induced me to steal for you——"

"You didn't need much inducement." Her air was contemptuous.

"I did not; you are right. There was nothing I would not have done for you at your wish. At last, at a word from you, I committed murder."

"Put it that way if you like. From my point of view you made a mess of the whole thing; I never wanted you to actually kill the man."

"No, you wanted me to play him some infernally clever trick which would result in his killing himself—as you afterwards killed that old woman. That was as much a murder as mine was. And then you denied me my reward."

"I never promised you anything."

"Not in so many words; you were much too clever. But you know what you wished me to understand that you had promised me, and how afterwards you robbed me of the price which you had made me believe I was to receive."

"Listen to me." Her attitude became all at once that of a person who was giving utterance to a final decision. "You have been to me a continual nuisance—not practically all your life, but actually all your life. There was a time when I tried to put up with you, though it wasn't easy. You've always been a penniless beggar, so that if you wanted to make me a present you had to steal it; now you throw it in my face. Afterwards—you know when—I explained that if a certain person were to die before a certain time it might be an advantage both to you and to me."

"Especially to you."

"Yes—especially to me—that is obvious." The air of scorn with which she said it! "Now you have the assurance to send me that telegram! It came to me last night, in the middle of a dinner-party, ordering me to come and meet you here. And now that I've come, what is it you want me to do? You want me to desert my husband, to throw away everything for which I've worked and struggled, and —think of it!—to come and live with you. Let me tell you this—I wouldn't live with you if there wasn't another man in the world. I wouldn't willingly stay in the same house in which you were, or even in the same town. I've grown to hate you—if you only knew how I hate you as I see you standing there, and how willingly I'd see you tumble dead at my feet!" She drew a great breath—the glasses made it perfectly plain. "I believe I should go back to Eastbourne almost a happy woman again if I knew that you were dead."

"You mean that?"

"I never meant anything half so much."

"Then—you shall go back a happy woman."

They were standing within a few feet of the cliff. The turf sloped downward. He ran down this little slope; when he had run as far as he could, he gave a sort of jump and sprang into space more than five hundred feet above the rocks below. The woman was left alone on the knoll. I was so taken aback by the horror of the thing that my joints seemed to have got locked; my limbs seemed rigid.

"HE GAVE A SORT OF JUMP AND SPRANG INTO SPACE."

There stood the woman, alone, and there I lay watching her through the glasses. For several seconds we remained motionless, as if incapable of movement. Then, with what seemed to me to be a violent effort, I scrambled on to my feet and went rushing towards the woman across the intervening grass. When she turned and saw me coming she staggered, and I thought she would have fallen. But, recovering herself just as she seemed to have lost her balance, she stood awaiting me. When I got to her I took her by the arm; I was beside myself with a strange sort of passion.

"You've murdered him!" I gasped. "I've a mind to send you after him."

"Send me." Her face was white; her great eyes glared at me; but she never flinched. "I am perfectly willing that you should send me after him. He's better off than I am."

Still gripping her by the arm, I turned and shouted, "Help! Help!" Two men came running out of the coastguards' station; they were followed by a third, and then a fourth. When she saw them coming she asked me, as coolly as if it were the most casual question:—

"What are you going to tell them—lies? He jumped over of his own accord."

I said nothing to her, but when they came within hail I called to them:—

"A man has just jumped over the cliff—he was with this lady."

The coastguards took her address and mine; then began to search for what was left of the man. I took the woman back with me to Eastbourne, holding her by the arm all the way.

"You needn't hold me," she said, when we were half-way down. "With you holding me like this it is not easy to walk on this rough ground. I sha'n't run away."

But I kept my hold. My friends had a private sitting-room at the hotel on the ground floor, to which admission was gained by a separate entrance. I led her to that sitting-room and rang the bell.

"Send up to Mr. Stephens, in No. 120, and tell him that I shall be glad to see him here as soon as he can make it convenient to come. And tell Mr. Ward I wish to see him."

"Who's Mr. Stephens?" asked the woman as soon as the waiter had gone. "And what are you going to say to my husband? Who are you? Let go of my arm."

She spoke savagely, trying to shake herself loose. But she was weaker than I and she could not do it.

"I am Judith Lee," I told her. "I am going to tell your husband everything I know about you."

"And what do you know? I only saw you once before in my life."

"Only once. You will presently hear what I know about you, if you have not already guessed."

I think she had. I saw it in her face. Almost immediately her husband came hurriedly into the room. He seemed disturbed.

"I am told Miss Lee wants to see me—are you Miss Lee? What are you doing here with my wife?"

I told him everything—his wife never even attempted to interrupt. As I pieced my story together I think she began to have a feeling that I was something almost supernatural—that she was afraid of me. I fancy that she recognized in me the pointing finger which, though it sometimes seems to move so slowly, touches the criminal on the spot at last; showing that from the very first, when all seemed most secure, there was already starting in pursuit the avenging hand of Justice.

I told about that interview on which I had tumbled in the tea-shop; about the experiment with the handkerchief illustrating the signals which might be made with a blind. How her eyes seemed to distend as she heard me! I spoke of the chance meeting with the red-headed youth, who was staring at the crooked blind, and then of the murder which was done two hours afterwards. I passed the next two years and came to the interview which I had witnessed in the Boscombe gardens; when I narrated what the dead man's wife had said to her friend, Mr. as well as Mrs. Athelstan Ward stood there like images of guilt stricken by their own consciences. Then came the story of what had happened that morning. When I repeated, word for word, the conversation which had taken place between the guilty pair, the woman sank on to the floor and the man seemed dazed. Then came the horror of the suicide which she had prompted.

"I am aware," I said, that it would be difficult, Mr. Ward, to bring home against your wife the full measure of her guilt to the satisfaction of a criminal court. I admit the dexterity with which she has eluded responsibility. On one condition I am willing to let her go with you, to wherever you may choose to take her, and to hold my tongue. She has done all these things to gain possession of the fortune left by the late Mrs. Dawson. Render an account of the money she left, resign all claim to it, transfer it in its entirety to the woman to whom it rightfully belongs, and I will leave Mrs. Ward

"THE WOMAN SANK ON TO THE FLOOR."

to her conscience. I do not at this moment suggest on your part complicity with your wife, though I cannot but feel that at some period you have probably had some sort of guilty knowledge. I may add that I communicated last night with the authorities at Scotland Yard, and that a detective is coming to Eastbourne by the first train which leaves London. If this matter is settled as I have suggested before he appears, so far well; if not, the matter will pass out of my hands into his. I have sent a message to a friend who is staying in the hotel, Mr. Arthur Stephens, a solicitor of high standing. He will probably be here in a minute or two, ready to draw up a formal assignment to Mrs. George Ryder of what ought to have been hers at the beginning. I must ask you to give your answer, Mr. Ward, at once. How is it to be?"

I could see that his lips were dry; with the tip of his tongue he moistened them. His voice was husky.

"I—I'm willing to do what you wish, Miss Lee. I am willing to do everything, and anything, if only you will say nothing to anyone else of what you have just now been saying to us."

Then I knew that my surmise had been correct, and that he had at least some sort of guilty knowledge of his wife's nefarious conduct. Arthur Stephens entered.

"I am very sorry to have disturbed you, Mr. Stephens, but I am in pressing need of your services. This is Mr. Athelstan Ward. He is in possession of certain property to which he has no title; at any rate, no moral title. Conscious of that fact, he wishes to assign it to the rightful owner. I want you to draw up a short form which shall give legal and valid expression to that wish of his. Afterwards, I may have to request you to go with him into matters of account; that you will be able to do later in the day. At present, all I ask you to do is to draw up a brief form which shall have the effect I have mentioned. Here are pen, ink, and paper."

Within a very few minutes that form was drawn up. As Mr. Ward was in the act of affixing his signature the door opened, and someone else I knew came in.

"This," I explained, "is Inspector Ellis, of Scotland Yard. Inspector, this is Mr. Athelstan Ward. He is about to sign a document; perhaps you wouldn't mind acting as one of the witnesses to his signature?"

The paper was signed and witnessed. Then I made certain other explanations; I kept within the letter of my bond, but I gave Mr. and Mrs. Athelstan Ward to understand that if they did not keep strictly within the letter of theirs, their trouble was only just beginning. After breakfast the inspector and Mr. Stephens went up to London with that undesirable husband and his still less desirable wife. In the evening they returned to Eastbourne. They rendered their report.

Mr. and Mrs. Ward had been called to a strict account; in the course of the day they had been stripped of every farthing of their ill-gotten gains. Berths had been booked for them on a steamer which was leaving the very next day for a South American port. They were informed that a certain amount of money would be credited to their account when they landed; with that they would have to begin the world afresh. Whether they succeeded or failed, they would return to England at their peril. I do not think that either of them is ever likely to set foot on English soil again.

Soon after the quartet quitted the hotel on their way to London, I kept the appointment which I had made the day before. A woman who was carrying flowers was shown into the sitting-room. I met her on the threshold.

"Come in," I said. "I am very glad to see you."

She seemed alarmed, as if the way in which I tried to be friendly and treat her as an equal was a thing she was unused to.

"Please don't look so frightened; there's nothing to alarm you. I have asked you here because I want the flowers I see you have brought, and also because I wish to tell you something which I fancy you will think very wonderful, and also, I hope, very pleasant. I believe you are Mrs. George Ryder?"

At once she turned to flee, but I had her by the hand.

"Please—please don't call me by that name—please don't!"

"Why not, since it is your name? Is it not your name?"

"How do you know it's my name? Who told you it was my name? Is it written on my forehead?"

Her looks were so wild that she seemed almost like a person who was out of her senses. When I began to tell her, in her turn, my story—the change that took place in her! Many times have I been thankful for the gift which God gave me; never, I think, more thankful than I was then.

When I explained that she was to have the money which was meant for her husband after all, and laid before her Mr. Athelstan Ward's assignment, she broke into dry-eyed sobbing.

"Do you know"—the words broke from her between her sobs —"my child is dying for want of sufficient and proper nourishment? She is dying of starvation—and now—thank God!—thank God!"

"UNCLE JACK"

Why are some men so silly—so many men—nearly all of them? I was once almost prevented from doing a man a very signal service by the singular delusion he was under that I was in love with him.

I was staying at the Cliftonville Hotel at Margate[1] with a Mr. and Mrs. Hastings and their daughter, Netta, who was a pupil of mine. Netta, although deaf from birth, was an extremely intelligent young lady of about eighteen, and by no means ill-looking. She and I were having tea one afternoon in the gardens on the cliff. She could speak quite well when she chose—although she had never heard a sound in her life; but there were occasions on which, if only for convenience' sake, she used the sign language. She used it then. She said to me:—

"Watch those two women who are having tea at the table under the tent."

I had noticed the pair. They were under the shade of a big umbrella, which rose from the centre of the table at which they were sitting. As I glanced round I saw one say to the other:—

"What about John Finlayson?"

The other was smoking a cigarette as she stirred her tea. She withdrew the cigarette, expelled the smoke, and I saw her say:—

"I don't know whether or not to marry him."

"My dear," rejoined the first speaker, "if you are ever likely to get a chance of marrying him, take my advice and do."

The smoker considered; then she smiled—rather as if she sneered.

"I'm not so sure. You can pay too dear even for a husband with money. Finlayson would bore me stiff inside a week. What I want is a little ready cash."

"You bet! I could do with more than a little—I could do with a lot."

The smoker sipped her tea; then asked, as if she were putting a very serious question: "Meg, what do you say to a thousand golden sovereigns—could you do with them?"

[1] A seaside town in Kent, South-East England.

The other glanced sharply at the speaker. I never saw a woman whose eyes were more flagrantly made-up in the broad daylight. I thought they were dreadful. She answered:—

"Could I do with a thousand golden sovereigns? Just couldn't I!"

"You wouldn't stick at a trifle to get them?"

"My love, I'd stick at nothing—I'd rob a bank!"

"I wouldn't for anything suggest your doing that. Besides, I think we could get them easier out of Finlayson than out of a bank." Then she added something which rather startled me. "See how those two creatures at the next table are watching us; they can't possibly hear what we are saying, but suppose we talk of something else."

Netta laughed outright—she can read lips almost as well as I can; I taught her how to do it. I could have shaken her. I did not look again in their direction. A few minutes after I got up with Netta and walked away.

"Did you see what they were saying?" she asked me as we went. "It was of Uncle Jack that they were talking."

That was precisely the point—it was because of that that I had watched. Mr. John Finlayson was Mrs. Hastings's brother, Netta's uncle, a bachelor of about forty years' standing, with a good opinion both of himself and of his money.

Some persons might think that the one who had been smoking was beautiful; and she certainly was what I believe is called "a very fine young woman." She was probably nearly six foot high; she held herself very straight, her figure was perfect, her features were regular, her hair wonderful, her clothes expensive. Mr. Finlayson had taken her and her companion out with him in his motor-car; he had dined at their table; and, very much to his sister's disgust, had associated himself with them in more ways than one. All the same, I had been startled to see the young woman hint that if she chose she could marry him; I had no idea that matters had gone so far as that. Keen-witted Netta seemed to read my thoughts.

"I shouldn't wonder if Uncle Jack did marry Miss Parsons. I believe I nearly caught him kissing her last night on the veranda."

Before I could reply her mother came towards us down the steps, with Mr. Finlayson himself at her heels.

Mrs. Hastings bore Netta off into the town; Mr. Finlayson returned to the balcony of the hotel, and I went with him. He was a scanty-haired little man, inclined to stoutness. A monocle was rarely absent from his right eye, and he wore two tiny tufts of hair upon his upper lip, which he had once confided to me he thought made him look French, and which I thought made him look ridiculous. He had inherited a large fortune from a relative, and had never done anything useful; so far as I could see, his chief occupation was changing his clothes. I do not know how many suits he had, but I do not think it is any exaggeration to say that he changed from head to foot half-a-dozen times a day. Yet, since his sister and her husband had shown themselves very good, and thoughtful, and generous to me, and I owed them many kindnesses, I felt that I could not allow his simplicity to make him the victim of that intriguing young woman who called herself Parsons, without at least attempting to put him on his guard.

The veranda of the Cliftonville Hotel runs along the road, being raised a few feet above the pavement. As I stood there with him, Miss Parsons and her friend, coming out of the garden across the way, passed close by us. Mr. Finlayson acknowledged their presence with a sweeping bow, and Miss Parsons smiled—a smile which evidently pleased him.

"Most attractive young lady, that—don't you think so? Very odd how strange some ladies are. My sister, now, has taken up a most extraordinary position as regards Miss Parsons; she simply doesn't like her."

"I fancy Mrs. Hastings's instinct in such matters is generally to be relied on. In spite of your wider knowledge of the world, Mr. Finlayson, I hope you won't mind my suggesting that it might be the part of wisdom to be on your guard against Miss Parsons."

His rejoinder was so preposterous that I could have shaken him.

"What I said to my sister, I say to you—jealousy in a lady's breast takes many forms. Eleanor is jealous of Miss Parsons, and so are you."

"On what conceivable grounds do you say that I am jealous of —that woman?"

He gave a sort of little hop.

"There you are—'that woman'—the very phrase betrays you. Now, Miss Lee, permit me for one moment. I've had—shall we say —an idea for some time past that your feelings towards me were

" I WALKED OFF THE BALCONY AND LEFT HIM."

—of the most flattering kind. I have known you, off and on, at frequently recurring intervals, for about three years. I discussed you
with my sister——"

"You discussed me with your sister!"

"Yes, and with her husband; and they both agree that, since
the period has arrived at which it is desirable that I should have an
establishment of my own, although the difference in our fortunes
is immense, you are a young lady eminently fitted to become the
head of it. Therefore, your jealousy of the fascinating Miss Parsons
is excusable; but, I assure you, baseless. My choice, Miss Lee, is fixed
on you; there is no reason why I should not take advantage of this
opportunity to tell you so; it may relieve your mind. I have cause
to know that the announcement of our engagement will relieve

my sister's mind. Therefore, with your permission, I will make that announcement this—no, not this evening at dinner—I happen to have an engagement this evening" (he wore a slight air of confusion)—"but—on the first occasion which offers."

When he stopped, which he did just as I was wondering when he was going to, I could only gasp. I saw that it was necessary to make myself quite plain to this little man.

"Mr. Finlayson, I won't pretend that I don't understand what you have been talking about, though anything funnier I never heard. You seem to be under the impression that you have only to throw your glove at my feet and I will pick it up and be grateful. I don't know what gave you that impression; you are quite mistaken if you suppose that I ever meant to."

Then I walked off the balcony and left him there. It so chanced that as I entered the hotel Miss Parsons came into the hall. Not a little to my surprise she addressed me.

"I should like to say two or three words to you, Miss—I believe it is Lee. May I ask why, since you are quite a stranger to me, you take such an interest in my movements?"

Her assault, coming so quickly after my surprising interview with Mr Finlayson, took me aback. I had no answer ready. She went on:—

"This afternoon, to give an example of the sort of thing I mean, you and that deaf-and-dumb young woman, whose governess I believe you are, watched my friend and myself while we were having tea, as if you were doing your very best to overhear every word we said. I don't like that sort of thing; don't let it happen again, or I may show my displeasure in a way you won't like."

She walked off with her nose in the air, very much as I had just walked off from Mr. Finlayson.

I could hardly have said, when I reached my bedroom, with whom I felt maddest—with her, Mr. Finlayson, Netta, or myself; Netta, for calling my attention to them first of all; Mr. Finlayson, for his astonishing stupidity; Miss Parsons, for her studied insolence; myself, for ever having had anything to do with any of the three.

It seemed to me Cliftonville was no longer the place for me. Mr. and Mrs. Hastings were leaving in two or three days in any case. I had had a letter that morning from an aunt who was passing through London, and who wanted me, if I was in town, to meet her. I resolved that I would be in town that night. I packed my trunk, scribbled a note to Mrs. Hastings, and departed.

I reached the station several minutes before my train was due to start. The arrival platform was crowded with passengers; a train had just come in from London. As I went towards the bookstall to buy some papers, I passed two men whose appearance had a curious effect upon me. I was conscious of what I call one of those premonitory little shivers which I say are sent to me as warnings. That shiver went all over me as I passed those two men, and it startled me. Close behind them were two other men. I saw one of these say to the other:—

"See those two? The one on the right is Chicago Charlie. It isn't often he's walking about; if he'd had his rights he'd have been strung up long ago. I wonder what his game is down here? Someone's in for trouble. I could tell you some tales of him."

At the bookstall I turned and looked after the two men who had passed me. A woman was coming down the platform to meet them; it was the woman who had been having tea with Miss Parsons at the next table to ours. She greeted the pair with an air of a familiar acquaintance. Was "Chicago Charlie" Miss Parsons's friend as well as her own?

Under cover of the paper I had bought I watched them coming; the woman was too engaged in talking to her companions to notice that a female was holding her newspaper up in front of her face. I saw Chicago Charlie ask:—

"What's the fellow's name?"

"John Finlayson. He's soft as butter—one of Nature's own mugs. She says he's good for fifty thousand pounds—if properly handled."

"Soft as butter, is he? And he'll be handled by a master. If there's anything left when I'm through with him he can keep it."

Apparently, since they paid no heed to the cabman who hailed them, they intended to walk to wherever they might be going. What was I to do? I had my ticket, my luggage was labelled, my train was due; I had advised Mrs. Hastings of my departure. I had washed my hands of Mr. Finlayson for ever and a day; what might happen to him was no concern of mine. The obvious course was for me to carry out my intentions and go to town. And yet—that was it—and yet!

There was the sound of a whistle; a train was steaming into the station—my train. I should have to hurry if I meant to catch it; they would send my luggage by it, since it was labelled, whether I went or not. That consideration did start me moving. I rushed over to the departure platform, caught a porter—my porter—in the act of putting my luggage into the van, stopped him—explaining that I had changed my mind and did not propose to travel by that train —induced him to take my luggage back and put it on to a cab, and then looked to see if the three persons on whom my interest was centred were still anywhere in sight. They were; they were at a distance of perhaps two hundred yards, and were moving at a leisurely pace towards the town. I said to the cabman:—

"I suppose your horse can go slowly? I want to read my paper and enjoy this beautiful evening. You go straight along at not more than three miles an hour, until I give you further directions."

That cabman carried out my instructions to the letter; we certainly did not exceed the limit I had imposed, and I pretended to read my paper. The trio in front were going about as fast as we were —straight on, with us still about two hundred yards behind. Presently I saw them turn into an hotel overlooking the sea. When we reached it I stopped the driver.

"Pull up, please. I want to see if they can let me have a room here."

They could—rather a pleasant one, looking towards Clifton-ville. Then it struck me that it was about time to consider. I was quite aware that I had done an eminently foolish thing. I had given way to my irresistible inclination to meddle in other people's affairs without having the faintest notion what sort of meddling it was going to be. What sort of mental standard Miss Parsons's friend might have I did not know; unless she was extremely unobservant, she had taken sufficient stock of me that afternoon to know me again. Even if she had not noticed me before, I had noticed her several times, and had an idea that she was supposed to be a Mrs. Hammond. Miss Parsons had a room at the Cliftonville; where Mrs. Hammond was staying I did not know—she might not be residing at the hotel in which I had taken a room, but might merely have entered, with the two men, for the purpose of refreshment. I had to risk that.

I took out of a case which was in my trunk an article which is known as a "transformation." It is simply amazing what an alteration is produced in a woman's appearance by a change of hair—if the change is well done. My hair is very dark brown; it has been called black. When I am crowned with scarlet a casual acquaintance would have to stare and stare, and yet be in doubt. "Transformation" is a polite synonym for a wig; the one I donned that night was scarlet. I touched my countenance here and there—I did not want the contrast between my complexion and my hair to be too striking; attired myself in my most gorgeous robe—I had a notion that a red-haired, unattached young woman in an hotel at Margate ought to be gorgeous—and I went down to dinner. The first thing I saw when I entered the dining-room was a table at which were seated Mrs. Hammond and her two male acquaintances.

As I entered Mrs. Hammond bestowed on me the glance which, in such circumstances, every woman does bestow on every other woman. But for that I was prepared. I was pretty nearly certain that she did not recognize me as a person whom she had ever seen before. The waiter gave me a seat at a large table which occupied the centre of the room. There were seats at the table for, I suppose, a dozen people; I was quite content, at least on that occasion, to be one of a crowd. The table with which I was concerned was directly in my line of vision; I had only to lift my eyes from my plate to see perfectly the three persons who were at it, while I was behind a quantity of flowers and foliage which made it impossible for them to see me at all without a special effort.

Mrs. Hammond had on a not unbecoming dress of violet silk; her hair was fair—I fancy it was as much hers as my scarlet crown was mine. Chicago Charlie had what seemed to be rather a nice diamond in the middle of his shirt-front. His companion was a big, bullet-headed man, who looked as if he were something in the prize-fighting line. "Charlie" was a lean, hatchet-faced man, with an over-large nose, too wide a mouth, and a protruding chin. He had small blue eyes, which had the fixed, stony stare of the glass beads which you see in the head of a doll. Had he only known it, his mouth was his most unfortunate feature; every word he uttered was so distinctly shaped on his long, thin lips that, from my point of view, he might as well have shouted. The first words of his I saw were sufficiently startling.

"What did I do to him? I killed him, that's what I did to him. They think nothing of that sort of thing out there; it's a man's business to see that he isn't killed."

He raised his glass of champagne and emptied it. Mrs. Hammond and the other man exchanged glances; I fancied they were asking each other if the speaker was to be taken seriously. Mrs. Hammond remarked, as she carefully removed the head and tail from a smelt on her plate:—

"You know, Charlie, there mustn't be any killing here. As some French gentleman said—I believe it was a Frenchman—in England that's not a crime, it's a blunder;[1] no man's life is worth to you so much as your own."

Charlie's reply was characteristic.

"I'm not so sure of that. I have met men—and women—for whom I'd be glad to swing. How long has Finlayson been here?"

"Baby says that he came down last week, but it doesn't necessarily follow that he did. She's a curiosity, Baby is. She's been down here about a month; I've been here nearly three weeks. It seems that she began planning this almost directly after she came, but she never so much as breathed a word about it to me till this afternoon. For keeping a thing dark I never saw her equal."

"Baby Parsons can hold her tongue better than any woman I ever met." This was the bullet-headed man. "I've been in more than one little game with her when silence was everything, so I know."

"There are times when a dumb woman is more precious than rubies."

As he delivered himself of this profound sentiment Charlie smiled. Mrs. Hammond retorted:—

"Then in that case there's a girl stopping up at the Cliftonville who ought to suit you—she's deaf and dumb. She's in charge of some governess kind of creature, whose neck I'd like to wring."

[1] This statement ("C'est pire qu'un crime, c'est une faute") upon the execution of Louis Antoine de Bourbon, Duke of Enghien, in 1804 has been attributed to a number of French soldiers and diplomats, including Antoine Boulay de la Meurthe, Joseph Fouché, and Charles Maurice de Talleyrand-Périgord.

It was at those latter words I smiled. It was towards the end of the meal that the trio began to touch upon the topic which interested me most. Probably what they ate and drank loosened their tongues; or they might have been excused for taking it for granted that, speaking together in lowered tones at their own particular table, they were as private as need be. The table had been cleared for dessert, when, without any preamble, Chicago Charlie plunged into the very middle of things.

"So Mr. Griffiths, or Miss Parsons, or both of them together, have taken a house in a retired neighbourhood, at a convenient distance from this town, in a position in which uninvited interruptions need not be feared; and to this house the excellent Mr. Finlayson has been invited for a little evening party?"

"Prefaced by a little dinner for three, like ours—Bob Griffiths, Baby, and Uncle Jack." So Mrs. Hammond—for she was the speaker —had picked up the Hastings trick of speaking of him as "Uncle Jack." "There was some idea of having the Kitten in for dinner, and so making the party square, but it was felt that even Uncle Jack might find her a little hard to swallow. The Kitten will eat with her knife, and is never quite sure whether to use her fork or her fingers."

"MRS. HAMMOND EXPLAINED, LEANING OVER THE TABLE WITH A CIGARETTE."

"The Kitten," observed the bullet-headed man, who seemed to answer to a variety of names—I had seen them address him as "Lobster," "Arthur," and "Puncher"—"is a child of Nature. If it weren't that she will get outside the contents of a bottle, I know few women I'd sooner have beside me in a row."

"I presume," continued Charlie, "that the programme is that Mr. Finlayson is to be well done at dinner, so that he can be done better afterwards, when we come in to complete the party?"

Mrs. Hammond explained, leaning over the table with a cigarette between her lips.

"Baby has found out all about him; he is so fond of braying that any woman can do that who likes. I don't know any girl who's better at that sort of thing than Baby is. It seems that he has been telling her all about himself, the silly ass! A mortgage of over fifty thousand pounds has just been paid up; the money is lying at his banker's. He's going to buy something with it when he's made up his mind what—stock, I mean. In the meanwhile, as Baby says, there's a chance for someone."

"That certainly is so; when we have got the confiding Mr. Finlayson to ourselves, there ought to be a chance for all of us. I'm not greedy; so long as I get my fill that's all I want," said Charlie.

The bullet-headed man looked at his watch. "Isn't it about time we start? What time are we supposed to get there?"

"No particular time, Baby said; somewhere about ten. They dine at eight. Uncle Jack is very fond of his food, and of his wine; to do him really well, as Charlie put it, takes time. The idea is to get him just drunk enough to make him think that he is still sober."

"It's past half-past nine; how are we to get there?"

"Taxi-cab. Baby's got a friend who drives one. He's going to call for us."

"Hanged if Baby doesn't seem to have friends everywhere. At what time is this particular friend of hers to call? Perhaps he's come. Waiter, see if there's a taxi-cab outside."

The waiter presently returned with his report: "There is a taxi-cab outside, sir."

"Good; we'll be with him in a minute."

This was the bullet-headed man. Charlie struck in:—

"I don't promise that I'll be with him in a minute. When I've had a decent dinner I hurry over my coffee for no man; as for gulping my liqueur, you may as well throw it down the sink." Then he asked a question which solved for me what I had been fearing might become a problem. "By the way, where is this house at which the party is to be held?"

Mrs. Hammond gave him the information he wanted, and at the same time she gave it to me.

"The house is called the 'Wilderness'; it is off the Broadstairs Road;[1] lies back, perhaps, two hundred yards; is approached by an avenue of trees. Everybody about here knows the Wilderness; it's a house which has had a history."

"To which another page is to be added tonight." If Charlie had only known how true that was his smile might have been less suggestive of amusement.

I left the trio at table. Mrs. Hammond and the bullet-headed man wanted to go, but Charlie declined. I fancy that after a good dinner he was not a very persuadable person. The three pairs of eyes were fixed on me as I went out. I saw Charlie say:—

"That's rather a fine girl; bit of a stepper."[2]

Mrs. Hammond said: "I can't think where I've seen someone like her before."

If only she had cultivated the faculty of observation! Her puzzlement tickled me. I was in the highest spirits, foreseeing that, quite possibly, I was in for the sort of adventure that I loved. I slipped on a long black coat, with a hood attached, which I drew over my head, and sallied forth to choose my taxi-cab. I did not wish to light, if I could help it, on another of Baby's many friends. There was a taxicab waiting at the door of the hotel; I eyed the driver. I even noted the number of his vehicle.

There were plenty of taxis on the rank. I did not hail the first, but walked past them all until I saw a lonely taxi in the distance, moving slowly, with its flag up. I advanced towards it.

"Do you know a house called the Wilderness?"

"On the Broadstairs Road?—Mr. Macfarlane's?"

"Mr. Macfarlane is not there now, is he?"

"I couldn't say. I fancy he's about the town. I saw him only the

[1] It is approximately four miles from Margate to Broadstairs, another seaside town.
[2] High-spirited, "fast" woman (slang).

other day. He's a gentleman what's very well known, Mr. Macfarlane is. I know the house you mean. I don't know that I care to go there at this time of night; there's my fare back. It's a lonely place, his house is. There won't be a soul about. I shall have to come back empty."

"Don't you worry about that; I'm going to keep you; I'll see that you have a fare back. Are there more roads to the house than one?"

"Well, in a manner of speaking, there is; but one of them isn't a very good one; it gets to the back of the house, the servants' entrance."

"You take me by that road—and move. I suppose you can move?"

He grinned. "She can do about forty—a bit more if she's pressed."

"Then—I think you might press her. By the way, is there a lodge at the back entrance?"

He shook his head. "No lodge anywhere that I know of. The grounds are large, and the house stands in the middle."

"In the house would they hear a taxi-cab approaching along that road?

"It depends; you see, it's lonely out there, and in the country, at night, sound travels. There's no reason why they should know it was me coming along."

We started. I do not know at what pace we travelled, but we did move pretty fast. I know that the vehicle stopped before I expected. The driver came to the door. "Here's the house, miss, and this is the back entrance—through the gate. Do you want me to drive you in?"

I alighted. There was no moon, but it was a starlight night, and I could see the gate quite plainly.

"Thank you. I want you to wait here till I come back. I suppose if I go through the gate and follow the path I shall have no difficulty in finding the house?"

"Not a bit, miss; you've only got to go straight on."

"I may be some time, perhaps an hour; but if I'm more than an hour, you had better come up to the house and knock until someone answers. I may require assistance."

He stared at me as if he did not understand my words. I quite expected him to ask me for a deposit which would at least guarantee his fare; but I imagine that he was of a trusting disposition, or that I inspired confidence; he let me go without a hint of the kind, just touching his cap as I walked off.

It was darkish along that avenue. When—as in places they did —the trees met overhead, I had simply to grope my way. The house came rather with the force of a surprise. There were no lights at the windows; I was near a door before I knew that it was there.

I waited and listened. There seemed to be no sound on the other side. I tried the handle—the door yielded at once; I slipped through it without a moment's hesitation. "Nothing venture, nothing win," was ever a motto of mine. Speeding along the passage, I reached a flight of steps, which I ascended. There was a glass-panelled door at the top; on the left a sort of recess into which it opened. As I reached it I heard steps approaching; I drew back into the recess. Two women appeared; they pushed back the door wholly unconscious of me.

"I thought I heard someone come up the stairs," said one.

"It was your fancy," replied the other. "There's no one down there to come upstairs."

They descended; I waited some moments, then slipped through the door. I was in quite a decent-sized hall, lighted by incandescent gas. I could hear voices, but could see no one. Advancing, I came upon rather a good staircase, with lights above. Up I went. The door of a room stood wide open; the brilliant lights came from within. On the left was another door, closed. I chanced it and went through. Where I was I had no idea; all was dark. I had a small electric torch in my pocket and I switched it on. Apparently I was in a sort of sitting-room; there were double doors on the other side. I went to them, switching off my torch. All at once I heard voices— and a laugh. I had had my doubts about the voices; I had none about the laugh. Anyone who had heard Uncle Jack's queer little cackling laugh could scarcely fail to recognize it when heard again. Mr. Finlayson was entering the adjoining room with at least one companion. I could only catch one other voice besides his—a woman's. It was Miss Parsons's. Were they two alone? I listened, but could not make sure. I should have liked to try the handle of that door and peep. Just as I had almost decided that I might venture there was the sound of other voices—at least three or four. Then a man said, in what I should have called rather boisterous tones:—

"These people have found their way here at last. I believe, Mr. Finlayson, you know Mrs. Hammond?"

"Oh, yes," Uncle Jack's rather ringing voice replied. "I know Mrs. Hammond—of course I know Mrs. Hammond. Pleased to see you."

"Not so pleased to see me as I am to see you, Mr. Finlayson—I pay you no compliment in saying that."

"It's very good of you to say so; I always like people to be glad to see me—especially if it's a lady."

The boisterous voice was heard again.

"Mr. Finlayson, allow me to introduce you to my two friends—Colonel Stewart, of the United States army, a distinguished officer whose name is no doubt well known to you; Mr. Arthur Poyntz, a first-rate sportsman, like yourself."

I took it that Colonel Stewart was Chicago Charlie, and that Mr. Arthur Poyntz was the gentleman with the bullet-head. There was a good deal of loud talking, all joining in paying the most egregious compliments to Mr. Finlayson, he swallowing them all with continual little cackles of laughter. I felt sure that he must have been very well done at dinner. Then I heard Miss Parsons ask:—

"What are you gentlemen going to play? I believe poker is your game, Mr. Finlayson?"

Uncle Jack laughed—I doubt if he would have been able to explain why—and, as if it were a signal, the others broke into a simultaneous roar of laughter. Then the boisterous voice exclaimed:—

"Mr. Finlayson, you're bad to beat; I've no doubt all games are the same to you. I shouldn't wonder if you learnt poker on your mother's knee."

"No, no, no; I assure you I did nothing of the kind. I have played the game—oh, yes; as you say, I've played a good many games, and I don't say I mightn't be able to hold my own."

The boisterous voice spoke again.

"Hold your own! I don't pretend to be a poker-player, Mr. Finlayson; in the presence of a man like you I'm timid—I expect we all are."

"There's no reason why you should be—not the slightest. You will find me merciful —not a bit alarming."

"I've got some poker chips somewhere. Ah, here they are! Now, boys, to business. I tell you quite frankly, Mr. Finlayson, I'm frightened of you. Miss Parsons, may I ask you to see that we have something to drink? You've got all the chips you want, gentlemen? Good! One blue chip is worth five whites, one red is ten whites, and one green fifty whites. Now, who deals?"

For several minutes the voices were subdued. There were occasional bursts of Uncle Jack's cackling laughter.

"You're clearing us all out, Mr. Finlayson. I shall want more chips. How goes it, Colonel?"

"More chips for me. Mr. Finlayson plays the game as I never saw it played before, and I thought I had seen it played most ways. Mr. Finlayson, you're a remarkable player."

Uncle Jack cackled and said:—

"I do seem to have most of the chips, don't I? I don't know how much these chips are worth."

The boisterous voice rejoined: "You've got nearly ten thousand pounds' worth of chips in front of you, Mr. Finlayson, and here am I buying two thousand five hundred more. We'll be ruined if this goes on."

"What!" There was a vibrant note in Uncle Jack's voice which suggested that the speaker's words had got through the vinous mists which fogged his brain. "Ten thousand pounds' worth of chips! You don't mean to say——What is the value of each chip?"

"The white are ten pounds, the blue are fifty, the red are a hundred, the green are five hundred. We started with two thousand five hundred pounds' worth of chips each, and you've got them nearly all."

"But I—I had no idea." In Uncle Jack's tremulous tones there was no hint of an inclination to cackle. "Really, you know, this kind of thing is quite out of my line—altogether out of my line. I—I never gambled in my life. I'm not a gambler."

"I don't know about being a gambler, Mr. Finlayson. You've won several thousands of our money."

"But I—I had no notion we were playing for such stakes. What am I to do with these—these chips? We've none of us paid for them."

"I'll pay for mine right now, sir, if you don't mind. It's the general custom for gentlemen in the circles in which I move to pay for their chips at the end of the game. But since you put it that way, I'll put my money up." This was unmistakably Chicago Charlie. I wondered how much money he really had—that was money. "Here, Mr. Griffiths, is two thousand five hundred pounds in Bank of England notes." Although I could not see them, I doubted. "You're banker; perhaps you'll just go through them, and at the end of the game pay this gentleman with that money for any of my chips he may have won. And while I'm at it, I'll have two thousand five hundred pounds' worth more. And here are the notes, sir."

The tone of Uncle Jack's voice, when he spoke again, gave me some notion of the expression which was on his countenance as he beheld Chicago Charlie's offhand manner of dealing with such enormous sums.

"But, my dear sir, I repeat that I never dreamed of playing for such stakes."

"If the stakes are not large enough for you, Mr. Finlayson, the value of the chips can be raised. We are not children, sir. It may be but a trifle that you've won, but, as my friend Griffiths remarked, you have won our money, so what's the use of talking? Arthur, it's you to deal. Mr. Finlayson, your very good health; I like a good game once in a while; I've brought a little money with me here tonight, and may you win it all—you'll find me all smiles if you do. Won't you drink to me, sir?"

I fancy Uncle Jack did drink to him—in imagination I could see his state of fluster, his tremulous hands causing him to take a bigger drink than he had meant to—and he was in a state in which every thimbleful counted. I supposed the cards were dealt. Several hands were played. I could not make out who won; comparative silence reigned. Then, after an interval of several minutes, the boisterous voice was raised.

"I say, you know, I don't mind a rousing good game, but isn't this getting rather serious? I don't know, Mr. Finlayson, if you're keeping count of the losses—Miss Parsons keeps ladling out the chips—and now you're cleaned out again. How much has Mr. Finlayson had?"

"I've got it all down on this piece of paper." It was Miss Parsons who replied. "That last lot makes twenty-eight thousand six hundred and fifty pounds."

.

"What!" This was a sort of shriek from Mr. Finlayson.

"Sure you're right?" This was the man with the boisterous voice.

"I don't pretend to be very good at addition. I put down the figures as I gave him each lot of chips; you'd better add it up yourself."

I took it that a paper was handed to Mr. Griffiths, who cast up the various amounts which were on it.

"That's all right—twenty-eight thousand six hundred and fifty, didn't you say? There were ten thousand which he had from me. I don't know how far you're prepared to go, Mr. Finlayson, but that makes nearly forty thousand."

"I'm good to go on all night. I'm spoiling for a rousing gamble. What's forty thousand pounds?" This was Chicago Charlie.

There was another silence; then Mr. Finlayson began to speak in weak, quavering accents which made it impossible for his words to reach me. The crisis was approaching—I had to hear what he said. I resolved to risk opening the door. I turned the handle noiselessly—to find that it opened inwards, and that it was screened on the other side by curtains, so that I was even able to glance between them and observe what was happening in the room beyond.

It was a large room, well lit by several inverted incandescent gas-burners. There was a card-table in the centre, at which four men were seated—Chicago Charlie, on his left Mr. Poyntz, opposite Mr. Finlayson, on his right a bullocky sort of man, whom I took to be Mr. Griffiths. There was a little table between each two men, on which were glasses; evidently Mr. Finlayson, for one, had been drinking more than he should have done, possibly assisted by Mrs. Hammond, who sat on his left to see that his glass was kept filled, and possibly also to inform the others what sort of cards he had. On his right was Miss Parsons, with a box divided into partitions, in which were ivory counters of different colours, which are used for the game of poker, and are known as "chips." Chicago Charlie was leaning back, a big cigar in his mouth, on his face an insolent grin. Poyntz was eyeing Mr. Finlayson as a dog might a rat on which be proposes presently to spring. Griffiths was apparently cast for the part of the genial host, who desires above all else to avoid unpleasantness. The only unhappy-looking person present was Uncle Jack. The others eyed him with amusement, as he did his best to make his position plain.

"You must understand, gentlemen, that I am no gambler—never was. It's against my principles. My idea was a little friendly game. I had no intention to play for high stakes, so let's hope there's no harm done."

"Certainly there's no harm done; what's forty thousand pounds to a man like you?" This was Charlie; the insolence of his grin grew more pronounced; I wondered how often he had played the same sort of part in similar scenes. Uncle Jack tried to wag his finger at him.

"Excuse me, sir—I beg your pardon, Colonel; I forgot for the moment that you were a military gentleman. I say, excuse me, but forty thousand pounds is more money than I ever had in my life."

Charlie took his cigar from between his lips and carefully knocked off the ash. "And will you excuse me, Mr. Finlayson, if I say you are a liar?"

"Come, Colonel," Griffiths interposed; "isn't that sort of thing a little irregular? We're all friends here; Mr. Finlayson is both a gentleman and my particular friend."

"Mr. Griffiths, I'm a man of peace, as you're aware, so I merely make this remark—Mr. Finlayson has lost to me twenty-three thousand one hundred and fifty pounds; if Mr. Finlayson will hand me his cheque for that amount I will consider the matter closed."

"Very handsomely said, Colonel, very handsomely indeed. How do you stand with Mr. Finlayson, Poyntz?"

"Mr. Finlayson has lost a few hundreds to me, but, as he seems to be a bit on the wrong side, they can stand over."

"I say the same, Mr. Finlayson. You're just on sixteen thousand down to me, but I'll wait," said Griffiths.

"I won't wait; it has always been my rule to play for cash, as all my friends are aware."

"It's quite right, Colonel, and a very good rule too. So all you need do, Mr. Finlayson, is to give Colonel Stewart a cheque for the twenty-three thousand odd you are down to him, and we'll leave the other little matters for friendly discussion later on. You have your cheque-book on you, Mr. Finlayson?"

"No, sir, I have not, sir. And if I had it would make no difference. I—I—I give you my word—I'm not a fool."

"What do you mean by that, sir?" The Colonel rose in sudden wrath.

"Now, Colonel—gently." This was Griffiths, the peacemaker.

"Are you prepared to pay me, Sir, the twenty-three thousand, one hundred and fifty pounds you owe me in cash?"

Drink seemed to be having the effect of making Uncle Jack sleepy; he looked up at the irate Charlie with heavy eyes.

"I am not, sir—I am not prepared—to pay it—at all."

"This is too much, you dirty little hound!"

Charlie, leaning over the table, lifted Uncle Jack off his chair and bore him across the green cloth, as if he were but the small quadruped he called him. The action suggested that Charlie was strong. Then, laying him flat across the board, he ran his fingers through his victim's pockets with a swiftness and dexterity which hinted at much practice. He held up a pocket-book.

"We'll see what you have in this, sir." He proceeded to do so. "You may not have a cheque-book on you, sir, but you do appear to have a cheque." He unfolded one which he had taken from the pocket-book. "Now, sir, pen and ink will be given you, and you will fill up that cheque in my favour for twenty-three thousand one hundred and fifty pounds, at once, without any further nonsense." He picked him off the table and sat him on a chair. "Griffiths, where's a pen and ink?" Those requisites were produced by Miss Parsons. "Here, sir, are pens for you to choose from; find one which suits your hand and fill up this cheque. Try this one, sir. If you don't take hold of it——!"

It was not necessary for Charlie to finish his sentence, because Uncle Jack did take hold. A woeful spectacle he presented, after the ignominious manner in which he had been handled—a fuddled, muddled, frightened little man, with those three great men and two big women looking down at him. Charlie continued to play the part to which he was accustomed.

"Now, sir, have you got well hold of that pen? Draw that cheque in favour of Colonel Frederick Stewart for twenty-three thousand one hundred and fifty pounds, put your usual signature at the bottom, and leave it open. Why aren't you doing as I tell you, sir?"

"I—I'd rather not," stammered Uncle Jack.

"Then you're a thief, sir. As it is the custom in the part of the world in which I was raised for a gentleman to shoot a thief at sight, if you don't get a move on you and fill up that cheque, I'll put the contents of this gun inside you."

Charlie, producing a revolver from some part of his person, pointed it at Uncle Jack, whose terror was so great as to be almost ludicrous.

"Don't shoot! Don't shoot!" he wailed. I'll draw the cheque."

He made haste to do as he was bid. Charlie checked his enthusiasm.

" ' DON'T SHOOT ! DON'T SHOOT !' HE WAILED. ' I'LL DRAW THE CHEQUE."

"Steady, sir, steady, or your handwriting will be all shaky, and you'll spoil the cheque. Just you fill up this cheque, without a shiver or a shake, in your usual handwriting, and you'll make a friend of me for life."

Whether the prospect held out to him by the other's words charmed Uncle Jack I cannot certainly say; he filled up the cheque with what appeared to be a surprisingly steady hand. The others watched him. Charlie picked up the cheque when he had finished. He handed it to Griffiths.

"Seems all right?"

The two women and Poyntz came and looked at it over his shoulders as he held it between his fingers.

"It does seem all right," he admitted, "as far as seeming goes."

"I'll see that it is all right. You keep him here all night. I'll go up by the first train. If they make any fuss at the bank, I'll put them on to the telephone. You see that he tells them to cash it. They probably know his voice. Only don't you let him play the fool by seeming to hesitate."

"I'll make it my business to see to that." This was Poyntz, who smiled as he spoke. "Trust me. Hadn't you better put him to bed straight off, perhaps with something which will help him sleep?"

"There's no reason why we shouldn't; we've done with him." Griffiths turned to Miss Parsons. "You can manage a little something, can't you?"

Drawing a tiny bottle from her corsage, Miss Parsons took from it what seemed to be a minute globule, which she dropped into a glass, drowned in whisky to which she added soda, and held it to Uncle Jack.

"Drink that up, old man," she told him. "It's a nightcap."

It seemed to me that the time had come for me to interfere. For a minute or so I had been conscious of certain sounds without the house for which I had been waiting. While the dashing lady was endeavouring to induce her poor little dupe to take the tumbler, with its drugged contents, between his tremulous fingers, drawing the curtains asunder, I stepped into the room. Mine was quite an effective entry. They stared at me as if I were some strange object dropped from the skies. Before either of them had a chance of speaking or of moving I whistled. I am rather a good hand at whistling. My whistle rang through the house. Before it died away, or they had an opportunity to recover from their amazement, half-a-dozen men came streaming through the door —uniformed policemen, with an inspector at their head. Him I addressed.

"That man, inspector, with the revolver in his hand is Chicago Charlie, a well-known American crook, for whom, I have no doubt, the police have had inquiries."

Charlie's stupefied astonishment was almost funny. For once in his life he had been caught napping. He stared at the inspector, then his glance came back to me—which was where he made a mistake, for while he glared in my direction two policemen stole on him from behind; one gripped the wrist which held the revolver and snatched it from him, while round the other wrist, his colleague snapped a handcuff. His surprise was complete; he did not even attempt to struggle. He merely thundered, ornamenting his words with adjectives which I am unwilling to reproduce:—

"Who in the name of all that's wonderful are you?"

"I'm a person," I informed him, "who takes a great interest in characters like you and your friends. I am already well known to Mr. Finlayson, not so well to Miss Parsons, and only slightly to Mrs. Hammond. Allow me to recall myself to their recollection. I am Judith Lee."

As I spoke I removed the scarlet transformation. And how they stared! It is surprising what a difference a little thing like that does make, in certain circumstances, to unobservant eyes. While seated at dinner, watching what the trio were saying, I had been scribbling a note on the back of a menu-card, which I slipped into an envelope brought me by the waiter. When I left the dining-room I gave instructions that it was to be taken at once to the police-station. In that note I had made it clear what I expected in that remote house, rightly named the Wilderness, and requested that adequate assistance might be sent; a certain signal was to advise me of the arrival of that assistance; my whistle was to serve as a signal for the police to enter. Everything worked as smoothly as could have been desired; that little party had quite a different ending from what had been intended. Uncle Jack was taken back to the hotel; his cheque was retrieved. The two ladies and three gentlemen who had proposed to share the proceeds of that cheque between them spent the night as His Majesty's guests.

The unfortunate part of the business was that later the ridiculous little man expressed himself, to me as well as to others, as absolutely convinced that my action in the matter was inspired by the affection I felt for him. I have reason to doubt if even the plainest possible language from me sufficed to drive the preposterous notion wholly from his head. As I asked at the beginning—why are some men so silly?

THE RESTAURANT NAPOLITAIN

One of my most thrilling adventures was the result of my desire to look out of as many of life's windows as one may. My friend, Dr. Rodaccini, an Italian physician, practising among his compatriots in London, being aware of my insatiable curiosity, suggested to me that I might find something of interest in a function to which he had been invited. It was a ball given by the restaurant-keepers and waiters who had come from a certain district in Italy, and who associated themselves into a sort of club. Dr. Rodaccini invited me to go with him, and I went.

The ball was held in a street off Leicester Square,[1] in a series of good-sized rooms, which I understood were, in the ordinary way, used by theatrical companies for purposes of rehearsal. The rooms were filled by as cheerful, light-hearted, well-dressed an assembly as one might wish to see.

Not long before I had been to Italy on one of those errands which sometimes did take me abroad; an institute had been established for the oral instruction of the deaf and dumb, and my services had been retained to assist the staff in putting the work on a sound footing. I have, as I may have remarked before, what is called the gift of tongues, and I had come back to London knowing Italian almost as well as my mother tongue.

The band was playing a waltz. I had noticed all the evening an extremely pretty, fair-haired girl who had been an object of much attention from the men. When an Italian girl has fair hair she is nearly always worth looking at—this one was lovely. Her partner of the moment was, in his way, almost as good-looking as she was. As I watched them a short, broad, stout man, with a round, bald head and no neck, took the girl's partner by the arm and drew him away from her. The girl's face had been all smiles and gaiety, but at sight of this man she changed countenance, shrank away from her partner, and slunk off towards the other end of the room. Her

---

[1] Situated in the heart of London's West End, Leicester Square is surrounded by theatres, restaurants and hotels.

act was eloquent. The big man drew the younger towards the wall and, going close up to him, whispered in his ear. No doubt his intention was that his words should be private and confidential, but as I had my eyes upon his face, and he had one of the most easily-read mouths I ever saw, what he whispered was plain enough to me.

"It is not enough to warn you? Good! You have been warned for the last time. I do not waste words on such as you."

The big man gave the youngster a contemptuous push which sent him cannoning against an advancing couple, and came, with the little, rapid steps of a short-legged, fat man, towards where I was standing. Just as he had nearly reached us the couple with whom the youngster had collided stopped within a couple of feet of where we were. The big man instantly addressed the lady:—

"Pardon, madam, if I speak to Gaspare—for one moment. It is important."

The lady yielded her partner with what struck me as a curious smile. Indeed, there was a meaning smile on Gaspare's face as he went off with the big man—and the big man himself was smiling. One felt, somehow, that with neither of them was it natural to smile. When the big man and Gaspare had passed through an open doorway by which I and my dancing partner were standing, I said to the latter:—

"Do you happen to know who that gentleman with the bald head may be?"

He replied, as if he knew him well:—

"That is Signor Alessandro, of the Restaurant Napolitain, in Greek Street.[1] His restaurant is well known. He is a rich man, Signor Alessandro—a man who is well esteemed."

He might be; but somehow I felt that he never would be esteemed by me. I disliked him still more when, a short time afterwards, I saw him walking off with the fair-haired girl, her arm through his, as if she were an unwilling captive. She was not looking very gay then. Her cheeks were white; fear was in her eyes. The good-looking youngster with whom she had been dancing stood against the wall

[1] A street in Soho, north of Leicester Square. The Soho area was home to immigrants, including many Italians and European socialists and anarchists, in the nineteenth and early twentieth centuries.

"'DOCTOR,' I CRIED, 'WHAT'S THE MATTER WITH HIM?'"

as she went past. She never glanced at him—I felt she dare not—but the big man whispered—I saw his words quite distinctly:—

"I will settle with you to-night."

The young man made as if he would have rushed after the vanishing pair, but he was stopped by someone who touched him on the arm—it was the lady with whom Gaspare had been dancing. She whispered in her turn, and I saw her words. She spoke the broadest Neapolitan:—

"Are you, then, in such a hurry for the finish?"

She just whispered her question and went on; and that young man seemed to cling to the wall as if it were a friend.

My instinct told me there was more to come, but I did not know that there would be so short an interval between the first and second acts.

When I had had enough of the dance I left. Dr. Rodaccini suggested that we should stroll a little before he put me into a cab. I was willing. He took me along a street whose name I do not know. Presently we came to a house with an archway which led, it seemed, into some sort of yard. In this archway someone was lying. I saw him first; I stooped to see what was wrong. It was the youngster who had danced with the fair-haired girl. He lay on his face, quite still.

"Doctor," I cried, "what's the matter with him?"

But somehow I knew before I was told—a knife had been driven into his back, and he was dead. The thing made me hot with rage; it seemed so hideous, so monstrous, so cruel, so out of harmony with all that had gone before—that he should have been struck down and killed almost on the threshold of the ballroom by a coward who had not even dared to attack him from the front. When others came to render what assistance they might I stole away. The sight of that dead young man recalled Signor Alessandro, of the Restaurant Napolitain; how he had whispered that he would settle with him that night. He had kept his promise within a few minutes of its being given—this was the settlement. Now I would settle with him.

I had no evidence to take to the police. They would want more evidence than a whisper that I had not heard, but seen. I meant to get that evidence in my own way. I had some idea of the whereabouts of Greek Street—I would find the Restaurant Napolitain.

I had to be directed twice—by a policeman and the driver of a taxicab. At last I came to it. There was the name on the wall at the corner.

As I stood there I became conscious that a man was on the pavement on the other side of the road. A window opened in the house in front of which he was standing. A woman put her head out. I knew her—she was the woman who had been dancing with Gaspare. Then I knew that the man on the pavement was Gaspare. The electric light shone on the woman's face, so that I saw it as clearly as if it had been the brightest day. She began with a question:—

"Well, is it done—the little business with Emilio?"

He said something which I could not see, since his back was towards me; but I could guess what it was from her rejoinder.

"That is fifty pounds in your pocket—and also mine—eh, Gaspare?"

Then, diverting her attention for a moment from her friend, she saw me.

"Hush!" she said. "There is someone opposite. I will see you tomorrow, at the usual time." She withdrew her head, then instantly put it out again. "Bring the money—my share!"

Grimly she laughed, and again withdrew. This time the window shut and the blind came down, and the man on the pavement turned and stood and looked at me. Then, with his hands in his coat-pockets, he strolled off down Greek Street. I turned and watched him as he went. He paused under a lamp which, attached to a building, projected over the pavement. He rapped at the door with his knuckles, and was almost instantly admitted.

When he was in I strolled up the other side of the road. Over a small window, which was divided into three long panes, was a board: "Restaurant Napolitain. Alessandro." Almost exactly opposite was an entry which ran by a picture theatre. I drew a little back into it and waited.

Not very long—hardly ten minutes. Then the door of the restaurant opened. Two men came out—Signori Gaspare and Alessandro. I could hear their voices, but I could not see their faces. After a few words they parted. As Alessandro was about to return indoors I quickly crossed over to him.

"I want to speak to you," I said.

"Pardon?" It was a question; he was probably wondering where I had come from.

"I want to speak to you," I repeated. "I'll come inside."

I was inside before he guessed my intention and he was still on the door-step. Clearly this was a restaurant; in the uncertain light I could see the marble tables. Presently he followed, coming closer to me than I liked.

"What do you mean by coming into my place like this? I will have no nonsense. You make a mistake if you think so."

I had no clear plan of action; I just felt that I wanted to strike— and I struck.

"That fellow Gaspare, with whom you were talking, has just killed a young man named Emilio."

I could not see his face very clearly, but I think it very probable that he was startled.

"Of what are you talking?" He spoke very quietly. He was one of those big men with soft voices, whom a wise woman never trusts.

"You know very well of what I'm talking. He killed him at your instigation; you've just paid him fifty pounds for doing it."

I rather lost my head, or I should have chosen my words more carefully. I knew the man was dangerous. He pushed the street-door to; it shut without a sound.

"Don't you dare to touch me!" I was a little scared; the darkness was like a shroud—the silence was ominous.

"Come," he said; "I want to talk to you."

He gripped me by the wrist and began to pull me along. I was powerless to offer any effectual resistance. I caught at a marble table as we passed. He snatched me away without pausing in his stride.

We came to a door, which he opened. We were in a passage with stairs and a light somewhere above.

"I advise you to release me," I told him, "and to be careful what you do. However it may be in Naples, you can't commit murder with impunity here."

He said nothing, but he caught me in some way by the shoulders, and began to run me up those stairs as if it had been level ground. I am agile, but his agility was amazing.

We came to a landing; he swung me round a corner and along a passage. At the end there was a door, through which he thrust me; having done so, he shut it, and I heard him turn the key. He himself remained outside.

It would be futile to attempt to describe my feelings—they were chaotic. For some seconds I stood shaking with rage and gasping for breath. I realized what an idiot I had been in saying nothing to Dr. Rodaccini, to the police, to anyone, before turning out on this mad adventure. No one had a notion where I was.

When I again became, in some degree, mistress of myself I tried to think what was the best thing I could do. If I had been a man I should have had matches about me somewhere, and thus have been able to see in what sort of place I was. Being a matchless woman I had to feel. First along the wall. I was in a good-sized room; I took twelve fairly long steps before I came to a corner which showed I was at the end of it. When I came to the table something caused me to put up my hand. I touched something overhead; it was the bulb of an electric light. I pursued my investigations, and found what I sought. In an instant the room was lit in a fashion which, after the previous darkness, was almost dazzling.

It was a sitting-room. There were two doors; one which I took to be that through which I had been propelled, and a second, by the fireplace, which perhaps led to an adjoining apartment. What I took to be the window was guarded by iron shutters, painted white.

I sat down on a chair feeling rather bewildered. Soon my courage, which had gone a little at the knees, stood up straight again. Probably, if I stayed there, sooner or later Signor Alessandro would return, and I ought to be prepared to meet him. There was a poker standing up against the fireplace, but I did not fancy that a poker would be of much service against him.

I examined the doors—first the one through which I had come. It was as solidly constructed a door as I have met; it would need a great deal of breaking down.

Then I went to the other door. There was a small brass bolt on my side. I drew it back—nothing resulted. I got that poker, gripped it hard, and brought the point with all my force against the panel. I did it twice—the third time the point went through. I used that poker as a lever, and broke away enough of the woodwork to enable me to insert my hand and arm. I felt for the bolt which I believed to be on the other side and found it, slipped it back, and the door was open.

It was a sleeping apartment. There was a bed with the usual

equipments of a bedroom. The room was certainly empty. By aid of the light which came from the room I had just left I saw that there was a switch near to the bed. When I got the room lighted I saw something which pleased me almost more than anything else could possibly have done.

In that bedroom there was a telephone, with the receiver on the mantelpiece. I rushed to it. With what anxiety I waited to learn if my call had been heard! In a second or two there came the operator's familiar query:—

"What number, please?"

I asked for a number which I knew very well. There was another interval of waiting, then there came a voice:—

"Who are you?"

I daresay my voice trembled as I asked a question in my turn:—

"Is that Scotland Yard?"

"Yes; who is speaking?"

I fancy I very nearly jumped. I knew I was within reach of a friend.

"Judith Lee. Can I speak to Inspector Ellis?"

"If you'll hold the wire, Miss Lee, I'll ascertain."

I held the wire—I did hope they would not cut me off. What seemed to me at that moment to be the faintest voice I had ever heard answered before they had a chance:—

"I'm here; just come in and just going out. Where are you?"

"I'm in the Restaurant Napolitain, in Greek Street, which I believe belongs to a man named Alessandro."

"We know the gentleman very well. What on earth are you doing there?"

"There's been murder done—in a street near Leicester Square."

"How do you know that? The report has only just come in."

"A young man named Emilio has been murdered by a man named Gaspare, at the instigation of the Alessandro who owns this restaurant. I can't stop to tell you how I know it, but perhaps you can guess. I was idiot enough to think I could tackle Alessandro single-handed. He has locked me in a room on the first floor of his restaurant."

A cheery voice came back.

"That's all right. We've had an eye on Signor Alessandro and his

Restaurant Napolitain for a good long time. I'm obliged to you for putting the game into our hands. We shall probably be with you inside ten minutes."

They seemed to me to be a pretty long ten minutes. I had no means of knowing how the time was passing. Suddenly I caught the sound of a footstep in the passage without. It was not a very audible footstep, but my ears were wide open. Then I heard someone turning the key in the lock.

I had still that poker in my hand, and something in the feel of it not only set my courage up but gave me an idea. First of all I switched off the light, then I stood by the side of the door at which it opened, and I held that poker tight; and the moment the door began to open, and I dimly saw the figure of a man without, I raised that poker above my head and brought it down with all my might.

Something had happened to someone—someone who went down on to the floor with quite a thud. I leaped right over him. There, in the passage beyond, was Signor Alessandro; I knew him —and that time I was on to him before he knew that I was coming. I struck him with the point of that poker in the chest, and I think I hurt him, because he made a curious sound, staggering back without making any effort to seize me as I passed.

Seeing a staircase beyond, I made for that. There was a light on the landing at the top; a passage to the left, one to the right. I chose the one to the right. There was a door at the end. I did not stop to consider what might be beyond, but I caught hold of the handle and turned it. The door yielded. I found myself in a room with the fair-haired girl whom I had seen dancing with the youngster who was dead.

That did startle me. I had been occupied with so many other things that, at least for the time being, I had forgotten her existence. It was a bedroom. A ball dress was thrown over a chair—the dress in which she had been dancing. Her hair was hanging loose over her shoulders; even then I thought what beautiful hair it was. She was standing in a stooping position, with her arms held out as if to ward off a blow. Apparently she had taken me for quite another person, from whom she had reason to fear the worst.

Having realized on whom I had intruded, I paid attention first not to the occupant of the room, but to the door. There was no key.

"Where's the key to this door? I asked.

"Who are you?" she replied. "What do you want? What do you mean by coming in here?"

"' WHERE'S THE KEY TO THIS DOOR?' I ASKED."

I persisted in my inquiry.

"Haven't you a key to this door?"

She shook her head. "No; they won't let me have one."

"Haven't you anything with which you can keep the door fastened against intrusion—even for a few moments? Help me with that chest of drawers and the bed. If we can get them up against this door we may manage to keep them out just long enough."

Without understanding what it was I would be at, she did as I asked. Together we rigged up a sort of barricade. As she helped she rained questions.

"Who are you? Who is coming? Of what are you afraid? What has happened? Tell me, I beg of you."

She spoke quite good English. She was getting almost as excited as I was.

"They have killed Emilio."

She stared at me, her hands against her breast.

"Emilio! I feared it! Alessandro swore that he would do it. When I saw him speak to Gaspare I feared still more."

"What is Alessandro to you? Are you his wife?"

"He is the patron; he wants me to be his wife, but I do not want to marry him. It is my mother who would force me. If it were not for him she would starve. He is a rich man, Alessandro. He says to my mother: 'If Lucrezia will marry me'—I am Lucrezia—'all will be well. I will give you a regular income; you may live in comfort for the rest of your life. If not, out into the street you go; you die in the gutter, you starve, besides the other things you know I can do to you.' He can do many things, Alessandro. 'As for the nonsense Lucrezia talks,' he says, 'young girls do not know their own mind. You bid her to marry me; I will see that she obeys her mother.' But I do not want to marry him—I do not."

"What position do you occupy in this place?"

"I am the cashier. I have been here nearly a year. I wish I had never come at all. Until lately Emilio was a waiter. He is from the same village from which I come; we have known each other all our lives. How can I help being fond of him, since he is so kind, so generous, so tender, and so thoughtful? And also he is so handsome."

"Are you the only woman in the house?"

"In general there are two others. We had, all three of us, a holiday until the morning. I was to sleep with my sister, whose husband has a restaurant at Brixton.[1] But when Alessandro saw me dancing with Emilio he said that I must come home with him. I did not dare to disobey. He threw Emilio out of the restaurant, not yet a fortnight ago, because of something he thought he had discovered—I don't know what. Since then he has been scolding me all the time. Gaspare told me only the other day that if I was not more attentive to Alessandro's wishes, more careful to keep him in a good temper

[1] A suburb in South London.

—I know what he meant—he was afraid that something might happen to Emilio."

"Who is this man Gaspare? It is he who is the actual murderer."

"Oh, yes, I know; it is always like that."

"Always like that? What do you mean? Who is this man?"

The girl dropped her voice still lower; she glanced round as if fearful that a listener might be hidden in the corner. Clearly the girl, with her susceptible Sicilian temperament, was half out of her mind with fear and grief, and other troubles besides.

"I don't know who you are, or why I tell you; but I feel you may be a friend, and I am so much in need of a friend. I have not one friend in all the world, for even my mother is against me. And now that you say Emilio is dead, it is still worse. I will be revenged on them—I will be revenged! You ask me who Gaspare is. I will tell you. I care not what they do to me; since it is he who has killed Emilio, I will tell you. He is of the Mafia—Alessandro is of the Mafia; all of them are of the Mafia. This house, this Restaurant Napolitain, this is where they meet; I will show you the room in which they have their meetings. Gaspare is just back from America. It is not the first time he has been there, not the first time he has been chased by the police. I know! They think I don't, but I do. As for Alessandro, with him it has come to this—he scarcely dares to show his face in the street for fear of the police. They are after him all over Europe, and if they once catch him—rich or poor—ah! it is all over with him. I know, and he knows I know. It is partly because he knows that he so wishes to make me his wife. He thinks to shut my mouth; but now that they have killed Emilio I will open it to its widest. I care not what they do to me! No, no, I care not!"

I do not remember to have ever before seen anyone in such a whirlwind of passion, None the less, she had her wits about her. Suddenly, with a gesture, she requested silence.

"There are footsteps on the stairs. Who is it coming?"

"There are two of them. Alessandro is one; I think Gaspare is the other, but I am not sure. Whoever it is, I hit him with this poker."

"That is good. I hope you hit him hard. I will hit him hard when I have a chance, I promise you. I also have a knife."

To my amazement she stooped and whipped a gleaming blade out of her stocking. I foresaw lively times ahead. I did not wish

Inspector Ellis to come and find me engaged in a fight to death with understudies for carving-knives. I deemed it desirable to get that knife from the fair-haired damsel.

"Do not use that. Let me have it."

"Why should I let you have it? No, no; I will keep it for myself. I can use it better than you."

As she spoke someone without tried the handle. When it was found that the door would not yield a soft voice demanded, in the broadest argot of Naples:—

"Lucrezia, what have you against the door? Don't fool; open at once."

The girl said nothing. She beckoned me to the other side of the room.

Throwing back a door which was covered with the same paper as the wall, she disclosed an aperture behind. "That is a door at the back; it is locked; they do not think I have the key, but I have."

While she took a key from some curious hiding-place in her corsets she burst, as it were, into a sudden flood of explanation.

"This house is very old. It belongs to the Mafia; it is their head-quarters in London. Strange things have happened in London—they happen still, though the people of London do not think it. This house could tell them tales. The police—they guess—but have no proof. What can the police do without proof in London?"

While words had been pouring from her at the rate of I do not know how many a minute she had been unlocking that door. At last it stood open—just as the door of her bedroom yielded to the vigorous attack which was being made on it from without. As I passed through the door at the back of the cupboard I saw Alessandro rush into the bedroom, and behind him Gaspare. I thought they would catch the girl, but she was too quick for them. With surprising speed she had whipped the key out of the lock, was through the door, had shut it, and was locking it again on the other side. The closing of the door had left us in pitch darkness; some vigorous Sicilian adjectives were coming from the other side of it.

"Where are we?" I asked. "I can see nothing."

"This is a recess—here is another door; it is not locked." She opened it, but it did not make things much clearer. "These steps lead down into the restaurant. Be careful, they are steep."

Those steps were certainly steep. I went down backwards, as down a ladder. In the darkness it was not easy. The girl's voice as she followed came from above.

"At the bottom is a door. They think it is locked, but it is not. I am not so simple as they suppose."

I began to be of that opinion myself. There, sure enough, was a door, and it was not locked—it yielded to a turn of the handle. I could not see her, but I felt her arm. Her voice seemed less confident.

"This is the restaurant. I do not know what we can do now. The door into the street is certainly locked and shuttered. I promise you I will use my knife. Have you a knife?"

"I want no knife," I told her, "nor must you use yours. We shall not improve matters by making bad worse. Besides, the police are coming."

She stopped suddenly.

"What do you mean by the police are coming? Who has told them?"

"I sent a message to a friend of mine at Scotland Yard—through the telephone."

"The telephone! Then—you have been in that room?"

"I don't know what you mean by that room. I have been in a room—a bedroom. Alessandro locked me in a sitting-room. I broke down the door which divided it from the next room, which is a bedroom; and there was the telephone."

"There is only one apartment in the house in which there is a telephone, and that is the one which belongs to the chief of the Mafia. He is there sometimes for days without anyone knowing he is in the house—or, I fancy, even in England. There has been history made in those two rooms. I know it, although I am only a girl. Here's a knife for you."

She thrust something into my hand, which I refused to take.

"Thank you, I would rather do without it. Inspector Ellis promised that the police should be here within ten minutes. They will be here before any harm can be done to us."

"You think so? We shall see. Gaspare and Alessandro move quickly—they will hide us where the police will never find us. For my part, I have no faith in the police; they always come a little too late—I know. I have a knife, and I will use it. If you are wise you will take this one and use it also."

I still refused to take the knife, though there was that, both in her tone and in her words, which grated on my nerves. When, presently, a door at the back opened, I was more than ever disposed to wish that my adventurous spirit had not lured me into the Restaurant Napolitain.

I did not need the girl to tell me what the opening of that door portended; I knew it for myself; but she did tell me.

"You see now they are coming; we shall soon know which it is to be—us or them. Down behind my desk."

We were standing behind the sort of counter which served as buffet and caisse combined. She drew me down as the door opened, but I peeped round the corner. Alessandro came in, and behind him Gaspare. I fancied the latter held himself as if he were in pain; that poker, which I still retained, had not come down for nothing. Alessandro held an electric torch above his head. It tickled me— even then!—to see them whisper to each other, wishing to remain unheard, while all the time the flare of that torch upon their faces told me everything they said.

It was Gaspare who whispered first. "They are not here." His glance travelled over the restaurant.

Alessandro's eyes also searched. "They must be here. If they are not here, where are they? They could not get out of the house."

There was a moment's pause, then Signor Alessandro added, with what I had no doubt was genuine feeling, "I will cut both their throats when I get them."

"Lucrezia's? Her pretty throat?"

"From ear to ear. I will send her to Emilio; and that black-faced devil's spawn, only let me get her within reach of my hand."

The last delicate allusion, I took it, was to me. Even allowing for the poetic licence which one associates with the language of Sicily, the prospect which these two gentlemen offered to the imagination was not alluring; to say nothing of the fact that I was solemnly convinced that they would do their best to be as good as their word.

The girl behind me did something—tried to change her position, or to keep under cover; anyhow, she moved, and a board creaked just loudly enough to be audible. Alessandro heard. Leaning

towards Gaspare, I saw him whisper: "They are behind the caisse—
we have got them—quick! You go one side and I the other."

"Look out," I whispered to the girl, "they know where we are.
We will give them a chase before they get us." I stood up straight,
and by way of a little diversion I brought the poker down on the top
of the counter. "You pair of murderous villains!" I cried; "do you
think you have us at your mercy? We'll teach you better!"

In my excitement, giving the poker a flourish, I swept half-a-
dozen bottles off the buffet, and they fell crashing to the floor.

"Is that your black-faced beauty?" inquired Gaspare, aloud. "It
looks as if she means to ruin you; she starts to destroy your stock-
in-trade."

"Be careful how you come." This was the girl, who was standing
by me, even more excited than I was. She was flourishing a knife
in either hand. "For each of you I have a knife. I will pay you with
them for Emilio."

Acting on Alessandro's advice, they came at us from either side.
As Alessandro passed, leaning over the counter, I knocked the torch
out of his hand, and in the same instant, turning towards Gaspare,
I struck him with the poker a blow which was more than own
brother to the first. He staggered back with curses which were deep
but not loud. I was past him in a flash. I hesitated whether to make
towards the door which I knew led to the staircase; but he made a
grab at me and almost caught my skirt. I rushed across the restaurant among the marble tables.

"Gaspare! Gaspare!" It was Signor Alessandro's voice, considerably raised. Apparently he was having a little argument with Lucrezia, of which, in the darkness, he was not getting the best. There
was a crash—what had happened I did not know; it sounded as if
more bottles had fallen to the floor. Then I knew that Lucrezia,
following my example, had got past Alessandro and was seeking
refuge among the marble tables. Then there was silence, broken by
Alessandro's voice:—

"Gaspare, I believe that cat has knifed me in half-a-dozen places;
my fingers are wet with my own blood."

Then came Gaspare's voice; he seemed angry. I should not like
to report his exact language; your true Sicilian can be vigorous; but
in effect he said:—

"That black-faced friend of yours has struck me for a second time with that poker. I swear to you by all the saints that she shall not strike me again. Give us some light, we can do nothing in this darkness. Where are your switches?"

Alessandro said something which I could not catch; but I could hear him moving, and presently the whole place was flooded with electric light.

"Can they see these lights outside?" asked Gaspare.

"Not a glimmer. The door and windows are so constructed that from the street nothing can be seen."

"Then to business!" And Gaspare started to carry out what I presume was his idea of business.

There ensued a scene as remarkable, I take it, as any which was ever enacted in a London restaurant. They chased us, those two men. In the hand of each was a knife. I daresay Gaspare's was still stained with Emilio's blood. I knew quite well what would happen if he got that knife within reach of me. I also knew that at any moment the police might be knocking at the door. If Inspector Ellis had carried out his undertaking literally they would have been there before. I scouted Lucrezia's idea that they were always too late. Then Gaspare came towards me.

I suppose in that restaurant there were a dozen marble-topped tables—oblong, round, and square. Most of the chairs had been piled upon the tables; I was entrenched behind a row of them. When Gaspare came towards me at one end I pushed them towards him; he swept the lot of them upon the floor, and came round my side of the table towards me. I retreated as he came, but I could not get away from Gaspare. Among the tables we twisted and twirled; sometimes I vaulted them, sometimes I ran round.

I had pushed a chair in his way, and he fell over it, and in falling he caught me by the skirt with so sure a hold that he all but dragged me over with him. I lifted the poker and struck him again and again; but, though he was still in difficulties with the chair, I could not make him loose his hold. He held me with his left hand. Suddenly I felt something prick me; he had struck me with the knife which was in his right. Frantically I lashed out again at him with with the poker. I fancied I had struck the wrist which held the knife, but I was not sure. I was straining every nerve to tear myself loose, when all at once the skirt did give way—but not with the result I had hoped for. As it yielded, the strain being unexpectedly relaxed, I slipped, and he, probably without intention, gave an unlooked-for jerk. Down he went on his face, and down I went on him.

" I LIFTED THE POKER AND STRUCK HIM AGAIN AND AGAIN."

At that same moment there came a hammering at the front-door

"HE SAW A MAN ON HIS KNEES, WITH A KNIFE HELD ABOVE HIS HEAD, AND A WOMAN IMMEDIATELY IN FRONT OF HIM UPON THE FLOOR."

—a loud, insistent hammering—and I knew that Inspector Ellis's ten minutes had expired.

With the sound of the knocking there came a scream from Lucrezia and something very like a roar from Alessandro. I was conscious that they were striking at each other with their knives, and that each was getting home in turn. Then I felt Gaspare's knife in my shoulder. I twisted myself round; I felt it again. I caught him by the wrist. He slipped the knife from his right hand to his left—I do not know how, but he did it. It pricked me again.

Out in the street they were breaking down the door. The force of their blows shook the building. That door was not easy to break down. In my agony—because Gaspare's knife hurt—I wondered how long they would take to do it. Those men were like two wild beasts; if they could kill us first they would care nothing for what might happen to themselves afterwards.

Gaspare got at me with his knife again and again, but he never had a chance to get home with a good, straight blow. Somehow I managed to break the force of each one before it reached me. But he had cut me all about the neck and shoulders. I was a reek of blood; I saw it falling on his face and on his hands. If they did not get that door down in a second or two, it would be too late. Then I reeled, and Gaspare got up—I thought it was too late.

That I am still alive to tell the tale is sufficient proof that it was not too late—I have been told by the merest fraction of a second. Inspector Ellis informed me that when he and his men succeeded in forcing an entrance he saw a man on his knees, with a knife held above his head, and a woman immediately in front of him upon the floor; that he rushed forward and caught Gaspare's wrist just as it was in the act of descending. When Gaspare turned and saw him, somehow he slipped from his hold, stood up straight, buried the knife in his own bosom, and fell down across me—dead.

Lucrezia had even a worse time than I had—and I was nearly three weeks in the ward of a hospital. They took Signor Alessandro alive; all the world knows that he expiated his crimes upon the gallows. There are still three marks upon my chest in front which I am told will never pass away, so I am not likely to be without reminders—if any were needed—of my adventure at the Restaurant Napolitain.

"8, ELM GROVE—BACK ENTRANCE"

This story is, in many respects, such a strange one that it is not easy to know how to set it down—whether to tell it backwards, or to commence at the beginning. It is on that account that I preface it with a remark that when, one afternoon, I was at the Arnolds', and the parlourmaid came into the room with a tea-tray in her hands, at the sight of her I was so startled that I nearly dropped the pastel I was holding.

But the story did not begin there. It began when I was returning from spending an evening with some friends at Blackheath. I came back by the Greenwich tram;[1] I believe it was the last tram. It was most dreadful weather. I had the vehicle to myself until it was boarded by two men whom I should have described as of distinctly suspicious appearance. They sat in perfect silence till one of them rose to get off, when the other said to him, in tones which were inaudible to me:—

"Now, don't you make any mistake—8, Elm Grove[2]—back entrance. Got it right?"

"Of course I've got it right. What do you take me for? Think that in my position I'm likely to make a mess of a thing like that?"

The speaker had a large, square bag, made of what was apparently a piece of old red carpet. It seemed to be full of something which was so heavy that it was all he could do to carry it. The car stopped. He got off; the other man remained. He was a square-faced, dark-visaged person; his cloth cap was pulled close down over his head. As was the case with the man who had just departed, there was nothing to screen his lips, so that to me the words which they had uttered had been obvious.

Presently the car stopped again; a policeman got in. At sight of him the man started. If it had been possible, he would undoubtedly have got off; but it was too late. The policeman shook, as well as

[1] Situated in East London, south of the Thames, these wealthy Eastern suburbs are some ten miles from Lee's home in West London.
[2] Probably a street in Peckham, South London, near New Cross.

he could, the rain off his cape, then entered and took his seat. He looked about him. He saw the black-visaged man, and the man saw him; plainly they knew each other. The man looked murder; the policeman grinned.

"So it's you," he said. "I didn't know you were out."

The man replied with a sort of venomous fury.

"Who asked you what you knew? You mind your own affairs, and don't you talk to me when you're not wanted to. That's not your duty. You do your duty and leave me alone."

"All right, Chippy; no harm intended. I hope you'll keep out longer this time than you did last."

The man made no reply. I wondered what had been the meaning of that reference to 8, Elm Grove, back entrance, and what had been the contents of that bag. I should rather have liked to ask a question or two. The car stopped in the Westminster Bridge Road.[1] The three of us descended. I should probably have forgotten the incident had it not been for something which happened not many days afterwards, which brought it all back to my memory with a rush.

I was standing in Piccadilly,[2] waiting for an omnibus. A shabby, unpleasant-looking individual was standing not very far from me. Suddenly someone came hurrying across the road. He was an undersized youth, whose attire was in the last stage of decay. Apparently he wore no shirt; his coat was buttoned up to the neck, the collar turned up. He kept his hands in his jacket pockets as if he were unwilling to expose them to the air. I had a feeling that in one of those pockets there might be something about whose safety he was anxious. He went straight to the unpleasant-looking gentleman. The man's lips formed themselves into a question:—

"Got it?"

The youth nodded, casting quick glances behind him and on either side. The man went on:—

"Then I told you what to do with it. If I was you, the sooner the better. Remember what I said? 8, Elm Grove—back entrance. Don't you make any mistake."

[1] A street leading to Westminster Bridge on the south side of the Thames, opposite the Houses of Parliament.
[2] A fashionable thoroughfare in the West End.

The youth passed into an entry which leads into Jermyn Street,[1] and was gone before I had realized where I had encountered that unpleasant-looking person's words before. "8, Elm Grove—back entrance"—that was what the black-visaged man had said in that Greenwich tramcar to his companion, who got out carrying the heavy carpet-bag.

I daresay it was a fortnight afterwards that I was at Waterloo Station. There had been a race-meeting down the line. The race-goers were returning; a cheap train was in. I drew away from the horde of men who all at once crowded the platform. As I looked about me I noticed a man in a fawn-coloured overcoat go up to a short and sturdy person, who, with his legs wide apart and his hat cocked on the back of his head, immediately accosted him. I saw quite distinctly what he said:—

"Halloa, George! I've been waiting for you. What luck?"

The other replied. He had had no luck; he had not been within ten miles of a winner; he had come back stony-broke. The other looked at him—he had a toothpick between his lips, which he shifted from side to side.

"Then it's about time we did something, ain't it, George? As far as coin goes, I'm about where you are. How about the girl? We're ready for her."

"She comes out of Holloway Prison[2] to-morrow morning at eight sharp, and I'm going to be there to meet her."

"I suppose she'll be all right?"

"You bet she will; I'll see to that. She does what I tell her, or—she'll be sorry; she will."

"Are you going to marry her, George?"

"Marry her? Me? Me marry her? She won't dare to ask me."

"Suppose she cuts up rough? Girls do sometimes, you know."

"Yes, and so do men. That girl cares for me—I'll show you how she cares for me before we've done with her." The speaker smiled —a thin, horrible smile. "She'll do just as I tell her without so much as a whimper."

"She comes out to-morrow morning? Perhaps she'd better stay inside."

[1] A fashionable street in the West End, associated with the gentlemen's club scene.
[2] A women's prison in Islington, North-Central London.

"They won't keep her; not this time they won't. I shouldn't wonder if next time she makes more of a stay. When a woman's been really useful to you it's just as well to have her for once in a while out of your way."

"But this one's very young, ain't she?"

"All the better; you can work them easier when they're young —and when they're young they are so fond of you, that makes it easier still."

The two men grinned, and I could have struck them for it. The man who had been racing stood closer up to the other and showed him something which was in his overcoat pocket. What it was I could not see; but I saw him say, in tones which were clearly meant to reach the other only:—

"I've got a little something here—out of a lady's bag."

"Seems to me you're always fond of the ladies, George. I suppose it's another case of 8, Elm Grove—back entrance?" Again the two men grinned.

The pair moved off to the refreshment-room. I had been a spectator of one of those strange scenes of which I see more than I like. And again there had been that reference to "8, Elm Grove—back entrance." I could guess at what was the nature of the something which the fellow had in his overcoat pocket; but what stuck in my mind—what hurt me most—were their allusions to the girl who, the next morning, was coming out of Holloway Prison. To what a fate she seemed to be coming! As the short man had hinted, she had much better stay inside. The fellow in the overcoat was, to a superficial eye, not bad looking. His features were fairly regular; he had a tiny moustache; but, apart from the fact that he had those whity-blue eyes which I, sometimes perhaps unjustly, associate with cruelty and treachery, there was in his whole expression a something mean, underhand, cunning, which would have made me, had I stood near him in a crowd, look after my belongings very carefully. The idea that he was going to get a young girl into his hands at the moment she was coming out of the jail to which she had been sent for what probably was her first offence—this was an idea which I found it very hard to digest. The result was that at an early hour the next morning I set forth on a quixotic errand. Before eight o'clock I was outside the gates of Holloway Jail.

Early though it was, I was not the first arrival. Perhaps a dozen people were there before me—such specimens of humanity! There was nothing to be seen of the man in the fawn overcoat. While I was glad enough that he was not there, in his absence what was I to do—when the discharged prisoners began to come out? I decided to await events.

The prison clock had struck eight some minutes when the great gate which fronted us swung back—and a procession came out. Such a procession! Probably chance had it that a number of sentences should terminate together; I should say that more than twenty persons emerged through the gates. I presume that they were liberated at such a matutinal hour in order that they might

"ALL AT ONCE SHE WAS IN HIS ARMS, CRYING AS IF HER HEART WAS BREAKING."

re-enter the world before people were up and about to observe from whence they came; yet, early though it was, nearly without exception each prisoner was met by someone at the gate. For those who had no personal friend there was a Salvation Army lass and a bearded individual who bore the insignia of that great organization. A slight, grey-headed man in tweeds, who had a notebook in his hand, was, I took it, a representative of some society.

I kept my eye on the gate. No one at all resembling the person I sought had so far appeared. Then, at the tail of the procession, she came; I knew her in a moment. Just then there appeared—I could hardly have said from where—the man in the fawn-coloured overcoat. He was dressed precisely as he had been on the previous afternoon. He lifted his hat to the girl, took her hand, and kissed her before us all; and all at once she was in his arms, crying as if her heart was breaking.

It was a delicate situation—by me wholly unexpected. I could hardly interfere in such a tender meeting. On what grounds? Because of something I had not heard but seen the man say the previous afternoon? If I proffered such a reason I might be laughed to scorn; I might have misjudged him; I might have got the thing all wrong. How she cried! How tenderly he soothed her! He led her to a taxi-cab, which was standing by the kerb at a little distance. As they entered and the cab drove off I recognized what a wild-goose errand I had come upon.

The procession ceased; the gates reclosed; prisoners and their friends went their several ways. I moved off, with the feeling strong upon me that I might just as well have stayed away. I went so slowly that the others, who went with brisker steps, before I had gone any distance, were out of sight. Just as the last of them had vanished round a corner, round that same corner there came a woman running—a matronly woman, in a state of what, to me, seemed frenzied agitation. When she got to me she stopped, her breath failing her.

"Have they—have they come out?" she gasped.

"Do you mean the prisoners—from the jail?"

"Of course I do. What else would I mean?" She spoke like a person from the country, setting her old-fashioned bonnet straight with trembling hands. "I meant to have been here before, and I ought to have been, only my train was late. Do you know if they've come out, young woman?"

"Some minutes ago. They've all of them gone their different ways."

"Then—my daughter—has she come out?"

In her voice there was a note of anguish and of terror. Her agitation increased. An idea occurred to me.

"Was your daughter a slight, dark-haired young woman, with big brown eyes?"

"That's my Mary, miss. Did you see her, miss? If she's out, where is she? She knew I was coming. She might have guessed my train was late. Where has she gone?"

"If she's the young woman I suppose, she was met by a slightly-built man with very light blue eyes, who took her away with him in a taxi-cab."

The woman shrieked—positively shrieked—out there in the open street. I have seldom been more startled.

"You don't mean to say she's gone with him? She can't—she can't! Not when she knew that her mother was coming to meet her and take her home! I'm her mother, and I tell you she's my girl."

Before we parted I had heard her story, and the story of her daughter's downfall. A painful one it was, though I am afraid it is one which is only too common. The poor old lady was nearly broken-hearted. I saw her to the railway-station, into the train which was to take her back home—alone. I promised that I would make all the inquiries that could be made, and, though I was occupied with very many matters, I did my best. But more than three months passed, and I learned nothing of the whereabouts of her erring daughter, until that afternoon when I was at the Arnolds' and that parlourmaid came into the room with the tea on a tray. She was the young woman I had seen that morning emerge from the gates of the prison whom her mother had been too late to meet. It was not surprising that I nearly dropped the pastel I was holding. Which brings me to the real beginning of my tale.

Mrs. Arnold's drawing-room is a charming room; in the best sense of the word, a feminine room—delicate, refined, delightful. Amy Arnold had had her portrait done by a fashionable pastellist. It had just come home; I had been looking at it when tea appeared.

That parlourmaid struck such a jarring note; she, as it were, projected me into another world. Those doubtful characters on the Greenwich tram, the young thief in Piccadilly, the pair of rascals at Waterloo, the scene at the Holloway Prison gate, that dreadful procession with the girl at the tail, the despairing mother who had lost her child—all these things came back to me in a series of discordant notes as the parlourmaid put down the tea-tray.

It was undoubtedly the girl; her uniform made a difference, but there was no mistaking her. I doubted if she had noticed me, or what an effect her entrance had had on me.

When she had left the room I hardly knew what to say. They continued to speak of the pastel; my thoughts were with the maid. As I thanked Amy for the cup of tea she gave me I asked if the servant who had brought it in was not a fresh one.

"Do you mean Jane?" she asked.

"Is her name Jane?" I inquired.

"Jane—or, to give her her full style and title, Jane Stamp. I suppose she has been with us about six weeks."

"Nearly two months," chimed in her mother; "and a very nice girl she is, and a good servant. She is quite refined for a servant, yet not a bit above her place. Don't you think she's pleasant looking?"

"I think she looks pale."

"She is pale. I fancy she has troubles of her own. I have suspected her, more than once, of crying."

"Where did you get her from?"

"Through an advertisement. I got tired of the creatures they sent me from the registry offices, so I tried an advertisement in the *Post*. She was the result."

"Did you have a character with her?"

"Of course I had a character." Mrs. Arnold opened her eyes as if I had suggested something utterly monstrous. "Does she look to you like a girl who hasn't a character? She was three years in her last place; she only left it just before she came to me."

"Where was her last place?"

She was with some people named Reynolds who had a flat near the Marble Arch[1]—9A, Waterman Mansions."

[1] A triumphal arch located at the western end of Oxford Street in the West End of London. The residential district immediately to the north and north-west was

"Did you see Mrs. Reynolds?"

"Of course I saw her. Do you suppose that I should be satisfied with a written character? My dear Judith, what are you thinking about? I called one afternoon. She was rather a florid-looking person, but the character she gave Jane was excellent. She only parted with her because they were giving up the flat. I have found that sometimes servants don't come up to the characters I have had with them, but I am venturing to hope that I've found a jewel at last."

We returned to the subject of the pastel. Amy thought that the artist had given her a little too much colour; but while we talked my thoughts were with the parlourmaid. I was wondering what I ought to do. I knew that her name was not Jane Stamp—nor Jane anything; I knew that she had not been three years in her last place, nor, at any time, with people named Reynolds. I knew, in short, a great many things about her which would have surprised Mrs. Arnold not a little. The question I had to answer was—was it my duty to tell her what those things were? That would mean instant dismissal for Jane Stamp. No mistress would keep her in her house after such a revelation. And that would mean something of which I did not care to think for the maid.

I went away from Mrs. Arnold's leaving these questions unanswered. I admit that I was desirous of avoiding the responsibility of arriving at a too hasty decision. A few hours could make no difference; I would employ them in making certain investigations of my own.

The first thing I did when I reached home was to get out a directory. I looked up the Elm Groves; as I had expected, there were plenty of them; there seemed to be Elm Groves in all parts of London. One at New Cross[1] attracted my attention. My knowledge of that locality was not very exact, but I took it that that tramcar had been somewhere about New Cross when that man with the carpet-bag got out. So far as I could judge, there might be an Elm Grove within quite a short distance of where he had alighted—and

---

both respectable due to its proximity to Hyde Park and slightly dubious due to the transitory nature of the population in rented properties.

[1] A residential district in Lewisham, South London, approximately halfway between Blackheath and Westminster Bridge Road.

No. 8, at the time that directory went to press, was empty. It might have become occupied since then. At any rate, I thought I would go and see—and I went, by the Greenwich tramcar. When we had gone some little distance I asked the conductor if he knew of any Elm Grove in that district. He did not; but there were persons who had heard my question who were able to supply me with the information I required. I received the most precise directions from more than one of my fellow-passengers as to how I was to reach Elm Grove; but it did not prove an easy place to find.

Elm Grove was one of those surprises which one often encounters in suburban London. It was a relic of the past; a street of old-fashioned, solidly-built houses, each standing in its own garden. There seemed to be about a dozen on either side. I came to No. 8—there was nothing to show that it was to let. A person came out of what I took to be No. 10, whom I addressed.

"Can you tell me," I asked, "if this house is to let?"

"That's more than I can tell you," he replied; "and, so far as I know, more than anyone else can tell you, either. I have been here going on for five years, and it was like that when I came, and it's like it still. I believe that some of the rooms are furnished, and I have heard that people have been seen going in and out. Between ourselves, round about here that house is looked on as a bit of a mystery."

He went his way and left me thinking. The front gate was locked. Remembering that there had been some mention of a back entrance, I went to the end of the road and turned to the right, and presently came upon a sort of narrow lane, which I proceeded to explore. These were evidently the back doors to the houses in Elm Grove. Clearly some of them were never used; one or two were boarded up. Then I came to a door which did show signs of occasional usage. It was not easy to determine the number to which it belonged, but I tried the handle. It yielded, and the door was open. Trusting that my boldness might have no serious result, I passed through, to find myself in a garden which was a mere wilderness of weeds. It was only after momentary inspection that I perceived that there was a sort of pathway, one which I fancied had been lately used. Pursuing my way along this apology for a path, I found that it led to what had probably once been a solidly-constructed outhouse, but which was now nothing but a ramshackle shed. The door, which hung on a single hinge, looked as if, were it moved in either direction, it might fall off. I looked to see what might be on the other side of that door. The shed was littered with all sorts of discarded rubbish, mostly so buried under a wealth of dust and dirt and cobwebs that it was not easy to guess what they might once have been.

There was one exception to this state of dust and dirt, and that instantly caught my eye. In the corner stood what might have been a huge corn-bin; it was painted a dark green, and was covered by a lid which seemed to be still intact. On the lid was an old packing-case. That green-painted bin would have been all the better for another coat of paint, but in other respects it was in such a good state of preservation that it piqued my curiosity. I removed that packing-case and found that in the lid there was an aperture something like the slit in a post-office letterbox, only on a slightly more generous scale. It almost looked as if that packing-case had been meant to conceal its presence. I had shut the garden-gate as I had entered. As I was wondering what that slit might mean I heard the gate softly opened and closed. There was a quantity of rubbish at the other end of the shed. Bolting towards it, I used it, so far as the thing was possible, as a cover, crouching down behind it.

Steps were approaching. I did not know how much of me was visible, but I did not dare to risk the noise which would result from an attempt to alter my position. Someone came quickly into the shed—a decently-dressed boy of perhaps thirteen or fourteen years of age, not at all the sort of person I had expected to see. He had a good-sized leather bag in his hand. Going straight to the bin in the corner, taking a key out of his pocket, he slipped it into a lock which I had not noticed, and part of the front came away in the shape of a door—of sufficient size to enable him to thrust his entire body into the bin. When he came out again his hands were filled with a number of different-sized packages, done up, for the most part, in the rudest fashion—some in pocket-handkerchiefs, some in grimy rags, some in scraps of newspaper. One or two were secured in grimy-coloured sheets of brown paper, but generally they were innocent of string or of anything which could secure whatever they contained.

"PART OF THE FRONT CAME AWAY IN THE SHAPE
OF A DOOR."

The boy made no attempt to examine them. He quickly counted them—I could see his lips moving as he did so; nine he made the number. He dropped them into his leather bag, which he shut with a snap, re-locked the door of the bin, and passed out of the shed as quickly as he had come in, without once glancing in my direction.

So soon as I heard the garden-gate open and shut again, regardless of the state I was in, making the best of my way through the nettles and the thistles, I was after him. When I reached the entry he was already turning the corner. I quickened my pace, determined, if possible, to see where that bag was going; but it proved not to be possible, for when I caught sight of him again he was getting into a taxi which stood waiting by the pavement. I believe I would have boarded that cab if I had had a chance, and made a snatch at that leather bag, but before I had an opportunity to do anything the vehicle had passed from sight, and I was left lamenting. Pursuit was out of the question. The only means of locomotion seemed to be the tramcar, and by that I returned to Westminster Bridge.

My rooms were at the bottom of Sloane Street;[1] Mrs. Arnold's house was in an old-fashioned square within five minutes' walk. My impulse, when I arrived home, was to go round to her at once and warn her against Jane Stamp. But for two or three reasons I did nothing of the kind. I was dirty, tired, and hungry, and it was dinnertime, and also I was in rather a mystified frame of mind. I felt that when I had washed and changed and had something to eat, I might be able to look at the position with clearer eyes.

After dinner I decided that I would do nothing—at any rate, until the morning. I had half a mind to get on to the telephone and talk to them at Scotland Yard about "8, Elm Grove—back entrance." I had very little doubt about the meaning of that bin in the corner of the shed, and as to the contents of the parcels which the boy had taken out of it. The bin, I fancied, represented an ingenious system of dealing with stolen goods. I wondered how many of them were scattered over London. Who were the enterprising persons who had their contents cleared, as if they had been pillar-boxes, at stated intervals?

At what to me was an early hour I went to bed. However, going to bed I found was one thing; going to sleep was another. That night, for what I have since thought must really have been some occult reason, I could not sleep. I had to think—and when, in bed, one starts to think, it is nearly always fatal. As the minutes slipped by I became conscious of what I cannot but call an extraordinary obsession—it seemed to me that someone was calling to me at Mrs. Arnold's. Of course, the feeling was a ridiculous one, but there it was. Worse—it became stronger and stronger. At last, getting out of bed, switching on a light, donning a dressing-gown, I went into the sitting-room to read. But the feeling followed me there—it was really too absurd.

Then something curious happened—I thought so then, I think so now. I daresay it will read like nonsense written down in cold blood, but the actual thing was indescribable. All at once it was borne in on to me that my presence was needed at Mrs. Arnold's house—that

---

[1] A fashionable thoroughfare in Chelsea, one of the best residential districts in London. In "The Affair of the Montague Diamonds," Lee names her address as Sloane Gardens, a small street situated just south of Sloane Square, at the end of Sloane Street.

something was happening which made it necessary that I should be there. I put away the book which I was reading; I returned to my bedroom, dressed myself, and went out into the street.

I had glanced at the time while dressing, and noticed that it was after two. It was not a pleasant night—or rather morning. The air was filled with a hazy dampness; it did not exactly rain, but everything was wet. So far as I was able to judge, not a soul was in sight; nor was there anywhere a sound. I walked round to Mrs. Arnold's without seeing a creature on the way. So soon as I had gained the street the poignant feeling that someone stood in need of my instant help had passed away. Its going was quite a relief; while it lasted it had seemed to press upon some nerve in my brain. I stepped out quickly, but when I came to Tedworth Square[1] I slackened my pace.

I cannot explain the motives which prompted me that night; I can only say that directly I reached the square something told me that, if it were possible, it was of the first importance that I should not allow my movements to reveal my presence.

When I was close to Mrs. Arnold's I paused—if only because my ears were so wide open that I became conscious of a sound. Two voices were speaking—in what was little more than a whisper. Soft though their utterance was, I knew that they were angry—that one of the speakers was more angry than the other. The voices came from the garden; the gate was open. I wished I could have seen the speakers; it was impossible to hear. Suddenly one of the voices was raised—not much, but just enough to enable me, with my wide-open ears, to catch what was said.

"I tell you she says that she won't open. How the something do you think I'm going to make her? If I could get hold of her it would be dead easy, but how do you suppose I'm going to get at her when she's the other side of the window?"

The second voice was audible—I fancy expostulating with the other for speaking so loud. I slipped through the open gate on to the grass—Mrs. Arnold's old-fashioned house is detached and has quite a garden in front. A sudden idea had come to me. I guessed at the identity of those two speakers, and at what they were doing there. They were so absorbed in what they were saying, and I was

---

[1] A Chelsea square, approximately a quarter of a mile southwest of Lee's home.

so noiseless, that I saw them long before they saw me—a tallish man and a shorter one, carrying on an animated discussion beneath their breath.

The shorter man seemed all at once to lose control over his temper; he slightly raised his voice. I strained my ears.

"If she won't, she won't, there's an end of it—I'm off. No wild-cat games for me—that wasn't in the bargain. Her letting us into the house and putting everything ready is one thing; what you are after is quite another—and not for me. It wouldn't be for you if your monkey wasn't up."

The other man blazed out: "By Heaven, I'll kill her!"

"Yes, I daresay you'd like to—and expect me to take a hand in that. No, thank you, not for me. There'd be trouble if we were found here, and as we've already been here longer than I like, or bargained for, I'll say good night. You'd better come along with me."

"As she won't let me into the crib, as she swore she would, I'll get in without her; and if I once have my hands on her throat——"

He left his sentence unfinished. The other continued to remonstrate. Both were speaking louder than perhaps they knew.

"Now, don't you be a fool. You don't want to get into trouble, do you? The idea was to get her into trouble and keep out of it ourselves. You'll be able to get hold of her before very long and give her all the handling she needs. Now you come along with me. What's that?"

I had been standing under the shadow of a tree; unconsciously I had touched one of the lower branches. Both men spun round.

"Look!" exclaimed the shorter man. "There's someone there."

He stood not on the order of his going; he went at once,[1] before he had really finished speaking, and so quickly that in the same instant, as it seemed, he was through the gate and out of sight. The other hesitated, then he would have followed; but that I would not have. The tale which the girl's mother had told me, the facts with which I was myself acquainted, the threat which I had just heard him utter against his miserable dupe, the conviction which I had that it was his set purpose to use her for his own horrible ends, to ruin her body and soul, and then to cast her aside, caring nothing if

[1] A reference to *Macbeth*, 3.4.119-20: "Stand not upon the order of your going, / But go at once."

"I RUSHED OUT OF MY HIDING-PLACE AND CAUGHT HIM BY
THE COAT."

she spent years of her life in jail to pay for his misdeeds—I say that
these things rose up within me, so that when he tried to follow his
shorter friend I would not let him.

I rushed out of my hiding-place and caught him by the coat—he still wore that fawn overcoat, and I yelled with the full force of a healthy, vigorous pair of lungs:—

"HE DRAGGED A REVOLVER OUT OF HIS POCKET AND FIRED AT THE SHRIEKING WOMAN AT THE WINDOW."

"Police! Police! Help! Murder! Thieves!"

It was perhaps not the most dignified course I could have taken, but there was no time to consider. I did the only thing which, on the spur of the moment, it seemed to me I could do—I yelled and I stuck to him. For some seconds he let me hold him without making the slightest effort to break away; whether it was because he was dazed by the suddenness of my attack, or amazed at the penetrative quality of my voice, I cannot say.

"It's a woman!" he ejaculated, as if that great truth had only just burst on him. "Stop that noise and let go of my coat, or—you'll be sorry!"

I remembered that those were the words he had used on the platform at Waterloo to illustrate what would happen to his unfortunate victim if she dared to call her soul her own, and the memory inflamed me.

"Oh, no, I sha'n't be sorry," I told him. "I shall be glad. It is you who will be sorry. Police! Help! Thieves!"

Loudly I yelled again. He tried to shake me off; then, finding that it was not so easy, he caught me by the wrist. As he did so I heard the window open in the house behind him, and a woman's voice cried out:—

"George, don't hurt her! Go, George, go—go!"

The last repetition of the word "go" rose through the air like a trumpet, or rather like a frenzied shriek. The woman's whole force was in the injunction the word conveyed. He released one of my wrists, put his hand into his overcoat pocket, swung round—I was for the moment stunned by the unexpected report of a pistol. Before I had even the dimmest suspicion of his intention, he had dragged a revolver out of his pocket and fired at the shrieking woman at the window. Just one queer sound came from her, then all was still.

"I said I would give you something for yourself," he remarked, speaking to the place where the woman had been, as coolly as if he were making some commonplace observation, "and that's it. I don't think you'll want any more."

"You've killed her!" I screamed. "You murderous villain, you've killed her!"

I tried to grip him by the throat. Had I been cooler I might have done it and held him fast; I might at least have been upon my guard. But I was in such a storm of rage that I neglected the most simple precautions. He was not the kind of man with whom, at such a moment, it was safe to do that. He swung suddenly back towards me and struck with the muzzle of his pistol at my forehead. Down I went, and, to use a famous phrase, the further proceedings interested me no more.

Nearly all the rest of the story was in most of the papers. What my screams and shouts had begun the report of his pistol finished; the whole neighbourhood had been alarmed. So soon as he had felled me, before he could even attempt to escape, the police were on him. It was the girl who had called herself Jane Stamp who appeared at the window, and, aiming perhaps better than he knew, he shot her dead. She probably never spoke a word after his bullet struck her. For her it was perhaps as well. It is easy to be optimistic, and even sentimental, if you have no actual experience of the hard facts of life; if you have, it is difficult to see what promise of happiness life could have held for a woman who had begun as she had done.

They hanged him. At the last moment strength had been given the girl to refuse to play the despicable part he had planned. She was to have let him into her mistress's house. It contained many valuables. She was so to arrange matters that they would be placed within easy reach. She was even to drug, not only Mrs. Arnold and her daughter, but also her fellow-servants. While they were drugged the house was to have been ransacked. But the girl refused, after all, to carry out the programme he had planned, or even to admit him into the house—and for that he shot her. The first time I ever appeared in a witness-box was to give evidence against him. The judge complimented me on what he called the courage which I had shown; I congratulated myself on having been the means of bringing such a wretch to justice.

As to "8, Elm Grove—back entrance," I told that story to certain officials at Scotland Yard. That same afternoon the messenger was trapped as he was dropping the contents of the bin into his leather bag. There was nothing on him to show who he was or whence he came. Even when they questioned him he told them, with unnecessary plainness, what would happen to them before they got anything out of him—so they got something out of the driver of the taxi-cab instead. The lad tried to give a warning whistle, but even as his lips were shaped to whistle a hand was clapped across his mouth. The vehicle was waiting, as before, by the pavement. Instead of the small boy, two adults went up to the driver, in whom one of them instantly recognized an old acquaintance.

They induced him to talk. To begin with, they made him drive to Scotland Yard. There it was made plain to him that unless he supplied certain information he would find himself in an extremely unpleasant position. So plain was this made to him that, after what was really only natural hesitation, he supplied it. He placed the police on the track of one of the greatest combinations for dealing with stolen goods which the criminal world has ever seen.

As is so often the case in these cosmopolitan days, the heads of the business were abroad. To begin with, the police had to content themselves with the tails. As I had surmised, "8, Elm Grove—back entrance," was only one of a dozen branches in all the different parts of town; so that when a man stole, let us say, a watch, he had only to go to the nearest, attaching to it his name or pseudonym, and within a very short space of time there would come to him, at an address which was previously arranged, its value in cash.

Thief and receiver never saw each other. On the face of it there was nothing to show that the thing was stolen; while the person who had "found" it never knew who had rewarded him for his ingenuity. The business had gone on for years; it might have gone on for years longer had not those two men had the misfortune to have me as a fellow-passenger in the Greenwich tramcar.

MANDRAGORA

I had returned from weekending with a friend, and was having lunch at the railway-station dining-room before returning to my work. The place was crowded with that miscellaneous assemblage which is the peculiarity of such places. Just as the waiter had brought me what I ordered two men, coming hurriedly in, took the only vacant seats in sight—at a little table next to mine. Something in their appearance attracted my attention. They were of different ages. One was about thirty, tall, dark, square-faced; the other was possibly nearly twice that age, a little, white-haired man, who looked as if his health was failing. What caught my attention chiefly was that he seemed to be in such a curious state of nervousness; watching him gave one the jumps. At last his companion commented on it—they were sitting sideways to me, so that I could see both their faces.

"If I were you, Hutton, I should take something for it."

It was the first time either had spoken; perhaps it was the unexpectedness of the remark which caused the elder man to give a sort of lurch in his chair. He looked as if, for a moment, he did not grasp the other's meaning; then he sighed.

"Ah, Walker, I wish I could take something for it; but—who can minister to a mind diseased? Mandragora[1] would have no effect on me."

An unpleasant look came upon the other's face as he said:—

"I wish you wouldn't talk such nonsense. What do you suppose is the good of it?"

"There is no good in it—that's the worst of it; there'll never be any good in anything any more—we've murdered goodness. You're a different type of man from me."

"Thank Heaven!" The speaker took a long drink from his glass.

---

[1] Mandrake, a type of plant with hallucinogenic qualities used in magic and witchcraft. Hutton appears to be referencing Shakespeare indirectly: "Not poppy nor mandragora/ Nor all the drowsy syrups of the world/ Shall ever medicine thee to that sweet sleep/ Which thou owedst yesterday" (*Othello*, 3.3.333-336).

"For one thing, I am nearer the grave than you are; perhaps that's why I'm so much more disposed than you to think of what's beyond it. I never thought that I should go to the Judgment Seat with such a crime to answer for. I don't know what I shall say when I get there."

"If you don't stop talking like that, taking up that pose, you and I will quarrel."

"IF YOU DON'T STOP TALKING LIKE THAT YOU AND I WILL QUARREL."

"I'm not afraid of that, Walker; I'm inclined to wish that you and I had quarrelled before. Rather Dartmoor[1] with Young than torment with you."

"Hutton, I can't think what's come to you; you used not to be this kind of man. You'll worry yourself into actual illness if you don't look out."

"I'm a sick man already—sick unto death."

Although they were unaware of the fact, I had become more absorbed in their conversation than in my lunch. I thought, as he said that, how he looked it. There was a quality in the coming shadow which seemed to be upon his face which went to my heart. His companion went on:—

"Of course, if it pleases you to feel like that, I can't help it, can

---

[1] A men's prison in Devon, South-West England.

I? Only let me give you a tip. You played a trick on George Young; don't you try to play a second on me. It won't benefit you to go to the Judgment Seat with two crimes to answer for."

"That's true. Don't I know it? That's what holds me in bonds. I'd have made a clean breast of things before this if I were the only one who would have to suffer."

The younger man regarded his companion fixedly, a savage something coming into the expression on his face.

"Hutton, we did this thing together, but the first suggestion came from you. If I thought that because of any sophistical nonsense, or because your digestion was out of order, you were meditating putting me where we put him, I'm not sure that I wouldn't kill you."

"I wish you would kill me, Tom; if it weren't that you'd have to pay the penalty, I'd say do it at once. I dare not determine my own life, but—God forgive me for saying so—if someone would do it for me I'd be grateful."

His sincerity seemed to impress his younger companion, who looked at him as if seeking words with which to answer; then, as if finding none, he summoned the waiter, paid their joint bill, and rose from his chair.

They went out. They had got through had their lunch in a very few minutes. Since their entry I had barely touched mine. I had, before I knew it, become a confidante in a tragedy in circumstances which had deprived me of the little appetite I had had. I sat with that old man's face in front of me long after they had gone.

For days afterwards I kept asking myself what was the nature of the tragedy which made that old gentleman so willing that his companion should kill him.

In the late summer of that year I went to a seaside town, which I will call Easthampton.[1] I believed it to be an obscure hamlet, until on getting there I found it impossible to rent a bed and sitting-room, either for love or money. It seemed that every house in the place was crammed to the roof. When I had received the same answer for about the twentieth time, I asked the fly-man, who was taking me from one likely house to another, if there was still another he could think of.

"I can't say, miss, that there is—at least, there is a cottage in the

[1] An imaginary town.

fields about half a mile along the shore in which you might find accommodation; but I can't say that I know much in its favour."

There was something in his tone which, ordinarily, might have prompted me to ask him what he meant; but there was my box, and there was I, and neither of us wanted to go back to town. I told him to drive me to that cottage. It turned out to have just the accommodation I was looking for, and to be quite a charming cottage in itself. It was not overburdened with furniture, but there was all I needed, and the rooms were spotlessly clean. Then I liked the landlady; she was quite a pretty woman, possibly not more than twenty-six years old. She told me she had one child, a girl of six, and kept no servant, but did all the work herself.

I was never in more comfortable quarters. I had been threatened by one of those nervous collapses which do come to me when I have been overworked, and rest, comfort, and fresh air were the three things of which I had need. I found them all three at Laurel Cottage. And my landlady was a most charming person; no make-believe lady, but a very real one. She was very reticent. She told me that her name was Mrs. Vinton, and that she was a widow; her husband had been dead three years. Since she was practically my sole companion, I saw a good deal of her. Mine being the only sitting-room the house contained, I asked her to share it with me —she and her little girl.

I never met a woman who had a finer gift of silence. She would sit for hours and say nothing. Not because she had nothing to talk about; she was not only a highly-educated woman, but she had seen a great deal of the world. What cause she had for silence I could not tell.

One evening, as I was going to my room to change my blouse for dinner, the door of the bedroom which she shared with her small child was wide open. She was putting the maid to bed. The child, kneeling at her mother's knee, was about to say her prayers, and the mother, bending over, said to her:—

"I want you, Nellie, to pray for papa to-night very specially indeed; it's his birthday."

Tears fell from her eyes on to the child's fair hair. I had left my walking shoes downstairs and was moving very quietly; I suppose that was why she had not heard me come.

The very next day something else occurred. I made another intrusion on her confidence—I protest, quite unwillingly. It was when I was passing the kitchen-window, which, like the bedroom-door on the previous evening, was wide open. I could not help seeing that Mrs. Vinton was on her knees beside the kitchen-table, that she had a photograph in her hands, that tears were streaming down her cheeks, and that her lips were forming words.

"My dear, my dear! May the Lord God bless and keep you, and send you back to me before my heart is quite broken."

Plainly there was a skeleton in this lady's cupboard. Why did she say her husband was dead, if she prayed the Lord God to send him back to her? It struck me that if he were to come back to her before her heart was broken he would have to be pretty quick. That some secret grief was eating into her soul was pretty clear.

It was the following evening, after dinner. We were at my sitting-room window, looking out across the wheat-field which divided us from the sea. Although she had done her best to hide it, I felt pretty certain that she had been crying nearly all day long.

"If you are not careful, Mrs. Vinton, you will make yourself ill."

With this remark I broke a silence which was becoming almost painful. She started, and her cheeks were flushed.

"Why do you say that?" she asked, with startled eyes.

"Because it is so obvious. I wonder if you'll forgive me if I say something? Do you know that each of us has been keeping a secret from the other?"

"What do you mean?" Her surprise seemed to increase.

"The secret I have kept from you is that I have the gift of seeing what people say by merely watching their lips, even if they are speaking to themselves."

"I don't understand. How can you possibly do that?" Her eyes seemed to grow larger; they were very pretty eyes.

"The secret you have been keeping from me is that your husband is still alive."

I had done it then. She got off her chair with quite a jump.

"Miss Lee!"

I thought she was going to say things to me—pointed things; she would have been quite justified. What she actually did was to collapse in a sort of heap on to the floor, pillow her head on the seat of the chair on which she had been sitting, and burst into tears. It was my turn to be startled. Kneeling beside her on the floor, I put my hands on her shoulders, whispering:—

"I am so sorry to have intruded on your sufferings, but I could not help it. I would not have said a word about it, only I felt you were in such trouble, and I thought that I might help."

"SHE PILLOWED HER HEAD ON THE CHAIR AND BURST INTO TEARS."

She stood up, the tears still streaming down her cheeks.

"I am ashamed of myself, Miss Lee. I have been ashamed ever since I told you I was a widow, and afraid because I knew you would find out. I suppose someone has been telling you something?"

"Not a word; all I know you have told me yourself."

I explained to her how it was. Her tears ceased to fall; the expression on her face was like a note of exclamation.

"You see, it is because of this gift I have of reading people's most secret thoughts—sometimes, as in your case, even against my will

—that I thought I might be of some little help to you. That gift of mine has been of help to people now and then."

"I don't see how you can be of help to me. It's quite true, as you say, that my husband is alive; but he might as well be dead, because he's in prison."

She said it with what I dare say she meant to be an air of defiance; but even as she spoke she shuddered, and she put her hands up to her face.

"I beg your pardon, Mrs. Vinton; I did not guess it was that way. Please forgive me. Still, perhaps I can be of help to you."

"My husband was sentenced to fourteen years' penal servitude; he has served three. In those circumstances I don't see what help you, a perfect stranger, can be to me. I had a little money when—when it happened, but it is nearly all gone. I thought to make a little by letting lodgings, but I have not made enough to pay the rent even of this cottage."

"I might at least be able to send you some lodgers."

"Do you think people will come and lodge with me when they know who I am? They whisper all sorts of things about me in East-hampton, I know. I don't suppose anyone knows the whole truth about me. I have done my best to hide it, but even as it is they shun me as if I were the plague."

I was at a loss for things to say, the situation being one for which I was so utterly unprepared. Presently she gave me unlooked-for help, while inflicting on me what was very like a snub.

"This is a subject, Miss Lee, on which you have forced my confidence—I am not sure quite fairly. Whether you go or stay, on one point there must be no misunderstanding: it is a subject on which you must never speak to me again. But before quitting it for ever, I should like to make myself clear to you on one matter: the jury found him guilty, the judge sent him to prison for fourteen years, the world thinks that punishment well merited—but I know that my husband is innocent."

She turned to leave the room, but something made it impossible for me to let her go.

"Mrs. Vinton! One moment, please! Don't you see that if your husband is innocent that is just the point on which I might be able to help you?"

Again her manner was not encouraging.

"Help me? You? How can you help me? You will have to work a miracle to restore my husband to his former place among his fellow-men. Yet I tell you he is innocent."

"Even miracles may be worked. You say that he is innocent. I have sufficient confidence in your judgment, Mrs. Vinton———"

"My name is not Vinton; nor is my husband's—his name is George Young." I suppose it was because I started that she added: "Now you will probably adopt a different tone; in common with all the world, you held my husband to be guilty."

"I know nothing either of your husband's innocence or guilt. Nearly four years ago I left England for a long tour round the world. Your husband's trial must have taken place while I was away. If there was an account of it in any of the few English papers I saw during my absence I never read it."

"I saw you start when I said my husband's name was George Young. If you did not know it, why start as if you did?"

Her tone was suspicious, even resentful.

"You have heard how the mouse helped the lion," I said. "I honestly think it is within the range of possibility that I may be able to help you. You say your husband's name is George Young. Tell me about him. With what was he charged?"

Abandoning her intention of quitting the room, she had sunk upon a chair. Her words limped a little.

"My husband was managing clerk to a firm of solicitors. He was about to be made a partner when it was discovered that, among other things, a large number of securities which had been entrusted to his principals for safe keeping were missing. They were very fond of George, and for his sake as well as their own they did their best to try to conceal the facts in hope of restitution. There was a trust fund of rather more than twenty thousand pounds, of which they were custodians; when the trustees wanted the money it was gone. They charged George with taking it. Other charges were made against him in the course of the trial, but it was on that charge that he was found guilty and sentenced to fourteen years' penal servitude."

The story, told thus baldly, did not sound very lucid, but my thoughts were travelling in a direction of their own; they were in that railway refreshment-room in which two men were lunching at a little table next to mine.

"What was the name of the firm by which your husband was employed?"

"Hutton, Hutton, and Walker. Young Mr. Hutton had died some time before the discoveries were made. The firm consisted of old Mr. Hutton, the senior partner, and Mr. Walker."

"Was his name Thomas Walker, and did Mr. Hutton sometimes call him Tom?"

"You know the firm—or do you know Tom Walker? His name was Tom. I was almost engaged to him once, and should have been quite if George had not—well, you know."

A faint flush tinged her white cheeks. I wondered if that had had anything to do with the position Mr. Walker had taken up.

"Is Mr. Hutton a little man, all a bundle of nerves?"

"His nerves were strong enough before the trouble began; he was a very able man. His health broke down after it was over; he grew old all of a sudden. Now he is ill and, I believe, unhappy—at least, he says so. It seems to have been almost as great a trouble to him as to me. Once he found out where I was and came to see me; he was so changed that I hardly knew him. I cannot help thinking that he has my movements watched, because when I came here I not only concealed my address, but I changed my name. Yet the other day he wrote to me a curious, rambling letter, parts of which almost suggested that he was in his second childhood. He is at Torquay,[1] and hints that he does not expect to leave it again alive."

"What is his address at Torquay? It is just possible that I may go and see him."

When she had given me old Mr. Hutton's address at Torquay, and had gone to bed that night, I was convinced that something like a gleam of hope had come into her life, the responsibility for which lay on me.

I went to Torquay the very next day, and a tedious journey it was. On arrival I put up at an hotel on the Strand,[2] dined, spent a very dull evening, and went to bed. The next morning, when, waking up, I remembered where I was and what I was there for, I asked myself

---

[1] A fashionable seaside resort in Devon.
[2] The street immediately fronting Torquay beach.

what on earth I was to do. However, I dressed and had breakfast, then went into the public gardens on the other side of the road, armed with a book and a newspaper. After I had had enough of reading I began to walk about. There were not many people in the gardens. There was an elderly woman alone on one seat, who was certainly an old maid, and a very old lady alone on the next, who looked as if she never could have been young, and on the third there was an old gentleman——

I stopped as I was approaching that old gentleman, suddenly conscious of a little catching of the breath. I had seen that old gentleman before—once; it was to see him a second time that I was there. He sat back in his seat, with his eyes closed; but not even the most unobservant could have supposed that he slept—there was a look upon his face which no sleeper ever has. He looked to me like a very sick man indeed—smaller than when I had seen him first, as if he had lost both flesh and vitality.

I was wondering whether or not to address him, and what method of address to employ, when I had another little shock of surprise. Someone else had entered the gardens—a tall, upstanding, quite young man. It was the square-faced man who had sat with the other at the adjoining table. He struck me as being the kind of man who does observe. I had an uncomfortable feeling that he had noticed me on what was likely to prove that momentous occasion. He eyed me as we passed each other, as if my face was not entirely unfamiliar, as if he were asking himself where he had seen it before.

He went one way, I the other. I had no doubt that he was making for the old man on the seat. Turning into a side-path upon the left, I turned again into another narrower path which ran parallel with the broad one I had left. I retraced my steps along it. Between the intervening shrubs and trees I could see the seats on the broader walk. When I came abreast of the one on which the old man had been sitting he was talking to the new-comer. A clump of rhododendrons was between us, high enough, unless particular search was made for a suspected presence, to serve as a screen. Standing as far back as I could without losing sight of the two men's faces, I made it serve as a screen for me, and I watched, so far as I could, what was being said between the two.

The younger man came up while the elder still had his eyes

"I WATCHED, SO FAR AS I COULD, WHAT WAS BEING
SAID BETWEEN THE TWO."

closed. He stood for a moment observing him, then he greeted
him, "Good morning."

The old man opened his eyes, looking up at him as if he were not quite sure who he was; then he said:—

"It will never be a good morning to me again—never—never!"

The other smiled ironically.

"Isn't that rather a strong thing to say on a morning like this, when the sun's in a cloudless sky?"

"Nor will there be any sun again for me—ever; for me there is only outer darkness."

I could see from the look on the younger man's face that he sneered.

"Aren't you slightly melodramatic? Didn't you sleep well?"

"I have not slept well since the day on which George Young went to jail; his going murdered sleep.[1] All night I lie in agony."[2]

"You were saying the other day how you longed for something to give you sleep; here is something."

The speaker took out of a waistcoat-pocket a small blue phial, offering it to the old man on his open palm. The old man looked at the phial, and then up at the face of the person who offered it.

"What is it?"

"Mandragora."

"Will it give me sleep?"

"If you choose, sleep which will know no waking."

The two men exchanged looks—such strange ones; then the elder took with tremulous fingers the phial off the other's palm. Then, when he had got it, he shut his eyes again. The younger, without another word, left the gardens.

I waited. If I could help it I was not going to lose sight of the phial which was in the old man's hand. Presently an empty bath-chair[3] came down the walk. The chairman, assisting the old man to enter, began to draw him away. I followed. They stopped at what I recognized to be the house in Belgrave Road[4] which Mrs. Young

[1] A reference to *Macbeth*, 2.2.35.

[2] A reference to Thomas Hood's 1831 poem 'The Dream of Eugene Aram, the Murderer', in which the speaker, like Macbeth, is prevented from sleeping by guilty thoughts.

[3] An early version of the wheelchair, originating in Bath, England and often used by invalids at spa resorts. A light carriage or a wheeled chaise, the bath-chair could be pushed by an attendant or drawn by an animal.

[4] A major street west of the Strand in Torquay.

had given me as Mr. Hutton's address. The old man entered the house leaning on the chairman's arm. I walked up the road, then back again.

Twenty minutes had elapsed since the old man entered. It was one of those lodging-houses in which the hall-door proper is never closed in the daytime. Turning the handle, I passed into the hall. I had noticed that the bath-chairman had led the old gentleman into a room on the left. After momentary hesitation I turned the handle of that room and, without any sort of ceremony, passed in. It was, as I had expected, a sitting-room. There was a big arm-chair on one side. On this, propped up by cushions, was the old man. I perceived in an instant that my intuition had not been at fault, that I was only just in time. He had a small blue phial in his hand; the cork was out; he was in the very act of raising it to his lips. I crossed the room, and it was in my hand almost before he knew it. There was no label on the phial, but one sniff at its contents was enough to tell me what it was.

"Do you imagine, Mr. Hutton, that by committing suicide you'll escape the consequences of crime? That when you stand before the Judgment Seat you'll be able to excuse yourself by pleading that you murdered yourself because you had murdered another?"

He stared at me as if I were some supernatural visitant; his jaw dropped open, his head fell back, he was one great tremble. I went on:—

"When you allowed George Young to be sent to prison for the crime of which you were guilty, you practically committed murder; you slew the better part of him, his character and reputation—to say nothing of the unceasing torture which you propose to inflict on him for fourteen long years. Conscience has you by the throat; God punishes in this world as well as the next. Do you think this will save you from the wrath to come?"

I alluded to the phial. He stammered out a question:—

"Who are you?"

"I am the voice of the avenging angel, calling you to account for the evil you have done and still would do. You foolish old man! Are you so ignorant as not to know that only through repentance comes forgiveness? Repent—there is still time—and God's infinite mercy will give you peace at last."

He gasped; I thought every moment he would collapse.

"If I only thought it! If I only could believe it!"

"Surely your own common sense must tell you that there is at least more chance that way than this?" I held out the phial.

"I do not know who you are, where you come from, what you want with me; but—if I only could believe that by doing what you say—I could be at peace again with God and man!"

He did believe before I had done with him, or, if his faith was not so perfect as it might have been, he did as I wished. He made a complete confession of the whole painful business. I wrote down every word he said. Then I read over to him what I had written; the landlady was called in, and in her presence and mine he signed it.

When I was alone again with Mr. Hutton I was struck by what I have noticed on other occasions—that there is some truth in the saying that "open confession is good for the soul." Confession had done him good—visible and obvious good; he owned as much. His tongue once unloosed, he became positively loquacious. He told me many things about himself which enabled me to understand the situation better than the bare outlines of the formal confession he had just now made.

His son had been the thief, his only child. When detection threatened, to escape punishment he had poisoned himself. How he had obtained the poison remained a mystery. And not only so, the tragedy had been handled in such a fashion as to make it appear that George Young had been to blame for it. At the trial certain evidence was produced that made it seem that he had been Young's victim; that he was of such a sensitive nature that, rather than face what must be the result of George Young's villainy, he preferred to die. As I heard this part of the tale I thought of the phial which had been given to the old man, and I drew my own conclusion.

When I left Mr. Hutton I returned to my hotel, to find a telegram awaiting me. It was in answer to one I had sent while I had been following that bath-chair. I smiled as I read it; I glanced at the clock —and I thought I saw my campaign finished. I had learnt from Mr. Hutton where Mr. Thomas Walker was staying; he was in a house in the higher part of the town, which belonged to a relative of his, and of which, in his relative's absence, he was, with the exception of some sort of servant, the only occupant. About a quarter to four, at which time the London express reaches Torquay, I went to call at Mr. Thomas Walker's, leaving at my hotel a note for a person whom I told them I presently expected.

The address the old man had given me was Tormohan, Ilsham Road.[1] Any idea I might have had of introducing myself to Mr. Walker as I had done to Mr. Hutton vanished directly I saw what kind of place Tormohan was. It was shut off from the main road on which it stood by a high wall. Admission was gained by a gate which opened on what was presumably some sort of passage. The way to get that gate to open was to pull at the old-fashioned bell which hung beside it. I pulled; when nothing particular happened I pulled again. I pulled four times before the door was opened a few inches, and the square-faced man looked through the opening. Rather an odd dialogue took place, which I commenced:—

"Mr. Thomas Walker?"

"Who are you? What do you want?"

"I wish to see you on very important business, and my name is Judith Lee."

"Haven't I seen you somewhere before?"

"It is possible; but I think I shall be able to satisfy you when you have allowed me to enter."

He opened the door just wide enough to allow me to enter, and I went in; the moment I was in he closed it. We were, as I had expected, in a sort of passage covered with a glass roof. He led the way to the house; I followed. We passed through another door, which this time was opened by turning a handle. We went into a dark hall, and then into a room at the back which was shadowed by a big tree, which grew nearly up to the window. When we were in the room he eyed me with what I felt were inquiring glances.

"Did I understand you to say that you are Miss Lee? On what business, which is of such great importance, do you wish to see me? I should have told you, if you had not said your business was so very important, that I was alone in the house; the woman who acts as servant is out, which explains why you were kept waiting at the door and why I answered your ring myself."

The thought of the innocent man, despairing, desperate with a

---

[1] A major street east of the Strand in Torquay.

sense of wrong, wearing his life out within the prison walls, which must seem to him like some hideous, mocking, unending nightmare, and of the woman, young, pretty, gentle, delicate, refined, with her white face, hopeless eyes, broken heart, longing with a longing which she knew never would be gratified for the beloved husband of whom she had been so foully and cruelly bereft—these rose before me, moving me to sudden rage, so that I broke into language which amazed Mr. Thomas Walker.

"The business which has brought me here is to tell you that you are a contemptible, cowardly, murderous scoundrel, and that the hour is struck in which your sins are going to find you out. That, in the first place."

He stared as if he wondered if I were mad; then he smiled oddly.

"That, in the first place. And in the second?"

"In the second, I am going to enter into details, by way of recalling certain facts to your recollection." Then I jumped at my fences without stopping to consider what was on the other side. "How many years ago is it since you began to incite young Frank Hutton to rob his father?"

At that he did change countenance; I had found a safe landing on the other side of the fence.

"What on earth are you talking about? Who are you, and what do you want with me?"

"You taught Frank Hutton to be a thief; in a small way at the beginning, on a large scale later on. You shared his ill-gotten spoils; yet, when detection threatened, you so played upon his fears that you induced him to commit suicide, in order to escape the consequences of what were more your misdeeds than his. Did you, a lawyer, forget that when A assists B in committing suicide A is guilty of murder? When you put the poison within Frank Hutton's reach, knowing perfectly well the use he was about to make of it, you committed murder; for that murder the law is presently going to call you to account."

The way in which he looked at me! I already began to suspect that his fingers were itching to take me by the throat. He merely said:—

"Is that so? May I ask from what quarter you have acquired the facts on which you base your rather surprising observations?"

The feeling was growing momentarily stronger in me that this man was one of those unspeakable creatures who are dangers to whoever they are brought in contact with.

"Not content with destroying young Frank Hutton, soul and body, to cover your own offences, you proceeded to wreck his father's happiness and to lead him into crime. You lied to him about his son; you were so skilful as to be able to make him believe that his boy was the sole offender, and then, pretending that it was your desire to spare him shame, you put it into his head to lay the burden upon an innocent man. You were so skilful as to make it seem that the suggestion came from himself and not from you. You unutterable thing!"

This time when I paused he said nothing. I was aware that he was all the more dangerous on that account.

"You made black seem white; you manufactured false evidence; you lied, and lied, and lied—and George Young was sentenced to fourteen years' penal servitude. Thief, murderer, liar, you have succeeded in doing that! I have no doubt you hoped that you were safe at last, you short-sighted fool! The mills of God grind slowly, but they grind exceeding fine—your sort they grind to powder. You are already being slipped between the stones; your course has run."

The grimace which distorted his face was rather a grin than a smile as he asked:—

"In the name of all that's marvellous, from what mad-house have you been permitted to escape?"

"When you planned that grand *coup*, putting the onus of all your guilt upon an innocent man and shutting him up for fourteen awful years, you overlooked one small point: that all men are not devils, that to some is given the saving grace of repenting their sins. And so poor a judge of character are you that you were unaware that your own partner, your first victim's unhappy father, was one of them. From the moment he sinned he began to repent."

He interrupted me, speaking, for the first time, savagely.

"Have you been talking to old Hutton? Has he been coaching you in this tissue of nonsense?"

As before, I left his questions unanswered; I simply went on.

"Fortunately for himself, your partner was one of those who cannot know happiness unless his conscience is clear and he is at peace with God. Better be whipped in this world than through all eternity. You had his son in your mind. By inciting him to self-murder you believed yourself to have escaped one danger. You hoped, by inducing the father to imitate his son, you would escape another. To-day—only a very little while ago—you murdered him."

His skin became livid, his lips trembled, words stuck in his throat, fear touched his heart.

"What—what do you mean?"

I believe he meant to say more, but could not. He shrank back from me as if in physical terror. I gave him no quarter. I held out my right hand, palm uppermost. On it was the small blue phial.

"Do you recognize that?"

He looked at it as if it were some dreadful thing; again he stammered his question:—

"What—what do you mean?"

"This morning I saw you give that phial to your partner, Michael Hutton. He has long had it in his mind to escape from the weight of remorse which has made life intolerable to him, as you are well aware. I saw you give him this phial a few hours ago in the public gardens. He said to you, 'What is it?' You replied, 'Mandragora.' He asked, 'Will it give me sleep?' You said, 'If you choose, sleep which will know no waking.' You let him take the phial between his shaking fingers, and you walked off, knowing that you had left death behind you."

There was a momentary silence; he cast shifty glances round him, as if he sought on every side some way of escape, finding none. Presently he asked, moistening his parched lips with the tip of his tongue before he was able to pronounce his words:—

"Is—is old Hutton dead?"

"Do not imagine that that will profit you. He made complete confession. The whole story is set down in black and white, signed by his own hand. This phial will avail you nothing."

Suddenly I realized that he was eyeing the tiny glass bottle with a new expression in his glance.

"I don't believe it's empty." He said it almost as if he were speaking to himself. He drew closer. "I don't believe the contents have been touched."

He made a sudden grab at the phial; I withdrew it just in the nick

"HE HAD ME BY THE THROAT BEFORE I HAD EVEN REALIZED THAT DANGER THREATENED."

of time. There was the sound of an unmusical bell.

"Who is that?" he asked.

I said: "Had you not better go to the door and see?"

He looked at me. I suppose he saw something on my face which set his own thoughts travelling.

"Is it someone for you?"

"It is someone for you—at last!"

"Is that so? Someone for me—at last."

He stopped; there was silence. The bell rang again. I was just about to suggest again that he should go and see who was at the outer door when—he leaped at me. And I was unprepared. He had me by the throat before I had even realized that danger threatened. I was to blame; I ought to have been on my guard. As it was, so swift were his movements, so strong his grip, that I was already finding it hard to breathe before I had a chance to pull myself together.

I am a woman, but no weakling. I have always felt it my duty to keep my body in proper condition, trying to learn all that physical culture can teach me. I only recently had been having lessons in jiu-jitsu[1]—the Japanese art of self-defence. I had been diligently prac-tising a trick which was intended to be used when a frontal attack was made upon the throat. His preoccupation, his insensate rage, his unpreparedness, which was even greater than mine had been —these things were on my side. Even as, I dare say, he was thinking that I was already as good as done for, I tried that trick. His fingers released my throat, and he was on the floor without, I fancy, under-standing how he got there. I doubt if there ever was a more amazed man. When he began to realize what had happened he gasped up at me—he was still on the floor: "You—you ——"

While he was still endeavouring to find adjectives sufficiently strong to fit the occasion the inspector for whose attendance I had telegraphed to Scotland Yard came into the room. In the note I had left at the hotel I told him to follow me at once, and if he was not able to obtain instant admission to the house, then he was to use means of his own to get in quickly. I had had a premonition that I might have trouble with Mr. Thomas Walker. The inspector had some skeleton-keys in his pocket which had once been part of a skilful burglar's outfit; when there came no answer to his ringing he promptly opened the front-door with them.

Mr. Thomas Walker understood what the new-comer's presence

[1] A Japanese martial art, allowing an unarmed combatant to defeat an armed opponent.

meant; he needed no explanation. In the struggle I had dropped the blue phial, a fact which he realized quicker than I did. Before I knew it had fallen he, still on the floor, had snatched it, had the cork out, was putting the bottle to his lips.

"Stop him!" I cried. "It's poison!"

I cried too late; before we could reach him he had emptied the phial. He was dead, as quickly as if he had been struck by lightning. The phial had contained sufficient cyanide of potassium to kill fifty men. The death he had meant for his partner was his instead.

The following morning I returned to Easthampton. I had told myself, more than once, what a foolish person I was to meddle in such unpleasant matters, which were no concern of mine; but when I explained to Mrs. Young what had happened, and saw the look which came upon her face as she listened and began to understand, I was not so sure that I had been foolish after all.

Representations were made to the authorities. Michael Hutton's confession was placed before them, together with certain facts which came to light when examination was made of Thomas Walker's papers. George Young was pardoned—for what he had never done. Old Mr. Hutton was arrested; he died before the magistrate's examination was concluded. It was found that he had made a will by which all he possessed was left to the man he had so cruelly injured.

THE AFFAIR OF THE MONTAGU DIAMONDS

Passing through the Embankment Gardens[1] one cold, bleak after-noon in March, I saw a man accost a woman who was some little distance in front of me. As he spoke she turned her head, and, having looked at him, started running as for life. The man stopped, stared after her, and laughed; then, turning on his heels, began to retrace his steps. I saw his face quite clearly. Words which he mut-tered to himself were framed upon his lips, sufficiently obviously for me to follow them.

"Very well, my dear, you wait a bit. You haven't quite learned your lesson yet."

He was a nondescript-looking sort of person—indeed, although he was, perhaps, not more than thirty, in a sense the whole man showed signs of wear. As he neared me he had the impertinence to smile. I decided that there was something about him which I did not like at all.

When I got on to the Embankment[2] I saw, on the other side of the road, the woman who had run away. She was leaning against the wall beside the river, holding one hand against her side, gasping for breath. My curiosity aroused, I asked her:—

"What's the matter? Are you feeling ill?"

"A man—spoke—to me, and—frightened me—nearly—out of my senses," she answered, brokenly.

"What did he say to you? What sort of man was he?"

"He—was the man—who—was the cause—of all my trouble. I—lost my situation—because of him."

"How was that?"

---

[1] Victoria Embankment Gardens, a small green space just north of the Thames between Waterloo Bridge and Hungerford Bridge.

[2] Victoria Embankment, a major thoroughfare running along the north side of the Thames from the Houses of Parliament to Blackfriars Bridge. The construc-tion of the Embankment in 1865-70 was a major engineering project, involving improvements to sanitation and traffic congestion and the creation of a cut-and-cover underground tunnel.

"He—made them think—I had stolen things, and—I hadn't. They—turned me away—without a character. I—haven't been able —to get—another situation since, and—I'm nearly starving."

I believed her; I had seen hungry women before.

"Come with me," I said; "we'll get something to eat."

I took her to a popular restaurant in the Strand.[1] I had to take her arm in mine to enable her to get as far.

In reply to my questions, she told me that her name was Maggie Harris. She had been a nursery governess in a family named Braithwaite in Camden Town.[2] They lived over a sort of fancy shop, from which they got their living. She had been with them nearly a year. Then things began to be missed, both from the house and the shop. Suspicion began to fasten on her. She herself did not know why. There was an assistant in the shop named Turner. This man made overtures to her, which she resented. One day a number of new goods were missing from the shop. While she was out with the children her master and mistress searched her room; she felt sure it was at Turner's suggestion. The missing articles were found in her box. Her employers turned her out on to the pavement there and then. That was six weeks ago. She had been trying to find other employment ever since, and had failed.

Her father, she said, was dead. She had a stepmother, who lived near Wisbech, in Cambridgeshire.[3] She left her stepmother's house because of some dispute over a young man. Practically she was without a friend in the world, without a penny, and with no prospects of earning one. So I took her home with me.

I was at that time in occupation of a flat in Sloane Gardens.[4] Fifteen or sixteen days had gone by when, one morning, there was a ringing at my front door, and Miss Marshall came rushing into the sitting-room, where I was at work with Maggie Harris. Miss Agatha Marshall had the flat immediately below mine. She was a rather eccentric person, somewhere in the thirties, who, although pos-

---

[1] A major thoroughfare 300 yards north of the Embankment, connecting Trafalgar Square and Fleet Street.
[2] A suburb in North London.
[3] A market town in the Cambridgeshire Fens.
[4] A small street of town houses and mansion blocks just off Sloane Square in fashionable Chelsea.

sessed of considerable means, found it difficult to induce a servant to stay with her.

"Oh, Miss Lee," she exclaimed, "there have been thieves in my flat. I was alone; they might have cut my throat from ear to ear, and no one would have been any the wiser!"

"'OH, MISS LEE,' SHE EXCLAIMED, 'THERE HAVE BEEN THIEVES IN MY FLAT.'"

"Are you quite sure, Miss Marshall, of what you say?"

"Miss Lee," she replied, "they have taken my mother's pearl necklace."

"I expect," I said, "you have mislaid the necklace. You will find it presently, when you have searched again."

"Miss Lee, you don't know what you are talking about." All at once her tone was angry. "Last night I placed it in the biscuit-box. I filled it myself with biscuits and put the necklace at the bottom. Just now, when I went into the dining-room. there were the biscuits on the table, the box was empty, and the necklace was gone! And the worst of it is that something woke me in the middle of the night; I couldn't imagine what it was. I lay listening, and I suppose before I made up my mind I dropped off to sleep again. Perhaps it was just as well, because, had I gone into the dining-room and found thieves in the act of robbing me, goodness knows what would have happened."

I gave one or two directions to Maggie Harris and went downstairs with Miss Marshall.

Her story seemed to be correct. The pearl necklace did appear to have gone, and other things besides.

The mystery was how the robbery had been effected. Presently we had up Wheeler, the hall porter, and a policeman who was fetched off his beat. Both these persons were of opinion that entry had been gained by the simple process of unlocking the outer door of the lady's flat, while the porter was certain that no suspicious character had entered the building after the lady herself had returned, just before midnight.

When I went back to my own sitting-room I found Maggie Harris still writing. My intention was not to keep her in my employment, but I felt that a month's rest would not do her any harm, and at her request I had given her work of my own to do. The more I saw of the girl the more I liked her.

Directly I appeared she said a very singular thing.

"Wherever I go a robbery immediately follows. It's happened again and again. I'm not a thief. But it seems I might just as well be. You had better have me locked up or turned into the street."

As she looked at me I was struck, not for the first time, by the pallor of her cheeks, her bloodless lips, and her shining eyes. I knew that, while she was not exactly hysterical, she was super-sensitive.

"I take it, Maggie," said I, "that you did not steal Miss Marshall's pearl necklace and the rest of her belongings?"

"I didn't! I didn't! Don't you know I didn't?"

"I never suggested that you did, which makes it harder for me to understand why you should use such extremely foolish words as you did just now." As I saw that words were about to drop from the girl's eager lips I stopped her. "Please don't let us discuss the subject, Maggie. Miss Marshall's losses have nothing to do either with you or with me."

The mystery of the robbery in Miss Marshall's flat remained unsolved. Nothing was heard about the articles which she professed to have lost.

Some ten days after the robbery Wheeler, the porter to the flats, stopped me as I was entering the lift.

"Before I take you up, Miss Lee, if you don't mind, there are one or two things which I should like to say to you."

"What is it, Wheeler?" I asked.

"'HERE,' I SAID, 'YOU CAN'T COME IN HERE!
WHAT DO YOU WANT?'"

"I was thirty-two last week, Miss Lee," he began, with rather unexpected candour. "My mother died more than twelve months ago, and left me quite a tidy bit of money. I'm going to set up in business on my own account, but before doing so I want a wife, someone who can look after the house and the accounts while I look after the customers and the shop, and, with your permission, Miss Lee, I was thinking of Miss Harris."

I was a little startled as well as amused. He was a big, strong-looking fellow, with an honest face and nice manners.

"Does this mean that you have spoken to Miss Harris, Wheeler?"

"In a manner of speaking, Miss Lee, I have, and also I haven't. She won't listen to me because of a hulking chap with whom she has got herself mixed up, and who, I am dead sure, means her no manner of good."

"This is news to me, Wheeler. I wasn't aware that she had any masculine friends in London."

"She's got two, Miss Lee. She's frightened out of her life at the sight of one, and she ought to be at the sight of the other."

"Are you sure of what you say? How did you find out these things?"

"One afternoon Miss Harris came running in here as if for dear life. She ran up the steps without waiting for the lift, and she cried out: 'Don't you let him touch me!' The very next moment a fair-haired, thinnish, shabby chap appeared in the doorway. 'Here,' I said, 'you can't come in here! What do you want?' His eyes went all over me. I didn't fancy his looks at all. 'Does the young lady who just came in live here?' he asked. 'What young lady?' I said. 'You take yourself off. It's not my business to answer questions asked by chaps like you. If you've got anything to ask, you take yourself to the office and ask it there.'

"Three or four days afterwards Miss Harris went out, as she generally does of an afternoon. I was going out myself. Barr"—that was the name of another porter—"was taking my place. I stood here talking to him with my hat on. I spoke to her as she went past; she paid no more attention to me than if I wasn't there. I don't mind owning that I followed her. There was something about her looks I didn't understand. She walked down to the corner of the Pimlico Road.[1] There she met a tall, thin chap, in a long black overcoat and a big, soft, black felt hat. A motor landaulette[2] was standing by the

[1] A street just south of Sloane Gardens.
[2] A chauffeured convertible limousine.

pavement. He didn't speak to her and she didn't speak to him; they just got in and the thing went off. She came back about six o'clock, looking white and ill, and I could see that she'd been crying. 'I hope there's nothing wrong,' I said. She looked at me for a moment or two, as if she couldn't make out who was speaking to her, and then she said, 'Everything's wrong—everything. I wish I'd never been born.'"

Wheeler paused for a second or two, and when he continued, his tone was almost oddly serious.

"I've reason to believe, Miss Lee, that she's been to meet that chap twice since then, and each time she's come back in the same condition. My feelings about her being what they are, I thought the best thing I could do would be to speak to you. I've got a feeling for her about which I don't care to say more than I can help. I'm convinced she's the very wife I want, and I'd make her a good husband; if, Miss Lee, you wouldn't mind speaking a word to her."

I liked the man; I liked the girl. I felt that they might not make at all a bad pair. The first chance I had I hinted as much to the girl. Instead of improving in health as I had expected, she seemed to me to be wasting away. She seemed always to be listening; it gave one an uncanny feeling to watch her.

One day, while she sat typing some papers, I noticed that absorbed look upon her face which I had come to know so well.

"What are you trying to hear?" I asked her, with a smile.

She looked round at me with startled eyes.

"I can't think what it is," she said. "Do you know, I'm always catching myself trying to listen to something—sometimes in the middle of the night—and I always wonder what it is."

I changed the subject by saying:—

"Do you know what I think you want? A husband."

"What do you mean?" she asked.

"Has Mr. Wheeler never spoken to you, or dropped a hint?"

She was silent. Presently she leaned over the typewriter and covered her face with her hands. Then she stood up and turned to me a face on which there was a mysterious something which was beyond my comprehension.

"You had better kill me—than talk to me like that."

She scarcely spoke above a whisper; then she left the room. The young woman mystified me, gave me curious ideas. I had heard of dual personalities; I was beginning to wonder if hers was such a case.

The following morning I was walking up Sloane Street when I saw in front of me a figure which I recognized as that of the man who, by accosting Maggie Harris in the Embankment Gardens, had first brought her to my notice.

I thought of Wheeler's story of the fair-haired man from whom the girl had fled as for her life. I decided that I would see where this gentleman was going.

When he reached the top of the street he entered a restaurant. I unhesitatingly went in after him. He had gone right down the room, and had joined a man who sat at a small table which stood in a sort of alcove. Looking round, I perceived that another small table stood in such a position that, if I occupied a chair at it, I could get a good view of their faces.

The person I had followed was the man of the Embankment Gardens; I had only to get one glimpse of his face to be sure of that. But he was in better fettle than on that first occasion. As regards his companion, he recalled Wheeler's description of the man who had met Maggie Harris at the corner of the Pimlico Road. He was, if anything, a more unpleasant-looking person than the other. He was very dark, with a long, thin face, high cheek-bones, thin lips, and a pair of the most unpleasant eyes I have ever seen in a human head.

Their conversation was carried on, for the most part, in whispers; but they both had those peculiar mobile lips the movements of which are like printed pages to eyes like mine.

The dark man began by asking a question.

"Any news?"

"The best. It will have to be Saturday."

"Why? Any particular reason?"

"A very particular and excellent reason." The fair man leaned over the table so that his lips were closer to the other. "On Friday afternoon he brings home a parcel of diamonds, a bag full of money, and quite a number of other pretty things. The diamonds, the money, and the other pretty things are going to be put in the nice little safe which is let into the wall. There they will remain in quiet and safe seclusion while our Mr. Albert Montagu and his dear little wife run down to Brighton for the week-end. So now you see, my dear Professor Argus, why it will have to be Saturday—and that's where you come in. I suppose you will be able to come in?"

The dark man's features were contorted by a smile which did not appeal to me at all.

"I have her under my finger as I have that crumb; I can do with her as I please."

"You're a remarkable man, Professor," the fair man observed; "but—this is a pretty remarkable thing you're proposing to do."

"Is it any more remarkable than the other things? There was a certain pearl necklace. Wasn't it pretty remarkable how it came into our possession, without either of us moving a finger or incriminating ourselves in any way?"

"I dare say. But it does seem as if there were going to be unusual features about this little job. She's got to enter the place with a pass-key; she's also got to open a complicated safe with a very delicate and ingenious little instrument. That would take some doing if she were wide awake; in the state in which she will be it will be dashed difficult. I can't help thinking that nothing could be easier than for her to make a little mistake, and the slightest slip, from our point of view, would be fatal, because if she spoilt our tool—which she probably would do—she'd be done, and, what would be worse, so should we."

"You say you know the safe?"

"I do. At least, so far as the lock's concerned, I've got its double; it cost a pretty penny."

"Good! And you've got the key which will open it?"

"I have; you saw it yourself—both the lock and the key."

"And you saw her rehearse; you saw her take that key into her hand and open that lock without my saying a word?"

"I did; it was a wonderful performance. You are a wonderful chap, Professor."

"Then why do you worry? I've got that girl, body and soul. You may take it from me that if you've got your part of the business right, that little matter will come off on Saturday."

"Professor, you really are a marvel—here's to you, my boy. It was a stroke of luck my getting on her track again; and her having found such a comfortable home with our dear, tender-hearted, charitable Miss Judith Lee."

As I sat there following the conversation of those two scamps the whole diabolical conspiracy was plain to me before they had finished. They went first. I remained after they had gone, doing my best to decide on what would be the proper course to pursue. At last I came to the conclusion that the wisest thing for me to do would be to go to Dr. Riderman—so I went.

On the way I stopped at a public telephone call-office, rang up Scotland Yard, and requested Inspector Ellis to meet me at Dr. Riderman's residence in Harley Street[1] in the shortest possible space of time.

Horace Riderman is not only a great surgeon; he is also one of the leading authorities on certain psychological aspects of disease. Shortly after reaching Dr. Riderman's house Inspector Ellis was ushered in. I introduced them.

"Inspector Ellis—Dr. Riderman. I wish to tell you gentlemen a little story, and then to ask your advice—probably, also, your assistance."

I told them the story of my first meeting with Maggie Harris, and of the man from whom she had fled; of the account she had given me of herself; of how I had taken her to my home, and of what had followed. When I came to the robbery of Miss Marshall's pearl necklace Inspector Ellis interposed.

"It didn't come actually into my hands, but I remember hearing of that. I believe that, so far, the thief has not been found, nor the pearls either."

I said that was so. Then I described the effect the robbery had had upon Maggie Harris.

"Dr. Riderman," I continued, "the girl has been hypnotized. She's a hypnotic subject. That, to my mind, explains everything."

"If that is the case, Miss Lee, I can only ask for details."

Then I told of the interview which I had just witnessed in the restaurant, and of the conversation which followed.

"You remember that the girl told me that she had left her step-mother's house because of a dispute she had had over a young man.

---

[1] A street in Marylebone in Central London, associated since the nineteenth century with prominent private medical practitioners.

My theory is that the man who caused trouble with her stepmother, the man who met her in the Pimlico Road, and the Professor Argus, to whom I have just been introduced in the restaurant, are one and the same person. He probably found out quite early the power he had over her. That power has grown with the years, her capacity of resistance being so slight, until now, as I just now saw him say, he can do as he likes with her. This is a case, doctor, of hypnosis by suggestion."

"Is that sort of thing really possible?" asked the inspector.

I waved my hand towards the surgeon. "Ask Dr. Riderman."

"It's certainly possible; indeed, it is not easy, in the light of our present information, to say what in such cases is impossible. How far do your theories intend to go, Miss Lee? Are you asking us to believe that, at the suggestion of this man, Professor Argus, she took Miss Marshall's pearls?"

"I make no positive assertion. I'm merely here to tell you of a conversation which has just taken place. The man Turner spoke of persons named Montagu. Now, on the first floor in my block of flats there is a Mr. Montagu, and he has a wife. He is a diamond merchant in Hatton Garden.[1] It is his habit to bring home parcels of diamonds. He once told me that a parcel he had in his hand was worth nearly fifteen thousand pounds. When I asked what he did, in his flat, to ensure the safety of such valuable property he replied that there was a little hiding-place close to his hand where it would be as safe as in the Bank of England. That suggests the safe of which the man Turner spoke, and the instrument in the nature of a key with which the girl is to open it."

"Do you mean to say," struck in the inspector, "that a girl in the condition in which, according to you, Miss Harris is to be, could, with any instrument whatever, open so complicated a piece of mechanism as the lock of a really good burglar-proof safe?"

"That, again, is a point on which I prefer to say nothing. Mr. and Mrs. Albert Montagu are in the habit of going away for the week-end. If it is the intention of those two ingenious gentlemen that, while in a state of hypnosis, Maggie Harris is to make a burglarious entrance into their flat, nothing is easier than that you, and the

[1] A street in Holborn, Central London, which has been the centre of London's jewelry trade since the Middle Ages.

doctor here, and I should be there to see. We need not interfere—
we can just stand and watch. Afterwards, when she hands over to
the arch-villain the plunder which he has made her take—that will
be the moment for us to move. What is your opinion, Dr. Riderman?"

"I think, in the first place, it's a very remarkable story, Miss Lee.
Dr. Milne Bramwell[1] tells us of a woman who, being told while
in a state of hypnosis to do a certain thing at a certain hour in a
certain way, several days afterwards, being released from her hypnotic trance, did that exact thing, at the exact moment, exactly as
required, without being conscious that such a suggestion had ever
been made. I have seen that sort of thing myself more than once. I
think your notion, Miss Lee, that we should be on the spot to see if
she really does is not at all a bad one."

And we were there, all three of us—and another, making four.
The fourth person was Edward Wheeler; in my scheme he was
essential.

"I'll be there—you may depend on me, Miss Lee."

On the Friday afternoon Mr. and Mrs. Montagu got into a cab
and were driven away. Wheeler had been informed that the servants had been given a week-end holiday, and that the flat was to be
shut up. So far the man Turner's forecast of their movements had
proved correct.

During the early part of the Saturday I noticed that Maggie
Harris seemed to be in an acutely sensitive frame of mind. Towards
evening she grew restless. She kept giving what seemed to be invol-
untary movements, as if suffering from a sense of physical discomfort. Soon after ten o'clock she went to bed; ten minutes afterwards
I went to the telephone and rang up Dr. Riderman. In less than half
an hour he appeared with Inspector Ellis.

We three sat in my room waiting and watching. At one o'clock
Wheeler came upstairs and joined us.

"Is everyone in?" I asked. He replied in the affirmative.

It was just past two o'clock before anything happened. We were
in my sitting-room; the door was open; Dr. Riderman said that if

---

[1] John Milne Bramwell (1852-1925), a Scottish physician, advocate of the use of
hypnotism in medicine, and author of several books on hypnotism and hypno-
therapy.

the girl were really in a state of hypnosis she would not notice such a trifle as the fact that my sitting-room lights were shining out into the passage. All at once the doctor held up a forefinger.

"A handle is being turned. Which is her room?"

"It's the next but one to this." I listened. In the utter silence a faint sound was just perceptible. Soft footsteps came along the passage, then a figure passed my door.

"It's she," I whispered; "and I believe she's dressed."

"Why shouldn't she be?" observed the doctor. "Do you think he'd be such a fool as to let her walk about the place in her nightdress?"

Someone had gone along the passage and opened my front door. We all rose.

"Now, recollect what I tell you," said the doctor. "If I think it safe to speak I'll let you know; till I do, be as still as you can. If he has her well in hand there'll be no risk of our being seen; so far as we are concerned she will be stone-blind."

When we got out on to the landing she was moving softly down the stone staircase.

"Do you mean to say," whispered the inspector, "that she doesn't know what she's about? She moves as if she were in possession of all her senses."

"Wait a bit," replied the doctor, "and you'll see."

He spoke louder than the inspector. At that moment the girl, pausing, put the fingers of her left hand up to her cheek and seemed to listen.

"She heard you," whispered the inspector.

"She didn't; she may have received a suggestion from someone who is at goodness knows what distance from this; she never heard me. I'll prove it to you presently. Unless I'm mistaken, this is the most remarkable case of hypnosis by suggestion that I've ever witnessed."

Maggie Harris descended those four flights of stone steps, holding herself very upright, well in the centre, with as much assurance—in Inspector Ellis's words—as if she had been in possession of all her senses. When she reached the first-floor landing, pausing in front of Mr. Montagu's flat, taking a key out of the bosom of her frock, with it she opened the door, as steadily and surely, as if she had been wide awake. We had followed her—a curious quartet—

from step to step, without her once looking round.

"Where did she get that key from?" inquired Wheeler, as the Montagus' door yielded to her touch. "There are only two other keys which fit that lock besides Mr. Montagu's: one I've got, and the other is in the office."

"That's a master-key which she has," murmured Ellis. "The man who is handling her is an artist. He's seen that she's provided with proper tools, and nothing's easier, if you know how to set about it, than to provide oneself with a master-key which will open every door in a block of London flats."

Dr. Riderman had hurried through the open door, and I was at his heels. Behind me was Inspector Ellis, with Wheeler in the rear. One thing we noticed at once: the girl had not switched on the light.

"That shows the state she's in—light and darkness are the same to her."

As he said this the doctor himself switched on the light. There she was, threading her way among the tables and chairs as if she could see them perfectly well—yet she did not give the slightest sign that she was conscious of the amazing change which had taken place when the doctor touched that electric switch.

Maggie Harris passed from the sitting-room to the bedroom. Some little time before Mrs. Montagu had been ill in bed. I had visited her on several occasions, but had seen nothing to suggest that a safe was in the room. Yet the girl, who, I should certainly say, had never been there before, went straight to it. There were twin beds in the room; the wall between them was covered with hangings. Maggie drew one of these aside, touched a spring, and a hinged panel flew back; behind was a small safe painted green. She did something to the lock, very much as a blind person feels for the Braille type with the tips of the fingers, then she inserted something into the keyhole, went through some further mysterious performances with the tips of her fingers, turned with the greatest of ease the something which she had put into the lock, and the safe was open. Within was a small black leather bag—we were within a few feet of her and could see it plainly. She opened it, took out a little paper parcel, a canvas bag, and a packet of papers; shut it, closed the door of the safe, returned the hinged panel; then, wheeling round, moved straight towards us. She came so close to me that I had to draw back to prevent actual contact. Her head was erect, her eyes open, but the pupils were fixed. I had seen hypnotized persons before that night; I recognized that I was looking at one then. We held our breath and she went by, though if we had made a noise it would have made no difference. Dr. Riderman proved it by exclaiming, just as she was passing into the sitting-room:—

"Young lady! Miss Harris!"

Obviously unaware that a sound had been uttered, she contin-

" MAGGIE TOUCHED A SPRING, AND A HINGED PANEL FLEW BACK."

ued her progress across the sitting-room, passed through the hall door, and shut it in our faces. That was certainly unlooked for. Inspector Ellis, for one, was visibly disconcerted.

"After all," he cried, "the whole thing may be a trap. What fools we shall look! If she's locked it from the outside she may be clear away with her spoils before we can get out."

"Yes; but as it happens it isn't locked on the outside," observed Wheeler. He showed it by pressing back the latch, and the door was wide open.

Ellis was first on the landing, but we were soon after him. There was the girl, two flights above us. We re-entered my flat, the girl in front, we four behind.

"Now, what's to be done?" asked Ellis. "That piece of sugar-paper she's carrying is a parcel of diamonds. As your friend said, Miss Lee, there may be fifteen thousand pounds' worth. There's money in that canvas bag which she's got in her left hand; by the look of it, quite a decent sum. Those papers she's carrying may be valuable securities. Hadn't we at once better make sure that they're safe?"

"If by that you mean," I replied, "that you'd like to take them from her, I will remind you that what we want to do is to make sure of the scoundrel who has engineered all this. The only way to do that is to catch him with that stolen property in his possession. We want to establish her innocence, to make it clear that she's the helpless victim of a nefarious plot, and, what is not least, remove her from his influence."

"All I want to do is to make sure that the valuables are safeguarded," said the inspector.

"I'll make sure of that," I told him. "I promise you that nothing which she has taken from Mr. Montagu's flat shall pass out of mine without your knowledge. If you like, you might leave a man here to keep an eye on things; I don't think it would be a bad idea if you did. But you've only seen the first act of the drama. Be here in good time to-morrow, and I fancy you'll see the second act—and the end. What you'll have to do will be to arrest Professor Argus and his confederate, the man Turner."

The next day was Sunday. Maggie Harris rose at the usual hour; she seemed tired and depressed, as if her night's rest had done her little good. At half-past ten she started out to church; so far as I was concerned, her Sundays were her own. While she was getting ready I opened her bedroom door to ask her a question. As I did so I was struck by the oddity of her manner. I spoke to her twice without her seeming to take any notice of what I said.

I put on my hat and gloves, sent a message over the telephone, and waited for her to go out. When I heard her bedroom door open I went out into the passage. She walked right past me without seeming to take any heed of my presence. She had a prayer-book in one hand and a green leather hand-bag in the other. I jumped to a conclusion.

"Mr. Montagu's property is in that bag. She's going to meet that —that creature."

I followed her down the staircase. Dr. Riderman and Wheeler

were in the hall, the latter in mufti. Both of them took off their hats to salute her as she appeared, an attention on their part which she utterly ignored. We all three followed her as she went out into the street. Inspector Ellis, in plain clothes, was on the other side of the road. Without crossing to us, he moved in the direction in which she was going.

"You'll find she's going to the corner of the Pimlico Road," said Wheeler to me. "I believe that's where she always does go; that's where he always meets her. If I could only get within comfortable reach of him——"

He stopped—in time. His agitation was obvious. Dr. Riderman deemed it necessary to address to Wheeler a warning word.

"Don't you let yourself go; control yourself, my lad. You leave the conduct of this business to others."

We were nearing the end of Lower Sloane Street[1] when Inspector Ellis motioned to us from his side of the road. We stopped short, letting the girl go on. The inspector, on his side of the road, strolled carelessly on. Crossing the street, the girl disappeared round the corner. The inspector vanished too. In another moment the inspector reappeared; when he beckoned to us we moved forward. A taxicab was standing by the kerb. The inspector explained.

"She's in that motor-car with the Professor, as you say he calls himself." We could see that a closed car was moving rapidly. "In you get; this cab's mine."

We got in; the cab started. The inspector continued to explain.

"Some of our men are shadowing our friend in front. I don't propose to take him single-handed."

The cab ran over Ebury Bridge into Warwick Street, turning into what I afterwards learnt was Alderney Street,[2] then suddenly stopped. We were on the pavement in an instant.

"There's that other motor going off in front," observed the driver. "It's put the pair down. There is the girl turning into Sussex Street.[3] She don't seem well. The man has gone into the house four

[1] The street connecting Sloane Square and Pimlico Road.
[2] Ebury Bridge leads from Pimlico Road to Warwick Street (now Warwick Way) and then Alderney Street in Pimlico; a journey of half a mile.
[3] A street crossing Alderney Street, leading either towards the river or towards Victoria Station.

doors from this; I fancy the door must have been kept open for him
—he slipped in so fast."

Four men were coming towards us down the street.

"There are my chaps," said Ellis. "What we've got to do is to get
into that house before the Professor gets out of it—perhaps by a
back door. For the moment, we'll leave the girl to herself."

This did not appeal to Wheeler at all, for he made a rapid
movement towards the street into which the girl had turned. We
approached the house of which the driver had spoken.

"ONE OF THE INSPECTOR'S MEN RAN ON TO THE BALCONY."

Inspector Ellis had in his hand a key, which he inserted into the
keyhole, and which opened the door as easily as if it had been made
for it. An elderly woman was in the hall.

"Who are you?" she asked. "What do you want? What do you mean by coming into my house without knocking?"

There came a sound from somewhere above, as if a heavy piece of furniture had fallen. Thrusting the woman aside, the inspector ran up the stairs with us at his heels. There were two doors on the first landing, which he threw wide open; then, turning, sprang up three more stairs which were on the left, to a door beyond. He turned the handle—then exclaimed:—

"The door's locked. He's in here. Pankhurst, drive this door open."

A great, big man, one of the four who had met us outside, went rushing forward, and by the mere force of his impetus carried the door away as if it were so much matchwood. In another second we were all of us swarming into the room. Then I heard someone shout:—

"Look out! He's going to jump through the window."

Just as I entered the man whom I had heard addressed as Professor Argus jumped, before anyone could stop him. There was an old-fashioned French window leading on to a little balcony; it was open when I got into the room. I saw a tall figure pass through it, then vanish. One of the inspector's men, running on to the balcony, looked over the low railing.

"He must have struck the spikes of the railings and fallen on the wrong side to the bottom of the area. He's lying all of a heap."

Inspector Ellis's voice, as he replied to this information, was cold and official.

"Two of you men go down and look after him." He turned to someone else who was in the room. "You are my prisoner; if you are a wise man you won't make any fuss."

The man addressed did not look as though he were likely to make what the inspector called a fuss—it was Turner, from whom Maggie Harris had fled in the Embankment Gardens, and whom I had seen concocting his hideous plot in the restaurant. His confederate was dead, the arch-criminal. Whether his intention was to commit suicide, or merely to make a wild effort to escape from the police, was not clear. In his pockets were that whitey-brown paper parcel which we had seen Maggie Harris take out of Mr. Montagu's safe, and which contained a large number of uncut diamonds; the canvas bag, in which there were nearly a hundred pounds in gold, besides bank-notes; and the bundle of papers. The two keys—the master-key with which the girl had opened the outer door, and the ingenious instrument with which she had manipulated the lock of the safe—were actually found in Turner's hands.

When I returned to Sloane Gardens I found Maggie Harris in my sitting-room crying as if her heart would break; and by her side, doing his best to offer her consolation, was the hall porter.

MY PARTNER FOR A WALTZ

I was introduced to him by Florence Emmett at one of a series of subscription dances[1] which were held at the Kensington Town Hall.[2] He put his name down for a waltz, the only one for which I was disengaged. He danced well, being that not too common person, a partner whose steps go with your own. We began at the first bar, and we danced right through. I quite enjoyed it. Then he brought me something cool during the interval, and as I was sipping it he said—

"It is not always easy to catch a name when you are introduced, but I believe yours is Judith Lee?" I acknowledged that it was. "I have heard a good deal about you."

I looked at him. There was nothing unusual about his appearance. He was probably in the early thirties, of the average height, clean shaven, with dark brown hair, not bad looking, his weakest point being his chin, which receded, and which was smaller than it should have been. It seemed to me that there was significance in his tone.

"Yes; have you? I hope you've heard nothing very greatly to my disadvantage."

"I am told that you have what I may call, for courtesy's sake, a very singular power, Miss Lee." I glanced at him, waiting for him to continue. I wondered what was the matter with the man; there certainly was significance both in his tone and manner. "I am informed that you act as—what shall I say—a spy on all the world."

"Yes—who told you that?" He was eyeing me with what looked very like hostility, not at all as one expects one's partner to do after an enjoyable dance. I wondered what I had done to him.

"Is it true that by merely looking at that man who is sitting with a girl over there you can tell what he is saying to her?"

---

[1] Subscription dances were semi-public balls held in a public hall and organised by a committee or a set of patrons rather than a private host or hostess. The subscribers could bring along a set number of friends and would expect to be introduced to other guests.

[2] Kensington, a wealthy residential area in West-Central London.

"It is—perfectly true; I teach the oral system to the deaf and dumb."

"Indeed! Is that all you teach?" He certainly sneered. "It seems to me that you ought to be labelled in order that innocent people might at least have fair warning of the inconvenience, to say nothing of the actual danger, with which your presence threatens them."

He walked off without another word, in what seemed to me rather an amazing fashion. It is true that my partner for the next dance was advancing, but that was no reason why he should turn sharply on his heel and stride off as if I were some contemptible thing. What had induced the man to address me in that fashion I could not think—but it spoilt that dance for me. He put into words what I had often thought myself, that it was a dangerous gift I had; there were many occasions on which I wished that it was not mine. But then, what a moment to choose to tell me so—after a nice waltz, which he might at least have had the grace to tell me he had enjoyed—and he a perfect stranger! When Florence had introduced us I had not even caught his name—he seemed to have known mine beforehand.

I looked about for Florence, but when I found her she was so surrounded by other people, and so many persons kept worrying me, that I had no chance of asking her who the curiosity was. He did not stay very long; I doubt if he danced with any one after that waltz with me.

Until he did go, wherever I was I seemed to see him, watching me with an intentness which I very much resented. I was on the point of telling him so, and was crossing towards him when, as he saw me coming, again he turned sharply round, marched to the vestibule, offered a check, for which he received in return a coat and hat, and strode out of the building.

"Well," I said to myself as I watched him go, "what an agreeable gentleman you seem to be! Was it conscience, which drove you to rudeness and made you run away?—I wonder!"

Two days afterwards I was walking down the Brompton Road when a masculine person took his hat off and addressed me.

"I believe you are Miss Judith Lee?"

I stood and looked at him; to the best of my knowledge and

belief he was a stranger. I was asking myself who he was and what he wanted when I heard a little click, and, glancing round, perceived that another male creature was standing within two or three feet, with a camera in his hand, with which he had apparently just snap-shotted me. Before I had quite realized what he had done, there was another click—and it looked as if he had taken me in a second position. Before I could ask him what he meant by such behaviour— because no one likes to be snapshotted against one's will—without even so much as a recognition of my presence, he walked to the edge of the pavement, got into a taxi-cab which was waiting there, followed by the man who had accosted me, and off the vehicle went.

I felt rather wild—apparently I had been made the victim of a little trick. These gentlemen were hunting in couples; the business of the one was to accost me and induce me to stop, so that the other might bring his camera to bear, and make a photographic record of me at an unexpected moment. What did they mean by such conduct?

I asked this question of myself still more vehemently when, a few mornings afterwards, a registered letter was brought to me while I was still in my bedroom, and which I found, on opening the envelope, contained two mounted photographs, both of myself. I had no doubt whatever that they were prints of the snapshots which had been taken of me in the Brompton Road, and not bad likenesses they were, as far as the likenesses went, but conceive what my feelings were when I saw that on the top of each mount these words were printed: "Warning! This is the portrait of a public danger"; and at the bottom, "Judith Lee, Spy"—then, in the corner, in smaller letters: "This photograph will be circulated broadcast. If you see any one at all resembling this portrait, shun her as you would the plague."

For some minutes I really could do nothing else but stare; it was as though some one had unexpectedly struck me a violent blow and knocked the sense clean out of me. Of all the outrageous things! That I should receive such treatment! This was clearly a plot; brief reflection showed that it must be. Those two men were tools of the man with whom I had danced—they must be. Could he have gone to that dance expecting to meet me, intending to treat me in this remarkable fashion? It looked as if he had. What had I done to him? Why had he taken such means to get my photograph? What did his conduct mean? Above all, why had Florence Emmett introduced me to such a man?

I would have that question answered at any rate. Directly after breakfast I went across the park to Linden Gardens,[1] where the Emmetts lived. Florence was just going out; she wanted me to go with her, but I declined. I told her there was something which I particularly wished to ask, and which, before she went out, she must answer. She took me into the morning-room.

"Good gracious, child!" she exclaimed. "What's the matter? Has the Bank of England burst? You look at me quite oddly."

"Florence, you introduced to me a man at Kensington Town Hall. What was his name?"

"Introduced a man to you at Kensington Town Hall? Did I? Oh, yes, I believe I did; but as for his name—what's the matter with the man? Has he tried to borrow money?"

"What was his name? Please tell me, Florence. Was he a friend of yours?"

"A friend of mine? Good gracious, no! I never saw him in my life before. Some one introduced him to me. I can't think who. Let me see, wasn't he a bald-headed man, with a ginger moustache?"

"He was not." I described the man. She seemed quite unable to recall him to her memory. "Do you mean to say you don't even know what his name was?"

"My dear, you know how things happen at that sort of dance. Some one introduces you to a man who asks you for a dance, and he asks you to introduce him to some one else—and there you are. Sometimes I don't know the names of half my partners, even in the houses of my most intimate friends. I do remember introducing some kind of a man to you, but what kind he was I do not remember. And as for your description—it leaves me cold."

"But you must have introduced him by some name—I'm sure you mentioned some name—think."

"I dare say; perhaps it was Brown. As Gus says"—Gus was her husband—"when in doubt about a man's name, say Brown; there

---

[1] A street in Notting Hill, just north of Kensington and Kensington Gardens.

are lots of Browns; he might be one of them. Why are you so keen about this might-be Brown?"

I explained. I told her what he had said to me, how badly he had behaved; about the two men who had snapshotted me in the Brompton Road; I showed her the prints which had come to hand in the morning. She commented on the inscriptions which adorned the mounts in a way which was rather unexpected; they seemed to amuse her.

"Well, you know, Judith, of course, it's perfectly horrid that any one should have treated you like this, but still the facts remain that I have asked myself if any one would ever dare to be so impertinent. I don't know if you realize that there are people who are positively afraid of you—who fly from a room when you come into it."

I had realized it, and I had suffered in consequence. More than once, when entering a room, I had felt a sort of blank silence descend on every creature in it. I told her so.

"But how can I help it? No one can say that I have ever made an unfair use of a conversation I may have seen."

Florence rubbed her chin with the tip of her glove in rather an exasperating manner.

"My dear, I never said you did. I have always stuck up for you through thick and thin. But all the same, if I wanted to say something to a person which was intended for that person's ear alone, I should take care not to say it while you were in the room. And, you know, there are lots of things, quite ordinary, innocent, funny things, which one likes to treat as secrets—what is life without its little privacies? And you know, you leave us none."

"Florence, I've felt that over and over again; there are things which I've seen said which I could have kicked myself for seeing—though I saw them without ever meaning to. Since I can't go about the world with my eyes shut, the only thing is not to go about the world, but to live the life of a hermit. This person, whose name you apparently never knew, has taught me a lesson which I shall not forget as long as I live. I will keep these photographs ever before me, so that they may become to me what the hair shirt was to the hermit in his lonely cell."

I suppose something like two years passed. It was May in Paris; in Paris May is sometimes the most glorious month of the year—

it was glorious then. The restaurants on the Champs Elysées[1] had their chairs out in the gardens—well filled chairs they were. I had been doing what I often do, giving lessons to would-be teachers of the oral system in an Italian city. On my way home I was staying for a few days in Paris. It was lovely weather; I thought I would lunch out of doors. I chose a restaurant whose name I did not know, not far from the Rond Point.[2] It had quite a nice garden. The chestnuts, which were already in full leaf, and of that delicious, delicate green which only lasts a few days, cast an agreeable shade. I looked about for a vacant table. In doing so, I passed behind one which was occupied by two men who were seated side by side. They were looking at something which one of them held in his hand. I gave but the most cursory glance in passing, but it was enough to show me that what they were examining was my photograph—one of the two photographs which had been taken by the ingenious gentleman in the Brompton Road.

The discovery gave me quite a shock. The memory of that photograph was still with me; I still regarded it as my hair-shirt. What could those two men be doing with it there?—so long after it was taken. I chose a table on the same side as theirs, but a little in front, so that I could not only see them, but they could see me. If they looked round and saw me, the recognition might be to them a pleasant surprise. But it gradually dawned on me, as I ordered lunch, that though they had seen me, and still had the photograph in their hands, they did not recognize the original. More, I gradually began to suspect that they believed that they saw me in an individual who was seated on the other side of the garden. Presently this individual got up and left the garden, and I saw one of them say to the other—

"Good-bye, Judith. May the lunch you have had poison you, and may you be run over by a taxi-cab just as you are in the act of dying."

The speaker uttered these Christian sentiments in French, but as French was as familiar to me as my own tongue, even when I was a child, there was no mistaking what they were. He was a rather

---

[1] A famous boulevard connecting the Arc de Triomphe and the Place de la Concorde in Central Paris.
[2] A circus halfway between the Arc de Triomphe and the Place de la Concorde on the Champs Elysées.

good-looking person, with one of those moustaches with waxed turned-up ends, which some young Frenchmen still favour. He turned to his companion, giving my photograph a little jerk in the air.

"Do you believe that any one can do what he says she can?"

His companion replied—and I at once recognized my limitations. He was rather a big, fair-haired man, with one of those hirsute countenances which are so often seen abroad and so seldom at home. He had a long, square-cut, carefully trimmed beard, quite a foot long, and a voluminous moustache which, from the decorative point of view, was a triumph of the hairdresser's art, and which effectively screened his mouth, so that, if it were open or shut, it was not easy to see his lips. Observing him as closely as I might, since his lips were to all intents and purposes invisible, by merely looking at him as he spoke, I could not get the faintest notion of what he said. I have sometimes thought that if all the people in the world were lip-readers, it would be necessary, for self-protection, to cultivate a beard and moustache. Here was a case in point. This man spoke to the other, who had arranged his moustache so that the whole of his mouth was visible—and I could not see a word he said. The other, laughing, answered him; there was no doubt about what he said.

"That is absolutely true—absolutely. I don't know how long I've had this photograph. Pattison sent a copy to every one of us. I do not know what his notion was—I do not know if he thought that Judith Lee was all over the world at once, with an eye on everybody's mouth. Between ourselves, I have thought that I have seen her more than once—in Vienna, Berlin, here in Paris, and in London —particularly in London. This is not an uncommon kind of face in London. I have compared this photograph again and again with women I have seen there, and I have said—well, it may be, or it may not be—as was the case just now. The lady who has just left—was she Judith Lee? Who can tell? What does it matter? I have come to the conclusion that if you have not seen the original a photograph, as a means of recognition, is of very little use."

I had come to the conclusion that perhaps this lively gentleman did not make sufficient allowance for the change in feminine fashions. Since that photograph was taken everything a woman wears had been entirely altered—as it were, gone completely round. Then we dressed our hair quite differently; I certainly did—and in a photograph that makes all the difference.

The bearded man was speaking—he might as well have kept silence for all the information he conveyed to me. He seemed to have a trick of scarcely moving his lips at all, so that, confronted by that thatch of hair, it was impossible even to guess at what he was saying. When his companion spoke again it was quite another matter. I do not know if my failure with his friend acted as a spur; I did seem to read his words with even unusual clearness.

"Two hundred and fifty thousand francs in five-franc pieces; a hundred thousand francs in franc pieces; two hundred thousand ten-sou pieces—that was a pretty large order; it is for you to place them, to deal with them—I have to hand them over to you. There, so far as I am concerned, the matter ends."

The bearded man said something—this time his companion's words gave me an inkling of what it might have been.

"My friend, the production is enormous, immense, altogether beyond what might be supposed. And it is all good money, mind you—standard value." He took something out of his pocket and held it out to his companion. "There are two five-franc pieces; they are in every respect precisely alike. No assayer,[1] by the most delicate tests, could tell one from the other—because there is nothing to tell; so far as he is concerned, they have both come from the French mint. But the expert at the mint, he can tell; that is to say, perhaps three, perhaps four, men in France—that is because they have a way of their own of distinguishing. It is like the man at Sèvres[2]—two pieces are placed before him, exactly alike; no dealer could tell one from the other, but he can. He knows that he made the one and did not make the other—that is all he does know. He knows because of certain minutiæ, so minute that to an uninstructed eye even a microscope will not reveal them."

Again the bearded man spoke—again the other's answer gave me a clue to what he said.

"What the exact profit is I of course cannot tell you. We let you have money—good money, at fifteen per cent. less than the face

[1] Someone who tests and analyses ores to determine their value.
[2] A French city known for its porcelain.

value. You are content, you ought to be; we also are content—so you see there must be something in it."

Once more there was what I can only describe as an interruption from the bearded man—then again his friend with the uplifted moustaches.

"Of course this sort of thing cannot go on, though it has already continued longer than you perhaps think. But that is where the great idea comes in—the idea of the great *coup*. Produce an enormous quantity at one time—silver coins, mind you, of all countries; flood the world with it before any one has a suspicion of what is in the air, and then, before discovery is made, retire from business—with what really, if all goes well, should prove to be a comfortable competence."

The bearded man nodded, as if there was a good deal in the other's words; as he uttered what appeared to be a brief sentence, I dare say he said as much. The other, drawing quite close to him, as if he whispered in his ear, waxed eloquent.

"You see there is no fraud in it, not a particle. If you give this five-franc piece to the waiter here, he cannot say it is a bad one—it is not a bad one; there's nothing wrong about it; it is in all respects exactly like every other good five-franc piece." In his ardour he struck his right fist against his open palm. "If he took it to the mint they would not dare to refuse it, because, if they did, the whole monetary system of the world would be disorganized—all the silver currency. No one would be able to tell what pieces had come from where—from our mint or theirs. The result would be that there would be a tendency everywhere to refuse silver pieces altogether. No, my friend, there is not the faintest suggestion of anything, in the true sense of the word, irregular about the business from first to last. The only thing is that ours is the manufacturer's profit instead of the Government's—why shouldn't it be? Why shouldn't there be competition in this sort of business as well as in any other? It seems to me that echo answers 'Why?' "

I fancied that the bearded gentleman glanced round him rather anxiously, as if he were conscious that very private things were being said. I imagine he dropped a hint to his friend.

"My good Philippe, no Judith Lee is here—what do you fear? I speak in a whisper; there is no one near us. However, time goes;

business calls; I must leave you. It is understood—to-night, at nine o'clock, 4, Rue Saint Herbôt."[1]

The pair shook hands in that demonstrative fashion which is common with their compatriots; the man with the upturned moustaches departed, the bearded one remained. He seemed in no hurry to go. Lighting another cigar, he ordered a waiter to bring him a liqueur and, taking a small notebook from his pocket, proceeded to make what was possibly a series of calculations.

The situation struck me as being rather humorous—in its way, so humorous that I was at a loss what to do. Here was a gentleman armed with a photograph of Judith Lee, so that he might be peculiarly on his guard against her, fancying he sees her again and again, all the while incredulous of the existence of the powers with which his principal has credited her, proving himself so unobservant, or so irresponsible, or both, that under her very nose he makes statements of the most delicate kind. As a matter of fact I had heard something about silver coins which had never seen a mint only a few days before at Milan. I was buying some trifles in a shop. An Italian friend who was with me, who was in the Government service, had asked me to let him look at a five-lire piece which I was tendering to the tradesman. I had done so. With a smile he had asked if I would exchange it for another—to which I, of course, agreed.

When we had got out of the shop he asked me where I got the coin from. I informed him that I had not the least idea; it was one of a number of others which I had got from some one somewhere. I inquired what was wrong with it. Then he told me, after some hesitation, what seemed to me to be rather a curious thing.

He said that there were silver coins in circulation which, while as regards the materials used in their composition they were good, at the same time were technically bad, since they had never been coined by the mint. That five-lire piece of mine was one of them. I could see that he was reluctant to say more than he could help, so I did not press him, but he left me with the feeling that there was something at the back of the business which was distinctly queer. This conversation, with one side of which I had been made so unexpectedly acquainted, threw a lurid light upon what my Italian friend

[1] Apparently imaginary.

had told me. These two men seemed to be trafficking in coins like that five-lire piece. From what I had gathered they were dealing with them in very large quantities. The bearded man was to take fifty thousand five-franc pieces, a hundred thousand franc pieces, two hundred thousand ten-sou pieces, which had been coined goodness alone knew where, and he was to take this immense amount of specie just by way of a single deal. I reckoned it up; it represented eighteen thousand pounds in English money. He was to have it at a discount of fifteen per cent., which meant a profit for him of two thousand seven hundred pounds. He must see his way to getting rid of it at a comparatively early date, or he would scarcely undertake such a risk. If other deals were taking place upon these lines in the currency of other countries, as that incredulous gentleman had hinted, before long the world would be flooded with what, let him phrase it as he liked, was really spurious coinage—and then what sufferings might not ensue? If what he had hinted was true, there must somewhere be a great factory, equipped with all the most modern appliances, which was about to let loose an ocean of bad silver coins, which it would be impossible to tell from good ones, which might play havoc with the monetary systems of the world.

The question for my consideration was—what was I to do? I did not want to be mixed up in affairs of that kind. I was not a thief-taker; I was not a detector of crime. I just wanted to enjoy a few days' holiday in Paris in this glorious May weather. If I were forced into relations with the French police, that would be the end of my holiday. I should probably find myself associated with unpleasantness of all kinds from which I might not be able to disentangle myself for ages to come. I did not at all relish the prospect. Still——

I will be frank—those photographs rankled. They did; it is no use pretending they did not. And then, that this moustached gentleman, with my photograph in his hand, and no doubt what his associate had told him in his head, should treat me with open contumely—for that I felt that I should like to give him a rap across the knuckles. I am a woman, and sometimes women are almost as illogical as men, though not often—and perhaps that is one reason why I felt bound to see the matter through.

I left the bearded gentleman still struggling with the figures in his notebook, and I went for a stroll. Inquiring my way to the Rue

Saint Herbôt, I was told that it was not far from the Gare de l'Ouest[1]
—so, as that is some way from the Champs Elysées, I commenced
my stroll by taking a taxi-cab. Alighting at the station, I did the
rest of the distance on foot. It proved to be one of those wide, old-
fashioned streets which are still to be found in that quarter of Paris,
occupied by a nondescript population—shops, private houses,
warehouses, *maisons meublées*,[2] all mixed up together, and none of
them very high class.

As far as I could see, part of No. 4 seemed to be some kind of
warehouse; a great gate was at one side, a big board ran across the
entresol, on which were painted the words: "Barrucand. Fournisseur. Gros et Détail."[3] "Fournisseur" is what I call an india-rubber
word; it can be pulled this way and that; it may mean any one of a
dozen things—it may mean them all. In this case it seemed that it
might mean that silver coins, stamped and struck in some private
mint, were supplied in quantities. There seemed to be not a soul
about the place just then. I was making up my mind to knock at the
door and put some innocent question, when the great gate swung
back and a man came out. I had just time to escape him by retreat-
ing into the establishment of a *charcutier*,[4] which stood on my side
of the way.

A meeting would have been awkward; he might have recognized
me, as he was the individual who had snapshotted me in the Brompton Road. His face was stamped very clearly on my memory; once
seen, never to be forgotten. He was rolling a cigarette as he walked,
stopping at the door of the shop in which I was to light a match. I
bought a sausage—I had to buy something; as it was being put into
paper, I asked if Monsieur Barrucand lived at his warehouse. The
effect of my question was rather unexpected. The oily person who
was enveloping my purchase paused in the operation to stare at me
with what struck me as startled eyes.

"Monsieur Barrucand? What do you know of Monsieur Barrucand?"

---

[1] A railway terminus in Montparnasse on the Left Bank of the Seine, now Gare
Montparnasse, about two miles south of the Champs Elysées.
[2] Furnished houses (French).
[3] "Barrucand. Supplier. Wholesale and Retail" (French).
[4] Butcher, specialising in sausages, patés and cured meats (French).

Possibly it was the oddity of the man's manner which caused me to say something which was not exactly true.

"I used to know a Monsieur Barrucand at Lille. I wondered if the one over the road was a relative of his."

"You used to know a Monsieur Barrucand at Lille? What Monsieur Barrucand was that?"

"You know the Monsieur Barrucand who is your neighbour? In what does he deal?"

The man stared at me for some seconds in silence. Then he finished rolling up my sausage, saying, as he handed it to me over the counter—

"I know nothing of Monsieur Barrucand; I am but lately come here. I wish madame good day."

I took the hint and departed, conscious that the oily man had come to the door of his shop, and was watching me as I walked down the street. Looking round as I turned a corner, I saw a small boy coming out of his doorway. I had not gone very far before I began to entertain the suspicion that it was the intention of that small boy to keep me in sight. That *charcutier* knew more about Monsieur Barrucand than he had chosen to say; if he got five-franc pieces for fifteen per cent. less than their face value, he might have sound reasons for wishing to keep his knowledge dark.

An idea struck me. I had given him a louis[1] for that sausage, having no small money. He had given me three five-franc pieces, besides other coins, by way of change. I immediately resolved to shake that small boy off, and with that intention dived into the Gare de l'Ouest, picked my way through the throng of people, and passing into the Place Loraine, jumping into the first taxi, bade the driver take me to the Café de la Paix.[2] Going into the interior, after first assuring myself that that small boy was nowhere in sight, I chose a seat at a table facing the door, and taking out the coins which that *charcutier* had given me, subjected them to a minute examination.

There was nothing peculiar about them so far as I could see. They were of different dates—1888 was on one of the five-franc

---

[1] A gold coin worth 20 francs, or just under a pound (colloquial).

[2] A famous café near the Paris Opera and serving the Grand-Hôtel, the Café de la Paix was opened in 1862.

pieces; none of them were of very recent coinage; and yet—I wondered.

The appearance of that snapshotting gentleman through Monsieur Barrucand's gate had enlarged the field of my doubts. Was it possible that my partner at the Kensington Town Hall had anything to do with this competitive mint? The man with the upturned moustaches had my photograph, which he could only have got from him; if he were connected with such a business as this, no wonder he resented the idea that any one could read what was being said by merely watching the lips. With agents of all sorts and kinds spread over the globe, the chance that one of them might encounter Judith Lee was not such a remote one as it might seem. One encounter with that dangerous creature might play havoc with the whole business. He was therefore but taking a simple precaution in making it his business to see that his associates were armed with a photograph which would serve as some sort of defence against this pestilent woman. Before I committed myself, if he had a finger in this pie, I should like to make sure of getting him. That would be a lesson to him not to go out of his way to be rude to his partners at a dance—even if she did not happen to know his name.

I had an acquaintance who was in the Paris office of a London newspaper. He was the brother of a girl with whom I had been to school; she had laid special injunctions on me when I was in Paris to look him up. So I looked him up, going straight from the Café de la Paix to do so. When I got to his office he seemed to be rather full of work. I explained that I had come to him at that busy hour of the day because I rather wanted to ask him a question.

"Do you know any one connected with the Mint here?"

"The Mint? You know the Mint here is at the Hôtel de Monnaie[1] —it's a sort of museum. As for the part in which the coining goes on, any one may get a ticket to view by applying to the director."

"That's not exactly what I mean. Do you know any one connected with the part of it in which coins are struck?"

"I'm afraid I don't, but there may be some one about the place who does. I'll go and see."

He went, and presently returned with a grey-headed man of

[1] The Hôtel des Monnaies, the Paris Mint, located on the Quai Conti on the Left Bank of the Seine.

distinguished appearance, whom he introduced as Monsieur de Brionne.

"De Brionne knows every one—it seems he knows just the very person I should say you wanted."

It appeared that Monsieur de Brionne did. He wrote a few lines on the back of his visiting card, put the card into an envelope, and addressed it to Monsieur Theodore Duglère.

"Monsieur Duglère," he explained, "is in the assaying department. He knows as much about the Mint as any man living. If you hand him this, I feel sure he will give you any information you may require."

I found that the Hôtel de Monnaie was on the Quai de Conti, next door to the Institute.[1] Addressing myself to an official in some sort of bureau which was in the vestibule, I entrusted him with my envelope to take to Monsieur Duglère. Within ten minutes I was being ushered into an apartment on the first floor, the windows of which looked out upon the Seine. A short, wiry man, perhaps fifty years of age, with shrewd eyes and a clever face, bowed to me from the other side of a large table.

"Miss Judith Lee? In what way can I do myself the pleasure of serving you, Miss Lee?"

"I am afraid, Monsieur Duglère, that it may turn out that I have come to you on a very foolish errand; before I touch on it, may I take it that anything I say to you will be treated as confidential?"

"You wish to speak to me on official matters—connected with our work here? What is it you wish to ask me?"

"You have not answered my question, Monsieur Duglère."

He looked at me with his shrewd grey eyes, and then he smiled.

"You understand that you may say certain things to me that it would be impossible for me to treat as confidential. I occupy an official position. I take it that it is not on such-like points you wish to touch? I have been in this place nearly all my life, Miss Lee. Monsieur de Brionne, who introduces you, would tell you that I am likely to be a pretty good judge of what may be regarded as confidential. I keep silence until I am forced to speak."

[1] The Institut de France houses the French Academy and the Academies of Humanities, Sciences, Fine Arts, and Moral and Political Sciences.

I considered him for some further seconds; he standing up on the other side of the table, Monsieur de Brionne's card in his hand, considering me. Then I decided not to try to make conditions. I took some coins out of my bag and laid them in front of him on the table.

"I want you to look at those three five-franc pieces, Monsieur Duglère."

He continued to look at me; then looked down at the coins— then back at me. He delivered himself of a monosyllable.

"Why?"

"Please look at those five-franc pieces first, Monsieur Duglère; ask questions afterwards."

He picked up the coins and examined them one by one: peering at them through a jeweller's glass, weighing them in the palm of his hand, feeling them with the tips of his fingers. Then he laid them down again and resumed his former occupation of considering me closely.

I thought that he was never going to speak; it was quite a relief when he did.

"Where did you get these coins, Miss Lee?"

I returned him question for question; there began a sort of verbal fencing match, each of us, as it were, remaining on guard.

"Is there anything wrong with them?"

"Have you any reason to suppose that there is?"

"I have come to you for information, Monsieur Duglère."

"Not to give it?"

"I give you the honour—precedence."

"With us, Miss Lee, the rule is—ladies first."

I pretended to sigh.

"Then in that case I'm afraid I must go."

"I'm afraid, Miss Lee, that I can't allow you to go just yet."

"Then there *is* something wrong? I thank you."

"That is rather neat—you score—*touché*. Now, Miss Lee, it is your turn. What do you suppose is wrong?"

"I merely wondered which of those pieces was struck in your mint, Monsieur Duglère."

"Sit down, Miss Lee; allow me also to sit." He sat on one side of the table, I on the other. "I have but to touch this button, Miss Lee, and this room will be filled with police. I am sure you would not wish for that."

I laughed outright—when I had recovered from my first shock of surprise.

"I should not mind that in the least; I should find it very amusing."

"You would not find it amusing—afterwards. The police are not so sympathetic to ladies as you may suppose. Two of these three coins, Miss Lee, are forgeries. Clearly you are aware of that. From whom did you get them?"

"They are part of the change I received for a louis."

"Indeed? Do not imagine for an instant that I doubt you; your manner tells me that you will be able to point out the person from whom you received these coins. That is not the point. These five-franc pieces are exactly like other five-franc pieces—exactly. Not one person in a million would be able to tell that there was a difference—how come you to know that there is a difference?—that is the point."

"Tell me what the difference is."

"I think, Miss Lee, that you know what the difference is—don't you? Do not fence with me, please. This matter is so serious that any attempt at trifling with it is inconceivable. Tell me frankly, do you not know what the difference is?"

"I know absolutely nothing, but I guess something."

"What do you guess?"

"I guess that those coins were manufactured in a private mint—from standard silver."

"Who are you, Miss Lee?"

"I am a teacher of the deaf and dumb."

"You are what? You are trifling with me again."

"I am not; that is exactly what I am."

There was a considerable interval before he spoke again. It tickled me to see what efforts he was making to find out by ocular inspection what kind of creature I really was. He failed; I puzzled him; he might have a wide knowledge of more worlds than one—I was in none of them. He recognized that I was something new in the way of specimens.

"You probably realize, Miss Lee, that nothing is easier than for us to find out who and what you are—what you do not adequately recognize is that this sort of thing"—he touched the coins —"might, quite conceivably, shake the whole fabric of society, and even destroy its foundations. You are an honest woman, I believe. Will you not be candid with me and tell me what your presence here means? These two coins represent a danger to the body politic which might bring injury to numbers of innocent people. Are you not aware of that?"

I reflected for an instant, and then I said: "I believe I am."

"In that case, Miss Lee, will you not now show the candour which I invite from you?"

Again I considered. He continued to watch me with an intensity which almost suggested that he could not have moved his eyes from my face if he had tried. Then I told him all about it—as well as he would let me with his questions. When I came to the incident of the two men in the restaurant gardens, he checked me with a movement of his hand.

"One moment, if you please. It is only right that I should tell you that everything which has taken place since your coming into this room has been both heard and seen by another person as well as by myself. There is the push piece of an electric bell under this carpet; when I press it with my foot some one opens a door which is on wall the other side of this and enters a little cupboard, which is divided from us by so thin a partition that every word which is spoken here is audible to the unseen listener, while he can see all that takes place through some peepholes which are specially provided—as I will now proceed to show you."

He did something to the wall with the tips of his fingers; part of it falling back, a short, squat man came into the room—and the wall was as it was. Exactly where that unsuspected door was it was not easy to perceive with the naked eye, though I had only a second before seen it open and shut. Monsieur Duglère introduced the new-comer.

"Monsieur Barron, one of the chief officers of our police. As you are aware, Monsieur Barron, Miss Lee has been favouring me with some very interesting statements."

"If Miss Lee will go on," was all that Monsieur Barron said.

I went on—under what I felt were disadvantageous conditions. I rather wished that I had not made use of Monsieur Brionne's introduction. Events were marching with a haste, and taking a form for which I had not bargained. However, I told the rest of my story, having at the end an uncanny feeling that those two elderly Frenchmen had me between their fingers and thumbs, and that, at a signal arranged between themselves, they could squeeze me to nothing.

They heard all I had to say, exhausting me with questions, some of them of the most inconvenient kind, but they gave me very little information in exchange. When I left that room, two facts had been impressed upon me; the first was that a raid was to be made upon No. 4 Rue Saint Herbôt, that evening at nine o'clock; the second that I was not to breathe a word touching on any part of the affair to any living creature. And as I crossed the quay towards the Pont Neuf,[1] it was with a feeling strong upon me that until I had left Paris behind me I should never be out of sight, except in the privacy of my own apartment, and quite possibly there might be in the wall of that a peep-hole of some agent of the police. I had spoilt my holiday.

I dined at my hotel that night, looking curiously about me to see which of the other diners suggested association with the police. I did not glean the slightest hint; yet that I was being watched I was as sure as that I was seated at that table. I lingered in the public rooms after the meal was over, gaining no information. I should have liked to treat myself to a trip to the Rue Saint Herbôt to see the fun, but I simply did not dare. I had a notion that I might spend a night in most uncomfortable quarters if I ventured on an escapade of the kind. It was borne in upon me that the Paris police had ways of their own. I realized this still more clearly when, soon after ten, my nerves a little on edge, tired with the silly book which I was trying to read in the deserted *salle de lecture*,[2] I retired to my own apartment, and had only been there a few minutes when there came a tap at the panels, and, without any invitation, two visitors came in, both of the masculine sex. It was not my habit to lock my bedroom door, but I felt, when those two gentlemen came in, just as I was beginning to undress, that during the rest of my stay in Paris it was a habit which must be changed. The visitors were Monsieur Duglère

---

[1] The oldest bridge in Paris, crossing the Seine at the Western tip of the Île de la Cité.

[2] Reading room (French).

and Monsieur Barron. Monsieur Duglère's greeting was, to say the least, unusual.

"Well, Miss Lee, what next?" He put the question as though he shot it at me. I was not flattered.

"What next? I should imagine, Monsieur Duglère, the door. Is it the habit for gentlemen in Paris to enter a lady's bedroom uninvited?"

He made a little contemptuous movement with his fingers, as if anything I might say was not worth noticing. He was a most unceremonious person.

"No stupidities, if you please, Miss Lee. Do you know what has happened?"

"It has happened that you two gentlemen have come into my room, and if you will not retire it will be necessary for me to ring the bell and have you shown out."

Monsieur Barron spoke in the smoothest, softest undertone, which was much more menacing than bluster.

"If we go, Miss Lee, we take you with us—as a prisoner."

"Certainly," snapped Monsieur Duglère. "You pretend not to know what has happened; I will tell you. We went to your Rue Saint Horbôt, not only at nine; we have been there ever since you left us this afternoon. Nothing has occurred which you led us to expect. We have searched the shop of your *charcutier*: every coin we found was a good one; you will now have to prove that you obtained your two five-franc pieces from him. As for Monsieur Barrucand, he is a wholesale dealer in delicacies for the table—sardines, anchovies, *patés*—all things of that kind. We shall expect you, in the morning, to give us a further explanation of that singular story of yours, Miss Lee. There is nothing about Monsieur Barrucand's premises which is in the least degree suspicious. Monsieur Barrucand will require an explanation from you, and so will the *charcutier*."

Monsieur Duglère opened the door; both he and Monsieur Barron stood on the threshold, observing me; then, with no more greeting than they had offered on their coming, they went and shut the door behind them. After what I had taken to be Monsieur Barron's threat, this abrupt departure was, as it were, another link in the chain of surprises. I concluded that the police of Paris had indeed ways of their own.

I spent a sleepless night. For one thing, I kept wondering if any one was stationed outside my door, and if I was virtually a prisoner in my bedroom. I cordially wished, as I turned and twisted between the sheets, that mine was not the gift of lip-reading. I called myself names for ever having gone with those two five-franc pieces to the Mint—by the way, Monsieur Duglère had kept them, so that at the best I was ten francs out of pocket. Could that man with the up-turned moustaches have been fooling me? Had he recognized me as the original of that photograph all along, and in what he said to his companion, had he been amusing himself at my expense? I did not believe it—he had not detected me; he had not been acting; he had meant every word that he had said, showing a frankness bordering on simplicity.

It was the *charcutier* who had found me out, how I could not say: possibly because my questions had roused his suspicions, he had set that small boy to watch me, and he had watched me better than I knew. It looked as if he had followed me to the Café de la Paix, then to that newspaper office, and lastly, to the Mint. If he had seen me enter the Mint he had, no doubt, got all the information he wanted; warning had been given; that *charcutier* got rid of his questionable silver; that appointment had never been kept—the result of which things was that Monsieur Duglère, and his friend, Monsieur Barron, suspected me of they alone knew what.

When, at last, as daylight was already beginning to peep through the curtains, I did go to sleep, I was roused after, as it seemed to me, I had only just closed my eyes, in a most singular and unpleasant fashion. I woke with a start, with the feeling strong upon me that something unusual had just been taking place in my room, though what I could not imagine. It was broad day; the sun was streaming in through the window; there was nothing to be seen; yet that there had been something a few minutes before I felt convinced. I got out of bed. After my experience with my uninvited visitors I had taken care to secure the door; it was as I had left it, both locked and bolted. No one—nothing—could have come in that way. I glanced at the window; then I understood—in part. It is my invariable custom to leave my bedroom window nearly wide open; some one had taken advantage of the fact to make me a present. On the dressing-table, which stood close to the window, was something which certainly had not been there the night before—a copy of one of the photographs which had been taken of me in the Brompton Road—mount, inscription, and all. It was fastened to the wood of the table by a knife which had been driven through the centre. Attached to the knife was a scrap of paper on which were the words, written with a pen in printed characters, "For the spy a knife."

There was no more sleep for me. That the photograph had been slipped through the window was clear. How the person who had put it there had gained the window was also clear. A narrow balcony ran nearly right across the back of the building. The different rooms were divided from each other by spiked iron partitions. Although the ordinary person would have found them difficult to pass, whoever had put that photograph on my dressing-table had come that way, whether from the right or from the left there was nothing to tell. Quite possibly what had woke me was the noise which he made as he drove the knife through the photograph into the table. I saw by my watch that it was just after six o'clock. I rang for the chambermaid. I asked for a cup of coffee, and for my bath to be prepared. Before seven I was out on the street, no one having attempted to stop me on the way.

Yet I had an uneasy consciousness that though, apparently, my movements were unimpeded, it was not because they were unobserved. My hotel was near the Place de l'Etoile.[1] The feeling was almost like a nervous affliction. As I moved up the Avenue du Bois[2] I kept giving what I was quite aware were silly glances in front and behind, and all about me, in search of I knew not what. It was perhaps because the weather was so fine that so many people were abroad.

When more than half-way up the avenue I decided to sit down. I chose a chair under a great chestnut tree. In front of me was one of those big houses which are a feature of the avenue. It had been recently repainted. Boxes filled with flowers decorated all the window-sills; what seemed to be some armorial bearings on the iron gates had been regilded. I wondered who lived there. A woman

---

[1] The circus around the Arc de Triomphe, where twelve straight roads, including the Champs Elysées, meet; now the Place Charles de Gaulle.
[2] Avenue du Bois de Boulogne, now Avenue Foch, a chestnut-lined avenue leading southwest from the Arc de Triomphe to the Bois de Boulogne.

alighted from a taxi, within a few feet of where I was, and walked quickly towards the gilded gates—and I stopped in the middle of my calculation to stare at her.

Could it be Florence Emmett? Something seemed to have happened to her if it was; perhaps it was the weird motor attire which obscured her from head to foot which lent her that appearance. I was on the point of jumping up from my chair and rushing after her, on the off chance that it might be she—when something occurred which caused me to do nothing of the kind. A man was coming rapidly up from the other direction, who, in spite of his huge overcoat and a cap the flaps of which hid his ears, I recognized at once—it was my partner for that waltz at the Kensington Town Hall. I had often told myself that if I ever did see him again I would favour him with a few candid observations; but his appearance at that moment was so unexpected, and what immediately followed so amazing, that I forgot all about what I had meant to do, and sat motionless.

The man and the woman were moving from different directions. They were evidently not only old acquaintances, but they had arranged to meet—they were even on such terms of familiarity that formal greetings were not necessary. He spoke to her as they met, and I could see his lips moving.

"Be careful—she is there; our friend the spy."

It seemed that the woman said something from behind her motor veil, to which he replied—

"Be easy; I'm not afraid of her; it is she who had better beware. If she had nine lives she'd lose them all before she finds us once."

The woman spoke again. He laughed, saying—

"Let them come in their battalions; we shall move quicker than they—behold our flying machine."

As he spoke a motor-car drew up in front of the house I had been observing. It was a big, covered car, and, as if its owner were afraid of its paint being damaged, it was enveloped in what seemed to be a loose, canvas cover. My partner for that waltz held the door open and the woman entered; he followed—they were both instantly hidden from me. As they entered the car on the one side, the great iron gates of the house I had been observing swung open, and a man, coming through, entered the car, which was drawn up within three or four feet of the gates, so quickly that I had no chance of seeing what manner of man he was. Instantly the car, beginning to move, went bowling down the avenue towards the Bois.

The entire episode had been like a happening in a dream; it had only occupied a dozen or twenty seconds. It left me in a state of confusion—what did it mean? Of the identity of the man who had greeted Florence I had no doubt—but was she Florence? Under ordinary circumstances I should have unhesitatingly said yes, but it was difficult to reconcile what I knew of her with her presence there. Then a thought, as it were, came sweeping over me.

What was Florence's husband—Cecil Emmett? Was he not, of all things in the world, a silversmith? Had not Emmett and Stacey some of the largest silversmith's establishments, not only in London and the big provincial towns, but also in Paris and other continental cities? Cecil Emmett would be in a position to handle large quantities of raw silver and to use them for practically any purpose without arousing the least suspicion. If my partner for that waltz was connected with this business of minting silver, as the man with the uplifted moustaches had put it, on competitive lines, and he knew Florence—was it not possible that Cecil Emmett, one of the greatest buyers of virgin silver, had a finger in the pie? Then, in that case, Florence herself—I tried to keep my brain from working; my thoughts, if I gave them rein, would perhaps lead me—where I very much did not want to go.

I was still glued to that chair; I was conscious that the motor was vanishing from sight; I was observing, with unseeing eyes, the gilded gates through which that other man had come, wondering hazily what manner of man he was, when something struck me sharply on the side of the head, so acute a blow that I sprang up with an exclamation of pain. For a second or two I could not imagine what had struck me. I looked down; at my feet was a shining strip of metal, the key to a Yale lock.[1] Could it have been that which had struck me? I picked it up. A label was attached to it, on which was written, "The key for the spy."

What did it mean? Had it been thrown at me? By whom? I looked around. As I did so, a man came running up, who, if I had permitted

---

[1] The pin tumbler lock, invented in 1848 by Linus Yale, Sr. and developed further by Linus Yale, Jr.

it, would have snatched the key from my hand, and who seemed unabashed as I drew it back.

"I insist," he exclaimed, "upon mademoiselle giving me that key."

"You insist!" I retorted. "Pray what right have you to insist? Who are you? Is this your key?"

"I am an agent of police, and I insist upon mademoiselle giving me that key at once."

I was conscious that other persons were advancing, both male and female; quite where they were coming from I was not sure, but I had more than a suspicion that they were all friends of the man who had accosted me.

"Where did this key come from?" I demanded.

"It was thrown at you by a young lad who took to his heels the moment he had thrown it, and who is now being pursued by an agent of police."

How long that agent kept up the pursuit I cannot say—he never caught that young man, so that I have never seen him except with the eyes of imagination. I wonder if he was any relation of the young gentleman who followed me from the *charcutier*'s. Why was the key thrown at me at all? I can only imagine that it was as a mark of contempt, and because it was taken for granted that I would inform the authorities of the episode of the motor-car, of the man who had been my partner for that waltz, of the woman I took to be Florence, and of the man who had come through the gates on which were the gilded armorial bearings; and that because of my information inquiries would be made at the house on the other side of those gates—to which the presentation of the key in that ignominious fashion could make no difference whatever. However that may have been, the key which that young gentleman had thrown at my head proved to be the key of the house which I had been observing.

Monsieur Duglère and Monsieur Barron arrived on the field in an extraordinarily short space of time. Messieurs les agents were rapidly very much in evidence. I approached the door of the house with Messieurs Duglère and Barron and a select number of their satellites. As we advanced we saw that something was on the centre of the door. When we came close to we realized that it was my photograph, one of those famous two which had been snapped in the Brompton Road—with the legend at the top of the mount, "Warning! This is the portrait of a public danger"; and at the foot, "Judith Lee, Spy." The lock yielded to a touch of the key which had scarred my cheek, and we entered the house. It was empty—save for the furniture.

There were cellars in the basement. In one there were many bottles of wine, in bins which covered the walls. At one point part of one of these bins had been drawn back, showing where it swung on hinges. Behind it was a door which stood open. On the other side of that cellar door was the mint in which silver was coined on "competitive lines": the up-to-date, well-equipped establishment of which the man with the uplifted moustaches had spoken to his bearded friend.

It certainly was a remarkable place; I know that my companions stared about them in speechless amazement. There were all sorts of what were to me strange machines, but which were familiar enough to them. How they ever came to be erected in that place was a complete mystery. They were, I believe, machines the secrets of which were supposed to be known to Government mints only.

In one respect that visit was a failure—the stocks of silver coins which my associates would have been glad to find were not in evidence. There were specimens of nearly every current silver piece in the world, which had, no doubt, been coined on the premises, bearing all kinds of dates at which they certainly had never been struck. They were actually laid out upon a table as if to enable us to admire the perfect art with which they had been fashioned.

Of the persons concerned in that "competitive" mint, nothing, so far as I know, has been discovered. It is true that the police authorities in Paris are in a position which enables them to keep silence when they choose. It is also true that the authorities of the various mints have what they might judge to be sufficient grounds for wishing to say as little on the matter as they can help. Still, I think if anything had been learned I should have heard of it by a side wind —especially as a side wind did blow one or two facts in my direction. It was discovered afterwards that there had probably been large stores of silver coin kept in the cellars of that house in the Avenue du Bois, which it was not unlikely had been removed the night before. The owner of the house was supposed to be a Monsieur Alvirez, a South American millionaire. He was supposed to have been giving a party the night before we came. From certain facts which leaked out, it seemed likely that motor-cars which were presumed to be bringing guests left the house laden with cases of specie.

Another little waft of that side wind told me of a discovery which had been made at the establishment of Monsieur Barrucand in the Rue Saint Herbôt. The warehouse was stored with cases packed with sardines in tins, and other comestibles. When these tins came to be opened by curious French policemen, it was learned that while there certainly were sardines in some of them, there were silver coins in nearly all, and in many practically nothing else.

Some time after I returned to London I met Florence Emmett at the house of a mutual friend—at what the cards of invitation called an "At Home, with Music." She was coming out as I went in. At sight of her I rather quailed, but she seemed perfectly at her ease. She said as she went by—

"Why, wherever have you been hiding? I haven't seen you for ages."

I replied—on the sudden impulse of the moment—

"And you? I haven't seen you since I saw you in Paris."

She stood still, staring at me with raised eyebrows.

"In Paris? Why, when did I see you in Paris?"

"Don't you remember that morning in the Avenue du Bois?"

"In the Avenue du Bois? When?"

"Oh, perhaps two months ago."

"Two months ago? Why, my dear child, I haven't been in Paris for close on two years; and I'll give you exact particulars of how I have spent every hour of every day for a good deal more than the last two months—when you come to see us in Linden Gardens."

I never have been to see them in Linden Gardens; I do not suppose I shall ever go. She would probably be able to give me all the particulars of which she spoke; all the same I have my doubts, and I fear that those particulars would not entirely clear them away. It was certainly the man to whom she had introduced me, pretending afterwards that she did not know his name, and the woman was very much like her. I am looking for the man still. One of these fine days he and I may meet again. In the meanwhile I seldom see a piece of silver money, whether English or foreign, in my hands or in those of another, without wondering where it was coined—especially since I have learned that in England sixty-six shillings are coined out of twelve ounces of silver which cost the Government just over a pound.[1]

---

[1] In England sixty-six shillings are coined out of twelve ounces of silver which cost the Government just over a pound: With the pound consisting of twenty shillings, the Government is making a substantial profit.

CURARE

It commenced on the steamer "Norse." We were a party of tourists on an excursion to Norway. We had pleasant weather nearly all the time, and we were, on the whole, a sociable party; the whole thing was a success from beginning to end. One morning, on the homeward journey, I was taking it easy on deck, when I noticed Mr. Bellasis and Mr. Tracey talking together at a little distance from where I was. I could not hear their voices, but I could hardly help seeing their lips. Mr. Tracey had a small, round, metal box in his hand, and was showing the contents to Mr. Bellasis.

"Do you know what that is?" I saw him ask. Mr. Bellasis was stooping over the box, so that for the moment I could not see his mouth, but apparently his reply was in the negative. Mr. Tracey went on—

"That's something which you won't find in Europe, except after a great deal of looking—I don't know where you'd begin—and then only in very small quantities. I'm told that it's used by doctors —or, at least, by some of them—in cases of tetanus; but I doubt if they use it in this form; it would be a little bit too risky. They probably have a pharmacopœial[1] preparation of their own."

I saw Mr. Bellasis ask a question: "Is it anything very remarkable? It looks rather like powdered ginger."

Mr. Tracey laughed. He was a grizzled bachelor of about fifty, who had been in all sorts of out-of-the-way places, from which he had brought some curious odds and ends of knowledge.

"I got that in South America, from a native who was piloting me in a dug-out on the Orinoco.[2] When we parted he presented it to me as a mark of esteem. I don't suppose it weighs half an ounce, but I've been told since that it's worth quite a lot of money. I don't know what use my pilot thought I should make of it; so I've made none. I have thought more than once of throwing it overboard,

---

[1] Related to the preparation of drugs and medicines.
[2] A dugout canoe or log-boat on the South American Orinoco River, which runs through Venezuela and Colombia.

or of destroying it somehow—it's such a very dangerous thing to have about one. I just found it in the leather pocket in my Gladstone bag.[1] I don't know how it got there. This box contains enough to kill every soul on board this boat, and probably half a dozen other boats as well."

"You haven't yet told me what it is."

"It's curare."

"And pray what's curare? I'm no chemist."

"Very few chemists would be able to tell you. Curare is the arrow poison which was once commonly used by the aborigines in certain parts of South America. Smear the tip of an arrow with that stuff: it has only to graze a man's skin and he is dead."

"What a very pleasant kind of article to carry about with you!"

"I didn't know I was carrying it about with me. I think, when I get to town, I'll see if I can sell it. I believe you could swallow quite a lot of it and suffer no especial inconvenience; but if you'd got a sore place—a scratch, a broken bruise—you've only got to touch it with this; you would almost instantly become rigid, incapable of motion, and you'd die of something very like suffocation. The fellow who gave it to me said that it was not seldom used by husbands who wished to rid themselves of troublesome wives. He said that he knew a gentleman who had been bereft of nine wives in succession. I thought that Providence seemed to have been unusually kind to him; but that is what he said."

Mr. Tracey, replacing the lid on the round tin box, slipped it into his jacket pocket as three or four people approached with what turned out to be a suggestion to get up some sort of game. It is amazing what games one does play on board ship.

The next day I was again the witness of rather an odd little scene between the same two gentlemen—Mr. Tracey and Mr. Bellasis. It was after breakfast. I was taking the air on the hurricane deck,[2] and Mr. Bellasis was leaning over the rail, looking down on the crew below. Mr. Tracey, coming up the companion,[3] looked about him,

---

[1] A small, rigid leather portmanteau, named after Prime Minister William Ewert Gladstone (1809–1898).

[2] The uppermost deck.

[3] The companionway, stairs connecting a deck with the area below.

as it seemed to me, a little anxiously. Seeing Mr. Bellasis, he strode over towards him and touched him on the shoulder. What he said I could not see, but I saw the other's answer, because he turned right round.

"Speak away, man. What's up? Another lovely day."

The first part of Mr. Tracey's rejoinder again I did not see; then, leaning sideways against the rail, he confronted Mr. Bellasis, and also me. I dare say he spoke in undertones, because the expression on his countenance suggested that he was speaking in confidence. But, willy-nilly, I saw quite plainly what he said.

"You know that stuff I showed you yesterday morning—that curare? You remember I put it in my jacket pocket? I left it there all day. It was there when I changed last night for dinner. This morning it was gone."

"Perhaps you dropped it out. I am always dropping things out of my pockets."

"This is the jacket I wore. It was in this pocket when I hung the jacket on a nail before getting into my dinner suit. Of that I'm sure. I couldn't have dropped it out in the night; and yet it's gone."

"You're not suggesting a thief? Surely no one would take a thing like that—a tin full of poison?"

"I'm not so sure. Some people might find it useful."

There seemed to be significance in the speaker's face; probably also in his tone. Mr. Bellasis appeared to be struck by it. He raised his eyebrows.

"What kind of people? Good gracious, Tracey, are you hinting that there's some one on the 'Norse' who might find it useful on board this ship?"

"I never ought to have brought it on board with me. Some one may have taken it for a lark: some petty pilferer may have laid hands on it without knowing what it is. Think of the damage that might be done if it got into the hands of some ignorant fool. It makes me shudder. I think I shall go and report my loss to the captain. He would at least be able to let its present holder know that he's in possession of something much more dangerous than dynamite."

I take it that Mr. Tracey did report his loss, because the captain announced at table that Mr. Tracey had lost a small tin box which contained a very deadly poison, and that therefore the finder was requested to return it with the least possible delay. A similar announcement was, I believe, made in the steerage and posted on the notice-board. Yet, when the time of parting came, I travelled with some of my fellow-passengers in the same train to London, and as we were bidding each other farewell on the platform of King's Cross Station,[1] I saw Mr. Tracey whisper to Mr. Bellasis—

"Never found that curare; so if you come across a case of mysterious poisoning, we may chance upon the finder."

He smiled as he spoke, but I fancied that his mood was not merely jovial. There was a suggestion in the glance which he bestowed on Mr. Bellasis which I noticed but did not understand.

When people travel together, as it were, in one large party, they are apt to make acquaintances, some of which develop into friendship. I liked a good many of the people I had met on the "Norse," and was quite willing to see more of them. Among these were a Dr. and Mrs. Ferrers—or, rather, the latter was not Mrs. Ferrers when I met her on the "Norse," because the doctor fell in love with her during the trip and married her afterwards. I was present at the wedding, and we became, after a fashion, quite good friends. He has a practice at a watering place in the South of England, within easy reach of town, and at which I occasionally spend week-ends. When I do I not seldom join the doctor and his wife at their evening meal on the Sunday.

This was the case one Sunday in June. We had finished supper —they dined early on Sunday—and Helen and I were settling ourselves in the garden—it was a warm, lovely moonlight night—when the doctor announced that he was going out.

"What, again!" exclaimed his wife. "My dear Stanley, you've been out all day. Can't you be allowed a little rest on Sunday evening? Where are you going to?"

"I'm going to see Mrs. Bellasis. That woman worries me."

"Bellasis!" said his wife. "I thought you saw Mrs. Bellasis this morning. Is she so ill as that? I thought you said it was nothing of any consequence."

"Superficially it seems to be. So far as I can see there is little or nothing the matter; and yet—well, there are features about the

---

[1] A major railway terminus in North-Central London.

case that I don't understand, and that's what bothers me. When I'm treating a patient I hate to be puzzled."

"Has your Mrs. Bellasis," I asked, "any connexion with the Mr. Bellasis who was on board the 'Norse'?"

"She is that man's wife. Perhaps you remember he used to speak of her? They've taken a furnished house here. Last week they called me in, without knowing who I was, and I am still in attendance."

The next morning, as I was sitting on the front listening to the band, I saw Dr. Ferrers on the roadway above; and when he saw me he came down.

"Miss Lee, you are the very person I'm looking for. Do you think it would be regarded as very scandalous if you came for a drive on my car? I haven't brought my man this morning, and there's room for you."

I smiled.

"I shouldn't care if it was scandalous; only I'm sitting here expecting to meet some one, so I'm afraid I can't come. Is there anything particular which you wish to say to me?"

He placed himself on the next chair. I had grown to know him rather well, and it struck me that he was not quite his usual self.

"There is, rather; and that's where it is. Quite a number of these people know who I am; some of them will expect me to speak to them. I can't sit here and talk to you with an air of mystery, to say nothing of the fact that there may be a Judith Lee on one of those seats with her eagle glance fixed on my lips—and then the fat would be in the fire. Very inconvenient persons, sometimes, are Judith Lees."

"In that case," I told him, "rather than that you should run any risks from such an impossible person, I'll come for a little way in your car. Then you can bring me back here; and let's hope you'll get me back before my friend arrives."

Dr. Ferrers had the usual two-seater which is patronized by the young general practitioner who has not as yet a very large and lucrative practice, so that when he was in it, and I was in it, there was not room for any one else. He took me slowly along the south cliff and towards the golf links; and as we went we talked. He did most of the talking, while I listened.

"You remember," he began, "that man Bellasis on the 'Norse'?

We said some free-and-easy things about our fellow-passengers now and then. Do you recollect some one once saying, in a spirit of jocularity, that he'd hazard a guess that his wife was a tartar,[1] and that was why he had left her at home?"

I nodded.

"I remember very well. I remember also that he made a confidant of some one who passed his confidence on to me. Mr. Bellasis had more than hinted that he was not the happiest of husbands."

"Well, I fancy he isn't. And that's it."

"What's it? What do you mean?" I asked, because the doctor had stopped. He appeared to find it difficult to make a fresh start. When he did start he was apologetic.

"You understand, Miss Lee, that I have no right to talk about my patients at all, but I'm rather in a peculiar position, and you're a peculiar person——"

"Thank you."

My interpolation was not received in the spirit I had intended. He only emphasized his previous remark.

"You're a very peculiar person, indeed; and that really is my excuse for saying to you what I'm about to say." As if spurred by my silence, his pace grew a little quicker. "I'm going to tell you all about it in as few words as I can. Mrs. Bellasis is years older than her husband. In his way he seems fond of her; and in her way I dare say she's fond of him. But her way is not a nice one. I had not been with her ten minutes before she informed me that she had all the money, that her husband had none, and that my bill was to be sent in to her. I have had that sort of communication made to me before; but not quite, I think, so brusquely. When a man marries for money he doesn't know what he's letting himself in for. He'd often do much better for himself if he went in for stone-breaking. That woman must give Bellasis the devil of a time. How he puts up with her I can't understand. I should have cut her throat long ago. But, then, I'm of a homicidal bent."

"You are. A doctor naturally is."

He looked at me; but I looked straight ahead. I believe he smiled.

"Thank you. Now we're even." There was a pause. When he

[1] A ferocious or formidable opponent or foe.

spoke again his tone was graver. "It's the consciousness of what I should have done had I been in Bellasis's position which makes me uneasy." He paused, as if seeking to clothe his thoughts in just the right words. "When I was called in to Mrs. Bellasis I was not sure that hers was not simply a case of malingering. Like most selfish and self-indulgent people, she is by way of being a hypochondriac. If anything really was the matter, I set it down as some form of indigestion. But the mischief is that it gets no better. If anything, it gets worse. There is either some remote functional derangement which escapes my diagnosis, or there is something else. And that's why I want your help."

I stared at him.

"Of what possible use can I be to you in finding out what is the matter with one of your patients? I have had no medical training."

"I don't want medical training. I want eyes—your eyes."

I stared at him, if anything, still harder, which was not so easy, considering that I had to turn nearly half right round to do it.

"Pray, haven't you any eyes of your own?"

He did something which caused the car to make a little spurt. His whole manner showed that there was something on his mind of which he found it difficult to be rid. His tone was quite irascible.

"Have you ever considered how difficult a doctor's position is in a case of suspected poisoning?"

"You don't mean to say——" I stopped. I began to see what he was after, and it startled me.

"I want to say as little as I possibly can; I want you to use your eyes. You would possibly be able to find out more in five minutes than I should in five months. You have met Bellasis. I want you to renew the acquaintance. I want you to pay a visit or two to 'The Deodars'—that's his house. Mrs. Bellasis, after a fashion of her own, likes my wife, and she'd like you. I want you to report to me anything unusual you may notice. Bellasis knows nothing about your parlour tricks, so you'll have a fair field."

"I see. You want me to play the spy. That's very nice of you."

We were on the road which runs across the links. There was a thicket on one side, a rising hill on the other. He stopped the car. He could hardly have chosen a more sheltered spot; and screwing himself round, spoke to me with sudden heat.

"I'll put the case to you. There's nothing the matter with that woman; yet she not only continues ill, she keeps on getting worse. When I got there last night she was just recovering from a sort of fit. She has had another this morning, before I came. Lately she has had several, always in my absence. They leave her in a state of curious weakness. Unless, I'll put it, some one is playing tricks with her, I haven't the faintest notion what they're caused by. She never had a fit in her life until I was called in. She's not the sort of person who is likely to have fits, and there's nothing in her condition which explains them. I have been reading up certain articles on poisons. Luckily, the average doctor doesn't have much practical experience of them. I have never seen a person under the influence of one; but, of course, the books give me a general idea of what to expect. Those fits of Mrs. Bellasis suggest to me a neurotic poison. They might be caused by one of a dozen things. What actually is the cause I cannot tell you. And that's why I'm appealing to you for help. I can't say straight out that I believe the woman is being poisoned. It quite possibly might turn out that she isn't; and, in any case, directly I said that the process of dosing her would most probably cease.

"I haven't a scrap of what the law calls proof. So where should I be? I should lay myself open to an action. I quite possibly should be ruined. People don't want to employ a doctor who, when he can't make out what ails a patient, hints at things of that sort without being able to prove it. So I'm in a cleft stick. If I hold my tongue the woman will very likely die; if, as things are, I say a word I incur a risk for which I have no liking. Now you understand why it is I wish you to use your eyes."

"I'm beginning to. But I should like to understand a little more. You have been so far frank; you may as well be franker. Whom do you suspect? Any particular person or persons?"

"That's a question to which I would rather not give a direct answer. But I will tell you what I know. I know that Mr. and Mrs. Bellasis had a serious quarrel. Theirs is a cat-and-dog life at the best of times; but this was something out of the common. From what I can gather the woman was in the wrong. She behaved like a female fiend. She drove Bellasis to such a pitch of exasperation that he was heard to declare that he would like to kill her. He said so in so many words. Two days afterwards I was called in. Mrs. Bellasis has attacks of a sort which I don't understand, which always come to her in my absence, and which may be caused by any one of a dozen neurotic poisons. There's the whole position for you so far as I've grasped it. Think it over while I take you back to the front." We had just emerged from the shadow of the thicket when he gave an exclamation. "Hallo! there's Bellasis crossing the links."

"Who is the lady with him?"

"That's Miss Orme. She's a sort of neighbour. In her way, I believe she is also an heiress. She owns the place she lives in. There are eighty or ninety acres of ground which one day will be worth a lot of money."

"She seems to be quite a pretty girl, and to be only a girl."

"That's all she is; she can't be more than twenty-two or three. My wife says she's the prettiest girl in the place."

"Your wife says that, does she? I see.... Do you know what they're saying to each other?"

They were coming down a slope which was at a distance from us of perhaps rather over fifty yards. They were so absorbed in each other that they looked neither to the right nor to the left, and were quite oblivious of our presence. The sun shone full on their faces, so that I could scarcely have seen them plainer had they been seated with me in the car. I was conscious that Dr. Ferrers was glancing at me sharply.

"You don't mean that you can see what they are saying from where we are?"

It was my turn not to give him a direct answer. When I spoke I was aware that, in spite of myself, something had happened to my voice. My tone had changed. Something had disturbed me.

"Now I am playing the spy. Would you mind driving on? I have seen all I want to see—and rather more."

The car progressed. The pair coming down the slope must have heard the noise it made; but if they did, they never glanced in our direction. We had gone right past them before my companion spoke again.

"What's up? I see there's something up. You may as well tell me what it is. You surely couldn't make out what they were saying from where they were."

"I wish that were so. I am sorry to say that I made it out only too plainly. We came at what was for them a very unfortunate moment. Dr. Ferrers, if Mr. Bellasis and that girl are not lovers they are something very like it."

In his surprise he did something to the car which made it give a little jump.

"Lovers! Bellasis and Miss Orme? You say that simply because you saw them alone together. I confess that they seem very much interested in each other; but to draw such an inference——"

"I will tell you what I saw them say. It's a trespass on their confidence which, in the face of what you have just been saying to me, I am inclined to think is justified. You'll be able to draw your own inference. When I first caught sight of them she was in the middle of a sentence. I saw the end of it. 'I—— truly mean it—truly, Frank?' That was the fag end of her sentence. He replied—I saw every word he said—'If Poppy dies—— Of course, that's rather a large "if." When she dies, I'll marry you the day after—or after what you consider to be a sufficiently decent interval.' 'I'd marry you the day after,' she answered, 'if you'd have me.' 'Madeleine!' he rejoined. 'If I'd have you!' It was at that point that I ceased to look at them and asked you to drive on. I did not know what he might be going to say next, and there are limits even to espionage such as mine. Now, before you speak, permit me to make a remark or two, lest you should doubt that I actually saw what I did. He used the name 'Poppy.' I don't know who Poppy is. Do you?"

"That's the name he calls his wife. I believe her name is really Florence; but I have heard him call her Poppy.... But that you should see him say it at such a distance!"

"That is nothing. Distance doesn't count—nothing counts—if I can see at all. I saw him call her 'Madeleine.' Is that her name?"

"I have no idea. I shouldn't wonder." He gave a sort of little gasp. "No one's safe. I shall have to give Helen a tip to try even to stop thinking—lest her thoughts should shape themselves on her lips— while you are about."

"You tell me about the curious case of Mrs. Bellasis; you ask me to use my eyes. When I use them you talk like that. I think, Dr. Ferrers, you had better call in the assistance of another medical man. I'll return to town this afternoon."

He seemed to be alarmed.

"Don't do that, for goodness' sake! See what you've done already. Don't you see how much more serious the position becomes in the face of the discovery you've just made? There was motive before. Bellasis was on bad terms with his wife; he was heard to threaten to kill her. But when he talks to that girl about marrying her directly his wife is dead, I'm afraid, Miss Lee, that things look even uglier than I thought."

That afternoon, instead of returning to town, Mrs. Ferrers took me to call on Mrs. Bellasis. I do not think Helen had any idea of the suspicions which were in her husband's mind, or of the purpose which really took me to "The Deodars." The maid kept us waiting in an empty room for a moment or two, then told us that Mrs. Bellasis would be very glad to see us in her bedroom. Hers was rather a pleasant chamber. I took in all of it I could directly I entered. There were four windows in the room, one of them a French window. They were all wide open. It was a glorious day. The patient's bed stood by one of the open windows. The blind was drawn, screening the sun from her face. Mrs. Bellasis was sitting up in bed with an arrangement of cushions behind her—a thin, grey-faced woman, with a wisp of hair twisted tightly on the top of her head. She looked as if she were not very far from sixty. I should have put down her husband as barely thirty. I could not help feeling that when he married her Mr. Bellasis must have been in a very tight place, or that she must have a very great deal of money.

We did not find her unpleasant. She seemed very weak. She said she had just recovered from one of her attacks. I pricked up my ears at this, getting her to tell us what form it had taken. She said that they generally came on when she was dozing, before she was quite asleep. All at once, as she put it, something had seemed to happen to her. She tried to wake, but couldn't; she ceased to breathe, her muscles became rigid. She did not think she ever quite lost consciousness, yet she could neither speak nor move nor see. How long the attack would last she could not say; it seemed to her that if some one did not come to her assistance soon she might be dead. As it passed away she would break into a profuse perspiration; she trembled all over, as again she put it, inside and out; she would begin to cry simply because she could not help it.

Mr. Bellasis came in while we were there. He had not altered since I had met him on the boat; but it struck me that he was nervous and flurried. He was very friendly to me. I wondered what he would have felt like if he had known what I saw that morning. And his manner towards his wife was excellent—much better than hers towards him. The woman was self-conscious, jealous, irritable, as well as ill. She was too clearly aware of the difference between them in years, in looks, in health—in all those things in which youth triumphs over age. She did not say a word to him which was not intended to sting. He could not help wincing now and then—else he would have been more, or less, than human. But on the whole he bore himself very well.

Helen Ferrers said to me as we left the house—

"I hope you won't be very shocked, but if I were in Mr. Bellasis's shoes I doubt if I should offer up very earnest prayers for his wife's recovery. However came he to marry such a woman? The mystery seems greater every time I go there. Unless he was actually starving, I do not see how he ever could have done it." She added, after a momentary interval, as if she had been reflecting deeply: "If anything did happen to her, I wonder if he would marry again?"

There came a note from "The Deodars" soon after Helen and I had returned. Helen read it first, and then passed it to me.

"DEAR MRS. FERRERS," it ran, "will you and Miss Lee come and dine to-morrow night? I shall not be able to be present at the actual meal, but I shall be with you in spirit, though upstairs. Two sisters of mine are coming, and I must do something to entertain them. I am sure they will be very glad to see you. Mr. Bellasis has been telling me what good company he found Miss Lee on that Norwegian cruise of his. I am sure he will be delighted to see her, so tell her she must come—and you also; and, of course, the doctor. Don't suppose because I am an invalid in bed that I will take a refusal from either of you. I shall expect you all three.—Yours sincerely,

"FLORENCE BELLASIS."

Helen eyed me as I read it. She said, when she saw I had finished—
"Don't you think that's rather a curious epistle? Let Jack see it."
I handed it to the doctor, who had just come in. She went on: "I

suppose you won't feel like going to the house of a perfect stranger, with the hostess in bed?"

"I'm not so sure." I was regarding the doctor. "My inclination is to go."

I do not know if the lady was aware of it, but her husband and I exchanged glances.

"I also am disposed to accept," he said; "that is, Helen, if you don't very much mind."

Helen seemed puzzled, which I did not consider surprising.

"I can't quite make you two out. However, if you've any special reason for accepting this very singular invitation, don't let me stand in your way. I'll come with you; though I think it will be the first time I ever had dinner in a strange house when I knew beforehand that my hostess was ill in bed."

I exchanged a few words with Dr. Ferrers as I was going to dress for dinner—we met on the landing.

"Did you find out anything this afternoon?" That was the question he put to me.

"That depends upon what you call 'anything,'" I replied. "By the way, you and I had better understand each other. What do you want? Do you want your patient to get better and run no risk of ever falling ill again from the same cause? And having satisfied yourself as to the patient's recovery, will you take my word for it that there is no danger of a recurrence, and ask no questions? I have my own odd ways of doing things. I am going to try to do this thing on lines of my own. I promise you, on my part, to do my best, and all that I feel you ought to know I'll tell you; but you, on your part, will have to promise that you'll use no effort to make me speak when I'd rather not, that you'll let me keep silent when I want to, and—as I said just now—ask no questions."

He looked at me very hard and very straight.

"I want no scandal, if that's what you mean."

"That's what I do mean; and I may have to take steps to produce the result which we are both of us aiming at of which I'd rather not say anything to you."

He smiled; he eyed me so steadily that I feel sure he thought he knew what was passing through my mind. If that was what he did think, I fancy he was wrong.

"I certainly want to know nothing about any course of proceeding which is not in the strictest order. I think you can be trusted to be reasonably discreet; and on the understanding that you are responsible for your own actions, that whatever you may do has nothing to do with me, you may count upon my being absolutely dumb."

It was very kind of him. He seemed to think that in allowing me to do his work in my own way he was condescending, but I did not mind—men are such queer things. I was prepared to accept responsibility.

The next evening there was quite a party at "The Deodars." Mrs. Bellasis's sisters proved to be two bustling, elderly spinsters, full of life and go, and, at least on the surface, very much pleasanter than their married sister. When Mrs. Ferrers began to talk of how strange it seemed to come to dinner when the mistress of the house was in bed, they pooh-poohed her altogether. They said that their invitation to "The Deodars" was of long standing, that Mrs. Bellasis had promised them a good time, and they did not see why they should be destined to dine alone with Mr. Bellasis every night because his wife chose to stop in bed. The elder Miss Wetherell—their name was Wetherell—whispered to Helen, it seemed to me rather gratuitously, that it was just as well, sometimes, that Florence should stay in bed.

There were also there as guests a Mr. and Mrs. Sydenham, a Mr. Sewell, and Miss Orme.

The latter young lady looked lovely, and she was beautifully dressed. She seemed to be without a chaperon, and under the circumstances I could not understand her being there at all, but since Mr. Bellasis was given an opportunity of comparing her with his lawful wife, I did not wonder that in the comparison Poppy suffered. As I looked at the girl's face it seemed difficult to believe that the relations could exist between her and her host which I more than suspected; she seemed so flowerlike, so sweet, so pure, so innocent.

At dinner I sat at my host's left, facing Mrs. Ferrers. The Misses Wetherell were at the other end of the table on either side of Dr. Ferrers. Miss Orme sat between Miss Wetherell and Mr. Sydenham. So far as I could see, she talked chiefly to her feminine neighbour, who had clearly fallen in love with her at sight. Mr. Bellasis talked to me. He recalled incidents of our trip on the "Norse." I asked if he had seen anything more of Mr. Tracey, and I kept my eyes on him as I put the question. He said that he had not; that he and Mr. Tracey had exchanged cards, that he had meant to continue the acquaintance, but that somehow he had not.

"He was a very decent fellow," he observed; "I liked him. The fact is, I don't know what became of his card—what does become of all the cards one gets? If I ever come across it I shouldn't wonder if I asked him to look us up."

Mr. Tracey had given me his card; I knew where it was. I should not wonder if I looked him up. I had at that moment a certain incident with which Mr. Tracey was connected very much in mind.

"It's very unfortunate," I said, "that Mrs. Bellasis should be unwell; I feel quite guilty coming to her house while she's in bed."

"It is unfortunate," he agreed, "and the worst of it is that I don't know what's the matter with her; and between ourselves"—he leant towards me—"I doubt if the doctor does, either."

I hardly knew what to answer. I could scarcely tell him, right out at his own table, that certain suspicions were entertained. I changed the subject suddenly.

"What a lovely girl Miss Orme is." I was mistaken if I expected him to change colour, or to show any sign of discomposure. He just glanced at her and smiled.

"Isn't she? And she's as good as she is lovely. Some men have all the luck!" I did not ask him what he meant. I fancied I could guess.

After dinner there arose a not unusual difficulty of how to entertain the company. Helen played; Miss Orme sang, not very well; then there was an interval, in which nothing was done. There was talk about bridge, about a round game—no one seemed keen on either. Mr. Bellasis got out a pack of cards and did some tricks; then Mrs. Sydenham volunteered to tell fortunes—and told them very badly; I could have done it much better myself. It was while she was making an exhibition of her incompetency to do what she pretended that a rather brilliant idea occurred to me.

"I don't know if any one here is aware," I observed when the lady had got herself into a hopeless muddle, "that I am by the way of being a witch, a magician, a kind of hereditary dealer in magic and spells."

"No, are you really?" asked Miss Orme, her beautiful eyes seeming to have grown all at once to twice their usual size. "Oh, do do something, please."

"Do all of you know," I continued, "that my name is Lee, and that the Lees are the greatest family of gipsies in England, perhaps in the world—the purest Romanies still surviving are Lees? My father's father was a pure Romany; my father lived under canvas till he was a well-grown lad—I heard him say so; my mother was of Romany extraction. When I was young my parents taught me many things which I don't think are taught to ordinary English children. Although my father and mother were two of the most intellectual persons I think I have ever met, they had, both of them, what it is the fashion to call superstitions. My mother used to say that if she had been born two hundred years ago she would have been burned as a witch. To my knowledge she had what people would call some very singular powers. I won't say anything about myself, but, is any one here a spiritualist—if it is not asking an impertinent question?"

"A spiritualist!" exclaimed Miss Orme, with her eyes still opened to their widest. "Why?"

"At any rate, does any one here know anything about table turning, or believe in it? I have produced some very singular results from a table, even in the presence of unbelievers; and as this room contains what seems to be quite a suitable table, I'll give some demonstrations with it now if you like."

I fancy that the people hardly knew how to take me. There was at one side of the room a round, old-fashioned table, which was attached to a sort of pedestal which served as a support.

"Mr. Bellasis," I said, "do you mind our having this table somewhere where we can all sit round it? As a repository of Romany wisdom I think I might be able to show you something rather curious."

The table was brought out; we all of us sat round, resting our extended finger-tips upon the top. Most people have at some period of their lives been present at a séance of table turning, and know what the preliminaries are.

"Now," I observed when everything was ready, "I must ask you to keep silence, and not to press upon the table—just rest the tips of your fingers. This is such a heavy table that I doubt if we could move it by any amount of pressure on the top; but, anyhow, I don't want the results I may have to be produced by any sort of pressure."

I spoke so seriously that the company had grown serious also— at least, outwardly. If the Misses Wetherell showed an inclination to giggle, I fancy it was because they were unwilling to be impressed.

"Perfect silence, please." And every one was silent. Miss Orme's eyes seemed to be almost as large as small saucers; the Misses Wetherell ceased to simper. There was a perceptible interval, and then I asked, in what I imagined to be portentous tones: "Are the spirits present?"

The words were scarcely out of my lips when the table began to tremble, as if it had the ague; there was an odd sound like the rending of wood—thrice repeated. The company seemed startled. I spoke again—

"Do you hear? The spirits are present; those three raps mean yes."

"Oughtn't we," inquired Mrs. Sydenham in a mysterious whisper, "to have the gas lowered? I thought that these sort of things were always done in the darkness."

"Not by me," I informed her. "By me they are done in the light. I wish to be suspected of no trickery; to have everything open and above board."

"Do you really think," asked Miss Orme, with a most singular look in those wonderful eyes of hers, "that there are spirits present?"

"You must judge for yourself; I say nothing. Suppose some one puts a question, you will be able to judge from the answer if any occult force is present. I'd better explain to any force that may be present that when a question is put I will repeat the alphabet aloud, so that all of you can hear, and when I come to the proper letter we shall esteem ourselves favoured if the fact is signified in the usual way. Is there a sheet of paper and a pencil handy? Perhaps, Mr. Sydenham, you wouldn't mind taking down the letters in order as they come, then when the answer is finished we shall be able to see if anything can be made of them. Now what would you like to ask, Miss Orme?"

The girl hesitated; then a faint tinge of colour came into her cheeks—I had no doubt that she was serious enough. When she spoke there was a little tremor in her voice.

"I should like to know if the dearest wish I have in the world will ever be fulfilled."

It might have been my imagination, but my impression was that as she spoke she and Mr. Bellasis exchanged glances; they were such flitting ones that perhaps it was only fancy.

"That," I remarked, "is a question which can be answered by a mere negative or affirmative. Miss Orme wishes to know if her dearest wish will ever be fulfilled. Force that is present, please tell her."

Again there was an interval of silence—rather tense silence, then the table began to tremble. "Oh-h-h!" The exclamation came simultaneously from Miss Orme and the elder Miss Wetherell.

"Hush," whispered Mrs. Sydenham, "that means that it's going to speak."

"When a question has been asked," I observed severely, "will no one speak until it has been answered. Force that is present, please tell us if Miss Orme's dearest wish will be fulfilled."

The table wavered more and more; all our fingers were shivering; then there came two loud insistent crackling sounds, and the wavering ceased.

"I'm afraid, Miss Orme, that that's a negative; it looks as if your dearest wish were not to be fulfilled. You had better wish for something else instead, something not so utterly out of reach, something which every girl has a right to wish. Has any one else a question to ask?"

The girl said nothing, but an odd change had taken place in the expression of her beautiful face. She looked as if she had just received some dreadful tidings and was unable to conceal the fact.

"Don't believe a word of it," said Mrs. Sydenham; "these sort of things always tell lies."

Still the girl said nothing. She seemed all at once to have become incapable of speech.

"Suppose," cried Dr. Ferrers, as if to break through the uncomfortable feeling which had all at once settled on the company, "I ask a question—if I may, Miss Lee."

"You may ask anything you please; the answer doesn't come from me."

"Is that so? Well, then, I've got a patient upstairs in whom I am naturally very much interested, and whose condition I find rather puzzling; can your friends, the spirits, tell me exactly what ails her? I should like to know, on good authority, wouldn't you, Bellasis?"

"I should, very much indeed."

If, as he spoke, a shadow of what might have been anxiety passed across the speaker's face, it was capable of a quite simple explanation.

"That's very interesting," cackled Mrs. Sydenham. "Now let the spirits tell us what's the matter with Mrs. Bellasis. I shall have a much better opinion of them if they do."

Miss Orme kept her glance on the table. Her long, slender fingers were twitching as if she were suffering from an attack of nerves.

"Spirits," I said, with all the solemnity of which I was capable, "Mrs. Bellasis is ill; can you tell us, please, what is the cause of her illness? Silence! and listen."

They were silent; for some moments there was not a sound. Then again the table began to waver, to shake, to tremble—I scarcely know how to describe it—so violently that it gave one an odd sensation to watch the shivering hands. I began to go through the letters of the alphabet, aloud, in the orthodox fashion. When I came to "M" there ran through the room that strange, tearing, rending sound which seemed to proceed from the very heart of the wood out of which the table was fashioned.

"The first letter, Mr. Sydenham, seems to be 'M'; kindly put it down."

And so I went on, until Mr. Sydenham had a long line of letters on his sheet of paper. Every now and then there came a double sound, signifying that the word was ended. Then, at last, three sounds, signifying that the answer was complete. The cracking sound ceased, the wavering died away; all was still, till Mrs. Sydenham spoke, in tones of awe.

"How very extraordinary. I never saw anything like that before."

The elder Miss Wetherell asked, in a shaky whisper: "Can there really be something supernatural present? Are you in earnest, Miss Lee?"

I left her question unanswered and spoke to Mr. Sydenham.

"Can you make anything of what you have written down?"

I had noticed that the expression on his face was growing more

and more peculiar. My inquiry seemed to add to his mental disturbance.

"This is most unpleasant. I am sure I have got the letters as you
gave them me. I think, Miss Lee, I had better give you the paper and
see what you make of it."

"What have you got?" twittered the elder Miss Wetherell. "What
is there strange about the answer?"

"I will read it to you, and then you'll be able to judge for yourself.
I asked what was the cause of Mrs. Bellasis's illness. This, according
to Mr. Sydenham, is the answer that has been given: 'Mrs. Bellasis is
being poisoned.'"

"What a horrible thing to say." This again was the elder Miss
Wetherell. There were several rather awkward moments. I did not
like the look on our host's face at all. He seemed to me to have had
a sudden scare. Miss Orme had raised her eyes and was positively
glaring at me. One might almost have said that her bearing was
intended to convey defiance.

"And pray," she asked, as if she were daring any one to answer,
"by what is Mrs. Bellasis being poisoned?"

I put her question then and there. I think that my promptness
rather took her aback. Silence had returned; on all the faces was a
suggestion of gravity; people were taking the matter much more
seriously than they had meant to. The tremulant movement of the
table recommenced. I recited the alphabet, again and again, up to
a certain point, till I was stopped by that mysterious sound, which
was all at once thrice repeated.

"The answer," I observed, "seems to consist of a single word.
What have you got there, Mr. Sydenham?"

"I presume I have got it correctly," replied the gentleman
addressed. "I took down the letters as they came, but if I have got it
right, I don't know what the word means. It seems to be 'Curare.'"

I imagined that the word was as strange to the larger part of the
company as it was to Mr. Sydenham; if the word was unknown to
Miss Orme her singular behaviour became the more inexplicable.

Rising from her seat she gave the table a push; she must have
exerted considerable strength, because she almost knocked it over.

"Lies! Lies!" she exclaimed, apparently in quite a paroxysm of
rage. "Nothing but lies! I won't stop here and listen to your silly,

wretched stuff. It's an insult to our intelligence. I'd sooner play blind man's buff. I think, Mr. Bellasis, that it's time I went home. Good night, every one."

Her movements were so rapid that, before we could realize her intention, she had not only reached the door, but had gone through it, having included us all in one curt farewell greeting. We were, all of us, I fancy, a little troubled, but our host's agitation seemed almost painful, as if he found it difficult to express himself coherently.

"I—I must go and see—what's the matter—with Miss Orme," he stammered; he also passed through the door as if he fled from the room.

"What does it mean?" gasped the elder Miss Wetherell. "What is the matter? Surely—surely——" She stopped to raise her hands as if in an appeal to Heaven. "I don't like to think—— I never did hold with trying to find out what we were never meant to know. This should serve as a lesson to us never to countenance this sort of thing again."

I looked at Dr. Ferrers; the expression of amazement and distress on his face struck me as almost comical. But then, I was not so much taken by surprise as he was. While they were all talking together, I, in my turn, slipped from the room. As I had half expected, I found Mr. Bellasis standing in the open doorway which led into the garden. He turned to me as if bewildered.

"I can't find Miss Orme," he exclaimed. "She must have run away."

I went into the garden; he followed me. The moon was so bright that I could see how the muscles of his face were working. I saw that he was in the frame of mind to suit my purpose. I did not beat about the bush, I went straight to the point.

"Mr. Bellasis," I said, "can there be anything in what has just now happened? Mrs. Bellasis told me this afternoon a strange story about the kind of attacks she has; and—curare! Do you remember the curare which Mr. Tracey lost on board the 'Norse'? Surely—surely——"

I purposely left my sentence unfinished; he completed it for me.

"I found it—yes, I found it; and—I've lost it again, and that's the trouble. I can't think who can have found it."

"Are you sure that you lost it?

"Am I sure? What do you mean by asking if I'm sure? One would think from the way in which you look that you were accusing me. What do you mean? It isn't possible that you think——"

It was his turn to leave his sentence incomplete, and for me to finish it.

"You tell me that you found the tin of curare which Mr. Tracey lost. But I happen to know that you did not tell Mr. Tracey so, and that he went away under the impression that no one had found it. If, as you say, you did find it, when did you find it, and why did you not return it to its owner?"

"I did not know until after I had left the ship that it was in my possession—that I had found it. It was contained in an ordinary round tin, very much like those used for tooth-powder. I dare say once it had been used for tooth-powder. My impression is that whatever he may have thought about having left it in his jacket pocket, he must have dropped it in one of the bath-rooms, because I took away from one of them a tin which I thought was my tooth-powder. When I got home I was about to dip my tooth-brush into what I supposed to be a tin of powder, and found to my surprise that it was nothing of the kind, that it was a tin full of resinous-looking stuff; and then all at once it jumped to my mind that it must be Tracey's curare; it gave me the cold shivers when I thought how near I had been to using it as tooth-powder. I told you at dinner that I had mislaid Tracey's card and didn't know his address. I've been hoping to come across him some day so that I can return him his property."

He seemed to be earnest enough; I believed him to be speaking the truth.

"And you say that it is now no longer in your possession, that you've lost it? Knowing what dangerous stuff it was, how came you to do that? Did you speak of it to any one—your wife, for instance?"

"Not to my wife, but"—he seemed to add it with difficulty—"I did mention it to some one."

"To whom?" I hazarded a guess. "To Miss Orme?"

"Yes, to Miss Orme. How did you know it?"

"I didn't; I—just wondered. Under what circumstances did you mention it to Miss Orme?"

"I told her the story of what a narrow shave I'd had—the same morning on which I came across it. I did as Tracey said he did, I put it in my jacket pocket—that was in the evening. I went indoors to change for dinner, hung my coat on a peg, thought next morning when I was going to put it on what an ass I'd been to copy Tracey, felt for the tin and it was gone."

"How long ago was that?

"That was two days after I'd left you all in town. I made what seemed to me all possible inquiries, but I've seen nothing of it ever since."

"And have had no suspicions?"

"Miss Lee, I believe you have a suspicion."

"Mr. Bellasis, I believe your wife is being poisoned by curare; I fancy you believe it also."

"It is impossible, absolutely impossible. I don't believe it; I can't believe it."

"Yet you do believe it, and you suspect Miss Orme."

"Miss Lee!" The way in which he glared at me. "How—how——"

I shaped his question for him. "How do I know that? Because your manner betrays you; as her conscience has betrayed Miss Orme. Tell me on what you base your suspicions."

He hesitated; he seemed to be undergoing a mental struggle; then he asked me a question which did take me aback.

"Miss Lee, do you believe that insanity is hereditary?"

"Under certain circumstances, undoubtedly. Why do you ask me?"

"Because——" He seemed as if he could get no farther; there came a look upon his face which it was not nice to see—a look of agony.

"Is there insanity in Miss Orme's family?" I had hit on it. Again his manner betrayed him. He spoke as if the words were being wrenched from him.

"Her mother is in an asylum—dreadful story; her mother's mother died raving mad; they are called 'the mad Ormes.' But I see no sign of anything of the kind in Madeleine, never; not one. I don't believe—I am quite certain——" I interrupted him.

"Then I am not quite certain; I have the gravest doubts. I am beginning to understand. Where does Miss Orme live?"

"The drive to her house is just outside our gates, but there is a short cut across the garden here, you know."

Just then Dr. Ferrers came out of the open doorway.

"I thought I heard the sound of voices," he explained. "What are you two people talking about out here? Every one is wondering what has become of you."

"Dr. Ferrers," I cried, "Mr. Bellasis and I are going to call on Miss Orme; will you please come with us? Come quickly, just as you are. I am afraid it is a matter in which we ought to make as much haste as we can. I've a feeling that it is."

I was right; although we could hardly have moved more quickly, we arrived too late. A footman told us, when we arrived at the front door of the young lady's house, that his mistress was not in. I pushed past him.

"Are you sure of that? I think you are mistaken. Is there no other way into the house beside the front door by which she may have entered without your knowledge?"

The man eyed me as if bewildered, which was quite excusable. Our eruption must have been unlooked for, and my manner probably seemed strange.

"Miss Orme may have come in through the conservatory, or by the drawing-room window; there are several ways into the house. I will make inquiries."

He was not put to so much trouble. There was a sound above of a woman screaming. A maid appeared at the head of the staircase; at sight of the footman she screamed again.

"Jackson, Miss Orme has had a fit. I believe she's dead."

She was dead. But the fit had not come in the ordinary course of nature. A tin box was beside her, which was familiar both to Mr. Bellasis and to me. With the aid of a curious form of hypodermic syringe, which it almost looked as if she must have had manufactured to her special order, having first torn open her bodice, she had injected some of the contents of that tin into the region of her heart, and must instantly have died.

Her conscience, roused by the cracks emanating from that round wooden table, had sent her to her death.

Mrs. Bellasis recovered. The presumption is that, having obtained possession of that deadly little box, Miss Orme had injected minute doses of the poison, whose potency—with the cunning peculiar to the mentally unsound—she had probably previously decreased, into her intended victim while asleep—her attacks always occurred just after she had been roused from slumber, especially when she had been dozing in the daytime. It was quite easy for the girl, who was regarded as an habitué of the house, to gain admission, and there was more than one way of reaching Mrs. Bellasis's bedroom unnoticed.

Possibly one day the dose would have been made stronger, with fatal results; the explanation would quite conceivably have been that the patient had died in a fit. Probably because—at least to some extent—of the pranks which were played with that table, at the present time of writing she still lives. I doubt if she has ever heard the word curare, or knows anything of the contents of that tin box. Those contents no longer exist. They were not returned to Mr. Tracey. I took upon myself the responsibility of their destruction. I burned them in the presence of Dr. Ferrers and of Mr. Bellasis, feeling strongly that it was the part of wisdom, since they had already been lost twice, to take care that they should not be lost a third time.

LADY BEATRICE

I was occupying a penny chair in Hyde Park one fine June morning, when there approached from the right one of the most beautiful girls I had ever seen. She was tall, slight, and stately; if her face had a defect, it was that her features were too perfect. She reminded me of what Galatea[1] might have been—a triumph of the sculptor's art come to life. Her dress was as perfect as her appearance. She seemed to know numbers of people, and as she strolled she nodded to this one and to that. As she neared me a man was approaching from the right—a tall, well-built man, broad-chested, head erect, who walked with a certain stiffness suggestive of a drill sergeant. His hat was set just the slightest shade on the side of his head, his moustaches were waxed. As this man neared the girl he eyed her with what struck me as an impudent stare. She did not glance in his direction at all, but was in the act of nodding to some friends who were on the other side of the railing; yet, as they passed each other, I saw her lips move and form the word "Clarice."

Each continued to stroll. No greeting had been exchanged; there had been nothing in their demeanour to show that they knew each other; yet I felt pretty certain that the girl had conveyed a message to the man—"Clarice." I wondered what the message meant, who Clarice might be; above all, why they wished the world to regard them as strangers.

A rather odd light was suddenly thrown on the little scene I had just witnessed. Among the usual loiterers leaning against the railing were two men, almost immediately in front of me. They seemed to be gentlemen, and to be there, like the rest of the world, to see the people and take the air. I saw the elder say to the younger—

"You saw that fellow who passed just now? That's one of the biggest blackguards in Europe."

His companion asked—

"Do you mean the man with his hat on the side of his head and the padded shoulders?"

[1] In Greek mythology, Pygmalion's ivory statue of a beautiful woman which comes to life.

"That's the fellow. He calls himself the Vicomte d'Aubry. He is one of those semi-demi-professional gamblers whom you always find taking the bank at baccarat at the Continental casino. He was suspected of funny little practices for years; then they nailed him at Aix,[1] and I believe somewhere else a little later. Still, I fancy, he plays the banker at places where he isn't known, or where little peculiarities are overlooked. A friend in the Paris police told me two or three years ago that they were after him for *chantage*[2]—and they got him, too; but the thing was hushed up, as those sort of things so often are. All the same, I believe he got the fright of his life. I wonder what the blackguard is doing in town?"

I also wondered. If what the speaker said was true, I could quite understand why that girl had been unwilling to advertise their acquaintanceship. Since she was so young, and seemed to be, every inch of her, a person of the great world, I wondered how she came to be on such intimate terms with him as to convey to him a secret message as she strolled through the park.

I had in my handbag at that moment a letter which the post had brought me that morning from a correspondent with whom I had some slight acquaintance—Lady Sarah Crawley. I had taken the letter with me so that I might have it at hand for further consideration—it told such a queer story, and contained such a singular request. Lady Sarah said that, for some time past, a series of petty thefts had been taking place in houses of her acquaintance. It was feared that the thief must have been one of the guests who, because exposure had not followed, had grown in boldness, since the articles stolen were increasing in value; until matters reached a climax a few days ago, when she was staying with her father, the Duke of Horsham. It was discovered, as one of the guests was about to leave, and her maid was packing, that a pearl necklace was missing from her jewel-case which had been there when she arrived. Lady Sarah went on to say that practically the same party was going to spend the week-end at a great house near London. Would I come down as one of the guests? If I exercised my gift, I might find out what no one else could. In other words, would I act as a sort of private detective? Lady Sarah was pleased to add, as delicately as possible, that

[1] Aix-en-Provence, a city in the South of France.
[2] Blackmail (French).

my services would meet with a handsome reward.

The proposition did not commend itself to me in the least. I never have done that sort of thing. I never want to. The adventures I have had in that direction have been more or less in the way of casual accidents; I have very seldom set out, from the very beginning, with the deliberate intention of conducting an investigation. I did not know what to say to Lady Sarah Crawley. I owed her more than one kindness. I did not wish to say, point-blank, "No"; yet I wished she had not written.

The presence of Lady Sarah's letter in my handbag was recalled very forcibly to my memory by the incident between that young and high-bred English girl and the foreign scamp of which I had been a witness. He had been accused of *chantage*. That meant blackmail. A simple, innocent, English girl might easily get herself sufficiently entangled with such an adventurer to enable him to make use of her in a manner which she had never dreamed was possible. I kept asking myself, over and over again, who was Clarice? Why had she, with such secrecy, breathed her name?

Tired of my penny chair, I joined the strollers. When I reached the corner by the statue, there, the centre of a group of persons who were chatting together like old friends, was the girl of whom I had been thinking. A superintendent of police with whom I had some acquaintance was standing a little way off.

"Can you tell me," I asked him, "who that young lady is?"

He looked at me with a twinkle in his eye.

"Got anything against her, Miss Lee? She's not in want of lessons. I don't think she's deaf and dumb."

"No," I admitted, "I don't think she is. She's chattering away just now. She's so very beautiful that I thought I'd like to know who she was—if you know, and it's not a breach of confidence to impart your knowledge."

"Oh, yes, I know. She's this season's débutante, the prettiest of the lot. She's Lady Beatrice Dacre, the youngest daughter of the Marquis of Putney."

I lunched that morning at the club. After lunch I had my coffee in the reading-room. On the table was one of those silly ladies' fashion papers which are nothing but a combination of advertisements. My eye caught a paragraph in one of the columns—

"We hear great things of that well-known professor of the recondite art which professes to see such wonderful things in the lines of the palms of our hands—Clarice. We hear Clarice spoken of on all sides. The names of those who consult a palmist are never breathed in public, or we might mention some very great names whose owners are among Clarice's most constant consultants. Rumour has it that Clarice's studio at No. 37, Airedale Street,[1] which is not a stone's throw from Bond Street, is crowded whenever it is open, and yet that room can always be found for more ardent inquirers after truth."

It was the name, I take it, which caused that paragraph to, as the French phrase it, "jump to my eyes"—Clarice. It was the name which Lady Beatrice Dacre had breathed to the Vicomte d'Aubry.

Did that mean that the palmist's was to be made the scene of a rendezvous? I had heard of such places being used for such purposes; yet Lady Beatrice Dacre would have to be careful, or she might find herself in serious trouble. I wondered if she had no near and dear relative or friend on whose advice and discretion she could implicitly rely. She would need one if she had much to do with the Vicomte d'Aubry.

I felt interested in M. le Vicomte. It is perhaps not generally known that there are in London certain sources of information open to the initiated, where something may be learned about almost any one. I gleaned no actual facts about that illustrious foreign nobleman, but certain suggestions were made which induced me that evening to pay a visit to a much-frequented restaurant within a hundred miles of Piccadilly Circus.[2]

It was, as usual, pretty full when I entered; there was only one vacant table within reasonable distance of the door. I looked carefully round before I seated myself. So far as I could see, if he was coming, the vicomte had not yet arrived. I ordered a cup of coffee. There was a solitary individual at a table nearly fronting me, with that unhealthy sort of complexion which marks a certain type of

[1] Apparently imaginary.
[2] The junction of Piccadilly, Regent Street, Haymarket and Shaftesbury Avenue in the West End; a fashionable district.

Frenchman—at least, to my mind. The man might have been made
of wax; he could scarcely have seemed more inanimate if he had
been. I had brought an evening paper. I held it up in front of me
as a screen. My *vis-à-vis*, in spite of his immobility, was impatient;
he kept glancing at his watch as if waiting for some one who did
not come. I began to have an idea that I had seen him somewhere
before; but I decided that the fact was that he was the croupier
type of man, that machine-like creature in whom humanity seems
dead, who is such a familiar figure in France in places where they
gamble.

My cup of coffee was drawing to a close. The waiter was eyeing
me; he would swoop on it in a minute. I should either have to order
something else or go. So I ordered a crème de menthe—one can
linger over a crème de menthe for an indefinite period. As the
waiter was pouring the bright green liquid into a tiny glass I saw the
Vicomte d'Aubry come through the door. I held up my paper. He
looked about him; then came striding towards my *vis-à-vis*.

He sat down on the red plush seat beside the wax-like individual,
so that both men fronted me. The greeting they exchanged was not
particularly warm.

"You think I am your plaything that you keep me waiting as long
as you please? You ought to have been here half an hour ago."

It was the waxen man who spoke. As might have been expected,
his lips barely moved; but they moved enough for me. Both men
spoke in French. Precisely what the vicomte replied I was not sure.
His face was sideways to me, so that it was not easy to be certain of
the movements of his lips. That he was volubly apologetic was clear
from the other's answer, which was frigidly contemptuous—

"You excuse yourself always. We all know your excuses. You will
please to understand that the time has come when something else is
required—something solid."

Again the vicomte's exact reply was lost to me; again the other's
rejoinder threw light on it—

"We do not require you to do what you call your best; we desire
from you a certain thing—that only. Nothing else in substitution.
Above all, no excuses."

Again the hiatus formed by the vicomte's answer. I began to
wish that he would turn his face round, so that I might not have to

guess at his words from the other's reply. The waxen man said very coldly, very dryly—

"You have the presumption to suggest it. You are under a bond to pay ten thousand pounds at least. You give me instead a necklace in which there are not a dozen pearls worth anything. You pretend that that shows the sincerity of your desire to pay. It won't do. We must either have the money or its equivalent before next Monday evening."

Then the vicomte did look round, all warmth, gesticulation.

"It is impossible! I give you my word of honour, it cannot be done."

"Your word of honour! That also is not required. As for impossible, I know better. Attend to me."

There was something in the waxen man's fashion of speaking which recalled a mechanical figure. He kept his tired, expressionless eyes fixed on the face of the Vicomte d'Aubry.

"You have a certain lady friend. I wish to mention no names; you understand—we also understand. She goes to a certain house on Friday for what here they call the week-end. To the same house are going two Americans, whom again I will not name."

"How do you know?" The vicomte asked the question with an eagerness which was in odd contrast to the other's phlegm.

"We do know; that is enough. The American woman is taking with her her jewels, among them her rubies. You have heard of her rubies? You know who I mean? I see you have heard of them. You do know who I mean."

How he had learned this from the other's face I could not tell. He moved his lips so slightly that while he was speaking, for fear of losing some essential word, I dared not move my eyes to observe the other. He continued—

"You may put pressure upon your lady friend, as you have done before; and before this time on Monday you will hand me those rubies. I will give you a quittance in full and five thousand pounds in cash. You will be a rich man."

I could now see the vicomte's face quite plainly. He seemed to gasp.

"But," he explained, "I have heard that those rubies cost a quarter of a million sterling—that there are no others like them in the world."

"Americans often pay more for their jewels than they are worth. These things are exaggerated. I have explained that we require from you ten thousand pounds by Monday, or ——" He paused; the vicomte winced. "I need not continue. I offer you an alternative —for us the rubies, for you a quittance and five thousand pounds. From no one else would you get so much; to say nothing of an assurance of absolute safety. You understand? It must be either one or the other. Nothing will be accepted in substitution; and certainly no excuses."

The vicomte sat up straight, breathing heavily, as one might do who is threatened with something he feared, yet could not escape. The waxen man had had a tiny glass of brandy in front of him ever since I entered. He took from it the tiniest sip; it was still half full. The vicomte had nothing in front of him. The waiter took advantage of the pause in their conversation to address him.

"What is it that monsieur desires?" He also spoke in French.

"Desires?" The vicomte looked at him with angry eyes. "I desire nothing; when I desire something I will let you know."

I was conscious that, a few moments before, a woman had entered—alone; that she had looked round her, and was now sailing towards the table at which the two men sat. Something caused me to glance at her; something caused the vicomte to glance at her also. When he saw her he uttered an exclamation and half rose. What he meant to do I could not say; she was on to him before he had a chance of doing it, whatever it was. Planting herself in front of him, she exclaimed in French, in a voice which was audible all over the restaurant—

"So, pig, wretch, thief, liar, cur, beast, it is you! It is you! It is you!"

She had in her hand a whip of some sort, with which, each time she said "It is you!" she struck at him. The first time, taken unawares, the lash caught him right across the face; the second and third times he warded it off with his hands. I never saw a man so utterly taken aback by the mere presence of a woman. He made not the slightest effort to snatch the whip, or to prevent her striking him. He did not even show any sign of resenting the volume of her abuse. When she had struck at him three times, still in the same very audible tones, she went on—

"I have paid you this little visit to tell you that I know where you are to be found, and that presently you will hear from me again—for the last time."

She stood confronting him for two or three seconds, then, turning, walked straight out. The place was in confusion; people had risen all over the room; persons in authority were hastening forward. But when it was seen that the incident was closed calm returned. The vicomte remained standing; he pressed with his handkerchief the place where the lash had touched him. Then, when he presently sat down, the waxen man observed—

"I think that makes it still plainer how necessary it is that before this time on Monday we should have the rubies."

I waited for no more. I had an idea. I hurried after that woman. When I got into the street I saw her some twenty or thirty yards away, walking leisurely. I hastened after her, caught her up, and fell in by her side.

The next day I called on Lady Sarah Crawley, instead of writing to her. When I had listened to all she had to say I accepted her invitation for the week-end on the understanding that I was not to go as a professional, with an honorarium of any sort in view, but as a simple guest. On the Friday, however, something occurred which would have rendered it very inconvenient for me to leave town. I telegraphed my excuses. On the Saturday, when I was nearly overwhelmed by the work which had come crowding in on me, demanding my immediate attention, a telegram was brought to me, with the intimation that the reply was paid. I tore it open. As my prophetic soul had warned me, it was from Lady Sarah Crawley—

"Unless absolutely impossible, please come at once. Something very serious has happened. Unless you can help, the consequences may be dreadful. I implore you to let me know by wire that you are coining at once.—SARAH CRAWLEY."

I read the telegram three times over. I considered for some seconds what it might mean; then, with a groan, I admitted that that work with which I had longed to deal after all would have to wait, and that I should have to go to Morebridge House. I could not easily forgive myself if dreadful consequences resulted because I refused to render such help as was in my power. All that part of the world which knows the upper reaches of the Thames knows Morebridge House. It stands in a prominent position on a treeless expanse of flat grass land which, when the Thames is in flood, is not seldom under water, close to the banks of the river. Possibly hundreds of thousands of people pass it and stare at it every year.

I arrived at about five o'clock on that Saturday afternoon. As I approached along the uninteresting carriage drive it struck me what a great barrack of a place it was. Architectural pretensions it had none; it was simply a huge, bare building. I felt that if I had been the Duke of Horsham I would have at least tried to make it outwardly more prepossessing.

But when the great doors were passed everything was changed. Within it was a fairy palace of delight; the beauty and splendour which are born of wealth and taste were on every side. I passed through three sets of doors before the hall proper was reached, and when it was I stared about me in amazement. The sun streamed through great windows of lovely painted glass on what seemed to me to be a crowd of people. Lady Sarah Crawley advanced to me with outstretched hands.

"I am so glad to see you." This she said out loud; then she added beneath her breath: "If you only knew how anxiously I have waited for you!"

I had tea; every one was having tea. Then Lady Sarah herself showed me to my room. The instant the door was closed she began—

"Oh, Miss Lee, if you only knew how glad I am to see you, and how earnestly I trust that you will be of help. I suppose no one ever was in a more unpleasant situation than I am. Mrs. Baxter-Raeburn's rubies have been stolen."

I was not a bit surprised. Lady Sarah seemed hurt because I showed that I was not.

"Of course, it doesn't matter in the least to you; but consider what it means to me. The Baxter-Raeburns have been most civil to us. My father was under actual obligations to them. They are his guests. As a compliment to him, Mrs. Baxter-Raeburn brings her famous jewels. She is not twelve hours in the house before her rubies are stolen." Lady Sarah sank on to a chair, as if distress had robbed her of the use of her legs. "They do say that Mrs. Baxter-Raeburn's rubies cost a quarter of a million sterling."

"That sort of thing is often exaggerated," remarked.

Lady Sarah stared. She did not know that I was a plagiarist.

"Even if they did cost less, it is quite certain that they cost an enormous sum and are immensely valuable. Quite apart from their value, the dreadful thing is not that they have been stolen, but that they have been stolen in my father's house. I almost feel as if I had taken them myself; while the duke told me this morning that, unless they were recovered, he would never again be able to look the woman in the face."

"As I don't suppose, Lady Sarah, that you have taken them, or your father, either, if you will tell me all about it I will see what I can do, though I warn you at the start, as I have warned you already, that I am no thief-catcher."

She told me all about it, at much greater length than it is necessary that I should use; the strength of her feeling was the cause of continual diversions. Mrs. Baxter-Raeburn was a very foolish woman, as so many very wealthy women are. She had worn her rubies on the night of her arrival, which was the night before I appeared upon the scene. When the house was supposed to have retired for the night, she had a sort of party in her bedroom; some of the feminine guests went to view those precious rubies at closer quarters. When they had departed, and she had retired to bed, Mrs. Baxter-Raeburn herself admitted that she had left them lying on her dressing-table. The next morning, when her maid appeared, they were gone.

"And if you don't mind my speaking plainly," I remarked, "I should say, Lady Sarah, that it served her right. A woman who leaves such valuable jewels lying about her room, without any sort of protection, deserves anything."

"I agree—in a sense, I quite agree; and if it had happened in anybody else's house I should have told her to her face that it did serve her right. But in my own house it's different. When a guest comes to visit me it is on the tacit understanding that she is not coming to a den of thieves, and that while she is beneath my roof she need fear nothing, either for herself or for her belongings."

"Who were the ladies who visited Mrs. Baxter-Raeburn in her bedroom?"

"Here is the list. You see, there were five of them." A glance at the paper she handed me showed that Lady Beatrice Dacre had not been one of the five. "It is impossible to suspect either of them. You see who they are. In fact, I have not dared to tell them that the jewels have been lost."

"Have you told any one?"

"No one as yet."

Lady Sarah betrayed the anxiety she felt by the manner in which, coming close up to me, she lowered her voice to a whisper, as if she feared that the walls might have ears.

"Not a soul—not one. I have induced Mrs. Baxter-Raeburn to keep still—luckily, she told me before she told any one else—by virtually promising that her rubies shall be returned to her before she leaves the house. You must perceive for yourself the scandal which the mere announcement that they were gone would make; it would be in every paper in the world, to speak of nothing else. I assure you that neither Mr. nor Mrs. Baxter-Raeburn is the kind of person to keep silent in the face of such a loss, and, for my part, I really can't blame them. I have heard so much about the wonderful things you do, Miss Lee, that I dare to count upon your assistance in getting me out of the most uncomfortable position a woman was ever in."

I thought that, considering all things, it was pretty cool of Lady Sarah. I did not, however, hint at what I felt, if only because just then I happened to be looking out of the window. A telegraph boy was going down the drive on his bicycle. A voice hailing him, he stopped. Some one ran towards him across the grass. It was Lady Beatrice Dacre. When she reached him she handed him what I had no doubt was a telegraph form. Possibly the message it contained had been scribbled with a pencil. To make sure that it would be understood, she apparently asked him to read it out to her, which he did, I staring at him with all my might. He stumbled over the first words, which were probably the address; I could not see her lips, but she probably helped him out. Then he got on better. I distinctly saw him say three words: "Clarice—four—Monday." That was all, but for me it was quite enough. Lady Sarah turned to see what I was looking at.

"The girl," she said, "is Lady Beatrice Dacre. She is only just out, and she is already engaged to Mr. Douglas Forrester—a most charming fellow, and, of course, from a monetary point of view, he is all that could be desired."

"She is engaged, is she?"

"It has not yet been announced, but it is just going to be. She, of course, has not a penny, but she has everything else which a man can want to have in the woman he marries. . . . Say that you think you can help me."

I had moved away from the window, and was turning things over in my mind. Lady Sarah watched me.

"I may observe," I told her, "that I don't think you are entitled to take it for granted that I can work miracles more than any one else; but it so happens that I think, by the merest chance, I may be able to help you. But we must understand each other at the start. My wish, Lady Sarah, is always, if possible, to keep matters out of the hands of the police."

"Miss Lee, I had really sooner almost anything should happen than that we should have to call in the assistance of the police. That is the one thing both my father and I wish to avoid."

"Then in that case I may be able to do something for you. What you want are the rubies?"

"That's all I want—the only thing. Place me in a position to return them to Mrs. Baxter-Raeburn before Monday, if possible, and you will make me your debtor for life."

"Suppose the thief, in carrying them off, had dropped them in the park, and we were to find them."

"What do you mean?"

Lady Sarah's eyes were open at their widest.

"You must ask no questions. If, as I say, you were to find them in the park, would you undertake to ask no questions, but be content with your find?"

"Am I not to know who took them?"

"You are to show no curiosity of any sort or kind."

"But these thefts, on a smaller scale, have taken place before. At least I think I ought to know whom I can trust and whom I cannot. I cannot ask my friends to form one of a party which contains a thief whose identity is unknown to me."

"I think I can undertake, Lady Sarah, that in future you will be able to trust every member of your present house-party as implicitly as yourself—if you will ask no questions."

I am not quite sure if, when Lady Sarah went, she had not at the back of her mind vague suspicions of me. That she was thoroughly mystified was obvious; but for that I cared nothing. I had her assurance that she would make no inquiries of any sort or kind, but would leave matters entirely in my hands. With that I was content. Before she left I had made her give me a sort of plan of the house, on which were the names of the guests, the rooms they occupied, and how they were approached. She had left me perhaps half an hour when I started on a little voyage of exploration. The plan showed that on the same floor on which I was, and not very far away, was an apartment occupied by Lady Beatrice Dacre. Having first made sure that the coast was clear, I went straight to it. I tried the handle; the door was locked. Then the lady was inside. I rapped at the panel sharply. A voice inquired—

"Who's there?"

"Please open the door at once. It is some one who wishes to see you on very important business."

Not nearly so much celerity was shown as I had requested. Two or three minutes elapsed before the door was opened five or six inches and a girl's face looked out.

"Who are you? What do you want?"

For answer I pressed the door farther back, entered, shut it behind me, and turned the key. The girl stared as if in speechless amazement. I thought she looked more beautiful even than when I had seen her in the Park, if only because the absence of a hat enabled one to realize how lovely her hair was. We fronted each other in silence for several seconds before she exclaimed—

"Who are you? What do you mean by this extraordinary conduct? How dare you come into my room like this?"

I saw that she was even more of a child than I had imagined —she spoke with a child's impetuous heat. I also saw that somewhere inside her was an uncomfortable something which made her heart beat faster. I spoke coldly, allowing no sign to escape me which would show how much I was affected by her girlish loveliness.

"When I tried your door just now, and found it locked, I think you were trying on Mrs. Baxter-Raeburn's rubies."

She had more courage than I had expected. She gave one violent start; then made a great effort to recover herself. She was not so successful as she would have liked to be. She was shivering, as it were, both inside and out.

"What—what do you mean?"

"Give me Mrs. Baxter-Raeburn's jewels at once; you were hiding them while you kept me waiting outside the door."

The chance shot had found the mark. She repeated herself with a piteous stammer—

"Who—who are you? What—what do you mean?"

"Last night—or, rather, early this morning—you entered Mrs. Baxter-Raeburn's room when she was asleep; you saw her rubies lying on the dressing-table, and you stole them."

She had fluttered back against the wall, like some hapless thing at bay. She tried to gasp out a denial—

"It's—it's——"

I stopped her.

"Don't say it is a lie, or I shall hold you to be a more despicable thing than I do already, because you know it is true. The other afternoon you met the man who calls himself the Vicomte d'Aubry at the rooms of the disreputable creature who calls herself Clarice, and who is an associate of his. He suggested that you should take advantage of your friend's hospitality to steal jewels belonging to a fellow-guest. You stole them. They are in your keeping now; you were trying them on when I came to your door; you propose to hand them over to him, in the palmist's rooms, at four o'clock on Monday afternoon."

She was, perhaps, at an age when one is easily impressed by what seems to be the marvellous. I fancy that she imagined herself to be in its presence then, and that I was a representative of the supernatural. Certainly, for some instants she was nearly paralysed by actual terror. She knew that what I said was true; she could have had no notion how I had acquired my information, and was terrified when it came, with what must have been such awful unexpectedness, from my lips. She stood close up against the wall, eyeing me as if I had been some terrible spectre. For nearly a minute she was incapable of giving utterance to an articulate sound. I was not going to help her out. Then all at once an idea seemed to come into her head and force from her a question—

"Are you—are you anything to do with the police?"

"That depends on you—upon whether there's anything in you which makes for good."

"Did he tell you—the Vicomte d'Aubry?"

"I have never spoken to him, nor he to me."

"Then how did you find out—what you have found out? Tell me who you are. Does any one—any one else in the house suspect?"

Before I could answer she was seized with a new and still greater fear—

"You won't tell—you won't tell Douglas? Please, please, please don't tell him. I'll do anything—anything you like—if you won't tell him."

"You are engaged to one man, yet at the dictate of another you play the thief. What sort of person can you be, Lady Beatrice?"

"I'm not so bad as you think. I'm not—I swear I'm not. Only—only I'm in a terrible mess, and—and I had to do what he told me."

"You wish me to believe that you had to play the thief—and such a mean thief—at the command of such a man as that? Pray, why?"

"It was—it was three years ago. I was—I was sixteen years old. I was sent to a school at Tours[1]—at least, it wasn't exactly a school; it was supposed to be a private family. Father wished me to learn French. The Vicomte d'Aubry was a friend of the person who kept the house. He paid attentions to me, and—— Oh, I was a fool! I was only a child—a silly simpleton. He pretended to care for me, and I thought I cared for him. I wrote him four letters—silly, idiotic, rotten letters. Then father took me away; he didn't like what he heard of the place. I wish he'd never sent me there. I forgot all about the Vicomte d'Aubry directly I got home; I never heard or thought of him until—until about four months ago. Then he came up to me in Hyde Park. I tried to cut him, but he wouldn't let me. He reminded me of the letters I had written to him. You see, I had forgotten all about them. I swear I never meant a single word I said in them. Don't you know what an idiot a girl can sometimes be, what romantic rubbish she can get into her head, and how in moments of absolute lunacy she can put it down on paper? That's what I did. I never dreamt that he would keep the letters. I thought he was a gentleman; I had no idea that any one ever did such things. When

[1] A city in Central France, known for the beauty of the French language spoken there.

he told me that he still had my four letters, and that if—if I didn't do something for him he'd send copies of them to Mr. Forrester, I—I was terrified out of my life."

"Were you engaged to Mr. Forrester at the time?"

"Of course I wasn't. I—I knew that he was—rather fond of me, and when that man spoke like that I knew that I was fond of him. I told the vicomte quite frankly that there was nothing I wouldn't do to keep Mr. Forrester from finding out that I had written such letters."

"You couldn't have said to him a more foolish thing. If you had told him that it was a matter of complete indifference to you what he did with the letters, he might not have thought it worth his while to waste his time in threatening you."

"I see that now—I saw it directly afterwards; but there it was. I—I did tell him, and never since has he left me alone. He's—he's been making me do all sorts of things which I—which I hate to think of. Oh, if you knew what I have gone through because I was such a simple-minded fool as ever to think that he was an honourable man! Then the other day Douglas asked me—asked me to marry him; and, of course, I said 'Yes,' though I was frightened half out of my life to think what the vicomte would do when he found out. So you can imagine what were my feelings when he told me that I must give him an interview at once. I knew what an interview with him meant. But what was I to do? I didn't dare to make him angry. So, as you seem to know, I met him at Clarice's rooms. And he told me that Mrs. Baxter-Raeburn was coming here with her rubies, and that if I got them for him he would give me back my letters."

"Rubies which cost a quarter of a million for four letters which are not worth the paper they are written upon! Does that strike you as a good bargain—for you?"

"Do you take me for an utter idiot? Of course it isn't. But he made it quite clear that if the rubies weren't in his hands by Monday the copies of the letters would reach Douglas that day. And that might have meant the end of everything to me—of everything. Douglas thinks that I'm the most perfect saint that ever lived, and, you know, no girl who ever lived was that. And if he found out that I was the kind of creature who could write such letters he—he wouldn't let me explain; couldn't explain even if he'd let me. I doubt if he'd ever speak to me again. And—and if things came to be like that—between Douglas and me, I'd—I'd commit suicide. I would!"

"Doesn't it occur to you that you have committed suicide?"

"Does that mean that you're going to tell him? Then—then——"

Rushing to the dressing-table, she took a tiny bottle out of a handbag. I had her by the wrist the instant it was out of the bag; and the bottle passed into my possession.

"You wicked girl! You admit that you have behaved like a simpleton, and something worse. Do you imagine that you will prove your wisdom by this sort of thing?"

"You may take that bottle from me, if you like, but there are plenty of ways of killing myself. If you do tell Douglas——"

She left her sentence unfinished. I had very little doubt that she would find out one of those ways, if the truth were ever told. I resolved then and there that, if I could help it, it never should be. After all, she was but a child; she was still more of a child when that scoundrel laid the trap in which he caught her. It was not difficult to understand how desperate her position must seem to her. I was not excusing her, but I made up my mind that it should not be my fault if she had not a chance to prove that in her there was the making of a good woman.

"First of all, Lady Beatrice, you will hand me those rubies."

"What are you going to do with them?"

"I am going to hide them in the park. An anonymous hint will reach Lady Sarah which will result in her discovering their hiding-place. She will never learn from whom the hint came, or in whose possession the rubies were. Not a word will be whispered which will point to a thief having been concerned in the matter. You will come with me to that palmist woman's rooms on Monday."

"Without the rubies? I daren't—I dare not! You do not know what he's like, what—what a brute he can be."

"It's not a question of daring. I say you will come with me. I know what the Vicomte d'Aubry is like a good deal better than you do. He will hand you over your letters in my presence. You will find that he will not even attempt to expostulate. That will be the last time in your life that you will either see or hear of him. . . . Give me those rubies, please."

She did not give them to me at once, but she did in the end.

She clung to me when I left, imploring me not to breathe a word to Douglas. It was only about him she seemed to care. I doubt if she altogether believed me when I assured her that she need fear nothing. After she had gone I went downstairs and said a few words to Lady Sarah. I begged her to excuse me from appearing among her other guests, especially as I should manage things much better if nothing were seen of me. She stared.

"But I thought you had to watch people's mouths, and that sort of thing, to see what they were saying. How can you do that if you can't see them?"

"It's a queer world, Lady Sarah; it is possible that I did all the watching of people's mouths that was needed before I came to Morebridge."

"But however could you? I don't understand."

"Our bargain was that you were to ask no questions and show no curiosity; perhaps in the course of to-morrow you will understand a little better."

I dined alone, and I spent the evening alone, and I did some of the work which I had brought with me. There was a project on foot for founding, at The Hague,[1] an institution for teaching the deaf and dumb by the oral system. I had been honoured by being consulted in the matter; certain papers had been laid before me on which my advice was required. Until I had thoroughly mastered those papers I knew perfectly well that I should not know a moment's peace of mind. I had brought some of them down to Morebridge House. I set about studying them then and there.

The next morning I was witness of rather an odd little scene which took place in the breakfast-room. Breakfast seemed to be a go-as-you-please meal in that establishment. I was having mine at a little round table, all by myself, when Lady Sarah Crawley came bustling in, and, crossing to Mrs. Baxter-Raeburn, whispered in her ear. The pair went together to a window. I saw both their faces.

"The most extraordinary thing has happened," began Lady Sarah. "Look at that!"

She handed Mrs. Baxter-Raeburn what I saw was a typed sheet of paper.

[1] A major port city in the Netherlands.

"What does this mean? However did you get this?"

"It came just now by the morning post."

The lady read the paper through and stared at Lady Sarah. She spoke with what was evidently considerable warmth.

"Some one, by way of giving me a lesson on the imprudence of leaving my jewels about, has taken them, by way of a practical joke, and hidden them. Do you know the tree indicated?"

"Not in the least; but the description is so precise that we ought to have no difficulty in finding it, if the thing exists."

"Precisely—if the thing exists, which, until it is proved, I shall take leave to doubt. Have you any idea who this comes from?"

"Not the vaguest. What we have to do, my dear, is to go and see if this is a hoax." She touched the sheet of paper. "If it isn't, and we do find the rubies hidden in the tree, what we shall have to consider is whether it wouldn't be wisest for us to keep our own counsel—to say nothing. You don't want to be made a laughing-stock of, and I'm sure I don't. If ever I do discover the identity of this practical joker, he and I will have an account to settle."

As Lady Sarah was leaving the room she perceived that I was there. I beckoned to her.

"I think," I told her, "I must return to town this morning. As I explained, I have work which must be done, and, frankly, I shan't be happy till I've done it."

"I suppose——" She had the typed sheet of paper in her hand which she had just been telling Mrs. Baxter-Raeburn had come by the morning post. I did not let her get beyond those two words.

"The understanding was that you were to show no curiosity and ask no questions."

"It's the most extraordinary thing of which I've ever heard," she said.

I believe she thinks so still.

I went back to town, did my work; and during the intervals, which will occur even when one is working one's hardest, I made certain arrangements. On the Monday I met Lady Beatrice Dacre at a point we had agreed upon, and together we went to 37, Airedale Street, the advertised address of the fool-snaring Clarice. I explained the programme I had arranged. Her lips quivered, but she only made one comment—

"I feel as I used to do when I was a small child and was going to the dentist's."

"It isn't all joy going to have a tooth extracted, even when one knows it's a very bad one, and that one will feel much better when the operation is over. Yet the dentist is not such a formidable figure, after all."

"But you don't realize," she said, "that during the last few months I've never thought of the Vicomte d'Aubry except with fear and trembling, and that night after night I have lain awake shivering at the thought of him."

"After to-day you will never be afraid of him again; you will presently be pinching yourself at the thought that you ever were."

When I rang at No. 37, Airedale Street the door flew back, opened by an invisible hand. A neat young woman ushered us into a room which was at the end of a passage. A big, flaxen-haired woman rose from behind a table. I addressed her—

"You are Clarice? . . . I am Judith Lee. You will go behind that curtain, and remain there until I tell you to come out. I have no doubt that you or your accomplices have played the listener there many and many a time before. After I have finished my business you will have twelve hours in which to leave England; if, after that time, you are still on English ground, the consequences will be on your own head."

The woman withdrew behind the curtain to which I had referred without a word. Lady Beatrice seemed to be amazed. Almost immediately an unseen gong was sounded twice. The sound had not died away when the door opened and the Vicomte d'Aubry entered. At sight of me he stared; there was something in his eyes which suggested to me that he was not so easy in his mind as he would have liked to be. I just looked at him, and an uneasy something rose up within him which made him bluster—

"What is the meaning of this person's presence here? I have told you on more than one occasion that it is always absolutely essential that I should see you alone."

He spoke in French; I replied in English—plain English.

"This is an occasion, my man, on which you will not see this lady alone."

I touched a bell which stood upon a table. A second man came through the door by which we had just entered, who simply came into the room and stood with his back to the door. The vicomte's concern clearly increased.

"Who is this man? Where is Clarice? This room is privately engaged by me. Lady Beatrice Dacre, I require from you an explanation."

I replied for Lady Beatrice—

"This, my man, is an inspector of police, of Scotland Yard. You have in the breast-pocket of your coat four letters. You will be so good as to hand them to me at once."

He answered in English which, although it was spoken with an accent, was almost as plain as mine was—

"So this is what you call a plant, is it? You think you have trapped me. We shall see. This is a conspiracy of which you will hear again, Lady Beatrice Dacre. . . . Stand away from that door, sir, and let me pass."

The vicomte ignored me utterly; I was more attentive to him—

"You will either hand over those four letters at once, or I will have you arrested. I will give you five seconds in which to make up your mind." I glanced at the watch at my wrist. "One—two—three —four—five. Inspector Ellis, arrest this man."

The thing was ridiculously easy. He meant to rage and to bluster and to shout defiance. Instead of which, the moment the inspector moved he crumpled into nothing. He tore his coat open, took an envelope out of his pocket, and threw it on the table.

"Here are your letters. What is all this fuss about them? I would have given them up long ago if I had been properly approached, if I had been treated with that courtesy which to a gentleman is due. It is to hand them over that I am here."

I said nothing to him; I spoke to the girl—

"Will you be so good as to open that envelope and see if it contains what you require?"

She opened the envelope with fingers which I could see were shaking. She took out some sheets of paper which were covered with writing.

"Yes, they're—they're my letters."

"You are sure of that?"

"Quite—quite sure."

"This man has nothing else of yours? You are absolutely certain?"

"He—he can't have."

There was a stand full of matches on the table. Striking one, I held it out to her.

"Had you not better——"

Taking it from me, she applied the flame to the corner of one of the letters. When they were all alight she laid them on a metal plaque which was on the table—for what purpose Clarice used it I cannot say. The letters made quite a little bonfire.

"That," I said, "is, I think, the end of them, and of Act I." Again a gong sounded twice. "That, I fancy, is the signal for the curtain to rise on Act II."

The vicomte's uneasiness increased; he moved to the door.

"You will now please permit me, sir, to pass, since this little matter is ended. I have business which requires my immediate attention."

I interposed—

"If you will have a moment's patience, my man, I fancy that you will find this a friend to see you."

"But I do not wish to see him. I do not desire——"

Before he could conclude his sentence there came into the room the man with the waxen face whom I had seen conversing with him at that restaurant within a hundred miles of Piccadilly Circus. Although he did not move a muscle, it did not need a very keen perception to see that he found himself in the presence of the unexpected. He said, in French, in tones of perfect suavity—

"It seems that I have made a mistake. A thousand apologies."

He turned to withdraw. Inspector Ellis blocked the way. I addressed him—in my usual plain English—

"I saw you the other night conspiring with this man to force a certain person, by means of threats, to commit felony. I need not tell you that this is a very serious offence; so serious that, for the common safety, I thought it wise to ascertain if anything was known of you. I found that a great deal was known." Again I touched the bell. Two men came in. When he saw them he almost changed countenance. "These gentlemen, who are members of the police in Paris, know a great deal about you. They are anxious to renew with you an acquaintance they have already had."

"Have I to thank you for this?"

The bitterness which the man with the waxen face put into the question!

The vicomte blustered.

"Upon my word of honour——" he began; but he did not finish. The other cut him short with vitriolic scorn.

"Your word of honour!" He turned to the agents of the Paris police. "You will find me, gentlemen, at your service. I believe you have been looking for me some little time."

"That," I observed, "completes the second act. Now for the third, and last."

I struck the bell again. Two women entered. One was the woman who had struck at the vicomte with her whip in the restaurant. She was cool with a coolness which was deadly. The other was a big, unwieldy female who was in a state of hysterical agitation. Behind them were two policemen. At the sight all the vicomte's bones seemed to turn to jelly; he became a mass of invertebrate pulp. Inspector Ellis moved towards him.

"I arrest you, among other things, for bigamy. I have a warrant in my pocket which will be read to you when we get to the station."

In another instant the Vicomte d'Aubry had a pair of handcuffs on his wrists, and stood between the two policemen, a pitiable wretch.

"Clarice!" I exclaimed. The woman came from behind the curtain. A pretty picture she presented. "You have now twelve hours in which to get out of England."

She went out of the room so fast that I am very much mistaken if she did not leave England by that night's boat. As we were leaving Airedale Street, Lady Beatrice said to me, with a sound which was rather a gust than a sigh—

"And to think that I was ever afraid of that man; and, what is much more awful, that I should ever have treated him, even in the days of my most childlike simplicity, as if he were a decent man, and written him those four letters!"

I quoted Paul—

" 'When I was a child I spake as a child, I understood as a child, I thought as a child.' "[1] Then I paraphrased him. "Now that you have

[1] 1 Corinthians 13.11 (KJV): "When I was a child, I spake as a child, I understood as a child, I thought as a child: but when I became a man, I put away childish things."

become a woman, I should recommend you to put away childish things, and try to be that sort of good woman who makes a good wife."

She looked at me, and she said nothing; but I think she thought a good deal.

The waxen-faced man was the head of a gang of jewel robbers who had been wanted by the French police for some time. He was sentenced in Paris to a long term of imprisonment. The Vicomte d'Aubry met with the same fate in England. He was charged with marrying an amazing number of women, not only in England, but in most of the civilized countries of the world. He had swindled each of them in turn.

The day after he was sentenced there came to me an invitation to be present at the wedding of the Lady Beatrice Dacre to Mr. Douglas Forrester.

In the envelope which contained the invitation card was a scrap of paper on which was written, in a sprawling handwriting with which I had lately become familiar—

"I have just been reading the verdict and sentence in to-day's paper. To think that I ever could! At the thought of it I writhe! Shall I ever forgive myself? Mrs. B.-R. told me the other day about the amazing manner in which she and Lady Crawley found her rubies in a tree in the park at Morebridge House. Shall I ever be able to repay you the debt of gratitude which I owe you?"

It was a question which I was incapable of answering. I felt, as I burnt it, that it was rather a dangerous scrap of paper to enclose with a card for her wedding; and I caught myself wondering if she would ever learn to be quite discreet in the use of pens, ink, and paper.

THE FINCHLEY PUZZLE

As I cut the string, and, unfolding the brown paper, saw what the little package contained, some trick of memory bore me back to an incident which had happened nearly two years before. I had been with a girl friend to the theatre, and had come back alone in an omnibus which put me down at the corner of the road in which I then had rooms. There had been a promise of rain all day, and just as I descended from the vehicle, something seemed to happen to the clouded heavens which caused water to descend in pailfuls. I was lightly attired; owing to some stupidity I had omitted to take an umbrella. I had to take refuge somewhere; I found it in the entry to a mews which was at the beginning of the street.

It did rain! I wondered what would happen if it kept on. I was only a couple of hundred yards from my dwelling-place, but if I had to approach it in that downpour I should be drenched before I got there. All at once I heard footsteps coming along the pavement from the direction in which my rooms were. Presently a man came quickly past. He had no umbrella; his billycock hat[1] was pressed close down on his head; his coat collar was turned up to his ears —he must have been soaked. Just as he passed the entry in which I stood a man came rapidly across the road, who wore a waterproof and carried an umbrella. At sight of him the other paused. There was a lamp-post on one side of the mews; in spite of the deluge they paused under its glow to exchange a few sentences, standing in such a position that both their faces were visible to me. I heard nothing, but I saw quite plainly what the new-comer said.

"Did you give it her?"

The other shook his head. "She wasn't in. I said to the girl who opened the door, 'Give this to Miss Lee directly she comes in.'"

"If the girl does and we have any luck, Miss Lee will be where there are no deaf and dumb in the morning."

The man with the umbrella held a part of it over the other, and the two went striding off as if they were walking for a wager, leaving

[1] A bowler hat; a hard, rounded felt hat.

me to wonder. I was quite certain that they had mentioned my name, and, though I had heard nothing, something in the expression of their faces convinced me that it had been in no friendly fashion. I was sure that they were strangers to me. The wet man was an undersized, pale-faced, mean-looking youth, whose appearance did not appeal to me at all; the other was a scarlet-visaged, bloated individual, who looked as if he might have been a publican. What had he meant by saying that if they had luck I should be where there were no deaf and dumb in the morning? I was quite sure that those were the precise words which he had used. I am not a supersensitive person, but—something made me shiver.

When at last I did get in—I could not wait for the rain to cease entirely, but so soon as it showed signs of slightly slackening, I made a dash for it—among other matter lying on the table in my sitting-room was a small, oblong-shaped package, addressed in a bold hand, "Miss Judith Lee." In those rooms a maid always sat up to let in late-comers; she had admitted me. As she commiserated with me on the state I was in—I was rather damp—I asked her, since it had clearly not come by post, how that packet had got there. She said that a young man had brought it who said it was most particular that she should give it to me directly I came in.

When the maid had gone I looked at that parcel for some moments before I even touched it. Although to the superficial glance it was the most commonplace-looking little parcel, there was something sinister about it to me. Had its contents anything to do with that red-faced man's observation about my being where there were no deaf and dumb in the morning? I opened my other letters first, and left that parcel to the last. Then, telling myself that my hesitation was absurd, I took a pair of scissors, clipped the string, removed the wrapping, and there was an ordinary, white cardboard box within, bearing the imprint of a well-known manufacturer of sweet things. I opened it. It was filled with chocolates; on the top was a scrap of paper on which was written, in the same bold handwriting: "To Miss Judith Lee, from a Humble Donor. This Little Present Long Overdue."

Nothing could seem more innocent. I did receive presents at times from anonymous givers, to whom, I presume, I had been so fortunate as to render services for which they felt they would like to make some sign of recognition. Had I not seen those two men under the lamp-post I should probably have put one of those chocolates into my mouth at once and scrunched it thankfully; but I had seen them, and I did not wish to be where there were no deaf and dumb in the morning.

I took one of the chocolates out of the box. I could hardly receive any hurt from the mere touch. It was a good-sized chocolate, looking as if it might contain a walnut. I was really curious as to what it did contain, and was regarding it attentively when some slight noise behind caused me to look round. I suppose I started; the sweetmeat fell from my fingers, and as it reached the floor there was a blinding flash, a sudden, extraordinary noise, a most unpleasant smell. I was left in a state of doubt as to whether I was alive or dead.

The advent of the maid made it clear that I was still alive. In a few seconds, the whole household was there to learn what was the matter. I could not explain; I was myself without information, and actual, tangible information I have remained without until this day. Who sent that box I have never learned; what was the secret of the construction of that toothsome delicacy I do not know. I sought light from a friend who was a famous chemist; he declared that that seeming candy was a bomb in miniature, and that if I had put my teeth into it it would have blown my head off; so it was lucky I had refrained. It was the only candy in the box about whose construction there was anything peculiar; it had been so placed that it was nearly certain that it would be the first I should take. Analysis showed that all the other contents of the box were simple, albeit excellent chocolates, manufactured by a well-known maker, and were in the exact state in which they had left his hands.

Some one had tried to murder me. I caused inquiries to be made on lines of my own, but since nothing came of them, and for reasons of my own I was unwilling to place the matter in the hands of the police, the affair remained "wrapped in mystery"; and now, nearly two years afterwards, under altogether changed conditions, there had come addressed to me another seemingly innocent package—whose innocence I gravely doubted.

Two or three evenings before I had been with some friends in a box at a popular variety theatre. Glancing round the crowded house through an opera-glass, the lenses had rested for a moment on two men who were leaning over the partition in the promenade, and in that brief instant I distinctly saw one of them shape my name upon his lips, "Judith Lee": just those two words. The lenses passed on before he had a chance of saying more. It was a curious sensation —to see my name being uttered all that distance off. I brought the lenses back again, just in time to see the second man asking a question, rather a full-flavoured one.

"Who the blazes is Judith Lee?"

I had been right; no doubt the first man had pronounced my name, because here was his companion doing it also. I allowed the glass to rest upon his companion's face. He was in evening dress, a crush hat[1] was a little at the back of his head; he had a cigar between his lips, which he took out to answer the other's inquiry. I saw as clearly what he said as if he had been in the next box.

"Judith Lee is a young woman who calls herself a teacher of the deaf and dumb; in reality she is the most dangerous thing in England. The police aren't in it compared with her: they make blunders, thank God; she doesn't. If she catches sight of your face at a distance of I don't know how many miles, and you happen to open your lips, you are done. The other day she saw—I won't mention his name; he was talking business to a friend; before he knew that she was there he said something—only in a whisper, to his friend, you understand—which, when dealing with a sharp young devil such as she is, was enough to give himself clean away. He's had the fidgets ever since, and I'm bound to say that I think he's right. I shouldn't like her to have half that hold on me."

"What's he afraid of? Is she connected with the police?"

"Not ostensibly; one would know where one was if she were. She has spoilt more good men and more good things by not being connected with the police than I should care to talk about. There has been more than one try to get her out of the way; now there's to be another. It's her or—him; and it's going to be her. She's going, and she'll never know what struck her." The other man looked round. "Take care, there's a chap behind who seems to be all ears. Let's stroll."

---

[1] A crushable hat; a collapsible top hat.

They strolled, or, at least, they moved away from the partition and passed from my sight leaving me not at all in a suitable frame of mind to enjoy that variety show. That I should have lighted on such a conversation in such a place and in so odd a fashion was amazing. By what fortuitous accident had my opera-glass rested on that spot at just that moment? What would that speaker's feelings have been had he known that quite unintentionally I was watching him from below, and that he was furnishing an illustration of his own words, that I had only to catch a glimpse of a man's face, though only from afar, and if he opened his lips he would give himself away.

Whom the speaker had in his mind when he spoke of the man whose name he would rather not mention, and to whom I was supposed to have given the fidgets, I had not the vaguest notion. I have an idea that since more people know Tom Fool than Tom Fool knows, I might often give the "fidgets" to persons who might suppose that I had obtruded myself upon their confidence without my having, actually, done anything of the kind. Possibly the speaker, being himself a person of doubtful character, had acquaintances like himself; if I had given one of them a scare it served him right; only—I did not relish that reference to getting me out of the way. As he said, there had been "more than one try," though I did not know how he knew it, and I did not desire that there should be another—just yet awhile.

Nearly two years before some one had tried to "get me out of the way" by means of a bomb in the shape of a chocolate bonbon; a shiver would go all over me when sometimes I thought of how narrow my escape had been. It was not the sort of thing one is likely to forget, so when I received that little package, of which I have already spoken twice, I hesitated before I inquired into what it contained.

It had come by post, the address was typed, the post-mark Fleet Street,[1] the wrapping coarse brown paper, within was a box of stiff brown cardboard. In the box there were four roses, arranged so as to form a shall bouquet. Whether they were real I was not sure, imitations are, nowadays, so exquisitely done. They looked like four lovely Maréchal Niel[2] blooms which had just been taken from the

---

[1] A major thoroughfare in the City of London, associated with the press.
[2] A large yellow rose that requires careful tending, named after a French military hero.

bush, deep golden yellow. It might seem very silly, but I was reluctant to take them out of the box. I raised it to enable me to eye them more closely. They must be real, imitations could not be so perfect. I had a strong impulse, as any woman would have had, to take them out and smell them; it was absurd to be afraid of roses.

I took them out and was advancing them towards my nose, when I saw something gleaming in the very heart of them, something which sprang out towards me. I gave the roses a swift twirl, and something went whirling out of them to the floor, a curiously coloured something which lay for a moment as if stunned, and then began to move across the carpet. About a week before some one had given me a Pomeranian puppy, the queerest, daintiest morsel of living jet. It had been asleep on a cushion. The noise of that thing being thrown to the ground disturbed him. He jumped up. Seeing the thing wriggling across the floor, imagining, I take it, that it was some new plaything, with its funny little bark the puppy dashed towards it. The thing on the floor reared itself, leaped at the puppy, not once or twice, but again and again.

It all happened so quickly that I hardly grasped what was taking place. Then all at once I realized that that simple-minded puppy was being attacked by that hideous little snake which had been contained in my bouquet of roses. When I rushed to its assistance it was already too late. I struck the creature with a poker I had snatched up, and with that one blow killed it; but the puppy was dead.

That was one of the most dreadful moments I have ever known when it was borne in on me that the puppy was actually dead, and how easily its fate might have been mine. I am not fond of snakes; to die from the bite of one—that is not the sort of death I would choose at all. If I had advanced those roses only a few inches nearer that creature would have struck me in the face—the puppy's fate might have been mine. This was the second time I had been saved from attempted murder by what seemed very like a miracle. If I had not seen through the opera-glass those two men talking in the promenade I should have known no hesitation, I should have at once advanced those roses to my face, as most women would, and I should have been dead.

The whole episode, as may be imagined, set me furiously thinking. When something of the same sort had happened before I had not taken any special pains to discover the guilty party. But this time I had a feeling that it was a sort of challenge, that I was on my mettle; I had got off scot free, but my puppy had been slain, and for that some one should pay dearly. The question I had to put to myself was—who?

As I was casting about in my mind to find an answer, I had what seemed to me at the time to be almost an inspiration, though, as I realized afterwards, it was open to the most commonplace interpretation. I recalled a fragment of a conversation I had seen when crossing on the boat from the Isle of Wight.[1] Two men had been walking up and down, talking together, apparently in undertones and very earnestly. I had been seated. I glanced in their direction while they were still at some distance, but were coming towards me along the deck. One was a shortish man with very fair hair and pink-and-white complexion. It was he who was speaking. He had a slight moustache, which was so fair as to be almost white, and which did not prevent my seeing his lips distinctly; his words came back to me from some forgotten cell in my memory with a vividness which—as I surveyed that dead puppy—almost frightened me. I had paid scarcely any attention to them at the moment; how they had got themselves stored in my brain I had no notion. Now they seemed so apposite.

"Get a man asleep, or unconscious, introduce the proper kind of snake to the proper part of his body, and that man will be dead inside sixty seconds, and I doubt if half a dozen doctors in the world would be able to tell you what had happened. Look at Finchley——"

I remembered that at that point he looked towards me, and, seemingly for the first time, saw that I was there. As he did so he brought himself up with a sudden jerk, put his hand in his companion's arm, turned him right round, and led him off the upper deck somewhere down below. At the time I was idly amused. The man was a stranger to me; I had no reason to suppose that I was not a stranger to him. Perhaps, conscious that he was talking in rather a curious strain, unwilling to be the object of a stranger's observation, he had taken himself and his friend away. If I thought about it

[1] An island off the south coast of England, a popular holiday destination.

at all, that was the hazy conclusion I arrived at. But such episodes are so common. I endeavour not to look at people's faces, since I suffer from a sort of obsession which suggests that, becoming conscious of my glance and the revelation of self which it portends, they remove themselves to where I cannot see them. I more or less vaguely took it for granted that this fair-haired man might be a case in point. I do not remember seeing him again on the boat, or when we landed. I never thought of him again until, all at once, he and his words came back with such terrific suddenness as I was looking at my dead puppy.

He had been speaking of how very easy it was to kill with the proper kind of snake. I had seen that fact illustrated. I wished he had not seen me; I might have heard more. Could the man in the promenade at the music-hall by any chance have been alluding to him? Could he have been the man to whom I had given the fidgets? Experience had taught me that coincidences are the rule rather than the exception, but what an astounding one that would be! And, in any case, why should he have been fidgety because of me?

Then, with the same odd suddenness, something else occurred to me. What was the word he had pronounced when, at sight of me, he stopped short? Was it not Finchley? I was sure that it was Finchley. But if that were so—again, how odd! Were not the newspapers still referring to what they had christened "The Finchley Puzzle"?

A Mr. and Mrs. Le Blanc had lived in a house called The Elms, in Hill Avenue, Finchley.[1] They were elderly folk, of rather eccentric habits—he was a naturalized Frenchman, and she was a Frenchwoman who had not been naturalized. One morning both of them were found dead in bed, each in a separate bedroom. They were alone in the house. They generally kept a French maid, but were for the moment without one. The question was how they died; it came out at the inquest that nobody was able to give a clear explanation. They had died, said the doctors, of shock, but of what sort of shock, and how it chanced to visit them simultaneously, there was the puzzle. The vital organs were fairly healthy, they had no congenital disease, they had been seen together the night before, they were

[1] The street appears to be imaginary, but Finchley is a North London suburb, some nine miles from Central London.

supposed to have retired to bed about ten o'clock; according to the medical evidence about two hours afterwards they were dead. The medical theory was that while they lay asleep in bed something had happened to them of so astounding a nature that both of them were smitten with death. Eminent authorities were called, not one of whom was willing to bind himself to an exact definition. The inquest had dragged on, and finally the jury, acting under the coroner's direction, had returned what he called an open verdict.

I regretted that that fair-haired man's discovery of my presence on the boat had caused him to cut his observations short; he might have added something about Finchley which would have shown that the Le Blanc tragedy was not in his mind. I did not say, even to myself, that it was. I picked up that snake, put it back in the box in which it came, concealed in those Maréchal Niel roses, and paid a visit to the Zoological Gardens.[1] I went straight to the snake house, and made inquiry of an attendant if there were any one about who might be regarded as an authority on its occupants. The chief authority, it seemed, was not there, but I was introduced to an elderly gentleman who, I was told, knew probably as much about snakes as I wanted to know. Opening my box I showed him what was in it. He regarded it with considerable interest, took it out, turned it over and over, examining it closely from tip to tip.

"Where did you get this from?" he asked.

I told him it had come to me that morning through the post.

"Alive?"

"Very much alive," I said. "I killed it after it had killed my puppy."

"Your puppy? It might have killed you. I can't tell you exactly what it is, because I have never seen one quite like it before. There are probably a large number of snakes of which we have no record; I fancy this is one of them. But I can tell you it is one of the *Viperidæ*,[2] and possibly West African. I have never seen one anything like so small before, but I have no doubt that it's one of that family, and I should say all the more dangerous because it is so small. But I can tell you who might be able to give you information, that's Dr.

---

[1] Originally opened as a scientific establishment in 1828, the London Zoo was opened to the public in 1847. It is situated in the north of Regent's Park in North-Central London.

[2] Commonly known as vipers, a family of venomous snakes (Latin).

George Evans. He is not only an authority on snakes in general, he has made the *Viperidæ* his special study. He doesn't live very far from here; he is always in and out. Here is his address." He wrote something on a card. "Although it may seem odd to you, snakes are the things he chiefly lives for, and he's always glad to see any one who wants to know something about them."

I called on Dr. George Evans then and there, with the snake in the box. His house was within a quarter of a mile of the Zoological Gardens. He was at home, and came to see me at once: a big, burly man, with a quantity of grey hair which hung over one side of his forehead like a sort of mane. I told him what I had come about, showing him the snake, and asking what it was. The sight of it affected him in a manner which, by me, was unexpected. His naturally sanguine countenance turned purple.

"Good God!" he exclaimed. "Where did you get that from?" I told him. His surprise seemed to grow. "That thing came to you by post? But, my dear young lady, how came it to do that?" I told him that that I hoped shortly to find out. "You don't know? What object could an anonymous person have had in sending it to you? I don't know your name, but, my dear young lady, are you aware that if that dreadful creature had bitten you it would certainly have killed you on the spot?"

I told him how I had escaped being bitten, and how it had killed the puppy. He dropped on to a chair and seemed positively gasping for breath.

"It's one of the most terrible things of which I ever heard. It almost looks as if some one had designed to do you mischief; but what a terrible means to have chosen!"

I had already felt that myself; as I listened to him I felt it more strongly every moment.

"This is a hitherto quite unknown member of the *Viperidæ* family. It is the smallest I ever met, and what is worse, I believe one of the most deadly. Until a little time back I was the owner of what I supposed to be a unique specimen. It was brought to me from the West Coast of Africa. It killed a native, and then, while trying to escape, got entangled in a quantity of calico which lay upon the ground, in which it was made a prisoner. The man who captured it was a friend of mine, who, knowing my tastes, and being aware that it was something unusual in snakes—although he knew the district well, he himself had never seen one like it before—refused to have it killed. At considerable risk to himself he transferred it to a metal case, in which he brought it home, and in due course presented it to me, and in my keeping it has been until a month ago last Sunday. I had it on the Sunday evening, but on the Monday morning it was gone; and do you know I am half inclined to suspect that the one you have here in this box is the one I had. I cannot see any other solution, since I am convinced that mine was the only specimen of the kind which has been seen in England."

"How do you account for its getting out of your possession, since it was clearly a very dangerous thing to handle? Do you think that it escaped?"

It struck me that Dr. Evans seemed to be very curiously distressed.

"My dear young lady, that's—that's the trouble. I—I'm afraid that it was stolen."

"Stolen? A thing like that? For what purpose—by whom? I should have thought that an attempt to steal it must have meant death to the thief."

The doctor got up from his chair, he brushed the mane of hair off his forehead; his manner became what I should have judged to be more normal.

"Exactly; you put the case correctly. Under ordinary circumstances it would have meant sudden death to the thief. Have you no idea who can have sent it to you, not even a remote suspicion? I have not your name. May I ask who you are?"

"I am Judith Lee." He stared at me hard.

"Not the—the young lady of whose lip-reading capacity I have heard so many tales which seem to me to border on the miraculous?"

"The same. I don't know what tales you may have heard, but I assure you that there is nothing about me which is in the least miraculous."

Then I told him all about it—about two men whom I had seen talking in the promenade. He stopped me at once.

"My dear Miss Lee, you say there's nothing about you that's the least miraculous, and then you tell me that you followed a conversation between two men who were removed from you by the whole auditorium of a great theatre, and that without hearing a word they said. That seems to me to be a miracle to start with."

I laughed. "I assure you it is nothing of the kind. I assure you it is simply a question of constant practice. Given ordinary perception, and as much practice as I have had, with the greatest ease you would be able to do just the same."

"I doubt it. I very gravely doubt it. However, that is by the way; that is a matter about which I should like to have a long talk with you presently. In the meantime, do I understand you to suggest that from what you saw those two men saying you draw the deduction that they may have had something to do with this?" He touched the box in which the snake was.

"Dr. Evans, I am making inquiries. I do not like to draw deductions, I prefer to deal with facts. Will you please to tell me, so far as you can, just how that snake came to pass from your possession? You see what importance anything you may say may have for me, and under the very peculiar circumstances of the case you must have your suspicions."

"I don't like suspicions any more than you like deductions, Miss Lee." He turned quickly towards me. "Do you know anything about snakes?"

"No more than the average person, and you know that that is practically nothing. A little while ago I saw—not heard—a man say something on a boat about a snake, which was news to me. He seemed to hint that an artist in murder might find one rather useful."

I told him precisely what I had seen. It seemed to me that the doctor's eyes opened wider as he listened.

"What sort of man was this you saw—not heard?" I described him as well as I could. The doctor's eyes grew more expansive. He plumped down on his chair again. "And yet you say, Miss Lee, that you are no dealer in the miraculous. What you saw I have heard him say. Because of him I have been suffering what I really believe to be much more than I deserve."

The doctor looked furtively about the room as if in search of an unseen listener. He went to the door and looked outside; closing it carefully he came towards me with what was very like an air of mystery. He even lowered his voice as if he feared that the very walls had ears.

"Miss Lee, what I am about to say to you I perhaps ought not to say, and in any case I must beg you to let it go no farther. Have I your assurance?" He looked at me with an odd sort of disquietude.

"I tell you quite frankly that I would rather give you no assurance till I know what you are going to say to me." Perceiving that he was about to speak, I stopped him. "Permit me to explain. You say you know this man who was on the boat; you are probably thinking of telling me something about him. Is it not possible that it may have something to do with this?"

I placed the tip of my finger on the box which contained the snake.

"Well, that was not at the moment in my mind; at least, not quite in that form."

I had one of those inspirations which do come to me every now and then.

"Has it anything to do with Finchley?"

The bow had been drawn at a venture, but the arrow hit the target; he obviously started. He positively glared at me.

"With Finchley? What—what do you mean by 'Has it anything to do with Finchley'?"

"I mean what you mean, Dr. Evans. Is it not odd that the same embryonic thought should have taken root in both our minds? That snake was meant to kill me; is it not possible that it killed some one else before it was sent to my address, two persons, say, at Finchley?"

"Miss Lee, what a horrible thought; how you jump at conclusions! I thought you liked to deal with facts?"

"So I do. I am about to deal with them. With your permission, Dr. Evans, we will deal with them together. The same thought in embryo is in both our minds; let's leave it there. Now, tell me, please, all you know about the man I saw on the boat. I have only to go to the police—I have had a good deal to do with them in my short life—and tell them my suspicions. You will find it more agreeable to answer my questions than theirs. You must see for yourself that I have been in danger of my life, probably from your snake; I think I am entitled to ask you to help me from running a similar risk again."

When Dr. Evans and I had said all we had to say to each other —and it took us an unconscionably long time—I paid a visit to The Elms, Hill Avenue, Finchley, the residence of the late Mr. and Mrs. Le Blanc. There were certain theories which I wished to test by an actual inspection of the premises. Hill Avenue proved to be a broad, old-fashioned road, in which private houses were interspersed with shops. I walked straight past The Elms—I saw the name on the gate-post as I went—because, just as I reached it, a young lady alighted from a taxi-cab which had stopped at the gate. There were four more houses, and then a stationer's shop. As I stopped to look at the window I kept one eye on the young lady who had descended from the taxi-cab. She was a distinctly pretty young person, about eighteen or nineteen years old, with something about her which told me that she was probably French. She appeared to be in a state of much agitation. From my post of vantage I saw her say to herself, in French—

"Why is the gate locked?" She had tried the handle and found that it refused to yield. "I have never known it locked before. And all the blinds are down. What does it mean?"

An elderly woman came out of the adjoining house.

"Why, Miss Le Blanc," she exclaimed, "so you have appeared at last? I have been wondering what had become of you." She stood on the pavement in front of the house with her mouth sufficiently visible to enable me to see what she said. The girl turned towards her; I could see her plainly.

"Oh, Mrs. Green, what is the matter?"

The woman turned more towards her so that her lips were hidden. I had to guess at her words from the other's reply.

"Dead!" said the girl. "My parents dead!" She seemed to reel. "Since—since when are they dead?"

Again I had to guess at Mrs. Green's words from her answer.

"How could I know? I have been staying with my friends in different parts of France. My parents do not often write, they are not fond of writing, but when I had no letters from them at all I supposed they had gone astray because of my so often moving about. But when I could get no answers, not even to my telegrams, I began to wonder if anything were wrong. I hurried back to see. I have been staying in a little village where there come no news at all. It is now more than a month since I heard from them, and when I did last hear they were both well. I could not guess that they were dead, I only imagined it was too much trouble to write. I knew they did not like writing, especially when they had nothing to say."

The girl's distress was evident; she seemed bewildered by the sudden shock of the news which she had learnt from Mrs. Green, too bewildered to know what to say, think, or do. Mrs. Green said something. I fancy she was urging the girl to come into her house, but before the girl could reply another taxi-cab drew up in front of the house, from which still another woman alighted. This was a very gorgeous person indeed, very tall and big, dressed in the very latest fashion. The fact that she wore a veil rather obscured her mouth, but I saw enough of it for my purpose. She was all warmth and enthusiasm.

"My dear Freda," she began. I could fancy the affectionate emotion which was in her voice. "Of all the lucky things, to have come on you like this. You poor, dear darling, to think that you have only just come home—to this!—without the slightest warning of what you were coming to."

It was, perhaps, small wonder that the girl burst into tears. There was quite a little scene on the pavement. Mrs. Green was apparently urging her to go into her house, a suggestion which the new-comer did not endorse.

"My dear Freda," she said—if here and there I missed a word because of that veil of hers, I did my best to fill in the hiatuses —"you must come home at once with me. A little bird whispered that you would be here to-day, so I simply had to come in the hope of catching you. And now that Providence has brought me here in the very nick of time, I am not going to lose sight of you for a single instant. I will tell you everything there is to tell when we get home. If you only knew how anxious Harold has been. Have your luggage put on my cab and we'll start at once."

"But can't I get into my own home?"

"My dear, I believe the police have the keys and they've locked the whole place up. When you've heard what I have to tell you, you'll know what it will be best for you to do. Come, let's lose no more time. Driver, put the young lady's luggage upon my cab."

The driver did. The cab, with the gorgeous lady and the girl in it, departed. The other was about to start when I hailed it. The position was developing along unexpected lines. So far as I could recollect there had been no mention at the inquest of a daughter. It seemed terrible that she should come back in this haphazard way from a pleasure jaunt to find both her parents dead, and her own home shut by the police against her. I could quite understand how news from London might never reach a remote French village. I wondered who the lady might be who had turned up at such a very opportune moment. I thought, as I was making investigations of my own, that it might be worth my while to see where that fine lady was taking her. I asked the driver of my cab to keep the other in sight. He did. The vehicle in front took us right across London, but we never lost sight of it; my driver did it very well.

The cab ahead led us to Warwick Gardens, Kensington,[1] stopping before an old-fashioned, detached house, guarded in front, as it were, by lofty iron railings. My cab drove on; the occupants of the other cab got out. My driver took me home. I, at that time, had a flat in Sloane Gardens. I had made a note of the address of the house at which that other cab had stopped. I looked it up in the directory. According to that encyclopædia of knowledge the tenant's name was Harold Cleaver. I found the news a little startling. According to Dr. George Evans that was the name of the fair-haired man whom I had seen saying how easy it was to use a snake as an instrument of murder while crossing on the boat from Ryde to Portsmouth.[2] Matters were beginning to take rather a peculiar shape. My search for the person who had sent me that specimen of the *Viperidæ* was taking me where I had never expected to go. I had to collect my thoughts, to put two and two together, from such facts as I had collected to draw—in spite of what I had said to Dr. Evans—my own deductions.

On a certain day Dr. George Evans missed a snake which, the night before, had been in his possession—a very deadly snake. Only a few persons knew that he had it; they knew what a very dangerous thing it was to handle. A few days before, Mr. Harold Cleaver, a

---

[1] A street south of the western end of Kensington High Street; a prestigious address.

[2] Ryde, the largest town on the Isle of Wight, is about four and a half miles from Portsmouth on the mainland.

well-known taxidermist, had brought back a case of stuffed snakes which he had been preparing under the doctor's direction for exhibition in a museum of natural history. The doctor had shown him the West African snake. Mr. Cleaver had regarded it with singular interest. It appeared that he knew more about it than the doctor himself. He spoke of some of its peculiarities, pointing out that though it was a very deadly creature, whose bite was instantly fatal, yet it scarcely left any mark, and the poison it had injected into its victim's body vanished almost directly it had done its work, leaving practically no traces behind.

How the snake was taken the doctor was unable to determine. He kept it in a glass case; the case was left, the snake was gone. He thought at first that in some inexplicable way the creature had escaped, and had some very anxious minutes while searching for its whereabouts. After a while he came to the conclusion that its escape, unassisted, was impossible. It is true that the case was found open, but the creature was so small—less than ten inches long—and so slender that it could be concealed in a bouquet consisting of four roses, that the idea that, unaided, it would force the case open was absurd.

The doctor's ophidians[1] were housed in a sort of conservatory, which was heated by hot air. Close observation led him to suspect that the door which opened into the garden had been tampered with. Since it was extremely unlikely that a thief would care to enter a building which contained such singular inmates, he was content, at night, simply to turn the key in the lock of the outer door. When he looked into the matter he found that the key was missing. He could not remember if he had locked it the previous night, which was Sunday. What had become of the key he could not learn—he never learned. The door was locked; he had to summon a locksmith to open it. It was an ordinary lock, the workman had no trouble in finding another key to fit it. The door was open.

Dr. Evans said nothing about his loss. The members of his household were already sufficiently nervous on the subject of his pets; he had difficulty in getting servants to stay. If he had mentioned that a dangerous snake was missing, quite possibly his staff would have left him on the spot. Snakes are not popular; no maid would

[1] Snakes.

like to run the remote risk of finding a particularly deadly specimen between her sheets at night. A few days afterwards Mr. and Mrs. Le Blanc were found dead in their beds. The more Dr. Evans read about the Finchley puzzle, the more uncomfortable he grew. At one time he nearly applied for leave to view the bodies. He had received from his friend a very vivid account of how the negro had looked whom that little snake had slain. He was haunted by a gruesome notion that Mr. and Mrs. Le Blanc would be found to look very much as that black man had done. He remembered what Mr. Cleaver had said about the snake leaving no marks, and the vanishing of all traces of poison from its victim's body.

Then he told himself it was absurd; the whole notion was too far-fetched. He did not know what had become of his snake; strange things had happened to his specimens before, which he had not plumbed to their deepest depths. How could that missing reptile have played such a prominent part in that Finchley puzzle? So, in spite of his first impulses, he said nothing, and he did nothing, until I appeared upon the scene.

Now I was confronted with the new fact that when they died the Le Blancs were alone in the house, not only because they were without a servant, but also because their daughter was visiting friends in some remote part of France. Somebody must have known of this; quite possibly some one knew her address, yet no communication was made to her until she stumbled on the truth on her return. It also looked as if some one knew that she was coming back. That gorgeous lady had talked about the whisper of a little bird, but little birds do not impart information which enables people to appear on the scene quite so pat as she had done.

There was one new fact, or series of facts; but there was still another, and that was the most curious of all. The gorgeous lady was presumably a relative of Mr. Harold Cleaver; she had actually taken Miss Le Blanc to a house of which he was the tenant.

So, to string facts together, the case stood thus: Mr. Cleaver shows interest in a snake with whose deadly properties he is better acquainted than its owner; that snake vanishes; shortly afterwards two people die in a lonely house without any doctor being able to give an adequate explanation of the cause of death; Dr. George Evans almost applies for permission to view their bodies, but is restrained because there is nothing to show what has become of his snake, because he has no reason to associate his interference with any act of Mr. Cleaver's, because he has no notion that Mr. Cleaver has any acquaintance with the Le Blancs. Then, all at once, I discovered that he must have some acquaintance with the dead husband and wife, because their only daughter is taken to his house.

There was the man on the boat. He was Mr. Harold Cleaver. Was it not possible that he was the unnamed person whom the man in the promenade had said had the fidgets because he had given himself away to me? Quite possibly he knew very much more about me than I did about him. If, having something on his mind, having said what he did say to his companion on the boat, seeing me, all at once, sitting there and watching him, might he not jump to the conclusion that I was there for a purpose, and that, inadvertently, he had supplied me with the missing clue? He had certainly vanished with remarkable rapidity. Dr. Evans thought he recognized the snake. If it had been used in Hill Avenue, and the man who used it had afterwards had reason to suspect that I was aware of the fact, might he not, in desperation, have sent it on to me, to do again what it had done at The Elms?

At this point I drew a long breath. Once more events seemed to be shaping themselves after a fashion of which I had never dreamt, as I had learned they had a trick of doing. I might, and probably should, never have concerned myself with the Finchley puzzle had it not been that the criminal's conscience caused him to make a horrible attempt to destroy a peril which only existed in his own guilty imagination. I should never have touched the business had my hand not been forced in such a fashion. Now that I had been compelled to move I would not stop until I had seen the matter through.

As the day went on I paid another visit to the neighbourhood of Warwick Gardens, certain vague ideas floating through my head which I had a notion to develop. But when I got in sight of the house at which Miss Le Blanc had taken refuge, they went by the board. I had gone by rail to Earl's Court Station,[1] and from thence had proceeded on foot. As I entered Warwick Gardens I saw an old-fashioned four-wheeler cab approaching, on the top of which was

[1] A station on the south-western edge of Central London, half a mile south of Warwick Gardens.

piled a quantity of luggage. A feminine head protruded from the window, giving directions to the driver. It was when I saw that head and that luggage that, all in an instant, an idea came to me. I hastened forward; I stopped the cab; I addressed the feminine head.

"Pardon me, but are you the new maid who is expected at Mr. Cleaver's?"

"I am," she said. "I am Eliza Saunders, the new house-parlour-maid. Are you from Mr. Cleaver's?"

"Will you allow me to get in the cab with you for one moment? I have something to say to you which is of very great importance."

She allowed me, not too willingly, but she at least offered no active resistance. About an hour afterwards a second four-wheeled cab drew up at the servants' entrance of Mr. Cleaver's house, from which I descended. I flatter myself I was a good deal altered. I rang the servants' bell and announced myself as Eliza Saunders.

"That's all right," the maid said. "Come in; we expected you before this." So I went in.

Presently I was taken to a room upstairs—in the roof—a minute, scantily furnished apartment, in which, if there was only a tiny window, there were two beds.

"That's for you and me," said the maid who had answered my ring. "It isn't a large room, but we at least do have a bed each, and that's something. You'd better be as quick as you can and come downstairs. Miss Cleaver is sure to want to see you when she comes in."

I was not afraid of Miss Cleaver. I had learned that she was Mr. Harold's sister, and that the brother and sister formed the household, together with a Miss Le Blanc, who had arrived earlier in the day as a guest. I had made myself up to resemble the real Eliza Saunders as nearly as I could. I had little doubt that so far as appearance went I should be able to pass muster with the lady; it was from her brother's keen eyes that I feared detection. I was put to the test almost directly. As I went downstairs there was a knock and ring at the front door, and the maid who was to be my room mate informed me that I should have to answer the door. I answered it, to find on the doorstep the fair-haired man whom I had seen talking on the boat, and, of all persons in the world, the man whom I had seen leaning over the partition in the promenade.

To find myself so suddenly confronting such a pair was rather nerve-shaking. I had not the slightest doubt that together they had planned the attack upon my life, and deemed it extremely probable that if they penetrated my identity I should find myself in a very parlous position. Luckily, neither of them so much as glanced at me. They came into the hall; and both marched off and disappeared through a door which was at the other end of the hall.

"What an escape!" I told myself. I found that I was positively trembling. "Don't be an idiot," I added. "How are you going to get even with that pretty pair if you shake at the mere sight of them?"

A few minutes afterwards Miss Cleaver entered by the same door, which I opened to admit her. With her was Miss Le Blanc; apparently they had been out to buy mourning, for the girl was attired from head to foot in black. Miss Cleaver looked me up and down, as I never had been looked at before.

"So you've come." Her manner was distinctly curt. "I thought you were taller and not so thin. I hope you are strong. I will talk to you in the morning; in the meanwhile the housemaid will give you an idea of what your duties are."

I said nothing; plainly I was not expected to. The two ladies passed up the stairs, and I was left with a feeling that I did not like being talked to in quite that tone. I wondered what the room was into which Mr. Cleaver had vanished with his companion. It might have been by accident that, instead of returning to the kitchen I found myself in what I took to be the drawing-room. It opened into a conservatory, which I entered for purposes of exploration. It was rather spacious; in the centre was a bed which was full of magnificent Maréchal Niel roses. The sight of them gave me quite a shock. Had four of them been sent to me that morning? Proceeding a little farther I came upon a window which looked into a room in which were Mr. Cleaver and the man of the promenade. Had I taken another step they must have seen me. As it was I drew up just in time, where I could see them without their having the faintest notion that they were observed. The man of the promenade was drinking something out of a tumbler. As he removed it from his lips I saw him say—

"Any news of the fair Judith?"

Mr. Cleaver was less courteous.

"Darn her, none; at least, as far as I know."

"The roses reached her?" The speaker grinned.

"So far as I know, unless something happened to them on the way. In which case, something probably happened to a Post Office official. It would be quite in the order of things if something did. Luck is on her side."

"I shall believe it if she gets off this time; she certainly can have had no warning, and she couldn't possibly guess what was in that box, and you say that what was in it was quick enough."

"No mistake about that; it would probably be at her as soon as she had the lid off; one touch on the hand, wrist, anywhere, would be enough."

"That young woman has got on your nerves."

"She has, and she'll keep there till I've got on hers, once and for ever. I doubt if there's anything I wouldn't do which would result in wiping her off the face of the earth."

"I believe you," said the man of the promenade.

And I believed him also. As I drew away from the window—for the two men had moved, and I had certainly no wish to be discovered at that particular moment—I told myself, not for the first time, that I would not stick at a trifle to dispose of him; my presence there proved it. Shortly afterwards, as I was on the landing of the floor above, the door of that room opened, and the two men came out. Mr. Cleaver himself opened the front door and said good-bye to his companion on the doorstep. When he had gone Mr. Cleaver came upstairs; he went into what I had learnt was his bedroom. I hurried to the apartment half of which was mine, then I hurried down again, bearing in a piece of tissue paper the body of the snake which had sprung at me from among those Maréchal Niel roses. I went into the conservatory; I cut four roses; the French window which opened into the room in which the two men had been sitting was open. I passed through it. On a table in the centre I placed those roses with the snake in full sight on the top of them, and I left it there.

It was perhaps half an hour afterwards when a bell sounded in the kitchen, which I was informed came from Mr. Cleaver's study, and it was my duty to attend to it. I started to do my duty with my heart beating a little faster than it is wont to do. I knocked at the door, a voice bade me enter. I went in. Mr. Harold Cleaver was dressed for dinner; in his black suit he seemed fairer than ever. It needed but a moment's glance to see that he was in a state of agitation. A paper was lying on the table in the centre of the room; I wondered if what I had placed there was underneath it.

"Who are you?" he asked.

"I am the new house-parlourmaid, Eliza Saunders."

"Indeed? Come a little farther into the room, Eliza Saunders, I should like to have a look at you."

I hesitated. He had his hand on an oblong box. I moved a little farther into the room; we eyed each other. He spoke again.

"Come a little closer, I can't quite see you."

I knew better. I vaguely wondered why he kept his hand upon that oblong box, as if it contained something precious. I was not afraid of him; the sight of him seemed to serve as a tonic, to brace me up. He might not know it, but I knew that his hour had come. I went right forward and I lifted the paper off the table. As I had expected, the four roses and the snake were underneath.

"Do you know anything of these?" I asked.

"You are Judith Lee!" he cried. "Of all the sluts——"

"And you," I told him—I was less afraid than ever—"are the coward who tried this morning to kill me with the same weapon with which you murdered Mr. and Mrs. Le Blanc. Here the weapon is, I have brought it back to you."

I pointed to the snake. He never took his eyes off my face.

"So you know, do you?"

"I didn't know when I saw you on the boat coming from Ryde, but you told me this morning when you sent this." Again I pointed to the snake.

"Did I? That's how you put it, is it? And now what are you going to do, or what do you think you're going to do?"

"They know at Scotland Yard that I am here, and on what errand. When I put those roses on the table I sent them a message by your telephone to come here at once. In a very few minutes the officers of the law will be here; they'll deal with you; they are the only sort of people who can."

"Are they? Will they? When they come—if they come—they'll find you dead."

"I think not."

"And I am sure. Can't you see murder in my eyes? You see so many things, can't you see that? You hell-cat! The man who rids the earth of you will perform a service to humanity. You are everybody's enemy. By getting rid of you I shall prove myself to be everybody's friend. I have tried once and failed. I shan't fail again, this time I'm going to do it."

"I tell you again that I think not."

"Don't you? Then I'll show you, if there's time."

He lifted his arm off the oblong box; the lid flew off; a dreadful-looking head sprang out of it, attached to a sinuous body. A huge snake, as if it had been specially trained, made a rush at me across the table. I had a revolver in the pocket of my apron. As the reptile raised its head, opened its jaws, showed its hideous fangs, I struck it with the weapon. Exactly what I did to it I do not know, I only know that I struck it. It whirled right round. In his eagerness Mr. Cleaver leaned over the table as if to urge it on. As it wheeled the creature seemed to come right against his face. The man gave a strange cry; with both his hands he gripped the reptile by the throat. The serpent seemed to fight the man; it was like a nightmare. I did not know what to do. I dared not fire, I dared do nothing. My eye caught sight of a metal rod which was in a corner of the room. I rushed to it. I hurried back, the rod in my hand, and with all my force I struck the snake. As it seemed in that same instant the man fell to the ground, and the snake, limp, lifeless, broken-backed, fell with him.

Mr. Harold Cleaver was dead. The cobra had struck him again and again when once would have been sufficient. The death which he had meant for me was his.

I telephoned to Dr. George Evans, who arrived almost as soon as Inspector Ellis from Scotland Yard. A medical man was already there. There was no necessity for him to declare the cause of death, it was self-evident. Dr. Evans informed us that that particular cobra was almost as dangerous a plaything as that other specimen of the *Viperidæ*. It had once belonged to him. Acceding to his reiterated requests, he had sold it to Cleaver on the understanding that he was going to destroy it and stuff it, and dispose of it in the ordinary way of business.

For what seemed to me to be obvious reasons, nothing was ever made public. We had no positive proof, but there was a very strong presumption that Mr. Harold Cleaver had killed the Le Blancs. He had what probably appeared to him to be sufficient motives. Old Le Blanc was by way of being a usurer; Cleaver owed him a considerable sum; he was pressing for payment; Cleaver was in no position to pay. Cleaver knew that both the Le Blancs had made wills leaving all they possessed to their daughter. He had made surreptitious love to Freda Le Blanc, who, a simple-minded girl, had in a way encouraged him. After a fashion they were engaged—in secret. It was old Le Blanc's discovery of the engagement which had caused him to put pressure on Cleaver, and to send his daughter away to friends in France, which action on his part brought about Cleaver's opportunity.

No doubt he stole the doctor's snake, which was of so small a size that it was easy to carry in his pocket; no doubt that with it in his pocket he gained entry to The Elms; no doubt he used it to slay both the husband and the wife; he thought that with the father and mother both dead—safely dead—he would be able to marry their daughter and sole heiress, and all that they possessed would be his.

Freda Le Blanc went with her fortune to France—to her relatives. I do not think she has any suspicion of how her parents came to die. The shock of her lover's death had been a great blow to her. She had no notion that it had been his intention to kill me.

The entire episode was still another illustration of the power which conscience has. If, on the Ryde boat, a suddenly startled conscience had not caused him to behave in a fashion which caught my attention, if the same pricking conscience had not prompted him to send me that message of death, I should not have been aware even of his existence. It would scarcely be speaking figuratively if one said that his conscience slew him.

TWO WORDS

It was at a dinner party given by the Prices in Gloucester Terrace.[1] I was taken in by a tall, grey-headed man, whose name I had not caught, but who I was rather disposed to think was a doctor, until he said, as the *entrée* was being served—

"I don't know if you know who I am, Miss Lee. I know who you are very well."

"Do you? I am afraid I am more ignorant. I do not even know your name."

"I am Philip Collier. Does the name convey anything to you?"

"Philip Collier! Isn't there a lawyer of that name?"

"There is, and I am he. You, Miss Lee, are the victim of a plot. I begged Mrs. Price to give me an opportunity of meeting you, and this is the opportunity she has given me."

"I suppose you expect me to say you flatter me. Was there any particular reason why you wished to meet me, Mr. Collier?"

"There was—a very particular reason. You are the wonderful person who, having eyes as well as ears, can see what people are saying by watching the words as they form upon their lips. I can fancy, Miss Lee, that such a gift is not an unmixed blessing."

"It is not; quite the contrary. I often see things said which I would much rather not see, which the speakers, if they had guessed I should see, would much rather have left unsaid."

"I can believe it. I suppose, without using your ears, you could tell what every one was saying by merely glancing round the table?"

"Exactly. Which explains why, at a dinner party, I often keep my eyes upon my plate."

"I wish you would exercise your gift for me: because, on the other hand, there must be occasions on which you can render price-less services, not only to individuals, but to society at large. If you will allow me, I can offer you such an occasion."

[1] A street in Bayswater, running north from Lancaster Gate; a prestigious address due to its proximity to Hyde Park.

"Do you want me to look round the table and report what every one is saying?"

"Not at all. Have you heard of the Blindley Heath[1] mystery?"

"I do read the newspapers, Mr. Collier."

"Then, since it has been their chief item of news during the last few days, you have probably heard a great deal more about it than is true. You know that the police have arrested Charles Sinclair—that they charge him with Gerald Tansley's murder?"

"I have already told you, Mr. Collier, that I do read the newspapers. I am aware that he has already been three times before the magistrates, and now I recollect that you are acting as his solicitor —if you are Philip Collier."

"Charles Sinclair is much more than a client, Miss Lee. His father was one of my best friends, his mother is a sort of second cousin, and I like the youngster himself."

"He is quite young?"

"He is twenty-five; he made his first appearance before the magistrates on his birthday. Then, he is engaged to the daughter of another dear friend, Gertrude Alloway; and, what is not of the least importance, I am absolutely convinced of his complete innocence."

"That is not precisely the impression the evidence which has been given, so far, before the magistrates conveys to the public mind."

"I know. I don't deny for a second that matters, so far as they've gone, look bad. I wonder if I can enlist your sympathy on his behalf, Miss Lee? It is because I should so much like to do so that I was so anxious to meet you—so now the murder's out."

I was more than a little astonished. I told him so.

"What do you take me for, Mr. Collier? A professional detective, or what? I am a teacher of the deaf and dumb; I take the profoundest interest in my profession. My interests in it are so wide that they occupy all my time. I pass not only from city to city, but from country to country, engaged—much deeper than I ever meant to be—in a perpetual propaganda. Last month I was in Madeira, last week in Paris; next month I go to New York, then to Chicago —instructing people how to teach the dumb to speak. I am continu-

---

[1]   An isolated district of Surrey, some 25 miles south of Central London.

ally in receipt of requests like yours, Mr. Collier. I am not quite sure that it was altogether fair of Mrs. Price to ask me here to dine if she knew what was in store for me. I have read, in common with the rest of the world, about the Blindley Heath mystery, and how Charles Sinclair has become associated with it, but I really don't think, Mr. Collier, that I care to have anything to do with it, except in the newspapers. I have already one or two matters on hand, besides my ordinary daily work, which just now engrosses all my time and energy. What is this we are eating, Mr. Collier? I can't make up my mind."

My right-hand neighbour kept silent while I consulted the menu. Then he asked—

"Am I to accept that answer as final, Miss Lee? Won't you allow me at least to state the grounds on which I solicit your sympathy?"

"I would rather you didn't. How much sympathy do you suppose I have? Sometimes I receive more than a dozen appeals to it in the course of a single day; probably seventy or eighty a week. If I were to listen to them all I should be dead, or mad; so I shut my ears and close my eyes and pay no attention to them at all. I have to, in self-defence. I see we are supposed to be eating some preparation of sweetbread, but I don't recognize it in the least—do you?"

"I never, on principle, make inquiries into what I am eating; so long as it is palatable I am content. I will try to be content now."

His last words were spoken with an emphasis which I understood: he meant that he was willing to accept as final my refusal to allow my sympathies to be actively enlisted on behalf of Charles Sinclair, and was prepared to be as content as circumstances permitted. I heard not another word that night about the Blindley Heath mystery, and for the next few days took it for granted that, so far as I was concerned, the matter was closed. Then I was, I will put it, the victim of rather a curious incident.

I was considering a telegram which I had just received to say that my presence was urgently required at a conference dealing with certain pathological aspects of the deaf and dumb, which was taking place in Berlin, when a maid entered to inform me that a lady —a stranger—had called to see me on very important business, and begged that I would see her, if for a few minutes only. I hesitated; then, having listened to the maid's description of the visitor, said yes. A young girl came in, well and quietly dressed, whose appearance prepossessed me in her favour, although the strained look which was on her face suggested that she was suffering from some great mental trouble. Directly she entered she drew herself straight up and announced, as if defiantly—

"I am Gertrude Alloway." I was aware that I had heard the name before, though for the moment I could not place it. "I have come to entreat you to—to save my lover."

As, with a break in her voice at the end of her sentence, she made that remarkable statement, it all came back to me. Gertrude Alloway? Of course! She was the young woman who—so Mr. Philip Collier had told me—was engaged to be married to Charles Sinclair, the young man who was charged with having murdered Gerald Tansley in his house at Blindley Heath. It looked as though I had been made the object of another little plot. A feeling of resentment rose within me. I stood up.

"I believe I know who you are, Miss Alloway, and while regretting——"

She cut me short, holding out her hands toward me with a gesture of earnest appeal.

"Please hear me for a moment, Miss Lee, before you refuse. Please do." I could not help myself; she went on so rapidly that for some moments I seemed to have no chance of interposing. "This was to have been my wedding day—my wedding day! It was settled months ago. Now, instead of standing at the altar with me, the man I was to have married is in jail. And he's as innocent of wrongdoing as the most innocent child—however appearances may seem to be against him, I am sure of it. Charles is sometimes hot-tempered —the best of us are sometimes that. He thought Gerald Tansley was not using him well. He quarrelled with him that night, but he never touched him. When Charles left him, Mr. Tansley was as well as he ever was. And as for Charles having taken anything from his house, the idea is too absurd. Such a judge of character as you are, if you knew him I am sure you would see that written on his face. They were associated in all sorts of inventions—although Charles had more than once suspected Mr. Tansley of sharp practice. The subject of their quarrel was an aeroplane, one which could move in any direction, regardless of wind, or storm, or anything, just as easily as if it were on land. The original idea came from Charles, but they were perfecting it together. I beg you to let me tell you——"

I had to stop her. There was a clock upon the mantel, and that telegram from Berlin in my hand. She might go on for hours, for all I knew. If I went at all, it would have to be directly; I told her so.

"Whatever you may have to tell me, Miss Alloway, I cannot possibly listen to you now. I have to leave for Berlin in less than an hour. Before I go I have all these letters to answer, and there is nothing ready."

Her face fell; she went white. As she clasped her hands I could see that she trembled. Stammering words came from her quivering lips.

"I—I—I—had hoped so much—and you won't listen."

"My dear Miss Alloway, it isn't a question of won't, but of can't. I leave for Berlin at once; I arrive there to-morrow; I stay, probably, two days, perhaps three. Directly the business on which I am going is done, I return. I ought to be back here certainly within a week. If at the end of that time you are still of opinion that any good can be gained by my listening to what you have to say, I shall be to that extent at your service. But I tell you frankly, as I hinted to Mr. Philip Collier, that I know of no reason why I should intervene in this case any more than in fifty others like it, and I think it highly probable that I should not be in the least disposed to do so after I had heard all that you may have to say."

That girl's face haunted me all the way to Berlin. I had seen many sad faces in my life; there must have been a special quality on hers which struck a sympathetic chord. It certainly was not nice to think that her wedding day should have had to be postponed for such a very unpleasant cause; on the other hand, if it should happen that Mr. Charles Sinclair was more guilty than she supposed—and her eyes were likely to be prejudiced—then she was really more fortunate than might appear on the surface.

That Berlin conference was very exciting—at least, to me. Every second of my time was occupied for three days instead of two. When, at the close of the third day, the proceedings were terminated and every one was leaving, my thoughts could scarcely have been farther removed from Miss Gertrude Alloway and her affairs —till, all in an instant, they were brought back to her in a fashion which affected me more than I should have cared to admit. A big, brawny, broad-chested man was leaving the room—I suppose my eyes had singled him out because of his physique—when he was accosted by a grey-haired individual who was almost as small as the other was big. They only exchanged three or four short sentences, and, my attention being really occupied elsewhere, they would have gone unnoticed had it not been that all at once two words caught my glance. They were spoken by the bigger and younger man to the smaller and elder. They came at the end of a sentence which I had not caught, and apparently referred to some subject of which they had been speaking. "Blindley Heath"—those were the two words. Having uttered them to complete his sentence, the young man nodded, strode out of the room, and the elder returned to a group of persons with whom he seemed to be intimately acquainted. For an instant I could not have said what the two words "Blindley Heath" conveyed to my mind; then it came to me with a rush: the *cause célèbre* which was the topic of the hour in England. The mysterious death of Gerald Tansley; the accusation of Charles Sinclair; Mrs. Price's dinner party; Philip Collier's little plot; Gertrude Alloway—all these were associated in my mind with the two words "Blindley Heath." How came those two words to have been spoken in that room?

I had never been to Blindley Heath in my life, but I knew it was a remote Surrey common, on what I understood was the best road for motorists from London to Eastbourne. That big young man was undoubtedly a German. I turned to an acquaintance to make sure of the other.

"You see that short, grey-haired man who is talking to the stout man with the glasses—do you know who he is?"

"That is Major Schrattenholtz, whose position in the army, it is understood, is, so to speak, much higher than his rank. He is entrusted with many delicate affairs."

My informant told me various things about Major Schrattenholtz which set me thinking. I should have liked to go up and ask him what he knew about Blindley Heath, but time pressed, and I had to do several things before attiring myself for the banquet which was to be offered as a compliment to certain persons who had been present at the conference. After the banquet there was a reception, which was attended by all sorts of eminent personalities of both sexes resident in Berlin. Among the first persons I particularly noticed after my entry on the scene was the big young man of the afternoon. Major Schrattenholtz had been at the banquet. He was at the reception, in a dark blue uniform which made him look smaller than ever, when there advanced towards him a striking figure in the gorgeous uniform of some cavalry regiment, the big young man. I could see both perfectly from where I was, and I watched attentively each word they uttered. They did not say much, but to me each syllable of what they did say was pregnant with meaning.

Clearly it was a rendezvous—possibly the appointment had been made that afternoon. They, of course, spoke in German, but as I know that language about as well as I do my own, and had expressly gone to Berlin to make a few remarks on the peculiar structure of certain German words with reference to the oral instruction of German deaf and dumb children, I found no difficulty whatever in following what those two gentlemen said. To begin with, the big man produced from the sleeve of his coat something which was wrapped in what looked to me like oiled silk. This the major transferred to the same part of his attire—so quickly that only those who were watching closely would have noticed that anything passed between them. As he slipped the package up his sleeve I saw the major whisper—

"You have examined it?"

To which the big man replied also in a whisper; they spoke in whispers throughout; evidently they wanted to keep what they were saying to themselves, and were sublimely unconscious of what a dangerous person—from their point of view—was present in the shape of a black-haired young woman who wore a biscuit-coloured frock.

"Closely; it is all right. I believe it to be not very far from perfection for its purpose—certainly better than ours. I am sorry it should have cost so much."

Replying, Major Schrattenholtz put into German a proverb which was originally French.

"'You cannot make omelets without breaking eggs.'[1] Besides, is

---

[1] "On ne fait pas d'omelette sans casser des œufs", often attributed to Maximilien de Robespierre.

it so sure that it is a misfortune"—he glanced about him as if fearful that his faint whisper might be overheard—"that he is dead? If this other one also dies, as from the latest advices seems likely, then the secret will be ours only. I fancy it will prove to be worth a great deal more than it cost, even if you appraise the cost from the sentimental point of view. That will do. Adieu."

The big young man was curtly dismissed. Major Schrattenholtz, with that package up his sleeve, passed on; the other was left to do as he liked. A few minutes afterwards I was introduced to a gentleman with whose family I already had some acquaintance—Captain Otto von Arnheim, who was himself in a cavalry regiment, an extremely good-looking young fellow; I thought how well his uniform became him. Presently I saw the big young man crossing the room with a lady at his side.

"Do you know who that is?" I asked my new acquaintance.

"Perfectly well. That is Gustav von Hertzheim, a particular friend of my own. He is in the aviation department, and has done some very wonderful things."

"But I thought from his uniform that he was in a cavalry regiment, like you."

"So he is; but with us one is often detached from one's regiment and detailed for special work. Gustav is becoming quite an authority on flight. Last month a cousin of mine was married to his sister."

"And was—this gentleman present at the wedding?"

"Of course he was. Since his father is dead he was his sister's chief supporter."

"Last month? Let me see, this is July; that was June. Do you happen to remember what day of the month the wedding was?"

"Very well. It was the fifth. I have good reason to remember it, because that same evening my horse put its foot in a hole and cut a knee. It was a Monday—the end of the fine weather. A thunderstorm came that same night, and it seems to have been raining ever since. Of what are you thinking? You look as if you had a great deal on your mind."

I had at the moment, though, after so brief an acquaintance, his question was perhaps a trifle impertinent. I was trying to think what was the date on which Gerald Tansley had been found dead in his house on Blindley Heath. I knew it was at the beginning of last month. Captain von Arnheim's statement that the fifth had been a Monday placed it at once. It had been a Sunday; it must have been the fourth—the first Sunday in June—somewhere in the middle of the night, possibly on the early morning of the fifth. And on June the fifth Captain Gustav von Hertzheim had been in Berlin and present at the marriage of his sister.

"What time of the day," I asked, "do marriages generally take place in Berlin?"

"Pretty nearly all times. My cousin, if you are thinking of him, was married in the morning, quite early, about eleven o'clock; but not in Berlin, in Cologne—they have a house there. They had to catch the afternoon train to Switzerland, to which, in English fashion, they were going for their honeymoon."

"Then you do sometimes have honeymoons in Germany?"

He told me all about it, and while I seemed to listen I was thinking that before eleven o'clock on the morning of Monday, June the fifth, Herr Gustav von Hertzheim was in Cologne.

The following day I left Berlin, returning via Brussels, where I stayed the night with some friends who had journeyed with me. The next day I went straight on to town, where for the next three days I had scarcely time to breathe, so engrossed was I with a hundred things that had to be done upon the instant. During my absence the affair of the Blindley Heath mystery had dragged itself to an end, so far as the magistrates were concerned: Charles Sinclair had been sent for trial. Public opinion already judged him guilty. It was a conversation which I saw taking place in a railway carriage between three men who spoke to each other in whispers, each of whom declared himself to be of opinion that Sinclair was guilty, which brought back to me the anguished face of Gertrude Alloway and certain memories of Captain von Hertzheim and Major Schrattenholtz. The following afternoon I paid a visit to Blindley Heath.

The weather was July at its best; under such a sky I thought the heath looked lovely—it was a common, by the way, rather than what I understand by a heath. Right at one side was one of those old houses which are much better to look at than to live in. I imagine that people take them because, seen under a blue sky, they are so picturesque; then, when the rains and storms of winter come, wish they had not, because they are so ill-lighted, ill-drained, and in every respect so inconvenient. The house stood in the midst of a good-sized, old-fashioned garden which, it struck me, was in imminent need of a gardener's care, and the garden was surrounded by a tall, ill-kept hedge.

In this delectable abode, remote from the habitation of man—the nearest cottage was a mile away—Gerald Tansley had dwelt, to all intents and purposes, alone. Servants refused to stop with him; they came and went. He tried to keep a cook and a couple of housemaids, but tried in vain. For various reasons no good servant could be induced to stay with him. On Sunday, the fourth of June, his only domestic was a Mrs. Keith, the wife of a labourer who dwelt in a cottage rather more than a mile away, who came in by the day to "do" for him. On that day she left at five o'clock; after that hour the only person who was known to have seen him alive was Charles Sinclair. When Mrs. Keith came on Monday morning she found doors and windows open, and Gerald Tansley lying dead on his study floor.

Inquiries which were set on foot elicited the fact that persons passing the night before had heard the sound of voices in the house raised in angry tones as of persons quarrelling. James Reid, a young country lout, stated that he was passing there a little before ten, when he heard the most dreadful language coming from the house on the other side of the hedge—and not only bad language, but the sound of blows. He admitted that he was so afraid that he did not dare to stop, but went hastening on. An aged man, Isaac Denman, at about the same time, had seen some one rushing out of the gate, and tearing across the heath as if for life. From the nearest railway station, three miles off, on a Sunday night the last train for London left at ten twenty-five. Among the passengers that night was a man without a hat, who arrived at the station in such a condition of heat and disorder that he was the observed of all observers. A hat had been found on the floor close to where the dead man was lying, the lining of which was stained with blood. The presumption was that it belonged to the man who had been heard quarrelling with Gerald Tansley, who had been seen flying across the heath, and afterwards, still half beside himself with excitement, at the local station. He was searched for and found: he proved to be Charles Sinclair.

He made a statement, when arrested, which was not so satisfactory as it might have been. He admitted that he was the person who had been heard quarrelling with Gerald Tansley, but he stated that when he left him Gerald Tansley was still alive. He had heard through the newspapers of his death, but had remained in the background for the simple reason that his tragic end had had nothing to do with him. Further investigations had by no means established the certainty of this. One piece of incriminating evidence was produced after another. His solicitor, Philip Collier, had professed to me his belief in his innocence, and his sweetheart, Gertrude Alloway; these were prejudiced persons. All the rest of the world seemed persuaded of his guilt. It seemed extremely likely, if no fresh evidence turned up, that the jury at the trial would find him guilty, and that he would be hanged.

It so happened, however, that on the subject of the guilt or innocence of Charles Sinclair I had theories of my own, which I had journeyed down to Blindley Heath to investigate.

After I had gone over the house—where I learnt nothing except that it was the kind of house in which I would rather not live—I passed on to the heath and looked about me. I spied at a little distance a man who was working on the road which bisected it. Him I accosted, and from him I learnt in a few moments all that I wanted.

He told me that he lodged at a little cottage at the other side of the common. He had given no evidence in the mystery case because he had none to give, but he remembered very well the night of the fourth of June; it was imprinted upon his memory because twice in the course of the night he had been woke up by a motor-car. He had never heard such a noisy motor-car on Blindley Heath before. I pricked up my ears at this. He was disturbed for the first time about midnight—he "never did hear such a noise as that there thing did make." He must have dozed off again, and in the course of another hour or so, as well as he could judge, he was disturbed again—"that there motor-car was making more noise nor ever." He did not sleep again; his night's rest was ruined, and, since he generally slept like a top, that was something he resented. There were motor-cars about there, he said, plenty of them, but he never did hear one make a noise like that. He heard it coming from afar, so he declared, then he heard it long after it had started. His impression was that the car had pulled up somewhere on the common. As evidence in support of his idea, he took me to a spot where the ground was all cut up, gorse and brambles being torn right out of the ground. He believed the "dratted thing" had come off the road and stopped there. He had noticed the place on the Monday morning, and had picked up a piece of paper which had been caught in one of the uprooted brambles. He had it on him then. He took a metal tobacco box out of his pocket, and from it a sheet of fine tissue paper, which was neatly folded so as to fit into the lid. When I opened it and saw what it was, my heart seemed to give quite a jump: that sheet of tissue paper was quite a compliment to my powers of perception. To my mind it proved the theory I had formed up to the hilt.

I asked the road mender if I might have it for half a crown.[1] He hesitated as if surprised at the largeness of my offer, then said that I might and welcome. He added that he could not make head nor tail of what was on it, and did not know that it was worth anything to anyone. He had just kept it because he had found it on that particular spot.

I returned to London, having learned even more than I had hoped, and spent that night in consideration. In the morning I had arrived at a resolution. Daniel Fletcher was acting in the case of the Blindley Heath mystery as solicitor for the Crown. He was by way of being a particular friend of mine; I had found him one of the most interesting men I knew. After breakfast I telephoned to him at his offices in Lincoln's Inn Fields[2] to ask when was the earliest moment at which I could see him. In consequence of the answer I received, shortly afterwards I was sitting in a great big, old-fashioned room, with Daniel Fletcher on one side of a great writing-table and myself on the other.

"I haven't come here on business," I told him. "What I am going to say is between ourselves."

His eyes twinkled. What he lacked in height he made up in breadth. In the huge head, set on a short neck between broad shoulders, were a pair of the most curious eyes I knew.

"You pay me an unexpected compliment," he replied, "in making

[1] A coin worth 2s.6d.
[2] A large square in Holborn in Central London, taking its name from the adjacent Lincoln's Inn, one of London's Inns of Court, or barristers' professional associations.

me the subject of a confidence which is to go no farther than ourselves; you who are the most secretive soul alive."

"I am not secretive, as I have told you before." It was a subject
which we had discussed again and again, and on which he was more
outspoken than polite. "I have not come to wrangle; I have come to
say something and go."

"That's right—speak and be off. Don't stay a moment longer
than you can help in a solicitor's musty office. And I hoped that you
would lunch with me."

"I can't. I will some other day, but this morning it is impossible."

"Mention the day on which it will be possible; I'll make a note
of it."

He had a pencil in his hand, with which he was about to write
something on a pad. I ignored his suggestion.

"You have charge of the case against Charles Sinclair in that affair
at Blindley Heath."

"It's in the papers; what is in them is sometimes true."

"He is innocent—of the death of Gerald Tansley."

The twinkle died out of his eyes, giving place to a light of quite
a different kind. He watched me. It was some seconds before he
spoke.

"You are sure of that? I ask you, although I know you would
not say so unless you were, you being one of the few women who
appreciate the meaning of words."

"The average woman appreciates them better than the average
man. However, you happen to be right when you say that I should
not say such a thing if I were not sure."

I told him of the two words which I had seen the big young
man utter as he was quitting the conference room at Berlin; of the
brief sentences he had exchanged with Major Schrattenholtz in the
evening; of the package which had passed from one to the other; of
my visit to Blindley Heath; and of the piece of paper which the road
mender had found entangled in the brambles. That sheet of paper
I laid on the table in front of Mr. Fletcher. He examined it carefully,
then leaned back in his chair and looked at me.

"I wonder if you are aware what a wonderful gift this is of yours?
I fancy sometimes that your very familiarity with it has bred something like contempt. To me it is a constant marvel. The whole

machinery of the law is put into action, goes lumbering along; after great cost of time and labour it takes things very little farther than they were at the beginning. Then, with those seer's eyes of yours, you glance round a crowded room, see a man pronouncing a couple of words, and what the whole resources of civilization fail to accomplish is done in a twinkling—the mystery is solved. After those remarks of mine you will not be surprised to learn that I think it quite possible this is the key to the whole thing." He flicked that sheet of tissue paper. "The thing is, how are we going to prove it? As you are aware, in a case like this assumptions, or presumptions, go for nothing. We want cold facts. Can you get them?"

I told him that I thought I could, and how. He positively beamed. I do not understand why Daniel Fletcher always seems to find me so amusing.

"Do you know," he exclaimed, "why I believe I like you? Because you remind me of those plays of which I was so fond in my youth and the likes of which one sees so seldom nowadays—you are so full of surprises. That most surprising notion of yours is not only a first-rate joke, it's both practical and practicable. As an assistant, count me in. Let me know when my services are required, and they're yours to command. Only please to bear in mind that time is of the first importance, and to be of use your friend must be brought to the scratch at once."

"I think I may promise that he will; probably the day after to-morrow."

"And if he declines to be brought to the scratch—what then?"

"He won't." I had risen from my chair, and was refolding that sheet of tissue paper. "This"—I held up the sheet of paper—"puts him in the hollow of my hand. You'll see."

"I hope I shall—and soon. Now how about that lunch? I'll give you quite a banquet."

"Thank you, I don't like banquets in the middle of the day. Then it is agreed that you fall in with any arrangements which I may make?"

On that understanding we parted, and one of the first things I saw when I got into the street was a newspaper-boy with a placard held in front of him on which was printed in thick black letters "The Blindley Heath Mystery. Fresh Developments." Although I was becoming much more interested than I had meant to be in that so-called mystery, I was not in the least interested in that paper's promise of fresh developments. I wondered what its editor would say if I walked into his office, told him certain things, and placed before him that sheet of tissue paper with leave to print it. He would then indeed be able to appeal to the public on the grounds of "Fresh Developments." His presses would be hard put to it to turn out copies fast enough for people to buy.

When I returned to my rooms I penned a letter to Captain Gustav von Hertzheim, which I sent to him at an address which I had procured before leaving Berlin—the rough copy I made for that letter had to be re-written perhaps half a dozen times before I arrived at the epistle which finally went. When I had stamped and posted it the only thing I could do in the matter was to await events. Everything went as I had expected. Captain von Hertzheim could not have received the letter before the evening post on the following day, yet on the evening of that same day I received a telegram to say that he would be in England on the evening of the day following— he would be with me about eleven o'clock.

Clearly the moment he had received my epistle the captain's mind was made up. He must have gone straight off to send that wire, and then made haste to catch the Nord Express,[1] which left the Schlesischer Bahnhof[2] at 10.45. Possibly it was not necessary for him to go through any formalities in the matter of taking leave, but where the call, as he deemed, was sufficiently urgent he could go and come as he pleased. That call of mine was possibly the most urgent he had ever received in the course of his official life; an instant answer was the only way in which he could possibly save the situation. I went to bed that night realizing that a very important person in the German military service was speeding across Europe as fast as express trains could carry him, bringing with him the explanation of what had happened that Sunday night in that remote corner of a Surrey common.

On the following night it was considerably past eleven when a knock at the outer door of my flat in Sloane Gardens announced

[1] A train service which from 1896 connected Paris with St. Petersburg, via Brussels, Cologne and Berlin.
[2] A major railway station in Berlin, now Berlin Ostbahnhof.

that the expected visitor had arrived. It was an uncanonical hour for a single woman to receive a visit from a solitary man, but the porter below, having been apprised of what was about to happen, was prepared for his coming, and everything was in readiness for the traveller who had come with such flattering speed to see me.

Captain von Hertzheim was admitted by my maid. I stood up as he came in. He slightly inclined his head, and we remained for some seconds observing each other; he was casting about in his mind for a clue which would tell him where he had seen me before. He was attired in a long grey coat which covered him from head to foot. It became him very well; I thought what a fine figure of a man be looked. As regards his face, he was a trifle coarse-featured, as young Germans of his stamp are inclined to be, but there was strength in every line. He addressed me at last in English which was marked by only a slight accent.

"You are Miss Lee?" I nodded an affirmative. "I have a good memory for faces—I do not remember to have seen you before." I remained silent. "Where have I seen you before? Where have you seen me?"

"That is not a point which matters. Captain von Hertzheim, you were in England on the night of June the fourth."

"How do you know that? Who told you? June the fourth? Let me remember. Was that not a Sunday?" Unbuttoning his paletot,[1] he took a notebook from a pocket of the coat beneath. He consulted its pages. "June the fourth; that was a Sunday. I find that on that evening I supped with my regiment. On the next day, Monday, was the marriage of my sister Bertha, at which I assisted. How, then, please, can I have been in England on the night of June the fourth?"

"You flew here—from Cologne, where, on your return on the Monday, your sister was married."

He did not start—he was not that kind of person; if anything, he grew more rigid, but there was a something in his eyes which suggested that if he had had me in some place where interruption was not to be feared I might have been subjected to some very singular usage. His tone was peremptory; he might have been reprimanding an awkward squad.

---

[1] A long overcoat, a greatcoat.

"What absurdity is this? Who put such ideas into your head? How can one fly from Cologne to England and back in the course of a single night?"

"You can tell me better than I can you, since you did it. I have a notion, Captain von Hertzheim, that it may have been rather by way of a trial flight. You may have had a new aeroplane with which you desired to experiment—one which was built for long flights at high speed." I could see by a look which was on his face that I had hit on the truth. "You supped with your regiment—good; sometimes one sups early in Cologne—perhaps you had finished by eight. You went quickly to the flying-ground, where you had previously seen that everything was in readiness. Soon after eight the new aeroplane was two thousand feet up in the air. Was that not so? You do not answer in words, but, all the same, you answer. From Cologne to London, as the crow flies, is rather over three hundred miles. You must have known your way very well. I am inclined to think that it was not the first time you had flown the course; I dare say a great many flights take place at night of which the world hears nothing. That branch of the secret service to which you belong, Captain von Hertzheim, has no doubt its own way of doing things. You flew fast; that new aeroplane was specially built for speed. Your objective was not London, but—Blindley Heath."

I paused. One could see he was annoyed. He glanced round the room, using language which was not becoming from a gentleman to a lady.

"Who are you? How do you happen to have become acquainted with the things you pretend to know? You talk nonsense, nothing but lies!"

I paid no attention to his annoyance or even to his discourtesy; I went quietly on. As I continued, his imperturbability, which was part of the discipline which had been drilled into him, became decidedly less.

"In a remote house on Blindley Heath resided one Gerald Tansley. You know all about it, Captain von Hertzheim, probably better than I do; I am only recalling certain facts to your memory. Mr. Tansley was an inventor whose attention at the moment was concentrated on aeroplanes. He had been in communication with the German Secret Service Department, of which you are so distinguished a member. He had offered to sell the patent of a new aeroplane which would manœuvre so quickly, was so steady, and was so little affected by climatic conditions that it promised to be an almost ideal weapon of war. Of that you, and your superiors also, were convinced. The negotiations reached a certain point, then there came a hitch; they threatened to come to nothing. Since the matter had been entrusted to your hands, that would be for you a very serious state of affairs. In Germany, in such a matter, failure is regarded as almost an offence. You were expressly informed by Major Schrattenholtz, the superior officer to whom you were directly responsible, that if the affair did fall through there would be a black mark against your name."

He positively approached a state of agitation. His language was even worse than before.

"How in the name of all that's damnable do you come to know all this? It is impossible that any one could know it—impossible! You are amusing yourself with a tissue of inventions. There is no living creature who could have breathed a word of what you talk about—not one."

When he paused I went on—

"You dropped a hint to Major Schrattenholtz of what it was you proposed to do. In return he gave you a look which you took to mean approval if you were successful."

"Clearly you talk balderdash. No one could have told you that."

"So you went at a hundred and fifty miles an hour through the air that Sunday night—what sort of machine it was which carried enough petrol to take you there and back I do not understand. Even if you carried a Swift compass and knew your way very well, you still must be an excellent pilot, because you alighted within two hundred yards of Mr. Tansley's house, coming down rather badly. In alighting you not only cut up the ground, but tore up the bushes and brambles."

"How the devil do you know that? How the devil!"

All at once the German guttural accent showed very clearly in his speech. He actually banged his clenched fist on my table within two feet of my nose.

"You hurried into Mr. Tansley, who had not yet gone to bed, and who must have been very surprised to see you, and there ensued an angry scene. When you went you left him lying dead on the floor, and you took with you the plans of that aeroplane. I doubt if you paid him for them; possibly, since he was dead, you did not think it necessary. In England killing is murder, even when a distinguished officer kills an insignificant civilian. Don't you know that, Captain von Hertzheim?"

His answer was to go to the door through which he had entered, and then stand confused.

"There is no key in that lock. It was removed before you came, with the express intention of preventing your making it fast against intrusion. The folding doors on the other side of those hangings at which you are glaring open into my bedroom. The door is unlocked; I don't see how I can prevent your seeing who is on the other side. What good do you suppose you would gain by doing so? I have brought you here for a particular purpose."

"Then what is contained in this letter is false?"

He held out a sheet of paper which I knew very well.

"Not necessarily, by any means. Like your new aeroplane, you move almost too quickly. Are you aware that Gerald Tansley had a partner?"

"I am aware of nothing, of nothing—you understand, of nothing!"

"That is the attitude you propose to take up. I see. Before we part you may change it. You are aware that Mr. Tansley had a partner. You are also aware that it was because of his partner that he hesitated about accepting the German offer for the plans of his new aeroplane. You also, Captain von Hertzheim, know perfectly well that that partner, Charles Sinclair, stands accused of the murder of the man you killed."

"I did not kill him."

"You did not kill him! You are aware, at least, of that? Perhaps presently you will become aware of a little more. If you did not kill Mr. Tansley, who did? He was alive when you entered his house, and dead when you left."

His answer was both brusque and uncivil.

"I am not to be caught with salt—by a woman who is all lies. Tell me what truth there is in what is contained in this letter."

Again he held out that sheet of foreign post.

"We are coming to that presently, Captain von Hertzheim. I have my own way of proceeding, which on this occasion must be also yours. I am about to place before you alternative, Captain von Hertzheim. There are certain persons watching this building, by my direction——"

"Are you an officer of police? Tell me what you are—tell me!"

"I have only to give them a certain signal; you will be arrested before you leave this building for the murder of Gerald Tansley, which means that you will find yourself placed in a very delicate position. Your department will not regard with favour one of its officers who gets himself charged with murder while upon its service, to say nothing of the damaging revelations which may result."

"So you think you have me in a trap? I see! And, by God, you shall see!" His language was most violent, especially when one remembers that it was addressed to a lady. "I was prepared for this kind of thing. You will find I am not so simple as you supposed."

"Of the second alternative you have already been advised."

"What do you mean by I have been advised? Of what have I been advised? I have been advised of nothing."

"You informed Major Schrattenholtz that your mission had been entirely successful, that you had obtained what you sought, that you had examined the plans of the new aeroplane which Germany was so anxious to buy, that they were perfectly all right. When you said that you lied."

The expression on his rather coarse features was remarkable. It might have been his intention to frighten me; if it was, he failed. I smiled at him, which seemed to make him still angrier.

"I believe you are a devil—I begin to believe it. No one but a creature who employs supernatural means can know what you pretend to know. I wish to be polite to you."

"You don't succeed; not very well, do you?"

"Will you tell me what exactly it is you pretend to know—tell me at once."

The man shook his fist at me—actually! I believe if I had been a man he would have struck me. And when I continued merely to smile he seemed nonplussed.

"You have been travelling some time, Captain von Hertzheim;

you must be tired. Wouldn't you like to sit? Perhaps you will not feel so excited if you establish yourself on a chair."

My soothing words did not seem to have the effect of calming him.

"I will not sit—I do not want a chair! I insist upon your telling me at once what you know."

"The word 'insist' as coming from you is out of place. I am in a position to insist, not you. I am going to tell you just what I choose to tell you—no more—when I choose. And I don't intend to tell you anything until you take a chair. Your violence distresses me."

He hesitated, he glared, he even gasped. I have no doubt he was telling himself what he would have done had I been a man. I believe that what exasperated him most was the fact that I was a woman, and that, therefore, he could not even challenge me to fight. At last he took a chair, placed himself on the extreme edge—I fancy he thought that his sword was hanging at his side, and that he had to give it room. Seeing that he had observed my wishes at least to that extent, I continued—

"When you told Major Schrattenholtz that you had examined those plans and that they were perfectly all right, you omitted to mention that when you returned to Berlin on that new aeroplane, about five o'clock on the morning of the day on which your sister was married, you discovered, with feelings which I won't attempt to describe, that a sheet of those plans was missing—which was the most essential sheet of all. Was your language very dreadful, Captain von Hertzheim, when you made that discovery? I fear that it was."

He did not answer my question; he asked one of his own—

"You have that sheet?"

"When you ask that question, do you not perceive how much you give yourself away? It is tantamount to an acknowledgment that you were at Blindley Heath on the night of the fourth of June; that you did enter Mr. Tansley's house; that when you quitted it you had in your possession the plans of that aeroplane; that the breeze carried one of them from between your fingers without, in the darkness, your noticing it—and it is that sheet which you have come to England to recover." He was about to speak, but I checked him. "That brings me to what I call the second alternative. You have lied to Major Schrattenholtz. You told him that you had left Gerald Tansley lying dead——"

"How do you know that I told him? How do you know any of these things? Tell me how you know it. What sort of creature are you? Are you a witch? I cannot believe that it is from any human source that you got your information."

"I repeat, Captain von Hertzheim, that you told Major Schrattenholtz that you left Gerald Tansley lying dead in the house; but you did not dare to tell him that you had not brought to Berlin what you knew to be the most essential part of the drawings of that aeroplane. You concealed its absence; you forged the missing sheet; you had had a hasty glance at the original; you thought you knew more or less what was on it; you trusted that it would turn out all right, and that luck would be on your side. But luck was against you, Captain von Hertzheim. Suppose I inform the major that that sheet is missing—what explanation will you be able to offer of the lies which you have told him? Suppose I place it before him—what will that mean to you? I am sufficiently acquainted with the German military system to know that that would be the end of you."

My visitor looked at me in a fashion which made it clear that he would not have been averse to taking me by the throat if my silence and the missing sheet could not be secured in any other way; but he had himself pretty well in hand. He got the better of his impulse. He merely observed, in tones which were more guttural than before—

"You talk of two alternatives. What do you mean by an alternative? You have not offered me one."

"Would you rather I handed you over to the police to be tried for murder, or should I send a little explanatory note to Major Schrattenholtz? Those are the two alternatives I offer you. Choose one, Captain von Hertzheim."

"I choose neither. There is a third; I see it on your face."

"You have good eyes. There is. I believe you to be, in the common acceptation of the term, a man of honour; that as a rule you do not lie. Answer me one question: How did Gerald Tansley come by his death?"

"I do not know. He was in a great rage; he swore, he shrieked at me. I do not say he was not right to be in a rage; I only tell you the truth. All at once he fell forward. In falling he struck his head against the edge of the table, at which he caught with both his hands. He drew himself nearly upright, then fell again, backwards, on to the floor. I had not touched him; I was not within six feet of him. He lay still. When I went to look at him I thought that he was in a fit. I knew where the plans were. I thought when his senses returned there would be another scene—besides, I was pressed for time. I took them out of the drawer, and carried them away with me. I had been willing all along to pay the sum originally agreed. I could send him the money from Berlin. What I wanted was the plans. When I heard afterwards that he was dead, I was amazed—I was very sorry."

"'One cannot make omelets without breaking eggs.'"

As I said that he jumped up.

"That was what——" He paused. Then, as he leaned over the table, I did think he was going to strike me. "Where did you hear that said?"

"Was it not said by a very famous Frenchman?" I inquired.

"It was said——" He checked himself. "You are a devil—or a witch, which is the same thing. Well, I have told you that I do not know how Gerald Tansley came by his death. What then? What is your third alternative?"

"This. I have reason to believe your story. Medical evidence shows that he had a weak heart. Charles Sinclair, who is at present charged with his murder, asserts that Gerald Tansley was alive when he left him. That assertion, if I had not discovered you, might have hanged him; because, as the case stands against him, the presumption is that he struck his friend and is unwilling to acknowledge it. In Tansley's condition, that blow, though a comparatively slight one, was enough to kill him, which would make Sinclair guilty of murder. You explain everything. You came after Sinclair went; you corroborate his story in every detail; you found Gerald Tansley alive; you explain how, when you left him, you thought he was in a fit. I repeat, I believe your story to be true. If you will go into the witness-box and tell that story simply, I think I can promise that no harm will come to you—that no charge shall be made against you; and as a reward you shall be placed in possession of the missing sheet, which has not left my keeping since I found it. Is that a bargain? Perhaps the presence of some friends of mine may assist you in arriving at a decision."

I touched a little handbell which was on my table. Two men came from my bedroom, a third from the little hall without. Von Hertzheim eyed them with rather a disagreeable look.

"So there were listeners, after all. I thought as much. That is why you were so brave."

I bestowed on him what I hoped was one of my sweetest smiles.

"Pray think so if you like. This is Mr. Daniel Fletcher, who in the case against Charles Sinclair has charge of the prosecution; this is Dr. Arnecliffe, a well-known medical authority, who was present at the autopsy on the late Gerald Tansley; this is a gentleman from Scotland Yard, whose personal acquaintance I trust you may not find it necessary to make."

Practically the whole of the remainder of the story is public history.

Captain von Hertzheim did not tell all the truth, but he told as much of it as was actually required in some brief and pithy sentences.

He told how Gerald Tansley was an acquaintance of his, with whom he had been negotiating for the purchase of the plans of an aeroplane; how a hitch had occurred in the negotiations; how he had left Berlin on an aeroplane early on the evening of Sunday, June the fourth; how he had arrived about midnight; how he had had an interview with Gerald Tansley, which became rapidly more and more heated; how Gerald Tansley stumbled and fell, in what witness took to be a fit; how, in ignorance of the fact that he was alone in the house, being anxious to get away before he recovered sufficiently to renew the discussion, he had hurried off with the plans in his hand. After another question or two, having carried the witness so far, Counsel for the Crown sat down. Counsel for the defence had no questions to ask.

Major Schrattenholtz followed. He corroborated Captain von Hertzheim's statement about his flying from and returning to Cologne, and he was allowed to go. Then came that aged road mender, who told of the noise he had heard, which he took to be a motor, and how he found the ground all cut up. Dr. Arnecliffe concluded with an expression of his conviction that the actual cause of

Gerald Tansley's death was a sudden attack of heart disease, of long standing, which had been brought on by excitement. A few minutes afterwards the case was at an end. Charles Sinclair was free.

As had been arranged, Captain von Hertzheim called on me immediately afterwards for his reward. He glanced at it; then broke into exclamation—

"What is this written on the margin? You have read it? It is written here that these plans are obsolete, that a defect has been found in the working of the engine which makes it impracticable; the whole thing is no good."

"I told you," I blandly observed, "that that was the essential sheet. In your judgment does not that note in the margin make it so?"

Captain von Hertzheim looked quite angry.

"So I have done this for nothing! You have made a fool of me!"

He strode from my room, and joined Major Schrattenholtz in the street. Of what the major said to him when he saw that pencilled note upon the margin I have no record.

Shortly afterwards I was going to stay with some friends in the neighbourhood of a Scottish moor. At Euston I encountered Mr. Daniel Fletcher. As we were chatting I saw a feminine figure coming along the platform which I recognized—it was Miss Gertrude Alloway. I accosted her when she came near.

"I congratulate you, Miss Alloway," I said, "on the completeness with which Mr. Sinclair was able to establish his innocence."

"It is very good of you." Her manner was cold—I might almost write disdainful. "It is extremely fortunate that we were able to manage, Charles and I, without your assistance, for which I so foolishly asked and which you so peremptorily refused. As for the German and his ridiculous story—if it was true!—the plans he took, if he took any, were worthless. Charles discovered a defect in that machine at the very last moment which rendered it impracticable; he pencilled a note to that effect on the margin of one of the plans. He then discovered how the defect might be remedied; it is a wonderful discovery. It was about that he quarrelled with Gerald Tansley. An aeroplane of his invention is now being built which will be the most wonderful engine of war the world has ever seen—which Germany will not have. For that also England owes no thanks to you!"

"Serves you right!" remarked Mr. Fletcher in his sympathetic way. "You wouldn't let me breathe a word to anyone that you were —shall I say the man behind the gun?"

As we took our seats in the carriage I smiled at the thoughts which were in my mind.

"It's a very queer world we live in," I said. "Charles Sinclair's life was saved by two words which I saw a stranger utter: 'Blindley Heath.'"

Mr. Fletcher looked at me for a moment before he answered. His words, when they came, were oracular.

"It's my profound conviction," he declared, "that you're one of the very queerest things in this very queer world. You may put that in your pipe, Miss Lee, and smoke it."

THE GLASS PANELS

The first time I took an active, intentional interest in a criminal matter was in what afterwards came to be known as the "Fergusson Case," and my association with that took, ultimately, what I cannot help calling a distinctly irregular form. The Fergusson Case had also for me an unusual feature. I see people talking, and, without hearing, I know what they say. But, as I may safely assert that more than ninety per cent. of what every one says is undiluted rubbish, this is rather a misfortune than a blessing. In the Fergusson Case, on only three occasions, apart from hearing, did I see things spoken, and on each of those occasions not only were the words uttered of importance in themselves, but they were probably the most important utterances which their speakers, among very many thousands, had made.

I knew Dugald Fergusson very well, and his mother still better. His father was dead; he was his mother's only child. He was what that respectable lady often spoke of as a "feckless loon"; in plainer Saxon, he was an impetuous, hot-headed young man of twenty-five or twenty-six, who I dare say meant well, but generally did badly. There was a time when he favoured me with his attentions; he gave me more than one opportunity of saying that I would be Mrs. Dugald. But as at least on one of these he had drunk more than was good for him, apart from all other considerations, the prospect was not a tempting one.

I had not seen anything of the Fergussons for some months, when, happening to be in the neighbourhood of their house one afternoon, I thought I would call and see the old lady. I found her in great tribulation; something had happened to Dugald—he had disappeared; she had had no news of him for more than a fortnight. Unfortunately it was not unusual for him to vanish without notice for two or three days at a time; he had never before been away for so much as a fortnight. And in this instance his absence was the more remarkable because he had promised to take his mother away to visit a relation in the North, and the day which had been appointed for her to start had been passed more than a week. She was sure that something was wrong with him. She had thought of going to the police, but the fact was that he resented too close interest being taken in his movements, and she was only too well aware that the less she knew about some of his habits and companions the happier she would be.

I tried to reassure her, but it was not easy. Anxiety had affected her health. Dugald had some friends named Hutchings. Mrs. Fergusson had an idea that if she could only get to see them, and bore herself as a diplomatist, she might obtain from them some data which would put her on the track of her absent son. But she could not get to see them: rheumatism crippled her; she could hardly move from her chair.

As I saw how she was fretting, I volunteered to see these people for her. She gladly consented. The Hutchings—there was a Mr. and a Miss Hutchings, who were brother and sister—lived at Mortlake.[1] The following afternoon I paid them a call. They had rather a pretty cottage, although it was quite a small one. It stood in its own garden, and was so constructed that to a stranger it was not quite clear which was the front door. There were two or three doors. I went to one at the side which had glass panels; it opened into a room. In the room a girl was writing. While I hesitated whether to knock or find some other entrance, the door of the room was opened, and a man entered, slamming the door to behind him with what I had no doubt was a bang.

His action had a singular effect upon the girl who was writing. She sprang to her feet, and she shrieked; then, when she saw who it was, she pressed her hands to her side, and I could see the man was trembling as with ague. His mouth was turned away from me, so that I could not see what he said, but I have no doubt he asked what ailed her, because she replied—I could see what she said, she spoke with hysterical violence—

"You mustn't slam doors; you mustn't! That door—how it clanged! I'm always hearing it clanging, always. Every time a door is slammed I hear it clang again. You must not slam doors unless you want to drive me mad."

[1] A riverside suburb approximately eight miles west of Central London.

Although not a sound was audible I could see with what passionate intensity she was speaking. Before either of them could speak again, I rapped with the small brass knocker on which I had had my hesitating fingers. Both started at the sound and stared at me.

"Who is it?" I saw the girl say. The man said nothing, but he strode up to the door and looked at me through the glass panels. Then he opened.

"You should not have knocked here," he told me. "This is not the front door."

"But there's a knocker. I couldn't tell which was the front door."

"Oh, the knocker! I'd forgotten there was a knocker. That knocker is where it is owing to a practical joke of a friend of mine." He stared at the knocker as if he saw it with surprise. "Of course there's a knocker." He turned to the girl. "Ellen, you've never had the knocker put back again."

"I had forgotten all about it," she replied.

I thought their conduct rather singular; and how they came to have forgotten the presence of a knocker on their own door was beyond me altogether. I told him my name, and that I wanted to speak to Mr. or Miss Hutchings. He asked me in, introducing himself as Mr. Hutchings, and the girl as his sister. I told him that I had come from Mrs. Fergusson, who was confined to her room by illness, and would be very glad if he could give her any news of her son.

Both of them were silent. The girl sat down and resumed her writing. I wondered what she was writing, because, apart from the discourtesy of the act, I could see that her hand was shaking, so that I was pretty sure that, whatever it was, it would be pretty hard to read. Mr. Hutchings stood by the table, drawing patterns with the tips of his fingers on the cloth. Then he looked up at me.

He was not bad looking. I suppose about thirty years of age, but he had the appearance not only of one who lived an irregular life, but also of one who suffered from insomnia. Those caverns about his eyes meant sleeplessness, unless I erred.

"I have been wondering where Dugald is, Miss Lee, as much as anyone, because, to speak quite frankly, he owes me money which ought to have been paid some time ago."

The girl looked up from her writing.

"He owes every one money," she said.

I thought her tone was curiously sullen.

"I'll not go quite so far as that," rejoined her brother; "but he certainly does owe one or two, who have been promised their money and want it. I know that I want mine. As nothing has been seen of him in his usual haunts, we have been wondering—to be quite frank, Miss Lee, again—if he has been keeping away because he does not mean to pay up."

I received, to be brief, no information as to Dugald Fergusson's whereabouts from them; they both protested that they would like to hear of him from me, or, indeed, from anyone. Yet I came away from their cottage with the impression strong upon me that, if they had chosen, they might have told me something, much more than I could have told them—though what I had not the faintest notion. Those words which I had seen the girl utter when her brother slammed the door kept recurring to my mind. I repeated them to myself over and over again. What door was it that had clanged? Why did she always hear it clanging, so that every time a door was slammed she heard it clang again?

Those very odd words of hers about some particular door which had "clanged" might merely be the utterance of a hysterical young woman—yet I wondered.

Two days afterwards I had a telegram from old Mrs. Fergusson asking me to go to her at once. I went, putting aside my own business to enable me to do so. I found her, though still tied to her chair, in a state of great excitement. She had found, among some of her son's papers, the address of a man of whom she had heard him speak, and to whom she had written. She had had a reply from the man. She showed it to me; it was because of the reply that she had telegraphed.

The letter was from a betting man—a bookmaker. It was rather a characteristic effusion—

"22, Beaconsfield Avenue,
"Wandsworth.[1]

"DEAR MADAM,

"Your favour duly received. I have been wondering what has

---

[1] An imaginary street in Wandsworth, a riverside suburb in South-West London.

become of your son myself. He is an old customer of mine, and I expected to have seen or heard of him before this, because I owe him money. If he owed me money, as he often has done, the boot would have been on the other leg. I should not have expected to have seen or heard of him.

"The last time I saw him was at Lingfield,[1] at the Spring Meeting. He won off me close on five hundred pounds. He wanted me to pay him in cash, and I did give him three hundred, and was, of course, prepared to pay balance on settling day. I have always settled with him at the club. If he was not going to turn up in person he has always let me know to what address to send the money. He did not turn up at the club, and I have had no address from him to which to send; whenever he does turn up and wants the money it is waiting for him.

"Again thanking you for your favour, I am, yours obediently,

"TOM BOWER."

I knew nothing of betting men, but I had a feeling, when I read that letter, that Mr. Tom Bower was a character.

"You see what he says about the Lingfield Spring Meeting," said the old lady as soon as she saw that I had reached the end of the page. "That was the day on which he left me; he must have gone straight from here to the races. There are all sorts of bad characters about those racecourses, sinks of iniquity they are. If that Mr. Bower paid Dugald three hundred pounds, who can say what those racecourse folk wouldn't do to get hold of a sum like that?"

I perceived her point, and realized that she was right enough. Men returning from a racecourse have been murdered for much less than three hundred pounds. The first thing we had to do, as I explained to Mrs. Fergusson, was to ascertain with whom he had gone to Lingfield, and, what was much more important, with whom he had probably left. She wished to make these inquiries from Mr. Bower, but for some reason, which I could hardly have explained, I felt that, in the first instance, I would rather make them at that cottage at Mortlake. I had told the old lady about my fruitless visit there, but had said nothing about those curious words

[1] Lingfield Park, a race course in Surrey, some thirty miles south of Central London.

which I had seen coming from the girl's lips, nor about the feeling with which I had left, that the brother and sister knew more than they had cared to say.

"I will go," I told her, "first of all to Mortlake; then, if I find out nothing from either Mr. or Miss Hutchings——"

She interrupted me.

"The girl knows nothing. How should the girl know anything? Dugald was never one for girls."

I had my doubts, but I did not contradict her. I merely observed that I had a sort of feeling that I should like to pay another visit to Mortlake, and that, if I failed in that quarter a second time, then I would apply to Mr. Bower.

The next afternoon I paid a second visit to Mortlake. That time, when I reached the cottage I did not hesitate. I went straight to the side door with the glass panels. I wondered if the knocker was still there. It was not; it had been taken away, but on the paintwork there were still the marks of the place where it had been. I was about to take the hint, and go in search of the door to which the knocker had been removed, when, glancing through the panel, I saw that in the room on the other side was Mr. Hutchings. It was the middle of the afternoon, yet he was fast asleep; the explanation was within reach of his hand. On the table close to his chair was a hypodermic needle. To such a stage, it seemed, had his insomnia reached that he had to resort to such desperate means to get a snatch of sleep, even in broad day.

Yet, although he had drugged himself, his sleep was not undisturbed. He was in what seemed to me to be a very uncomfortable position in a great arm-chair. Though it was not turned towards the door at which I was standing, I could see his face very clearly. He appeared to be in the grip of a nightmare, of some horrid dream, in which he was suffering from unknown terrors. He was talking in his sleep; broken words were coming from his lips, so broken that they were unintelligible even to me. Presently he sat more upright in the chair, in a sort of spasm, and at least part of a sentence was formed by his lips—

"Don't go by Three Bridges[1]—don't go!"

[1] A village on the Brighton-London railway line, some 30 mi. south of London and 9 mi. west of Lingfield. Marsh had lived at Three Bridges since the mid-1890s.

The words burst from him by what seemed to be a muscular effort, so acute that it woke him up. His eyes opened. He looked gapingly about him, as people do when suddenly aroused from haunting dreams.

I did not wait to see what followed. I did not announce my presence. I withdrew as unnoticed as I had come.

I went home, and I hunted up a time-table and maps of Surrey and Sussex. With their aid I strove to make sense of the few words which had escaped from Mr. Hutchings in his dream. He had said, "Don't go by Three Bridges—don't go!" What baleful vision had forced him to say it? The words in themselves were simple, innocent enough; yet I had seen with what agony they were wrung from him. Something uncomfortable was underneath them, I felt sure. I made it my business to learn what that something was.

Three Bridges station, as a station, I knew very well. I had often passed through it on the road to and from Brighton. But from the time-table I learned something more: I found that it was one of the routes by which one could return from Lingfield. The direct route to London was via Oxted and Croydon,[1] but one could, if one missed a train, or preferred it, go on to East Grinstead[2] and return to London by Three Bridges. It was rather a roundabout way, but not necessarily much the worse on that account; nor, it seemed, if one caught connecting trains, was it bound to take much longer.

Nothing had been seen or heard of Dugald Fergusson since Mr. Bower had paid him that three hundred pounds on Lingfield racecourse. Mr. and Miss Hutchings had both denied that they knew anything of his whereabouts, but in their statements I had no faith whatever. Miss Hutchings had spoken of a door which had "clanged" to so much purpose that it still haunted her a fortnight afterwards; her brother, in the agony of a dream, implored some one not to go by Three Bridges—I wondered why. I had two or three free days. I decided to devote them in making inquiries, on lines of my own, as to the route by which Mr. Dugald Fergusson returned from Lingfield.

I began with Lingfield itself, a straggling, country village, and,

[1] Oxted is a town some eight miles north of Lingfield and twelve miles south of Croydon, which is eleven miles south of Central London.
[2] A town some four miles south of Lingfield, and eight miles east of Three Bridges.

as I had expected, learned nothing there; then I went by train to East Grinstead, which seemed to be quite a flourishing town, and still learned nothing; then, still by train, to Three Bridges, which seemed to be a mere congregation of not particularly prepossessing modern cottages, and still achieved no results.

That occupied the first day. On the second I tried another method. I had noticed, when travelling from East Grinstead to Three Bridges, a distance of some seven or eight miles, that the train passed leisurely through what, for the most part, was a garden of wild flowers. I spent the night at Three Bridges. The next morning, following directions I had received, I found myself, after some little walking, in a narrow lane which passed under a railway arch. There was a stile on my left, which I crossed; then scrambled over a fence, up a bank, and gained access to the line. I proposed to explore, on foot, until I was turned off, the strip of railway line between East Grinstead and Three Bridges. If anyone tried to interfere with me I proposed to explain my presence there by a desire to gather wild flowers. I have seen it stated somewhere that the strips of land running beside railway lines are the only places left in England in which wild flowers can be seen at their best. Certainly I never saw them in greater profusion than on the piece of line which I traversed that morning. Trains were not frequent. One—a motor train—went bustling by when I was on the top of a bank sampling what seemed to be a thicket of fern; another—a luggage train consisting of three empty wagons and an engine—passed in the other direction as I was gathering watercress from a tiny stream which was as clear as crystal.

I was enjoying myself hugely, forming a famous posy of pretty wild things, but I had achieved nothing towards the end I had in view. I reached a spot where the line ran between high banks, carpeted with Nature's own wild flowers. A little distance ahead an archway carried a road across. When I gained this archway I saw, coming along the line towards me, a man, evidently a workman, carrying a tool of some kind over his shoulder. There was a footpath of sorts leading up the bank to the road above. I thought that it might be advisable that I should use it before that workman came up and ordered me off. In the bank some nine or ten feet above the line, was a sort of shelf. As I reached it I was seized by a most curious sensation of dizziness. The arch, which was made of brick, rose from that shelf—that is, its outer span. In the brickwork itself, directly fronting me, was a door, an iron door. What caused my dizziness was that the sight of that door recalled Miss Hutchings's words; it was just the kind of door that would "clang," and it was on the road from Lingfield to London, via Three Bridges.

In spite of the odd feeling of bewilderment which the discovery of a door in such an unexpected place occasioned, I was perfectly conscious that my imagination had a tendency to move too fast, and that I was on a false track altogether. So conscious was I of this that my second impulse was to continue my ascent up the path and gain the road before that advancing workman was upon me. As I moved my foot struck against something. I looked down. There was something shining in a cluster of anemones. I picked it up. It was a gold locket. I had just time to conceal it in the palm of my hand when that workman was upon me. He addressed me very civilly—he was a big, round-shouldered man, with a pronounced stoop and a ragged black beard.

"You know, miss, you are trespassing here; the public aren't allowed upon the line. There's a notice-board to say so."

"I have been stealing your flowers," I told him, holding out my posy, but saying nothing about what was in the palm of the other hand. "What quantities of wild flowers you seem to have. Surely you can spare some?"

"There's no doubt about that, miss, as far as sparing goes; you're welcome to the flowers, but it's against the rules to allow trespassing on the line. If people get hurt, or maybe killed, by passing trains —it's very easy—they blame the company, and that's where it is. No trespassing is allowed—it wouldn't do."

"I was wondering," I said to the man—he seemed to be a decent creature, and not indisposed, even in the execution of his duty, for a little conversation—"what that door is doing in the brickwork of your arch. Isn't it rather a queer place in which to put a door? Is there anything on the other side of it?"

"I was wondering," he replied, "how it comes to be closed. The last time I saw it it was wide open enough. They have been putting fresh clinkers[1] in the six-foot way, and, it coming on to rain, some

---

[1] Dense, heavy, partially vitrified bricks, used in building and road construction.

of the chaps left their tools under cover. When they came for them a day or so after, they couldn't get at them because the door was shut; that's more than a fortnight ago, they've been there ever since. I told them I'd get the key and unlock the door. They'll be coming along directly to get their tools again—the company's tools they are."

He had a huge piece of iron in his hand which was in the shape of a key. His words had increased my feeling of dizziness. He did not know how the door came to be closed; it was wide open enough when he saw it last, then it had been shut on the workmen's tools. It was rather more than three weeks since Dugald Fergusson ought to have returned from Lingfield. Might not his more than a fortnight mean more than three weeks? I watched him fitting his monstrous key into the clumsy lock with sensations of which he certainly had no notion, and I slipped that gold locket between the buttons of my blouse.

When at last he had succeeded in opening the door he stood for a moment looking at what was beyond him, and then exclaimed excitedly—

"What's this? In God's name, what's this?"

I knew before he told me. His tone gave me all the intelligence I wanted—and more. On the other side of that iron door, which rang with a clanging sound each time he touched it with his key, in the chamber formed by the brickwork of the arch, was all that was left of Dugald Fergusson.

I have no wish to dwell on unpleasant details. One glimpse of him was too much for me; a hint will probably be enough for others. He had been lying there dead for more than three weeks.

While we were still in doubt as to what had better be done, four other workmen came along the line in search of the tools which the company provided for their use. The man with the key who had made the discovery appeared to be a ganger.[1] Acting on his orders, two of them set off to give information in the proper official quarter of what had been found; two of them remained with the ganger to keep watch and ward, and I was allowed to go. It never entered the heads of any of those men that I could have any possible connexion

[1] Foreman (of a gang of laborers).

with the grim discovery. The ganger saw the condition to which it had reduced me—how white I had grown, how unhappy I looked—and he said, with well-meant awkwardness—

"This ain't no place for you, miss; if I was you, I'd take myself off. You don't want to get mixed up in anything like this."

I most decidedly did not; at least, at that particular moment. I had found out all I wished to find out there; further discoveries would have to be made in another direction, unhampered by official interference. I climbed with uncertain steps up the remaining portion of that precipitous bank, gained the roadway, and walked rapidly along what was little more than a cart-track through the fields to the road at the other end.

Just before I reached the road, on one side of the cart-track, was a little spinney, formed, I believe, for the most part, of firs and beeches. Under the shade of this I paused; there was no one about. I took the locket from my blouse. It was of gold, with flat sides, large, and oval shaped. I opened it—my portrait was inside. I could scarcely believe, for an instant, that it was my portrait; then I remembered. I had given his mother my photograph. She had told me once, half jestingly, that Dugald had stolen it. I could hardly ask him to return it; so far as he was concerned I took no notice of what his mother had said. It looked as if he had cut my head out of the photograph, and fitted it into that locket.

I went straight back to town, with that locket in my handbag, which I had retrieved at Three Bridges station. I reached Victoria station at four o'clock on a summer afternoon. An hour later I was entering the garden of the Mortlake cottage. It was my intention to strike the iron while it was hot. I had been told by some one, of whom I had asked the shortest road, that there were two means of reaching the cottage, one by an alley-way which entered the garden at the back, the other by the main road along which, on my two previous visits, I had gone. I chose that way again.

I went, without hesitating, to the side door with the glass panels. There were two persons in the room beyond—Miss Hutchings, and a person whom I recognized as an acquaintance of Fergusson, to whom he had introduced me, and whose name, if I remembered rightly, was Pomeroy. It was an instant or two before I recalled who he was; he presented such a curious spectacle. The whole of his head was enveloped in bandages, his face looked out of a sort of frame. I recalled him as a big, fine-looking young man, by whose manner and appearance I had been favourably impressed. Now, with those ghastly bandages round his head, and his colourless face, he looked like some huge ghost. Evidently he had just risen from a bed of sickness. I was not sure that he ought not to have been on one then; he was clearly so weak that it was with difficulty that he stood on his feet.

I was so struck by the contrast he presented to the handsome, debonair person I had known that, before I could carry out my intention of announcing my presence, I saw his lips form words which caused me, almost involuntarily, to stay my hand.

"What's become of Fergusson? For God's sake, tell me, Nell."

He asked the question as if his life depended on the answer; his physical condition was so weak that, as he asked it, the tears were rolling down his cheeks. For some reason or other the man was but a caricature of what he had been. He was a pitiable spectacle. They were standing sideways to the door, so that I could see both their faces quite clearly. The girl's was white and tense and drawn; it struck me that she was making a great effort to bring herself to a desired point. Her lips moved once or twice, but I was sure that no words came from them; it looked as if her throat were so parched that, for the moment, she was incapable of speech. Then I saw her say—and such a look came on her face—

"Fergusson's dead."

"Dead? Then—it wasn't a dream."

"I wish it had been."

"Nell!" He just uttered her name, and then he stopped. I could see his muscles working underneath his skin. This man certainly ought to have been on a sick bed. "You know, Nell—I've been very queer." She nodded; apparently she could not trust herself to speak. "I've been—in bed over there, having an awful time."

"I know. I—I've been having an awful time, too."

"I—I suppose I've been unconscious for I don't know how long. I wish I'd remained unconscious. When I got my senses back I began to try and think of what had happened, and—I haven't been able to." The man shut his eyes; on the girl's face was such a look of pity. His eyes were still closed as he asked her a question, as if he were afraid to look her in the face while she answered it. "Nell, who killed him?"

If he had seen the look which was on her face as she struggled to answer I believe that even he would have been startled. Her lips moved several times; it was only after a perceptible interval two words came from them.

"You did."

Then he opened his eyes and looked.

"Nell! For God's sake, don't say that—don't say it."

"You asked me—so I had to tell you."

The big man looked at her, then he sank on to the chair by which he was standing, his head fell on to the table, and he cried, not like a child, but like no one I had ever seen cry before; his were not tears, they were convulsions. The girl stood watching him; although she was dry-eyed, I did not doubt that her emotion was almost as great as his. She touched him on the shoulder. I saw words come from her as if by a series of shocks.

"George, please—please don't do that. You—you'll make yourself ill again. Don't, George—don't. Please—please don't!"

His sobs continued to shake his great frame just as they had done before she uttered a word. Then I saw a change come over her face as she watched him, a surprising change, as if something had entered into her all at once and made of her another woman. She still had her hand upon his shoulder. She bent down, and she said, speaking now quite calmly, with no outward show of emotion, save for the strange, new look which was in her eyes—

"George, you must not cry. You have no reason to cry. What I told you was not true; you did not kill Dugald Fergusson."

I could not tell how loudly she had spoken; not a sound reached me; not a sound seemed to have reached him. He still cried on. So she knelt on the floor beside him, and the sun, shining through a window, seemed to add a new beauty to her face.

"George, listen to me—listen. What I told you was not true. You did not kill Dugald Fergusson. Don't you hear me, George?"

It seemed, that time, that he did. He lifted his tear-stained face, all blurred with weeping, with the tears still on it, and he looked at her with his half-blinded eyes.

"You are only saying that—to comfort me."

There was a great gulp in the middle of his sentence. She moved a little closer so that their faces were nearly touching.

"I'm not, George! I'm saying it because it is true. What I said before is untrue. You did not kill Dugald Fergusson—you never touched him!"

"Who killed him then?" I could see that he asked in a whisper.

And in a whisper she replied—

"I did!"

There was silence in the room—silence so profound that I was conscious of it even where I was. I held my breath, as if fearful of intruding on what, to both those persons I was watching, must have been an awful moment. Presently he asked her, still in a whisper, with his face so close to hers—

"Is that true, Nell?"

"Perfectly true, George."

"You—did kill him?"

"I did kill him!"

It was strange what resolution was on her face, and how unfaltering her tone was. He seemed to doubt her, staring at her as if he would look into her soul.

"You are sure you killed him?"

"Quite sure. I wish I weren't. I've never had a happy moment since."

"Why did you say that I killed him?"

"Because—because—— Oh George!" She gave a great sigh. "Saying that was worse than killing Dugald. When I saw that you didn't know who killed him, I thought I might escape that way." Her face was lit by the queerest, wannest smile. "I think, George, if you would have killed me I might be happy. I suppose you couldn't?"

He drew himself a little away from her, and he said, three times over—

"I don't understand! I don't understand! I don't understand!" speaking as a man might do who was groping for light in a fog.

She replied—

"And yet it's perfectly simple."

I think she was going to add something more, but her ear heard something which mine did not catch. Evidently he had heard it, too. They both remained in an attitude of listening. Then the door at the back opened, and the girl's brother came in. I took it that he had entered the house by the gate leading out of the alley-way at the back. I had not been conscious of his approach. He had not stayed to remove his cap; his agitation was such that he was apparently still unconscious that it was upon his head. He stared at Pomeroy in seeming surprise.

"So you're here, are you? I'm pleased to see you. I've been wondering where you'd got to."

Pomeroy did not answer. The girl seemed to see something behind her brother's agitation. She asked him—

"Edward, what is the matter?"

He rested both his hands on the edge of the table, and leaned over it towards them, and I saw him say—

"They've found him."

That was all he said, and the girl, at least, did not seem to need any more. She looked at him with comprehension in her eyes, and again there was silence in the room.

I, personally, did not know what to do. I was so absorbed by the tragedy which was being enacted on the other side of those glass panels that I had become oblivious of the purpose which had brought me there. It may seem strange that I had continued so long unnoticed; as a matter of fact, it was not. About the door was trained a fine wistaria, which at that period of the year was a mass both of leaves and flowers. I had only to draw myself a little back into the foliage to become nearly invisible to those within. And, moreover, they were so engrossed in the dreadful thing of which they talked that, wholly unsuspicious that anyone was in the neighbourhood, they had no faculty of observation left for me.

The tragedy continued to be played inside that little room while I still remained in a state of indecision as to the course of action to pursue; willy-nilly I had to play the part of audience. Never before, I think, had I been so conscious of the strange nature of that gift of mine which enabled me, without hearing a sound, to become a sharer of the secrets which these three people supposed they told only to each other.

A motor-car was passing on the other side of the privet hedge, when the silence was broken by the girl. She got up from her knees; she looked her brother in the face, and she asked him, in tones which I judged did not falter—

"Do you mean that they have found Dugald Fergusson?" The expression on his face was apparently for her a sufficient reply. "How came that door to be opened?"

"I don't know. I can't say. I went down to Rowfant,[1] meaning to see how Pomeroy was getting on, and I found he was missing. They told me he had got up this morning, and insisted upon going away; they had told him that he was not in a fit state to go, but he insisted. They did not know where he had gone; he refused to tell them. When I left Cooper's cottage and was walking to the station, some children who were coming home from school stopped me, and informed me, quite gratuitously, that Mr. Garnett had just found —I learned afterwards that Mr. Garnett is a ganger—a dead man in an arch on the line; they seemed to think that they were giving me quite a pleasant piece of news. By the time I reached the station it was all over the place; they even knew that his name was Fergusson; some envelopes had been found in his pockets on which were his name and address. I do not know what is the usual course in these cases, but I suppose a warrant will have been issued by now."

"Whose name will be on it?"

This question was asked by the girl. Her brother looked at her sharply, as if he read intention behind her words. He answered—

"How do I know? Some poor devil's, I suppose."

She, perceiving that he had misunderstood her, proceeded to explain.

"You needn't be afraid of speaking plainly—George knows."

He started as if her words took him by surprise; for the moment his back was towards me, so that I could not see what he said. But her answer enabled me to guess. I saw her say—

"I told him."

Hutchings plumped down on to a chair, staring at her as if the statement she had made was wholly beyond his comprehension.

Pomeroy asked—

"Is it true—what she says?"

The girl said—

"You can tell him, Edward."

[1] A wooded area some three miles east of Three Bridges.

Hutchings inquired of Pomeroy

"What has she said?" Then of the girl—"What have you told him?"

The girl replied—

"I've told him that I killed Dugald Fergusson." She and Pomeroy both waited for Hutchings to speak. He thrust his hands into his trouser pockets, as men so often do in all sorts of unexpected moments; he tilted back his chair, and I saw him say—

"That's true enough—worse luck—though why she told you beats me altogether!"

Pomeroy looked at her; then, moving, he held out his hands as if he would take her in his arms. But she drew back.

"Don't touch me; don't come near me. I'm going to tell you exactly how it was. Don't interrupt me, and don't speak a word until I've finished. Edward here will tell you if I speak a word which isn't true." Pomeroy made as if to speak; the girl motioned him to be silent with an impatient movement of her hand. "Don't you say a word until I've done, till I've quite, quite done; then you can say what you like. I want to get my thoughts in order so that I can tell you everything just as it happened."

She stood for a moment as if thinking, both men watching her —her brother with his chair tilted back, and both hands still in his pockets; Pomeroy with one hand resting on the table, as if in need of its support. It was strange to watch the lights and shadows which passed across his tear-stained face, and the changes which took place in it as the girl proceeded with her story. The play of varied emotions on her face fascinated me as nothing of the kind had ever done before. I felt, before she began to speak, that she was standing there as a witness of truth; as I saw her lips form words, which came from her as if they had been drops of blood drawn from her heart, she impressed me with a conviction that her one desire was to give accurate expression to exact facts. If, sometimes, strength of feeling made the words which she chose seem strong ones, considering the theme on which she was engaged it was not strange.

"You remember the morning when he came and wanted us all to go to Lingfield—you haven't forgotten that? You can speak."

She made a little gesture which seemed meant to give Pomeroy permission to use his tongue.

"I do remember so much."

"You had been spending the night here, and were just going when he came. He had been drinking, though it wasn't eleven o'clock. He made such a fuss that we all agreed to go. I stood out. I wanted to do some work, but he made me go, too. While I was upstairs getting ready he took the knocker off the front door, and put it on the one with the glass panels—that one."

She waved her hand towards the door outside which I was standing. I drew quickly back, but neither of the trio even glanced in my direction; they took what she said for granted.

"Edward was very angry when he found what he had done; it was such a fool's trick, and there was very nearly a quarrel before we started. Dugald kept drinking all the way to Lingfield, every chance he had. By the time we reached the course he had had more than enough. He betted—Edward told me afterwards that he had betted recklessly."

Her brother remarked, chair still tilted, hands still in his pockets—

"Reckless wasn't the word for it; he betted like an idiot—backed outsiders at short prices, most of it with Tom Bower. I fancy Bower thought he had a soft thing on, but he hadn't. I'm not sure, but I fancy that everything Fergusson backed came off; it was one of those days of miracles which every fellow knows. Then he began ragging Bower about payment; he wanted him to give him cash. It ended in Bower giving him three hundred pounds in bank notes; he was to let him have the balance, whatever it was, on the usual settling day. There would have been a fight if Bower hadn't met him; he was obviously spoiling for a row."

The girl took up the thread of the story where her brother had dropped it.

"That three hundred pounds was his undoing. We had a fine time of it. I wanted to go a dozen times, but he wouldn't let me. I wish I had gone."

"There would have been a free fight if you had." This was her brother.

"That would have been better than what followed."

"I'm not so sure; he looked like murder then. He generally did when the drink was in him."

"You know what he was like when, as Edward says, the drink was in him. We missed the special train from Lingfield, then we took a local one to East Grinstead. There he started drinking again at the refreshment room on the platform, treating all who would be treated. I believe he gave the girl behind the bar a sovereign."

"He did; then he wanted to toss her for another. When she declined he began to make hay of all the things on the counter. He was stark mad by the time he got into the train."

"He was. Oh, how ashamed I felt! I was pretty mad myself. Do you mean to say, George, that you don't remember what trouble we had getting him into the carriage?"

"I've some hazy recollection; it may all come back some day, but at present it's just haze. Was I sober? I have been haunted by a sort of horrid idea that I had been drinking."

"He made you; he made us all drink something. I don't know how many times he paid for drink for me which I never touched. I can't say how much you'd had, but you and Edward were both perfectly sober. In the train his mood changed. He had a big gold locket on his watch chain. In it was a portrait of a girl. He insisted on showing it to us—the girl of whom he was always talking, whom he used to call 'the miracle worker'—Judith Lee."

Judith Lee winced outside the window; it was so strange to see oneself spoken of like that. "Miracle worker," he had called me. I felt as if I were in a place of miracles then. The girl went on. I began to find that I had played a part on that memorable night of which I had never dreamed.

"The stuff he spouted about Judith Lee! To begin with, she was the most perfect creature the world had ever seen. He told us, with tears in his eyes, that he had asked her again and again to be his wife. Then he began to storm at her at the top of his voice because she had very wisely refused his offer. The language he used! He worked himself into a blind rage; then he wrenched the locket off his watch chain and threw it out of the window—and the very moment he threw it the train stopped. I have often thought how queer that was. I suppose the explanation was that the signals were against us, and that the train had been slowing down without our noticing it. But it seemed to Dugald that the stopping of the train at that particular moment was a miracle caused by his throwing the locket through the window. Before we had guessed what he was going to do, he opened the door and fell out on to the line. You jumped after him to see if he was hurt, and Edward went after you. I was left alone in the compartment. I couldn't have that. I had no ticket, no money, nor anything. So I went after the rest of you."

She paused for a moment, as if to visualize, to reconstruct, what must have been a singular scene.

"Two things about that business have since struck me as odd. I didn't close the carriage I door. I wonder what they thought when the train came into the station with the door wide open. Then I don't believe we were seen: that anyone in the whole train knew that four people had got out and been left standing on the line. I can only explain that by an idea which has since occurred to me. I do believe that, with the exception of ourselves, the train was empty: certainly the latter part of it in which we were. Very few passengers got in at East Grinstead, and I dare say they got out at the two stations at which we had stopped. Possibly the engine-driver was looking for the signals on the other side of the line, and the guard had got his head out on that side also. Anyhow, there is the fact that we four got out, the train went on, and left us standing on the line, and no one seems to have been aware of it—not even to this hour."

Again she stopped; her eyes seemed to be looking at something which was at a distance, which yet she saw quite plainly.

"I shall never forget the place in which we were—how it looked in the moonlight. The line ran between two high banks; close to us it was spanned by an arch, which, with the moon shining behind it, looked quite beautiful. One of the strangest parts of it all was that I noticed, distinctly, that in the side of the arch was an open door, and I wondered what was beyond it. I must have noticed all this in the flash of an eye, because directly I realized that the train had actually gone I had something else to occupy me."

Although I could not hear her, I knew that her tone became more serious.

"You and Edward had helped Dugald to his feet, but he had misunderstood the situation. He was fighting, mad drunk, and though he did not seem to be seriously hurt, I dare say he was badly shaken. He was under the impression that you had pushed him out of the carriage on to the line; he swore he would kill you for it, and he proceeded to do his best to put his threat into execution. You know what a great, strong man he was, and how impossible it was to do anything with him when he was excited and bent on some act of wrong-headedness."

"He carried his drink worse than any man I ever met," struck in her brother. "He was one of those men who ought to have been a teetotaller from his cradle; no one's life was safe who came near him when the drink was in him."

When the girl continued, as if unconsciously, she illustrated her narrative with gestures which lent it a grim significance.

"On the bank, close to the line, some workmen had left their tools—iron crowbars, and things of that kind. Fergusson was struggling with you, swearing he would kill you, when all of a sudden he stopped and picked one of these up; it looked like a long bar of metal. He struck you with it on the shoulder. You went down with a crash, and when you were down, without giving you a chance to get up or to move or to defend yourself, he struck you again and again. We couldn't stop him; he was a madman, and he meant murder. Edward clung to his arm, but he shook him off as if he were nothing. I suppose madness had made him stronger than ever."

"You must remember one thing," interposed her brother, "he was above and I was below. I couldn't get at him; he didn't give me a chance to get on to the bank where he was—there wasn't time."

"But I got on to the bank, and I snatched up another of those iron things. I could hear the thud that the thing he had made each time it came down on you. I wasn't going to stand there and see you beaten to a pulp, so, as I tell you, George, I caught up one of those iron things—it was a great, heavy thing, and it was all I could do to lift it, but I did lift it, and I struck him with it. I don't know where —I struck blindly. My only thought was to stop him striking you. And he went tumbling down—and that's all I remember. I think I fainted."

"You did faint, for the first, and I hope for the last, time in your life." This, of course, was her brother.

"When I came to, Edward was bending over me. The first thing he said was that Fergusson was dead. At first we thought you were dead, too; but you moved, so we knew you weren't—quite. But Edward said that Dugald had never moved after I had struck him."

The girl passed her hand before her eyes as if to brush away something which she did not wish to see.

"We had to do something; we couldn't stop there and do nothing. I was clear witted enough by then. I looked round, trying my hardest to think of the best thing to do, and I saw that open door. I told you about the door which I saw on one side of the arch. I went up to it. Edward asked me what I was going to do. I said, 'I'm going to see what's in here.' Beyond the opening it was all in shadow. I could not see what was there, but I could see that there was plenty of room. I said, 'We'll put Dugald in here,' and we did, Edward and I between us. And when he was in I pushed the door to, and it shut—with a clang. I shall never hear a door shut again without that clang coming back to me."

The first words which I had seen her say recurred to me; those first words which had put me on the scent of Dugald Fergusson.

"Edward said to me, when the door had shut with a clang, 'They'll hear that down the line; you'll have them on to us.' I don't know if they did hear it, but we saw no signs of anyone. Edward knew that part of the world quite well."

"I used to stay there a lot when I was a kid," explained her brother. "I used to know every creature for miles round; there weren't very many to know, anyhow, in my time."

"He remembered that an old racing man, whom he knew very well, used to live close to there."

"Cooper," explained her brother, "used to be in a stable over at Lewes[1]—training stable; got savaged by a horse, and took a job as under gamekeeper on some shooting near Rowfant, which, of course, was close to where it all happened. His cottage wasn't more than a hundred yards from that cutting. I knew he was the sort of chap who would ask no questions and keep his mouth shut, so——"

His sister continued—I could see that she took the words almost out of his mouth.

"So we carried you up the bank and to Cooper's cottage—it wasn't very easy—and we left you there. Mrs. Cooper had been a nurse, and knew something about dressing wounds, and she started dressing yours at once. Mr. Cooper undertook to go at once for a

[1] A town nine miles northeast of Brighton.

doctor, and tell him some cock-and-bull story about your having been in a row, and I don't know what besides. I wanted to wait and hear what the doctor had to say, but Edward would not let me. We walked to Three Bridges station and caught a late train up to town. And you've been at Cooper's cottage ever since, and Edward and I have been here, and we have both of us been haunted. Edward hasn't been able to sleep, and I—I have been haunted whether asleep or waking. And now it seems that you are better, and Dugald has been found; so all that remains for me to do is to go and deliver myself up to the police and let them hang me."

She made a movement as if she would have started upon that errand then and there. Pomeroy caught her by the arm. He seemed to have gained vigour since I had seen him first, to be better able to play the man, as if the story which the girl had told had braced him.

"You'll do nothing of the kind. They wouldn't hang you if you did; no judge or jury would ever find you guilty of having done anything wrong. What you did was to prevent murder."

"But I did kill Dugald Fergusson!"

"To save my life, and all the rest of my life I'm going to devote to proving to you that I'm not ungrateful. I'll never go on to a race-course again, and I'll never touch another drop of drink. But I'll make no protestations; I'll do—or, at least, I'll try to do." He drew himself up straighter, and I could see what a big man he was. "Nell, you're going to be my wife."

"Your wife—George! When—when——" She held out her hands in front of her, as Lady Macbeth does in the play, as if to show the stain which was on them, which nothing might ever remove. He took her hands in his and drew her to him.

"Nell, you're going to be my wife. We'll be married to-morrow."

"To-morrow? George, are you—are you daft?"

Her face was towards me, and I could see how she was trembling. I have no doubt he held her closer to stay her tremors.

"I tell you we'll be married to-morrow. People can be married in four-and-twenty hours, and you and I will be. Listen to me—now you keep still until I've finished. You know I've got a goodish bit of money; I can get hold of all of it to-morrow if I want it. You and I are going to emigrate; we're going to start afresh in a new world, and start fair; and, please God, Nell, we'll continue fair and keep the slate clean. Edward, why shouldn't you come with us? You're as movable a man as I am; you can get everything ship-shape in a few days. Come with us. Nell and I will be married to-morrow, and we'll start next week for Australia. I know something about things out there; it's a real white man's country. Edward, you come with us; there's nothing to keep you here."

Mr. Hutchings lowered the front legs of his chair on to the ground. He got up; he took his hands out of his pockets, and he stretched them above his head instead, as a man might do who is trying to rouse himself from the heaviness of sleep.

"You are quite right, my boy, there is certainly nothing to keep me here—and wouldn't I like to come! But I'm a householder, and a man of property; this cottage isn't much, but it is my own, and all the things that are in it. How is it to be done? Especially in the time you talk about."

"I tell you it is to be done, and I'll show you how." Mr. Pomeroy banged his fist upon the table with sudden vigour. "Nell and I together will show you how it's to be done. Each second he seemed to be growing more and more of a man. A thought all at once occurred to him. "Nell, you've never kissed me—never once in all your life. You're going to kiss me now!"

I moved quietly back from that door with the glass panels, along the little garden path, into the main road on the other side of the privet hedge, and so away from Mortlake.

I might have stayed their going, but I did not. I might have gone to the police and told them this, that, and the other; but I did nothing of the kind. That was the first criminal case in which I had intentionally meddled, and I proposed to conduct it on lines of my own; and I did. What I had seen through that door with the glass panels was not evidence. I had not heard a single word; I had not been witness of a single overt act. I might have misunderstood everything which had been said in that little room. I might be tolerably satisfied that I had done nothing of the kind, but my satisfaction was not evidence; I could produce no proof.

I have since learned, by what one may call a side wind, that those three people did go to Australia, and are there still, doing very well; that they promise to be good and faithful citizens, a credit to the land of their adoption. With all my heart I wish them well; my hopes and my prayers are with them.

So far as I am aware the Fergusson Case remains a mystery. How his body came to be in that strange hiding-place has never been made clear, or how he came by his death. That the object could hardly have been robbery was established by the fact that in his pockets were found notes and gold to the amount of considerably over three hundred pounds, besides personal belongings of all sorts and kinds. It was obvious that nothing he possessed of the slightest value had been touched. He was recognized, rather vaguely, as a person who had made a disturbance at East Grinstead station, and it was there believed that three other persons were then in his company. But on this point no one seemed certain; nothing was ever heard of these three persons, so the belief remained a mere surmise.

About a week after the day on which I was at Mortlake I saw a copy of a local paper which was published at East Grinstead. It contained an account of the death and funeral, at Rowfant, of an old man named Cooper. A line at the bottom stated that his wife, a very old lady, had left the neighbourhood and gone to reside with some friends at Lewes. Because of the old man's death and of his wife's departure, I take it, nothing came of what might have been a clue, if the story had got abroad of the sojourn of the injured Pomeroy at Cooper's cottage.

Dugald Fergusson's mother, though she could hardly be expected to admit it, is, I think, happier with him dead than living. Alive he was a constant cause to her of anxiety, and often of shame; now her mind is at rest. And not only so, she has enshrined him with a sort of halo. She regards him almost as a martyr, who met his death at the hands of wicked persons, under circumstances which were greatly to their discredit and his honour. If the whole truth were ever to be known, it is possible that that halo would have to come off, and that she would be the poorer and sadder for the loss of one of her most cherished illusions.

I believe that I am the only person, except his mother, who has a memento of that most erratic young man; and of the existence of that no one knows—not even his mother. It is a large, flat, oval-shaped locket made of gold, within it what I would describe as the portrait of a young lady. I have it in a drawer among other odds and ends, and sometimes, when I come upon it, I ask myself if it would not be the part of rectitude to hand it over to Mrs. Fergusson. But I tell myself that the act of handing over would have to be accompanied by such a vast deal of explanation that I doubt if I ever shall.

ON TWO TRAINS

I have scarcely ever become engaged in what I will call a case of set intention. I have nearly always drifted, the thing—to vary the word —has been thrust upon me. When, for instance, after having spent a very pleasant time with some friends in the north, I started on the journey to London, my only object was to reach my destination in the shortest possible space of time. I had work awaiting me in town; nothing was farther from my mind than to allow anything to divert my attention on the road. Yet, before the train drew up at the platform at King's Cross I had become—although I did not know it at the time—engaged in what was destined to be one of the most singular experiences in my life.

At Peterborough,[1] where the train stopped, a girl got into my compartment, which hitherto I had had all to myself. She was attended by a man; I say man, although he struck me as being little more than a boy. He was fair-haired, sunny-faced; as he stood chatting to her at the open carriage door it seemed to me that he had the sweetest smile I had ever seen. Neither spoke in very subdued tones, so I could not help hearing some of the things they said. Just as the train was about to start she said to him, in what was a high-pitched rather than a loud voice—

"But I don't know what address to write to."

He smiled—that wonderful smile of his.

"Of course, how absurd of me! Here, I'll write it down." Taking a card from his pocket he wrote something on the back, which having written he proceeded to read aloud. "George Winnington, Old Times Club, Jermyn Street." He handed her the card. "That address will always find me."

"I never heard of the Old Times Club," she said.

"No, very few people have. It's a little nook where a few kindred spirits rub ideas together. I shall be there in the morning, so mind you write me to-night."

She nodded. She stood in the open door glancing at the card

[1] A city some eighty miles north of London.

he had given her. Just then some one called out, "Take your seats, please"; he got on to the foot-board, and I feel sure before she had guessed his intention, drew her down towards him and kissed her. Then he got down on to the platform again, the door was shut, he stood with his hat in his hand, smiling, repeating his previous words, "Mind you write to-night!"—and the train started.

The girl, whom he had left to be my companion to town, presented a picture which, from one point of view, was amusing; I do not think I ever saw a damsel in such a state of confusion; that young gentleman's kiss had unhinged her utterly. She stood by the window till the train had moved clear of the platform; I believe it was only when she realized where she was that it occurred to her she might as well sit down, which she did in the corner at the opposite end of the carriage, facing me. Conscious of her condition, I hid myself behind the pages of an illustrated paper, so that she might not feel that she was the object of too close attention; yet I was sufficiently human to feel bound to peep at her occasionally round the edges of my journal.

She was extraordinarily pretty, and beautifully dressed; those two facts I grasped at once. She was very tiny—I doubt if she was over five feet—with a profusion of hair which was of a pretty shade of brown, big, dark grey eyes, a charming mouth, and a complexion which certainly owned none of its delicacy to art. She was perhaps twenty years old, yet there was something about her which, in these days of bachelor young women, was unusual, a suggestion of freshness, sweetness, simplicity, which nowadays is not often the attribute even of a child, and very seldom marks a young woman.

As I glanced at her from behind my paper I was not sure that it would not have been just as well for her if she had borne herself more like the modern young woman of her years; if she had, I doubt if that young man would have mounted the foot-board to surprise her with his kiss. That her surprise had been so great as almost to overwhelm her was obvious. It was not only that a mantle of scarlet seemed to have settled permanently on her cheeks, but she seemed so dismayed, as if something had happened which for her had all at once turned the world upside down. All the way to town she never moved, but sat in her corner like a startled thing, staring straight in front of her at something which was so strange as to be incredible. It was only when we were nearing the terminus that it seemed to occur to her that she had in her hand the card which that young gentleman had given her. Its discovery seemed to occasion her another start. She glanced at it as if amazed to find it there; then up from the card towards me. I do not know if she had realized my presence before; she seemed to find the sight of me not only amazing, but alarming. Hurriedly opening her handbag, cramming the card inside, she turned her face towards the window and her back to me, and unless I was mistaken she was positively trembling. What became of her when we reached King's Cross I do not know. Appreciating her desire to evade my scrutiny, I busied myself with my own affairs and was careful to pay no attention to her. I should possibly never have thought of her again had it not been for an incident which occurred a few days afterwards.

I went to a great London hotel to see Mr. and Mrs. Hastings, whose deaf and dumb daughter had more than once been in my charge. Failing to find them in any of the reception-rooms, I went to look for them in one of the lounges below. There are two lounges just outside the smoking-room, a large open one on the left, a smaller and more secluded one on the right. As I stood at the smoking-room door, wondering if at any rate Mr. Hastings was within, I glanced round, through the entrance of the small lounge which was on my right, and as I did so saw a man pronounce a name which seemed familiar—George Winnington.

Two men were seated at a table on the opposite side: a tall, lean man, with a long face and lantern jaws, and a shorter, plumper person, with one of those round faces through whose skin the blood vessels are unpleasantly conspicuous. It was he who had pronounced the name which struck me as familiar—George Winnington. My attention aroused, I caught the end of a sentence as it was framed on his loose lips.

"... If George Winnington don't look out we'll show him that there's a thing or two he's still got to learn."

The lantern-jawed man replied, "His money or his life—is that the sort of thing you mean?"

"That's what it comes to, only we'll have something more than his life if we don't get his money."

"You'll get his money fast enough, by way of his little lady."

The fat man, laying his hand upon the other's arm, said with an air of great solemnity—

"If he has got her, really got her, my boy, our fortune's made: we are rich men."

The long man seemed to be amused by the other's solemnity. He said with a grin—he had one of those big mouths on whose long, thin lips it always seems to me that every word ought to be as plain as print to the merest tyro—

"I should like to see the colour of some of our riches if we are."

The words were scarcely spoken when some one, passing me, entered the lounge. It was the young man who had kissed the girl at the door of my compartment at Peterborough station. Of course that was where I had heard the name before: it came back to me on the instant; it was the name he had read aloud from the card on which he had written it—"George Winnington, Old Times Club, Jermyn Street." The expression on his face was very different from that which I had seen at Peterborough. I was struck by the difference. His sweet smile had gone; the sunshine, the look of careless, boyish happiness had vanished from his face; instead it was white and haggard; his eyes seemed to be inflamed; it was the face of one who was possessed by some overmastering, terrible anxiety. He had no eyes for me, although I stood quite close to him I doubt that he even realized that anyone was there. When he saw the two men seated at the table he paused, then took a few steps forward, exclaiming in a perfectly audible tone of voice—

"So there you are, two thieves together! You're a nice couple of blackguards! Damn the pair of you!"

The sentence was such a curious one, and seemed to presage a conversation of such an intimate character, that realizing that this was certainly an occasion on which auditors were not desired, I moved away from the entrance to the lounge, out of sight and hearing.

About a week afterwards I was at a dance in Lowndes Square.[1] A waltz had just finished; my partner was leading me to a seat, when I caught sight of a face in the crowd of dancers which rather startled me: it was the face of the girl whom George Winnington had kissed

[1] A residential square in the eminently respectable Belgravia district; the home of Paul Lessingham in Marsh's bestseller *The Beetle*.

on the foot-board of my compartment. I seemed destined to run against that pair. She was on the arm of a man with whom I had some acquaintance—Sir William Berry. I was taking my seat; she was lost in the crowd almost as soon as I had a glimpse of her. I should possibly have thought no more about her had it not been for a brief conversation which I saw taking place between two elderly ladies who were at some distance from me on my right. One, the elder, was on a chair; the other was standing close to her in such a position that her full face was turned towards me. I saw her ask the elder lady—

"Who is that lovely girl who is dancing with Sir William Berry?"

I could see all sorts of things which were being said about me: banalities mostly; it was that one question which seized my attention. I watched for the answer. It was spoken in that confidential tone in which one does say such things in a ballroom; had I been seated by the speaker I should probably not have caught a word. As it was, from where I watched I saw each syllable distinctly.

"My dear, that's the Braxham girl—Miss Beatrice Braxham."

The other lady inquired, speaking just as confidentially—

"Not of *Braxham's Balm*?"

"The same, my dear—the young lady of the ointment and the millions. I understand she's been brought up in the most extraordinary way. Her mother died when she was a child; her father, who was a person of imperfect education, had sense enough to distrust his capacity to bring up a girl unaided, so he transferred her to a convent somewhere in the wilds of Brittany, and there she's been immured till quite the other day."

"When did Braxham—the original Braxham—die?"

"Some six months ago—suddenly, without warning, on a chair in his office. When the girl came to England he was already buried. Practically he was an utter stranger to her; I'm told she only saw him three or four times in her life, and then only for a few minutes at a time. I've been informed that she knew absolutely nothing whatever about him, not even the business he was in. She had lived very simply in her convent all the year round, with very little money to spend, and nothing to buy if she had had heaps."

"And did her father leave her all his money?"

"My dear, so far as a will was concerned he left her nothing, because he made no will—he died intestate. So, since she was his only child, and I believe his only known relation, everything is hers to do with exactly as she chooses. Although no formal announcement has been made, I hear he left several millions, and *Braxham's Balm* is bringing in an enormous amount of money every year. There's a situation for you—a simple child, who has possibly never had more than a five-pound note at a time, and who has probably never done anything of her own initiative, the sole possessor of untold wealth; no wonder London is asking what will she do with them. Will she throw her sacks full of sovereigns into the sea as if they were so many pebbles on the shore, or——"

The elder lady stopped; the other completed her sentence on lines of her own.

"Or will she dower some impecunious and probably undeserving gentleman with the treasures which that singular father of hers —he must have been a singular sort of person—spent his whole life in amassing?"

"I need not tell you," resumed the elder lady, "that the eyes of every fortune-hunter in Europe are fixed upon her. She'll be lucky if she gets through the season without being caught by a scamp."

The two ladies parted: the elder remaining on her chair, the younger moving off among the crowd. I am afraid my partner found me inattentive to the remarks with which he was endeavouring to entertain me. Indeed, later in the evening, I happened to glance at him as he was talking to a friend, and I saw him say—

"Miss Lee can dance all right, but as a talker she's a frost; it seems impossible to get a word out of her. One generally does find it difficult to know what to say to a girl at a dance, but from a conversational point of view she's the absolute limit."

I did not feel flattered. He is quite a nice man. I did not want him to have so poor an opinion of my capacity; I should have liked to explain to him that while he had been talking to me my thoughts were elsewhere, which is really why he had found it so difficult to get words out of me. I could have assured him that as a rule I can talk nineteen to the dozen; but that when he was wanting me to prove it I was thinking of Miss Beatrice Braxham, of *Braxham's Balm*, that wonderful ointment whose merits are proclaimed on every hoarding and in the advertising columns of all our journals

—the simple, inexperienced, convent-bred girl who, while still only a child, had the uncontrolled disposal of all those millions. Small wonder London was asking what she would do with them.

There was one question which I was disposed to ask myself —although it was no affair of mine, but then I am always interfering in the affairs of other folks—who was Mr. George Winnington; how came they to know each other; what were the relations between them? That she had been more than amazed by the liberty which he had taken at the door of that compartment in Peterborough station I felt convinced. My one question had become several. Although the affair was no business of mine, I should have liked to find answers to them all. I should like to have known also who those two undesirable-looking men were whom I had seen seated in the lounge at the hotel; what hold they had over Mr. George Winnington; what they had meant by their allusion to "his little lady." Why had Mr. Winnington been in such an agitated state of mind as he approached them? Why had he addressed them in such unparliamentary language? Were they, indeed, a couple of thieves? If so, how came they to be associates of his—who had had the temerity to kiss the unsophisticated representative of *Braxham's Balm* before a perfect stranger on a railway platform?

When I was going away from the dance I waited for some moments in the hall while some one was finding for me the electric brougham[1] which I had jobbed for the occasion. People were coiming down the stairs. Among them Miss Beatrice Braxham on the arm of a man who was nearly a foot higher than herself. They made a singularly ill-assorted couple. They were talking as they descended. Apparently he had asked if he might be permitted to call, for I saw her say—

"I shall be very glad to see you. I'm at home every Thursday after four; 37, Curzon Street[2] is my address."

She dismissed him when they got into the hall.

"You really needn't come any farther," I saw her tell him; adding, when he was unwilling to be sent away, "I'm expecting to meet some one, if you don't mind."

---

[1] An electricity-powered motor vehicle in the shape of a horse-drawn brougham carriage, used in town driving in the early twentieth century.

[2] A street in Mayfair in the West End; a very prestigious address.

He took his dismissal with, I thought, not a very good grace. I was standing close to the open door; looking through it I understood why his escort had been declined: on the pavement, looking at the people as they came out of the house, was the young gentleman of the train. He was in evening dress, his coat collar was turned up, his hat was pressed far on to his head; it struck me that he was in a state of curious agitation—as he had been during those brief moments when I had seen him in the hotel. He started as Miss Braxham appeared on the steps; then hesitated, as I fancied, to learn if anyone was with her. When he saw that she was alone he moved quickly forward. His agitation seemed to infect her: at sight of him her cheeks went crimson, as they had done in the train. He met her when she was half-way down the steps. I saw her whisper to him, as he held his hat in his hand—

"You ought not to have come."

"Ought not!" He replaced his hat with a defiant flourish. "I had to, you know I had to.

I would not have come if I could have helped it."

I wondered what he meant; his manner did not suggest that he was merely conveying a compliment. He seemed possessed by some overmastering excitement. I saw the startled look she gave him; unless I erred she trembled—they did not convey to me the idea that they were just a pair of lovers. Crossing the pavement they entered a big Limousine, the door of which was held open by a resplendent footman. My brougham had been found; the big car was starting just as I got into it. I said to my chauffeur—

"You see that Limousine? Do you think you can keep it in sight until I tell you?"

The man said nothing, he merely touched his hat. I got in, and off we started.

Why I had told my driver to follow that Limousine I had myself only a very vague idea; I knew quite well that it was not exactly a legitimate thing to do, but the fact was I was devoured by curiosity —I sometimes am. Somehow I was convinced that that young man was not at all the sort of person who was entitled to ride alone at that hour of the night, or rather morning, with a young woman who was possessed of millions. She must have had a chaperon—a girl in her position would hardly go to Lady Bulkeley's ball alone;

what had become of the dame in whose charge she was supposed to be? Had she given her the slip and stolen away without her knowledge, in order to be alone with that very singular young man? It must have been a rendezvous—I had seen her tell her tall escort that she expected to meet some one. But, to put it mildly, what a bold thing to do—to make an appointment to meet that ineligible young man—I felt sure he was ineligible—on the pavement outside Lady Bulkeley's house at half-past two in the morning. It seemed to me that they must have courage, those two. I wondered—I could not help it—what was taking place in that Limousine in front of us: what those two were saying to each other.

Suddenly my coupé stopped. I put my head out of the window to speak to the driver. He said—

"That Limousine in front has just pulled up."

I asked, "Where are we?"

"This is St. James's Street;[1] the Limousine has stopped at the corner of Jermyn Street."

Jermyn Street! I recalled the address which Mr. George Winnington had scribbled on the card: Old Times Club, Jermyn Street. My driver went on—

"A gentleman is getting out, miss—he is saying good-bye to a lady; I fancy the lady is crying, miss."

"Crying!" I was surprised. "How can you tell she's crying, at this distance?"

"Well, miss,"—the man's tone was apologetic—"she's got a handkerchief to her eyes. The gentleman's turning into Jermyn Street; the car with the lady in is moving off. Do you want me to follow it, miss?"

That was precisely what I did not know. To be candid, I was feeling a little confused: almost, I may say, a trifle ashamed. What business had I to be playing the spy? What had those two people to do with me? I had not the slightest right to be interested in their movements. And yet—well, I find it hard to explain. But there are moments in my life in which my sense of intuition becomes so keen that it almost approaches what might seem to some to be the verge of the supernatural. With me it was one of those moments then:

[1] A street south of Piccadilly, associated, like Jermyn Street with which it intersects, with the gentlemen's clubland scene.

I was convinced that there was something about those two young persons which called to me. For what, or why, it called, as yet I could not tell; I only knew that within me was something—altogether different from mere vulgar curiosity—which insisted upon my concerning myself in the affairs of these two utter strangers.

It was 3 a.m., certainly time for me to be in bed; probably my driver, being human, also stood in need of sleep. Yet something which was stronger than I was suddenly began to tell me to follow that young man; it may seem ridiculous, but there was the fact. I sat still for a minute, then I asked my driver—

"Do you know the Old Times Club in Jermyn Street?"

"The Old Times Club?" He repeated my words. "No, miss, I can't say I ever heard of it. That Limousine has turned round and gone up into Piccadilly; where shall I take you to?"

It seemed to me that his words conveyed a hint; it was as good as saying that he was anxious to get home, and no wonder. I came to an instant resolution, I would take pity on the man.

"Drive me home," I said.

We turned; re-entering Piccadilly we ran along towards Sloane Street. It was odd what I suffered directly that driver began to obey my orders; each yard he went seemed to cause me positive pain. I became all at once possessed by the most singular feeling that something had happened to that young man in Jermyn Street, and was still happening, which it was my business to prevent. It was no use my struggling against the feeling: my struggles seemed to make it worse. As the car went on and on I began to endure positive agony. We were nearing Knightsbridge[1] when I came to the conclusion that I could stand it no longer. I turned the pointer of the index in front of me to Stop. The car came to a standstill. I was ashamed to put my head out of the window; I waited till the driver came to the door.

"You stopped me, miss?" he said.

I had—of course I knew I had, but there was that in the man's tone which made it hard for me to admit it. I was conscious that he was eyeing me curiously.

"Anything wrong, miss?" he inquired.

[1] The district south of Hyde Park, approximately half a mile from St. James's Street.

"No; there's—there's nothing wrong, only"—I was aware of an unwonted tendency to stammer—"only—I should like to go back to Jermyn Street—please."

Looking back, I am not surprised that he stared at me as if he could not make me out. The indecision in my tone, amounting to timidity, I have no doubt struck him as strange—to say nothing of the singularity of my request. Having just left Jermyn Street, why, at that hour in the morning—since my own abode was in Sloane Street—in such very quavering tones, should I ask him to take me back to it? I dare say he used strong language to himself—under the circumstances it was excusable; but fortunately he kept it to himself. Returning to his place, he took me back to Jermyn Street.

The moment the car went round the strange feeling of which I had been conscious assumed another phase: pain became excitement. When the car stopped I had become obsessed by a singular state of expectation; though what it was I expected for the life of me I could not have said.

"Wait," I said, and I got out of the car. Outwardly the driver remained silent, but I think it quite possible that he was full of speech within. The weather had changed: clouds obscured the sky, drops of rain were falling, there was a chilly little breeze, the atmospheric conditions were hardly inviting for a young woman attired in a ball dress. I held my skirt up well off the ground, drew my long blue wrap closer, and passed into Jermyn Street. I had hardly gone twenty steps when I almost stumbled over something which was lying on the pavement. It was the body of a man. He lay on his back, with his face turned towards me—it was the shorter of the two men whom I had seen talking in the lounge, the one on whose lips I had first seen George Winnington's name.

While I hesitated, conscious that my heart was beating faster, a door opened in a house a little farther down the street. There was a deep doorway on the other side of the road: hardly knowing why, I made a rush for it. As I gained its shelter a man came out on to the pavement opposite. He paused as if to consider the state of the weather, spoke to some one in the house, then started to walk quickly towards St. James's Street. He reached the recumbent figure. He bent over it, then called aloud, "Hallo, Jukes!"

Another man came out of the house, apparently some sort of

servant. He went to the man who had called. Together they bent over the figure on the pavement. Close to them was a lamp, which cast so bright a light that their faces from where I was were plainly visible. Some of their words escaped me, but I caught enough to be able to supply their places.

"I believe he's dead," said the man who first came out. I have no doubt he spoke in lowered tones because I could not hear a sound; I had to rely upon my eyes. The other man rejoined—

"This is a bad business. There has been foul play. Take care how you touch him; he's a reek of blood—look, my fingers are wet."

There was silence—the silence of awe. Then the first man said, in what I felt sure were quavering tones—

"Young Winnington has done this."

"I shouldn't wonder," agreed the other. "He owed Mr. Haseltine one; I heard him tell him that he'd pay him. They were having a few words just now; it looks as if this is what has come of them."

Another period of silence; perhaps they were thinking of what young Winnington had done. Then the first man suggested—

"Jukes, you'd better get on the telephone to the police—and to a doctor." He seemed to add the last words as an afterthought.

"Right," said Jukes, "I will. I fancy that this is a job for the police, and that a doctor will be too late. It looks to me as if Mr. Winnington had done him in."

Jukes returned to the house; the other man remained on guard. He had his back towards me. Coming out of my doorway I walked quickly towards St. James's Street; that man was so absorbed in eyeing the figure at his feet, and probably with his own reflections, that I doubt if he even saw me. I got into my coupé, and that time I went straight home.

I got into bed, but I did not go to sleep. I cast about in my mind as to what I ought to do. Having begun to meddle in matters which were no concern of mine it seemed to me that I must keep on. Mr. George Winnington might go red-handed to Miss Beatrice Braxham and, keeping her in ignorance of the thing he had done, might induce her to take some rash step which, at its very outset, might spoil her life for ever. It seemed to me that I must keep her from running such a risk as that. And I tried to. I had made a note of the address which I had seen her give to her tall escort as he brought her down the staircase at Lady Bulkeley's, and soon after ten o'clock I was asking for her at the door of her house in Curzon Street. The servant who answered my ring seemed to regard me as if I might be something in the millinery line.

"You can't see Miss Braxham now," he assured me; "it's impossible, Miss Braxham is in bed."

"Take my name up to Miss Braxham," I told him, "and tell her that I must see her on most important business at once. I will come up to her bedroom if she likes, but, for her own sake, see her I must."

The man, after ushering me into a little anteroom, departed with my message. Presently a woman appeared.

"I am Miss Braxham's maid," she informed me. "Miss Braxham wants to know on what business you wish to see her—she does not know your name. She is not feeling very well this morning and would rather not see strangers."

There was some note-paper on a side table. I wrote on a sheet just two words—"George Winnington." I put it into an envelope, which I handed to the maid.

"Give that to Miss Braxham at once. Tell her that she will find the subject on which I wish to see her inside this envelope."

Three minutes after she returned.

"Will you please come this way," she said; "Miss Braxham will see you."

She led me to a smallish room on the first floor, which was apparently used by its owner as a sort of boudoir. While I was looking about me, a door which led into an adjoining apartment opened and Miss Braxham entered.

Plenty of girls look well at night, when they are dressed in their best clothes, and seen by artificial light; many girls look well in the afternoon, when attired for out of doors, or for receiving guests at home; but the number of young women who present a pleasing appearance when, taken by surprise, they jump out of bed in the morning, is not so large as the unsophisticated may suppose. If only they all of them made such a charming picture as Miss Beatrice Braxham did as she stood at the door of her bedroom looking at me!

"What do you want with me?" she asked as she came a step or

two into the room with that sheet of note-paper in her hand. "They woke me out of sleep to tell me you were here; then—they brought me this." She held out the sheet of paper. "I do not think I know you—do I?"

"At least you have seen me before—I travelled up with you from Peterborough."

She regarded me with wide-open eyes.

"Oh dear!" she exclaimed, as suddenly it came back to her. "I remember you—of course; you were in the carriage. But how did you find out who I am, and where I live and what do you know about George Winnington?"

"I'm inclined to put the question in another way—what do you know?" She started back with what was a very natural gesture of resentment. I hastened to add, "Pardon me, Miss Braxham, but I must beg you to believe that it is very far from my wish to be in the least degree impertinent; but it so happens that facts have come to my knowledge which—make me anxious for you. Is Mr. Winnington an old friend of yours, or is he a mere chance acquaintance?"

She stood at her straightest, with what I am sure she meant to be an air of dignity. I thought what a dainty little thing she was; she did not need to be framed in her father's millions for men to fall in love with her.

"I have known George Winnington," she said, "ever since he was a little boy. I was at a convent in Brittany where his father was consul. Whenever I had a holiday I used to spend it with his father and mother, and of course with him. Now that his father and mother are dead I think I may say that he is the best, indeed the only, friend I have in the world. That is what I know of Mr. George Winnington. Now what do you know?"

There was a ring as of defiance at the end of her sentence, but it was the pathos of her words that appealed to me—that a girl in her position should feel herself entitled to say that that young gentleman was the only friend she had in the world. Yet, as I looked at her, I felt that it might be true; I suppose that is why I wanted to put my arms about her and kiss her. I had been aware all along that in her presence mine would be a delicate position—I was more conscious of it then than ever. That consciousness making me hesitate caused her to repeat her question.

"I have told you what I know about George Winnington, now perhaps you'll tell me what you know. It must be something very particular, since you have come to me at this hour and sent me such a message."

"I'm afraid that even you will find it, as you put it, something very particular that I've come about," I told her. "Indeed, it is so particular that it is not easy to find words in which to say it. Do you know if Mr. Winnington is in any financial trouble?"

She changed colour; drawing a little back she eyed me in silence. Then she asked, very properly—

"What business is that of yours? What have Mr. Winnington's private affairs to do with you? You are a complete stranger to me, and for all I know you are the same to him."

"I am; indeed, I am more of a stranger to him than I am to you. You did see me in the compartment of that train; I don't think he ever did."

"Then how dare you come here asking me such a question? Pray, Miss Lee, who are you? What has Mr. Winnington, or what have I, to do with you?"

With her dainty head held well back, her pretty cheeks flushed, her big eyes sparkling, somehow her air of injured dignity reminded me of an outraged bird of paradise.

"If you'll let me tell my story in my own way, I think, Miss Braxham, you will admit that I am more of a friend than you are willing to suppose."

"I don't see how you can possibly be a friend when I don't know you."

But she saw better before I had finished. I told her just everything, as it is written down here, and I believe in nearly the same words; and as my tale—such as it was—continued her eyes seemed to grow wider open. When I explained how it was that I had seen what those two men said to each other in the lounge of the hotel, and the two ladies at the dance the night before, and her words to her escort as she had come with him down the staircase, and what she had said to Mr. Winnington and he to her when she had met him on the pavement, her expression, her attitude, was like on big note of exclamation.

"But," she observed, when I had got to the point where I had made my driver take me back to Jermyn Street, "although what you say is very interesting, and full of the most curious coincidences, I don't see that it suggests that there's anything in it which entitles you to say that you have something to tell me about George Winnington which is so very wonderful."

"Have you heard anything of, or from him, since you put him down at the corner of Jermyn Street?"

"How could I, since that was at nearly three o'clock this morning, and now it is only just past ten?"

"Do you know anything about a Mr. Haseltine?" I inquired, and I described the round-faced man I had seen in the lounge.

"I only know," she said, "that he and George are not on the best of terms. I don't think he can be a very nice man. What do you know about him?"

"I know that I saw him soon after three o'clock this morning lying dead on the pavement in Jermyn Street, outside what a reference to the directory shows must be the Old Times Club."

"Miss Lee!" She uttered my name as with a gasp of horror.

I described the scene which I had witnessed, the brief sentences which I saw the two men exchange. When I told her what I saw them say about that young man her manner changed: she became almost white with rage, reminding me of nothing so much as an infuriated kitten. Even the tone of her voice had changed.

"Is it possible that you dare to hint that—that George Winnington had anything to do with—with what happened to that horrible man?" Then she suddenly seemed to do her best, as it were, to scratch me. "What a wretch you are!"

I was a little taken aback; the attack was as unexpected as uncalled for. I said so.

"I don't think you're entitled to speak to me like that, Miss Braxham. I'm only telling you what has happened, what I saw those two men—who seemed to know what they were talking about—say about a person in whom I knew you were interested, and I came here actuated by the best possible wishes for your welfare, to put you on your guard."

"Against what? You really are an extraordinary person!" She positively seemed to scintillate sparks—again like a kitten whose fur has been rubbed the wrong way. "Do you imagine that anything you could possibly say would induce me to believe that George Winnington did what you are hinting he did? What you are capable of, of course I can't say, but I can guess. But I do know that nothing in all this world could ever cause George Winnington to do anything of which he was ashamed; as for—as for killing a man, under any provocation—oh, that you should have the courage, and the impudence, and the cowardice to come here and breathe such things! I think it's very possible that you're the sort of person who is capable of doing anything—anything! But George Winnington! Will you please take yourself out of this room and out of this house before I do something which I may afterwards regret."

What she supposed she would do to me I cannot say; I should not have been a bit surprised if she had started scratching me in real earnest—and I should have liked her none the worse for doing it. It did me good to hear her champion the cause of her absent lover —that he was her lover was clear. Her heat warmed me. I felt that there must be good in the man in whom she had such entire faith. I was about to say so when the sound of a voice behind me caused me to look round. A tall, portly lady stood just inside the door.

"What new story is this about Mr. George Winnington? Of what fresh disgraceful act has he been guilty?"

Whether the lady's questions were addressed to me was not clear; Miss Braxham took it upon herself to answer them. The maiden seemed, if anything, angrier than ever.

"Pray, Lady Gill, what right have you to speak of a friend of mine like that?"

The portly lady rejoined: "If that young man is a friend of yours, my dear——" Miss Braxham cut her short, really speaking like a small virago, which, in fact, for the moment she was—

"Don't you call me 'my dear,' and don't you speak of Mr. Winnington as 'that young man,' my good woman. You mistake the position, Lady Gill. I am your mistress, you are not mine; you are paid by me to act as a chaperon when I want one. When I don't, you have no more right to interfere with what I choose to do, or so insult my friends, than this impertinent person here." I was the impertinent person alluded to. "I've just told this young woman"—that, again, was me—"to leave this room and this house, and while I'm about it, I'll extend the same invitation to you. If you will let me know what I owe you, your account shall be settled; kindly understand that your residence beneath my roof is at an end."

With that the little lady flounced back into what I presumed was her bedroom, leaving the portly dame and me to regard each other. I was disposed to smile; she certainly was not.

"Ill-bred little upstart!" Her tone was grim enough. "Of what fresh outrage has that Winnington scamp been guilty?"

I emphatically did not propose to take her into my confidence; I was frigidity itself.

"For information on that subject, Lady Gill, I will refer you to Miss Braxham."

With that I went out of the room, down the stairs, and out of the house. I felt like pinching myself when I got on to the pavement.

"This comes," I told myself, "of meddling in matters which are no concern of mine—it serves me right. If that furious little thing had had me thrown down the steps it would have been no more than I deserved. This ought to be a lesson to last me the rest of my life. If ever I interfere in what doesn't concern me again——"

I pulled up before I committed myself too far—before I vowed a vow which I was sure to break. I know myself sufficiently well to be aware that there are occasions on which I find it absolutely impossible to keep my fingers out of other people's pies—so what was the use of pretending? And the point of the joke is that before I was through with Beatrice Braxham I had justified myself, even to her, for putting my fingers in her pie.

I had not left the angry maiden very far behind before I came upon a boy who was selling the early editions of the evening papers. On the placard which he had in front of him was the announcement, "Murder of a well-known sportsman in Jermyn Street." I bought a copy of each of his papers. The well-known sportsman, as I had expected, was the round-faced person whom I had heard spoken of as Mr. Haseltine. He had been found stabbed to death that morning outside the Old Times Club. According to the paper the police had a clue which was presently expected to result in the capture of his murderer. When that came about, I told myself, it was possible that Miss Beatrice Braxham might be disposed to talk to me in a different tone.

"If the police once lay their hands on Mr. George Winnington it will go pretty hard with Miss Beatrice Braxham."

It might have done if the police had laid hands on him, but they never did. Events began to follow each other so fast that I was in the midst of a wild tragedy almost before I knew it.

The next day I paid a visit to some friends at Windsor.[1] Returning, just as the train was leaving the platform, two men came scrambling into my compartment. I resented their presence; judging from their appearance I doubted if they had first class tickets, and quite apart from their attire they really were such an evil-looking pair. They began whispering together almost as soon as the train was clear of the station. I had had enough of playing the unintentional eavesdropper; such persons could have nothing to say which would interest me; I studiously held my paper up in such a fashion that I could see nothing of their faces. The journals, by the way, were full of what had become known as "The Jermyn Street Mystery." The clue which the police were supposed to have had so far resulted in the arrest of no one. I wondered if by some lucky chance George Winnington had managed to get clear away; I wondered also, in the light of what I had told her, what Miss Beatrice Braxham was feeling.

For my part, I did not find my paper pleasant reading. I had already had more than enough of the Jermyn Street Mystery. I sincerely wished that I had never told the chauffeur of that jobbed electric brougham to drive me back again. I almost resolved that this should be a lesson which would induce me in future to confine myself rigorously to my own affairs, and just as I was at the point of arriving at this resolution, glancing from my newspaper, I looked for a second at those two whispering men, and as luck would have it I saw what one of them was whispering to the other. I saw just one word—Haseltine.

Having had no intention of observing them, the accident that he should have just been uttering the name with which my own mind was already too much occupied was a little startling. Really unwittingly I watched to see what else he might say—I say unwittingly because in my case I sometimes do that sort of thing without consciousness or intention. I did then. The one man had come to

[1] A town 21 miles west of Central London, associated with royalty because of Windsor Castle, an official residence of the Royal Family.

an end of his sentence, and the other spoke. He was a little, mean-looking creature, with foxy hair, and a foxy face, and an old, brown cloth cap, which he wore on one side of his head.

"I should have liked to have treated Mr. Thomas Haseltine to six inches of knife myself, I would that—the——!" He added some words which were not nice to see.

The other replied: "That Winnington lad gave him what he deserved, I will say that; he was a pretty——, Haseltine was."

By this time my attention was on the alert. Those two men were speaking as if they were acquainted with both the parties they had named. I watched to see what else they would say. The foxy man, glancing in my direction, leaned closer to his friend, and so brought his face a few inches nearer to me. Although I was pretty certain that he had seen nothing in my attitude to arouse his suspicion, he was clearly about to speak of subjects which, in his judgment, required to be spoken of with the profoundest secrecy. He scarcely breathed his words, but so long as he framed them on his lips that made no difference to me.

"Young George Winnington?" I saw him whisper. "He done it? What do you think!"

"I don't think nothing," replied his foxy friend, "I only know what everybody's saying."

"He no more put that knife into John Haseltine than you or me, but if I was asked I could tell who did."

"How do you know?"

"I don't know, if it comes to that; but I tell you what, I'm betting, and what's more, I'm laying the odds."

"Who did it if young Winnington didn't?"

"Why——" again the speaker glanced in my direction; I had just time to avert my eyes and get them back upon his face before he continued to speak—"what price Lantern-jawed Jack?"

"What, John Dutton of Rudgeton?"

"Don't mention no names, you fool."

"That young woman can't hear."

"I don't say she can, but all the same I don't want to have no names mentioned in a job like this."

"What makes you think he did it?"

"I don't say I do, I only say I'm betting. However, that's enough of it. I'm sorry I've said as much as I have; you get out of your head that I've said anything at all." The foxy-faced man drew farther away from his friend; plainly he regretted the indiscretion of which he had been guilty, though he could scarcely have guessed how indiscreet he really had been. He abruptly changed the subject. "Nice thing," he said, "our getting into a carriage where you can't smoke."

"Suppose," suggested his friend, "we was to ask the lady if she minds our smoking."

"It would make no difference if you did ask; I should object."

The two men stared at me; I had lowered my paper and was looking at them.

"Excuse me, miss," said the foxy man, "but what was that you said? Was either of us speaking to you?"

"I saw you grumbling to your friend because you had not got into a smoking carriage, and I saw your friend suggest that you should ask if I minded smoking; I merely wished you to understand that I do object."

"But—but——" The foxy man looked from his friend to me, and from me back to his friend; he was apparently suffering from some confusion of mind. Leaving the remark which he had commenced unfinished he addressed a question to his associate. "Charlie, did you say anything to the lady?"

"Not me, not a word; I haven't spoke to her; you know I haven't spoke to her."

"That is correct," I agreed, "you neither of you spoke to me; it was not necessary. You merely whispered to each other; you might as well have shouted, since I saw—and understood—every word you were saying."

There came that expression upon their faces which I was so used to seeing—a muddled, hazy look, as if they wondered if I were in jest or earnest.

"I don't know if you're getting at us——" the foxy-faced man began. I interrupted him.

"I will tell you what I saw you say and then you will be able to answer that question for yourselves. You were talking about the Jermyn Street Mystery, of how that man Haseltine deserved his fate. Your friend spoke of George Winnington as the one who killed him; you hinted that he was innocent, and were willing to lay odds that the guilty man was John Dutton of Rudgeton.[1] Now I should like to ask you if what you said was mere idle chatter, or if you have any grounds on which you based your insinuation. Who, in the first place, is John Dutton of Rudgeton, whom you spoke of as Lantern-jawed Jack?"

I have seen some startled people in my time, but I don't think I ever saw any quite so moon-struck as those two unpleasant-looking persons. Their jaws had dropped open, their eyes were distended; what would have happened if the train had not begun running into Paddington station I cannot say. When they realized that our speed was slackening they made a simultaneous rush for the door. While the train was still moving at a dangerous speed they flung it open and sprang out upon the platform. Porters shouted—whether they heeded them or not I cannot tell. When I looked out to see if they had come to grief, the pair had already vanished out of sight. As I was about to alight, an official came up to me as I stood framed in the door.

"Did those two men jump out of your compartment?"

I nodded. "They seemed in a hurry," I said.

"It's a wonder they didn't break their necks," he growled. "What was the matter with them? Have you any complaint to make of them?"

"Not I; but I rather fancy that they were travelling in a first class compartment with third class tickets, which might explain their haste."

"Weren't the tickets collected at Windsor?"

"Not from them; they got in just as the train was starting—too late for the collector to reach them."

"Then probably they had no tickets at all—that's about the size of it."

I crossed the departure platform to find a telephone box. As I was coming out I all but ran into Mr. George Winnington—be seemed to be in as great a hurry as those two men had been.

"Mr. Winnington," I exclaimed.

"Hallo!" He stopped to stare; then took off his hat. "I beg your pardon, but I'm afraid I don't remember who you are."

"I am just going to see Miss Braxham."

[1] Apparently imaginary.

"Are you? Then I'm afraid you won't see her. I've been trying to, but they told me a very queer story about her having gone to see me—into the country somewhere, no one seems to know quite where—in consequence of a wire I'm supposed to have sent—a wire to ask her to come and see me. Now, I never sent her a wire. Who has been forging my name, where she's gone, what it all means, is beyond me altogether. Do you know anything about it?"

"I don't." While he had been speaking I had been noticing two men who were striding towards us. Suddenly one of them perceived us. I saw him say to the other—

"Look down there; there's our man, talking to the girl. We're in luck; we've got him."

I grasped the situation in an instant; they were constables. They were alluding to George Winnington—they were about to arrest him.

"Mr. Winnington," I said to him, "there are two policemen coming to arrest you—you haven't a moment to lose. Go to that address,"—I slipped a card into his hand—and wait till I come. Quick, or they'll have you."

He was as swift to understand the position as I had been—possibly one glance at the two policemen was enough for him—he was gone almost before I had ceased to speak. As he moved off the constables came rushing forward. One of them almost knocked me over—perhaps I did get a little in his way.

"You've been helping that man to escape," he said.

The other called to him. "Never mind her; push along, we ought to get him yet." The pair tore off. People standing about stared: those officers were two big men; folks perhaps wondered at the rapidity of their movements. Hurry seemed in the air. I caught the infection. Slipping through one door while they rushed through another, getting into a taxi, I was away from that station I should say in less than ten seconds. I gave the driver the first address which came into my head. "Hyde Park Hotel," I said. What became of those two policemen I do not know. I feel sure they did not attempt to follow me.

As my cab was nearing Knightsbridge I altered my instructions to the driver—I told him to take me home. As I opened the door of my flat my maid advanced.

"There's a gentleman named Winnington in the sitting-room, miss. He's just come; he says you sent him."

The young gentleman greeted me as one who was not quite sure of where he stood.

"Did they find out where I'd gone?" he asked.

"I cannot tell you positively, but I should say not. There's one question I should like to ask, Mr. Winnington, before I go any farther. What had you to do with what happened to Mr. Haseltine?"

"Nothing—absolutely nothing. I assure you, Miss Lee—I suppose you are Miss Lee,"—he was glancing at my visiting card which he had in his hand—"I assure you that I had no more to do with it than you had. I'd just had a row with him, I gave him a piece of my mind—I don't mind admitting that, because it's true, and I'm not ashamed of it; but I didn't know anything had happened to him till yesterday. It was only just now that I heard that I am supposed to have had anything to do with it. Off I tore to Beatrice—I mean to Miss Braxham—because the idea that such a lie should reach her almost drove me mad. Then, when I got to Curzon Street, I found that she had gone off somewhere into the country; what does it mean?"

I was unable to say; but I was beginning to get an inkling of one of the causes of that girl's faith in him. That he was telling the truth I was persuaded. That he had got himself into some tangle with the disreputable Mr. Haseltine was probable—young men will do such things; sometimes only after painful experience are they able to distinguish a rogue from an honest man. But that this eager-eyed lad in front of me was the soul of truth I was sure; I had only been two minutes in his company before I agreed with Miss Beatrice Braxham that he was absolutely incapable of such an act as was being charged against him. However, I did not tell him so; instead, I asked a question.

"Mr. Winnington, have you ever heard of a person who is known as Lantern-jawed Jack?"

Obviously he was mystified by my inquiry.

"Why, that's what they call long Jack Dutton—Mr. John Dutton, that is. I don't know if that's who you mean."

"Who is Mr. John Dutton?"

"Well, he's—he's a pretty bad lot. I don't like to say anything against anyone, but he really is a wrong 'un, upon my word, Miss Lee—that is if you mean John Dutton of Rudgeton."

"Where is Rudgeton? Is it a house or a place?"

"I'm not quite sure, but I fancy it's somewhere on the Sussex coast, somewhere near Pevensey,[1] I think. They tell all sorts of stories about it; most of them I expect are lies. Haseltine and Dutton, I believe, were intimates; but I've a notion they weren't over-fond of each other, for all that. What do you know about Jack Dutton? Indeed, what do you know about Beatrice, or about me? I don't remember to have heard of or seen you before; if it hadn't been for you I might have been—good God! I might have been in prison at this very moment." He shivered at the picture his imagination conjured up. "I should never have dared to look Bee in the face again; they might have handcuffed me—think of it! I'm nothing compared to Bee as it is—I've scarcely got a shilling, and she's got millions; but when I first fell in love with her I didn't know that, nor did she. On the very night that she heard her father was dead we had arranged to elope together. I was waiting by the convent wall, as we had agreed; but instead of her, the head of another girl appeared over the top of the wall—Felice Ramont, a French girl. She dropped me a note, 'From Beatrice,' she said, and then she went. I opened the note. She wrote that she had just heard that her father was dead, and so it was quite impossible for her to run away with me. She added in a postscript that she had heard that he had left her millions; what was she to do? I didn't know what she was to do; I didn't know what I was to do myself. I had got her railway ticket in my pocket: we were to have been married at Brest.[2] And now here am I, owing to the intervention of a perfect stranger, escaping by the skin of my teeth from being locked up for murder—and for all I know they'll have me yet. I suppose, as a matter of plain fact, I may as well be hanged as anything else."

It was a sort of philosophy which did not commend itself to me —I doubt if it did to him, only the poor lad was in such a desperate plight that he did not know where to turn for a glimmer of hope. The more I heard of him, the more I saw of him, the better I under-

---

[1] A village on the south coast of England, approximately seventy miles south of London.

[2] An important port city in Brittany, France.

stood how it was that Miss Beatrice Braxham had raged at me. I was at my old trick of rushing at my fences again. Instead of telling myself that I would never meddle with the affairs of other people, I had scarcely made that young gentleman's acquaintance five minutes before I had resolved that I would leave no stick or stone unturned in order that that couple of romantic youngsters should be brought together in what I was convinced would be a perfect union—though she had billions, and he had not a cent.

Arriving at such a resolution and putting it into practice were two quite different things. While I was trying to get some dim notion of what immediate steps it would be best to take, I started on what I intended to be a series of instructive observations.

"I don't like to hear young men talk like that, Mr. Winnington: I really think there may be some better fate in store for you than hanging——" I had got as far as that, and I fancy he was about to interrupt with some tragic remark to the effect that he did not know what there could be, when some one knocked and rang at my hall door. I stopped to listen. His attitude was gloomy.

"Perhaps that's the police after me," he said.

I heard the hall door open; then the door of my sitting-room was opened; some one came rushing past the maid, who was holding the handle—and there was Miss Beatrice Braxham standing just inside the doorway. Which was the most surprised, that young man, the young woman, or myself, I should not care to have to determine. The girl stared at my masculine visitor as if he had been a ghost.

"George," she exclaimed, "whatever are you doing here?"

"Bee!" he cried, and in an instant they were almost in each other's arms. Almost, but not quite, for just as his arms were about to close round her she drew back and motioned him from her with her outstretched hand.

"One moment," she remarked, "I should like some sort of explanation; I was not aware you knew this—lady."

"I don't," he declared; "I only know that she has just saved me from the police, and that if it hadn't been for her I should at this moment be the inmate of a felon's cell, perhaps with gyves upon my wrists. I was within an ace of being arrested for murder; if it hadn't been for Miss Lee I should have been."

His language was a trifle lurid. It had such an effect on Miss Braxham that it seemed she had to sink upon the nearest seat.

"I never thought," she said, "that she would have saved you from arrest; I supposed she would have made it her special business to give you in charge."

"Then you were all wrong; she gave me shelter—me, a perfect stranger. I don't know yet how much I owe her, but I do know that I owe her my liberty. And pray where have you been? What was the tale they told me about your having that telegram from me? I never sent you a telegram."

"Didn't you? Oh dear, then what an escape I've had! I've been in a frightful state of mind. I had a telegram, signed George—here it is, see it for yourself."

From her handbag she took a pink slip of paper, the contents of which he proceeded to read aloud.

"'For the sake of all that has ever passed between us meet me at Victoria Station, Brighton line, at once. Something dreadful has happened. I implore you not to fail me. George.'" He lowered the slip of paper to stare at her. "Well, I never did read such an effusion. Did you suppose such an effusion could have come from me?"

"I wondered. It didn't seem like you. I hadn't seen you for ever so long——"

"I had made up my mind that you should never see me again."

"George, however can you say such things!"

"I wasn't a fit person for you to see, a creature like me! I had taken money from you——"

"George, if you talk like that I shall cry!"

The threat awed him; she already had six square inches of cobwebby linen in her hand.

"Bee, for Heaven's sake don't do that. Don't make me feel a bigger brute than I do already. But, my darling child, when you got this ridiculous effusion, what did you do?"

"I went to meet you—of course I went to meet you; I'd have gone across the world to meet you if I'd thought you wanted me——"

"My angel!"

"And when I got to Victoria station you weren't there."

"Of course I wasn't there. How could I be there? I never meant to be there."

"And a man came up to me—a tall, thin man, with a big nose, and a horrid face—and he took his hat off and said, 'Miss Braxham? I come from Mr. Winnington.'"

"He came from me! The villain!"

"'Mr. Winnington,' he said, 'has had to leave town,' then dropped his voice and looked round, as if anxious that no one should hear. 'As you perhaps know, the police are making themselves unpleasantly active.'"

"Did he say that? The scoundrel!"

"The way he said it made me shudder. 'I'm glad to say,' he went on, 'that I've been able to give him shelter in a little house which I have in the country, at Rudgeton——'"

"Rudgeton! Had he a long chin and hollow cheeks?"

"He had, and he said his name was Dutton."

"Lantern-jawed Jack! It was Lantern-jawed Jack, Miss Lee. You suspected the man—but there's a villain for you! Then what did he say, this nice cup of tea?"

"He said you'd not dared to tell me where you were in the telegram, but that you'd asked him to take me down to you. He had got a ticket for me, and he took me to a train. I was trembling all over, and I was so frightened that I didn't know what to do. So I got into the train, and off it started."

The little lady gave a great sigh; the young gentleman seemed half beside himself with excitement.

"Did anybody ever hear the likes of that! Were you and he alone together in the carriage?"

"We were, that made it so much worse. There was something about him, the way he looked at me, the way he spoke, which made me feel that I'd do anything if only he'd sit at the other end of the carriage. But he wouldn't; he sat right opposite me, and leaned forward—the idea of being alone with him in that compartment for I didn't know how long was more than I could stand. When we got to Clapham Junction,[1] I turned the handle, which fortunately was inside the carriage door, and I was out on the platform before he even guessed what I was going to do. He did try to stop me, but just then one of the railway people came up, and I said to him, 'Guard,'

---

[1] A station approximately three miles south of Victoria.

—I don't think he was one, but I called him Guard—'this person is quite a stranger to me, will you ask him to leave me alone?' The railway person looked at him, and you should have seen how that dreadful man shrank back into the carriage! The train went on and I was left upon the platform. I didn't know what to do. I wanted advice and help from some one, and I didn't know who in the world to turn to. Then I thought of Miss Lee, who had made herself so officious and so disagreeable—I simply couldn't think of anyone else. I found her card in my bag, and I looked at it, and though I knew I was a perfect idiot, I came tearing off to see if she could help me."

The business of making matters even relatively clear took considerably more than an hour. By that time we had had tea—a really good tea—and we were on terms of something like friendship—those two young persons did move so quickly. We were still talking as hard as we could when the maid came in with a card, "Inspector Ellis, Scotland Yard." Before I could decide what to do the inspector appeared in the doorway.

"I must ask you to forgive my intrusion, Miss Lee," he began, "but I wish to see you on a very pressing matter and I did not gather that you were engaged."

I had become so convinced of George Winnington's entire innocence that I there and then took the bull by the horns—I introduced both my visitors.

"Miss Braxham, let me introduce to you Inspector Ellis. Inspector, this is Mr. George Winnington."

The inspector stared. "Not *the* George Winnington, and *the* Miss Braxham?"

"I fancy, inspector, that from your point of view, that's precisely who they are."

The inspector turned to me. "Then you know?"

"I know that there's some nonsensical notion among your people that Mr. Winnington had something to do with what happened in Jermyn Street the other morning, and I also know that he hadn't."

"That's correct, he hadn't—we also know it. That's what I've come to talk to you about. You travelled up from Windsor this afternoon in a compartment with two men?" I nodded. "I thought it was you from the tale they told. At Paddington station one of our men tried to arrest Mr. Winnington, and you gave him the office?"

"I did; that is, I told him they were coming."

"I thought, again, it was you. Our men were pretty mad. Just as they were giving up hope of getting their man they came upon a gentleman who is known in his profession as the Snide-Pitcher, who was wanted for quite a different job, so they buckled him. I fear the Snide-Pitcher is not much of a sportsman, and on the way to the station he began to hint that he knew who was responsible for the Jermyn Street murder, and that, if it were considered favourably in the matter of the charge which was about to be brought against him, he would turn King's evidence. They informed him that they knew as much about that as he did and thanked him for nothing. He said, 'You think it was George Winnington—well, it wasn't.' They pricked up their ears at that and asked him what he knew about it and who it was. Then he told a tale about how he had come up by train with a friend from Windsor, and how they had had a chat together, and how there was a lady in the carriage who had heard every word they said though they had never spoken above a whisper: and how the way she had sprung it on them had upset them altogether, so that for his own peace of mind he felt that he had better make a clean breast of it. When they got him to the station they telephoned for me, and he told me a pretty yarn."

The inspector, placing his hat on a chair, took out a pocket-book.

"I believe, Miss Braxham, that the other day you drew a cheque for a thousand pounds?"

"I did—what then? I suppose I can draw a cheque if I like."

"Certainly. You took it yourself to the bank and received bank-notes in exchange. The night before last those bank-notes were given by a gentleman whom I will not name to Mr. Thomas Haseltine at the Old Times Club. This gentleman said some rather plain things to Mr. Haseltine. After he had gone Mr. Haseltine, who had been drinking, ostentatiously made a list of the numbers of those bank-notes and handed it to the porter at the club. When, soon afterwards, Haseltine was found murdered, there were no bank-notes on his person. Yesterday morning Mr. John Dutton, also a member of the Old Times Club, gave the Snide-Pitcher a ten-pound note, in settlement of some sum which he owed him; there had been some very funny dealings between those two gentlemen. A few minutes afterwards, the Snide-Pitcher, according to his own tale, saw in a newspaper for the first time what had happened to Mr. Haseltine, and also the numbers of the notes which had been missing from his person. That note which Dutton had given him was one of them. Dutton had taken it from a large wad of others. The Snide-Pitcher had reasons for knowing that only the day before Dutton was impecunious. He naturally jumped to a certain conclusion. He was talking about that conclusion, as such men will—they can't keep their mouths shut—to a friend in the train when you startled him by telling him what you had seen him say. That seems to have frightened him half out of his senses; when our men arrested him that finished it—the whole tale came out, at much greater length than I have told it to you."

Returning his notebook to his coat pocket, the inspector picked up his hat.

"I wired to Rudgeton to instruct the local police to call on Mr. John Dutton. I've just had a wire back from them to say that they did call; that they came upon Mr. Dutton as he was entering his house; that at sight of them he took out a revolver, and before they could get near enough to stop him, he blew his brains out. So I thought, Miss Lee, that since it's a matter in which you had so considerable a hand, the least I could do was to call and post you in the latest news."

When the inspector had gone, those two young persons kissed each other, solemnly; and then, with equal solemnity, they both kissed me. George Winnington did it in accordance with instructions received. The lady saw them carried out. It was most embarrassing. Then the girl snuggled into my arms, and had one of those good cries which are so comforting to some young people. While the young gentleman danced about the room, and kept saying things.

There, again, was the result of putting my finger into other people's pies.

THE CLARKE CASE

He had cut the end off the cigar and was about to strike a match when the telephone-bell rang. The instrument was close to the matches, so that without moving he was able to take up the receiver. "Yes, who's there?"

A voice came along the wires.

"If the man with the red moustache offers you a cigar, don't smoke it."

"What's that? Who is it speaking?"

The voice came again.

"Are there three men with you—one with a red moustache, one with a scar on his cheek, and one with his hair parted in the middle? If so, you're in bad company. Be on your guard; and mind—this is very particular—if the man with the red moustache offers you a cigar, don't smoke it. That's all. Good-bye."

The voice ceased, but he remained where he was with the receiver still held to his ear.

"Who is that speaking?" he asked, but he was not surprised that no answer came. He still kept the receiver to his ear for an instant. He wanted to gain time, if only for a few moments, to think.

The voice which had come to him had been unfamiliar; he did not know if it had been male or female. It was strange how it had given expression to certain doubts which had been floating through his mind—so strange as to be almost miraculous.

Presently he hung up the receiver. One of his companions spoke to him, the one with the scar on his face, Fred Darlington; how was it that the person who had spoken to him through the telephone knew that at that moment there was in the room with him a man with a scar on his face?

"I don't like a telephone in the room in which I live," Darlington said. "You never know when it's going to worry you. I hope that wasn't anything worrying."

"No; it was only a reminder," replied the host carelessly. "You must excuse me for a moment while I attend to it."

He passed from the room.

The moment he had gone the man with the red moustache, Clifford Sayers, spoke—

"He took it with him, didn't he?" he asked, and as Darlington nodded: "I wonder what the message was? If it hadn't been for the telephone-bell ringing just then he'd have lit it."

"He'll light it all right when he comes back. What's the matter with you, man? You speak as if you'd got the jumps."

"I have; we are playing such a game of touch-and-go. Suppose he doesn't—we're done."

Charles Arnold, the man whose iron-grey hair was parted in the middle, remarked sententiously, as if he were giving utterance to a profound truth—

"There are other ways."

The three men looked at each other; there was something odd in the glances they exchanged. Gilbert Clarke returned. As if moved by a common impulse the trio glanced sharply at him. He still had the cigar in his hand, unlighted.

"Wasn't it my deal?" he observed as he was crossing the room. "Sorry to keep you waiting."

He put the cigar which he was carrying between his lips, and, striking a match, applied it to the end. As if unconscious of the interest with which the three men were watching him, he drew a puff or two.

"Sayers, this is a nice cigar of yours," he remarked. "Now let's go on with business."

He sat down to the table, drawing at the cigar with every sign of enjoyment. The three men eyed him with an interest which seemed to be momentarily growing—as if the spectacle of a man smoking a cigar were a strange one. He took up a pack of cards.

"Are these cards made?" he asked, and added as no one answered: "This is a rattling good cigar of yours, Sayers—top hole."

He took the cigar out of his mouth, drew it to and fro across his nose, and examined the ash with the air of a connoisseur. Mr. Sayers, watching him with a very peculiar expression on his face, put out the tip of his tongue as if to moisten his lips.

"That's not the cigar I gave you," he said slowly.

"My dear fellow, what do you mean? Not your cigar? It's the one you gave me."

"It is not."

"It is—of course it is; what else can it be?"

"I expect you put down the one I gave you somewhere when you were out of the room."

"Sayers—what do you mean?" Clarke demanded, and, resting his elbows on the table, he looked the man with the red moustache very straight in the face. "How on earth can you tell this is not the one you gave me? What was the matter with that cigar?"

Arnold struck in: "Don't be absurd. Why shouldn't it be the one you gave him? Aren't we going on playing?"

"Aren't we?" Clarke echoed the other's question.

At that moment a man came in with some things on a tray; he placed the tray on a sideboard. Clarke took something out of his waistcoat pocket which he held out across the table. "Sayers, have a cigar?"

"That's my cigar."

"Is it? Then smoke it."

"What do you mean by that?"

"Ferguson, lock the door and put the key in your pocket." The man who had brought in the tray, moving quickly to the door, did as he was told. Gilbert Clarke had risen.

"You're quite right, Sayers," he said. "This is your cigar, and before you leave this room you're going to smoke it."

Quite a perceptible change took place in Mr. Sayers' complexion. Darlington's scar seemed suddenly to gleam brighter. Arnold was the only one of the three who outwardly remained calm. He looked up at Clarke with what seemed quite natural surprise.

"Clarke, what is the matter with you?"

"Nothing is the matter with me. I just want Mr. Sayers to smoke his own cigar, and I'm going to see he does it before he leaves this room."

"Hand it over." Sayers held out his hand.

"Mr. Sayers, I'm quite willing to do what you call 'Hand it over,' but it's on the distinct understanding that you put it straight into your mouth, light it, and smoke it while I watch you. If you don't —if, for instance, you try to put it in your pocket, or break it up, or to play any trick with it—there'll be trouble."

"Mr. Clarke, have you suddenly gone mad?"

This again was Arnold.

"Why should you suppose that I have gone mad merely because I wish Mr. Sayers to smoke his own cigar?"

"That's not all you've done; you've ordered your servant to lock the door and pocket the key."

"Precisely; because I wish him to remain and see fair play. Three to one are rather bigger odds than I care to face. I'm going to waste no time, either. Mr. Sayers, you smoke this cigar at once or I telephone for the police."

"What was that call," asked Darlington quickly, "that you had just now on the telephone?"

"You've hit it, Darlington. That call was a warning not to smoke the cigar which Mr. Sayers gave me. That is why I would like him to sample it himself."

The three men stared at each other, amazed.

"I felt," cried Sayers, "the moment I heard that confounded bell begin to tinkle that there was something up."

"Your instinct guided you correctly, Mr. Sayers; there was something up. It looks as if there were going to be something more up presently. For the last time, are you going to smoke your own cigar?"

"If you'll excuse me, sir," interposed Ferguson, who was standing at the door, "the thing's pretty plain. I think, if I were you, sir, I should let them go."

"There's something, Ferguson, in your idea." Gilbert Clarke looked from one to the other of the three men as if they were curiosities, the spectacle they presented seeming to amuse him. "Ferguson, open the door. Gentlemen—save the mark—let me invite your attention to the open door."

"You've won my money!" exclaimed Sayers.

"That's perfectly true, Mr. Sayers. I think with the assistance of the cigar I didn't smoke, and you won't, it was your intention, presently, to win mine—Mr. Sayers, the door."

"You give me back my money!"

"I'm afraid I can't do that; but—your cigar?"

Sayers made a snatch at the cigar which the other held out. Breaking it in two, he began to crumble up the tobacco in his hands. Clarke watched him smilingly.

"Now that you've quite made an end of it, let me assure you

that that wasn't your cigar after all. It was one of my own. If you had smoked it, no results of any kind would have followed; only you didn't even dare to try. It suggests that there must have been something really peculiar about the cigar you gave me, which I have under lock and key—and propose to keep for future use."

Sayers held the remnants of the cigar which he had broken to his nose. He let them fall on to the floor with an oath.

"You give me back my cigar," he demanded.

"You recognize that that isn't yours? There must have been something peculiar even about the smell. No, Mr. Sayers, I shall not give you back your cigar; I never return a present. Let me again invite your attention to the open door."

Arnold spoke as he moved across the room—

"Come on, Sayers. I won't comment upon Mr. Clarke's behaviour, or on his notions of the duties of a host. We may have a few words to say to him on a future occasion—words which he will find very much to the point."

"But I want my money," persisted Sayers. "He's won nearly forty pounds from me; he's cleaned me out."

Darlington went close up to Clarke, looking him very straight in the face. He was a bigger man even than his host, who was no pygmy.

"Although, Mr. Clarke, you have your servant here to protect you, I've a mind to give you the soundest thrashing you ever had in your life."

"Have you, Mr. Darlington? Pray don't consider my servant. I am at your service—to thrash."

Arnold, who was standing near the door, called to him—

"Come away, Darlington. What's the use of making a scene? We'll talk to him, in our own fashion, later on. Let him flatter himself for the moment that he has got the best of us."

Clarke made a movement with his hand.

"You hear, Mr. Darlington, the voice of wisdom. May I ask, if you are going to thrash me, to do it at once; I want to be rid of you."

The scar on Mr. Darlington's cheek showed more clearly.

"It's easy for you to talk, my foxy kid; but I could kill you if I liked."

"Darlington!" exclaimed Arnold. "Come, don't be an ass!"

Clarke smiled a little grimly.

"Don't you think you had really better go—leaving me unkilled?" he suggested coldly.

Darlington moved still closer, raising his left hand. Gilbert Clarke did not flinch; he continued to smile. "If you touch me—— If you touch me——"

"If you're set on making an ass of yourself, Darlington," said Arnold impatiently, "you can do it on your own—I'm going. Come along, Sayers."

As he spoke Arnold quitted the room. Sayers followed after him. Darlington hesitated.

"You may think you have finished with me, Mr. Clarke, but I assure you I haven't finished with you. You've got my money, and I assure you I'll make you give full value for every penny."

Mr. Darlington followed his companions.

Three days later Gilbert Clarke was at Brighton. On the morning after his arrival he was on the West Pier listening to the band. He was leaning over the railing of the balcony when a voice addressed him from behind—

"Good morning, Mr. Clarke."

Turning, he found that the speaker was a quiet, nice-looking young woman, with big, bright eyes, and a clear complexion. She perceived that he was at a loss.

"No, you've never met me before, nor have I ever seen you; but the man you were talking to just now—I saw him call you Clarke."

"You *saw* him call me Clarke?"

"Why not? If you watch a man's face you can see what he says. I hope you didn't smoke that cigar?"

Gilbert Clarke stood with his hat in his hand, plainly more at a loss than ever.

"What cigar?" he asked. "I'm afraid I don't quite follow."

"Wasn't it you I recommended over the telephone not to smoke a certain cigar?"

Light seemed to be dawning on him, causing some very curious changes to take place in his expression.

"Was it you? Great Scott! You don't mean to say—but I don't understand. To whom have I the pleasure of speaking?"

The girl let his question go unanswered.

"The man with the red moustache is here," she went on quietly. "He's on the deck below. You seem to be quite a decent sort of person; I wondered if you were, and if it would be worth my while to telephone. How came you to be in such society? I hope you're not in the habit of choosing such companions."

Her frankness seemed to take him aback. Her big eyes were fixed on his face, as if she were trying not only to read what was on it, but what was behind it, too. He positively blushed.

"The fact is," he explained with marked hesitancy in his speech, "that I met them—that is, I met Darlington and Arnold—at Monte Carlo; you know how one does pick up men at that sort of place. But, I beg your pardon, I suppose, as you're a woman, you don't."

"You may suppose I do."

"May I? That's good. They seemed to know a lot of other men there, and, after a fashion, I chummed up with them. We came back together, and in London they introduced me to Sayers—and that's how it was."

"I see. Well—they are not nice men."

"May I ask what you know about them; and also I hope you won't mind my asking who you are? You have the advantage of me."

"Darlington is the man with the scar," returned the girl, ignoring the more personal question. "He would kill you at sight, and without warning, if you had something he wanted and he couldn't get it any other way. Arnold, the man with his hair parted in the centre, is more diplomatic; he would rather some one else killed you than do it himself. Sayers, the man with the red moustache, is a sneak; he would like to kill you on the sly. By the way, what have you done with his cigar?"

"I'm keeping it as a memento. One day it may come in useful."

"He is preparing another for you—or its equivalent. This time it takes the shape of a woman. Is there a fluffy, fair-haired lady staying at your hotel, to whom you have paid attention—say, just a little?"

Gilbert Clarke blushed again. He was only a young man, after all, and this girl's eyes never left his face.

"There was a lady who sat by me last night in the Winter Garden to whom I spoke a word or two," he replied hesitatingly.

"She has a private sitting-room?"

"I believe she has; she did say something about it. She is staying in the house with her husband."

"Her husband? Yes, quite so. Her husband wasn't there last night?"

"I understood from her that he had gone away for a day or two."

"Exactly; and you asked her to go for a spin with you in your car this afternoon?"

"How do you know that? Did she tell you? Is she an acquaintance of yours?"

"Never spoke to her in my life; but she's an acquaintance of the man with the red moustache."

"No! How do you know that?"

"She has just been talking to him on the front. He wanted to come on to the pier and listen to the band, but she told him that you were doing that already, so they had their little talk on the front instead. Apparently she has got rid of him," she added hurriedly; "isn't that she coming along the pier? A word of warning: Don't go into her sitting-room, and be careful where you go with her in the car."

The girl, laughing at him, held up a monitory finger; then, without the slightest warning, turned and walked quickly away.

"One moment," he exclaimed, and would have hastened after her. She turned into the pavilion; when he reached the door she had vanished from sight.

"Who on earth is she?" he inquired of himself, and what the goodness does she mean by tearing off like that?"

He glanced down the stairs, looked around the pavilion, went back to the balcony and stared on the deck below; there was not a trace of the girl to be seen. A lady coming down the pier, seeing him lean over the balcony, catching his eye, slightly waved her parasol to him.

"Hallo! There's Mrs.—didn't she say her name was Denyer? She's uncommonly good to look at." He took off his hat in recognition of her signal. "Who is that girl, I wonder? What does it matter? I shall do no harm by saying a few civil words to Mrs. Denyer, even if she has the misfortune to number Mr. Sayers among her acquaintances. And, after all, I actually have nothing against Mr. Sayers or his friends—that is, nothing substantial. It's only surmise. It looks as if she were coming up here. I don't see how I'm going to cut her if she does; I must be civil."

He was civil to her to such an extent that—unheeding the stranger's warning—he took her out for a spin in his car that very afternoon.

That was on the Friday afternoon. On the afternoon of the following Monday a young woman got out of the train at Bramborough[1] station—Bramborough is a village something more than twenty miles from Brighton—and put rather a singular question to the man who took her ticket at the door.

"Is there a house in the village, or near the village, with a very large sycamore tree in front of it?"

"Sycamore?" echoed the man. He looked puzzled as if he would like to ask what a sycamore was.

A man who was on the box of a fly, which was standing in the road, called out: "There's The Laurels, miss. That's got a sycamore in the front garden."

"How far is The Laurels from this?"

"I'll drive you there, miss, in ten minutes."

"Thank you; I think I'd rather walk, if you wouldn't mind telling me where it is."

"It's just outside the village, miss. It's an old-fashioned house, standing well back from the road; there's a laurel hedge and a large sycamore tree in the front garden. It's on your right as you go straight on; you can't miss it."

"Just outside the village" proved to be rather an elastic phrase. It seemed to her that she had left the village behind a good half-mile before she came to what she was seeking.

"This must be it," she decided. "He said the house with the sycamore; there are hardly likely to be two houses with sycamores in a place like this."

As she stood looking over the gate, she smiled to herself. "A nice wild-goose chase I'm on," she went on to herself; "compared to what I'm doing, chasing a will-o'-the-wisp isn't in it."

She pushed back the gate, which swung on rusty hinges. "That wants oiling. The house seems empty; it looks as if it hadn't been

[1] Apparently imaginary.

lived in lately. The windows look as if they hadn't been cleaned for ages, or the blinds drawn up. I wonder who's supposed to live there, anyhow." She pulled a comical face. "A pretty figure I'm going to cut."

She walked along the weed-covered path to the house; the nearer she came to it the more deserted it seemed. There was no knocker at the front door; she rang the bell, and could hear it clanging within. She rang three times, but no one answered.

"There's no one in here now, that's pretty certain. Somehow, the very way that bell clangs seems to tell you that the house is empty."

She walked around the building. All the blinds were closely drawn. At the back, a pane of glass in a French window was broken. She seemed struck by it.

"That window seems to be broken in a rather convenient place. I wonder if I were to put my hand in if I could reach the fastening? I can—there is the window open. Now, if I enter this house, shall I be committing burglary, or what crime shall I be committing?"

She stood with the open window in her hand, hesitating; then she passed the threshold.

"How dark it is in here! That's because the curtains are so thick and the blinds are all down. Shall I pull them up? Will that be a further offence, I wonder?"

While standing in the shadowed room—she still seemed to be of two minds—the silence was broken by a very curious sound. If for a moment she started, seeming about to retreat, it was but for a moment; almost in the same instant she recovered her presence of mind.

"What was that? I do believe I've not come on a wild-goose chase after all."

The room, which was filled with odds and ends of furniture, was apparently a drawing-room. It had folding doors, which were the only means of egress. Throwing one open she entered the room beyond.

"It isn't very long ago that some one was in here—some one, it would seem, who was having rather a good time."

On the table were two champagne-bottles, which seemed to be empty; a champagne-glass lay broken on the floor; another stood by a dish of grapes; a half-consumed cigar lay on the carpet; a box of cigarettes was open on a chair. Near them was a woman's glove; on this she pounced.

"That ought to be a piece of evidence, if evidence is needed." As she examined the glove that curious sound was repeated. "That comes from upstairs." She passed through the hall; at the foot of the staircase she halted. "I wonder what I'm going to see."

Then she ascended the staircase. When she reached the top she pointed to a door.

"It comes from the other side of that." Even with the handle between her fingers she stood to listen. "I wonder what is on the other side; I do hope it is nothing very dreadful." She threw the door of the room right back. "Oh, what a smell!" Then she went in. "You poor, poor thing!"

It was a bedroom, and something was on the bed. A figure of a man tied hand and foot with a variety of ingenious fastenings. The atmosphere could scarcely have been more unpleasant. There were two windows; she ran to them, drew up the blinds, raised the sashes. A pleasant breeze came through. Then, turning to the bed, she repeated her previous cry of pity.

"You poor, poor thing; what have they done to you?"

The man was not only secured so he could not move a limb, he was gagged as well. It was the gag that, in the efforts which he made to give vent to his feelings, made it seem such a curious sound. The gag took the form of a towel, which had been folded over his mouth and tied at the back. When she had removed this, the man made an attempt to speak, but failed.

"Don't talk; don't try to. Don't do anything till I have untied you," she commanded, attacking the knot. But it was not an easy job, the untying. "Oh, if I had a pair of scissors or a knife; these knots are terrible. I wonder where the knives are kept? It will take me hours to untie those knots. There must be knives in the house; I'll run downstairs and get one."

"Don't go," the man managed to gasp.

"I sha'n't be an instant; I'll be back before you know I've gone. I must get something to cut those cords with."

She was nearly as good as her word. Considering she was in a strange house, with no idea of where anything was kept, she was back with surprising quickness, with quite a collection of knives in her hands.

"I brought all these in case any of them should be blunt. Now we'll see! This one is not blunt, anyhow; that cord's cut, and that, and that. We'll have them all off in less than no—— Oh, Mr. Clarke! What's the matter? Surely I haven't hurt you?"

Something had happened which seemed both to startle and surprise her—the man on the bed had fainted. Momentary reflection, however, told her that that was precisely what might have been expected. The shock produced by the sudden removal of his bonds was more than he could bear.

It seemed to her that the best thing she could do was to remove those ligatures which still remained and do her utmost to recall him to consciousness afterward.

Before very long she was pressing on him the contents of half a tumbler of champagne which she had taken from still another bottle which she had found below—this time a full one—and some biscuits which she had found in a tin.

He disposed of both with a ravenous appetite which it was not pleasant to see. It was some time before he was able to tell his disjointed story, then the chief part of it was prompted by her.

"So you took Mrs. Denyer for a drive on Friday, and she brought you here?" she began.

The man made an effort at recollection.

"Yes; of course," he replied, the words coming from him awkwardly. "I remember—she brought me—somewhere."

"And then you had a drink with her?"

"Yes, I did. She opened a bottle of champagne and—I had a drink with her."

"And after that?"

He repeated her words. "And after that—after that—I—I don't seem to remember—after that." As if a thought had suddenly struck him, he asked a question. "How long have I been here?"

"Well, this is Monday. If you came here on Friday afternoon, you've been here practically three whole days."

"Good Lord!" His jaw seemed to drop open; it was with an effort that he recovered himself. "You don't mean to say that I've been here in this house three whole days—tied up—alone?"

"It looks like it, doesn't it—if you came here on Friday?"

"It doesn't feel like three whole days."

"No—fortunately for you, it does not. I rather fancy that that champagne was like Mr. Sayers's cigar—drugged. It would seem that the drug they used is such a powerful one that it has kept you here unconscious for three whole days."

"But what can she have done such a thing for? She could have nothing against me."

"I doubt if she did do it, on her own initiative. I expect Mr. Sayers was somewhere about the house when she brought you here, although she said nothing about that little fact and you did not guess it. Indeed, I may say that I know he was."

"You know he was? Who are you? Aren't you the girl who spoke to me on the pier and then tore off when I asked you what your name was?"

"I am that girl, and my name is Judith Lee. Quite by accident I learned that you had taken a lady out for a spin in your motor on Friday, and had not been back to your hotel since.

"I happen to be acquainted with the establishment which Mr. Sayers patronizes when he wants a little refreshment in the morning; it's a most respectable one. I go there myself sometimes for a cup of coffee. I went there this morning.

"As luck had it, Mr. Sayers was standing in the entrance hall talking to Mr. Darlington as I went in. He was in a hurry—just leaving. All I could see him say was——"

"'*See* him say'?" interrupted Clarke. "That's the second time you have used that expression. I don't understand."

"All I could see him say," repeated Miss Lee, smiling tantalizingly but ignoring his interruption, "was: 'The place is called Bramborough; all I can tell you about the house is that there's a great sycamore tree in the front garden; that's all I know about it.'

"Then he went, and Mr. Darlington with him. It didn't seem much that he had said, but I turned it over in my mind when I was drinking my coffee. Bramborough? I knew where that was; just a nice, short motor run from Brighton. You had gone out on Friday without your chauffeur, as he understood, for an hour or two.

"Nothing since had been heard of you or your car or of the fluffy-haired lady. Suppose, I said to myself, I were to go down to

Bramborough—I've nothing to do—and look for the house with a sycamore tree. So I came."

Gilbert Clarke did not present a pleasant spectacle. He badly needed shaving; he would have been the better for washing; his hair was dishevelled; his attire was in disorder. But as he stared at the girl the thing which struck one most was the look of amazement which was on his face.

"You say you came as if it were just nothing at all; but if you hadn't come, what would have happened to me?"

"I wonder; it does seem to be fortunate that I came." She went to the open window. "There is some one passing down the road. I'm going to hail him. Hallo! Hallo!" She waved her handkerchief. "He sees me—he's coming. He's quite an intelligent-looking boy."

Through the open window she spoke to the boy, who was in the garden below.

"Where is the nearest doctor? About a mile. Where do you live? Just down the road; that's good. Who is there at home? Your mother and your sister; that's still better. Do you think if you were to tell them that there was a gentleman lying ill here, and very much in want of some one to do for him, they would come to him at once, especially if they know that he would pay them well? You think they would; then there's half a crown all for yourself. Now if you'll go and send your mother and sister and go and tell the doctor to come at once to a gentleman who is very ill, when you come back with the doctor I'll make that half-crown five shillings. Off you go as hard as ever you can." She brought her head back into the room. "He's gone; for a boy he seems quite sensible. I shouldn't wonder if we have all the help we want in a little while."

The help she desired came in the shape of a man of medicine. When the doctor saw the patient, instead of pronouncing him very ill, he declared him practically well. To judge from his manner, he had expected to find him trembling on the verge of the grave. His bearing conveyed the impression that, in his judgment, if Mr. Clarke suffered from anything it was from over-indulgence in alcoholic stimulant. When he heard what had happened to him he whistled—a lapse from the proper "bedside manner" for which he instantly apologized.

"I beg your pardon, but the fact is that not only is your case an extraordinary one—that such a thing should have taken place in broad daylight, under our very noses, and nobody know it—but the most extraordinary thing, from my point of view, is that I probably saw the miscreant leaving the premises and that I practically bade him Godspeed on his journey."

The doctor, who was a little, bustling, bald-headed man with an inclination to rotundity, seemed quite excited.

"On Friday afternoon I was coming back from a patient; I was alone in my car—it's a two-seater which I've had five years, and is a bit noisy—when I saw a motor-car, big grey one, standing outside the gate of this house."

"That was mine," said the man on the bed—he was still on the bed, though that was more for the sake of his being at his ease than anything else. "It's a forty Daimler."[1]

"Oh, a forty Daimler, is she? I thought it was a very nice car. Just as I was coming round the bend I saw a man coming out of the gate with a woman in his arms——"

"A woman *in his arms?*" exclaimed Miss Lee.

"Yes, in his arms; he was carrying her like a child. He put her into the car and propped her up into the corner. I stopped when I came along. 'I hope the lady's not unwell,' I said. 'She's a bit off colour, that's all,' said the man, not noticing me.

"'Can I be of any assistance?' I asked. 'I'm a medical man.' 'I do not know what even a medical man can do for a lady that's been drinking; that's the complaint she's suffering from.' He said this in what I thought was quite an unpleasant tone.

"I looked at the lady; she was breathing heavily, and her appearance was quite consistent with what he said. 'You don't mean that she's intoxicated?' 'She's drunk as a lord,' he snapped; and as he said this he got on to the driver's seat and off he went."

"What sort of man was he to look at?"

"The chief point about him that I carry in my mind is that he had a heavy red moustache."

"Mr. Sayers—what did I tell you?"

The girl looked at Gilbert Clarke, who remarked—

"Anyhow, it doesn't look as though Mrs. Denyer was quite the

---

[1] A powerful 40 h.p. Daimler car, in this period the chosen vehicle of many royal families; thus, a superior car.

person you thought; it almost looks as if she did not know what was the matter with that bottle of fizz any more than I did."

"Have you any reason to suppose," asked the doctor, "that the outrage to which you have been subjected was prompted by robbery—or by what?"

That one, at least, of the motives was robbery was very soon made clear. To begin with, Mr. Clarke had been stripped of everything of value he had on him.

"Can you think of anything which has been taken," asked Miss Lee, "besides your watch and chain and sovereign case and gold pencil-case and gold match-box and gold cigar-case and links and studs and diamond tie-pin? I suppose they were worth taking. It seems as if a man can carry a good deal of solid value about him, if he doesn't wear jewellery."

"I suppose my pocket-book's gone."

"Was there anything in it?"

"As it happens, there was a good deal. I drew two hundred pounds out of the bank when I left London, and that was in my pocket-book. There was a blank cheque besides. I always do carry a blank cheque in case anything should turn up and I should want one."

"A very sensible custom. Something has turned up; probably that blank cheque of yours has been found very useful."

Mr. Clarke looked as if he would have liked to say something to the young woman, but could not think what. She, however, proved to be correct. That blank cheque had been found useful; it had been filled up for five hundred pounds, presented by a dapper young gentleman about whose appearance there was nothing in the least suspicious, and paid across the counter.

The motor-car was recovered, which was more than Mr. Clarke's other belongings seemed ever likely to be. Late on Friday night a car had been discovered by a policeman in the lane only a short distance from Harrow[1] station. The lamps were not lighted; no one was in charge; there was nothing to show where it had come from or to whom it belonged.

The policeman waited and waited. When, after quite a long

---

[1] A suburban district eleven miles northwest of Central London.

period of waiting, no one appeared, he gave information at the station-house—and the car was locked up. The owner was ultimately discovered; it was Mr. Clarke's forty Daimler, though how it got to Harrow and who took it there, as the police put it, there was no evidence to show.

Gilbert Clarke went back to Brighton, where he made quite a stay. One morning he was again on the West Pier listening to the band, when, as on a previous occasion, a voice addressed him.

"Good morning, Mr. Clarke. I hope you're feeling better, and I hope you have had no more adventures." He turned with a start. It was Judith Lee.

"It's you again!" he cried. "Why, I'd sooner see you than get back my seven hundred pounds. I'd sooner see you almost than anything. You're looking awfully well. That's a ripping hat, if you'll forgive my saying so. What became of you that afternoon? I thought you were downstairs somewhere and were coming back with me to Brighton; then when it came to the scratch, no one could find you anywhere: you'd vanished."

"I had gone back to town. I am glad you like my hat."

"I do; it suits you splendidly—but never mind your hat."

"But I do mind my hat; it cost quite a lot of money for me. You don't think it's a little big?"

"Not a bit too big; though, of course, it's a pretty good size, isn't it? It suits you down to the ground."

"I'm so pleased that you think it suits me down to the ground—though I don't quite know what degree in superlative that is."

"I was thinking of putting an advertisement in the paper for you."

"Why?" She was looking at him with something like laughter in her big, bright eyes. "You're looking perfectly all right again."

"Oh, I'm as fit as a fiddler. Miss Lee, I owe you an awful lot. First, the warning about the cigar; then the tip about that woman; then your coming to the rescue in that beastly house. I don't know what would have become of me if you hadn't."

"I dare say somebody else would have found you sooner or later —before you were quite dead."

"I believe if I'd remained there, gagged and bound, when consciousness returned, for many hours, I should have gone mad. I felt as if I were going mad when you appeared. I feel that I owe you more than my life. The queerest part is that I know nothing about you. I haven't the faintest notion why you've done all these things for me."

"You see, I'm a teacher of the deaf and dumb—that's why."

"Are you—are you—chaffing me?"

"Not on this occasion. I am a teacher of the deaf and dumb—the lip-reading system—and that is why. In my time I've had to make this explanation to a good many people. If all persons were like me there'd be a good deal less conversation. They would not only be afraid of being overheard, they would be still more fearful of being seen. I only have to see people to know what they are saying."

Clarke stared at her in amazement, but found nothing to say.

"On the afternoon of the day I telephoned to you," went on Miss Lee, "I saw three men sitting in a café—one had a scar on his face, one had his hair parted in the middle, one had a big, red moustache. I was rather interested in what they were saying. It's queer when people are talking secrets and you know every word they're saying; it's a sort of sublimated eavesdropping.

"The man with the moustache took a cigar out of his pocket. 'That's for Mr. Gilbert Clarke,' he said; 'that'll do his business!'

"'What time are you going?' the man with the scar asked.

"'He said, come after dinner, about nine.'

"'He didn't ask us to dinner?'

"'No, I noticed he didn't ask us to dinner. He said to come after dinner, about nine, and have a little poker.'

"The man with the moustache held the cigar out again. 'That'll give him all the poker he wants,' he growled. Then he put it very carefully in a case, which he placed in his pocket.

"Directly they had gone I asked for a directory, and I looked up Gilbert Clarke. I found that Clarke was spelled in half a dozen different ways, but that there was only one Gilbert Clarke, and he spelled his name C-l-a-r-k-e. He had a flat in Whitehall Court,[1] and he had a telephone. I got on to that telephone, and I sent you that message. I thought it possible it might reach you about the time that cigar was making its appearance."

"It did. I've had that cigar analysed since. It was loaded with some

[1] A street in Central London, near the river, between the Embankment and Westminster.

horrible drug, which would have had the effect of making me seem dead drunk. A few whiffs would have been enough, and while I was in that condition they would have been able to do with me what they liked—make me sign anything. It seems that not long ago a young fellow in Paris was made to sign cheques for large amounts under precisely similar circumstances, which were cashed before he knew anything about them. I have a large balance at my bankers; but they might have cleared me out."

"I'm glad they didn't. It's one of the pleasures of living to be able to do one's fellow-creatures little services."

"Do you call what you've done me 'a little service'? Could anyone have done me a greater? If you only knew how I feel about it—if I could only tell you."

"Don't bother to try; let's talk about the weather."

"I hope, Miss Lee, you'll lunch with me?"

"Thank you, Mr. Clarke; I'm afraid not. Frankly, one of the reasons why I hesitate to render people—little services is the fear of that."

"The fear of what?"

"The next man to whom I may render a little service may be that person down there with a big, black beard, his hands in his pockets, his hat on the back of his head, and his pipe in his mouth. It doesn't follow because, in pursuit of my hobby, I may render him a little service that I should want to carry it further, does it?" Her smile robbed the words of much of their sting.

"I think I understand," replied Clarke, flushing a little. "Then you are to place me under heavy obligations and I am not to be allowed to show that I am even conscious of what you've done. Is that quite fair?"

"You're a young man, Mr. Clarke, younger than you think," returned Miss Lee quietly. "I believe you are rich. You'll find all sorts of people who will be ready to take advantage of your youth and—I won't say innocence, because you might think I was insulting you —I'll say money. If you wish to show your consciousness of what I have done for you, consider one or two copy-book maxims: 'Be careful what acquaintances you make'; 'Don't ask people of whom you know nothing to your private apartments'; 'Don't play cards with strangers for money.'"

There was a brief period during which neither spoke. He seemed to be digesting her words, and to be finding the process not a very pleasant one.

"I fancy your three friends have deserted their usual trysting-place," she said at last, and there was a subtle change in her tone. "I have seen nothing of them since that Monday. Have you any news from the police?"

"The police!" He uttered the words as if he scorned what they stood for. "I don't expect to have any news from them. They seem to think that I dreamed the whole thing, and that, if I didn't, it served me right."

"It's certainly very wrong of them to think that."

He glanced sharply at her; on her face was an expression of perfect gravity. He was not sure even that there was a twinkle in her eye.

"I don't care what the police think. What I want is to find myself face to face with Mr. Clifford Sayers, just we two alone, and I shall one day; those things come by waiting. When I do, I'll hand over what is left of him to the police. This is a personal matter between him and me. At present he's one ahead; some day, I hope very soon, that he'll be one, or more, behind."

It was her turn to glance at him. There was a grim look on his face. She thought it suited him; she felt that in a hand-to-hand encounter with his enemy this young gentleman might be at his very best.

"You believe in the old-fashioned methods—redressing your own wrongs: an eye for an eye, and that sort of thing?"

"Exactly, that sort of thing. You'll laugh at me, but I never feel so much at home as in the thick of a row; it's on the way to it that I make an ass of myself."

"If that is the case, suppose—she glanced at him again —"suppose I were to put you in the way of having a little private conversation with Mr. Clifford Sayers—what then?"

"What then? I should say, thank you, and please make it as soon as you can."

"I rather fancy I saw Mr. Clifford Sayers strolling along the King's Road[1] a little while ago; he must be a courageous man."

---

[1] The road running along the seafront in Brighton.

"He must be. Would you mind strolling with me along the King's Road, the way he went?"

They went off the pier together. When they had gone a little way she stopped.

"If you really would like to have a little conversation with Mr. Sayers, I think you're rather fortunate. Isn't that he talking to a friend?"

A short distance from where they paused, the gentleman in question was waving a friendly adieu to an elegant young man.

"I do seem lucky," observed Mr. Clarke. "I hope he'll be pleased to see me. I fear it may be some time before that smart young man with the pink socks will see him again."

The allusion was to the hose worn by the elegant young man who had just parted from Mr. Sayers. Mr. Sayers was walking toward Kemp Town,[1] in happy obliviousness of the couple in the rear who were making it their business to keep him in sight. He bent his steps toward an hotel which looked out on to Castle Square,[2] and passed through the door in blissful ignorance that they had entered immediately after. He was going up the staircase as they went in.

"I wish to speak to that gentleman," said Mr. Clarke to the youth who was acting as hall-porter. "I'll go up to his room." He turned to Miss Lee. "Do you mind coming with me?"

The pair went up the staircase, the youth looking after them as if in doubt whether or not he ought to let them go. When they reached the passage on the first floor they saw Mr. Sayers opening the door of a room which was about half-way down it. He still had his back to them when Clarke spurted. Mr. Sayers had opened the door of the room, but by the time he had realized who was coming his recent victim was already on him, and he was assisted into the room with a swiftness which possibly surprised him.

"What the devil is the meaning of this?" he spluttered.

Mr. Clarke was standing at the still open door.

"Come in, Miss Lee, come in. I should like you to hear me say a word or two to Mr. Sayers, which won't require me to detain you more than a few moments. This appears to be only a bedroom, but perhaps you won't mind that."

[1] A district of Brighton to the east of the Piers.
[2] A location in Central Brighton.

Miss Lee did not seem to mind in the least. She came in, closed the door, and stood with her back against it. Mr. Sayers stood staring at his visitors with an expression on his face which suggested that he was very far from pleased to see them.

"What do you mean by forcing your way into a gentleman's room like this?" he demanded furiously.

"I am going to have a little conversation with you, Mr. Sayers," replied Clarke coolly; "and I hope you will enjoy it as much as I feel sure I shall. You tried to drug me with a cigar; and when you failed you tried something else. Had the cigar succeeded, you would certainly have robbed me; when the other way came off as you desired, you robbed me on that occasion instead.

"You took from me my watch and chain, various trifles which I had about me, two hundred pounds in cash, and you got another five hundred for another cheque, which you first stole, then forged, and then presented. Those various items, added together, represent quite a formidable sum, Mr. Sayers. For that amount you are in my debt; but when we have finished our little conversation I will give you a receipt for it in full."

The man had turned quite an uncomfortable colour; he showed white under his freckled skin. He seemed all at once to be short of breath.

"Don't you play any of your monkey tricks with me," he stammered.

"Not at all. I'm not going to play any tricks, Mr. Sayers; I'm merely going to teach you a little lesson."

The man made a dash in the direction of the bell, but Clarke caught him by the shoulder with a grip which made him wince.

"If you should succeed in ringing the bell, Mr. Sayers," he said quietly, "I should hand you over to the police, with the result that you would probably get a long term of penal servitude. I don't want to have the police interfering in a little matter like this; when I'm through with you, I assure you, you'll run no risk of penal servitude from me."

He turned to the girl. "I am obliged to you, Miss Lee, for favouring me with your attention while I explained matters to Mr. Sayers; now I think I need detain you no longer."

Miss Lee smiled and went out. As she went, the door was shut behind her, and she heard the key turned on the other side. The look which was on Mr. Sayers' face as Gilbert Clarke, gripping him by the shoulder, explained his intentions, haunted her as she moved along the passage.

Two or three days afterward she was entering a Piccadilly restaurant when she noticed two men standing in the hall. One of them, a man of unusual height, had a scar on his cheek. She saw him say to the other—

"So our dear old friend has had trouble."

"He's in the hospital," the other replied, with a smile which hardly suggested mirth, "if you call that trouble."

"It depends rather on the circumstances which have taken him there, doesn't it?"

"Mr. Gilbert Clarke stood for the circumstances in this case. I understand that he, as nearly as possible, broke every bone in his body, and that he won't be able to move for at least a month. A motor-omnibus could hardly have hurt him more."

"And I will tell you something else: from what I am told, if you were to meet that nice young man, I shouldn't wonder if you found him one of the toughest propositions you ever tackled. He may be a simpleton, but he's built on a steel frame, and he can use it."

The speaker made a little movement with his fists which was full of meaning.

"I have not the slightest wish to meet him, I assure you," the tall man replied; "not the very least. I've had enough of this effete old country, and between ourselves, the day after to-morrow I'm going to leave it for quite a while."

"I'm thinking of leaving it also," the other gentleman returned.

As she went in to lunch Miss Lee was smiling. She had heard from another source quite a spirited account of that conversation with Mr. Clifford Sayers. As she was choosing a table she was saying to herself—

"How strange it must feel to be a young man!"

THE BARNES MYSTERY

The Barnes Mystery was the topic of the day. It had the place of honour in all the papers. Mrs. Netherby was a widow lady who occupied, with a maidservant, a small detached house in the Shelbourne Road, Barnes,[1] called Oak Villa. She and the maid, whose name was Mary Freeman, were the only persons in the house. The maid was ailing. On the morning of Friday, March 22nd, the medical man in attendance, Dr. Anson, diagnosed her case as one of typhoid fever. The usual notices were at once sent to the authorities, and on the afternoon of that day she was taken away to the hospital. Her mistress, Mrs. Netherby, was left alone in the house. From the moment in which the ambulance took Mary Freeman away, no one ever again saw Mrs. Netherby alive.

On Saturday morning Dr. Anson called in the ordinary round of his practice to inquire how the old lady was getting on. The blinds were all down, the house seemed empty. He knocked and he rang, but, receiving no answer, he went away. He took it for granted that Mrs. Netherby had left the house to itself and gone to stay with her friends or relatives. Various tradesmen called in the usual way, but, no notice being taken of their presence, they departed again. So far as was known, no one else came to the house till the Tuesday following, March 26th. On the evening of that day her married daughter, Mrs. Penton, came with her husband, George Penton, to call on her mother.

The Pentons lived at Putney.[2] They had been away for the weekend to Westcliff-on-Sea.[3] From there Mrs. Penton had written to her mother, asking her to spend the evening with them on the following Tuesday. She received no answer at Westcliff; on her return home on Tuesday morning she found none awaiting her. When in

[1] The street appears to be imaginary, but Barnes is a wealthy riverside suburb in West London.
[2] A suburb in West London, approximately two miles east of Barnes.
[3] A seaside resort near Southend, some 34 miles east of London on the north of the Thames Estuary.

the evening she did not appear, she went over to Barnes with her husband to learn why it was her mother had taken no notice whatever of her letter.

It was about seven o'clock when the Pentons reached Oak Villa. When they entered the gate a light showed through the blind of the front room on the upper floor.

"Why," exclaimed Mrs. Penton, "there's only a light in mother's bedroom. Whatever is the matter?"

It was Mrs. Netherby's habit after nightfall to have a light in every room as well as in the hall. She would smilingly say that she liked lights for company. Mrs. Penton had a peculiar knock, which she used as a sort of signal to let her mother know that it was she who was there. Mr. Penton, who was standing at the foot of the steps, noticed that the moment she knocked the light in the upper room vanished.

"What's the matter with Mary?" asked Mrs. Penton. "She's generally so quick."

"The light in your mother's room has gone out," her husband said. "Perhaps she's coming down."

"She's pretty long about it." Mrs. Penton knocked again. Again there was no sign that she had been heard. She broke into nervous speech: "George, there's something wrong; I feel sure there's something wrong. Whatever can be the matter?"

They became alarmed. They went round the house to the kitchen at the back. It was in darkness; the back of the house was as dark as the front.

They were aware that Mrs. Netherby had all her windows secured with patent fasteners. It would not be easy to gain access to the house without resorting to actual violence.

"Whatever shall we do?" In the darkness and the cold Mrs. Penton drew closer to her husband's side, as if in the atmosphere of mystery which surrounded the shrouded house she felt that there was something uncanny.

"George, what's that? It sounded like——"

He cut her short. "It sounded like someone opening and shutting the front door."

"George!" He was rushing off; she clung to his arm. "Don't leave me! George, don't leave me!"

"Then for goodness' sake come too; only be quick about it. I'm going to see who came out of the front door."

"George!" She clung to his arm with a grip which he all at once recognized was hysterical. He did his best to calm her; by the time he succeeded it was too late. No one knew who it was who opened and shut the front door and went out of the gate. Had Mrs. Penton permitted her husband to do as he wished—to rush off to see—the mystery might have ceased to be a mystery that very first night.

In the adjacent house there was a family of four, a Mr. and Mrs. Thomas and their grown-up son and daughter. Mr. Thomas was a solicitor. He suggested that they should send to the police-station for some person in authority, and then take his advice about breaking into the house. In due course a sergeant appeared on the scene

" THE SERGEANT, MRS. PENTON, AND MR. THOMAS AND HIS SON ENTERED THE HOUSE."

with two constables. In his presence a pane was taken out of the kitchen window at the back. George Penton slipped through; then opened the back door.

The sergeant, Mrs. Penton, and Mr. Thomas and his son entered the house. The party went all over the house, lighting the gas in each room as they came to it, but found nothing. It was empty.

There was only one thing in the whole house which struck the searchers as peculiar. On the strip of carpet which ran along one side of Mrs. Netherby's bed there was a damp patch—not only damp, but actually wet, as though someone had quite recently spilt something on it. The Pentons had seen the light shining through the blind of that apartment. Someone had been in there when they knocked at the door and left that patch of wet. Who was it?

The strip of carpet was submitted to an analyst, who reported that there was nothing unusual about the carpet at all—for instance, that there was no trace of blood.

The problem presented was—what had become of Mrs. Netherby? She seemed to have vanished off the face of the earth. One or two facts made the problem more acute. On the Friday the maid had been taken to the hospital the old lady had been left in the house alone. On the Monday morning no fewer than twenty-three cheques bearing her signature had been presented in different quarters and cashed—not one of them at her bankers'. They had been drawn up for various amounts and changed by tradesmen with whom she had been more or less in the habit of dealing. She was a well-to-do old lady, and her credit was good in many quarters. Someone must have had an intimate knowledge of what those quarters were. In each instance the process had been the same. A woman had entered the shop, had announced that she had come from Mrs. Netherby, of Oak Villa, Barnes, had ordered goods which she paid for on the spot with a cheque which was always much larger than the bill, and had gone off with the change. In each case the woman had informed them in the shop that Mrs. Netherby had gone away for a little change, and the goods were to be sent to her at the address she gave, which was in each case a different address, but always at an hotel. It was afterwards found that the goods were at the hotels awaiting the arrival of the person to whom they had been addressed.

That was peculiarity number one. The aggregate of the twenty-three cheques reached a considerable amount—within a few pounds of the sum which was standing to Mrs. Netherby's credit at the bank. Apparently someone, knowing how much she had there, did not wish to cause friction by overdrawing.

A third significant fact came to light. On the Monday morning, being the third day after Mary Freeman had been taken away in the ambulance, a woman called at the offices of a safe deposit company, having with her what purported to be a letter from Mrs. Netherby, in which she stated that she was in bad health and unable to leave home, and requesting them to give the bearer access to her safe. The bearer had Mrs. Netherby's own pass-key; she gave her name as Mary Freeman. They permitted her to have access to the safe. When authority stepped in and the safe was examined, it was found to be empty; whatever it had contained "Mary Freeman" had taken away.

Many of the Press comments were by no means relished at Scotland Yard, as was shown by a conversation which took place one evening in a room of that national centre for the suppression of crime and the discovery of criminals.

"Well, Davis, have you seen the special *Evening Screecher*?"

Inspector Davis, to whom the question was addressed, made a sound which was scarcely suggestive of pleasure.

"I have seen the thing. It's easy enough for those newspaper fellows to talk and write. It's another thing to have to make bricks without straw."

"Which means, I suppose, that you've still no news of Mrs. Netherby, or of anything? The 'Barnes Mystery,' as the *Screecher* puts it, is still a mystery, and likely to remain so."

"I can only tell you, Mr. Ellis, that I've done everything which, while English law remains what it is, it is possible for a man to do. Any suggestion——"

"One moment; let me see who that is." The bell of the telephone which was on the table at which Mr. Ellis was seated was calling. He took up the receiver.

"Yes?"

A voice came to him. "What place is that?"

"This is Scotland Yard."

"Who are you?"

"I'm Stephen Ellis. Who's speaking?"

The question was ignored. "Do you want to solve the Barnes Mystery?"

Mr. Ellis returned question for question. "Who are you?"

The answer came. "If you want to solve the Barnes Mystery, be at the Regent Circus[1] entrance to the Café Poncini in half an hour. Wear some primroses with some violets in the centre in your buttonhole. Bring two or three plain-clothes men—not with you, and don't be seen talking to them, but let them be handy. You understand?"

The voice ceased. When Mr. Ellis spoke again he received no answer, although he tried three or four times.

"I wonder," he said, as he hung up the receiver, "if someone's playing another fool's trick?" He reported to the inspector the brief conversation he had had with someone unknown. "I'm going to the Cafe Poncini; I'll go myself. You'd better be there too, Davis, and have two or three men within call. I dare say someone is having another joke with us; but things are getting to a point at which I'm going to throw no chances away."

Half an hour later Stephen Ellis entered the hall of the Café Poncini. The moment he did so—before he had even time to glance about him—someone came up to him. "Good evening, Mr. Ellis. You're well on time."

The speaker was a woman, scarcely more than a girl; at the first glance she struck Mr. Ellis as distinctly pretty.

"Was it you who telephoned?"

"Come inside and have some coffee. We shall be able to do all the talking that's necessary better in there." She led the way into the *café*, with its long rows of marble-topped tables.

On one side of each row of tables a long settee runs from end to end of the Café Poncini, covered in red velvet. The woman selected a lounge; at her invitation Mr. Ellis seated himself beside her.

"Order some coffee; we can take our time over drinking it."

The coffee was ordered. While it was coming Ellis eyed his companion, she submitting to his keen scrutiny with what struck him

[1] The intersection of Regent Street and Oxford Street in the West End (now Oxford Circus).

as almost laughing indifference. She was pretty, distinctly, but her most prominent characteristic was vitality.

"Who are you?" he asked, when the coffee came, "and what have you brought me here for?"

"I'm a thought-reader," she replied.

"Then, if you can read my thoughts, I wonder what you think of them?"

"I don't care about your thoughts. I look at people's faces. I not only know what they are thinking, without hearing—I know what they are saying. Look at those two young men at the end table: the one with the moustache is telling the other about a girl who sat beside him on the seat of the omnibus on which he came from Walham Green.[1] He is saying that she gave him her address; he is reading it from the piece of paper which he has taken from his pocket; he is saying 'Ruth Dennis, 21, Barkham Road, Parson's Green[2]—see, that's the address she gave me. I wrote it down, so that there might be no mistake. I shouldn't be surprised if one of these days before long I looked her up'—I've reported the words exactly as he uttered them; if you doubt the accuracy of my report, if you'll go and ask him you'll find that you've done me an injustice. Here's our man—the one who just came in at the door, with the clean-shaven face. He's going to sit at that empty table on the left opposite us. He's given himself into our hands; at that distance a man with a clean-shaven face can hide nothing from me."

"Is this a trick you're trying to play on me, counting on the proverbial stupidity of the police? Who is this man? And, by the way, what's your name?"

"Never mind my name. I don't know our man's name, but he is our man, as you'll find. Presently he will be joined by a companion."

Even as she spoke someone entering stood for a moment to look about him. Seeing the man alone at the table, he hastened to him. The new-comer was a short, sturdily-built young man, with a square jaw.

"Bother him!" exclaimed the woman at Mr. Ellis's side. "He's

---

[1] A lower-middle-class residential district in West London.
[2] The street appears to be imaginary, but Parson's Green is the district immediately to the north of Walham Green.

placed himself with his back to us. I sha'n't be able to tell you what he says, but I dare say we shall get enough from the other."

The new-comer had placed himself on a chair fronting the first arrival. Apparently they exchanged no greetings, but plunged at once into subdued conversation.

"You drink your coffee," said the woman to Mr. Ellis. "Don't look their way. I'll do all the watching that's needed; they won't suspect me." There was a momentary interval. "He says he's got it."

"Got what?"

"You'll see for yourself before long—he's got what will hang them."

"Let me give you a word of advice, young lady. Don't push your jest too far; what do you take me for?"

To judge from his tone Mr. Ellis was getting angry.

"If you think I'm having a jest with you, you can always go. The best thing you can do is to keep still." After an interval she asked, "Did you bring those men with you?"

"I did. You yourself are likely to find their presence awkward if you push your jest too far."

"Don't be silly. Fetch one of them in here. Tell him to keep an eye on the man who came in first and, when he goes, to follow him. He's not to lose him, and he's to report to you his whereabouts. The other one is going presently; you and I will have to follow him. Send in your man—quick!"

The man who had entered last had risen from his seat. Something in the woman's manner influenced Mr. Ellis in a fashion which rather surprised himself. He rose also. The woman whispered:—

"He says he's going to the Empire.[1] We shall first have to follow him there. Wait for me outside."

Ellis went; something in her manner seemed to compel him. As she was settling with the waiter for the coffee, Inspector Davis came sauntering in. The square-faced man went out; the woman followed. She found Ellis without. The square-faced man was moving along Coventry Street, towards Leicester Square.

[1] An upmarket variety theatre, the Empire in Leicester Square had been attacked in 1894 by anti-vice campaigners as a haunt of prostitutes, forcing it to close for a short period.

"How do you know he's going to the Empire?" asked Ellis, as he walked by the woman's side.

"I saw him say so."

"I don't know what you mean when you say you saw him say a thing when you couldn't hear a word."

"IN THE LOUNGE THEY SAW THEIR QUARRY TALKING TO A WOMAN."

"These things may be unfolded to you later. In the meantime, you see he is going to the Empire, so thus far I'm right." The man turned into the entrance of the Empire Theatre. "We'd better go in after him. I don't fancy he will stay long; he's after other game to-night."

In the lounge they saw their quarry talking to a woman. It was easy for them to stand and watch.

"He's just said to her," observed Mr. Ellis's companion, "that he's very sorry that business has turned up which it is impossible for him to neglect. Now he's going. The question is—is it easier to follow a man in a taxi or a hansom?"

"In a taxi," replied Ellis.

He was becoming interested in this young woman, almost in spite of himself. He had no doubt that she was playing a trick on him of some sort. He was beginning to wonder what was the point of it, what was her object, how far she was going. Presently the square-faced man had gone off in a taxi, closed. Had it not been closed he might have become conscious that close behind him kept another taxi, whose top was open. After they had gone some little distance the woman in the second taxi said to Mr. Ellis:—

"Is there a big hospital near?"

"There's the Surrey Hospital just ahead of us."

"Can you pick up a constable or two as we go along? They may be wanted later."

The taxi in front turned into a side street. The second driver spoke to his passengers.

"The chap in front has pulled up—had I better wait and see what's going to happen?"

It was the woman who answered.

"Wait till I give you the word." She spoke to her companion. "We may have a minute or two to wait—now's your time to pick up your constables; they may come in handy very soon. There are a couple at the corner over the road."

Getting out of the cab and going to where a couple of policemen were standing on the other side of the street, he returned with them.

The policemen, acting on Mr. Ellis's instructions, managed to squat themselves on the bottom of the vehicle, holding their helmets in their hands. Hardly were they in their places when the driver said:—

"That chap's going off. What I know of this street, there's only one turning out of it, and that brings you back into the Southwark Road. If we go quietly on he'll come to us.

The man proved to be right. Soon a taxi came out of a turning a little way down the road, which the driver of the second cab declared to be the one they were chasing. The chase continued.

"I wonder if he's got it?" said the woman to Mr. Ellis, in tones which were only intended to reach his ears.

"Got what?"

"What will hang him."

Mr. Ellis's tone was irascible. "If you could only manage to be a little more explicit, and not deal so much in mysteries!"

They went on perhaps the better part of another mile. Then the second taxi slowed. The driver said to them:—

"That other chap's stopping at the hospital; his passenger is getting out."

The woman said to the driver: "Take us up to the door—and stop there." Then to Mr. Ellis: "We shall have to follow him into the hospital; you must make it clear to the porter that we must see him at once, before he's had a chance of getting rid of what he's got."

They got out of the taxi at the door of a great grey building. In the hall a uniformed porter advanced to meet them. Mr. Ellis addressed him in tones of authority.

"I want you to take me immediately to the gentleman who has just come in."

The porter hesitated. "What's your name and business? He may be engaged and not wish to be disturbed."

"I'm an officer of police from Scotland Yard. Your business is to take me to him at once without an instant's delay."

Still the porter dallied. "I believe he's gone to the dissecting-room."

"Where is the dissecting-room? Take us there at once."

The porter led the way and the others followed; the woman and Mr. Ellis in front, the two policemen behind. The porter paused outside a door.

"This is the dissecting-room."

"Stop!" said the woman. Then, to Mr. Ellis: "Let the two police-men stay outside until you call them in. Now open the door."

The porter did as he was told. Ellis and the woman went into the room. Only one person was in the room, the man they had been fol-lowing. He was standing by one of the tables, busy with something which he had taken out of a small, square parcel.

"Halloa!" he exclaimed, as he heard the door open behind him. "Who's that?"

The woman strode forward, Ellis at her side.

"You see!" she exclaimed, pointing to the ghastly object which the man was holding as nonchalantly as if it were some unconsidered trifle.

"'WHAT NONSENSE IS THIS?' CRIED DR. LINTOTT."

"Who the deuce are you?" he demanded. He turned to the porter. "Simpson, what do you mean by letting these people in here?"

"That," said the woman, "is Mrs. Netherby's head. I rather fancy it is all that is left of her."

The man stared at the woman. Something seemed to pass from her eyes to his. He changed countenance, looking all at once like another man—like one who was suddenly afraid. Words came from him.

"Who told you—Anson?"

"Anson! That's the name I couldn't catch," the woman cried. "What an idiot I am! I might have guessed—that's the name of the man who was in attendance on her at Barnes. Take this man, and then off for Dr. Anson—quick! He's the man you're wanting most. This gentleman will hardly deny that what he's holding is the head of the late Mrs. Netherby, of Barnes."

"What's your name?" asked Ellis.

"I'm Dr. Lintott. I'm one of the house-surgeons. What's the meaning of this intrusion? Who are you, sir?"

"I'm an officer of police, and I arrest you for being concerned in the murder of Mrs. Netherby, of Barnes." He called the two policemen into the room. "Take your prisoner."

"What nonsense is this?" cried Dr. Lintott.

"You need not answer my question; you need say nothing. You heard what this lady said. Is that Mrs. Netherby's head which you have in your hand?"

"How am I to know whose head it is? It's a subject which I brought here for dissection in the ordinary course. I'm going to give a demonstration on it to-morrow."

"I tell you it is the head of the late Mrs. Netherby, to his knowledge, and for that statement I accept full responsibility. Don't chop phrases with him—something tells me that if we are not quick we shall be too late for Dr. Anson."

In spite of his protests Dr. Lintott was handcuffed, and was presently borne off, a prisoner, in the same taxi-cab which had brought him, with the two policemen as companions. That dreadful human relic went with them in the cab.

Mr. Ellis dashed across London, the woman at his side, in the second taxi. It is a long way from the Surrey Hospital to Barnes.[1] Mr. Ellis plied his companion with questions to which he received no answers.

"What you have to do," she told him, "is to solve the Barnes Mystery. Before you go to sleep to-night you'll have done it. My

---

[1] It is approximately nine miles from Southwark to Barnes.

part in the business doesn't matter. I'll give you all the explanations you're entitled to—when we have finished. Something tells me, as if it were something in my bones, that the chief criminal is slipping away from us, even while we're rushing to him."

The cab stopped. Someone who was standing on the pavement came towards them. Ellis spoke:—

"Who's this? Why, Davis, is that you?"

"The man you told me to shadow was Dr. Anson."

"You traced Dr. Anson home?" asked the woman.

"I did. He came by train to Barnes Station, then walked."

"Do you think he knew that he was being followed?"

"I think he may have had his doubts. He stopped twice and looked round."

"And saw you?"

"That I cannot say."

"But you think it possible?" The inspector was silent. "I see; that explains my premonition."

Leaving the taxi where it was, the three approached the house on foot. The inspector remained at the gate, while the others went to the front door, which was almost instantly opened by a trim maid.

"Can I see Dr. Anson?" asked Ellis. The maid invited them in; she said she would see. "Where is he?" She pointed to a door at the other end of the little hall. "I will announce myself." Mr. Ellis moved to the door to which she had pointed. He turned the handle. "This door is locked." He tapped at the panel; no answer. Again, very loudly; no reply. He thumped it with the palm of his open hand. "Inside there! Dr. Anson!" Still silence. He turned to the maid. "You are sure Dr. Anson is in this room?"

"Dr. Anson went in there; I saw him go. I haven't heard him come out."

"You'll have to force the door," said the woman.

Ellis struck it a violent blow with his shoulder. It showed no signs of yielding. He went to the hall door and called out.

"Davis!" The inspector came across the garden. "The servant says Dr. Anson is in his study. The door is locked, and I can't get him to pay any attention to my knocking—I'm going to force it open."

"Let me see the door," said Davis. "There are very few rooms in modern houses which I can't open."

He was a big, heavy man, nearly six feet high. He wrapped a great handkerchief round his knuckles, then drove his right fist with all his might against the panel of the door. It went through it as if the panel had been made of paper. He glanced through the aperture which he had made.

"He's in there, on a chair at the table; but there's something wrong."

He enlarged the aperture by striking the panel a second time; then, putting his arm through, got down to the key, which was in the lock, turned it, and the door was open. They all went in; then they saw that, as Davis had said, there was something wrong. Dr. Anson was leaning back in his elbow-chair in a quite natural attitude, but he was dead. The inspector touched his skin.

"I'M A TEACHER OF THE DEAF AND DUMB—THAT IS THE EXPLANATION."

"He is quite warm; he can only have been dead a few minutes."

Ellis stooped to the dead man's mouth.

"It's cyanide; he probably took it when he heard me knocking. Death was no doubt instantaneous."

"As I said, he knew that he was followed, and he understood. He probably recognized your knock as the knell of doom. I think that my presence is no longer needed."

This was the woman. She turned as if to go. Davis interposed.

"Excuse me, but your presence is needed more than ever. There's a great deal that will have to be explained."

"That is easily done—probably in less than five minutes."

She looked at Ellis. Even in the grim presence of Death one could see that there was a twinkle in her eyes.

"I'm a teacher of the deaf and dumb—that is the explanation."

Ellis looked puzzled. "But, pardon me, I don't see that that explains anything."

"On the contrary, it explains everything. I teach lip reading; that is, I teach deaf and dumb people to speak and to understand other people speak by observing, and imitating, the motions which the lips make in pronouncing words. I'm an expert teacher. My father and mother are teachers. Wherever I am I have only to look about me at people's faces, and if they are talking I can tell you what they are saying."

"Is that really a fact?"

"I've given you one very good proof to-night. Last night I was in the Café Poncini. Two men were seated in front of me—one was this man, the other was Dr. Lintott. It was rather late. I fancy Dr. Lintott had been dining pretty well. It was the fact that he seemed to have drunk quite enough which caused me first of all to notice him. They had evidently both of them something to do with medicine, probably doctors. They were talking about subjects for dissection—the difficulty of obtaining them. Suddenly Dr. Lintott said something which struck me: 'I suppose we've nearly finished with your old woman of Barnes?' The other man said nothing. Dr. Lintott went on, ticking his words off on his fingers. 'She's been an educational force to all the hospitals in London. The way in which, without rousing the slightest suspicion, I've helped you to be rid of Mrs.——' The other man cut him short. 'I wish you wouldn't talk like that,' I saw him say. 'I won't,' said Dr. Lintott; 'but as an educational force you certainly must allow me to drink to Mrs. N. I saw him say 'Mrs. N.' most distinctly. I almost jumped as he said it. He had already spoken of the 'old woman of Barnes,' and I at once thought of Mrs. Netherby; there was an evening paper in front of me, in which the chief topic was the Barnes Mystery."

"How far," asked Ellis, "were these two men from you?"

"They were two tables farther down on the other side. I had a perfect view of their faces."

"It's a very uncanny power which you seem to have."

"It's not uncanny at all. But to continue about last night. I saw Dr. Lintott say, 'Now, tell me, have you got rid of the whole of her?' The other man hesitated. Then he said, 'There remains the head.' They whispered together for some moments. At last Lintott got up. I could see him say, 'Then to-morrow night, some convenient place?' 'Quite—where you can get it on your road back.' Then Lintott went away; then the other went; and last of all I went."

The woman held out her hands with a little, quaint gesture.

"The more I thought of it, the more convinced I became that the 'old woman of Barnes,' 'Mrs. N.,' was Mrs. Netherby, of Oak Villa, and that I held in my hand the key of what all the world was beginning to regard as an insoluble puzzle. That these two men were criminals, to my mind, was clear; but how was I to make it clear to the official mind? I hesitated, and at the last moment I telephoned. You are now in a position, I think, in which the Barnes Mystery is likely to continue a mystery no longer."

"There's one detail you have still omitted—your name."

"My name is Judith Lee."

"Still one moment." Mr. Ellis checked her as again she turned to go. "There seems to be something here which you may find of interest."

The dead man sat at his writing-table. In front of him was a large blotting-pad. On it were sheets of paper closely covered with writing. Over these was a half-sheet on which were a few lines. Mr. Ellis read aloud from the half-sheet:—

"'Three men got into my train at Waterloo. I had my suspicions directly I saw them. They got out with me at Barnes; they were the only persons who did. They did their best to conceal the fact, but I was aware that they followed me from the station home. I feel that in the pocket of each one is a pair of handcuffs. I understand. Every second I expect a knocking at the front door; when it comes, I go. I shall have gone before they get from the front door to this room. The MS. on which I am going to lay this half-sheet of paper contains notes which may save a certain amount of trouble.' He must have written that, Davis, while you were waiting for me in the road outside." Mr. Ellis took up the sheets of paper, which were covered with writing. "I presume these are the notes to which he refers."

They were. They are at present in the archives of Scotland Yard, forming as singular a document as is to be found in the annals of criminal literature.

From these notes it appeared that Dr. Anson, whose expenses far exceeded his professional income, was hard pressed for ready cash. A friend named Lintott, who was one of the house-surgeons at the Surrey Hospital, was in similar straits. They were boon companions; birds of a feather. One evening they had been discussing their common necessities. Lintott asked Anson if he had no patient of whom he could dispose, and by whose disposal they could replenish their exhausted coffers. The question was jokingly asked. Anson took it in earnest. His thoughts flew to Mrs. Netherby. She seemed to be very much alone in the world, and to be possessed of sufficient means. He might get a clearer idea of her exact pecuniary position in the course of a day or two.

According to Anson's own statement, the two men talked Mrs. Netherby over together as if she had been a lay figure who might turn out to be worth to them a considerable sum of money. It would be easy to kill her; the difficulty would be in the disposal of the remains. Lintott said that there need be no difficulty about that. If a reasonable amount of time might be reckoned on, she could be dismembered at her own house, and the different parts of her body could be distributed among the various London hospitals for the purposes of dissection.

On Friday, March 22nd, it became clear that the servant-girl had typhoid. Anson communicated with the authorities, and on the Friday afternoon she was taken away. He was present in the house at the time, remaining after she had been removed. He stated in his confession that it was only after she had been removed and he was left alone in the house with the old lady that it occurred to him what a magnificent opportunity it would be to put into practice what he and Lintott had talked about a few evenings before. He declared that the temptation came to him in a form which he found it impossible to resist. Ten minutes after the maid had been taken away her mistress was dead; he had killed her. He then overhauled her papers, to find that she had a satisfactory balance at her bank, and documents of considerable value in the vault of a safe deposit company. He put the body of the old lady under a bed which was shrouded by a valance which reached the floor, put her papers in his pocket, and went his round. The next morning he called, and, in the presence of his coachman, he knocked and rang, without any notice being taken. He said to his coachman that he supposed the old lady had left the house and gone to stay with friends.

He telegraphed to Lintott, who that night came to see him. He told him what he had done. When Lintott heard what a large sum she had left at her bank he seems to have acquiesced without remonstrance.

Dr. Lintott was an amateur actor. He had acted female parts in musical comedies with striking success. According to Anson he made almost a perfect girl. He was also an expert penman. He forged cheques for the lady's entire balance and, garbed as a woman, presented them at her various tradesmen's shops without suspicion having been once aroused. In another feminine disguise, with a forged order, he went to the old lady's safe in the vault of the deposit company and cleared it out. The securities, however, were of a kind which it would be dangerous to negotiate.

The old lady was dismembered by Dr. Anson at night in the empty house, and the various parts were handed to Lintott, who distributed them among medical students of his acquaintance. On the Tuesday evening on which Mrs. Penton called to see her mother Anson had gone to Oak Villa to perform a double task: to remove all that was left of his victim—the head—and to get rid of a tell-tale stain which, in spite of all his precautions, was on the carpet by the old lady's bed. His sensations when he heard the knocking at the door are graphically described. He instantly put out the light, and with the head in a cardboard box in his hand he hastened downstairs. When the would-be visitors went to the back of the house, he opened the front door and slipped out.

Whether, in all their details, the statements in Anson's MS. were perfectly correct has never been ascertained. Lintott was as prepared for emergencies as his accomplice. In spite of his handcuffs, on the road to the police-station he managed to reach his mouth. All at once the two policemen found that they had with them in the taxi-cab a corpse. He had left behind him no papers of any kind which threw light upon the story which Anson had told, but among his belongings was a large quantity of feminine wearing apparel. One of the dresses was recognized by some of the tradesmen who had cashed the cheques as having been worn by the woman who presented them. Officials at the safe deposit company had no doubt that a second had been worn by the woman who came in Mrs. Netherby's name.

9 781943 910229